BOOKED TWICE

BOOKED TO DIE
AND
THE BOOKMAN'S WAKE

JOHN DUNNING

SCRIBNER

New York London Toronto Sydney

SCRIBNER
1230 Avenue of the Americas
New York, NY 10020

First Scribner Edition 2004
These titles were originally published by Scribner.

SCRIBNER and design are trademarks of Macmillan Library Reference USA, Inc., used under license by Simon & Schuster, the publisher of this work.

For information regarding special discounts for bulk purchases, please contact Simon & Schuster Special Sales at 1-800-456-6798 or business@simonandschuster.com.

Text set in Sabon
Manufactured in the United States of America

1 3 5 7 9 10 8 6 4 2

Library of Congress Cataloging-in-Publication Data

Dunning, John, 1942–
[Booked to die]
Booked twice: Booked to die—The bookman's wake/John Dunning.—
1st Scribner ed.
p. cm.
1. Janeway, Cliff (Fictitious character)—Fiction.
2. Booksellers and bookselling—Fiction. 3. Antiquarian booksellers—Fiction.
4. Ex-police officers—Fiction. 5. Book collectors—Fiction.
6. Denver (Colo.)—Fiction. I. Dunning, John, 1942– Bookman's wake.
II. Title.

PS3554.U494B65 2004
813'.54—dc22
2003066787

ISBN 0-7432-6140-2

THE BOOK COLLECTOR

"After love," wrote Rosenbach, "book collecting is the greatest sport of all."

Books hide everywhere, sometimes for years, decades, centuries. Then one day a trunk is opened, a corner is turned, a garage sale brings up wonders from a dusty basement . . . suddenly an educated eye is cast their way after countless others have skimmed over them in ignorance, and a good one is revealed, brightening the heart of the hunter.

A bookscout I knew once walked into a yard sale just after the crack of dawn. He was not a rich dealer; not a dealer at all. He lived hand-to-mouth, hoping that something extraordinary would rise out of the muck, leap up and bite him as the saying goes.

He didn't know much, not then, but instinctively he understood one of the bookscout's basic tenets: you don't just look around and leave. You always ask, always.

"You got any books?"

The woman was busy unpacking old clothes, battered kids' games, and other assorted junk, but she hollered to a kid across the lawn, "Bring up those three boxes of books."

When the scout saw what was in those boxes, he almost fainted: thirty-two Oz books by Frank Baum and Ruth Plumly Thompson, all in gorgeous condition, many from the 1930s in dust jackets.

"How much you want for these?" he asked.

When he heard her price, a quarter apiece, he almost fainted twice.

The basic tenets: the things every bookscout, dealer, or you as a collector must know in order to effectively tap into the joys of book hunting.

- First, you must know how to tell one edition from another. With few exceptions, the first edition is the only one that matters, yet, incredibly, there are some dealers who can't tell a first from a later printing.

- Always buy the best copy you can afford. A superb copy of a scarce title can bring many times what the price guides advise, while a small tear can knock the book's value in half. 'Tis better to spend your grocery money on a grand copy and watch it appreciate on your shelf, sometimes by startling degrees, than to pay chump change for a hangdog copy no one will ever want.

- Often small "points" will affect value. Hemingway's novel, *For Whom the Bell Tolls,* had a photographer's cutline inserted onto the jacket in the middle of the print run. Though they are both firsts, the book without the agate line, "Photo by Arnold, Sun Valley," might sell for three times as much.

- Never, ever, ever write in a book. If you have one of those awful name-embosser gadgets, give it to someone you hate. Better yet, break it apart and scatter the pieces in the nearest junkyard.

- Put your dust jackets in protective plastic. It has been said that the jacket is the "soul" of a book. With a modern book, the jacket's condition can count for 90 percent of the book's value.

- Don't be too impressed by old leather on the face of it. Many old leather-bound books are worthless, while some books published in the last ten years can sell for hundreds of dollars. A lovely dust jacket from the thirties is worth any number of ratty-looking leather books.

- Remember that the long-range value of a modern book is questionable at best. The value will almost always follow the number of copies available. A good formula might be written as small-big: a small print run usually equals bigger value.

- Modern-first-edition collectors tend to go after hot new talent, but a poor second book, or even a good book poorly received, will sometimes dramatically diminish the first novel.

- Learn to use the Internet but, please, please, never become its slave. Don't assume, just because some faraway bookseller is asking $500 for a book, that (a) it is a true first edition, and (b), even if it is, it is a $500 copy. Get on www.bookfinder.com for comparative prices. Telephone the dealer and make sure the book is returnable. Pay by credit card.
- Beware of Internet auction sites. Flaky people sometimes use them, on both sides of a deal.

Yes, you can still find books. I find them where I've always found them: everywhere! The best place to start is with a reputable bookseller. I still go to flea markets and junkshops. Get a copy of *A Pocket Guide to the Identification of First Editions,* by Bill McBride. This booklet tells how English-language publishers, past and present, have identified their first printings. McBride also publishes a booklet on points of issue, though the lack of inclusion does not mean that there are no points on a particular book.

Enjoy the hunt. Savor its joys. It's such an old saying that it's probably a cliché, but buy what you love. It's hard to go wrong when you do that.

JOHN DUNNING
DENVER, COLORADO
2003

BOOKED TO DIE

To Warwick Downing,
who got me started again,
and
to the Denver antiquarian book trade:
the good, the bad, and the ugly

Bobby the Bookscout was killed at midnight on June 13, 1986. This was the first strange fact, leading to the question, *What was he doing out that late at night?* To Bobby, midnight was the witching hour and Friday the thirteenth was a day to be spent in bed. He was found in an alley under one of those pulldown iron ladders that give access to a fire escape—another odd thing. In life, Bobby would never walk under a ladder, so it would seem ironic to some people in the Denver book trade when they heard in the morning that he had died there.

You should know something about bookscouts and the world they go around in. This is an age when almost everyone scouts for books. Doctors and lawyers with six-figure incomes prowl the thrift stores and garage sales, hoping to pick up a treasure for pennies on the dollar. But the real bookscout, the pro, has changed very little in the last thirty years. He's a guy who can't make it in the real world. He operates out of the trunk of a car, if he's lucky enough to have a car, out of a knapsack or a bike bag if he isn't. He's an outcast, a fighter, or a man who's been driven out of every other line of work. He can be quiet and humble or aggressive and intimidating. Some are renegades and, yes, there are a few psychos. The one thing the best of them have in common is an eye for books. It's almost spooky, a pessimistic book dealer once said—the nearest thing you can think of to prove the existence of God. How these guys, largely uneducated, many unread, gravitate toward books and inevitably choose the good ones is a prime mystery of human nature.

They get their stock in any dusty corner where books are sold cheap, ten cents to a buck. If they're lucky they'll find $100 worth on any given day, for which an honest book dealer will pay them $30 or $40. They stand their own expenses and may come out of the day $30 to the good. They live for the prospect of the One Good Book, something that'll bring $200 or more. This happens very seldom, but it happens. It happened to Bobby Westfall more often than to all the others put together.

In one seventy-two-hour period, the story goes, Bobby turned up the following startling inventory: *Mr. President,* the story of the Truman administration, normally a $6 book unless it's signed by Truman, which this was, under an interesting page-long inscription, also in Truman's hand—call it $800 easy; *The Recognitions,* the great cornerstone of modern fiction (or the great unreadable novel, take your pick) by William Gaddis, also inscribed, $400 retail; *The Magus,* John Fowles's strange and irresistible book of wonder, first British edition in a flawless jacket, $300; and *Terry's Texas Rangers,* a thin little book of ninety-odd pages that happens to be a mighty big piece of Texas history, $750. Total retail for the weekend, $2,000 to $2,500; Bobby's wholesale cut, $900, a once-in-a-lifetime series of strikes that people in the Denver book trade still talk about.

If it was that easy, everybody'd be doing it. Usually Bobby Westfall led a bleak, lonely life. He took in cats, never could stand to pass up a homeless kitty. Sometimes he slept in unwashed clothes, and on days when pickings weren't so good, he didn't eat. He spent his $900 quickly and was soon back to basics. He had a ragged appearance and a chronic cough. There were days when he hurt inside: his eyes would go wide and he'd clutch himself, a sudden pain streaking across his insides like a comet tearing up the summer sky. He was thirty-four years old, already an old man at an age when life should just begin.

He didn't drive. He packed his books from place to place on his back, looking for a score and a dealer who'd treat him right. Some of the stores were miles apart, and often you'd see Bobby trudging up East Colfax Avenue, his knees buckling under the weight. His turf was the Goodwill store on Colfax and Havana, the DAV thrift shop on Montview Boulevard, and the dim-lit antique stores along South Broadway, where people think they know books. Heaven to Bobby the Bookscout was finding a sucker who thought he knew more than he knew, a furniture peddler or a dealer in glass who also thought he knew books. On South Broadway, in that particular mind-set, the equation goes like this: old + bulk = value. An antique dealer would slap $50 on a worthless etiquette book from the 1880s and let a true $150 collectible like Anne Tyler's *Celestial Navigation* go for a quarter. When that happened, Bobby Westfall would be there with his quarter in hand, with a poker face and a high heart. He'd eat very well tonight.

Like all bookscouts, Bobby could be a pain in the ass. He was a born-again Christian: he'd tell you about Christ all day long if you'd stand still and listen. There was gossip that he'd been into dope years ago, that he'd done some hard time. People said that's where he found the Lord, doing five-to-ten at Canon City. None of that mattered now. He was a piece of the Denver book world, part of the landscape, and the trade was a little poorer for his death.

He had been bludgeoned, battered into the bookscout's hereafter by a heavy metal object. According to the coroner, Bobby had felt no pain: he never knew what hit him. The body was found facedown in the alley, about three blocks from the old *Denver Post*. A cat was curled up at his feet, as if waiting for Bobby to wake up and take her home.

This is the story of a dead man, how he got that way, and what happened to some other people because of his death.

He was a gentle man, quiet, a human mystery.

He had no relatives, no next of kin to notify. He had no close friends, but no enemies either.

His cats would miss him.

No one could think of a reason why anyone would kill Bobby. Who would murder a harmless man like that?

I'll tell you why. Then I'll tell you who.

BOOK ONE

1

The phone rang. It was 2:30 A.M.

Normally I am a light sleeper, but that night I was down among the dead. I had just finished a thirteen-hour shift, my fourth day running of heavy overtime, and I hadn't been sleeping well until tonight. A guy named Jackie Newton was haunting my dreams. He was my enemy and I thought that someday I would probably have to kill him. When the bell went off, I was dreaming about Jackie Newton and our final showdown. For some reason—logic is never the strong point of a dream like that—Jackie and I were in the hallway at East High School. The bell brought the kids out for the change of classes; Jackie started shooting and the kids began to drop, and that bell kept ringing as if it couldn't stop.

In the bed beside me, Carol stirred.

"Oh, Cliff," she groaned. "Would somebody please get that goddamn telephone?"

I groped for the night table, felt the phone, and knocked the damn thing to the floor. From some distant galaxy I could hear the midget voice of Neal Hennessey, saying, "Cliff? . . . Cliff? . . . Hey, Clifford!" I reached along the black floor and found the phone, but it was still many seconds later before Hennessey took on his bearlike image in my mind.

"Looks like we got another one," Hennessey said without preamble.

I struggled to sit up, trying to get used to the idea that Jackie Newton hadn't shot me after all.

"Hey, Cliffie . . . you alive yet?"

"Yeah, Neal, sure. First time I been sound asleep in a week."

He didn't apologize; he just waited.

"Where you at?" I said.

"Alley off Fifteenth, just up from the *Denver Post*. This one looks an awful lot like the others."

"Give me about half an hour."

"We'll be here."

I sat for another minute, then I got up and went into the bathroom. I turned on the light and looked in the mirror and got the first terrifying look at myself in the cold hard light of the new day. You're getting old, Janeway, I thought. Old Andrew Wyeth could make a masterpiece out of a face like that. Call it *Clifford Liberty Janeway at thirty-six, with no blemish eliminated and no character line unexplored.*

I splashed cold water on my face: it had a great deal less character after that. To finally answer Hennessey, yes, I was almost alive again. The vision of Jackie Newton rose up before me and my hand went automatically to the white splash of scar tissue just under my right shoulder. A bank robber had shot me there five years ago. I knew Jackie Newton would give a lot to put in another one, about three inches to the left and an inch or so down.

Man with an old bullet wound, by Wyeth: an atypical work, definitely not your garden-variety Helga picture.

When I came out of the bathroom Carol was up. She had boiled water and had a cup of instant coffee steaming on my nightstand.

"What now?" she said.

As I struggled into my clothes, I told her it looked like another derelict murder. She sighed loudly and sat on the bed.

She was lovely even in a semistupor. She had long auburn hair and could probably double for Helga in a pinch. No one but Wyeth would know.

"Would you like me to come with you?"

I gave a little laugh, blowing the steam from my coffee.

"Call it moral support," she said. "Just for the ride down and back. Nobody needs to see me. I could stay in the car."

"Somebody would see you, all right, and then the tongues would start. It'd be all over the department by tomorrow."

"You know something? I don't even care."

"I care. What we do in our own time is nobody's business."

I went to the closet and opened it. Our clothes hung there side by side—the blue uniform Carol had worn on yesterday's shift; my dark sport coat; our guns, which had become as much a part of the wardrobe as pants, shirts, ties, badges. I never went anywhere without mine, not even to the corner store. I had had a long career for a guy thirty-six: I'd made my share of enemies, and Jackie Newton was only the latest.

I put the gun on under my coat. I didn't wear a tie, wasn't about to at that time of night. I was off duty and I'd just been roused from a sound sleep; I wasn't running for city council, and I hated neckties.

"I know you've been saying that for a long time now, that stuff about privacy," Carol said dreamily. "But I think the real reason is, if people know about me, I make you vulnerable."

I didn't want to get into it. It was just too early for a philosophical discourse. There was something in what Carol said, but something in what I said too. I've never liked office gossip, and I didn't want people talking about her and me.

But Carol had been looking at it from another angle lately. We had been seeing each other, in the polite vernacular, for a year now, and she was starting to want something more permanent. Maybe bringing our arrangement into the public eye would show me how little there was to worry about. People did it all the time. For most of them the world didn't come to an end. Occasionally something good came out of it.

So she thought.

"I'm going back to bed," she said. "Wake me when you come in. Maybe I'll have a nice surprise for you."

She lay back and closed her eyes. Her hair made a spectacular sunburst on the pillow. I sat for a while longer, sipping my coffee. There wasn't any hurry: a crime lab can take three hours at the scene. I'd leave in five minutes and still be well within the half hour I'd promised Hennessey. The trouble is, when I have dead time—even five minutes unfilled in the middle of the night—I begin to think. I think about Carol and me and all the days to come. I think about the job and all the burned-out gone-forever days behind us. I think about quitting and I wonder what I'd do. I think about being tied to someone and anchoring those ties with children.

Carol would not be a bad one to do that with. She's pretty and bright, and maybe this is what love is. She's good company: her interests broaden almost every day. She reads three books to my one, and I read a lot. We talk far into the night. She still doesn't understand the first edition game: Hemingway, she says, reads just as well in a two-bit paperback as he does in a $500 first printing. I can still hear myself lecturing her the first time she said that. Only a fool would read a first edition. Simply having such a book makes life in general and Hemingway in particular go better when you do break out the reading copies. I listened to myself and thought, This woman must think I'm a government-inspected horse's ass. Then I showed her my Faulkners, one with a signature, and I saw her shiver with an almost sexual pleasure as she touched the paper where he'd signed it. Faulkner was her most recent god, and I had managed to put together a small but respectable collection of his first editions. You've got to read this stuff, she said to me when she was a month deep in his work. How can you collect the man without ever reading what he's written? In fact, I had read him, years ago: I never could get the viewpoints straight in *The Sound and the Fury,* but I had sense enough at sixteen to know that the problem wasn't with Faulkner but with me. I was trying to work up the courage to tackle him again: if I began to collect him, I reasoned, I'd have to read him sooner or later. Carol shook her head. Look at it this way, I said, the Faulkners have appreciated about 20 percent in the three years I've owned them. That she understood.

My apartment looked like an adjunct of the Denver Public Library. There were wall-to-wall books in every room. Carol had never asked the Big Dumb Question that people always ask when they come into a place like this: *Jeez, d'ya read all these?* She browsed, fascinated. The books have a loose logic to their shelving: mysteries in the bedroom; novels out here; art books, notably by the Wyeths, on the far wall. There's no discrimination—they are all first editions—and when people try to go highbrow on me, I love reminding them that my as-new copy of Raymond Chandler's *Lady in the Lake* is worth a cool $1,000 today, more than a bale of books by most of the critically acclaimed and already forgotten so-called masters of the art-and-beauty school. There's nothing wrong with writing detective stories if you do it well enough.

I've been collecting books for a long time. Once I killed two men in the same day, and this room had an almost immediate healing effect.

I've missed my calling, I thought. But now was probably years too late to be thinking about it.

Time to go.

"Cliff?"

Her eyes were still closed, but she was not quite asleep.

"I'm leaving now," I said.

"You going out to see Jackie Newton?"

"If this is what it looks like, you better believe it."

"Have Neal watch your flank. And both of you be careful."

I went over and kissed her on the temple. Two minutes later I was in my car, gliding through the cool Denver night.

I crossed the police line and walked into the alley. The body was about thirty yards in. Strobe lights had been set up and pictures taken. The lights were still on for the benefit of the sketcher, and the narrow canyon was ablaze. The sketcher stood at the edge of things, working with a pencil and clipboard while two assistants checked measurements with a tape. The coroner had arrived only a short time before me, but an assistant coroner had been there for more than an hour. The two men stood over the body talking. I didn't interrupt: just hung back and watched. Hennessey appeared out of the gloom with two cups of coffee. I took mine and he filled me in on what little he knew. Police had responded to an anonymous call at 1:32 A.M.: report of a dead man, which checked out affirmative. Officers arrived at 1:37: homicide detectives had been sent over and the crime lab summoned. Then, because the case strongly resembled a series of such apparently random derelict murders, Hennessey had been called. Hennessey was my partner, and he called me. We had been working that chain of cases for two years; if this one fit the pattern, it would become ours.

There had been no one to interview at the scene. The caller, who was described by the dispatcher as a white-sounding male, probably under fifty, had hung up when asked for his name. Later we'd want to listen to a tape of that conversation, but I didn't have much hope for it. Chances were we'd never find the guy because, chances were, he was just someone who had stumbled over the body and didn't want to get involved.

The scene itself wasn't a good bet for evidence. The alley was narrow and paved. On one side was an old department store; on the other, an old hotel. The walls of the hotel were red brick, worn smooth by many years. The department store had a fake marble facade, which continued into the alley to just about the place where the body lay. Orange powder had been dusted on both sides, and it looked like they'd come up with some prints. In all probability they'd turn out to be everyone but the mayor of Denver and the guy we wanted.

That was all we had. That was all we ever had. The first murdered bum had been found in an alley much like this one two years and two months ago, April 1984. His head had been kicked in. There had been three more that year and two the next, all the same general method of operation: a helluva beating, then death. The guy's hatred for street people, winos, and the homeless seemed compulsive. Hennessey thought he might be a skinhead, one of those jerks with a brownshirt mentality and an irresistible need to take out society's lower elements. I thought his motives were simpler. He was a sadist: he didn't care who he killed, as long as he got his little shot of violence when he needed it. Street people were easy marks, so he did street people. If you murder women and children, society will try to track you down, but the best effort society gives the killer of a bum is a quick shuffle. Time is fleeting and manpower limited: we do what we can, and sometimes a killer gets away because we can't do enough.

It turned out Neal and I were both right. The guy we'd fingered for all these jobs was Jackie Newton, ex-con, refugee from the coast, a real sweetheart in anybody's book. Jackie wasn't a skinhead but he might as well have been: his mind worked the same way. We now knew all about his sadistic streak. Jackie hated everybody who didn't think, act, and look just like him. He particularly hated people whose personal, racial, or intellectual characteristics could be summed up in one cruel gutteral word. Queers, freaks, spics, shines, gooks, dopes— Jackie hated them all, twenty-four hours a day. And let us not forget cops. Pigs. Jackie was a product of the sixties, and pigs were the group he hated most of all.

The feeling was absolutely mutual on my part. There's something in the book, I know, about a cop keeping his feelings out of his work. If detection is a science, which I believe, it should probably be done with unfettered intellect, but God damn it, I wanted Jackie Newton dead or locked away forever. Don't tell me it shouldn't be personal:

we were way beyond that little phase of drawing room etiquette, Jackie and I. I had been working on him two years and was no closer to putting him away than I was when I first heard his name, almost three years ago.

He had blown into town, broke, in 1983. Today he was involved in two $30 million shopping center deals and owned property all over the city. There are guys who have a streak of genius for generating money, and Jackie, I will admit grudgingly, was one of them. He owned an estate in undeveloped Jefferson County, where he lived alone and liked it, and reportedly he was connected to what passes in Denver for the mob. This alone brought him to our attention before we learned that he murdered drunks for a hobby. It was a strange case that way: we knew who the killer was before the first victim was killed. A cop in Santa Monica told us not to be surprised by a sudden rise in derelict deaths. This had happened in California and in Newark, where Jackie lived fifteen years ago. We knew before the fact what Newark knew, what Santa Monica knew, and we still couldn't stop it and we couldn't prove it once it had started. It had almost seemed too pat, and we went through a phase of exploring other ideas—the skinhead, the unknown sadist—before we learned, without a doubt, that Jackie was our boy.

In the killing of Harold Brubaker, we'd had a witness. Jesus, you never saw such a beating, our boy had said: this guy has sledgehammers in his fists and what he does with his feet . . . it's like something inhuman. The witness was a highly credible young man who had watched from a dark doorway less than ten feet away: a kid working overtime who had stepped out for a smoke and seen it all. It was like Providence was suddenly in our corner. A light had come on and Jackie had looked straight up at it. The kid had seen him clearly, not a doubt in the world. I had the son of a bitch where I wanted him at last. I brought Jackie in and ran him through a lineup. The kid had no trouble picking him out: he was a first-rate witness all the way. I did everything according to Hoyle and the Miranda ruling: the last thing I wanted was for the bastard to slide on tainted evidence or technical bullshit. We threw a protective shield around the witness, for Jackie had friends in slimy places, but what can I say? Things happen . . . court dates get postponed, his attorneys drag it out, weeks become months, and in all that time there's bound to be a breach. They got to our boy, and when they were done he had no heart for testifying against anybody. They never put a hand on him, but they sure made him see things their way. He stammered in court, he hesitated, he wasn't sure . . . and the case against Jackie Newton went down the drain.

Jackie had been quiet since then: we had scared him with Harold Brubaker and he had been lying low. Now he was starting up again, and I'd bet there'd be another one before long. Success breeds success. There's nothing worse than a cunning killer who strikes down people he doesn't know, for no reason other than a blood lust.

3

I waited until the coroner was finished, then I moved in for a look at the body. They had turned him over, and he lay on the pavement with his arms crossed gently over his chest. He looked like he might get up and walk away. His eyes were closed and he had the unwashed, unshaved look they all had. But there was something different about this one, something vaguely familiar, as if I had known him once, long ago.

"What can you tell us, Georgie?" I said.

The coroner, a spectacled man in his fifties, spoke while his assistant looked on.

"It's a lot like the others, but there are some significant differences. As you can see, the victim is a guttersnipe, body not well nourished, white male, probably mid-thirties, five foot seven inches, hundred fifty, sixty pounds. Murder weapon was a heavy blunt instrument, a pipe wrench or a crescent wrench or some steel tool would be my guess. The victim was hit twice in the center of the rear cranium, once for business and once for good measure. There was no doubt in the mind of the killer what the objective was. I think the first one did it—we'll know more in the morning. Time of death was within the last three hours."

"Call came in about one-thirty," Hennessey said.

"He had probably been dead a little over an hour then," the coroner said.

I looked at the face of the dead man and again felt that disquieting rumble deep in my brain.

"There's some evidence he was killed somewhere else, then dumped here," the coroner said.

"That's new," Hennessey said.

"What evidence?" I asked.

"I think there's a good deal of blood unaccounted for," the coroner said. "Again, we'll know more in the morning, but let's say I'm about eighty percent sure. That pipe really opened his head up. A wound like that will bleed like a geyser, but this one didn't, or, if it did, where's the blood? This little puddle's just leakage, as if the heart had stopped some time prior to his being put here. I think that's what happened. Somebody did this man in somewhere else, then dropped him here."

"Any signs of a beating?"

The coroner gave me a look. "You don't consider this a beating?"

"I mean injuries to other parts of the body . . . indications that he was beaten severely before he was killed."

"Nothing so far. Looks like he was hit twice and that's that."

I shook my head. "I've seen this guy somewhere. I can't make him."

Hennessey asked the coroner if they had a name. The coroner looked at his notes and said, "The deceased had no driver's license. There was a fragment of a social security card. Most of the number had worn away, but we were able to get a name. Robert B. Westfall."

The name clicked. "Yeah, I know him," I said. "He's a bookscout."

"A what?"

"A guy that hunts for books. That's where I've seen him, selling books in the neighborhood stores."

"I always heard you were the intellectual type, Janeway," the coroner said.

"Is that what you hear?" I said dryly.

"It's a small world, my friend, and the night has a thousand eyes."

"You've been observed reading books again, Clifford," Hennessey said. "I guess I'm the man of action on this team."

I turned my attention back to the corpse. The coroner hung over my shoulder like a scarecrow. I was trying to place the guy, to remember where and when I had last seen him.

"In the bookstores they call him Bobby the Bookscout," I said. "He was pretty good, from what I hear."

"How does a bum get to be good at something like that?" the coroner asked.

"They're not bums in the usual sense. Most of 'em work like hell, don't drink, and stay out of trouble."

"What about the ones that don't like to work, do drink, and don't stay out of trouble?" Hennessey said.

"I guess there are some of those."

"I don't know much about this kinda stuff," Hennessey said. "You tell me, Cliff. Could one of these boys find something, say a book, since that's what they look for, that's so valuable another one might kill him for it? And where does that leave us with Jackie Newton?"

"I'll let you boys hash that out," the coroner said. "Call me tomorrow."

"Thanks, George."

We stood for a moment after the coroner had left. Hennessey's questions kept running through my mind. I felt a pang of disappointment that Jackie Newton might slide on this one for the plain and simple reason that he hadn't done it.

"Cliff?"

"Yeah, Neal. Just give me a minute."

I watched them cover the body and take it away. The sketcher had left and the lab men were packing up: the sad saga of Bobby the Bookscout was just about over. All that was left was the hunt for his killer.

"We sure can't rule out the possibility of Jackie," I said.

Hennessey didn't say anything.

"Let's go see the son of a bitch," I said.

"I'll call Jeffco."

As peace officers, we were empowered to investigate and arrest anywhere in the state of Colorado. Usual procedure when you went out of your jurisdiction was to take an officer from that district along, in case something happened. Thirty minutes later we had arrived at the Jefferson County Sheriff's Department, where Officer Ben Nasses was waiting for us. Officer Nasses was young and articulate, one of the new breed. He was also very black. Jackie Newton would love him.

Jackie lived in an expensive villa a few miles south of the town of Morrison. He wasn't quite in the mountains, but the house was perched at the top of a bluff where you could see most of Denver and the front range south, halfway to Colorado Springs. We pulled into the driveway. The house was dark, with no sign of life. I had a sinking feeling that we'd find Jackie Newton asleep, that he'd been asleep all night. I had the feeling, not for the first time, that I'd never be able to make him on anything.

But Jackie wasn't home. Nasses rang the bell three times and knocked, but no one came. "What now?" he said. I told him we would wait, if he had nothing better to do, and he said that was fine. "I'd like for us not to be visible when he comes home," I said, and Hennessey went to move the car on down the street. By the time Neal came back, Nasses and I had moved off the step and onto a gravel walkway that skirted the house. Hennessey was nervous. "I don't think we want to mess around here, Cliff," he said. He had been my partner for a long time; he knew all about my impatience with oppressive procedure, and he also knew how much I wanted to put Jackie away. Don't be stupid—that's what Neal was saying. But I was very much aware of the rules of evidence. I had never had a case thrown out because I was weak in court, and Hennessey knew that too. Sometimes you play by the book, sometimes you had to take a chance.

"I'm going to take a look in the garage," I said.

Hennessey whimpered but stayed with me. I moved around the house. "You boys're crazy," Nasses called. He wasn't going anywhere. Hennessey tugged at me in the dark. "Cliff, the kid's right. This makes no sense. Even if you find something you won't be able to use it. Let's get out of here."

"If I find something, I'll find a way to use it."

"The bastard's liable to come rolling in here any minute."

"Then let's do it quick."

The garage was locked but that was no problem: I had it open in less than half a minute. There were two vehicles inside, a Caddy and a Jeep four-wheel. There was an empty space for the third car, the one Jackie Newton was now driving.

I felt the hood of each car, then went through the glove compartments. There was just the usual junk—papers, ownership, registration. John Randolph Newton was listed as the owner of both vehicles, but I knew that. I knew where and when he had bought them, that he'd bought the Jeep on time, paid it off in six months, and paid cash for the Cadillac. I knew the salesmen who had dealt with him. *A real laid-back guy,* one salesman had said, *a pussycat.* Money wasn't anything to a guy like Jackie: he had made, lost, and made again three times over more money than those boys would see in their whole lives. That's one thing you could say for Jackie Newton: he was free with his money, and salesmen loved him.

There was an unpaid ticket on the seat of the Caddy. I took down the information. Jackie had been tagged for speeding—fifty-five in a twenty-five, a four-pointer. This was good news: the last time I'd looked at his record he had had nine points against his license. Jackie liked to drive fast, and it was costing him. I knew he hadn't paid the ticket because of the points: he'd have his lawyer go in and plead it down, try to get two points knocked off in the city attorney's office before it ever got to a judge. A word from me in the ear of the city attorney might not be out of order. Anything that hassled Jackie Newton was a good use of my time. From little things big things grow. Get Jackie's license suspended and I knew he'd drive anyway. Then I could bust him for something bigger. Al Capone never got indicted for murder, just tax evasion, but it was enough.

I put everything back the way it was. Hennessey was standing at the door, the man of action watching for headlights. I looked along the shelves. There were paint cans, tools, boxes of screws, all meticulously in their places. Jackie Newton was a neat man: the compulsively neat killer.

"Cliff," Hennessey said. His voice fluttered in his throat.

"All right," I said. "There's nothing here."

I turned off the lights and locked the door. We started across the yard but a vision brought me up short. I thought I saw a body hanging from a tree. It was one of those sights that makes you wonder if your eyes are getting old. "Look at that," I said, but Hennessey still didn't see. I took out a penlight and cut across the lawn, and slowly the thing came into focus. It was a dog, the Doberman, hung by the neck like some western desperado. "It's Bruno," I said numbly. Again I realized what an obsession Jackie Newton and I had become to each other: I knew everything about the guy, even the name of his dog. Supposedly, Jackie had loved the dog: the only thing Jackie Newton had ever been said to love. This was what happened if he loved you: you didn't ever want to give him cause to hate you, as I had.

"Looks like somebody's got it in for Jackie," Hennessey said.

"I don't think so, Neal. I think he did it himself."

I was playing my light around the barbecue grill, which had been turned over and spilled. There was a half-eaten steak in the grass, many hours old. The steak had been chewed as if by an animal. Beside it were two upset plates. "I'll tell you what happened here," I said, "you tell me how it sounds. Jackie had been entertaining somebody— probably a woman since there were just the two of 'em. Something happened to take him away for a minute . . . maybe the phone had rung . . . but something made him go inside. When he came back, the dog had turned over the grill and eaten one of the steaks and was starting on the other. Jackie went into a rage. We've seen him in action, we know how he can be. He strung the poor bastard up with the clothesline. Then he did what he always does when he gets like that. Took his fastest car, the Lamborghini, and went out for a drive. That's where he's been tonight, out in the country driving at a hundred and fifty miles an hour."

"You could make me buy that," Hennessey said.

"Then I'll tell you what else he did. He couldn't get rid of it, the rage just wouldn't go away. Nothing worked. He hated killing that dog, hated himself for doing it, so he went downtown and killed the bookscout. Somebody he didn't know or care about . . . just an out-let for all that murderous energy. That's why the bookscout wasn't beaten before he was killed: that's why he was different from all the others. Jackie didn't do this one for pleasure, he did it because he needed to."

"I don't know about that part," Hennessey said.

"What's the matter with it?" I snapped.

"For one thing, you want it too much. You want it to fit, Cliff. I know where you're coming from with Jackie Newton, you'd pin the goddamn Kennedy assassination on Jackie if you thought you could make it stick."

"It does fit," I said impatiently. "It fits, Neal."

Hennessey didn't say any more, which was probably a good thing. We didn't touch the dog except to confirm that it had been dead for some time. It was very stiff. Its eyes were open. If a dog's face can show feelings, this one showed shock, sadness, and, finally, disbelief. Its front paws had been clawing the air and had finally come to rest, frozen there, in a posture much like a man in prayer. I had to fight an impulse to cut it down. Hennessey was right: we had no warrant, no authority, no right to be here. This was very bad police work. The dog didn't exist for us, even assuming that it might be relevant to our case, until we established some proper groundwork.

We had pushed our luck about as far as it can go. We went around to the front of the house, where Officer Nasses again told us his opinion, no offense intended, that we were out of our minds. I still wanted to be here when Jackie came rolling in: I wanted to see what time it was, how he looked, what his car looked like. I wanted to see as much as possible of what he did, what the state of his mind was. I put Hennessey and Nasses out front, in the trees across the road, and I went around to watch the back. This could be a very long wait. Jackie might be in Wyoming by now: that's the kind of state a Lamborghini was made for, empty roads and wide-open spaces and cops who didn't care how fast you went. He might be gone for a week.

So I'd wait. If the wait got too long, I'd let Hennessey and Nasses go in, but I would stay. Jackie Newton was turning me into an eccentric. I had a disturbing vision of myself waiting here for days, then weeks, into the changing seasons, my beard coming in, my clothes becoming tattered and worn, Hennessey bringing me food and water once a day. I was like Fred Dobbs in *The Treasure of the Sierra Madre:* I had started out a sane and decent man and slowly the obsession had turned me crazy. I looked at my watch: the sky was getting light in the east. Sanity came with the dawn. I'd give him till eight o'clock, nine at the latest, then I'd go in and catch him later. Hennessey was right again: I had nothing on Jackie. It didn't fit, the pattern was broken. For once, Jackie Newton wasn't my man.

I snuffed that thought fast. One of my problems was beginning to resolve itself. In another twenty minutes it would be daylight: then, I thought, we could see the dog from the road. That would make it legitimate discovery, as long as Jackie didn't find out that we'd been here earlier. I wasn't going to tell him. Hennessey wasn't. Nasses was the unknown factor. I gave up the idea of confronting Jackie as he stepped from his car. I decided to do it by the book from here on out. I would join the boys in the bushes across the road. When Jackie did come home, we'd go get the car and pull up in front and ring his doorbell, as proper as Emily Post.

Let the fun begin, I thought.

4

We waited almost another hour before Jackie came home. We heard him first—the squeal of the tires, the angry, impatient growl of the engine. "Helluva way to treat a car like that," Hennessey said. The Lamborghini roared past in a swirl of dust. It made the turn and went behind the house and into the garage. Jackie came out, looking as he had the first time I'd seen him, like some plastic hero from Muscle Beach. He was a serious bodybuilder: his arms looked like a pair of legs, his chest like a fifty-gallon drum. He had grown himself a mustache and he needed a haircut. The image was formidable, a guy you don't mess with. He stopped for a moment and looked at the dog, and the anger began again. "Get out of that car!" he shouted, and the woman peeped meekly through the open garage door. "Come on, come on!" Jackie said. She was none too happy about it: I could see that even from where we crouched in the bushes. Jackie grabbed her by the scruff of the neck and pushed her toward the house. They disappeared inside.

We waited. Nothing happened.

"Looks like the ball's in our court," Hennessey said.

"Yeah. Let's go see the son of a bitch."

We walked down the road to the car; then we drove back and turned into Jackie Newton's drive, three officers of the law, proper to the bone. We stepped out and started up the walk. You could see the dog even from there, swinging grotesquely from the tree.

"Jesus, look at that," Nasses said. "You boys see that last night?"

"See what?" I said.

Nasses gave a dry laugh. "Play it that way, then. I'll help if I can."

"Translate it for us, Nasses."

"Don't ask me to lie to cover your ass. I won't volunteer anything, but don't ask me to lie."

"Ring the doorbell," I said.

I had my badge pinned to my belt, like some cop on a TV show. I was pumped up: I always was when I was about to face Jackie. I heard him coming. The door opened and he filled the space.

"Mr. Newton?" Nasses said.

Jackie had seen me right off. He looked straight through Nasses and locked eyes with me. He probably didn't even notice yet that Nasses was black.

"I'm Officer Nasses, Jeffco Sheriff's Department. These gentlemen are from the Denver police. They'd like to ask you a few questions."

His eyes cut to my badge. Nasses had taken a little involuntary step to one side. There was nothing between Jackie Newton and me but two feet of violent air.

"Hello, Jackie," I said.

"What the fuck do you want, Janeway?"

"You must be having trouble with your ears. The man just told you, I want to ask you a few questions."

"You arresting me for something?"

"Maybe."

"Go fuck yourself. Bust me right now or come back with a warrant."

"How do you know I don't have a warrant?"

"If you did you'd use it. Go away, you're wasting my time."

He started to close the door. I stepped past Nasses and put my foot in it. I started reading him his rights, thinking maybe it would throw him off, buy me a minute. At least if he slipped and said something, we'd be protected.

He listened, uncertain.

"Where were you last night?" I said.

"I drove out on the plains. I was gone all night and, yeah, I had company. I got an alibi for any goddamn thing you want to dream up about last night."

"Where's your alibi, Newton? I want to see him."

"Her, flatfoot, her . . . my alibi's a girl."

"Bring her down."

"Come back with a warrant."

Again he tried to close the door. Again I put my foot in it.

"I told you, Newton, you've got the right to remain silent. That doesn't mean you can keep me from a witness. Now bring the girl down here or I'll have your ass in jail for obstruction of justice."

It was a bluff and I figured Jackie would know it. He didn't know it, not for sure. He went and got the girl, who actually was a woman in her late twenties.

He had slapped her at least three times: there were that many distinct welts on her face. In another day she'd look like she'd been face-first through a gauntlet.

"Would you step outside, miss?"

She did. She was blond, and might've been pretty in a glassy kind of way. She wasn't pretty now.

"What's your name?"

"You haven't got to tell him one fucking thing," Jackie Newton said. There was an implication in his voice that she'd better not.

"What's your name, miss?"

"Barbara."

"Do you need help?"

She looked confused, scared.

"We can take you out of here if you want to go," I said.

"She doesn't want to go anywhere with you, cop," Jackie Newton said.

"Miss?" I tried for eye contact, but I couldn't get a rise out of her. "Did this jerk beat you up?"

"She ran into a door," Jackie Newton said.

"You'd better get that door fixed, Newton. Looks like she ran into it three or four times."

"She ran into a goddamn door, okay? You want to make something out of that?"

"Miss," I said, "do you want to go with us?"

"I don't know," she said shakily.

"We could go over to the car and talk it over. Come on, let's do that."

"She's going nowhere with you, cop."

"Don't pay any attention to that," I said. "If you want to go, you go. Fatso's got nothing to say about it."

I knew that would get to him. He balled up his fists and said, "I'll show you fat, motherfucker. Take off your badge and I'll beat your fuckin' head in."

I gave him a bitter, pathetic smile, the kind you'd give a talking worm. I kept looking at him the whole time I was talking to her. "I want you to be very sure, miss, what your options are. It's all up to you. If this jerk beat you up, you can file charges against him. He can do some good time for that. Maybe when he gets out he won't feel so frisky."

"I've had about enough of this shit," Jackie Newton said.

"I don't think so, Newton. You and me, we've got a long way to go with each other."

"You wanna go now, Janeway? You wanna go now, huh? What do you say, cop, just you and me, bare hands, an old-fashioned fight to the finish."

"I see you've been reading comic books again, Jackie. I wish I could accommodate you, I really do. You could show me how you beat up women and murder dogs. Or murder bums on the street."

"Is that what this is about? Are you still trying to stick me with that?"

"I'm going to stick you with it, pal. You watch me."

"Why don't you fight me, Janeway? Just pick the place and time."

"I wish I could. We don't do things that way."

"That don't surprise me. Now if you're all through, I'm going in."

I had been working my way slowly around, putting more distance between Newton and the woman. Now I put an arm out and moved her completely aside.

"Barbara," I said. "Why don't you come on with us?"

"All right."

"I wouldn't do that," Jackie Newton said.

"You wouldn't do anything unless it was stupid or mean," I said. I got my hand on her shoulder and guided her away from the house. We got her to the car and inside, and there she broke down in a fit of sobbing. Her whole body trembled. I took off my coat and covered her shoulders, but it was a long time before she was ready to tell us about it.

We let Nasses off in Jeffco and were coming down Sixth Avenue toward Denver when I started to get her story. Hennessey was driving and Barbara was huddled against the shotgun door. I was in the back, leaning over the seat. I started with the little things. Her last name was Crowell. She lived in a Capitol Hill walk-up near Eleventh and Pearl. She worked for one of the companies that did business with Jackie Newton. Yesterday was the first time she had seen him . . . socially. She was flattered that he had asked her: he was rich and some people found him attractive. No one had warned her what he was really like.

It had happened pretty much as I had figured. Jackie's idea of a date was apparent soon after they arrived at his house. He had a waterbed the size of a football field, with a hot tub, mirrors, the whole nine yards. That hadn't bothered her much: she wasn't entirely indisposed to going down with a guy the first time out, if she liked him. If a guy knew how to treat a girl, what was the harm in it? But then the dog ate the steaks and Jackie went crazy. You wouldn't believe how strong he was. That was a big dog, and he'd pulled it up over that limb like it weighed nothing. She had tried to stop him: she hated cruelty, she just couldn't stand there and watch that animal kick its life out. She had tried to cut the rope and Jackie slugged her. He was strong, all right, no mistake about it. With one punch he knocked her senseless.

The next fifteen hours were a nightmare. When she opened her eyes she was in the car. They were on the interstate heading east out of Denver. He drove the same way he did everything, always one inch from the brink of insanity. He kept his foot jammed on the floorboards—Jesus, you couldn't imagine a car could go that fast. Later he'd gone off the freeway into a narrow country road. Once they'd stopped in the middle of nowhere. She didn't seem to want to go into that, but I had started to taste blood and there was no way I was going to let her drop it.

"Barbara," I said softly. "Did he rape you?"

She shook her head.

"Because if he did, you know, we can give him a lot of grief."

"I didn't struggle."

"You don't have to struggle for it to be rape."

She took a deep shivery breath. I gave her a handkerchief and she dabbed her eyes.

"Barbara," I said.

"I just want to forget about it."

"I can see that you do, and I understand that. But if you don't do something he'll just do it again."

"Not to me."

We didn't say anything more for a minute. Hennessey drove smoothly into the city, turning north on Santa Fe. From there we could go easily to her place or to Denver General.

"We need to go to the hospital," I said. "Get you examined, get a doctor involved. You can make up your mind what to do later, but we need to get this done now."

"I want to forget it. I want to go home."

I sighed tiredly. "Jackie wins again."

"He'd win anyway. They'd let him off, and then where would I be?"

I couldn't argue with her. The way I had taken her out of there, without a warrant or probable cause, might give a judge fits. We could make the probable cause argument to some judges and win, based on what we had seen from our stakeout across the road. But there was another kind of judge who always held a cop's nuts to the ground, who'd view everything said and done after I'd stuck my foot in the door as tainted evidence. It was the luck of the draw.

We pulled up at her place on Pearl Street. She didn't want us to come in, but I had a few more questions. I wanted to hear all of it, everything they'd been doing since yesterday afternoon. Nothing much to tell, she said: he just drove like a maniac and she huddled in the car and expected death every minute. Once he had run over a flock of chickens. If there was anything on the road, a squirrel, chipmunk, any living thing, he'd swerve and crush it.

That car, though, was something else. That car was amazing.

She had been with Jackie Newton without a break since 3:00 P.M. yesterday. They had gone halfway across Kansas before he'd turned and come back.

She knew nothing about a dead man in an alley.

Sometimes when I get going, I can work thirty hours without a break. This is tough on my partner, especially a guy like Hennessey, who needs his beauty rest. Neal went home to catch up on lost sleep and I went running. I used to be a marathon man in college. I can still do thirty miles, but it's harder and I'm slower now. I'm not bad for my age and I go through a lot of pain to keep it that way. I run two, three times a week, and every year I run in the Bolder Boulder and finish respectably. I don't try to beat the world anymore: if I can just hold up my little part in it, that's enough. When I was young I had thoughts of a career in the ring, but the cops won my heart, and my mind and balls soon followed. You've got to be realistic, as people keep telling me. It's a long way from the Golden Gloves to any kind of fighting career, and I had seen enough of the fight game to know it wasn't for me. While I was at it, I was pretty good. I had people comparing me to Marciano. I was light for a heavyweight, just over one ninety, but so was Marciano. I was fast and tough: no one had ever been able to knock me down. It was said that I could hit like a mule and take any punch ever thrown. I liked it when they said that.

This is all by way of saying that I'd've been delighted to take on Jackie Newton some dark night. He had me by four inches in height, at least that much in reach, and thirty pounds that would never be called excess baggage. On paper he should whip my ass. But that's what they said about Jess Willard when he ran into another of my old heroes, Jack Dempsey. Dempsey put that lardbucket flat on the floor, and when it was over Willard's corner was screaming about plaster of paris and everything but the Rock of Gibraltar being in Dempsey's gloves. It ain't the size of the dog in the fight, is it? And I had a feeling that, under all that bullshit, Jackie Newton didn't have much heart.

The one sure thing was that I'd never find out. It got tiresome, always having to play by the rules while the other guy did his mugging and raping under a cloak of protections and rights. I jogged out Sixth Avenue, past expensive homes along the parkway. Somewhere, somehow, I was missing something: I didn't know what. I had stepped off the treadmill way back when and didn't know how to get on again. I was molded by a conservative father; I had rejected him and everything he stood for. I'd fought in the last stages of Vietnam, returned a fiery liberal, and slowly, over the past decade, I had watched those values trickle away as well. Today I'm a mess of contradictory political views. I believe in human rights: I liked Jimmy Carter for that reason alone, though I later came to believe that he had sold out his own cause in the game of pure politics. I think the Miranda ruling has generally been good, though the public will never know what a pain it can be to work with. I believe in due process, but enough is enough: I'm a fan of a just and swift execution where vicious killers are concerned. It's just ridiculous to keep a guy like Ted Bundy on death row for ten years. I don't believe it when psychologists tell me the death penalty doesn't deter—take a look at kidnapping statistics in the 1930s, when it was made a capital crime after the murder of the Lindbergh baby, before you start to argue with me. I think justice started collapsing under its own weight when they let shrinks into the courtroom. The plain fact is, for some murderers, I just don't care whether they were incapable of reason, were whipped as children for wetting the bed, or had a mother who bayed at the moon. Gacy, Bundy, Manson, Speck—you'll never make me believe the world is a better place with that quartet alive and kicking. I hate abortion, but I'd never pass a law telling a woman she couldn't have one. I believe in the ERA, find it hard to understand why two hundred years after the Bill of Rights we're still arguing about rights for half our people. I like black people, some of them a lot. I supported busing when it was necessary and would again, but there's something about affirmative action that leaves me cold. You can't take away one man's rights and give them to another, even in a good cause.

I was burned out, and never more than today. My police career had been solid, some said brilliant, but I was on a long slide to nowhere, a treadmill to oblivion, as Fred Allen called it. These are the days that try men's souls. I wanted to fight Jackie Newton with a broken bottle and a tire iron, and society, decency, and my own good sense said, *You can't do that*. There was something about gun law that was immensely appealing: it really cut through the crap and got to the heart of things. Barbaric? Maybe. But I'll tell you this: watching a guy kill people and not being able to do a damn thing about it, that's no bowl of cherries either.

My apartment, as always, was the great healer. I stripped off my sweats, turned on a light, and sat surrounded by treasures. I looked for a while at an old *AB:* my fascination with the life of the bookman was almost as acute as my interest in books, and I had been a faithful subscriber to the bookseller's trade journal for almost five years. I thumbed through Wyeth's Helga pictures, lingering on that lovely scene in the barn. Carol Pfeiffer, of course, had long gone: she had been gone when I had come in earlier and changed for my run. I took a cold shower and dressed slowly, planning my day. Barbara Crowell's statement seemed to alibi Jackie Newton nicely, which meant I had to start from scratch. It never occurred to me to call Hennessey, or to check downtown and see if we'd been assigned to the case. Hennessey would just be turning over for his second forty winks, and downtown they'd know we were on it. They knew all about my work habits.

I drove out Sixth to Colorado Boulevard, went north to Colfax, then east to the bookstores. This was my turf: I was as much at home along Book Row as I was in the world of hookers and pimps that surrounded it. Colfax is a strange street. It used to be known as the longest street in the world: people with more imagination than I have used to say, in the days before interstate highways, that it ran from Kansas City to the Great Salt Lake. Its actual length is about twenty miles, beginning on the plains east of Denver and dwindling away in the mountains to the west. Just about every foot of it is commercial space. About twenty years ago, urban renewal came in and ripped out old Larimer Street, and the whores and bums who lived there landed on Broadway south and Colfax east. Lots of whoring goes on on East Colfax Avenue. It starts at the statehouse, where they know how to do it without ever getting in a bed, and works its way through the porno shops between Broadway and Colorado Boulevard. From Colorado east, for about thirty or forty blocks, the street goes respectable in a chain of mom-and-pop businesses of every imaginable type. Here you'll find produce stands, garages, video rentals, fortune-tellers, antique dealers, 7-Elevens, liquor stores, and, of course, Book Row.

More than ten years ago, an old-time book dealer and his wife hung their shingle on an East Colfax hole-in-the-wall. Those people are gone now—the old man died and the wife lives in another state. Their store has passed along to a succession of younger bookmen: it has spawned other bookstores until, today, the area has become known as Book Row. This is the honey-draws-flies concept of bookselling: put two bookstores in one block, the theory goes, and business doubles for everybody. It seems to work: the stores have all stabilized where business was lean for one before. As a book collector, I did Book Row at least twice a month. A couple of the dealers knew me well enough to call me at home if something came in with my name on it; the others knew me too, though some of them were a little shy about calling a cop. Book dealers are like everyone else: they come in all sizes and shapes and have the same hangups that you see in a squad room or on an assembly line. If you picture a wizened academic with thick spectacles, forget it. Once they get in the business, they have little time to read. They are usually a cut or two smarter than the average Joe. I've never met a stupid book dealer who was able to make it pay. Some of them, though, are definitely crazy. There are a few horse's asses, a few sow's ears, but today's bookseller is just as likely to be an ex-hippie ex-boozer ex-junkie streetfighter like Ruby Seals.

I liked Ruby: I admired the old bastard for his savvy and grit. He had pulled himself out of the gutter the hard way, cold turkey and alone. He was a bottle-a-day drunk and he'd kicked that; he had been on cocaine and later heroin and had kicked that. He had been busted for possession, beginning in the days when, in Colorado, you could get two years for having a leaf of grass in your car. Ruby had served a year on that bust, another year for speed, and two years of a seven-year rap for heroin. By then the laws had been liberalized or he might still be languishing at Canon City. I had known him all this time because I was into books, and Ruby, when he was straight, was one of the keenest book dealers in town. A lot of what I knew I had learned watching Ruby work. "I'll tell you something, Dr. J," he had said to me long ago. "Learn books and you'll never go hungry. You can walk into any town with more than two bookstores and in two hours you're in business."

You did it the same way the scouts did, only on a higher level. While the scouts looked for $2 books that could be turned for $10, you looked for the $100 piece that would fetch a McKinley. You bought from guys who didn't know and sold to guys who did. If nobody in town knew, you wholesaled to people on the coast. You worked the *AB* when you could afford the price of it; you put a little bankroll together and before you knew it, you had three or four thousand books. Ruby had done this more times than he could remember.

Seals & Neff was the last store on the block, but I went there first. It was in their store, about a month ago, that I had last seen Bobby Westfall. I vaguely remembered it now: Bobby had come in to sell something, and there had been a dispute over how much and in what manner Ruby would pay for it. I hadn't paid much attention then: I was wavering on the price of a nice little Steinbeck item. There wasn't much to the argument anyway, as I remembered it: Bobby didn't want to take a check and Ruby didn't have the cash, so Bobby had left with the book. But that was the last time I had seen him and it seemed like a good starting place.

Ruby and his partner, Emery Neff, were sorting books from a new buy when I came in: they were hunkered over with their asses facing the door and didn't see me for a moment. The stuff looked pretty good: lots of fine modern firsts, some detective novels, a Faulkner or two. My eye caught the dark blue jacket of *Intruder in the Dust.* Carol's birthday was coming up: maybe I'd buy it for her, see how she liked it when she actually owned a book like that. A $100 bill flitted through my mind. That's what the book was worth, though I expected a good deal of preamble before we got to that point. I didn't like haggling. I wasn't one of those cheapskates always trying to pry a book away from a dealer for half its value, but I didn't want to pay twice retail either. I knew how Seals & Neff operated. They tended to go high with stuff they'd just bought. That sometimes worked with pigeons and sucker books. But then the rent would come due or the sheriff would call for the sales tax, many months delinquent, and they'd scramble around, wholesaling their best books for pennies on the dollar in a mad effort to keep from being thrown out or padlocked.

Ruby was dressed in his usual country club attire: jeans, a sweatshirt, and sandals. He wore a heavy black beard that was streaked with gray. His partner was neater. Emery Neff had blond hair and a mustache. Taken together, they were a strange pair of boys. Ruby was gritty, down-to-earth, real; Neff put on airs, oozed arrogance, and, until you passed muster, seemed aloof and cold. Ruby could sell birth control to a nun; Neff seemed reluctant to sell you a book, even at high retail. Neff wasn't quite a horse's ass, but he was close: I guess it was his deep well of knowledge that saved him. He really was a remarkable bookman, and I seemed to like him in spite of himself.

They still hadn't seen me: they were engrossed in the hypnotic, totally absorbing business of the bookman—sorting and pricing. I had seen the ritual before and had always found it interesting. Ruby would pick up a book and fondle it lovingly, then they'd bat the price back and forth and finally they'd settle on something, which Neff would write in light pencil on the flyleaf. They were just getting to the Faulkner when I leaned over their backs.

"Buck and a half," Neff said.

"Too high," Ruby said.

"It's a perfect copy, Ruby. I mean, look at the goddamn thing, it's like it was published yesterday, for Christ's sake."

"You never see this for more than a bill."

"You never see a copy like this either."

"Go ahead, if you want the son of a bitch to grow mold over there on the shelf."

"Buck and a quarter, then. That's rock-friggin'-bottom."

Neff penciled in the price. I cleared my throat and got their attention.

"Well, Dr. Janeway, I do believe," Ruby said, brightening. "We just got in some stuff for you."

"So I see. The masters of overcharge are already at work."

Neff gave me a pained look, as if the mere discussion of money was a blow to one's dignity.

"Always a deal for you, Dr. J," Ruby said, and Neff's pained look drifted his way.

I put the Faulkner out of my mind for the moment. I never could split my concentration effectively.

"I want to ask you boys a few questions."

"Jesus, Mr. Janeway," Neff said seriously. "This sounds official. Let me guess what it is. Somebody knocked off the sheriff and right away you thought of us."

I gave him a mirthless little smile. "When was the last time you saw Bobby Westfall?"

"Jeez, I don't know," Ruby said. "He ain't been coming around much."

"What's he done, rob a bank?" Neff said.

"See if you can pin it down for me," I said.

"Well," Ruby said, "he come in here maybe two weeks ago. Ain't that right, Em? About two weeks ago."

"About that," Neff said. "What's it about?"

"I told you, I'm trying to pin him down," I said. "Did he have something to sell when he came in?"

"Just a few turds," Ruby said. "Nuthin' I wanted."

"Bob was on a losing streak," Neff said. "He hadn't found much all month long."

"He was bitchin' up a storm about it," Ruby said. "Bobby never bitches much, but I guess he needed the money and for once in his life he couldn't find any books."

"You have any idea what he needed the money for?"

"Hell, Dr. J, I just buy books from these bastards, I don't go home and sleep with 'em."

"They always need money," Neff said.

"Who doesn't?" Ruby said. "But bookscouts . . . yeah, Em's right. Those guys're always scraping like hell just to get two nickels to rub against each other. But I'm not telling you anything you don't already know."

"When was the last time Bobby had a big strike?"

"Oh, Jeez," Ruby said, shaking his head.

"What do you call big?" Neff said.

"I don't know, Neff," I said. "What do *you* call big?"

"Big to him might be this Faulkner you're looking at. We'd give him thirty, forty bucks for that. Nothing to sneeze at if you got it for a quarter."

"Bigger than that," I said.

Ruby's eyes went into mock astonishment. "You mean like maybe he found *Tamerlane* in the Goodwill? Something like that, Dr. J?"

"Something like that."

"You're kidding."

They had stopped grinning now and were hanging on my next words. I let them wait, and finally Neff stepped into the breach.

"That's been done. Remember the guy who found *Tamerlane* in a bookstore for fifteen dollars a few years ago? Do you know what the odds are of that happening, anywhere in the world, twice in a lifetime?"

"I'm not talking about *Tamerlane,*" I said. "Just maybe something like it."

They both looked at me.

"What's going on, Dr. J?"

"Somebody beat Bobby's brains out last night."

"Holy Christ," Ruby said.

"Killed him, you mean," Neff said numbly.

I nodded.

"Now who the hell would do that?" Ruby said.

"That's what I'm trying to find out. Let's go back to what I asked you. When was the last time Bobby had a big strike?"

"Oh, hell, I can't remember," Ruby said. "Jesus, Dr. J, this's terrible."

"You're asking us when Bob might've had something somebody would kill him for," Neff said.

"Let's make like I'm asking you that."

"Hell, never," Ruby said.

Neff nodded immediately. "Even that big score he made a few years back, when he found all four of those big books in one weekend . . . I mean, that's the biggest score any of them ever make, and all four of those books don't add up to much more than two grand. Who'd kill a guy for that?"

"Some people, maybe," I said.

"Nobody I know," Ruby said. "Goddamn, this's terrible. I can't get over it."

"Let's say he had something worth two or three thousand," I said. "That's a lot of money to guys on the street."

"It's a lot of money to *me,*" Ruby said.

"But to a guy who lives like they live, it's more money than you'll ever see again in one place."

"You think that's what happened . . . Bobby found something and some other bookscout took it away from him?"

"I don't think anything," I said. "I'm trying to find out something and put it together with what I know. It's unlikely Bobby found anything worth a real fortune. You said so yourself. Pieces like *Tamerlane* don't just drop off trees into somebody's lap. The reason they're worth a quarter of a million dollars is because there are no copies out there to be found. A guy would have a better chance of winning the Irish Sweepstakes, right?"

"I'd give him a better chance," Ruby said.

"And yet it happens."

"In movies it happens."

"Once in a while it really happens."

"I'd sure hate to chase that down," Ruby said. "Talk about a needle in a goddamn haystack."

"On the other hand, if Bobby found something worth a few thousand, you'd have to ask yourself a different set of questions. Anybody might kill for a quarter of a million, but who'd kill for three grand?"

"Three grand wouldn't begin to solve my problems," Ruby said. "Hell, I owe the sheriff more than that."

"But it's a lot of money to a bookscout," I said.

"I see what you're saying."

"So," I said, "who did Bobby go around with?"

"Well, there's Peter. I've seen the two of 'em walking together, that's all. Doesn't mean they were fast and tight. Other than that, old Bob ran alone. I've never seen him with anybody else."

"Who's Peter?"

"I can't remember his last name. You remember it, Em?"

Neff shook his head.

"Just called him Peter the Bookscout, just like Bobby. Hell, half those boys never had a name, or don't want you to know it if they do."

"Does Peter come by often?"

"He was in here yesterday," Neff said.

"Comes in three or four times a month," Ruby said.

"When did you see Bobby and Peter together?"

"Oh, maybe a year ago," Ruby said. "They were going up to Boulder together, to a book sale. Bobby didn't drive, so he was hitching a ride with Peter."

"What do you mean Bobby didn't drive?" Neff said. "I've seen him drive. Don't you remember that old car he had?"

"That was a long time ago, pardner," Ruby said. "The cops busted him for no valid license, no insurance. He cracked up the car and ain't had one since. I know damn well he didn't have a license."

"I think you're wrong about that," Neff said.

"There was no driver's license found on the body," I said.

Neff shrugged. "Then I guess you're right."

"I know I'm right," Ruby said.

"Why would one bookscout drive another one up to a sale?" I said. "It sounds like cutting your own throat to me."

"That's what makes me think maybe they were friends," Ruby said. "At least as much as those guys get to be friends."

I made a note in my book. "Any idea where I can find this Peter?"

"The only time I see him is when he comes by," Ruby said.

"If he comes by again, tell him I want to see him."

"Sure, Dr. J. You bet."

I looked through my notes. There are many reasons why people get murdered, but 99 percent fall into four broad motive categories: love, hate, greed, insanity. I had looked at two of these.

"Did Bobby have any girlfriends?" I said.

"Not that I ever saw," Ruby said.

"He ever talk about women he knew, or might have known in the past?"

They shook their heads.

"Anybody you boys can think of who'd want to see Bobby dead?"

"Oh no," Neff said.

"He was the easiest of 'em all to deal with," Ruby said.

"Who'd he sell most of his books to?"

"Us, as much as anybody," Neff said.

"Not so much anymore, though," Ruby said.

"Why not?"

Neff gave a little shrug. "We've been going through some lean times, Mr. Janeway. We've had a few setbacks."

"Oh, let's call a spade a bloody fucking shovel," Ruby said. "We bounced a few checks on him. That's no big deal, people do it all the time. We always made it good. But these bookscouts hate to take a check anyway. They go all the way down to the bank and the check's no good. I know where they're coming from. I understand why they get pissed off."

"Then why do you do it?"

"You mean write a hot check? You know that, Dr. J, I know you do. It's book fever. You've got it just like I have. You see a book you want, you do what you have to do to get it. My intentions are honorable, it's my performance that lags a little."

"Where else did he go to sell his stuff?"

"Might be any one of a dozen places. You know the scene, Dr. J: hell, there's thirty bookstores in Denver. Probably half of 'em pay well enough for bookscouts to be able to deal with 'em. Not many places will pay forty percent across the board, but some do. You could narrow it down that way, I guess. Start with the boys up the street, see if they know anything."

I thought for a minute. Then I said, "Do either of you know where Bobby lived?"

"I do," Ruby said. "I drove him home a couple of times."

"You think you could show me where it's at?"

"Sure. You want to go now?"

"In an hour. I want to talk to the boys up the street first."

"I'll be here whenever you say. You better let me sell you this Faulkner before you leave. It's the world's best copy and it won't last long."

"How much?"

"For you . . . Today? . . . Ninety-five bucks."

Neff groaned as I reached for my checkbook. "Oh, what the hell," he said. "I get tired of selling Faulkner anyway."

6

I walked up the street carrying Mr. William Faulkner under my arm. The next store along the row was Book Heaven, owned by Jerry Harkness.

Denver is a young man's book town. In the old days there were only two dealers of note: Fred Rosenstock and Harley Bishop. Those boys died and the book trade fractured into twenty or thirty pieces. The new breed came in and the books changed as well. In Rosenstock's day you could still find documents signed by Abraham Lincoln or the framers of the Constitution. The trouble was, you couldn't get much for them. Forty years later, those papers and books are worth small fortunes but can't be found. What can be found, and sold for good money, is modern lit. We live in a day when first editions by Stephen King outsell Mark Twain firsts ten to one, and at the same price. You explain it: I can't. Maybe people today really do have more money than brains. Or maybe there's something in the King craze that's going over my head. I read *Misery* not long ago and thought it was a helluva book. I'd put it right up with *The Collector* as an example of the horror of abduction, and that's a heavy compliment since I consider Fowles one of the greatest living novelists. Then I read *Christine* and it was like the book had been written by a different guy. A bigger crock has never been put between two covers. What the hell do I know? I sure can't explain it when a book like *Salem's Lot* goes from $10 to almost $1,000 in ten years. That's half again what a near-perfect *Grapes of Wrath* will bring, if you need a point of reference. You can buy five copies of Hemingway's *Old Man and the Sea* for that, or six copies of Thomas Wolfe's *Of Time and the River.* You can buy first editions signed by Rudyard Kipling or Jack London for less money. So the business has changed, no question about it, and the people in it have changed as well. The old guard is dead: long live the new guard. But I can still remember old Harley Bishop, in the year before he died, stubbornly selling King firsts at half the original cover price. The big leap in King books hadn't yet happened, but even then *The Shining* was a $100 book. Bishop sold me a copy for $4. When I told him he should ask more, he gave me a furrowed look and said, "I don't believe in Steffan King."

Jerry Harkness most definitely did believe in Steffan King. He specialized in King and his followers—Dean Koontz, Clive Barker, et al., the little Kinglets. Behind every big ship you'll find a dozen little ships atrailing. Most of their plots make absolutely no sense, but again, they stand tall where it really matters in today's world, at the damn cash register. There's something seriously wrong with a society when its best-selling writer of all time is Janet Dailey. Don't ask me to prove it: it's just something I know. I don't mind a good scare story once in a while, but Jesus Christ, the junk that goes down! The stupidity of some of these plots that sell in the billions is the scariest thing about them. *The Exorcist* is a truly scary book because it only asks you to believe one thing—that Satan does exist. There are no talking dogs or curses lingering from antiquity: there's no literary sleight of hand, no metaphorical bullshit. Accept the guy's premise (and who can totally deny it?) and he's got you where you live. All it takes after that is talent. The trouble today (do I begin to sound like Mel Brooks's two-thousand-year-old man when I get on one of these soap boxes?) is that show biz is often mistaken for talent. Get to the end, though, and ask yourself what it all meant, what was it all about? The answer's usually nothing. Relieve the author from the obligation to make sense, and what's there to be afraid of?

I have come to the conclusion that the people who buy these books don't care much about books at all. You will seldom see a King guy or a Koontz guy browsing in a bookstore. I've been in Ruby's store and watched the action myself. A guy opens the door. He doesn't even come inside. He stands on the street with his head sticking in and asks his three questions. Got any King? Got any Koontz? Got any Barker? If the answer's no, he's gone. Ruby points him up the street, to Jerry Harkness, and later learns that the guy dropped two grand with Jerry. Unbelievable! What else can you say but absolute around-the-bend insanity? "All a guy needs to make it in this business," Ruby says, "is an unlimited amount of Stephen King."

Jerry Harkness had started in the book business as a teenager. He had worked for Harley Bishop and had learned the ropes, but had gone on to do things his own way. He knew his market and his people. His shop contained many items of general interest, but it was his horror, fantasy, and sword and sorcery sections that drew people from all over the country. Harkness had the only copy I've ever seen of the signed, very limited edition of King's *Firestarter*, a $3,000 piece.

Twenty years have passed since Harkness worked for old Harley Bishop. He must have been young then, full of dreams of this—his own business. I looked in the window and wondered, not for the first time, how the reality matched the dream. I might like it myself, if I weren't a cop, if I hadn't been born a cop. Where's the truth in that, I wondered: was I really born to wade through guts and mop up blood every Saturday night? Suddenly I had the strangest feeling of my life, almost what they call déjà vu in the superspook trade. *I have been here before. I have walked these paths and done these things.* I've missed my calling, I thought for the second time in ten hours. I've been a book dealer before, I'm a book dealer now, I already know more about books than 90 percent of the bozos in the trade. I've always thought I might be a book dealer someday, maybe when I retire. I had begun to put some things in storage for that distant day. Maybe it ain't so distant, I thought for the first time ever: maybe I'll just chuck all this crap and do it. I had already made one incredible buy, an act of good judgment that I'd be hard-pressed to duplicate. Almost fifteen years ago, I stumbled across John Nichols's *Milagro Beanfield War* on a B. Dalton's remainder table for ninety-nine cents. I read the book in a weekend and loved it, and I went all over town, to every Dalton's I could find, buying them up. They were all unmarked first editions. At the end of that week I had seventy-five copies. I was twenty-two years old when I did that. I've run into Nichols a few times over the years and he's always been happy to sign books. I had gotten about half of them signed. The book now goes for $150, probably $200 with a signature. I had at least $12,000 worth of books sitting in storage for my $75 investment. Maybe the time had come to do something with it.

Jerry Harkness was long and lean and still fighting the good fight against middle age. He perched on a stool behind his counter and watched me all the way past his front window and through the front door. He had been reading a Clive Barker paperback when I came along, and he put it aside for the customary greeting as I came in. I went straight to the counter and got to the point.

"When was the last time you saw Bobby Westfall?"

"You mean the bookscout? I don't see him, unless he's got something for me. He knows I don't buy stock from scouts. They want too much for the run-of-the-mill stuff. He comes in if he's got a King or a Burroughs, or maybe an early Gene Wolfe. He knows I'll pay him more than anybody if it's something good in my field."

"So you see him what . . . once a month?"

"If that. I did see him about two weeks ago. I think he was up the street trying to sell Ruby Seals some books. I don't know, he didn't bother showing 'em to me."

"Did he seem any different than he usually did?"

"I don't know how he usually seemed. These bookscouts are almost nonentities after you've seen 'em around awhile. I don't think about things like how they usually are. But since you asked me, I guess he seemed the same as ever."

"Which was what?"

"Quiet. Almost mousy. He just walked around looking at my stuff. That's how they learn, you know . . . look at the books on the shelves and see how they're priced. None of 'em ever have any reference books, they can't afford that, so they have to keep it all up here." He tapped himself on the head. "What's the matter? Bobby get himself in trouble?"

"Bobby got himself dead."

Harkness opened his mouth and it hung there for a moment.

"Did you ever talk to him?" I said.

"As a matter of fact, we passed a few words that day in the store."

"About what?"

"Usual run of stuff. How bad business is, on both his end and mine. This is the slow time of the year. I'm used to it. In the early summer, right after tax time, you'll go whole days without seeing more than ten people. Then a dealer will come through and drop five hundred, and in the end the figures balance out okay. But bookscouts have it tough. Books have been drying up. Even Goodwill is putting horrendous prices on their books lately. God, I wonder who'd kill Bobby."

I looked at him strangely. He got my drift and shrugged. "You're a homicide cop; I put two and two together and assumed he'd been murdered."

I nodded.

"I don't know what I can tell you. Bobby was singing the blues about those stupid asses at Goodwill. People are just plain greedy: they don't want to leave anything for anybody else, they don't want the next guy to make even a dime. Goodwill's trying to play bookstore again. They're a thrift store, for God's sake, and they put everything out at bookstore prices. They've got some clerk there who can't find her ass with both hands, and she's gonna figure out what a book's really worth. Right. Of course they get it all wrong. They go on weight and glitz. They'll put out some useless novel about two lesbians fighting for control of their dead aunt's cosmetics company for five dollars. Then they'll let a King first go for fifty cents."

"How does that hurt the bookscout?"

"It's the stock he makes his bread and butter on. You don't find Kings every day. What the bookscouts used to be able to do is grab up a handful of these glitzy titles for a buck apiece and double or triple their money in one of the big general bookstores. They can't do that anymore. Goodwill goes through this silliness once every three or four years. Somebody in the front office gets a wild hair up his ass and they start marking everything through the roof. After a while they learn they can't sell the damn things and they go back to the old prices. But while they're at it, guys like Bobby really hurt."

"So this is the gist of what Bobby was complaining about?"

"That's what he said to me."

"Did he give you any indication that he might've made a recent score?"

"Are you kidding? The way he was talking, he didn't have bus fare back downtown."

"Maybe he found something and hadn't had a chance to sell it yet."

"I doubt that. I don't think he had a prayer of seeing any money in the immediate future. He was just too down, too pissed off at the world."

"Who else did he do business with?"

"Almost everybody. You're gonna have to go to every bookstore in Denver if you want to touch all of Bobby's bases."

"But they have their favorite guys they sell to, isn't that right?"

"Sure. They all do that. They'll find a dealer who pays 'em well and they'll stick with that guy for a while. Then something happens— either they get pissed off or the dealer does—and they go somewhere else. But it's never perfect and eventually they come back. It's a vicious circle. When a book doesn't sell to anybody reputable, they wind up giving it away for pennies to jerks like the one two doors down."

"You mean Clyde Fix?"

"What an idiot. I wish we could get that junkman off the block."

"Can you think of anybody else Bobby might've sold to regularly?"

"I think he was in with Roland Goddard. Don't tell Goddard I sent you, though. He used to be my partner."

"I didn't know that."

"Oh, yeah. But don't bring it up. We don't get along now."

"How come?"

"You don't really want to get into that. It's ancient history."

"Humor me a little."

"When we were kids we both worked for Harley Bishop. Then we moved on to the Book Emporium, you remember, that big place that used to be on Fifteenth, across from Public Service? They closed it up and Goddard and I bought out the stock and used it to start our first store together. It didn't work out, that's all. We've got different aims in life, different tastes. At the bottom of it, we just didn't like each other. Sometimes you've got to go into business with somebody to find out how little you like each other. So we flipped a coin to see who would buy the other out. Goddard won. Or lost, depending on how you look at it."

"That's a pretty classy shop he's got."

"Yeah, but so what? Everything in life has a trade-off. He's got a great shop and a super location in Cherry Creek, probably makes two hundred grand a year. But the overhead's got to be unreal. Me, I was out of the business for a couple of years after the big coin flip, but I'm back again. I've got what I want."

"Can you think of anybody else I should see?"

"As a matter of fact, yeah. Go talk to Rita McKinley."

"Who's that?"

He raised his eyebrow. "You're a bookman in this town and you've never heard of Rita McKinley?"

"I guess I never did."

"Well, Officer Janeway, you've got a treat in store for you."

"Who's Rita McKinley?"

"She's got a closed shop in Evergreen. Appointment only, that kind of place. Operates out of her house."

"What's she got to do with Bobby?"

"I don't know, except when he was here he dropped a piece of paper with her name on it."

"You still got it?"

"Sure. I've been waiting for him to come in again so I could give it back to him." He reached into the cash drawer and took out a small sheet of notepaper. In pencil, someone had written the name and a phone number.

I looked at Harkness. "You ever met the lady?"

"She was in here once, a year or two ago. A real looker, young and pretty and sharp as a new brass tack. She knows books, brother. She knows as much as I do, and I'm talking about books in my field. You know what she did? Bought two copies of *Interview with the Vampire* out of here for fifty bucks apiece. That's what the son of a bitch was going for then. Now it's three hundred, and it's gonna go to five, I'll betcha. I'd love to have one of those babies back; hell, I'd pay her four times what she paid me. It's not often that somebody teaches me a lesson in my own field, but Rita McKinley did it. A real cool customer. And I got the feeling talking to her that she knows every field like that. And she can't be much over thirty."

"How long has she been up there?"

"A few years, I guess. I've never seen her place. She's goddamned intimidating if you want to know the truth. You don't just call her up because you're out for a drive some Sunday and you want to scout her shelves. At least I don't."

"How does she sell her books?"

"She's got clients who come in from out of town. Does mail order. And deals in very expensive stuff."

I wrote her name down.

"It doesn't sound logical, does it?" I said. "Her and Bobby?"

Harkness shrugged. "That's all I can tell you."

I believed him for the moment, and left.

There were two more dealers on Book Row. One was a specialist in collectible paperbacks, who kept odd hours. His store was closed. Near the end of the block was a junk shop called A-1 Books, owned by Clyde Fix. I had never dealt with Fix, for two reasons: I have never seen a book in his store that I wanted, and his hatred for cops was well known and documented. He and Jackie Newton might make a great pair that way, but that was the only way. While Jackie was carving out land deals, Clyde Fix was struggling to stay alive. Where Jackie had brains, Clyde Fix had only animal cunning. It was a safe bet that Clyde Fix had never heard of a Lamborghini: he clattered around town in a red '62 Ford that always seemed two miles from the scrap heap. He was in his forties, with thinning hair and a gaunt, consumptive profile. He had owned bookstores all over Denver in the last fifteen years, all of them dumps like this one. Ruby had known him for years. Before he had discovered books, Ruby said, Clyde Fix had been a seller of graveyard plots; before that, he had sold shoes. With books, he had found a way of keeping body and soul together without having to punch a time clock. There are lots of customers for cheap books, and a junkman in almost any kind of junk will usually make a living.

He had a deceptive manner: he could ooze charm and in the same moment turn on you like a snake. People who had never seen his bad side thought of him as a nice man; the rest of us knew better. Fix had been busted half a dozen times for disturbing the peace, and Traffic had pulled him in a few times for speeding. He always argued with the cop. He was his own worst enemy. Once, I knew, he had talked himself from a simple taillight violation to creating a disturbance and ultimately resisting arrest. Cops have a lot of discretion in things like that.

My interview was a short one. Fix was hostile, as I knew he would be, and he wouldn't give me much. He didn't seem to know or care that Bobby Westfall was dead. "Why should I worry over that fool? That's just one less fool out there working my territory."

"Where's your territory?" I asked.

"Wherever the hell I say it is."

I knew that mentality well. Beat me to a book and you're my enemy for life. Turn over all your best books to me. Sell that to me for ten cents on the dollar, and don't give me any damn guff about it either. Fix would intimidate if he could, cheat if he could do that. He'd buy a $1,000 book for a quarter, then laugh all year at the sucker who'd sold it to him.

It occurred to me suddenly that there was a lot of latent anger in the Denver book world. I could easily see Clyde Fix bashing Bobby's head in. But with Fix it wouldn't be calculated: more likely it would be a spur-of-the-moment thing, in broad daylight with fifteen witnesses looking on. They had had one run-in last year: the story had gone through the trade like a shot and quickly taken on the characteristics of an urban legend. I remembered it now and could almost see it: Bobby and Fix at the Goodwill store, both spotting a treasure nestled among the junk. James Crumley's *One to Count Cadence,* a $100 book then, two or three times that now. The mutual lunge, the struggle, the tumble into a counter of glassware, Fix coming up with the book, whirling and knocking a little old lady flat. The cops arrived, but Fix and Bobby were gone. So was the book.

I hassled him for a while: it was good for my constitution. Where were you last night, Fix? Anybody there with you? Can you prove where you were between ten o'clock and midnight? You didn't like Bobby much . . . did you kill him?

Pleasantries like that help get me through a dull day. If only I had something to do with my hands.

I moseyed back up the street. It was a quiet day on Book Row. At Seals & Neff a few customers had come and gone and the day was quickly settling into its inevitable, uneventful course. There was a young woman in the store, who had brought in a bag of books.

Bookscouts, like dealers, come in all sizes, colors, and sexes. This one was a cut above the others I had seen, at least in the category of looks, but it was clear from what was being said that she had more than a smattering of ignorance when it came to books.

Neff was explaining to her why her as-new copy of Faulkner's *The Reivers* wasn't a first edition. "But it says first edition," she protested. "Right here on the copyright page . . . look. First edition. How much clearer can it be than that? Random House always states first edition, right? You told me that yourself the last time I was in here. Now I've got a first edition and you're telling me it isn't a first edition. I don't know what to believe."

"Believe this, honey," Neff said. "I don't need the grief. If you think I'm trying to steal your book . . ."

"I didn't say that. I'm not accusing you, I just want to know."

"It's a Book-of-the-Month Club first," Neff said, enunciating each word with chilly distinction. "It's printed from the same plates as the first, or maybe the same sheets are even used; that's why it says first edition. But the binding is different, there's no price on the jacket, and the book has a blind stamp on the back board."

"What's a blind stamp?"

"A little dent, pressed right into the cloth. Look, I'll show you. You see that little stamp? That means it's a book club book. Whenever you see that, it came from a book club, even if it's written 'I'm a first edition' in Christ's own blood inside. Okay?"

She sighed. "I'll never learn this stuff. How much is it worth?"

"This book? Five bucks tops. There are eight million copies of this in the naked city."

"I *paid* more than that for it. Didn't I come in here last week and ask you what it was worth? You said fifty dollars. That's why I went and bought it."

"We're talking about two different animals. You asked me a question, I answered you. How was I supposed to know you couldn't tell one from the other?"

"I paid seven-fifty," she said sadly.

"You got rooked."

"Damn shit," she said.

"You tell her, Mr. Janeway," Neff said. "Lady, this guy is a Denver cop. Would a cop lie to you? He's a cop and he's also a damn good bookman. Show him the book."

She handed it to me. I looked at it and told her Neff was right. It was a $5 book and you had to pray mighty hard to ever get the five.

"Let me see your badge," she said. "You don't look like a cop to me."

I showed her my badge. She sagged in final defeat.

"It's a tough world, hon," Neff said.

"Don't give me that. I see some of the characters who sell you books. They don't look like any Einsteins to me. If they can do it, I know I can. I've got as much brains as they have."

"I'm sure that's true. The difference between you and them is that they've already made their mistakes."

"Seven dollars and fifty cents, shot to hell," she said. "Bet you won't even give me two for it."

"I can pick those things up in thrift stores all day long for fifty cents."

"Aw, give her the money," Ruby said, coming out from the back room. "We'll subsidize this mistake. Just don't make any more, and bring us all your good books first. Give her the seven-fifty, Em."

"No wonder we're going broke," Neff said.

"This'll pay big dividends down the road, I can feel it in my bones," Ruby said. "What's your name, lady?"

"Millie Farmer."

"Here—here's your money back. I'm taking a two-buck loss, that is if I ever sell the son of a bitch. Bring me a good book next time."

"I will," she said determinedly. "By God, you watch me."

"It's easy," Ruby said. "Like taking candy from a baby. When you see a box of books, don't take any bad ones and don't leave any good ones. That's all there is to it."

I had been taking all this in as a spectator. Now, at the end of it, I couldn't help shaking my head and asking her one question.

"Why would you want to be a bookscout?"

"I'm a teacher," she said. "Would you like to try to make it on what they pay you to teach third grade in this town? I need the extra money."

"All right," Neff said. "Stick around, I'll show you some ropes. It doesn't look like much else is gonna happen today."

"Ruby," I said, "I'm ready to go to Bobby's place if you are."

We picked up my car and headed down Seventeenth Avenue toward Capitol Hill. Ruby talked as we drove, a seemingly endless chain of stories about Bobby Westfall and his adventures in the book trade. Ruby knew all the scuttlebutt. "I can't believe the little bastard's dead," he said at one point. I told him he could believe it. "I sure hope you get the son of a bitch that did it, Dr. J," he said. I told him I would, but you never know about that. You just never know.

Bobby lived in one of those old tenements on Ogden Street. It was a garret, up three long flights of stairs. We stopped at the manager's on the ground floor. I showed him my badge and told him the news. He was shocked. The manager was about fifty: he wore a sweatshirt and had a dark, unhealthy look. His name was Marty Zimmers. I told him we'd need to see the apartment and he got his spare key. At the top of the stairs, I said, "I don't want you boys to touch anything. In fact, I think I'm gonna ask you to wait out here."

I opened the door and the cats came running. I went in alone.

It was a small place, one room with a kitchenette and a tiny bathroom. It was a maze of books, a veritable cave of books. There were books piled from the floor to the ceiling, books stacked around the hideaway bed he'd slept in, books on the toilet, on the kitchen counter. I could see at a glance it was mostly crap, the kind of things a bookscout buys on a wing and a prayer, because it's cheap, because he has a hunch that never pays off, because he makes mistakes. Millie Farmer ought to be here now, and see what it's really like, I thought. There were later printings and books without jackets and books with vast, unfixable problems. Later I'd have to go through every piece in this room on the off chance that, if Bobby had found something, it might still be here. For now the main job was to get the area secured.

"This the only key?" I called out into the hall.

Marty Zimmers stuck his head in. "Well, he had one."

"This is the only spare, though."

"That's it."

I gave the place one quick look-see before going down to call the lab. The only things that stood out were the cats and a cheap little notepad that he had used for a telephone book. I picked up the notebook carefully and thumbed through it. Everybody was in it, all the book dealers in Denver by name and address. For some he had home numbers. Ruby and Neff were there, both home numbers and the store. On the back page of the book he had scrawled "Rita McKinley," and a telephone exchange that I recognized as Evergreen, in the mountains. I checked it against the number on the paper that Bobby had dropped in Jerry Harkness's bookstore. The numbers were different. I copied the new number in my notebook and left Bobby's book on the rickety little table beside the bed.

In the manager's office I made my calls. The first was the new Rita McKinley number. It rang once and was answered by a machine. The cool female voice said, "You've reached 303-670-2665. No one's here now. Leave a message and I'll get back to you soon." The phone beeped. I didn't leave a message.

I tried the other number. A cutoff recording came on and said that the call could not be completed as dialed.

I called downtown. Hennessey had come in. I told him I was at Bobby's place and I gave him the address. "We'll need a crew over here to comb through things. You come supervise, will you? Tell them to leave the books for me. I want to go out and talk to some more book dealers."

"Will do. You had a couple of calls while you've been out. One of them might be important. Barbara Crowell."

"When did that come in?"

"Time on the message said one-fifteen. Just a few minutes ago."

"Did she say anything?"

"The dispatcher wrote 'urgent' on it, underlined in red. Said the woman sounded scared to death. But she wouldn't talk to anybody else."

"What's her number?"

He read it to me. I hung up and dialed it. Another goddamn answering machine.

"Hi, this's Barbara. I can't come to the phone right now, but . . ."

I slammed the phone down. I had a very dark vision suddenly. Jackie Newton walked over my grave.

"Ruby, I want you to stay here and keep Mr. Zimmers company. I'm leaving you the key, so you can give it to Hennessey when he comes. I don't want either one of you guys to go into that apartment. You understand what I'm saying?"

"I think I do, Dr. J."

"You boys need to vouch for each other that nobody's been up there between the time I left and when the cops came. Okay?"

"Sure. What're you gonna do?"

"I've got to be somewhere, right now."

Five minutes later I pulled up at Barbara Crowell's place on Pearl Street. The Lamborghini was parked out front.

The house where Barbara lived had two apartments on each floor. I parked in the loading zone behind Jackie Newton's car, got out, went inside, and started up the stairs. The place seemed like a mausoleum, still and deathly quiet. The steps creaked as I moved up, but that was the only sound until I got to the second floor and heard the radio. It was soft rock music, trickling faintly from above. I knew it was her radio playing—the apartment across the way was vacant. I took a grip on my gun and started up to the top. The radio came closer but still there were no voices. At her door I stopped and listened. Nothing. It was one of those *oh-hell* bad times in a cop's life. You want I should maybe knock on her door? Not this boy. I'd walk in and catch him in *flagrante delicto,* my only witness the terrified victim. Can't you just see it? *No, Your Honor. I didn't invite him in.* That's me she's talking about now, not Jackie Newton: we know from past experience what she'd say about a guy who could make her heart stop just by saying boo. *I asked Mr. Newton over to make up a quarrel we'd had. . . . I certainly didn't expect or want Detective Janeway to come walking into my bedroom. . . .*

Why couldn't she scream? Throw something against the wall? I'd take any help I could get, any way I could get it.

But there was only profound stillness and the refrain from *A Lover's Concerto* on the other side of the door.

Ah, fuck it. I turned the knob. It was unlocked. I pushed it just a crack, enough to see into the front room. The radio got suddenly louder and that was all. I could see it blaring away on a table across the room. I pushed the door a little wider and I could see through to the kitchen. Still nothing. Nothing. No . . . living . . . thing. The bedroom door across the room was closed. Here I come, ready or not. I pushed the door wide and stepped in, the gun pointing my way like a beacon. I saw that the wood had been shattered where she'd had a chain lock fastened. That had stopped him for all of twenty seconds. I took four long steps to the bedroom door and listened again. It wasn't going to happen, was it? They just weren't going to invite me to their little party. I stood on the verge of big trouble, a brilliant, silly line from James Jones running through my head. *They can kill you but they can't eat you.* I had news for Mr. Jones, whatever corner of Eternity he'd gone to. They could kill you, yes, and they could eat you too.

I opened the door. They weren't there.

They weren't anywhere.

The bed had been neatly made up, not a ripple showing on the pink-and-white spread.

I looked in the closet and found nothing I could call unreasonable. I looked in the bathroom. Finally I went into the kitchen and began to see what had happened. There was a door that opened onto an outside landing, and a wooden staircase that ran down the rear of the apartment house to a small parking lot. The door had been slammed open with such force that the glass was broken. I walked back into the main room, the gun still in my hand. The scenario was becoming fairly clear. The curtains were drawn back: the Lamborghini was parked directly below. Barbara had looked out this front window and had seen Jackie Newton down in the street. She had called me: when I wasn't there, she had hung up. The recorder had activated automatically, and here we were. She had panicked when she heard him coming up the stairs. She took the only way out—down the back way. The lock had bought her a few seconds, then he came through the door and went down after her. That's where they were now, playing a game of chase on the streets.

Probable cause had dropped in my lap like a plum. I had never been in here—that was my story before God, Mother, and the state of Colorado. I had come up on a response to a phone call. I had come to her door and knocked: when no one answered, I had gone away. If I happened to spot them in the course of cruising the neighborhood, if it looked to my casual eye like Barbara Crowell was being unlawfully pursued . . . well, events could take care of themselves.

I didn't think it would be hard to find them. Barbara had run without any money, it seemed—her handbag was still on the table beside the radio. She wouldn't be jumping into any buses or cabs, and I didn't think she'd be flagging any cops, either. There was too much fear in her: it was an old story to me, I had seen it so many times. As for Jackie Newton, he was out there in hog heaven. This was the kind of game he loved: the cat-and-mouse, the heading-off, the dodging up alleys and down side streets. Playing with people, working on their fear.

I went downstairs and opened my trunk. In the toolbox I found a rubber hammer and a punch. I flattened one of Jackie's tires and the Lamborghini sagged back on its haunch, hissing.

I drove in a widening circle, coming back to Pearl Street every few minutes to check on the Lamborghini. It took me twenty minutes to find them. I came upon Jackie on East Eighth Avenue, a few blocks from the governor's mansion. He was standing under a tree like a predator, watching. I drove on by. He didn't see me: like the leopard, his attention was fixed on the prey, on the place where the prey was hiding. I couldn't see it at first: all I knew was that she was there somewhere. I circled the block, parked the car, and got out. I walked to the corner and got behind a tree of my own. That's the way we did it for half an hour: Barbara hiding in a place unknown, Jackie watching her, me watching Jackie.

It was all a lot of fun till it started to rain.

I went back to the car and pulled into a vacant lot that had a clear view up Eighth. Jackie hadn't moved. He looked almost like a statue, every muscle chiseled in infinity. The rain fell. From a slight drizzle it had become a summer storm, water swirling in the street in the wind. It didn't seem to bother Jackie: he watched with an intensity that was almost scary, as if to watch all week, all year, wouldn't worry him a bit. Only once in that hour did he look up the street. But I was in an unmarked car, settled back with only my eyes above the dash, and he turned away none the wiser.

Rainstorms in Denver are often fast and furious. This one was over in forty minutes, becoming what had started it, a drizzle. I saw Barbara come out of a flower shop and look around nervously. Was he there? Of course. When someone scares you that bad, he's always there.

She had to do something, even if it was wrong. She walked to the corner, looked around again, and started up the block to the north.

Jackie leaped into action. He ran straight toward me, then doubled up the next block toward East Ninth Avenue. He was going to cut her off, try to get close enough to grab a wrist before she knew he was there. I started the car, drove up Eighth and hung a right. Barbara Crowell was half a block ahead, walking briskly. But she kept stopping and looking back, not trusting the evidence of her eyes that he was gone. Once she stood for half a minute, giving him plenty of time to get in place on Ninth. I had pulled to the curb about forty yards behind her, opposite side of the street. When she started up again, so did I.

I could see him now, a shadow behind a tree on Ninth near the corner. I don't think I knew what I was going to do until that moment. She had reached the corner and looked both ways. He was now no more than ten yards away and could have caught her easy. But no . . . he was waiting for the big shock when he could grab her after she thought she'd made it. He wanted to see the fright, the heartbreak on her face. She had stopped on Ninth to look around, and I got out of the car and gave her the high five sign.

I had my finger to my mouth, the universal gesture for quiet. I came up beside her and took her arm. With my other hand I got out my gun. I turned her east on Ninth, a course that would carry us right past the tree where he hid. She started to speak: I shushed her with a low hiss. The tree loomed up, then we were by it and Jackie leaped out. This all happened in less than five seconds. Jackie made a grab for my arm, still thinking it was Barbara he was grabbing. I said, "Hello, sweetheart," and jammed him in the ribs with the gun. I saw him start to swing and I brought the gun up and let him taste the barrel, hard. It knocked him down and split both lips. He rolled over in the grass and got to his feet. He stood like a panther ready to spring and I stood there waiting for him.

Then nothing happened. He didn't say a word: his eyes said it all. You are dead, Janeway, his eyes said, you are one dead cop. He had me quaking like Mount Saint Helens. With his eyes, Jackie said, I don't know when, I don't know how, but I am gonna bury you. With my mouth, I said, "I told you before, Newton, you better fix that door." He didn't think that was funny. He turned his evil eye on Barbara. She couldn't look at him: her skin had gone white with goose bumps. I stepped in front of her and locked eyes with Jackie for what seemed like forever. He turned and walked away first. He was going up the hill toward her place, where his car was parked.

"Come on," I said. "We'll go a different way."

Again she had been taken by a fit of shivering. I draped my coat over her shoulders. "I'm gonna have to start charging you rent for this coat," I said. It didn't cheer her up. We cut up alleys and went in the back way to her place. I sat her on the couch and put on a pot of water for instant coffee. While it was coming to a boil I went to the window and looked down where Jackie Newton had discovered his flat tire. I saw him throw his jack halfway across the street, then flip off a passing driver who had blown his horn. He was a bad son of a bitch, Jackie. All that remained to be seen was how bad.

8

I got the coffee down from a cupboard. I found her liquor cabinet and stirred in a generous shot of brandy. She sipped it, then sat staring at the oval rug under her feet. I went to the window to check on Jackie's progress. He was still in the stage of initial disgust and hadn't done much yet. I should've punched two out, or maybe all four, I thought.

"How you feeling now?" I asked without turning away from Jackie.

Numbly, she said, "Why is this happening?"

"You're letting it happen."

I turned in time to see the anger in her eyes. But she didn't say anything.

"You've got to play his game by his rules," I said. "He's like a bully in a schoolyard. Either you stand up to him or he kills you, piece by piece, day by day."

Her voice trembled, from anger, fear, or both. "How the fuck do I stand up to *that?*" she shouted.

"Start showing him you mean what you say."

She shivered, drawing my coat tight around her neck. "A week ago I'd never heard of the goddamn man. Now he's got control of my life."

"Take it back."

"You keep saying that. I'm sick of it. It's easy for you to say."

"I didn't say it was easy. But it may be your only choice."

"Then tell me, please, what exactly do you want me to do?"

"Show some guts, Barbara. Maybe it'll get you killed, but how do you know this won't?"

I got her some more coffee. She had finished the first cup and it seemed to be doing her some good. Her shivers had subsided and in another minute she let my coat hang loose on her shoulders.

"For starters," I said, "if he ever touches you again, get the cops involved. Don't just hang up because I'm not there. I'm a homicide cop; you don't need me here unless he kills you. There are other cops who handle this kind of stuff. I'll give you some names; I'll grease the skids downtown so you'll get priority treatment. In other words, I'll do what I can."

She shook her head.

"Look, you had a start on him this morning, then you let him get away. He raped you. What you should've done right then was go to the hospital. Swear out a warrant. Let him cool his heels in jail for a few hours. Take him to Denver District Court. Take him all the way. If you get one of those lemon-suckers on the bench, he gets off. But at least he knows you're ready to play hardball."

"Which means I go to the morgue next time."

"Or maybe there won't be a next time. I've got a theory about our friend Jackie. If you show a white flag, he'll tear you to pieces. Jackie takes no prisoners: he loves to take on people who won't fight back. If you do fight, he'll give you a hard look before he comes back again."

"I think you're wrong. I think he takes it very personally when you fight. I think he's going to kill you for what you did to him today."

"I'm not gonna argue with you. I didn't become a cop because of my grades in psych. You asked me what to do and I told you. Rack his ass if he blinks at you twice. Get yourself a restraining order and then the cops can bust him if he doesn't leave you alone. That's the first step."

"And the last. Oh, Christ, you can't protect me."

"We can try. We can do the best we can do."

"Then what? You can't take me by the hand and walk me to work. You can't sleep with me. . . ."

We looked at each other. She said, "What if you do the best you can do and it still isn't good enough? What do I do then, challenge him to a duel? Quit my job and leave my friends and start over in another state?"

"I got no guarantees, ma'am. All I can do is tell you this—I'm on your side and so is the police department. We got a guy out there who thinks he's one tough cowboy. Our job is to show him he isn't. There are many ways of doing this, and some of them you don't need to know about."

She took a deep breath. "It's really bad between you two, isn't it?"

I gave her my sour little smile in return.

I told her I'd be back in a minute. I had looked out the window and seen that Jackie Newton was now hard at work on his flat tire. I didn't want him to leave without saying good-bye.

I went down and sat on the coping and watched him work.

Jackie was into his silent act. It was supposed to be intimidating, and I guess it was. He knew I was there: I could tell by the way he breathed. He had scraped his hand and blood had oozed out between his knuckles.

I started a running line of chatter, thinking it would annoy him.

"I sure wouldn't leave a car like that on the street," I said pleasantly. "You never know when you'll come back and find a door kicked in."

He grunted over his lugs. I heard them squeak as he jerked on the lug wrench.

"There're gangs around who do stuff like that," I said. "Just bash up expensive automobiles."

His lugs squeaked.

"Scumbags," I said. "Everywhere you go."

Squeak.

"It's getting so you can't do anything without running into some scumbucket who wants to take away a piece of your life."

Squeak.

"Take the lady who lives here," I said. "There's a certain asshole I know who won't leave her alone. Tries to screw around with her head, make her wish she'd never been born. What do you think of a man who'd do something like that?"

Squeak-squeak.

"Some man, huh?"

Squeak.

"Tighten those things too tight and you'll have a helluva time getting them off again."

There was a sharp clang as he threw the lug wrench down on the street.

"Never know when you'll have another flat."

He came around and let the car's weight jiggle down off the jack. Then he stood up tall and gave me a look. His face was a mess: blood had dripped onto his fine white shirt and his hair for once was tousled. He threw the tire and jack into the car and made ready to go.

"When this guy comes back again, he's gonna pay a heavy price," I said. "A real heavy price."

He pulled up the door and stood there for a minute. I thought he might say something then but he didn't. He ducked his head and got in his car, and I stood up and backed away under the shadows of the front porch. You never knew when a guy might have a piece hidden in the car, and if something serious started I wanted some cover.

But he drove away. Calmly. Like a man of reason. He didn't even peel rubber.

A real scary guy, Jackie. A bad son of a bitch.

I knew an old man once who swore he saw a sailor beat the hell out of Gene Tunney in a barroom brawl. Tunney was at his peak then, the heavyweight champion of the world. Titles don't mean much when you're getting your lunch eaten.

The meanest son of a bitch in the world can only be the meanest while he's at his absolute peak and the other guy hasn't quite come up to his. Say a month on the long end, a few minutes on the short.

I know guys who could make Jackie Newton wish his mamma had never set eyes on his daddy. I grew up with one of them. Vincent Marranzino wrote the book on tough guys. I haven't seen Vince in a long time: his life and mine have taken different paths and we both understand that. But Vince still owes me one—a certain fight with knives in a north Denver backlot when we were sixteen. I had taken his side against a pack of wolves and the two of us had kicked ass against great odds. Guys like Vince never forget something like that: they have a streak of loyalty that goes to bedrock.

A simple phone call was all it would take. Before morning, Jackie Newton's anatomy would be rearranged.

Tempting, isn't it?

A nice hole card, if the system couldn't be made to work.

This was what I had meant when I told Barbara that there were things in life she'd be better off not knowing. The genie was out of the bottle, just a phone call away.

But of course I wouldn't do it. Like Brutus, I am an honorable man.

9

I spent another futile hour with Barbara Crowell. There's no way to talk common sense to someone who's that scared, so there wasn't much else to do but wait for the locksmith to come fix her door. While I waited, I made some calls on the Bobby Westfall case. I called Bobby's apartment and talked to Hennessey. Our boys had been there for an hour and weren't finding much. They had lifted some prints, probably the victim's, and had arranged for the pound to come pick up the cats. They had sent Ruby Seals back to his bookstore in a police car. It didn't look like the apartment was going to give us much. There were still piles of books to go through, but that would take a bookman's eye—my job, and I'd be at it far into the night.

I tried Rita McKinley: same answering machine, same message.

I sat with the telephone book opened to "Book Dealers, Used and Rare," and I went through the stores in my mind. Some eliminated themselves from my priority list—junk shops, paperback exchanges, dealers in comic books: these I'd get to, eventually, if something didn't pan out higher up. I called Roland Goddard in Cherry Creek and told him I wanted to see him tomorrow about the murder of Bobby Westfall. There was no use pussyfooting around anymore. The book world is amazingly tight, and even now the word of Bobby's death would be racing from one store to another. By tomorrow it would be all over town.

I called three or four other dealers who might have bought books from Bobby. All of them had. I told them I'd want to see them, and would try to stop in in the next couple of days.

This was going to be a long haul.

I tried calling Carol, to tell her I'd be late tonight. She was out on the streets and I didn't want to leave a message. The only world tighter than the world of books is the world of cops.

The locksmith had fixed Barbara's back door and was installing a deadbolt in the front. Nobody was coming through that door once that baby was put in, the locksmith said. I wasn't too sure of that, but I didn't say anything.

I went back to Bobby's place. The boys were gone, all but Hennessey. We sat and talked the case out, as it stood to now. It didn't stand anywhere. We had nothing: we were shooting in the dark. We might be dealing with something totally outside Bobby's book-dealing activity, and in that case it might never be solved.

Hennessey had talked to the coroner, and the guesswork of last night had been confirmed. Bobby was killed somewhere else, then dumped in the alley. Time of death was sometime between eleven o'clock and midnight. This told us nothing, as we had been going on that assumption anyway. "Let's forget about it till morning," Hennessey said. "Come on home with me, we're having a big pot roast tonight." I took a rain check: I wanted to get started on Bobby's things, and I knew that I wouldn't stop till the last scrap of paper had been sifted to the watermark. This is just the way I work. It made Hennessey feel guilty, but that's life. "I should stay here and help you, Cliff," he said. "I'd probably just get in your way. I don't know from Shinola about this stuff." I agreed and told him to go home. It was getting dark outside. I hadn't eaten in more than twelve hours, so I asked Marty Zimmers to call Domino's and have a deep pan pizza and a bucket of swill sent over. Then I got to work.

It was a long, thankless job. You wouldn't believe the crap that accumulates in a bookscout's den. Book after book came down from the pile and went into another pile that I had labeled "Junk" in my mind. I thumbed each piece carefully, I went page by page to make sure a $50,000 pamphlet wasn't hidden inside a $2 book. It wasn't. There were some real heartbreakers—a fine little Faulkner poem, original 1932 issue, paper wraps, a $250 piece that Bobby could've sold to me on the spot except that someone had lost his supper on the title page . . . an early Steinbeck, nice, except that somebody had ripped out the title page . . . Robert Frost's first book, inscribed by Frost on the half title, very quaint except that a kid had been at the book with crayons. There were so many books eaten by mold that I had to wash my hands after handling them. My pizza came and I washed my hands again. I went munching and sorting my way into the early night. At nine-thirty I seemed to be about half through. I went downstairs and called Carol, told her I'd be another two or three hours, and said she'd better not wait up.

I chugged my swill, burped, and went back to it.

I was resigned by then to coming up zero. I took a break at ten-thirty and let my eyes skim over the books as a lot. If there was anything worthwhile in that mess, I sure couldn't see it. I started on the books in the toilet. Nothing. I was mucking it out pretty good now. There were a few papers in the closet and some books in the kitchenette. No great secrets were hidden there that I could see. Nothing the Russians would kill for: nothing anybody would kill for. Slowly the one natural motive—that Bobby had found something valuable—was dwindling before my eyes. Of course, the killer might've taken it away with him: I was going on the slim, bare hope that he had killed Bobby and had failed to find what he had killed for. But I was beginning to believe it was something as simple, and insane, as an old grudge, or a sudden fight between rivals.

Then I found the good books.

There were two stacks of them in the cupboard in the kitchenette. They stood like sentinels, acting as bookends for the Cheerios and the Rice Chex. The first thing I noticed was the quality. There were some very good pieces, some real honeys. I took them into the living room and sat with them, browsing. There were fifteen titles, and I made a list, adding my own idea of what they were worth.

Gardner, Erle Stanley. Case of Dangerous Dowager. *$200*.
Finney, Jack. Time & Again. *$150*.
Uris, Leon. Battle Cry. *$150*.
Kennedy, William. The Ink Truck. *$200-250*.
McMurtry, Larry. Last Picture Show. *$200*.
Heinlein, Robert A. Glory Road. *$250*.
Cain, James M. Postman. *A biggie—maybe a grand*.
Bellow, Saul. Augie March. *Buck and a quarter*.
Jackson, Shirley. The Lottery. *$150*.
Bradbury, Ray. Illustrated Man. *$200*.
Miller, Henry. Books in My Life. *$100*.

Isherwood, Christopher. Berlin Stories, *signed by C. I. $150.*
Irving, John. 150-Pound Marriage. *$200.*
Bloch, Robert. Psycho. *$200.*
Rawlings, Marjorie. The Yearling. *$150.*

I did a quick tally. Call it three grand retail and put me down as momentarily confused. When we last saw Bobby Westfall, through the eyes of Jerry Harkness, Ruby Seals, et cetera, he was broke, pissed off, and without hope. Books had been drying up: Harkness doubted that Bobby even had bus fare back downtown. That was two weeks ago, and now I had discovered a stash of books, extremely whole-salable at a thousand dollars. There was simply no way for this stack to have been scouted in two weeks, probably not in two years. I looked at it again. No way, I thought. Even a titan of bookscouts couldn't've done it piecemeal. So where did they come from and what did it mean? Here were the possibilities that initially occurred to me.

Bobby had come upon them as a lot, sometime within the past ten days, and had stolen them from some ignorant soul for pennies.

He had literally stolen them.

He had been hoarding them for a long time.

It was possible, I guessed, though not likely, that he had been hoarding books. There are people like that, guys who pigeonhole things for a specific reason and then have the willpower—no matter how bad the times are—never to touch the stash. Say Bobby had been building this pile for three or four years. When he found a book he particularly liked, it went into the Good Pile marked NFS, not for sale. Sometimes he had to sell books that he'd like to've put there, but once a book actually went in the cupboard he never, ever took it out again.

That made sense, didn't it?

I looked at the books again, singly and as a group. Hoarding was possible, but thievery was likely. Bobby had shafted someone; then that someone had found out what the books were really worth and had come after Bobby with a crescent wrench. Maybe, maybe. I stared at the books and let my mind play with them. Common denominators, I thought. For one thing, they were all modern lit. They were all easily disposable—any bookstore worth the name would buy any or all at 40 percent. I revised my estimate of condition

upward. These were uniformly pristine. There wasn't a tear anywhere: even on the Cain and Gardner and Rawlings, the three oldest,
the jackets were fresh and bright and had minimal sun fading to the
spines. Three grand might actually be very low retail for stuff this
nice: books don't come along every day in this condition. So Bobby
had a standard, if I wanted to go back to the hoarding theory, and
that was another common denominator. Nothing went in here unless
it was damn near perfect. One hundred retail seemed to be the cutoff
point on the low end. There was a healthy mix of mainstream and
genre fiction, but you had to keep going back to one sure thing: the
books were all desirable, all eminently salable.

Now I began to examine them page by page. Tucked into a back
page of *The Last Picture Show,* I found the sheath of notes.

They were figures, chicken scratches, columns of multiplication
like a kid might have to do for homework. There were lots of figures
on four separate sheets. The sheets were small, the kind you might
tear off a memo pad. At the top of each was a printed name: Rita
McKinley. She had signed each with scribbled initials. One had some
writing at the bottom. It said: "These are the good ones. Not much
gold, I'm afraid, for all the mining. R.M." I took the papers, handling
them carefully, and dropped them into an envelope. Then I put the
books back in the cupboard, closed the door on them, and turned off
the kitchen light. I felt an almost physical pain leaving them there.

Good thing I'm an honest cop.

I drank the last of my swill, and that pretty well threw a wrap on it.

I picked up Bobby's little address book and put it in my pocket
along with the Rita McKinley notes. I turned off the light in the bathroom and felt the first wave of weariness wash over my aging bones.

Then I heard a noise, a creaking sound, like a man trying to be
quiet.

I waited. It came again, then died and went away.

I listened.

Rats, maybe?

Rats with two legs.

I took out my gun and eased up to the door. I put my head against
it and in a minute I heard it again. Someone had come up the steps
and was standing just outside in the hallway.

I leveled the gun and ripped open the door.

He let out a yell and cringed back against the stairwell.

"Jesus Christ, Dr. J! God Almighty, don't shoot me!"

I sighed and put the gun away. "Ruby, what the hell are you doing here?"

He held up his hand and with the other hand clutched his heart. "Jesus, you scared me out of ten years' growth. You better let me come in and take a leak before I lose it right here in the hall."

"Not in here you don't. What the hell are you doing here?"

"I came up to see if I could help."

I looked at him.

"Swear to God, Dr. J. I was over to some friends, shootin' the shit and listenin' to some old Dylan records. We just broke up. I drove by and saw the light on and I figured it was you. Thought you might be able to use a hand, you know, from somebody who's been around the Cape and knows his books."

"You know better than that. Look, I appreciate the thought, but you can't come in here. I thought I made that clear this afternoon."

"Yeah, but the cops've already gone through the place. What do I know about police procedure? I just thought a question might pop up that you couldn't pin down for yourself. The last thing I want to do is get in the way. I want you to catch the prick that did this, that's all I want."

"All right, Ruby. I'm sorry I scared you."

"Took ten years off my goddamn life is all."

"Just stay away from here. Don't even think of stopping here again. If I need any help, I'll come to you."

"That's all I want, just to help out. You know how tricky this stuff can be, trying to figure out what's what in books. I know you're pretty good, Dr. J, but a real bookman could maybe help you knock some time off the clock."

"All right," I said. "I'll call you if I need you."

"You think it'd be okay if I took a leak? I got a sudden urgent need, Dr. J, and that's no lie."

"I'll have to watch you."

"Hey, I ain't proud."

I walked him through to the bathroom. I lifted the lid on the toilet and stood back in the doorway while he did his business. His eyes ran down the book titles on the back of the toilet, a natural bookseller's habit.

"Some crap," he said.

"Yeah."

He zipped up his pants and flushed the toilet. "Thanks, Dr. J."

We walked back to the door. Suddenly, I said, "What do you know about Rita McKinley?"

"The ice lady?"

"Is that what you call her?"

"That's what everybody calls her. Once every year or so she makes a sweep through all the Denver stores. Drops a ton of dough. Buys anything unusual but cherry-picks like hell. She's got the best eye I've ever seen. Won't touch a book with a bumped corner, no matter how much it's got going for it. She won't take anything that's got even a little problem, but doesn't mind paying top money for those perfect pieces."

"And that, I guess, is why she's called the ice lady."

"That's part of it. The other part is that people in the trade think she's got a cold shoulder. She don't stand over the counter engaging in mindless bullshit. She don't seem to be interested in shoptalk at all."

"How do you like her?"

"Man, I love her. I wish she'd come twice a week; maybe then I could get out of the poorhouse. She's not bad-looking, either. Brightens up the joint while she's in there."

"How come I never heard of her before today?"

"Beats me. Maybe 'cause she don't do retail."

"How long's she been here?"

"In Denver? I don't know, a few years I guess."

"Where'd she come from?"

"Back east, I think. Hell, I don't know. I don't exactly ask her this stuff when she comes in."

"When was she in last?"

"It's been a while . . . maybe a year? Longer than usual. I remember that last time because we had some great stuff for her. She dropped six grand in our place alone. Man, what I could do with six grand now."

"What else do you know about her?"

"Not a damn thing, really. Is she mixed up in this?"

"That's what I'm trying to find out."

"It don't make much sense to me. I mean, Bobby Westfall and Rita McKinley? It just don't play in Peoria."

I had said the same thing a few hours before. But the human comedy makes some strange whistle-stops on the way to Peoria.

I kept looking at him, encouraging him.

"Look, Dr. J . . . almost anything you hear about Rita McKinley is gonna be rumors. Nobody knows her well enough to talk about her. That doesn't stop 'em from talking anyway, though. Sure, I hear some shit. You can't help but pick up stuff in this business, but I hate to spread trash about people when I really don't know. You see what I'm saying?"

"Ruby, I've got a dead man and no suspects. You see what I'm saying?"

He sighed. "Some people think she's a gold digger."

"What people?"

"Who the hell knows where something like that starts? One day you just start hearing it. If you hear it enough, you might even start believing it."

I looked at him.

He shuffled and said, "For one thing, she didn't always have money. Didn't always have books. She's got a lot of both now. I know plenty of rich book dealers, but very few who started with no money. It's hard to work your way up in this business without a bankroll to start with. There are damn few ways, inside the law, to get that much money and that many good books in that short a time . . . divine intervention excluded."

"Where do people think she got 'em?"

"Oh, everybody knows where she got 'em. There wasn't any mystery about that—it was all wrapped up in a big *AB* spread a few years ago. What nobody knows is the circumstances of that deal. That's what the mystery is. What I remember about it is this. She had been dating a book collector. She moved in with him. He died, and when he went he left her everything—books, estate, money—the whole works."

"Was this man old?"

"I don't think so."

"Do you know anything about when and where he died?"

He shook his head. "I can't remember. You could write to the *AB*, I'm sure they'd send you the article. There was another piece about Rita McKinley when she moved her stuff here and opened her business. I remember reading it. It wasn't much of a piece, just a little one-column job saying she had come here and was open for business . . . about three, four years ago. The guy's name escapes me just now . . . I ought to remember it; he was a good enough collector that the *AB* devoted two pages to his death."

"Did the article say how he died?"

"Sure. That's the part that keeps the tongues wagging. He killed himself."

10

Ruby's visit to Bobby Westfall's apartment bothered me, and on second thought I decided to take the good books along with me when I left. Carol was sitting by the bed reading Faulkner when I came in. I put Bobby's books on the floor and pushed the bag containing her birthday present behind the stack.

"Hi," she said. "What's that you've got there?"

"Just some stuff for the evidence room. I didn't want to leave it in that empty apartment."

She came over and looked. "These are valuable?"

"Yeah, but this is all of it. The rest is like total junk." I looked at my watch: it was one-fifteen. "What're you still doing up?"

"Couldn't sleep. What's your excuse?"

"Liftin' that barge. Totin' that bale . . . payin' my debt to the company store."

"So how was your day?"

"Ducky."

"Did I ever tell you, Clifford, that the thing I love best about you is your communications skill? Did you go out to see Newton?"

"Uh-huh."

She sighed and rolled her eyes. *"And?"*

"He's gonna be my date at the policeman's ball."

"Wonderful. You girls will look great together."

"Look, I'm sorry. I'd really rather talk about the cockroach problem some other time. Right now I'm gonna grab a shower and mount a major assault with heavy artillery on your body."

Later, in bed, she lay in the crook of my arm. She was a great lover, good for what ailed me after a twenty-four-hour shift. Now, I thought, I could sleep. But again I found myself thinking about us, our situation, permanence, and me. I was in the middle of a vast sea change. I wondered what she would think of me if I suddenly wasn't a cop anymore. She had been a tomboy: being a cop was all she'd ever wanted. She had never mentioned children: we had simply never talked of it. In my mind I could hear her saying, I've got to tell you, Cliff, I don't want kids—I'm just not cut out for the motherhood bit. I could see her staring in disbelief when I told her I'd rather be a bookman, I think, than a cop, and not thirty years from now. Maybe she wouldn't do any of those things. She had been in the department long enough now—almost eight years—to be building up her own case of burnout. Maybe she was getting ready to hear what I was thinking but was still not inclined to talk about it.

"What're you thinking?" she said.

"Think I'm gonna turn in my badge and become a book dealer," I said.

But I said this in a safe, singsong voice, the same tone you use when you say you're going to the policeman's ball with Jackie Newton. She couldn't do much with it but laugh.

Only she didn't laugh. She just lay there in my arm and we didn't speak again for a long time.

It was the telephone that finally broke the spell.

"God Almighty," I said wearily. "If that's Hennessey I'll kill the bastard."

"I'll get it," she said, reaching over me. "I'll tell him you've died and the funeral's the day after tomorrow."

She picked up the phone. I heard her say hello and then there was a long silence. Without saying another word, she hung up.

"What's that all about?"

"A guy trying to sell me a water softener."

"At two o'clock in the morning?"

She didn't say anything.

"What's going on?" I said.

"I seem to've got myself a heavy breather. That's why I couldn't sleep. It started about eight o'clock and he's been calling back every hour or two."

"Does he say anything?"

"He whispered once."

"What'd he say?"

"The usual stuff. Cunt, bitch, whore. Some other stuff."

"Did he say anything personal . . . anything to indicate that he might know who you are?"

"Why would he know who I am? Those kinds of calls are mostly random, you know that."

"I don't think this one is."

She sat up and turned on the light.

"What happened out there today?"

I told her about my day with Jackie. I could see it wasn't convincing her that Jackie had taken up telephone harassment for revenge.

"I'm taking the phone off," she said. "If you don't get some sleep you'll be a zombie tomorrow."

The phone rang.

"Let it go," she said. "He'll get tired of it and hang up."

But I picked it up. Didn't say anything, just listened. He was there, listening too. This went on for almost a minute. Then I said, "You having fun, Newton?"

He hung up.

"It's Newton," I said. "He hung up when I called him by name."

"That doesn't mean anything."

"All right, then, I can smell the son of a bitch, okay?"

"Okay, Cliff. I'm sure not going to argue about it at two o'clock in the morning."

"Listen," I said sometime later. "Jackie and me, we shifted gears out there today. There never was any love lost between us, you know that. But it's different now, it's on a whole new plain."

She had propped herself up on one arm, a silhouette against the window.

"He'll do whatever he can to get at me. I don't think it matters to him that I'm a cop, or that you are. I don't think anything matters. It's him and me."

"Hatfields and McCoys."

"Yeah. It's gotten that deep. I may've given Barbara Crowell some very bad advice today."

"Cliff, you need a vacation."

"I need to get something on that weasel. That's the only vacation I need. To get him good and make it stick."

"You're a classic type A, you'll die before you're forty. You need to go and lie on a beach and listen to tropical breezes blowing through luscious palm trees."

"And go crazy with boredom. That's not what I need."

"I'd go along too . . . try to keep you from getting too bored."

More long minutes passed.

"I'll do whatever I can," Carol said.

"As a matter of fact, there is something you can do."

"Just tell me."

"Get the hell out of here."

"Oh, Cliff, that's not going to help anything."

"I've been thinking about it all day, ever since I gave Jackie the thirty-eight-caliber lollipop. Newton doesn't know who you are. All he knows is, he called my place and a woman answered. Nobody knows about us. We've taken a lot of trouble to keep what's ours private."

She took a deep, long-suffering breath.

"Well? Will you do it?"

"Of course I'll do it," she said. "But God damn it, don't ask me to like it."

I patted her rump. "Good girl."

"You sexist bastard."

We laughed. At that moment I came as close to asking her the big question as I ever would.

It was a long time before we got to sleep. When I did sleep, I slept soundly, untroubled by dreams. In the morning we got her things together and I carried them down the back way and put them in her car. I watched the street for ten minutes before I let her come down and drive away.

She rolled down her window. "I'm not afraid, you know."

"I know you're not," I said. "But I am."

11

I called Rita McKinley and got the same recording. This time I left a message, telling her who I was and that I needed to speak with her on official business regarding a homicide investigation. I left both numbers, home and office.

I called the *AB* in New Jersey. Also known as *Bookman's Weekly*, the *AB* is the trade journal of the antiquarian book world. Each week it lists hundreds of books, sought and for sale by dealers everywhere. Thus can a total recluse operate effectively in the book business without ever seeing another human being: he buys and sells through the *AB*. In addition to the listings, which take up most of the magazine, there are a few articles each week on doings in the trade—obits, career profiles, book fair reports. Sometime during the past few years, I explained to the editor, a piece or pieces were run on Rita McKinley. He was a wise gentleman who knew his business, and he knew right away who McKinley was and about when the stories had run. He promised copies in the next mail.

I went to see Roland Goddard, in Cherry Creek. This is a neighborhood of high-class and expensive shops in east Denver. Nestled in the center of things was Roland Goddard's Acushnet Rare Book Emporium. Goddard had a cool, austere manner, almost like Emery Neff only somehow different. You could break through with Neff, if you were patient enough and gave a damn: with Goddard, you never could. He had an icy, slightly superior attitude about books and his knowledge of them, and he could intimidate a customer or a bookscout before the first word was said. If he had friends, they were not in the book business: no one I had ever spoken to knew Goddard personally.

It would be hard to imagine two guys less alike than Goddard and Harkness. At least with Ruby Seals and Emery Neff, their differences seemed to complement each other: Harkness and Goddard

were ill-suited for partnership in almost every way. It's hard sometimes to look back over twenty years and know why the boys we
were then did things so much at odds with the attitudes and philoso-
phies of the men we had become. Goddard was fastidious: Harkness
tended to be sloppy. Goddard disdained everything about the book
business that Harkness found interesting. Oh, he'd sell you a
Stephen King—whatever else you could say about Roland Goddard,
he was a helluva bookman and he knew where the money came
from—but you might leave his store feeling faintly like a moron.

Goddard dealt primarily in Truly Important Books—incunabula,
sixteenth-century poetry, illuminated manuscripts, fine leather stuff.
He had some great things. Even the name of his store simmered in
tradition. *Acushnet* was the whaler Melville served on in the 1840s.
I liked his store and I loved his stock, though I never did much business there. When I marry one of the Rockefellers, Goddard will have
a big payday, most of it from me.

Acushnet was one of only three bookstores in Denver that could
afford full-time help. The man who worked there was Julian Lambert,
a good bookman in his own right. Lambert bought and sold as freely
as his boss did: Ruby, in fact, had told me once that bookscouts pre-
ferred dealing with Goddard because he paid them more. Goddard
wasn't in when I arrived, but I busied myself looking through the stock
until I saw him come in through a back entrance. The morning rush
had waned: he and Lambert sat behind the counter cataloging. I knew
that Goddard issued catalogs a few times a year, though no one in Denver ever saw one. He had the best reference library in the state, but
played it close to the vest when it came to sharing information.

Goddard and Lambert were surprised when I introduced myself. I
knew they had seen me around—we had spoken a few times in
passing—but until this moment they had not put my face together
with the Detective Janeway who had called on the phone and asked to
see them. I got right down to cases. When was the last time they had
seen Bobby Westfall? The same questions, the same answers, with
Goddard doing most of the talking. It had been almost two weeks
since Bobby had been in. He had come in one day just about the time
he was last seen on Book Row. "He had a couple of books he was trying to sell me," Goddard said, "but they weren't the kind of things I

use." I told him I had heard through the grapevine that he had been dealing with Bobby rather heavily. He frowned and said, "That must be Jerry Harkness talking, and as usual he doesn't know what he's talking about. Westfall made one very lucky find about a year ago and I bought all the books he had on that particular day. I wouldn't make any more out of it than that. He had some books and I bought them."

"What were the books?"

"Oz books. Westfall stumbled over them in a garage sale. Thirty-two Oz books for a dollar apiece. Most of the time when you see those they're in poor condition. These were very fine, beautiful copies."

"Were they firsts?"

"Only a few were. None of the Frank Baum titles were, but there were a couple of Ruth Plumly Thompson firsts and the one Jack Snow. The main thing about them was the condition. Half of them still had dust jackets. All the color plates were fresh and unscuffed, even the plates on the covers."

"You got any of 'em left?"

"Oh, no. They didn't last the month."

"Nice little strike for both of you, then. What did you pay him?"

He looked offended and tried not to answer.

"I'd really like to know that," I insisted.

"I prefer keeping my finances private."

"You'd have every right to, if the man hadn't been murdered."

He hedged. "I don't remember exactly."

"Did you pay him in cash?"

"Not for something that big."

"Then you wrote a check. Which means you've got a record of it."

His eyes narrowed. "Do I have to talk to you about this?"

I didn't say anything.

"It's just that I don't want people knowing my business. Most of the time I pay more money per book than anyone in town. But you never want people knowing exactly what you're doing."

"This is a homicide investigation," I said. "I'm not gonna take out a billboard and plaster it with evidence."

"I just don't see how a transaction that we did a year ago can have anything to do with evidence. But if you promise me you'll keep it private, I'll tell you. I gave him seven hundred."

"You have the canceled check?"

"At home, yes. I can produce it if necessary."

"I'll let you know. How did the books price out?"

"I'm not sure exactly. Julian?"

"Twenty-two hundred dollars," Lambert said.

"So you paid him a little less than one-third," I said.

"Which was fair, under the circumstances," Goddard said. "He had thirty-two dollars in it."

"Which shouldn't matter. That is very salable stuff."

"Yes, it is."

"All right," I said with a little sigh. "You're right, it probably doesn't matter anyway, but if it does I'll ask you for that check. Now you say he was in here a couple of weeks ago. What happened?"

"Like I told you, he had a couple of books. One was a good book, but the condition wasn't there."

"So you bought nothing from him?"

"That's right."

"And that's the last time you saw him."

"That's the last time I saw him."

Something unfinished hung in the air. It took me a moment to realize what it was. Lambert, who had been busily engaged writing book descriptions on index cards, had looked up and caught his boss's eye.

"That is right, isn't it, Julian?"

"He did come in once since then," Lambert said. "You weren't here, and it was a busy morning, like today. He was only here for a few minutes. It was unusual because he didn't do anything. He didn't look at any of our books and he didn't have anything to sell."

"When was this?" Goddard said.

"Recent. No more than a week." Lambert closed his eyes and went into deep thought. "I think it may've been Thursday."

"What went on?" I said.

"Nothing. He just came in to see Roland. He said he had a deal cooking and he wanted to see Roland."

"Was that his exact language?"

"Just like that," Lambert said. "He had a big deal cooking and he wanted to see if Roland was interested."

Roland was far more annoyed than interested. "Why didn't you tell me about this?" he said.

"I was busy that morning; I didn't have time to talk to the man. Then I just forgot about it. I didn't think it was anything that would set the world on fire. You know how these guys are. Everything's important. Everything's a big deal."

"It's not like you to forget something like that," Goddard said.

"I should etch it in stone every time one of these characters opens his mouth? I was busy. I was running the bookstore. I assumed if it was important he'd be back. Then I forgot about it."

"If you guys don't mind," I said, "I'd like to get back to my questions. You can grumble at each other all day after I'm gone." I flipped a page in my notebook. "Have either of you got any idea what Bobby would be doing with Rita McKinley?"

Goddard just stared. Lambert laughed out loud.

"Who told you that?" Goddard said.

"Everybody."

"Well, it's the first time I've heard it."

I looked at Lambert. "How about you?"

His laugh had been cut off in the middle of a ha-ha, and his face had begun to turn red. He had busied himself with a book and was pretending to be somewhere else. That's a sure sign with a guy like Lambert that he knows something more—something he'd rather not tell.

"Don't fall all over yourself answering the question," I said. "It's just that a man has been murdered, and I'm supposed to make some kind of effort to find out who did it."

He looked up defiantly. "All right, I just this minute remembered. When he walked out that day, he was kind of angry. He had been waiting for Roland for more than an hour, and I finally said I didn't know how much longer it would be. That's the day you went to get license plates for your new car," he said to Goddard. "How can you ever tell in advance how long that's going to take?"

"I was there three hours," Goddard said.

"That would make it . . . what?" I said. "You thought it was Thursday."

"It was Thursday," Goddard said.

The day before the murder.

"So what happened?" I said, looking at Lambert.

"Suddenly Westfall gets impatient. He stalks over to the door like he's going to leave. But before he does, he turns and says to me, 'I guess Rita McKinley would be more interested in what I have to sell.' And he stomped out."

Goddard shook his head. "This just gets worse all the time. How could you forget something like that?"

"I told you," Lambert said. "The store was a madhouse that day. I can't buy, sell, and be a secretary all at once."

"Let's get back on the point," I said. "Did Bobby say, or even hint, what he might have to sell?"

"No, and like I told you, he wasn't carrying anything with him."

"Did he say anything else?"

"No," Lambert said.

We looked at each other for a moment.

"You've got to remember one thing," Lambert said. "You've got to consider the source. How many times have these guys come in thinking they've found a thousand-dollar book and it turns out to be nothing? I don't consider it my first line of business to keep up with people like Westfall. Especially when we're doing seven hundred in real business in the space of an hour."

"All right, forget it," Goddard said.

But it wasn't over yet. "What can you boys tell me about Rita McKinley?" I said.

"I can't tell you a thing," Goddard said. "I never met the lady, wouldn't know her if I saw her on the street."

"You're aware of her reputation, though?"

"I know she has some good books. That's what I've heard. But I don't scout the other dealers. I don't do business that way."

I looked at Lambert. Again he had gone red around the ears. He'd be a terrible witness in court, if he had anything to hide.

"It's a good thing you didn't kill Bobby, Lambert," I said. "All a cop would have to do is ask you."

He looked up shakily. "I went up there once," he said.

Then, after a long pause, he said to Goddard, "I didn't say anything to you because I knew you wouldn't like it."

Goddard didn't like it. The temperature in the room dropped another five degrees.

"I wanted to see her stock, that's all," Lambert said. "There's been so much talk, and I wanted to see what she had."

"I hope you didn't represent yourself as a buyer for this store," Goddard said.

"I didn't have to. She knew exactly who I was. She knows everybody."

"When did you go up there?" I asked.

"Last fall, before Thanksgiving."

"Could you show me how to get there . . . draw me a map?"

"Sure. It's not that hard to find. You'll need more than a map, though. There's a high fence all around her place, and nobody gets in without calling ahead. You have to call and leave a message."

"Is she pretty good about calling back?"

"She called me back. I heard from her within a couple of hours."

"What was she like?"

"All business."

"But she gave you no trouble about coming up?"

"Why wouldn't she have me up? She's in the business to sell books."

"I just heard that she doesn't exactly roll out the red carpet."

"You won't hear that from me. She's a real lady," Lambert said, his face reddening. "She's got perfect manners and I'll tell you this. She knows her stuff. I was damned impressed."

"Obviously," Goddard said.

"What did you think of her stuff?" I asked.

"Absolutely incredible. I've never seen books like that. She's got a *This Side of Paradise,* signed by Fitzgerald, with H. L. Mencken's bookplate and a personal note from Fitzgerald practically begging Mencken for a review. The book is in a bright, fresh jacket with no flaws. She's got a whole wall of detective stuff—prime, wonderful books. Have you ever seen perfect copies of Ross Macdonald's first three books, or the first American edition of *Mysterious Affair at Styles?* She's got a *Gone With the Wind* signed by Margaret Mitchell, Clark Gable, and Vivien Leigh. Gable wrote a little note under his name that said, 'And now, my dear, everyone will give a damn.' There's so much great stuff, you don't know where to start."

Goddard grunted.

"Here's another thing," Lambert said. "You remember that old rumor about Hemingway and Wolfe signing each other's books?"

It was a rumor I had never heard, so I asked him to fill me in.

"Sometime in the thirties, a woman in Indiana was supposed to have sent a package of Hemingway and Wolfe books to Max Perkins, begging for signatures. The books sat around in Perkins's office for months. Then one night Hemingway and Wolfe were both there and Perkins remembered the books and got them signed. But both of them were three sheets to the wind and Hemingway thought it would be a great joke if they signed all the wrong books. He sat down and wrote a long drunken inscription in *Look Homeward, Angel,* and signed Wolfe's name. Wolfe did the same with *A Farewell to Arms.* They started trying to outdo each other. Wolfe's inscription in *Green Hills of Africa* fills up the front endpapers and ends up on the back board."

"Thomas Wolfe never could write a short sentence if a long one would do just as well," Goddard said sourly.

"But the point is," Lambert said unnecessarily, for by then even I knew what the point was, "McKinley has all those books, with the handwriting authenticated beyond any question. She seems to look for unusual associations, offbeat signatures, and pristine condition. Hey, she's got a *Grapes* with a drunken Steinbeck inscription and a doodle of a guy, drawn by Steinbeck, who has a penis six feet long. I mean, a guy would fall on his face from the force of gravity if he had a schmuck like that. Under the picture, Steinbeck wrote, *'Tom Joad on the road.'* All I can say is, I've looked at a lot of books, but I've never seen a collection quite like that."

I had some more questions, mostly insignificant, which they answered in terms that were generally inconsequential. Then I had Lambert draw me a map to Rita McKinley's house and I left them to their unfolding squabble. I called headquarters and talked to Hennessey. Rita McKinley had not yet returned my call. I gave Hennessey the names of additional book dealers to check out, and twenty minutes later I was in the foothills, heading for Evergreen.

It was pretty much as Lambert had said, a waste of time. She lived near the top of a dirt road that snaked up the mountainside. You went through Evergreen, a bustling little mountain town about thirty minutes from Denver; then, eight or ten miles out of town, doubled back onto a road that was clearly marked PRIVATE. There were half a dozen places up there, McKinley's being at the far end. She had the entire mountaintop to herself. Her privacy was protected, just as Lambert had said, by a locked gate and a fence ten feet high. I wondered about covenants: I didn't know you could build a fence like that anymore, but there it was. I looked through the chain links and followed the fence through the woods, until it became clear that I was simply circling the mountaintop and the fence went the distance. At one point the trees thinned out and I could see her house, the glass glistening two hundred yards above my head. I called up through the break—cupped my hands to my mouth and shouted her name—but no one came.

I talked to people on the way down: stopped at each of the houses and asked about the mystery woman at the top. She remained that, a faceless enigma. No one knew her. She never stopped to chat. All people saw as they passed on the road was a figure, obviously female, in a car. One man had put together a Christmas party last year for all the neighbors on the mountain. Everyone had come but Rita McKinley, who had sent regrets.

In Evergreen, I called her number again and got the recording. I left her a stiff message, telling her I wanted to see her right away. But I had a hunch that I wasn't going to hear from the lady, that I'd have to track her to earth and pin her down. I had another hunch, that that might prove to be heavy work.

For all my alleged expertise, it was Hennessey who got the first break in the case. While I was spinning my wheels in the mountains, Neal had hit the streets and talked to more book dealers. He had come to a store on East Sixth Avenue where Bobby had sometimes been seen. The owner was a man in his forties named Sean Buckley. He had a good eye for books and he sold them cheap. His store was dark and was sometimes mistaken for a junk palace, but Buckley was no Clyde Fix. He knew exactly what he was doing. His books were priced intentionally low, sometimes drastically low. People talk when they find bargains like that, and Buckley's store was always crowded with eager treasure hunters.

It was not a place for a claustrophobic: it was dusty, shabby, disorganized; books were piled on the floor and shoved into every nook. Buckley was a pleasant man, easygoing, shy, well liked, highly intelligent. I had spent a rainy afternoon a year ago talking with Buckley about politics, police work, and the intricacies of the book trade. He had just sold a $250 *Naked and the Dead* to another dealer for $85, knowing full well but not caring much what the price guides said the book was "worth." The other dealer might eventually get that high-end money, but it wasn't easy. Norman Mailer has lost a lot of luster since 1948. People don't care much anymore, so let the other guy take the chance. If it worked, more power to him. The book had cost Buckley eight-five cents at a flea market. Buckley was the best example I had ever seen of the "keep the stock moving" school of bookselling.

I had put him fairly low on my list of people to see. Bookscouts didn't do much business there: they don't like to sell to a low retail man because the margin just wasn't good enough. But Bobby had come in about a week ago with his pockets stuffed with cash. He had flashed a wad bigger than a man's fist, and no small bills either. It looked like all hundreds from what Buckley could see: it must've been several thousand dollars at least. After much prodding, Hennessey had pinned Buckley down to a date. Last Tuesday it was, three days before the murder.

There was another thing. Bobby had been dressed to the hilt, three-piece suit and tie, hair and beard trimmed and combed, shoes shined. It had taken Buckley some time to recognize him. He had come to the store at quarter to five, just before closing. Buckley had been on the phone and hadn't paid much attention at first. Bobby just moved back into the store and started browsing the stacks. As time passed, Buckley began getting restless. He was a man who ran by the clock—he opened and closed on time and seldom stayed open late for anyone. At five-fifteen, Buckley began turning off the lights. At last he walked back and said, in a soft, apologetic voice, "I need to close now."

Bobby looked up and grinned. Buckley had to take a few steps back, so great was his surprise. No one had ever seen Bobby the Bookscout in a coat and tie.

"My gosh, Bobby," Buckley said. "Where you going, to a funeral?"

"Yeah," Bobby said. "Tonight I'm burying my old life."

You could see right away how much he was enjoying it, Buckley said. There was always a tendency in these street people to strut when they got a little money—delusions of grandeur, you know. "Tonight I'm making the biggest deal of my life," Bobby said expansively.

That wouldn't be much of a deal, Buckley thought, but he was too much of a gentleman to say it.

"I'm not gonna be a bookscout anymore, Buckley," Bobby said. "Not gonna be anybody's doormat."

"What are you gonna do?" Buckley said.

Bobby grinned, a sly that's-for-me-to-know look crossing his face. "You'll see soon enough. I'll tell you this much. After tonight I'll be a book dealer, same as you guys. That's all I ever needed, just a stake."

That's when he pulled the money out, just for effect.

"Well," Buckley said, "looks like you got it."

"This is just pocket money. I'll be shopping here a lot from now on, Buckley. It kills me to see you selling books for a quarter on the dollar and I can't buy them myself. That's all gonna change."

"Well," Buckley said, "whatever's happening tonight, I wish you luck."

"Don't need luck; just need to be there at seven o'clock. This is the biggest deal Denver's ever seen, and nobody even knows about it."

"Good luck anyway."

This was the gist of the conversation between Bobby and Buckley, as Buckley told it to Hennessey.

"So," Hennessey said, "what's it mean?"

"Exactly," I said.

"Looks like a motive anyway."

"You mean simple robbery?"

"Sure. The guy flashes a wad like that one time too many. There's plenty of people who'll kill you for a roll like that . . . especially out on the street where this guy worked."

"That might make sense if it had happened the same night," I said. "But he was going somewhere just to spend that money. He was due there in two hours: all he was doing in Buckley's was killing time. That's why he didn't buy any books there—he didn't have any money to spend."

"You mean the big wad was spoken for."

"To the last dime. In real life, Bobby was still broke."

"What's it mean, then?" Hennessey said again.

"Let's think about it. Where'd he get the clothes, for one thing? I went through his place, you know, and I didn't see anything that looked like a necktie or a three-piece suit."

"You were looking for books. I've seen you lose track of time when you're looking at books."

"Maybe. I'll go back and look again, but if there's a coat and tie anywhere in that apartment I'll eat your shorts."

"Whether there is or whether there ain't," Hennessey said, "the question still remains, what does it mean?"

"It means Bobby had a coat and tie for one night only. It means he either borrowed or rented it. It doesn't sound like a rental—not formal enough. Buckley didn't say he showed up in a tux, did he?"

Hennessey gave a little laugh. "Suit and tie is what he said."

"I think we'd better ask Buckley how well the clothes fit. I think he borrowed that coat and tie, from someone who was just about his size."

"Could be anybody," Hennessey said. "He was pretty average."

"It didn't have to be a perfect fit for one night. My guess is he got the coat and tie from the same guy who gave him the money. And I think he was as broke as ever two hours after Buckley saw him. Three days later he was in Goddard's store trying to sell something. Lambert says he didn't have anything with him, but maybe it was something small. The fact was, he didn't have that money anymore. He had given that to someone on Tuesday night, and they didn't have to kill him for it. I think the fact that he wasn't killed till Friday night rules out robbery as a motive."

"It might've still been robbery," Hennessey said. "Maybe not for money. Maybe whoever did it took what Bobby *got* for the money."

"That makes it robbery of a different kind, though, doesn't it? Not your garden-variety thug. The average thug would walk right past fifty thousand dollars' worth of books to lift twenty bucks from the cash register. This would've been somebody with a fairly sophisticated span of knowledge. And a damn cold motive for what he was doing."

"Well," Hennessey said, "there are guys like that."

"There are a lot of guys like that."

"I'll tell you how it looks to me. Somebody pays Bobby to do a job. Say he was taking delivery of some literary masterpiece. At this point we don't know how Bobby got involved—we don't know why whoever hired him couldn't've taken delivery himself instead of hiring a bookscout to do it for him. Maybe that part of it isn't important. The bookscout gets hired, then does a double cross and keeps the merchandise. It takes the client three days to track him down."

"Maybe," I said.

"How small can something like that be?"

I looked at him, not understanding the question.

"Bobby had several thousand dollars on him the night he went to Buckley's," Hennessey said. "Presumably he was going to buy something at a wholesale price."

"Okay, I'm with you so far."

"What's the retail valuation on something you'd pay up to five grand for?"

"Hell, Neal, it could be anywhere from ten to twenty-five thousand dollars."

"Could it be more than that?"

"If it gets to be much more than that, it stops being wholesale and starts being fraud. Most honorable book dealers figure twenty-five to forty percent as a fair wholesale price. Twenty would be rock-bottom. But for a big-money piece, sometimes you have to go higher than 40 percent. If you fall into a piece that's worth a quarter mil, you might have to put up three-quarters, maybe even eighty percent. That's still a lot of change for the book dealer."

"If he can sell it."

"On that level he can always sell it. The easiest thing in the world to sell is a truly rare book. The biggest problem would be getting the money to buy it."

I still didn't see where his mind was going. Hennessey tends to plod in his thinking—that's why we were a good team. I tend to leapfrog, and sometimes it takes a guy with a more fundamental approach to rein me in and make me see what's been in front of my face all along.

This time he didn't seem to know where he was going. He was groping, trying to find a handle.

"You said something a minute ago," he said. "That most honorable dealers figure such-and-such. How honorable do these guys tend to be?"

"As a group, they're just like everybody else. There are some old gentlemen straight out of the last century. Fewer of those every day. There are egomaniacs . . . more of those every day. There are shysters, a few scumbags, a nut or two. There are some guys who'll take your pants off if you don't know anything. But I think as a group they have a pretty good standard of ethics. They'll vary right up and down the scale."

Hennessey nodded.

"Neal, I still don't see what you're getting at."

He blinked and brought himself back to his premise. "Robbery. Bobby bought something and somebody brained him and took it away from him. That idea works, Cliff, if it was something small enough for him to carry it around with him. I think this is going to be a very stupid question, but does it sound feasible for something that small to cost so much money?"

"Hell yes. Why would you think otherwise?"

"It just seems like, for five g's, you ought to get something more than a booklet."

I told him the *Tamerlane* story—how some guy had found one in a bookstore for fifteen bucks and sold it at auction for two hundred grand.

"I hate to say it, but I don't know what *Tamerlane* is."

"Poe's first book. Just a booklet, like you said, but some of the most expensive stuff in the world is very small. Broadsides, pamphlets, papers . . ."

"Stuff you could put in a pocket."

"Sure. That's the first thing a dealer or a bookscout has to learn. Always look at the little stuff."

"So it's not far-fetched to think that the bookscout might have been carrying something that somebody would kill him for."

"Not at all. Just imagine that somebody had found a little piece of scroll signed by Jesus Christ. A silly example—I don't know who the hell they'd get to authenticate it—but for the sake of argument, okay? How much do you think something like that would be worth?"

"I get your point. And I guess that's what I've been trying to pin down . . . a motive for robbery. Something so tiny he could carry it in his pocket, but worth big bucks. That's what he was sent to buy, and somebody killed him and took it away from him."

"If that's true, it points back to the book trade. It wasn't a sudden fight or an old enemy. The answer is in the money. Where did the money go, where did it come from? If we can follow the money, we'll know a lot more than we know now."

"There's one more thing we could check," Hennessey said. "How about the religion angle?"

I saw it suddenly, what Neal had been pushing around in his head all day.

"They say our boy was religious," Hennessey said. "Found the Lord in prison a few years ago. That means he went to church somewhere. That means he had a life outside the book business. Maybe friends on a whole different level. Maybe a minister he'd confide in. You only see one side of him when you see him in a bookstore."

I sat up straight in my chair. "How the hell could I miss something like that?"

"You're too busy looking at the books," Hennessey said.

13

The body of Bobby Westfall lay unclaimed in the morgue: if there was a church in Bobby's life, it had not yet made its presence known. No one had stepped forward and offered Bobby a Decent Christian Burial. The coroner had done more for Bobby in death than most people had in life: his office had spent many man-hours on a long and fruitless search for next of kin. They had found a rumor of a sister living in Salt Lake City, but that had not checked out. Bobby had told people that his mother was dead and he never knew his father. He had mentioned Pennsylvania to several people, but that had not checked out. At seventeen, he had once said, he had been in the army: medical discharge, flat feet. Amazingly, that had not checked out. The army had no record of a Robert Westfall in its service at the time and place that Bobby would have been there. This was important, the coroner said, because if military service could be established Bobby would qualify for burial at Fort Logan. They still had a few leads to check: sometimes a body had to be kept on ice for weeks, until every-thing petered out. Lacking everything—church, service, next of kin—Bobby would go to an unmarked pauper's grave at Riverside, and have the earth plowed over him by a bulldozer.

In the morning, I went back to the bookstore beat and Hennessey began checking churches around the neighborhood where Bobby lived. I visited some new stores and went back to the old ones with new ques-tions. Did Bobby ever mention what church he attended? Did he ever mention any names of ministers or people he knew outside the book world? I talked to Ruby Seals, Emery Neff, Jerry Harkness, and Sean Buckley. I went back to Cherry Creek and talked to Roland Goddard and Julian Lambert. It was a wasted morning. Even two bookscouts in Ruby's store didn't know much about Bobby. One of them had seen him a few times with the scout called Peter, but no one knew where

Peter lived or what his last name was. I wrote down some stuff in my notebook, but I had a feeling that none of it meant anything.

Meanwhile, Hennessey found the church before noon. We thought it likely that Bobby would go to church in his own neighborhood. He didn't have a car, and probably wouldn't want to spend Sundays doing what he did every other day of the week—walking or riding a bus. We looked closely at churches that would appeal to born-again types rather than older establishment religions. Ruby remembered that Bobby had once referred to Catholicism disparagingly—"not a true faith," he had called it—so he wouldn't like the Episcopal church any better. He probably wasn't a Lutheran, and anything from the outer limits, such as Unitarianism, was unlikely. No, Bobby was probably caught up in some evangelical splinter group formed by a diploma mill preacher with a slick tongue and a ready supply of hellfire. It was easy: Hennessey found the church on the fifth try. It was one of those little chapels off University Boulevard, the Universal Church of God, it called itself. The preacher recognized Bobby's picture at once. Yes, Bob was a regular: he seldom missed a Sunday and usually came to Bible studies on Wednesday nights as well. He always came with a fellow named Jefferson or Johnson, good friend of his. They were always together. Hennessey asked if they had come last Wednesday. As a matter of fact they had, the preacher said. Suddenly Jefferson or Johnson became the last known man, except Julian Lambert, to have seen Bobby Westfall alive.

The preacher got the man's name from the church registry. Jarvis Jackson lived on Gaylord Street, just a few blocks away. The preacher didn't know either Jackson or Bobby well. They kept to themselves and were quiet and reflective in church. The preacher looked a lot like those birds you see on TV Sunday mornings: sharp and cunning, and dressed in an expensive tailored suit. Hennessey didn't like him much.

"What does the church do about burying its members?" Hennessey asked.

"That all depends," the preacher said.

"On what?"

"On whether they've made arrangements."

"In other words, on whether they've got any money."

"Money runs the world, Mr. Hennessey."

"It looks like old Bob's headed for a potter's field funeral, unless somebody stands the tab," Hennessey said.

The preacher cocked his head and tried to look sympathetic.

Riverside loomed a little larger for dear old Bob.

We met at Ruby's bookstore and went to talk to Jarvis Jackson together. Jackson lived in the south half of a shabby little duplex. He lived alone except for half a dozen cats. The cats, he explained, were what first drew him and Bob together. The place smelled strongly of sour milk and well-used kitty litter. There was a case of books in the front room and I gravitated toward them and let my eye run over the titles while Hennessey and Jackson went through the preliminaries. There wasn't anything in the bookcase—some condensed books and other assorted junk. The bottom shelf was well stained with cat piss, the books all fused together. I would've cried if there'd been a Faulkner first in there.

Jackson and Bobby had met a year ago at the church. They had sat on a bench after the service and talked cats. After that riveting conversation, Jackson had invited Bobby home for some lemonade and lunch. They had soon become friends. Jackson thought of himself as Bobby's best friend. He was fifteen years older, but age doesn't matter when the chemistry's right. They liked the same things, shared the same philosophy. They liked the Lord, books, and the smell of cat poop, in approximately that order. They never ran out of things to talk about. Twice a week they would meet in a café on East Seventeenth and eat together. They discussed the Lord and the Lord's work. Bobby had an idea that the Lord had something in mind for him. It was probably a surprise, I thought, when he found out what it was. Bobby had always wanted to do missionary work, but he'd spent all his life putting out brushfires. Jackson had heard of Bob's death only this morning, when he'd read about it in the paper.

"When did you see him last?" I said.

"Wednesday night. He always came by here. We'd eat something, then walk over to church. Neither of us drove. We always walked together."

"Did you talk about anything?"

"We discussed the Lord's work over dinner."

"Anything other than that?"

"Not then, no."

"Some other time, then?"

"After church we came back here and talked some more. Bob didn't seem to want to go home. Me, I'm retired . . . I don't mind staying up late to talk things over."

"What did you talk about that night?"

"He said he'd done a big book deal. But it wasn't working out like he'd thought."

"When had he done this?"

"The night before. He had been up all night."

"Did he tell you what the deal was?"

"Not exactly. He did say it involved a lot of money. But it wasn't working out."

"What did he mean by that?"

"He didn't go into any details. Just said things never seemed to work out right for him, somehow it just never went right. He couldn't understand why the Lord always wanted him to fail. The only thing he could figure out was that the Lord was still angry from the things he'd done as a young man. That's why he wanted to talk to me—he needed reassurance that the Lord is good, not vengeful, that the Lord doesn't always work in ways we can understand. He doesn't do things for our convenience or personal glory. There's a bigger purpose to His acts. We all need to be reminded of that on occasion."

"Yes sir."

"So I listened and we talked. It seemed to help him to talk about it. I think he was trying to make up his mind."

"About what, sir?"

"What to do about it. He was angry. I think he was even angry at the Lord until we talked about it. I think I got him to focus that anger where it really belonged."

"Where's that, Mr. Jackson?"

"At himself. At his failings and weaknesses."

"Or maybe at someone else?"

He shrugged. "I didn't tell him to do that. It would never be any advice of mine that one man should hate another."

"Did he say he hated somebody?"

"He was angry. He felt he'd been lied to and cheated. And I think he was trying to make up his mind what to do about it."

"But he never mentioned any names?"

He shook his head.

"Maybe a name you've half forgotten."

He looked at me blankly.

"Did he give you any idea where he'd gotten the money for the deal?"

"I assume someone gave it to him. I know he didn't have any money of his own."

"Did he say anything that might indicate where the deal was done?"

"No . . . nothing."

I looked at Hennessey. He gave a frown and turned his palms up.

"I'm sorry I'm such a dead end," Jackson said. "I want to help if I can. It's an awful thing, what happened to Bob. I want to help, but it was his business and I just didn't pry. All I know is that he worked all night on it. He borrowed a coat and tie from me . . . he wanted to make a good impression . . . said it was to be the first day of his new life. He was sorry later that he hadn't gone in his old clothes. There was too much work for him to be dressed like that. He brought the suit back in pretty bad shape."

"Could we see that suit?"

"It's right back here in the closet."

He went into a back room and returned a moment later with the coat and tie. The pants hung loosely under the coat. It had a vest, as Buckley had said, and it looked worn and limp in the light of day.

"He was sorry he had taken it," Jackson said again. "It's pretty well ruined, as you can see. He apologized and said he'd buy me a new one if he ever got enough money together. Bob was like that. He never thought ahead. He wanted to dress up and see what it felt like, and he never gave a thought to the work he had to do."

"Then there were a lot of books?"

"Oh, yes . . . that much I do know. It took him all night to move them."

I went through the coat pockets, then the vest. In the pants I found two receipts from a 7-Eleven store.

"Are these your receipts?" I asked.

Jackson looked at them and shook his head. "Must be something he left in there."

I showed them to Hennessey. "No telling which store," Neal said. "Must be hundreds of 'em in Denver."

Suddenly Jackson said, "It was on Madison Street. I remember it now, he went in that store late that night. He was hungry, he hadn't had anything to eat in almost two days. He had been working about four hours and was feeling faint. He went out on the upper porch for some air. He saw the sign, 7-Eleven, about half a block away. It was the only place open that time of night. It was unusual that way—usually they don't put those places in residential areas like that, but there it was . . . like the Lord had sent it just for him. He had two dollars in his pocket. So he walked up and got a soft drink and a Hostess cake."

I asked for his phone book. There was only one 7-Eleven on Madison Street. It was in the 1200s, only a few blocks away.

We found the house without much trouble after that. It was half a block north of the 7-Eleven, on the opposite side of the street. It was the only house in the block with an upper porch. The doors were open and there were people inside, pricing stuff for an estate sale. There were signs announcing that the sale would be this coming weekend. Inside were bookshelves. There were bookshelves in every room, all of them empty.

14

"Where're your books?" I said from the open doorway.

The man looked up. "We don't open till Saturday."

"I'm just wondering where all your books went."

"Come back Saturday and I'll tell you."

A smartass, I thought. I walked into the room and Hennessey came in behind me. I flashed my tin and said, "How about telling me now."

He looked at the badge, unimpressed. "So you work for me. Big deal. Am I supposed to hyperventilate and lose control of my body functions because you can't find a real job?"

"Look, pal, I'm not trying to impress you. I'm asking for your cooperation on a murder case."

"Oh yeah? Who's been killed?"

"How about letting me ask the questions."

I knew it was a bad start. I meet a lot of characters like him, cop-haters from the word *go,* and I never handle them well.

"You can ask all you want," he said. "There's nothing that says I have to talk to you."

"Are you sure of that?"

"I should be. I'm a lawyer."

Wonderful. So far I was batting a thousand.

"I don't owe you bastards one goddamn thing," he said. "I got a ticket coming over here this morning."

Now the woman looked up. She was in her mid-thirties, five to ten years younger than the man. Pretty she'd be, in a cool dress, relaxing by a pool: pretty in the bitchy way of a young Bette Davis, mean and intelligent and all the more interesting because of that. Now she was dirty and hot, doing a job that must seem endless—cataloging and sifting and finally putting a price tag on each of the hundreds of items of a man's life.

"You have just made the acquaintance of Valentine Fletcher Ballard," she said. "Charming, isn't it?"

I didn't know what to make of the two of them, didn't know if they were playing it for laughs or if I had come in in the middle of something. The look he gave her seemed to say that they weren't playing anything.

"You'd think the goddamn mayor of this goddamn city would have better things for the goddamn cops to do than sit in a speed trap with goddamn radar guns harassing the hell out of honest citizens," he said.

"Don't even try to talk to him," the woman said. "You can't talk to a fool."

The guy went right on as if she hadn't said a word. "Have you seen what they did on Montview? *Lowered* the goddamn speed limit all of a sudden to thirty miles an hour. It's four lanes in there, for Christ's sake, it ought to be fifty. You think the mayor gives a rat's ass about safety? Don't make me laugh. They bring ten cops in on fucking overtime just to write tickets and generate revenue. When you get your cost-of-living raise this year, copper, remember whose pocket it came out of and how you got it."

I hate the term *copper*, but I couldn't argue much. I've never liked the city's use of cops that way. If you have to bring a cop in on overtime, let him do the legwork on a murder case or chase down a rapist. Let him walk the streets in a high-crime area, where his presence might mean something. Don't put him in the bushes with a radar gun on a street that's been deliberately underposted. Don't make sneaks out of cops. The guy was right, people don't like that, and that's how cop-haters are born.

"Goddamn pirates," he said. "You fuckers are no better than pickpockets."

All I could do was try to lighten it up. "Hey, I'm doing my part," I said. "I'm looking for a killer."

"So I'll ask you again," the guy said. "Who's been killed?"

"The guy you sold these books to."

He blinked. The woman stood up and looked at me.

"You want to talk to me now?" I said. "Maybe we can get off on a better footing. I'm Detective Janeway. This is Detective Hennessey."

The guy finally said, "I'm Val Ballard."

He made no attempt to introduce the woman: wouldn't even acknowledge her presence. I thought it was strange that neither had spoken directly to the other, but maybe that was just my imagination.

It wasn't. She said, "I'm Judith Ballard Davis. The klutz you've been talking to likes to pretend he's my brother. Don't blame me for that."

He ignored her fairly effectively: all she got for her trouble was a look of slight annoyance. I was beginning to see a pattern emerging in the hostility. He ignored her: she heaped insults upon him, but only through another person.

I said, to anyone who wanted to answer it, "Whose house is this?"

They both began talking at once. Neither showed any willingness to yield, and the words tumbled over themselves in indecipherable disorder.

"Let's try that again," I said. "Eeeny meeny miney mo." Mo came down on her. That was a mistake, for Ballard began immediately to sulk, and in a moment he went back to his work. I'd have to warm him up, if you could call it that, all over again.

"The house belongs . . . belonged . . . to my uncle. Stanley Ballard."

"And he died, right?"

"He died," she said.

"When did he die?"

"Last month. Early May."

"What'd he die of?"

"Old age . . . cancer . . . I don't know." She didn't seem to care much. "When you're that old, everything breaks down at once."

"How old was he?"

"Eighty, I guess . . . I'm not sure."

"He was your father's brother?"

"Older brother. There was almost twenty years between them."

"Where's your father?"

"Dead. Killed in an auto accident a long time ago."

"What about your mother?"

"They're all dead. If you're looking for all the living Ballards, I'm it."

I looked at him. "What about you?"

"I told you what my name is."

Something was slipping past me. "Are you two brother and sister or what?" I said.

Neither wanted to answer that.

"Come on, people, what's the story? Do you inherit the old man's estate?"

"Lock, stock, and barrel," she said.

"Both of you?"

She gave a loud sigh. At last she said, "Yes, God damn it, both of us."

"All right," I said pleasantly. "That wasn't so hard, was it? You inherit the house and all the contents equally, right?"

"What's this got to do with anything?" Ballard said. "Whose business is it, anyway, what I inherit and what I do with it?"

"I have to watch every goddamn penny," Judith said to no one. "If he gets a chance, he'll screw my eyes out."

"Gee, but it's nice to see people get along so well," I said. "Have you two always been so lovey?"

"I hate his guts," she said. "No secret about that, mister. The only thing I'm living for is to get this house sold and the money split so I won't ever have to see his stupid face again."

"When you decide you want to talk to me, I'll be in the other room," Ballard said, and left.

"Son of a bitch," Judith said before he was quite out of the room.

I had this insane urge to laugh. She knew it, and did laugh.

"We're some dog and pony show. Is that what you're thinking?"

"Yeah," I said. "What's with you two?"

"Just bad blood. It's always been there. It's got nothing to do with anything, and I'd just as soon not talk about it."

"How do you manage to work together if you don't even speak?"

"With great difficulty. What can I tell you?"

"What happened to the books?"

"We sold them. You know that."

"You split the money?"

"You better believe it."

"Did you know the guy you sold them to?"

"Never saw him before. We were in here working and he just

showed up. Walked in on us just like you did. Said he heard we had some books and wondered if we wanted to make a deal for them."

"Did he say where he'd heard about it?"

"No, and I didn't ask. The man had cash money, that's all I care about."

"Did you go through the books before you sold them?"

"What do I care about a bunch of old books? Besides, I told you we were in a hurry to sell them. I don't want to stay around *him* any longer than I have to."

"So neither of you looked at the books, or had a book dealer look at them, before you sold them?"

"Look," she said shortly. "There weren't any old books in there, okay? It was just run-of-the-mill crap. Anybody with half a brain could see that."

She was angry now. The thought of blowing an opportunity will sometimes do that to people. She said, "Everybody knows books have to be old. Everybody knows that."

I shook my head.

"What do you know about it?"

"Not much. A little."

"What could a cop know about books? Don't come in here and tell me what I should've done. You see those bookshelves? They were all full. There are more like this in every room. He had the basement laid out like a fucking library. Do you have any idea how many books were in this house? I haven't got enough to do, now I've got to go through all this crap looking for a few lousy books that might be valuable?"

I shrugged.

"Besides," she said, "Stan did that."

"Did what?"

"He had a book dealer come do an appraisal. It was three, four years ago, when he first got the cancer. He had an appraisal done and it was there with his papers when he died."

"Do you remember the name of the appraiser?"

"I don't have enough to do without remembering names?"

"I'll need to see that appraisal." I made it a demand, not a request. "Do you have a copy?"

"You better believe it. I've got a copy of everything. With a son of a bitch like him around, I'd better have a copy."

Ballard, in the next room, had heard this, and he came in fuming.

"If you want to talk to me, talk," he said. "I've got things to do today."

I shifted easily from her to him.

"Did you look at the books?"

"Hell no. There wasn't anything there worth the trouble. Read my lips and believe it, there was nothing there. This joker wanted them, I say let him *have* the damn things. I told him he could have my half."

"Is that the way you sold 'em?"

"I sold him my half," Ballard said. He still refused to admit that his sister shared the same planet.

"He came here and took all the books," Judith said. "Is that what you want to know, Detective? The little man came and took *all* the frigging books, okay? He gave me some money and the rest went . . ." She jerked her thumb at her brother, who stiffened as if he'd just been slapped.

"Let's talk for a minute about the man who came and took the books. You say he just showed up one night?"

"We were in here just like we are now. I looked up and he was standing in the doorway. I thought he was full of shit." She lit a cigarette and blew smoke. "He was wearing this cheap suit that didn't fit and strutting around like one of the Rockefellers. He came in the night we started and said he wanted to buy the books."

"Who the hell is telling this?" Ballard shouted. He made sure he talked to me, not her. "God damn it, are you talking to me or what?"

"Oh, I don't care," I said wearily.

"I said the only way I'd sell the damn books before the sale started was all in one fell swoop. I didn't want any damn picking and choosing, you see what I'm saying? Get 'em all out of here, that's what I wanted."

"What did he say to that?"

He gave a sweep of his hand. "They're gone, ain't they?"

"I'm not asking you the question, Mr. Ballard, to belabor the obvious. I want to know what the man said when you told him he'd have to buy all the books. Did he act like he wanted to do that or not?"

"He didn't act any way. He just said put a price on 'em."

"And what price did you put on them?"

"In a sale I thought they'd be worth a buck or two apiece. For a guy to take 'em all, I told him I'd knock something off of that."

"Could we maybe get to what the final price was?"

"He gave me two thousand dollars. What he did with the other two thousand's none of my business."

I looked at Judith, who managed to look quite sexy smoking. "Did you get the other two thousand, Mrs. Davis?" I asked in my best long-suffering voice.

"You better believe it."

Ballard took me on a tour of the house. Judith followed at a distance, as if she didn't trust him long out of her sight. I tried to imagine what long-ago rift had ripped them so deeply and permanently apart. I tried to imagine them locked away in here for days on end, divvying up the old man's loot without speaking. The picture defied me. Only greed could motivate them, greed and hate and the all-powerful ego motive to come out on top.

The basement was impressive, but then, I could see what it had been with all the books in it. It was lined with bookcases, against the walls and in rows, library-style, in the center of the room. I did some quick arithmetic and figured that the shelves here and upstairs might hold as many as nine thousand books.

"The old man really loved his books," I said with admiration.

"Some guys like sex," Judith said from the doorway. "Stan liked books."

"So you sold the books for forty, fifty cents apiece?"

"I wasn't gonna quibble," Ballard said. "The guy came back with two grand. Two grand is two grand, and I wanted the crap out of here."

I took a picture of Bobby Westfall out of my notebook. "Is this the guy?"

"That's him," Ballard said. "That a dead picture?"

I nodded and showed it to her. She nodded and looked away.

"Who do you think killed him?" she said.

"We'll see," I said.

*   *   *

We talked some more, and it all boiled down to this:

They had struck a deal and Bobby had come one night last week and stripped the house of everything that remotely resembled a book. He had worn that same silly suit for the heavy work. They didn't know anything else about him—where he'd come from, where he'd gone—the only record of the transaction was the receipt that Ballard had written out (copy to her, and you'd better believe it) to keep it straight and legal. Bobby had signed it with an undecipherable scrawl and left his copy on the table. All he wanted was to get the books and get on the road.

He had come for the books in a huge truck, a U-Haul rental. Now we were getting somewhere. Ruby had said that Bobby had no driver's license: that meant someone else had to have rented the truck. I was hungry for a new name to be thrown into the hopper: I was eager to begin sweating that unseen accomplice. I felt we were one name away from breaking it, and I wanted that name and I wanted it now.

But Bobby had come to Madison Street alone. If someone else had rented the truck, why not ask that buddy to give a hand with the heavy lifting? The obvious answer was that Bobby wanted no one to know what he had really bought from Stanley Ballard's estate. He had insisted on loading the books himself, which was fine with the two heirs, who had no intention of helping anyway. Bobby had brought hundreds of cardboard boxes and had spent all night packing and loading the books. Ballard and his sister kept after their own work and before they knew it the night slipped away. Bobby loaded the last of the books as dawn broke in the east.

During all of this, Hennessey had not said a word. This is the kind of cop Neal is: he melts into the woodwork; he listens, he looks, he adds two and two, then stares at the number four to see if there's any broken type. I didn't notice when he'd stepped away: I found him on the front porch talking with a neighbor.

"Cliff, this is Mr. Greenwald. He and Mr. Ballard were friends for fifty years."

We stood on Ballard's front porch and Greenwald stood on his, and we talked easily across the hedge. Ballard was already living here when Greenwald moved in in 1937. They had a great mutual passion—books. In a very different way, they reminded me of Bobby Westfall and Jarvis Jackson—two lonely guys held together by honest affection and one or two deep common denominators. Ballard was an old bachelor: Greenwald's wife had died in 1975, and the two men took their dinners together at a place they liked, a few blocks away.

Greenwald was a leathery old man, bald with white fringe hair and a white mustache. I could see his books through the window. They had belonged to the book clubs together, Greenwald said: every month they'd get half a dozen books, read them and discuss them. They weren't collectors in the real sense, though both had accumulated a lot of titles over fifty years. It was a comfort, Greenwald said, to see a copy of a book you loved on the shelf. It didn't have to be a fine expensive edition. This was how they both felt: books were meant to be read, not hoarded. Both of them gave a lot of books away—to nursing homes, library sales, and other worthy charities. "What's the use of having a book that's too good to read?" he said. "Half the fun is giving the books away."

I could see his point, though I hadn't agreed with it for years. "Did Mr. Ballard ever have anything that might be called valuable?"

Greenwald looked away and shrugged his shoulders. "I can't imagine. We didn't do it for that reason."

"Still, sometimes people pick up things, sometimes by accident."

Greenwald shrugged again.

"Did Mr. Ballard ever go to estate sales or junk stores looking for books? Maybe he found something that way."

"Never, and I can tell you that with absolute certainty. He wasn't a book hunter, he was a book buyer. He never went to used bookstores. He bought them when they were new and read them all. He was in the Book-of-the-Month for as long as I knew him, maybe longer. I think he started soon after the clubs came in, in the early thirties. You can check on that—he kept all his records from the clubs, all the way back to when he started."

"Really?"

"Oh, yes. He kept all the flyers and bulletins . . . I know you'll find them there in his den, in that big filing cabinet. He used to keep the club flyers and write his notes in the margins. He'd never write in a book, of course, but he'd mark up those advance flyers they sent every month, little notes to himself—which books to buy, which ones to keep, which to give away. I do the same thing, but it's a habit I picked up from him. I've only been doing it about twenty years. His files go back much further."

"May I come over, sir, and see your books?"

"Certainly."

We walked across and went into Greenwald's house. It was like a branch library: row upon row, bookcase after bookcase, all cheap editions of great books. The two old men had fine taste. Anyone could see that.

"We had a lot to talk about, Stan and I. We had been around the world together many times, without ever leaving this block, if you know what I mean."

"I sure do," I said. "It's a wonderful hobby."

"Oh, it is. It's harder today, though. You can't find the good books, like you once could. People don't read anymore, or when they do read they read things that couldn't have been published in the old days. I don't know: my days are all in the past. Everyone I knew is dead, and no one is writing anything worth reading. This is a different world from when I was a boy. I can't read the stuff they publish today, can you?"

"Some of it," I said. "Every once in a while it still happens, Mr. Greenwald. I don't know how it happens, or why, but it still does. Sometimes a great book not only gets published but read, by one helluva lot of people."

"Stan would've liked you," Greenwald said. "He liked everybody who read and appreciated good things. He was an old gentleman, I'll tell you that. Not like those two next door, squabbling with their silly silent feud over every last dime. Stan's turning over in his grave this very minute. Money never came first with Stan. Honor, trust, friendship, those were the qualities he believed in. A great old man. His like will not come this way again."

We went back to Ballard's house. I told Judith I would have to see her uncle's files. The two of them followed us into the den and watched while I went through a great old filing cabinet. It was all there as Greenwald had promised—the entire record of Stan Ballard's love affair with the Book-of-the-Month Club: receipts, billing statements, flyers so annotated and footnoted that I groaned at the thought of wading through it. But Ballard came from a generation that was taught penmanship: his writing was small but precise and, in the final analysis, beautiful. It looked to me like the old man had kept the economy of Camp Hill, Pennsylvania, going strong since March 1931. He had bought the main selection and six other titles that month. The average price was around a dollar: not much in today's world of the $20 novel, but in 1931 there were men working a sixty-hour week for less money than Stan Ballard was spending per month on books.

"What did your uncle do for a living?" I asked.

"He was a stockbroker," Judith said.

"He got into the book club in 1931. That couldn't've been much of a year for stockbrokers, but he seemed to have plenty of money to spend on books . . . even in the Depression."

"He inherited money," Judith said. "I don't know how much; he sure didn't leave much cash in his estate. He probably spent it *all* on books. It didn't matter how the times were, he always had money for that."

I thumbed through the papers. "I'll have to take these files."

They didn't like that. They were on guard now, full of new suspicion. I could almost hear the wheels turning in their heads. Maybe the old man had kept his cash hidden somewhere. Maybe there was a big, juicy stack of thousand-dollar bills tucked into the book file— book money unspent.

"I don't think you should just walk out of here with that stuff," Ballard said.

"I can get a court order if I have to, and I think you know that," I said. "Why don't we make it easy on ourselves?"

"What is this stuff?" Judith said. "Is there anything in there worth any money?"

"I'd be amazed if there was. You can look for yourself while we pack it up. I'll give you a receipt and after this is over you'll get it all back."

"*Who'll* get it back?" Ballard said.

"Whoever the hell wants it."

We started packing the files. I could see it was going to take some time, because Ballard and Judith wanted to examine each file microscopically as we went.

"This could take all night," I said. "Let's try to cut to the chase. Where's the original copy of that appraisal he had done?"

"The executor has it," Judith said. "A lawyer named Walter Dreyfuss. I think he and Stan were soldiers together in the Revolutionary War."

"One of us ought to go see him," I said to Hennessey.

"I'll go. I'll have to take a cab."

"Good. If you hurry you might make it before his office closes. I'll call and tell him you're coming."

It was dark before I was finished at Ballard's. We packed all the contents of Stanley Ballard's filing cabinet into six big cardboard boxes and I loaded them into my car. Neither Ballard nor Judith offered to help. I thanked them and left them to their awful job. I hope I never hate anyone the way they hate each other, I thought as I drove downtown to fetch Hennessey. Then I thought of Jackie Newton, and the world was a darker place again.

Hennessey was waiting for me on Seventeenth Street. Under his arm he had a single folder, which contained Stanley Ballard's will and a copy of the appraisal. He had made no attempt to read the will—Walter Dreyfuss had given him a verbal summary—but he had looked the book appraisal over.

"What's it say?"

"Book club fiction, almost without exception. Worthless."

"Who did the appraisal?"

"That dame up in Evergreen. Rita McKinley."

I grunted.

"So where does this leave us?" Hennessey said.

"Right back where we started. It was something small, and Bobby had to buy the whole damn library to get it; something so tiny you could carry it in your pocket, but so potent it makes the hair stand up on my neck just thinking about it."

"How're we gonna find it?"

"I'm gonna dig. I'm gonna comb through every piece of paper in this state if I have to."

I dropped Hennessey at Ruby's store, where he had parked his car, and I started back to my apartment for what I thought would be another long night's work.

Then something happened that changed my life for all time.

15

I was full of nervous energy: I wanted something to break that would engage me fully and keep me going through the night. I had two possibilities, either of which ought to do it. I took the Ballard files up to my place, but when I started to work I decided to run down the U-Haul lead.

There are almost fifty places in Denver that rent U-Hauls. A lot of gas stations are subagents and rent them out of their backyards. I sat at the phone with a Yellow Pages and began to work. I did it the same way we had found the church, beginning at Bobby's place and working in a widening circle between there and Madison Street. This is what police work is all about: your trigger finger always gets more action on the telephone than in any gunplay. I hummed "Body and Soul" between calls, trying to get a hint of the way Coleman Hawkins used to play it. "Dah-dah de dah-dah dumm." It didn't work. Nothing worked. I gave them Bobby's name on the insane chance that someone somewhere might've had soup for brains and rented a $25,000 truck to a guy with no driver's license. You never can tell. Lacking a file on Westfall, they would have to look through all their receipts for the night of June 10. I waited through interminable delays. Most of the little places had no extra help—the guy who rented the U-Hauls was the guy who pumped your gas. Customers came and went while I dangled on the phone. One place took almost thirty minutes, and it turned out that they hadn't rented any trucks on the night in question.

The truck outlets themselves were, if anything, slower than the corner gas stations. Those places are all on computer now. This is supposed to make finding information faster and easier, but in real life it doesn't turn out that way. Have you noticed how much longer you have to wait in bank lines, and at Target and Sears stores, since the computer came in? I hate computers, though I know that without them police work would be like toiling in a medieval zoo. After three hours of being told that the computer was down, that there were no such rentals, that they'd have to check and call me back, I was ready to adjourn to my favorite beanery. I couldn't raise Carol, but when I'm that hungry I don't mind eating alone.

Before I could get out of there, the phone rang.

It was Barbara Crowell. Her voice was quaking, terrified.

"Janeway! My God, I can't believe you finally got off that phone!"

"Hello, Barbara," I said without enthusiasm.

"Can you come over here?"

"What's the matter?"

"It's . . . him."

"Ah," I said.

"I know he's out there."

"Out where?"

"Somewhere outside. I saw him."

"When did you see him?"

She breathed at me for fifteen seconds. Then she said, "I think I'm losing my mind. I see him everywhere. I don't know what to do. Everywhere I look I see his face. Then I look again and he's gone. Then he's there again. I hear a sudden noise and I freak out. I'm afraid of the dark. The telephone rings and I jump out of my skin. I answer it and there's no one there. I know it's him. All of a sudden I'm afraid of the goddamn dark. I've never been afraid of anything and now I see shadows everywhere."

"All right, calm down. I'll be over in a few minutes."

I parked a block away from her place and walked over. I came up carefully, keeping in shadow. For a long time I stood across the street and watched her apartment, and nothing happened. Her light was a steady beacon at the top. I walked down the street and around the corner and came up from the back. There was no one around: I could see quite clearly. I skirted the house and went in through the front, and I stood in the dark hall and watched the street. It was quiet: people were settling in for the night.

I climbed the three flights to the top and knocked on her door.

"Who's there?"

"It's me."

She clawed at the locks and ripped the door open.

"Jesus, what took you so long?"

"I wanted to walk around and look the place over."

"Did you see him?"

"Barbara, there's nobody there."

She closed her eyes and collapsed against me. I held her with one arm and closed the door with the other. Eventually I got her to the sofa and sat her down. Then I went through it all again, the same routine we'd done before: the coffee, the calming words, the lecture. She looked like a little girl, ready to explode in tears. I couldn't help being angry and sorry for her at the same time.

"Jackie doesn't need to torture you, honey," I said. "You do a good enough job on yourself."

"I know I saw him this morning. That's what set me off."

"Where did you see him?"

"I was on my way to work. I had stopped at a red light and he pulled up beside me. I could sense him there looking at me."

"What do you mean you could sense him? What does that mean?"

"I couldn't look at him."

"It might've been the man in the moon sitting there for all we know."

"It was him. I saw his car. There couldn't be another car like that, so don't tell me I'm imagining it. When the light turned green he pulled out ahead of me and turned the corner. I couldn't be mistaken about that car."

I left her alone for a while. I turned down the lights and went to the window and looked down in the empty street.

"While you're scaring yourself to death, Jackie's probably home watching TV," I said. Or breaking in a new dog, I thought.

"He's not home," she said. "He's out there somewhere."

I didn't say anything. There didn't seem to be anything to say.

"Call him up if you think he's home," she said.

I looked at her.

"Go ahead, call him and see. You're not afraid of him; call him and see if he's home. If he is, I won't bother you anymore."

"All right."

I didn't need to look up the number: I had known it for more than a year. I dialed it and waited. No one answered.

"I guess you're right," I said. "Looks like Jackie's hiding out there in the bushes, just waiting for you to show your face."

She shivered and the goose bumps started.

"I guess you can go hide in the bedroom," I said. "Tremble in the dark for the rest of your life."

She cried at that. She cried a good deal. I didn't want to hurt her, but I didn't know how to push her off the dime. What was worse, I wasn't sure anymore what Jackie was capable of, or what I wanted Barbara Crowell to do about him.

"God, I hate having you hate me," she said at one point.

"If I hated you I wouldn't be here. I told you before, this isn't my line of work. I should be well fed and home by now, settling in for a long night's work."

I kept looking down in the street. Softly, I said, "Jackie's probably working somewhere. Trying to figure out a new way to rip somebody off. Maybe he has a date tonight. Maybe he'll like her better than you. Maybe you'll get lucky and it'll be her problem."

"You bastard!" she cried.

"Yeah, I know. It's the company I keep. Pogo was right. We have met the enemy and it is us."

"I don't know what you're talking about half the time."

"It doesn't matter. You got anything to eat here?"

"I could fix you some bacon and eggs."

"Jesus, that sounds marvelous."

We ate. The coffee and the food warmed her up. I tried to get away from that judgmental tone I had taken with her, and after a while we were able to converse in a more or less normal way, the way men and women have always done. I even managed to make her laugh. When that was over, she said, "What do people call you . . . friends, I mean."

"Cliff usually does it."

She turned it over in her mind. "That's a good man's name. Can I call you that?"

"Sure, if you want to."

Suddenly she said, "Will you stay with me tonight?"

I was off duty. I didn't have anything better to do. The murderer of an unknown bookscout could wait till tomorrow.

"Sure," I said.

She was surprised. "Do you mean it?"

"Yeah, I'll stay," I said.

She looked at the bedroom, then at me. Clearly, she didn't know how to read me.

"It'll be all right if you want to . . . you know . . . if you don't hate me too much."

"I'm not staying here tonight for a shackjob, Barbara. I'll make you an even trade-off. I'll get you through the night, then you've got to do something for me."

The look of frightened warmth faded, till only the fright was left.

"I know what you want. The only thing you ever cared about was putting him away. You'll do anything for that, won't you?"

My silence was like a nolo plea.

"I can't do it," she said.

"Then I'm leaving."

I started toward the door.

"Wait!" she cried.

I stopped and turned.

"Please wait . . . please. Look, I'll try, okay?"

"You've got to do better than that."

"Help me, Cliff . . . please don't leave."

"I'm trying to help you. I don't know what the answer is. I may only end up getting you killed . . . I don't know. I know you can't go on the way you are. So tomorrow morning, accompanied by me, you will drive out to the Jeffco DA's office. You will swear out charges of kidnapping, assault and battery. I don't know, it's probably too late for the rape charge, but we'll tell him about it and let the DA decide. Then we come back to Denver and find us a judge and get you a restraining order. If the son of a bitch comes near you after that, you will call a number I will give you and we will come and bust his ass. If you won't meet me that far, there's not much I can do."

She didn't say anything. I said, "We just keep going over the same ground. It won't get any easier. One way or another, you've got to face it."

"Don't tell me what I've got to face. You won't be here, you won't have to face it. Why should you care? You just want one thing; you don't care what happens to me."

"That's not true."

"It is true. You hate him so much you'd use me to get him. At least be honest enough to admit that. Who was it that took me out of his place? If you'd left me alone I'd probably be fine now. He'd've done what he wanted and that would be the end of it. But you had to take me. You had to put me between you, and now you tell me there's nothing you can do. Go on, get out of here."

I couldn't go after that. I still didn't know what to say to her.

"I don't understand you two," she said. "How do two men come to hate each other that much?"

"I don't know. It's not covered in the police manual."

"It's called human nature," she said. "I guess they don't have writers for that."

Here's how it happened. I put Barbara to bed and settled down on her sofa. I watched TV till my brain went limp, then I turned it off and lay quiet with my own thoughts. At 2:30 I heard a car door slam. I went to the window and looked out. Jackie was across the street, looking up at me. I knew he couldn't see me with the light out, so I stood still and watched him. Poor Barbara, what a mess she's in, I thought. He really is crazy, I thought—here he comes now, across the street, into the dark places under the window, up the stairs. In another moment I could hear his footsteps. I had maybe twenty seconds to decide what to do. Whatever I decided, there wouldn't be any logic to it. None of this made any sense: it never does when you're dealing with a Jackie Newton. I will kill him, I thought: when he comes through that door I'll blow his brains out and take all the heat tomorrow. This was a rational, cold decision: in that twenty seconds all the consequences raced through my head. I saw it with crystal clarity: all the flak that would trickle down from City Hall to the cop on the beat. All over town tomorrow, guys in blue would be asking one question: *What the hell was Janeway doing there at that time of night?* Did I set Jackie up? Did I goad him, then execute him with no more thought than a gangster gives his enemy? Everyone knew I hated the man: even Barbara knew it, and she barely knew me. All this flashed through me with the power of instinctive knowledge, something as simple as your own name, something you don't have to ponder or weigh. Give me some time and I could describe every memo and phone call, everything they'd be saying tomorrow from the mayor to the manager of safety, and from there to the chief of police. Give me time, I thought.

Then Jackie came to the door, and my time was up.

I eased back into the bedroom and woke Barbara. "Don't make a sound," I said. "Just get up and put on a robe. Jackie's here."

I had to put my hand over her mouth to keep her from screaming. Luckily, I had anticipated that.

I got her up, though it wasn't easy. She had gone rigid with fear. I pushed her into the closet and closed the door. Then I got in her bed and pulled the covers up to the top of my head. I'm as crazy as she is, I thought: I'm as nuts as Jackie. Is this police procedure? Is this the way you catch a guy? All I can say is, it felt right. I took out my gun and held it like a hot water bottle, tight against my heart. I savored the surprise Jackie had coming: I could hardly keep from laughing.

Nothing from then on seemed real.

I heard him kick the door in. It's amazing how quiet that can be when it's done in one swift blow. The unbreakable deadbolt ripped through the wood like so much cardboard and he was coming fast. He crossed the room in four giant strides and came into the bedroom. He jerked back the covers and even then I didn't know whether to kill him. I came up with the blanket, the gun leading the way. "Kiss me, sugar," I said, and I cracked steel against his head. He went down like I'd shot him, and before he could move I had the light on and the gun cocked against his head.

I had him facedown on the floor beside the bed, the gun jamming him behind the ear. One move and Barbara Crowell would have Jackie Newton's brains for a throw rug. He knew it too: the blow had dazed him but he was coming out of it now. He kept trying to look back at my gun. He was bleeding out of the left eyebrow where I had opened his head to the bone. I kept him there, kissing the floor for another minute while I patted him down. He wasn't carrying any-thing, the arrogant bastard. I backed off slowly. "Just stay where you are, Newton. Don't even think about getting up."

When I was ready, I told him to get up. "Get against that wall," I said, "face-first." He didn't say a word, just let his eyes rake me over like before. I was terrified so it must've worked. "Turn around," I said again. I shoved him against the wall and jerked his hands behind him. Then I got the cuffs and shackled him. I made it tight; I didn't care much about chafing him. I called Barbara out of the closet but she wouldn't come. I called her again, louder.

"Just stand there, punk," I said. "Keep your face to that wall and you might make it downtown in one piece."

I went to the closet and opened it. Barbara was sitting with her hands over her eyes. I took her by the arm, but she looked to be in shock. I told her it was okay, she could come out now, but she didn't seem to believe it.

"Come on," I said. "You've got to get dressed and go downtown with us."

She didn't seem to understand simple English. She couldn't look at Jackie, who had turned slightly so he could see her. Jackie knew what intimidation was: he knew what a hold he had over her. I kicked him in the ass, hard enough to break a bone, and he turned slowly back to the wall. Blood was everywhere, on the wall, on the floor, and all over Jackie.

"Get dressed," I said to Barbara.

She didn't move. I went to her closet and took out a blouse and a pair of jeans. "Go in the bathroom and put these on," I said. When I looked in her face, I saw a picture of fear and despair so absolute it was heartbreaking. "C'mon, Barb," I said, as gently as I could. "Get dressed, hon, we've got work to do." She shook her head and dropped the clothes on the floor. I picked them up and guided her to the bathroom. I left the door open a crack, and every so often I peeped in and tried to talk her into her clothes. Put on the jeans, Bar-bara. That's good. Now the blouse. Real fine.

Suddenly she found her voice. "Tell him to go away," she said through the door. "I don't want him here."

When she came out of the bathroom, I took her under my arm and gave her a big hug. It only got the tears started again. She began to tremble and whimper and I didn't know what to do with her.

Jackie began to laugh.

I knew how to stop that. I whipped him around and cocked the gun and rammed it in his mouth. "Laugh now, asshole," I said. He didn't seem inclined to. I held him like that for a full minute, my eyes burning into his: I let him see my hand tremble, my finger waver on the trigger. "I may kill you yet, Newton," I said. "Just give me an excuse, just any at all, and they'll be picking pieces of your head out of that wall for a month. You got me, pardner?"

Jackie got me. I turned him to the wall and tried to work on Barbara. She had begun talking again, dangerous, mindless drivel in monologue, nonstop. "I think we could just let him go," she said. "Just make him promise not to come back if we let him go this time." The same thought came up, over and over, in different words. Let him go. Turn him loose. Get him out of here. Do this and Jackie, I guess out of gratitude, would leave her alone in the future. Bullshit, I said. She talked over my one-word argument as if I weren't there. "Bullshit, Barbara," I said, louder. This was not looking good: she'd make the worst kind of witness, assuming I could get her downtown to sign the papers in the first place. I don't know what else I expected: the fact was that, for the first time in my career, I hadn't thought far enough ahead to deal with even the most obvious problem. The victim was going to let Jackie walk: I had to've known that, so why was it making me so angry? I was almost beside myself with rage.

"Bullshit!" I shouted, loud enough to wake the block.

Barbara just stared at the floor and said she was sure he'd leave her alone if we let him go this time.

And Jackie was laughing again. He wasn't, really, but I could hear him anyway.

Something frightening happened inside me. Sometimes it happens to an old cop when one asshole too many has been patted on the head and turned back on the streets—you want to go out and take care of a few of them yourself, the fast and easy way. A few cops had done it: maybe I would too. I grabbed Barbara by the scruff of her worthless neck and pushed her to the front door. Jackie I handled a good deal rougher. I pushed them down the dark stairs and into the deserted street. Barbara was still muttering about turning him loose. I told her to shut up and walk, and a moment later we reached my car.

I opened the trunk and got a roll of electrical tape out of my tool-box. I fished a handkerchief out of Jackie's pocket and told Barbara to bind up his wound with that. I didn't want his crappy blood all over my car. But Barbara wouldn't touch him, so I wrapped the tape myself, right over his hair. Then I pushed his head down and forced him into the front seat. Barbara said she didn't understand why we couldn't just let him go, if he'd just promise not to come back. I told her to get in back. I got behind the wheel and started the car. I made Newton roll over with his head against the door. Then I drove up to Speer Boulevard and turned north.

We weren't going downtown, that much was certain. Jackie didn't say anything, but there was a feeling of tension in the car, of an act yet to come. He had misread me all the way: I had seen the fear in his eyes when I stood him up with the gun in his mouth, and he waited now for a telltale sign. You assume when you're dealing with a cop that everything gets played according to Hoyle. It doesn't always happen that way. Cops roll with the tide like everyone else. The good ones don't let the tide swamp them and so far I had been one of the good ones. But tonight I hadn't even read Jackie Newton his rights.

I hit the interstate, heading north, then east. Now they were both quiet, waiting to see what I was going to do. I didn't know either. I was driven by long frustration and the dim outline of a foolish idea. As a cop I had only two choices—let Jackie go or take him downtown and try to make a good case out of bad evidence—and I was quickly pushing myself to a third choice that, as a cop, wasn't mine to make. Procedure was out the window, but as I drove that mattered less and less. All I can do now, as I look back on it, is plead temporary insanity. It works for the assholes, why not for me? Answer—I'm supposed to be better than that. I'm supposed to know what the law says. I knew this much: there comes a point when a cop stops breaking procedure and starts breaking the law. An arrest becomes an abduction, and blame shifts easily, almost casually, from his shoulders to mine. Go far enough and you might as well go all the way.

The city limit slipped past us and so, in my mind, did that fine line.

Ahead lay five hundred miles of open prairie. We were playing on

Jackie's court now, with his rule book. That didn't seem to please him much. I didn't blame him; it wouldn't've pleased me either, in his place. I understood suddenly that this was a solitary thing between Jackie and myself: Barbara had no place in it; she was simply the instrument that had pushed us over the limit. I'm not thinking clearly, I thought—should've left her home. But by then we were fifteen miles out of town.

I pulled off the road. The morning was still very dark. I bumped along a dirt trail until I came to the river. There I told them to get out of the car.

Jackie found his voice. "What do you think you're doing, Janeway?" His big bad silent act was finished. He was trying to sound tough but it wasn't working: his voice was thick with worry. "What the hell do you think you're doing?" he said. Barbara said, "What are you gonna do, Janeway?" as if she hadn't heard the question just being asked. There was no fear in her now, just wonderment. They had both glimpsed the shadow of my foolish idea.

"I think I'll kill him for you, Barbara," I said. "Would you like that?"

She didn't say no. Again I told them to get out. Jackie was convinced: he turned to me and his mouth moved in the dashboard light as if to form a word, but nothing came out. He looked a lot like Barbara had looked back at the apartment. I guess real fear is the same all over.

We got out. A streak of light had appeared in the east and we began to see each other not as dim shapes but as people, faces, types. The thug, the brittle beauty, and me. What type was I?

I gave Barbara my keys. "Here. Take the car and get out of here. Park in your spot behind the house. Lock it up. I've got an extra set of keys. . . . I'll come by for it later."

She looked reluctant, suddenly unwilling to leave. "What are you gonna do?"

"Don't worry about me."

"How will you get back?"

"Barbara," I said, anger rising in my voice, "get out of here, right now."

She got in the car and drove away. Jackie Newton and I stood alone on the empty prairie and looked at each other.

I pushed him down toward the river. He was trying to talk again—
"Listen, Janeway," he said—but I told him to keep walking and shut
up. We came to a little grove of trees. Daylight was coming fast: I
could see the fear working at him. I took off my coat. Jackie Newton
watched every move I made. I folded my coat and put it on the
ground. "What are you doing?" he said, his voice suddenly shrill. I
was taking off my gun, unstrapping the holster from under my arm.
I draped it over a low-hanging branch. "Head down that way," I
said, pushing Newton along a path by the river. We went about thirty
yards. He turned and his eyes went past me, to the gun hanging from
the tree. It dropped like a piece of deadly black fruit.

He began to grin as he realized that I wasn't going to shoot him.

Slowly, he understood.

I had circled him a couple of times. The last time, I came in close
and unlocked the cuffs.

All that stood between Jackie Newton and the gun was me.

"Okay, tough guy," I said. "There's the gun. Why don't you go
get it?"

He took a deep breath. The old arrogance came rippling back. He
flexed his hands, rubbing the circulation into his chafed wrists. He
threw the handcuffs to the ground and stood up tall.

"That's the biggest mistake you ever made," he said.

I walked up through the trees, alone. I had come with a question and
was going home with an answer.

What type was I?

You're a killer, Janeway. Oh, what a killer you are. I knew what
Kong felt like after the big tyrannosaurus fight, how the soul of David
must've soared when he cut down Goliath. I felt the joy of victorious
underdogs everywhere. It was a crummy fight, if I have to hang a label
on it. Jackie hit me with everything he had: when I didn't go down,
that was the end of it. His little chicken heart crumbled and broke into
a thousand pieces. I ducked under his next punch and pounded his
guts on the inside. He exploded in a hurricane of bad breath. I came
up fast and got him on the button. He tottered and I punched him
again and he went down. He sat on his ass in the dirt and I knew he

wanted to quit but he couldn't. I let him get up in his own time and I moved in and let him hit me. I started to talk to him. *Fuck you, Jackie, I thought you had some balls.* I punched his stomach into great swollen slabs of meat, then went upstairs, for his eyes and chin. He toppled and went down. He rolled in the dirt and I waited for him to get up. Three more times he got up, just enough to salvage some pride and get his face caved in. I punched him with both hands, butted him with my head, and put him down for the count.

Hallelujah, brother. I had no illusions about what this would cost me, and it felt great.

I looked back once. He was still lying in the dirt. I thought he had a broken nose and two or three cracked ribs. I had the skin peeled off my knuckles and a mouse under one eye. It didn't hurt a bit.

A killer. God, I shoulda stayed in the ring.

The thug, the beaut, the killer.

Me.

I was finished as a cop. I strapped my gun on and threw my coat over my shoulder.

Soon I was on the highway, heading west. The morning rush hour was getting started and there was a steady flow of traffic into Denver.

I walked for a while, not wanting company.

My police career was over. I didn't need a mystic to tell me that. A line kept running through my head, that famous speech of Lou Gehrig's when he was losing not only the job he loved but also his life. *Today I consider myself the luckiest man on the face of the earth.*

For the first time in years, I knew where I was going.

I flagged a state cop, showed him my badge, and let him drive me home.

16

Ruby Seals and Emery Neff were working late, still pricing books from their big score.

They hadn't been listening to the radio. The newspaper accounts were still twelve hours away, but the TV and radio guys already had it.

I wanted to buy something I couldn't begin to afford.

"What's the best piece of fiction in the store?" I asked.

Ruby showed me a *Catcher in the Rye,* crisp, lovely in its first-state jacket. I stared into the impenetrable eyes of J. D. Salinger and bought it.

Four hundred dollars, a steal.

"What else've you got?"

Ruby looked at Neff and Neff looked back at Ruby. They cleared their throats and went to work.

"Got some King, but I know you don't care about that," Neff said.

"Which ones?"

"*Carrie, The Stand,* and that book of stories . . . ah, *Night Shift.*"

"I'll buy 'em if you want to wholesale 'em," I said.

"We'd consider that," said Ruby, his face a wall of dignity. "Yes sir, I believe we would. We bought these right, didn't we, Em? I think we could do a little wholesaling and still come out on top."

I gave a little laugh. "I'll bet you could."

"Screwed a little old lady out of her life savings, kicked her shins and took her books away," Ruby said.

"Now I don't feel so bad, offering you three-fifty for the three of 'em."

"We'll take it," Ruby said in a heartbeat.

"Not so goddamn fast," Neff said. "Ruby, these books don't just walk in here every day."

"Do I need to remind you again that the Greeks are at the gate?" Ruby said. "That's not a wooden horse they're knocking with, that's a battering ram. And that's not Helen of fucking Troy I hear calling my name."

Neff just stared.

"Sold to American," Ruby said. "Now, Dr. J, since you're in such a buying mood, take a look at these." He pushed a *Lie Down in Darkness* at me, the most beautiful copy I've ever seen of the only salable Styron. There was an *Out of Africa* in the same condition, and a great copy of Pynchon's *V.*

"God damn it, you're wholesaling the heart of this goddamn collection," Neff said.

"There'll be another collection, but not if we don't get the sheriff paid. This gentleman is gonna help us get well again."

"Oh, we're never gonna get well," Neff groaned.

"That's because you guys've got too many bad habits," I said.

"Yeah," Ruby said, "we like to eat."

I took the Styron, the Dinesen, the Pynchon. I took the Kings, too, and wrote them a check for $1,000.

"Don't it feel great to buy good books?" Ruby said.

"Yeah," I said, and it did.

"So when are you opening your place?" Neff said suddenly.

"Why the hell would I do that? Maybe I'll stake somebody, just to get my hand in."

"You want to stake somebody, stake us," Ruby said. "We are, after all, the most knowledgeable sons of bitches we know. Besides, I know where there's twenty thousand good books just waiting to be picked up for pin money."

"What kind of pin money?"

"Twenty-five grand. You might even get 'em for a buck a book, cash money."

Twenty thousand dollars was just about all I had in savings. Such a coincidence.

"Why don't you tell me where those books are, Ruby? You know, for old times' sake."

Ruby grinned through his beard and waved at me with his most prominent finger.

Neff, from on high, said, "The books are in a very safe place, Mr. Janeway. They'll be there when we've got the means to go get them."

"Maybe they will, maybe they won't," I said. "Who knows when somebody else will come along with twenty grand?"

"Not . . . very . . . likely." Neff peered through his glasses at a cracked hinge he was gluing, then smiled at me without much humor.

"Not where these books are hidden," Ruby said. "You couldn't root out these babies if you had the Lost Dutchman himself to lead you there."

"Must be in Arizona," I said. "You know . . . Lost Dutchman . . . Arizona?"

"Dammit, Ruby, don't screw around with this," Neff said. "This man is a detective, for Christ's sake."

But Ruby was enjoying the game. "Arizona's a big state."

"With not much going on in the empty spaces," I said. "There can't be many places to hide twenty thousand books in the Petrified Forest, so we must be talking about . . . ah, Phoenix."

Ruby chuckled.

"Tucson," I said, watching his eyes. "Tucson, Phoenix . . . or Flagstaff."

"Guess," Ruby said.

"Tucson."

Neff sighed with disgust.

"Your eyes moved when I said Tucson," I said. "Just a little, but it was enough."

"They're sittin' in a Tucson warehouse where they've been the last twenty years. There's nothing startling in there, just new blood; fresh faces that people in Denver haven't seen over and over for the past hundred years. Damn good stockers that you'd price in the seven-to-ten-buck range. Biography, history, some scholarly religion, some anthropology. I've known about 'em since the day they were put in there and never had the money to do anything about it. If you can spring those books, Dr. J, more power to you."

"I think I'll quit this business and take up something easy, like rolling queers in the park," Neff said.

"Em, it just don't make any difference. You see us *ever* having twenty grand? Why shouldn't somebody make use of those books, and why shouldn't it be a good guy we both like? I hate to see good books sit. And I think Dr. J would treat us right. Hell, I know an honest cop when I see one."

Neff's mind was shifting to that place where Ruby's had already gone. "I suppose we could release any claim we'd have on first dibs," he said, "for a finder's fee."

"What would you want?" I asked. "Assuming I'd be interested and the books could be sprung."

"Oh, I think a thousand dollars would be fair."

Ruby brightened suddenly. "I got a great idea. You go down there, Dr. J, and take me with you. Let me do all the talking. This is a weird bird that's got these books and you gotta stroke him. I'll get those books for fifteen grand, sixteen tops. You give me a two-grand finder's fee and let me pull out fifty books. You get out for eighteen and I get a new lease on life."

"Until next month," Neff said with a sigh.

"And what do I do with twenty thousand books?" I said, knowing the answer so thoroughly it seemed I'd always known it.

"I don't think I have to tell you that," Ruby said.

"We've seen it coming, Mr. Janeway," Neff said. "We know all the signs. You're hooked, you just don't know it yet."

"We've got a bet going, if you want to know the truth," Ruby said. "Em's betting you'll go this year. Me, I think you'll spend your whole life dreaming about it. A guy'd have to be crazy to give up your job—good money, prestige, interesting work, ten years already on the greasepole. And you're gonna give up that for this?"

"Ruby jests, of course," Neff said. "This is God's own occupation and he knows it. What would you rather be, Rubes, a bookseller or a cop?"

"Rather be a stinkin' garbageman if it put a beefsteak on my table tonight."

"Every day is like a treasure hunt," Neff said. "You never know what might walk through that door five minutes from now."

"Most likely it'll be shit," Ruby said. "Neff don't tell you about that side of it—the jackoffs that come through your front door every day and grab off a piece of your life."

"Are you talking about our beloved customers?" Neff said.

"My beloved ass. I'll tell you what a customer is, my friend. That's a guy who comes in here and knows what he's doing. He knows as well as I do what the damn book's worth, so I don't have to waste my time justifying the seven lousy bucks I'm asking for it. If you don't have a book he wants, he goes on about his business: he don't stand in your face for two damn hours telling you about it—how his grandma read it to him when he was five years old, over and over till they were both brain dead. On the other hand, there are the jackoffs. You got any idea how many jackoffs you see in the book business on a given day, Dr. J?"

"This man is trying to win a bet, that's all there is to it," Neff said. "Trust me: he wouldn't be caught dead doing anything else."

The door opened suddenly and a ragged man in jeans came in.

"Hiya, Peter," Ruby said.

"You buyin' books?"

"Does a cat have an ass? You ever known me when I wasn't buying?"

The bookscout opened his bag. I knew enough about bookstore etiquette to move away while they did their business. Their voices dropped to a dim hum. I heard Neff say, "Where'd you get this book?" Then the bookscout said something, then they were all talking at once, the scout lost in the flanking din between Seals and Neff. It turned angry. Ruby cursed and walked away. Neff continued to negotiate with the scout, who quietly stood his ground. "It don't matter where it came from," the bookscout said. "I didn't steal it, but I don't have to tell you my sources either." Ruby came back to where I stood, shook his head, rolled his eyes, turned, and walked back into battle. The fray went on for some time. At last it was quiet, but I could still hear them breathing up there.

"Dr. J?"

I came up from the shadows.

"Wanna buy a book?"

"I just bought a bunch of books, Ruby."

"Wholesale, man. All of a sudden Peter here don't trust our check."

"I need the cash," Peter said stubbornly.

"The hell with it," Ruby said. "You guys are all alike. I'm tired of the bunch of you. Maybe this gentleman will buy your book for cash money."

I looked. The book on the counter was a fine American first of Golding's *Lord of the Flies*.

I wasn't sure what to pay for it. But when I looked up, Ruby had moved behind Peter and was holding up two fingers, pointing with his other hand to the ceiling. The signal seemed to mean two hundred, high retail. I had two bills in my wallet, a hundred and a ten. Peter took the hundred gratefully.

When he had gone, Ruby said, "You paid him too much. You don't want to go over forty percent when it's a wholesale deal. Eighty bucks you shoulda paid. You're still thinking like a customer. You gotta be mean and lean if you're gonna make it in the book biz."

Neff's hand trembled as he picked up the book. "On the other hand," he said in a dull voice, "this is such a nice copy, I think I'd mark it three."

"Two seventy-five, that's the perfect price for it," Ruby said.

I looked at the book, and at the seven others I had bought. "There sure are a lot of good books showing up all of a sudden."

"It goes like that," Neff said. "You get a run, then it peters out. When that happens, you can't find a goddamn Dr. Atkins diet book."

"Millie Farmer found the Kings," Ruby said. "She's gonna be a good bookscout yet. I told you we'd get our seven bucks back."

I nudged the Golding. "This one's yours. Your store, your book, I'll take your check, if you want it for a hundred."

Ruby had already started reaching for the checkbook. Neff said, "Can't do it."

"The hell we can't."

Neff reached across the counter and snatched the checkbook away. Ruby bristled and for a moment I thought a fight was coming. The moment passed and Ruby laughed it off, though his face was still flushed with anger.

"Everybody in this business is crazy, Mr. Janeway," Neff said. "That probably includes me. But I'm not so crazy that I'll let my partner write a hot check to a cop. You keep the book."

"I'll tear up my check," I offered. "Write you one for a hundred less."

Neff sighed. "We need every dime of that check, Mr. Janeway."

"I just remembered something," Ruby said. "I just plain forgot about it in the heat of battle. That's Peter the Bookscout . . . you wanted to talk to him about Bobby, remember? If you hurry, maybe you can catch him before he gets to the bus stop."

We went outside, but Peter was gone.

I guess we all had a lot on our minds that day.

"When he comes back, tell him to call Hennessey," I said. I packed my books carefully in a small box and again opened the door.

"I'm not on that case anymore," I said.

The press was ugly. You could avoid radio and TV, but those news-paper headlines, when they came, were everywhere.

I had made the decision to go light on myself. I would read each paper once, to know what I was up against: then I'd forget it.

The *Denver Post* was simple and sweet: COP CHARGED WITH BRUTALITY, it said. Beneath that, in a smaller headline: HAND-CUFFED AND BEATEN, JEFFCO MAN ALLEGES.

The *Rocky Mountain News* wanted me shot at sunrise: COP'S BADGE DEMANDED IN WAKE OF BRUTAL ATTACK was what *News* readers read over their morning coffee. Nice objective slant.

I had made top headlines in both daily rags.

They were, as usual, about ten hours behind the tubes. The later developments, I knew, would help keep the story on the front pages for another day.

I had been summoned to Internal Affairs to give my statement on the charges of John Randolph Newton. I told it to two steely cops I barely knew, and they took it down without comment and asked only a couple of questions at the end.

It all sounded silly and unjustified a day later. I must seem like a character out of a 1945 movie: a cop with an Alan Ladd complex. And that was according to *my* version, which was supposed to make me look good. Jackie's version was another story. In that, I had beaten him with his hands cuffed behind him. He had the scars for evidence—the chafed wrists, the broken nose, the hamburger face. And he had a witness, Ms. Barbara Crowell, who was prepared to back up his version in court.

Let no one doubt that this was going to court. Even as I gave my statement to Internal Affairs, Jackie and his lawyer—a tough New Yorker named Rudy Levin—were still in the building raising hell.

Boone Steed, chief of detectives, was not happy. Boone was a tough cop who knew the ropes. He told me what to expect, what I already knew. Jackie would sue. He would sue us all, but it was me he really wanted. He would break me if he could. The department would do what it could for me, but I had acted illegally and that gave our insurance a loophole. I might end up having to mount my own defense, at my own expense. Goddamn lawyers and insurance companies, Steed said. I could run up a $20,000 legal tab in no time. And the weights of the system were all on Newton's side: they were always on the side of the guy with the dough. Newton would drag me over every bump in the courts: he'd stall and prolong it so that he could drain my account of its last dime.

I was called to Steed's office again at the end of the day. I had been suspended with pay pending the outcome of the investigation by Internal Affairs.

That night I went out to Ruby's and dropped another grand on books.

I bought wholesale, and I bought well.

By the time the second-day stories appeared I was hardened to it: COP SUSPENDED, they both said. There was a picture of Jackie, looking like the sole survivor of Nagasaki. There I was, too, plastered next to him, one mean-looking bastard. They had used my old mug shot, my killer pose. You'd never know from just a look which of these two guys is the real hood, I thought. Take a look and guess.

I didn't get much comfort from my friends. I talked to Hennessey and that was okay—Neal never changes: he reminds me of a Saint Bernard dog, always there with a keg of cheer at exactly the right moment. Others in the department weren't so hot. Somebody leaked the gory details of my long feud with Jackie, and the papers picked that up and ran with it. It looked like I had had a long vendetta against the guy, without a helluva lot in the proof department. All the times I had picked Jackie up were examined and dissected. It didn't look good.

Finally there was Carol. We talked several times over the next few days and nothing came of it. She wanted to come over but somehow it didn't happen. There was a coolness now, a distance between us. I thought I knew how that was going to turn out too.

18

In the middle of the third day, my phone rang.

"Dr. Janeway, I presume."

"You got me."

"Rubio here. That's quite a beating you took in the papers this morning."

"You should see the other guy."

"I did, my friend. His nose looked like one of my legs flopping down between his eyes. But look, I didn't call just to be sociable. I've got three questions for you. Ready?"

"Shoot."

"Number one. You want to make a fast two bills on that Golding item?"

The book happened to be on the table before me. I looked at it and thought. *No, hell no, I'll never see another one this nice.*

Ruby, catching my drift, said, "If you're gonna deal books, Dr. J, you can't fall in love with the bastards."

"Sure," I said, and my rite of passage began.

"Number two," Ruby said. "Will you let me make a little money on it?"

"That seems fair."

"All the right answers so far. Now for the big one. You ready to take the plunge?"

"I might be."

"I thought you might after I read the papers. A lot of things started coming clear after that."

"What've you got in mind?"

"Tell you when I see you. Meet me at the store in an hour, and bring the book."

The client was a man in his fifties who had been looking for the

Golding for a year. "Pickiest bastard you ever saw," Ruby said. "He'll pay top dollar, but it really has to be the world's nicest copy." He had seen and rejected half a dozen copies, Ruby said, and was primed for this one. Ruby had warned him that the tariff would be four hundred dollars.

The guy bought it without a whimper. He paid with a check to Seals & Neff and left a happy man.

I felt strangely elated, inexplicably confident. In that moment, every book I had was for sale.

"Mr. Janeway, it looks like you're a book dealer after all," Emery Neff said. "All you need now is a place to hang your shingle and the guts to take the leap."

"Which brings us back to that third question," Ruby said. "The place on the far corner has been empty about six months. It used to be a Greek restaurant and nobody thinks of it any other way. But man-oh-man, what a great bookstore that'd be. Plenty of room, lots of atmosphere—I'd rent it myself if I had the money and wasn't tied in here with a five-million-year lease."

I walked up the street and looked in the window.

It was one of those old places with alcoves and side rooms and high ceilings. The house had been built, I guessed, around 1910: a residence long ago, before East Colfax had hardened and become Hustler's Avenue. When the hustlers had moved in, the place had gone commercial: the porch had been stripped away and bricked up; a storefront had been added and grates put over the windows. The last tenants had not been kind: there was grime on the walls and grit on the floor; the ceiling sagged and the carpet, where it existed, was a nest for all the rats and bugs of east Denver. But if you could see past the dirt to what it could be, none of that mattered.

I copied the number from the sign in the window, went back to Ruby's and called the man. He wanted $800 a month and a two-year lease: he would maintain the outside and I'd take care of the inside. The place was 2,500 square feet, which included two rooms in the basement. I told him I was interested, and we agreed to meet later in the afternoon and talk some more.

"If I do it we'll be in competition," I said to Ruby.

"That never scared me any."

"Do it and in a year this block will be known from coast to coast," Neff said.

"Believe that, Dr. J," Ruby said. "Believe it. Have faith. Know that the good guys always win."

"I've been a cop too long to buy into that, Ruby."

"Believe this, then," he said, holding the check between two fingers.

"He made the check out to us," Neff said. "If you'll allow us fifty for selling it, I'll write you our check for three-fifty and we're square."

"Things must be looking up," I said cheerfully. "You're writing checks again."

"Cash it fast, Dr. J," Ruby said. "There's still a little left over from your check the other day. I'm goin' down to the bank and put this in right away. But you cash that check real fast."

19

I met the guy and signed the lease. Then I quit the department.

I called in and told Steed. We talked for ten minutes. Most of what he said could be wrapped up in a couple of short sentences.

You've been a damn good cop, Janeway: don't throw it all away because of a stupid mistake. Fight the bastards.

I didn't have the heart for that fight anymore. I went home and put it in writing.

It swept through the department like wildfire. My phone started ringing and didn't stop for three days.

20

I wanted to build it myself. I wanted to feel it going up around me. I had no sense of urgency: I hadn't touched my savings yet, and what I'd get in mustering-out pay, back vacation, and my refund from the retirement pool would more than keep me going. I bought lumber, paint, and carpet. There was a bank less than a block away, perfect for a book fund checking account. Bookscouts, who hated checks, could cash them on the spot. I knew I'd need a name and I didn't want the obvious: Clifford L. Janeway, Books. I wanted something soft and literary, not cute. I settled on Twice Told Books, and I called a sign man and told him what I wanted.

I knew it would take at least a month to get it ready. The first night I spent getting rid of the old carpet, a rotten job. Ruby came by and pitched in, unasked. He had been a carpenter in the old days, long before books, before booze and dope had jerked him screaming through life's most ragged porthole. He wasn't fast anymore but he was good. We walked through the store and he pointed out things and made suggestions, and he said he'd be back now and then with his tools to help. I slipped him a double sawbuck. He said he wasn't doing it for money and I knew that, but he was too broke to refuse. He came two or three times that first week. Our evenings settled into a routine. I had pizza brought in and we worked till ten. We talked and laughed and I felt the first faint stirrings of a new camaraderie.

In the second week the book editor of the *Denver Post* called. He wanted to do a story on the cop-becomes-bookman motif. I wasn't thrilled at the idea, since the papers were still gorging themselves on my resignation under fire, as they called it, but I knew I'd need all the help I could get. The piece ran in the Sunday supplement. The headline said, HE SWAPPED HIS BADGE FOR A BOOKSTORE. The picture of me looked almost human. "Look at that," I said to the empty store.

"I ain't such a bad guy after all." The article was okay, too. There were a few disparaging remarks from unnamed sources within the department: there was a brief recap about the two guys I had killed, and a couple of lines about Jackie Newton. All this I could've done without. But there was a quote from Ruby, too. Ruby Seals, longtime Denver antiquarian book dealer whose store is half a block east of Janeway's new establishment, said, quote, Janeway is the best bookman I've ever seen outside the trade; I know he's been thinking of this move for years, and he'll do extremely well. He has an eye for books that will carry him to the very top of his new profession. Unquote. "Aw damn, did you really say that?" I asked incredulously. He gave me his scholar's profile and farted loudly. "I think what I said was, he ain't bad for an old flatfoot. Jeez, that shrimp curry does it every time."

I never saw Emery Neff at all that week. "Neff don't like to sweat," Ruby said with a laugh. He told me he and Neff had become partners a few years ago after an on-and-off ten-year acquaintance. "Man, we thought we'd grab the book business by the ass," Ruby said. "Neff knows everything about early books. He knows seventeenth-century English poetry like I know the whorehouses of St. Louis, Missouri. Neff's an expert on magic and ventriloquism. He used to perform and give shows but he don't do that anymore. Too much hassle, not enough pay. He had one of the best collections of magic books in this state, but like everything else he sold the high spots and the rest just trickled away. Me, I know illustrated books, American lit, and off-beat stuff. I like books about strikes, headbusters, radical politics. I got a real feel for what can be milked out of a good book that nobody's ever heard of. Both of us have good juice in all the other fields. Turn the two of us loose in a store that hasn't been picked in a while and it's tantamount to rape. We're damn good bookmen, Dr. J: between us, we thought we'd have all the bases covered. The problem is . . . well, you know what the problem is. You said it yourself. We got too many bad habits, especially together. We see a book we've got to have and we pay too much. Then we've got to wholesale for less than we paid to cover the rent. You can't keep doin' that, but we can't seem to stop. Books're like dope, and me and Neff seem to feed off of each other's worst habits. We egg each other on."

"Then why don't you split?"

He shrugged. "For one thing, we really like each other. I've still got the feeling we could be the most dynamic duo since Batman and Robin if we could just get our shit together. And we'd damn near have to declare bankruptcy and start all over again if we split. I'm too old for that. So we keep after it, day after day, trying to keep from losing too much ground, looking for the big score."

"Big scores don't come along every day, Ruby."

"Tell me about it. They do happen, though. They happen when you least expect 'em. But I'm beginning to believe what Neff's always said, the big score always happens to the guy who isn't looking for it."

We were at the end of another night. I was packing the tools and putting things away.

"And then there's the problem of gettin' old," Ruby said. "I can't do this forever, I can't keep hauling books all my life. Frankly, I don't care if I never see another ten-dollar book. I want to do expensive stuff, like Rita McKinley. But almost everybody I know who does that has money to begin with. The rest of us just break our backs and get old."

"You sure find your perspectives changing."

"Ain't that the damn truth. Everybody gets old in different ways. Me, I'm just slowing down. Neff's becoming a recluse. His uncle died a year or so ago and left him a scruffy broken-down ranch in Longmont. He lives up there on weekends now, and you know what? . . . He won't even give me his goddamn phone number. He's like Greta Garbo, he vants to be alone. He says if the store burns down he don't want to know about it anyway, and he doesn't want to be bothered for anything less. But I'll tell you a secret, Dr. J, if you don't tell anybody you heard it from me. I think he's gettin' in that Millie Farmer's pants. She let something slip last week about the ranch, so I know she's been up there. She thinks Neff's the most brilliant bastard she's ever met. Hard to believe, considering she's also met me."

*   *   *

I was still at least two weeks from opening, but already the books were piling up. Bookscouts were coming by at all hours, tapping on the glass, offering their wares. People were curious and that was good. Neighbors looked in and some gave me a thumbs-up gesture as they walked away.

I knew I would open with good stock, but it wouldn't begin to fill the place up. I had to decide about the books in Arizona. Ruby waved his hand, a gesture of dismissal. "I'll tell you something, Dr. J, and I'll tell you this in good faith because you and me, we're becoming friends, I hope. You don't need that stuff. I would really give my left nut for that finder's fee, but if I were you I'd build this mother from the ground up. That's how you learn, that's how you keep deadwood off your shelves. Trust me. You'll be up to your ass in books before you know it. As soon as people find out you're paying real money, you won't know where all the damn books came from."

We had barely begun work that night when the girl arrived. It was still midsummer and the door was open to catch the early-evening breeze. I looked up and she was standing in the doorway, looking about seventeen in her spring-green dress. She had long coppery hair and when she spoke her voice had Scotland stamped all over it.

"Is this the bookstore? The new one the paper wrote about?"

"You've found us," I said. "You're a little early, though. I haven't put out the Shakespeare folios or the Gutenbergs yet, and we won't open for another week or two. What can I do for you?"

"I'm looking for a job. I'm honest and I work hard, I'm pleasant to be around and I like books."

"You're hired," Ruby said from across the room.

"Pay no attention to this street rat," I said. "I'm the boss."

"I knew that from your picture. I did think when he spoke up so forcefully that perhaps he's the power behind the throne."

"Hire this kid, Dr. J," Ruby said. "In addition to all the obvious stuff, she sounds smart."

"I am smart. I've got a brain like a whip. Ask me something."

"What's your name?"

"That's too easy. Ask me something bookish."

"What's the point on *The Sun Also Rises?*" Ruby said. "Every bookman knows that."

"What's a point?"

We laughed.

"You can't expect me to know something I never learned. But tell me once and I'll never forget it. Oh, I forgot to mention one other thing. I work cheap."

"Hire this woman, Dr. J, before the word gets out," Ruby said.

"Don't pressure the man, I can see he's thinking it over. Why don't you make yourself useful and tell me what a point is."

"Three p's in 'stopped,' page 181," Ruby said. "That's a point."

"In other words, the first edition has a mistake and the later ones don't. Now that I know that, I'm a valued employee."

"How old are you?" I asked.

"What difference does that make?"

"I'd like to know I'm not aiding and abetting a runaway."

"For goodness sakes! I'm twenty-six."

"In a pig's eye."

"I am twenty-six. What are you looking at, don't you believe me? That's another of my virtues—I never lie. My judgment's good, I'll always give you a sound opinion, and I'm compulsively punctual. What more do you want for the pittance you're paying me?"

We looked at each other.

"I have a great sense of humor," she said.

"You don't look a day over fifteen," I said.

"I'm twenty-six. When I come back tomorrow, I'll bring you something to prove it."

"We won't be open tomorrow. I won't be ready for a couple of weeks."

"I know that. I'm coming in to help you paint and stuff."

"Look, miss, I haven't even opened the door yet. I don't know if I can afford an employee."

Ruby cleared his throat. "May I interject, Dr. J?"

"I haven't found a way to stop you yet."

"A word to the wise is all. You don't want to shackle your legs to the front counter. You don't want to be an in-shop bookman. You want to keep yourself free for the hunt."

"Exactly," the girl said.

"You need to be out in the world. Meet people. Make house calls."

"House calls are important," the girl said.

Our eyes met. Hers were hazel, lovely with that tinge of innocence.

"If you're twenty-six, I'm Whistler's mother," I said.

"I'm nineteen. Everything else I've told you so far's the truth, except that I do fib sometimes when I have to. I'm hungry and tired and I desperately need a job. I need it bad enough to lie, or to fight for it if I have to. I'll come back tomorrow in my grubbys if you'll let me do something—no charge, just a bite to eat during the day. I'm wonderful with a paintbrush. I could save you a lot of time staining those shelves."

I started to speak. She cried out: "Don't say no, please! Please, please, *please* don't say anything before you at least see what I can do! Just have something for me tomorrow; in a week you'll wonder what you ever did without me. I promise . . . I promise . . . I really do."

She backed out the way she had come and hustled off down the street.

"Well," I said. "What do you make of that?"

"I told you what I think," Ruby said. "She's a Grade-A sweetie, right off the last boat from Glasgow. She's just what this place needs, the pièce de résistance. She might even be two pieces."

We went back to work. After a while Ruby said, "Remember what Neff told you about the book business, Dr. J? Honey draws flies. Truer words were never said, and it works on more levels than one."

"She never even told us her name," I said. "Five'll get you ten she'll never come back."

But there was something relentless about her, something that didn't give up, something I liked. She was sitting on the sidewalk in the morning when I got there; she was wearing an old gingham dress that had seen better times.

"You're late," she lectured. "I've been here since eight. Here, I brought you a plant for the front window."

She handed me a tin can in which grew a pathetic little weed.

"It's a symbol," she said. "It starts out little and insignificant, almost nonexistent, like your business. Both will get strong together."

"If this thing dies, I guess I can give up and close the doors."

"It won't die, Mr. Janeway. I won't let it."

I opened the door and we went inside. The early-morning rays from the sun came through the plate glass, making everything hazy and new. The place smelled like fresh sawdust, tangy and wonderful.

"Are you gonna tell me your name or is that some deep secret you're keeping?"

"Elspeth Pride." Her hand disappeared into mine. "What friends I've had have called me Pinky, for my hair. You may call me Miss Pride."

I laughed.

"I believe in keeping things professional," she said. "Don't you?"

"Absolutely."

"Let's get to work."

She started in one of the back rooms, staining while I worked the shelving up front. In a while the smell of the stain mingled with the sawdust and made a new smell, pleasant but strong. I propped open the front door. The sound of the saw buzzed along the street: people stopped and looked in and some of them asked questions. I've never been good at idle chatter, but these were potential customers and I was now a businessman. I didn't get as much done as I might have, but Miss Pride worked steadily through the morning and never took a break. At noon I went back to ask if she'd like some lunch. She had done two-thirds of the room and her work was excellent.

I went to a fast-food joint and brought back some sandwiches. We ate together in the front room. She was very hungry, and it didn't take long and she didn't say much. Personal questions were put on a back burner. Now there was just the job: the work finished and the work yet to come. She was relentless. When she spoke it was to make suggestions about color schemes and decorating and what the walls would need. "Are you going to do art as well as books?" she asked. When I told her I believed in learning one difficult trade at a time, she said, "Then you'll need a picture for that wall, not for sale, for show." The interest she took was personal and real, and by midafternoon I found her promise coming true: I was beginning to wonder what I'd have done without her.

At three o'clock I looked up and Peter was standing in the door. "I got a box of sports books, Dr. J." They had all taken to calling me that, taking their cue from Ruby. I went through his books and bought about half. I bought with confidence and paid fair money. I knew what I wanted and nothing else qualified. I would buy no book that had a problem: no water stains, no ink underlined. I set a standard that still holds: if one page of a book is underlined, that's the same as underlining on every page; if the leather on one volume of a fine set is chipped, the whole set is flawed. I would have only pristine copies of very good books. I would do only books of permanent value, not the trendy cotton-candy junk that's so prevalent today. I paid Peter out of my pocket and reminded him that Hennessey still wanted to see him about Bobby Westfall's death. "I don't know nuthin' about that," he said, and went on his way.

When I turned back to my work, Miss Pride was standing there. "I'm not sluffing off, you know. I wanted to see how you bought these things. I'm going to be your buyer someday, so you might say this is my first lesson. Why did you buy these and not something else? Why pass up the Jane Fonda book? I thought that was an enormous seller."

I sat beside her on the floor and went through them book by book. Some of it Ruby had told me. *Baseball books are all wonderful, Dr. J. Football books are a waste of paper. For some reason baseball fans read and football fans drink beer and raise hell. Basketball sucks and hockey can be slow. But always buy golf books, any damn golf book that comes through the door will sell. Buy anything on horses or auto racing. Buy billiards and chess, the older the better, but don't ever buy a bowling book.* On my own, I added this: a good biography on Jackie Robinson is worth ten books on Joe Namath. Robinson's story had conflict and drama and racial tension, not to mention baseball. It would still be interesting a hundred years from now.

And as for the *Jane Fonda Workout Book,* phooey! There are two distinct kinds of book people, best-seller people and the others. Sometimes they cross over, but usually a best-seller like Jane Fonda or Dr. Atkins lives and dies on the best-seller list. Every single person who wants one gets it while it's hot: six months later you can't give them away.

We worked on toward evening. I could see she was getting tired, but I was just coming into my second wind. Every so often she'd come out and stretch, then go back in for another hour. She asked if Mr. Seals was planning on coming tonight. I said I didn't know: Mr. Seals came and went according to his own whim. That night Mr. Seals did not come. At eight o'clock I told her to go home: I'd stay and putter around a little more. She said she'd stay and putter with me. We ate a late supper, delivered, and I pushed on to eleven o'clock. I could've gone another three hours, but it's no fun working with a zombie. She was making a heroic effort, however, for a dead person.

"Come on," I said, "I'll drive you home."

"You don't have to."

"I know I don't have to. But it's midnight and you've worked hard and this is East Colfax Avenue. Get your stuff and let's go."

"Well, the fact is, Mr. Janeway, you're embarrassing me. I have no home. There's no place to drive me to."

"Then where are you staying?"

"At the moment I'm, um, between things."

"What the hell are you doing, sleeping in the park?"

"I hadn't quite decided yet, for tonight." She went into the back room and fetched the little valise she'd been carrying. "The fact is, I just got to Denver an hour before I turned up on your doorstep. I got here with five dollars and spent half of that in the Laundromat. That's how I found out about you—there was an old newspaper there from Sunday. Fate, Mr. Janeway."

"Well, Miss Pride, tonight you sleep in a good bed." I reached for my wallet.

"No, you don't, I'm not taking any money for this. I told you—"

"Pardon my French, Miss Pride, but bullshit."

"I want a job, sir, not day wages."

"Day wages would look pretty good to me right now if I had two bucks in my pocket. Besides, nobody works for me free, not now or ever. So take the money"—I shoved $60 in her hand—"and we'll go find you a motel."

"I will take it, then, but only if you agree that it's a loan against wages."

"Don't push me, Miss Pride. You've been real good today; don't try to back me into a corner at the last minute. Now let's button it up and get out of here."

*   *   *

It had been a good day. We had gone from strangers to those first
halting steps into friendship. We had sat on the floor and broken
bread together, which is a fairly intimate thing: we had talked about
books and points, and about hope. What we didn't know about each
other would fill its own book: what we did know was a simple broadside. I sure liked what I did know. I liked her. She brought out something I had never felt before, an unexpected sensation of paternity. I
felt suddenly responsible for her welfare.

The motel we found was a few blocks from the store: she'd be able
to walk back and forth easily. I gave her a key so she wouldn't have
to wait on the sidewalk in the morning, and I went into the motel and
paid her up for a week.

The next day was a copy of the first: we worked, we ate, we said
little. Bookscouts came to sell their wares, and Miss Pride stood and
watched over my shoulder. In the evening Ruby joined us and we
worked till ten. I paid them both and Miss Pride did not argue. Ruby
never argued when money was coming his way.

The three of us got along fine. The place was shaping up. "Lookin'
booky, Dr. J," Ruby said. It felt solid, good; it felt great. We talked
and laughed, especially at dinnertime, and I paid the tariff and was
glad I had these people around me.

Miss Pride was from Edinburgh, "Auld Reekie," she called it. In
natural conversation she spoke a Scotch dialect that was all but
indecipherable: I was *so* glad she had learned English as well. Her
story—what she chose to share of it—might have been one of those
Horatio Alger tearjerkers of the 1890s. She was an orphan, desperately poor in her own land. America had always been her big
dream. She was here on a one-year work visa, which, she hoped,
could be extended. She had been here six months, mostly in New
York, but the last three weeks on the road. New York had disappointed her: her sponsor had died suddenly, leaving her to cope
in the tough Big Apple. But Denver felt right. She felt good about
Denver. Denver was where her version of the American dream was
to begin.

Ruby draped himself in a drop cloth and stood with his paintbrush pointing up. "Send us your tired, your wretched, your book-scouts," he said, and we got a good laugh out of that.

We finished up one night ten days later. The place looked like new; it looked truly marvelous. Miss Pride went over it with a vacuum while Ruby packed his tools for the last time. I just walked from room to room, unable to remember when I'd last felt such peace and satisfaction.

Now came the books. I emptied out my apartment and brought in everything from storage. Ruby was astounded at what I had. "I'm tellin' you right now, Dr. J, this fiction section is gonna be the most important one in the West. Good God, look at the *Milagros!* I can't believe it. John Nichols hasn't got this many." I told him I thought I'd make a pyramid of *Milagros* in the glass case, but he shook his head. You put these out one at a time, he said: in a rare book section, you never put more than one copy out, it would undercut the illusion of scarcity. You wanted that feeling of urgency to always be a customer's companion, the notion that he must act now, *today,* else it be gone for-ever. The three of us sat up all night pricing. Miss Pride priced the common stock using the standard ratio: she'd look it up in *Books in Print,* and if ours was a perfect copy she priced it half of the in-print tariff. Ruby and I priced the collectibles, arguing incessantly about high retail and low, scarcity, demand, and, always, condition. "Remember, Ruby, I don't want to be high," I would say, and Ruby would look at me with great disgust. "You still haven't learned anything," he would say. "You still don't know that it's easier to sell a good book high than low. Dammit, people like to think that what they're buying is worthwhile. Price it too low and it looks like you don't value your own stuff." He would hold a book against his head and close his eyes as if the book could speak. When it spoke to him, he would make his pronounce-ment. "Seventy-five bucks," he'd say, and I would argue, and he'd throw up his hands. "Seventy-five dollars, Dr. J, you can't *sell* the son of a bitch for less than that. Do you want to look like a fool?"

And so it went, till well after dawn. The night had passed in a wink and suddenly it was over. "It's always that way when you're lookin' at books," Ruby said. "An hour goes by in a minute: you don't know where the hell the time went. It's like making love to a woman . . . the most hypnotic business a man can do."

Then they were gone. Ruby went home for a few hours' sleep and Miss Pride went to her room. I walked through the store and only then did it hit me—what I had taken on, what I'd left behind, how drastically my life had changed in only one month. I took a deep breath. The place smelled of paint fumes and sawdust. It smelled like a new car, though the actual odor was nothing like that. It was real, it was alive, and it was mine. It was sweet and exciting. I had a sense of proprietorship, of direction. I had a lifetime of work ahead of me, and it was very good.

21

That was all some time ago.

We had a sensational opening week. I sold two signed *Milagros* the first day, and did almost $1,000 before the day was out. The three Stephen Kings flew out the door on the second day. By the end of the week I had taken in $3,000. I started a beard, shaved it, started it again and shaved it. I never, ever, wore a necktie. People said I was in danger of becoming a bohemian.

Jackie Newton sued me for $10 million. It looked like something that would drag on for years. I had a lawyer who was also a friend, and he said not to worry, we'd work it out.

I didn't worry. I had one or two regrets: occasionally I dreamed about Bobby Westfall and his unknown killer, but I told myself I was out of the worrying business forever.

Today it seems as if my years as a cop were all part of another lifetime. I never hear sirens in my sleep, and even a report of a gunfight in progress between police and drug dealers leaves me strangely detached. I've gone to a few funerals since I quit the department, but as time goes by I'm treated more and more like an outsider. I still run. I keep in good shape because it makes good sense. I keep my gun because that makes good sense too, but I've got a permit now, just like any other law-abiding citizen.

I see a few old friends a few times a year. I never see Carol. I hear she's living with a sergeant over on the west side. Hennessey's the same old buffalo. We sit and drink beer and talk about old cases, old times.

I get the feeling he doesn't try as hard these days. He never did talk to Peter. He never found Rita McKinley. The U-Haul lead fizzled and went out.

The cops weren't about to solve the Westfall case. As it turned out, I had to do that.

BOOK TWO

22

My days settled into a glorious routine. I was up at seven; I ate breakfast in a café a few blocks from my apartment, I read the paper, had my coffee, and was on the streets by nine. I left the opening of the store to Miss Pride. She had her own apartment now, still within walking distance; she was there faithfully by nine-thirty, leaving me free for, as Ruby put it, the hunt. From the beginning I was amazed by the stuff I found. In the old days I had gone into thrift stores and junk shops occasionally and never found anything. From the moment I became a book dealer, good things began to happen. Suddenly there were real books on the shelves of those dust palaces where there'd been only dogs before. I know two things now that I didn't know then. Then I had been looking with a much narrower eye, seeking out titles in my area of interest only. Now I bought a medical book on eye surgery, a fat doorstop with color plates, circa 1903, that I never would've touched in olden times. It cost me $1: I lowballed it to an out-of-town medical specialist for $100. I bought a two-volume set on farming from the early 1800s, very technical, for $10; I think $125 would be very reasonable for it in a store. The second thing I learned is that books are seldom found on a hit-or-miss basis. The hunt is not a random process. I had to be where the books were, and I had to be there all the time. A good book placed in the open for a small price could be expected to last only hours, maybe minutes—then a bookscout would come along and pick it off. I tried to be there first, and I was, a fair number of times. I drifted across town and sucked them up like a vacuum.

I bought extensively and well in my chosen field, first edition lit and detective fiction. I read the trades and saw trends coming. I got on the Sue Grafton bandwagon, though I don't care much for her stuff, at just the right time. Her first book, *A Is for Alibi,* has been going crazy in the used book world, appreciating at around a hundred percent a year until now people are asking $300 to $400 for a fine first. Grafton is breezy and readable, entertaining but never challenging. Her father, C. W. Grafton, once wrote one of the cleverest, most gripping novels in the literature. His book, *Beyond a Reasonable Doubt,* is by most accounts a cornerstone, but if I want to sell it I have to do it on *her* popularity. I put one away for a more enlightened time. I discovered Thomas Harris when people were still selling *Black Sunday* for $6.50. His *Red Dragon* put me on the floor, even if he did make a sophomoric break-and-enter mistake with a glass cutter in the early going. You can't break into a house that way, you might as well use a hammer and knock the glass out, but writers and the movies keep the myth going anyway. *Gimme my glass cutter, Doc. I'll just cut a little hole in this here glass case and pluck the Hope diamond out.* Uh-huh. Try it sometime. Somehow it didn't matter. *Red Dragon* was such a good book that Harris could've fed me the untreated discharge from the Metro Denver Sewer Plant and I'd've been standing there like little Ollie Twist with my gruel-bucket in my hand, begging for more. *More? You want MORE!* Even then he was putting the polish on that big riveting pisser of a book, *Silence of the Lambs,* simply the best thriller I've read in five years. I thought of old Mr. Greenwald all the time I was reading it and I wondered if he'd like it. It proves, I think, the point I was trying to make that day, that wonderful things can come from anywhere, even the best-seller list. Thomas Harris. All he is is a talent of the first rank. I hope the bastard lives forever, but in case he doesn't, I've been squirreling him away. Collectors are starting to find him now: in recent catalogs I see that *Black Sunday* is inching toward the $100 mark, and I've got six perfect copies hidden in a safe place.

Janeway's Rule of the Discriminating Bookscout was born. Buy what you like, what you read. Trust your judgment. Have faith. The good guys, like Melville, might die and be forgotten with the rest, but they always come back.

I was practicing what Maugham has called the contemplative life. At night I read some of the books I'd found. I read things I had never imagined or heard of, and I listened to good music, mostly jazz, and studied incessantly the catalogs of other dealers. I learned quickly and never forgot a book I had handled. This is how the game is played: you've got to be part businessman, part lucky, part clairvoyant. The guy with the best crystal ball makes the most money. The guy in the right place at the right time. The guy with the most energy, the best moves, the right karma.

I had been here before: I knew things that hadn't yet happened. I was home at last, in the work I'd been born for.

I had been in business three months when I was pulled back suddenly into that old world. It started a few days before Halloween. I had two visitors in the store: Jackie Newton and Rita McKinley.

23

I had come to the store late that day after a tough round of fruitless bookscouting. The days were getting shorter: we were off daylight saving time and darkness had fallen by five o'clock, the time we normally close for the night. Usually I tried to get in by four—Colfax is a rough street and I didn't like leaving Miss Pride to close up alone—but that day I had scouted Boulder and had run later than expected. It was almost five when I pulled up in front of the place and parked. I saw Miss Pride, alone in the front room, adding up the day's receipts. When I came in she rolled her eyes toward the back rooms, and when I came closer she held up the calculator to show me what she'd done that day. The total was $1,425, my best day ever. I gave a little whistle. "Couple of high rollers," she said. "They're still here, in back."

She showed me the receipts. They had bought John Stephens's *Incidents of Travel in the Yucatán,* a very nice 1843 first edition in the original boards, and the expensive Louise Saunders-Maxfield Parrish *Knave of Hearts,* which I had bought from a catalog only last month. The tariff for the two items came to almost $1,200.

"Just an average day if it wasn't for them," I said.

"They are definitely strange ducks, Mr. Janeway," she said, keeping her voice down. "But when they spend this kind of money, who's going to quarrel?"

"Strange how?" I asked.

"Well, they came in here about three-thirty. The one did all the talking. He asked for you right off. When I told him you weren't in, he asked when you'd be back. I said probably before five. He asked to see the best books in the house. I showed him the Stephens and the Parrish. He said, I'll take these, just like that. Paid with hundred-dollar bills." She cocked the cash drawer open slightly, so I could see the wad of money. "Then he wouldn't take any change. He gave me twelve hundred-dollar bills and said keep the change. I told him it was against policy, we didn't accept tips, but he went on as if he hadn't heard me. I thought he was going to leave but he didn't. He walked all around the store. Like I said, he's in the back room now."

I shrugged. "No accounting for people, Miss Pride. I'll take his money."

"I thought you would."

I sat where she had been sitting and started looking through the other sales. "You can take off now if you want."

"Oh, I'll hang around a bit. Mr. Harkness is coming by in a few minutes to take me to dinner."

I sat up straight. "Jerry Harkness?"

"Something wrong with that?"

I went back to my bookkeeping. Far be it from me to tell her who she could see. But yes, dammit, now that she mentioned it, there was something a little wrong. She was a sweet young girl and Jerry Harkness was a relatively old man. Honey draws flies, remember? And yeah, I was a little ruffled and I didn't like it much. Hell, *I* was too old for her, and Harkness had me by a good eight years. I had gone around the horn to keep my relationship with Pinky Pride on a purely professional level, and she was going out with Jerry Harkness.

"Mr. Janeway? Is something wrong?"

"It's your business, Miss Pride. He just seems to be a bit old, that's all I was thinking."

"Funny, I never thought of him that way. But you're right, he's got to be almost as old as you are."

I stared at the ceiling.

"I'm kidding, Mr. Janeway, where's your sense of humor? Of course he's too old for me, I'm not going to marry the man . . . unless . . ."

"What?" I snapped. "Unless what?"

"I might consider it if he'd be willing to do one of those convenience things that would let me stay in the country permanently. I might consider anyone who'd do that for me. But Mr. Harkness isn't going to do that. He wants to buy me a supper and I said yes: nothing more to it than that. If you've got something for me to do, though . . ."

I shook my head. "Just don't get in any dark corners."

"I never do, sir, unless they're of my own making. I hope he'll tell me some of the finer points of his specialty."

"I'm sure he will," I said dryly.

"I want to know it all."

"Someday you will," I said, and meant it.

She was learning fast. It'll be a national tragedy if we have to send her back to Scotland, I thought. The enormity of the book business—the fact that most of the books that even a very old dealer sees in a year are books that he's never seen before—simply did not faze her. She was fearless and confident at the edge of the bottomless pit. A genius, confining himself to the narrowest possible specialty, could not begin to know it all. This was the task Pinky Pride had set for herself.

She had learned so much in three months that I had her added to my book fund as a co-signer. She bought from bookscouts and signed away my money as freely as I did. She made mistakes but so did I: she also made at least one sensational buy a week. I knew that someday, in the not-too-distant future, she'd be gone, if not back to Scotland then away to a place of her own. For now, for this short and special time we shared, my job was to keep her happy.

"By the way, I'm giving you a raise," I said.

She considered it for a moment, as if she might turn it down. But she said, "I guess I deserve it."

I heard a laugh from the back room. It had a familiar ring, like something from an old dream. I heard the two guys talking in low voices, and again one of them laughed.

Then they came up front.

It was Jackie Newton, with some gunsel straight out of old Chicago. Jackie wasn't carrying anything, but the enforcer was packing a big gun. You learn to spot things like that. My own gun was on my belt, in the small of my back. I couldn't get it easily, but I'd get it quick enough if something started—probably a lot faster than Jackie would believe.

The gunsel was a bodyguard, a bonecrusher, a cheap hood. They circled the store together and pretended to look at books. I fought down the urge to say something cute ("No coloring books in here, boys" would be a nice touch) and let them do their thing. Miss Pride inched close to the counter and I saw her pluck the scissors out of our supply box.

She was no dummy, Miss Pride.

I looked in her eyes and said, "Why don't you go home now?"

"Uh-uh. Harkness, remember?"

"Go home, Miss Pride."

She didn't move. Jackie turned and looked at her and she stared back at him.

"Wanna go for a ride in a big car?" he said.

She shook her head.

He started coming toward her, looking at me all the time.

"How ya doin', fuckhead?" he said.

It was the opposite of our little meeting the day I had flattened his tire. Now I was playing it mute and Jackie was doing the talking. "I sure wouldn't want to have a place like this . . . all these valuable books . . . such a rough part of town. I hear there're gangs who don't do anything but go around smashing up places like this."

When he was three feet away, he stopped and said, "There's always a scumbag waiting to tear off a piece of your life."

He was doing all the talking.

"Broken window . . . somebody throws a gallon of gas in at midnight. Poof!"

Then he opened his bag and took out the two books he had bought. I knew what was coming and couldn't stop it. He had paid for the books: he had a receipt; the books were his.

He opened the Stephens, ripped out the 140-year-old map and blew his nose in it.

He ripped out two pages of the second volume and did it again.

He tore a page out of the $800 Maxfield Parrish, set it on fire, and lit the cigar the gunsel had been chewing.

"No smoking in here," I said calmly.

"Oh, I'm sorry, I didn't see your sign," Jackie Newton said. He dropped the flickering page on the floor and stepped on it. Then he opened the Parrish and held it out, and the gunsel dropped his soggy cigar inside it. Jackie rolled the book up in his hands and passed it to me over the counter.

"You got a trash can?"

I took the book with two fingers and dropped it into the can.

They headed toward the door.

"Come again," I said.

Jackie laughed as they went out. Miss Pride let out her breath. The scissors slipped out of her fingers and clattered on the floor.

"I recognized him too late," she said. "I didn't know who he was until I remembered his picture just now."

"It's okay."

"Pretty expensive way to show his contempt, wouldn't you say?"

"Depends on your perspective. He can afford it."

"What a terrible way to use your money, though."

I saw Jerry Harkness come to the window. Go away, I thought, I'm not in the mood for this.

But of course he wasn't going away. He opened the door and came in. He had slicked his hair and put on a tie and he wore an electric blue blazer. He looked like the well-dressed man of Greenwich Village, Mr. Cool of 1968.

"You ready?"

Miss Pride got her coat and wrapped her neck in a scarf. Harkness shifted his weight back and forth. His eyes met mine and the cool image melted and flushed. He looked uneasy.

"Okay with you, Janeway?"

"Hey, I'm not her guardian. Just watch your step."

We looked at each other again. What passed between us didn't need words: it was sharp and unmistakable. We were both years away from puberty: we had those years and that experience and a male viewpoint in common. I knew what he wanted and he knew I knew, and I was saying *Don't try it, pal, don't even think about it,* and my voice was as clear as a slap. Only Miss Pride didn't hear it.

I faced a bleak evening alone. Happy Halloween, Janeway. A light snow had begun falling. Tomorrow, I thought, I'd mosey up the block and have a little visit with Mr. Harkness. I shelved that plan at once. Mind your own business, I thought: make her mad and she may just quit and go to work for him. But the night was dark and so was I. Newton had put me on the defensive, Miss Pride had put me on edge, and I didn't know where to go to get a shot of instant light. I didn't want to read, work, go home, or stay where I was. I was at one of those depressed times when nothing seems to help.

It was then that the door popped open and Rita McKinley walked into my life.

24

I knew it was her. I had this vision of her in my head, and she seemed to fit it. Weeks ago I had received a package of photostats from the *AB,* but they contained straight news articles with no pictures; I had read the material through once and passed it on to Hennessey. It wasn't my job anymore, and yet, at odd times of the day or night I'd find myself thinking about her. Somehow she was at the crux of what had happened to Bobby Westfall. We had damn few hard facts, but my gut told me that. Almost everything about her fit the picture I'd had: she was damn good-looking, with dark hair and hazel eyes. I had been told that much by those who knew her, but my mind had filled in the blanks with amazing accuracy until the vision formed that now stood there in the flesh. The only thing I hadn't got right was the wardrobe: I had seen her in furs and jewels and she wore neither. What I could see of her dress under the old and rather plain coat looked common and conservative. She wore a little hat, tilted back on her head. It couldn't've been much protection against the wind. Her cheeks were rosy from the cold. In her hand she carried a cloth bag (I had pictured her with leather) that opened and closed by a frayed cord that looped through it. She was everything, and nothing, that I had imagined her to be.

"Are you Mr. Janeway?"

I said I was.

"I'm Rita McKinley."

I felt at once what others had felt in her presence—small and insignificant in the bookseller's cosmos. I'd like to know how she does that, I thought: I'll bet it's a helluva advantage in certain situations. Then I did know. She projected an aura that was totally real. You could look in her face and see it: not an ounce of bullshit anywhere. She came to the counter and said, "That was a blunt message you left on my machine a while back."

"I tend to get blunt when I don't seem to be having any effect. Don't you ever return calls?"

"I'm very good about returning calls. This time there was a mix-up. I've been out of town."

"You've been out of town a long time."

"I've been out of touch almost six months. I'm supposed to be able to get my messages when I call in, but it didn't work."

"What'd you do, take a world cruise?"

I didn't expect an answer to that, and I didn't get one. She went right to the point. "What can I do for you?"

"Nothing, now."

"The phone said something about a murder."

"I thought you didn't get the message."

"My machine recorded it, I just didn't get it when I called in. Now what's this about a murder?"

"I'm not in the murder business anymore."

"So I see."

She looked around at the store, and again I felt small and insignificant. I felt irritated too, for reasons I only half understood.

"Don't pay any attention to this place," I said. "This is just something to while away my golden years."

"You've done a nice job."

I looked at her for traces of sarcasm, but I couldn't see any. She browsed her way around the room, glancing into the back as she passed the open doors. "You seem to know what you're doing," she said.

"Does that surprise you?"

"Sure. It's not something I'd expect a policeman to know."

"Don't worry, I know how to beat up people too. There's a good deal more to me than pure intellect."

My sense of humor was lost on her. "This is very nice stuff," she said without a hint of a smile.

"Thank you," I said.

"You must've been putting it away for a long time."

I didn't say anything.

"You have very good taste."

"For a cop," I said. I grinned to blunt the mockery and turned my palms up.

"I guess it proves that a good bookman can come from anywhere. Even a librarian has a chance."

"You don't like librarians?"

"I used to be one. They're the world's worst enemies of good books. Other than that, they're fine people."

She fingered a book, opened it, and read something. But her eyes drifted, came up and met mine over the top edge. She had the deadliest eyes. I'd hate to have to lie to this lady with my life at stake, I thought.

"If you don't know it yet, there's an endless war going on between libraries and book dealers," she said. "At best it's an uneasy truce."

"I didn't know that."

"Oh yes; we really hate each other."

"Why is that?"

"For obvious reasons. We're all after the same thing: in some cases, things that are unique. They see us as mercenaries, motivated by greed and excessive profits."

"That's a laugh."

"Sure it is. Try to convince them of that."

"And how do we see them?"

"I know how I see them, having worked with them. I can show you libraries that would make you cry. Priceless, wonderful books given to the library, then put in some moldy basement to rot. Old-timers die and think they're doing the world a favor when they leave their books to the library. They might as well take them out and burn them. Public libraries particularly. They just don't have the staff or knowledge to handle it. And after all, the public's got to have its Judith Krantz and its Janet Dailey. So the library buys fifty copies of that junk and then cries that it has no budget."

"Where'd you work?"

"I started in a library back in Kansas, a good case in point. That library was given a gorgeous collection thirty years ago. It's still right where they put it then, in a basement room. Part of the ceiling came down five years ago and the books are buried under two thousand pounds of plaster. I'd give a lot of money to get that stuff out of there."

"Why don't you try that? Most people respond favorably to money."

"Forget it. There are all kinds of complications when you get into deals like this. Sometimes you win and save some fabulous things. More often you lose. But that's another story. What did you want to ask me?"

"I think you better talk to the man who's handling that case." I wrote Hennessey's name on the back of a bookmark and gave it to her.

"What's it about?"

"I think I should let Hennessey tell you that."

"You said something on the phone about a man named Westfall?"

I nodded. This was tricky water we were navigating. I knew I shouldn't be discussing it with her, but I had been curious for a long time.

"Am I supposed to know him?" she asked.

"Are you telling me you don't know him?"

"Never heard of him before this day."

"What about Stanley Ballard?"

"Him I know. I did an appraisal for him. Nice old man."

"You looked at all his books?"

"Every bloody one. A colossal waste of time."

"You found nothing there?"

"He was in two book clubs, and that's where ninety-nine percent of it came from. You know as well as I do what that stuff's worth."

"The history can be okay."

"But Mr. Ballard wasn't a historian, was he? He was literati, and it was all book club fiction."

Junk, I thought.

She said, "When he called for the appraisal, I told him it wouldn't be a good use of his money unless the books were worthwhile. I don't work cheap, Mr. Janeway. My expertise is every bit as specialized as a lawyer's and just as hard to come by. When I get a call like that, cold, I tend to ask some questions before I jump in the car and go racing down the hill."

"What questions?"

"The same ones you'd ask if you were me. Why they want the appraisal done, for starters. This eliminates most of them right out of the gate. Most of the time they say they just want to know what they're worth. They're just fooling around, wasting their time and mine. When I tell them that the fee for an appraisal starts at sixty dollars an hour, they back off fast. Once in a while you get a real one. He wants to get his books insured and he needs an appraisal before a policy can be written. Maybe he's had a loss, a flood in a basement, and the insurance company doesn't want to pay off. I do a lot of work like that. I don't like insurance companies—they all try to low-ball: some of them even claim that the books were never worth what they were insured for. That's where I come in. I'm not shy about telling you, there's nobody better at sticking it to a shyster insurance company. But I'm sure you know all this."

"I don't know any of it. I'm too new at it; I haven't done any appraisals yet."

"It's like money from heaven. Take my advice and the next time you run a Yellow Pages ad, put 'appraisals' in big letters. You go out, look at the stuff, do a little research, write up a report, and collect more money than an auto mechanic makes in a week. These days, that's substantial."

"Do you do mostly insurance claims?"

"No, but I do get a lot of them. I had one just before I left town. It was typical. The guy had lost his whole library in a flood. The pipes broke, the guy was visiting a friend . . . you know the story. There were books in the basement that this man had collected for twenty years. The books had never been appraised, they were supposed to be covered by his homeowner's policy . . . the replacement value, you know the clause. Well, the company wouldn't pay. The guy submitted a bill for two lousy thousand dollars and they rejected it. That's the biggest mistake they ever made. The guy called me and I went over and looked at the stuff. Christ, all he wanted was what he had in them, which was a fraction, believe me, of what it would cost to replace them today. There were some wonderful books; it broke my heart to see them all scummy and ruined. But I went through them and when I was done the guy had a retail valuation of thirty-five thousand dollars."

"And on your say-so, the insurance company rolled over and coughed up."

"They did what they always do, they sent some hot dog up the mountain to challenge my competence. You can imagine how I got along with him. So it looked like we were going to court. That's okay with me if that's how they want to play it. But all of a sudden somebody in that company got his head straightened out. All of a sudden they wanted to settle. They called and asked me to make up a book-by-book manifest, giving retail and wholesale values chapter and verse. I was delighted to do that. Suddenly I'm working on the company's nickel. If I had a cup of coffee while I was putting that list together, it cost the company five dollars. I don't mean to sound crass, but that company could've done what was right and got out of it cheap. When they decided to cheat, the bill went way up. So I gave them a list with references and footnotes and comparatives that they couldn't possibly challenge. It ran sixty pages and took me three days to put together, at eighty-five an hour. They settled with my guy for a little more than a third of the appraised value, eleven-five. What really killed them was having to pay my bill on top of that."

I did the mental arithmetic. "You must've cost them just about what the guy had originally submitted as a total bill."

"Two thousand, forty dollars. And people say there's no justice in the world."

"So what about Ballard?"

"I went through the whole routine with him. Asked him why he wanted the appraisal done, so I could be sure it was a good use of his money. That's what it's all about. If you've got any ethics, this is the first thing you've got to find out."

"What difference does it make, if you find out and you still do the appraisal?"

She recoiled from the question as if a snake were wrapped around it. Her eyes narrowed in anger. "Don't sit there and judge me, sir. It makes a hell of a difference."

"What difference?"

"Are you trying to needle me, or do you really want to know?"

"Like I told you before, it's none of my business anymore."

"Fine. Then I'm wasting my time."

I thought she was going to leave then, but she didn't. She did the store, looking more carefully now at items that had caught her eye earlier. I went back to my bookkeeping and let her browse. It took more than half an hour for her to work her way around the room.

"Look, I'll tell you something and then I've got to go," she said. "I don't care what you think of me or why, but here's what happened. The man told me he'd been in the clubs for fifty years. In all that time, he had bought only the fiction. I told him my bill would be higher than the whole library was worth. He said he didn't care about the money, he just wanted a record left for his heirs so everything would be easy after he was gone. I took it from what he said that the heirs don't get along."

"That's the understatement of the year."

"Well, there you are. He didn't care about the money, he just wanted them to have one less thing to fight about after he'd gone. God damn it, that *is* a good use of his money, if that's how he decides to use it. As long as they know what they're getting into, who am I to tell them they can't do it. I still didn't want to do it. This isn't the kind of work I usually do, and there are plenty of people in Denver who'd be glad for the job and do it well and for a lot less money. If you want to know the truth, I just can't get excited about looking at five million book club books, even if I'm getting paid for it; I don't need the money and I don't do anything anymore unless it excites me. But this old gentleman wanted me. He wanted a document that wouldn't be questioned. It may sound arrogant, Mr. Janeway, but he made it sound like a man's last request."

"It doesn't sound arrogant, it's probably true. He died this summer."

"I'm sorry to hear that. He was a grand old man and I liked him."

"Everybody says that."

She seemed to thaw a little. "He was like . . . my grandfather . . . only his taste in reading was better. There were some fantastic titles in there, but they just won't sell in those cheap editions. What more can I say?"

"You did the appraisal?"

"Yeah; three weeks later I drove down and did it. It didn't take long and I didn't charge him much—just enough to keep it on a professional level."

"How did you do it?"

"What do you mean, how did I do it? I looked at the books and wrote them up. There wasn't anything in there that needed to be itemized individually. They needed to be counted and we did that: rather, he did it before I got there. I told him to do that. There's no sense paying an appraiser for something you can do yourself. All I had to do was look at them. There wasn't a single book that needed to be researched. It took me about four hours to go through it and I was really moving."

"Was there a chance you might have missed something going that fast?"

"There's always a chance with a library that large. All I can tell you is, I looked at every book on those bookshelves. It was just what the man said it was, book club fiction top to bottom. Not worth the paper it was printed on."

"What did your written appraisal say?"

"Just that. No value, except as salvage books. Maybe a decorator might want them, to fill shelves in model homes."

This was her statement and it was now finished. What she had told me so far was harmless: it was what she would tell Hennessey tomorrow or the next day. This was where the questioning began, for a cop. I wasn't a cop anymore and I had to be careful of what I said to her. You don't tell someone what questions the cops are likely to be asking: it sets her on edge, gives her an advantage.

But I couldn't resist this. "Would it surprise you to know that someone bought that library, Miss McKinley? Thought he was getting a helluva deal."

I saw the anger again, but this time she kept it in. "Nothing surprises me," she said. "There's always someone who'll buy something, and there's always someone who'll pay too much. You'll find that out when you've been in it awhile."

I gave a little shrug. "This guy knew books," I said, and my alarm went off and that was the last thing I was going to say to Rita McKinley about the Ballard books until she had given her statement to Hennessey.

Her anger simmered to the surface. "Maybe he didn't know them as well as you think. Maybe he lost his mind, Mr. Janeway. Maybe I was in cahoots with someone. What do you want me to say?"

"Nothing."

"Do you think I lowballed the appraisal just so somebody could buy it cheap? Is that what this is all about?"

"It doesn't matter what I think. I'm not the police anymore."

"I've got to go," she said again. "Show me a couple of things in your glass case first."

I took the books out and she looked at them carefully. "Let me see those too, please." She was all business now. I tried to be too. I showed her the books and eventually she put most of them back. What she finally bought were Saul Bellow's two rare novels, perfect copies I had bought from Peter less than a month ago. Ruby had priced them, high retail I had thought at the time: *Dangling Man* at $400; *The Victim* at $250.

She didn't ask for a discount: money seemed to mean nothing to her. I gave her the usual twenty percent and she wrote a check for $520.

And I fell into the pit of aimless chatter. Suddenly the night looked very long and dark, and I hated to see her go.

"I'm surprised you bought those: an old bookman I know said I'd probably die with them. Bellow's supposed to be like Mailer and Roth and Henry Miller. Nobody cares enough to collect them."

"I guess your friend was wrong. At least about these Bellows."

She was heading for the door. I wanted to grab her by the sleeve and show her something. It didn't matter what, as long as it was interesting and she hadn't seen it before.

How would you like to see how a cop really interrogates, Miss McKinley?

What I said, though, was "Look, I didn't mean to imply anything."

She turned at the door and gave me a look. I gave up the fight and made my betrayal of the Denver Police Department complete.

"I knew the books weren't worth anything," I said. "We saw the statements from the club. He kept them all, a complete record, all the way back to the beginning. I could've done that appraisal, just from the records he'd kept."

"Well, then," she said crisply. "I guess I won't go to the electric chair after all."

She had the door open. Now or never, I thought.

"How about dinner some night?"

"I don't think so," she said in the same heartbeat. "Thank you for asking, but no."

The door pulled shut in her wake. I stood again in an empty room on an empty world. A faint trace of her cologne lingered. Her memory lingered a good deal longer.

25

I dreamed about her. We swam together through a sea of books, in my dream. This was wonderful stuff. I hadn't had much to do with love, quote-unquote, in a very long time. Perhaps a bachelor heading into senility doesn't believe in the quote-unquote; maybe it's the one thing he's truly afraid of. But Rita McKinley had lit a fire under me and I knew it. I had gone up like an ember doused with gasoline. This may be normal for an adolescent, but for a man in his thirties who deals in "relationships" rather than "love," the feeling was heady and strange. It wasn't an unpleasant feeling, but with it came the unease of knowing that it would probably turn out to be.

In the morning I called Hennessey to square things away. I was still enough of a cop to do that. I told him about McKinley's after-hours visit, what we'd said, and how much I'd given away. He didn't seem to care much. The mayor wasn't exactly demanding that cops be called in on overtime to solve Bobby Westfall. He would be happy to talk to McKinley, when they made connections, but he wasn't hopeful that anything would come of it.

Two hours later, he called back and said McKinley was coming in around eleven o'clock. After that she was fair game.

Fair but elusive.

I called her number around two. She had the recording on, but she called back less than an hour later.

Her voice was cool and distant. "Well, Mr. Janeway, have you figured it out yet?"

"Figured what out, the murder or the book business?"

"If you ever get the book business figured out, let me know how you did it. What can I do for you?"

"Help me figure it out."

"I told you last night, and I told your Mr. Hennessey again this morning, I don't know anything about it."

"I was talking about the book business. I'd like to come up and see your books."

I felt completely transparent, stripped before the world. I braced for another rebuff and got it.

"There's no margin for you up here," she said. "Everything I've got is very high retail."

"I bet I'll find something."

"I don't think so. You couldn't possibly make any money, and look, I'm very busy now. I just got home, I'm still tired, and I've got a million things to catch up on. Add to that the fact that I'm just not feeling very hospitable. I don't feel like having company."

"Well, that's plain enough."

"I'm sorry. Good-bye."

Strike two on Janeway: bottom of the ninth, two out, and the fans begin to head for the turnstiles. I left the store in Miss Pride's care and made my rounds. I reached the DAV on Montview just as books were being put out. It looked like crap. I looked at it through Rita McKinley's eyes, and all I could see was crap: small-time books eagerly coveted by eternal small-timers. Book club mysteries. Book club science fiction. Dildo books: the *Cosmo Book of Good Sex, How to Make Love to a Man,* screwing seven ways from Sunday, blah blah blah. I hope these aren't the books we're judged by, by archaeologists of the future.

I'd been staring, thinking of Rita McKinley, when my eyes focused on the title *JR* and the name Gaddis. I reached out and plucked it just in time. A shadow loomed over my right shoulder.

"Hiya, Dr. J."

I turned. "Hi, Peter. How's tricks?"

"Could be better. Y' almost missed that one. What's it worth?"

I opened the book, took off the jacket, sniffed for mold. It was a nice enough first: the flyleaf had been creased and some bozo had written his name in it.

"Oh, for this copy, thirty, forty bucks."

Miss McKinley probably wouldn't pick it up, even at $2. But to a guy like Peter, it was a little shot of life.

"Damn," he said. "Another minute and I'da had it."

"You can have it anyway," I said, and I gave it to him.

"Jesus, Dr. J . . ."

"Merry Christmas, two months early."

"Jesus."

We walked out together. In the parking lot we stood and chatted for a moment. I asked if he was finding any books. He said yeah, he had some nice stuff to show me. One or two real honeys. Maybe he'd come in later in the week.

Then he seemed to go stiff. I looked at his face and thought he might be having a heart attack. He tottered and would've fallen if I hadn't grabbed his arm.

"Hey, Pete, you okay?"

"Yeah, sure."

He didn't look okay. He looked like a gaffed fish.

"I gotta go," he said.

"Come on, I'll give you a ride."

"No . . . no ride. Here comes the bus."

He broke away and ran across the street. A car swerved and almost hit him. He spun around and without breaking stride ran full-tilt to the bus stop. He had dropped the copy of *JR* at my feet.

I picked it up and watched the bus roll away. What the hell was that all about? I wondered.

It was about fear. Peter had been so scared of something that his mind had stopped working. Something had scared the hell out of Pete.

I stood where I was and looked around. A busy but harmless intersection: cars raced through on four lanes and people hustled along the sidewalk. Two convenience stores faced each other across the street. On the third corner was a little shopette and a Mexican café. The thrift store took up the fourth corner. I tried to remember what Peter had been doing, where he'd been looking, when it had happened, but I couldn't be sure. I walked across the street and went into one of the convenience stores. I bought some gum. Then I shrugged it off and went back to work.

"Rita McKinley called," Miss Pride said when I came in. "About fifteen minutes ago."

I played it cool. Checked the day's receipts. Verified my suspicion that it had been a lousy day. We had barely broken a hundred: cleared expenses was all.

I walked up the street and visited Ruby. He was getting ready to pack it in. Neff had gone home for the day. The firm of Seals & Neff had taken in less than fifty dollars.

It had been a lousy day on Book Row all around.

I didn't go down as far as Jerry Harkness. I could see a light coming from his window, so I knew he was there. I could see a light in Clyde Fix's place as well.

Night had come with a vengeance. I felt alone in the world and I had a hunch that, whatever Rita McKinley had to say to me, it wouldn't make that feeling go away.

But it did. When I called her, she was full of apologies.

"I'm not usually rude to people, Mr. Janeway. Put it down to jet lag."

"I didn't notice at all," I lied.

She spoke into the sudden yawning silence. "If you still want to come up, of course you're welcome."

"Just say when."

"Tomorrow afternoon would be as good a time as any. Make it late afternoon and that'll give me time to wind down from the trip."

I felt light-headed, almost giddy. Janeway's still at bat, folks: as incredible as it is to believe, he's been standing at the plate popping fouls into the bleachers for more than twenty-four hours, and the game's still hanging in the balance.

Miss Pride was watering her plant, which had been repotted twice and was growing into a small tree. I had never seen anything grow like that in just three months.

"What kind of thing is that?" I said.

"I have no idea. Just something I dug up myself."

"If it grows teeth, kill it."

We began to go through the nightly ritual, preparing to close.

"So you didn't tell me," I said. "How was Harkness?"

"A dear. A perfect gentleman."

I sighed.

"I know you'd love an excuse to go up there and tear his head off, but I'm afraid I can't give you one. He was just fine. His manners were beyond reproach."

"Just watch your flank, Miss Pride, just watch the water fore and aft, port and starboard. Now what do you say we lock this baby up and call it a bad day?"

"It *was* pretty dreary. I'll get the lights and put the recording on."

She disappeared into the back room. I locked the front door and began counting the money. I had just got started when I felt my hackles go up. I turned and looked through the glass. Jackie Newton was sitting in a car at the curb, watching me. It was a long black car, not one of his. The gunsel was behind the wheel.

"Uh-huh," I said.

Miss Pride, coming from the back room, said, "Did you say something to me?"

"I said we've got company."

"Oh, God."

"Don't even look at 'em; don't let 'em faze you at all. Just go on about your business and get ready to leave."

I turned the sign around, in case they had any notions of coming in. Miss Pride bustled about gathering her things.

"Are we ready to go?" I said.

"I am."

"Good. I'm driving you home tonight, by way of west Denver. Don't argue with me, let's just go. We'll walk right past the sons of bitches and get in my car and drive away. Got that?"

"I got it."

I flipped the front room lights. The telephone rang.

I heard the machine kick on and then begin recording. I don't like machines that answer telephones, but Miss Pride had talked me into it, so we wouldn't miss anyone with a big library to sell. As usual, she was right: the damned machine had made its cost back, three times over.

"I'm gonna see who that is," I said. "You wait here. Don't look at those guys and don't look worried. I'll be right back."

By the time I got into the office, the recorder had cut off. It was probably Rita McKinley, I thought, canceling tomorrow. I rewound the tape and played the message.

It was Peter. His voice was tense, strained. "I need to talk to you, right now," he said.

I waited. I knew the line was still open, but he didn't say anything. He was like a man whose attention has suddenly been captured—like the poor scared fool he'd been in the thrift store parking lot.

"Oh, shit," he said, and hung up.

I ran the tape back and replayed it. It didn't make any more sense than anything else he had done that day. I had no idea where he lived or how to reach him. Maybe Ruby knew.

I reset the tape, went up front, killed the last of the lights, and took Miss Pride by the arm. "Let's go."

I locked the door and we walked past the car where Newton and his thug sat waiting. The gunsel started the engine and the car rolled along beside us. I'm gonna put up with this about ten seconds, I thought; then I'm gonna kick some ass. I walked up to Ruby's. The store was closed and locked. I walked past Harkness's, which was also closed. Only Clyde Fix was still open: he sat in the window and watched the street like a vulture.

We went around the corner to the small lot where everyone on Book Row kept their cars. The headlights of the gunsel's car swung behind us in a slow arc. I held the door for Miss Pride, then I walked back to the gunsel's car, which was sitting still with its motor running.

I tapped on the window. Jackie rolled it down a crack.

"That's all for you, Newton. If I see your ass again tonight there's gonna be trouble."

"Izzat so," the gunsel said.

I kept looking at Jackie. "Does this guy speak English? Keep your hands on the wheel, dogbreath; touch that gun and I'll blow you right through the door." There was a long quivering pause. The gunsel's fists clenched around the steering wheel. "Now I'm gonna tell you something, Newton, and this goes for you too, Anton. If you want to live to celebrate your next birthday, don't fuck with me. You want to put that in Mongolese, Jackie, so the ape can understand it? Don't . . . fuck . . . with me."

"Tough guy," the gunsel said. "I'm gonna walk on you, tough guy."

"You couldn't walk the plank without losing your way. Now get this crate down the street."

Jackie wanted to look amused, but he couldn't sell that. He rolled up his window and motioned with his finger and the car pulled away from the curb. I watched the taillights go and thought again of Vinnie Marranzino. I stood for a long moment after they'd gone, watching the empty street.

Just another day on Book Row.

The next day began like every other. How it ended was another matter.

I made my rounds and found nothing of interest. The entire day was colored by my coming meeting with Rita McKinley. I was on edge, nervous and apprehensive and, in a very real but strange way, thrilled. I had an early lunch with Hennessey and we talked a little about the Westfall case. Hennessey liked Rita McKinley and was inclined to believe everything she said. The line from the police department now seemed to be that Bobby Westfall had been killed by a petty thief, who was likely to remain unknown until he was caught for another crime and confessed to this as well. "Right, Neal," I said, and he gave me a look over a ten-pound sandwich and decided to say no more about it.

I had time to kill and I didn't want to go into the store. I called in instead, and told Miss Pride I was heading west and probably wouldn't see her till tomorrow. "Well, that's going to be a problem for Peter," she said. "He was here a while ago looking for you. He seemed quite put out when you weren't here. I told him to come back at closing time, you're always here by then."

"Well, tonight I won't be. Did he say what he wanted?"

"No, but he certainly made it sound urgent."

"When he comes in, try to help him. He mentioned to me yesterday that he might have some pretty good books to sell. If he needs some money, give him some. Give him up to a couple of hundred if that's what it takes. Write him a check on the bank up the street and tell him I'll square it with him tomorrow."

"Well, all right, but I don't think that's what it's about. He didn't have any books with him and he didn't say anything about money."

"All right, if worse comes to worst, have him call me up at Rita

McKinley's place. Now, one more thing. Call your friend Harkness and let him know you're gonna be alone at closing tonight. Tell Ruby and Neff too."

"I'll be fine, Mr. Janeway."

"Listen to me. Do what I tell you. That's the most dangerous time of day for businesses run by women alone. Just let the others on the block know that you'll be closing up alone tonight. That way they can keep an eye on you."

I heard her sigh with feminist impatience.

"Miss Pride? Are you listening to me?"

"Yes, Mr. Janeway."

"Do it."

"Yes, Mr. Janeway."

I decided to scout west Denver, work my way through Golden and Morrison and let my momentum carry me to McKinley's place by late afternoon. For some reason, west Denver is a bookscout's ghetto. There are a few thrift stores, but nothing to write home about, and Golden is a complete wash. Morrison is an interesting little mountain town, full of antique stores that will sometimes cough up a garnet in the sea of junk. It was, however, less than a blue-ribbon performance: the sum total of the day's work was less than a dozen books, none even on the fringe of greatness. Some days are like that.

It was almost dark when I drove up the road to Rita McKinley's. The clock in my dashboard said 4:53. I was running a little later than I'd planned—a place in Evergreen had caught my eye, and you know how bookscouting is. She had left the gate open and I drove right through. She was working when I arrived: she had a fire going in the yard and huge piles of trash waiting to be fed to it. It was chilly. She wore faded jeans and a red flannel shirt and a heavy coat. The house was perched on top of the mountain, a great stone building with a porch that looked east, toward Denver. You couldn't see the city from there, but that didn't hurt the view. Miss McKinley gave a wave as I came into the yard. I parked beside her car, a plain Dodge about four years old.

From a distance she looked very young, an illusion that dissolved as I came closer. She was one of those women who look better with some age. She'd be a knockout at forty, about six years from now. We said our hellos and I apologized for intruding. She waved that off and led me inside. "My books are all over the house," she said. "It'll take you a long time to see them all. Maybe we should confine ourselves to the big room today."

The house smelled musty, the way a place gets when it's been closed for six months. Her living room was long, with a fireplace and a high ceiling. She had an enormous print of a whale, the picture Rockwell Kent had done for the 1930 edition of *Moby Dick*. There were other whales about—knickknacks on the shelves, pictures on the walls, paintings, photographs. Over the fireplace she had a blown-up photograph of a lone man standing on the bow of a speed-boat. A larger boat was in the background, bearing down. I knew what it was: someone from Greenpeace, putting himself between an unseen whale and a boatload of modern whalers.

There weren't many books in the living room, and these she said were junk, "just things I'm reading." The main event was two rooms removed. The whole east wall was made of glass. There were heavy drapes, open now, which she used, probably in the morning, to pro-tect her books against the sun. All the other walls were lined with books.

"Before you get started, there was a call for you about ten minutes ago. It may've been your girl at the store. It sounded pretty confused. Here, I got part of it on the tape machine."

She flipped a small cassette player. The first thing I heard was Peter's voice. He was in the middle of a sentence, as if he'd been talk-ing over the recording. I couldn't make out what he was saying, but his voice sounded almost panicky. He turned away from the phone and there was a jumble of voices. A woman's voice said, "Let me talk to him, Peter. . . . Peter, would you give me that phone . . . give it to me, Peter, right now." There was a click and a bump and Miss Pride came on. "Mr. Janeway, are you there? Hello?" Then I heard her say, lower, as if she'd turned away, "There's nobody on the line, Peter, are you sure you dialed it right?" Then Peter screamed—literally screamed—"It's a fucking tape recorder!" and I heard him shout something but I couldn't make out the words. They were both talking for about ten seconds; then Miss Pride came back on and said in a low voice, "Look, I'm sorry, someone's come in. . . . I'll call you back."

The line went dead.

"You certainly know some strange people, Mr. Janeway," Miss McKinley said.

"I can't imagine what was going on there."

"I think you'd better call her back."

She went out of the room while I called. The phone rang and rang. The clock on the wall said five twenty-five: the store had been closed for twenty-five minutes.

I sat for a moment and stared at the machine. Miss McKinley poked her head in.

"Everything all right?"

"I don't know. Could I hear the tape again?"

But there was nothing on the tape that hadn't been there the first time.

I called Seals & Neff. Ruby answered on the first ring.

"Hey, Rube, this's Janeway. Listen, would you walk up the street and see if everything is okay at my place?"

"Sure. What's wrong?"

"Peter was just in there. I'm afraid he may've been giving Miss Pride some grief."

"Sure . . . gimme your number where you're at. . . . I'll call you right back."

I hung up and sat down to wait.

"How about some coffee?" Miss McKinley said. "I've got some whiskey if you'd like a drink."

"As a matter of fact, it is almost decent time for a bourbon."

"How do you like it?"

"Just like it comes."

She came back with the drink just as Ruby called. She motioned to the phone, that I should answer it, and I did. Ruby said, "Place looks shipshape to me, Dr. J. All locked up tight and the night-light on."

"Did you try the doors?"

"All both of 'em. Walked around, rattled the windows, sang three stanzas of 'The Battle Hymn of the Republic' through the keyhole.

Nobody's there, Dr. J. Whatever the bug up Pete's ass was, she must've handled it and got him out of there."

"Okay," I said in a doubtful voice. "Thanks, Ruby."

I looked at Miss McKinley. "What a crazy thing."

"There's probably a simple explanation."

"Yeah . . . but you'd think she'd call back."

"Maybe it slipped her mind. She did say someone had come in. Anyway, there's nothing you can do about it now. Might as well do what you came for."

28

Everything Julian Lambert had said about her books was true, except that even then you weren't prepared for them. You just don't see that many sensational books in one place. It was all literature, published since the mid-1800s, and it was all letter-perfect. You need a book-man's eye to appreciate what a perfect copy of a fifty-year-old book looks like. It does not look like a new book—it looks so wonderfully like an old book that's never been touched. Never been touched by human hands—that's the feeling her books gave you. There were things in that room that I knew hadn't been seen in that condition in half a century. She had a shelf of Jack Londons in crisp dust jackets from before 1910. She had a little poetry piece that had ushered Ernest Hemingway into the book world. She had Mark Twain's copy of *Kim,* signed by Kipling when he and Clemens had met, in 1907. There were so many signed books, variants, unique pieces, books with unusual associations, books from authors' personal libraries, letters, and manuscripts that mere first editions seemed unexciting and trite. She had factory-fresh copies of *Look Homeward, Angel,* and Steinbeck's first, awful, but extremely scarce novel, *Cup of Gold.* After a while this becomes meaningless: it degenerates into a simple list of the great, the rare, the wonderful. When I came upon Hawthorne's copy of *Moby Dick,* inscribed by Melville in great friendship and lavishly annotated in Hawthorne's hand, I heard a long deep sigh fill the room. I realized a moment later that it had been my own voice.

The phone rang, and I thought of Miss Pride. I heard the recorder kick on and Rita McKinley's voice repeating the message I had heard so often. At the beep, a man said, "Rita, this is Paul. . . . Call me back when you can." It rang again, almost immediately. The recorder played and beeped and a voice said, "This is George Butler the Third calling from New York. I have decided to buy the four books we discussed yesterday. Would you please ship and bill as soon as possible?" Of course I knew who Butler the Third was. I saw his self-aggrandizing ads in the *AB* all the time. "Mr. George Butler III announces his acquisition of . . ." That kind of thing. George Butler was one of the so-called big boys of the book world. You read his ads and you knew he never put on his pants like a mortal man, he just drifted up and floated down into both legs at once. I wondered what four books George Butler had decided he couldn't live without, and what the tariff would be. Ten thousand? Twenty? Just routine business for Ms. McKinley, who was certainly operating on a high level from her ivory tower in the mountains.

I took a break and called Miss Pride's home number. She wasn't home. I looked through some more books. I had done most of one short wall and still had the long wall and another short one left. I felt light-headed, like a drunk just coming back from a three-week bender. It had been too rich, this feast of her books, and I decided to pack it in for the night. I got up, stretched, and moved to the door. There was no sound in the house, other than the grandfather clock ticking in the hallway. The clock said it was eight-thirty. I went through the dark hall, drawn by the light at the end. Suddenly I smelled food cooking. When I came into the kitchen, I saw that she had set a table for two.

I didn't see her at first. She was standing by the glass door, perfectly still, lost in thought, looking away into the night. I cleared my throat. She turned. There was a pensive, lonely, almost sad look on her face. I didn't know what else to call it but a window to the soul. It disappeared at once and the mask came up. She looked surprised, as if she'd forgotten I was there.

"Well, Mr. Janeway. You all finished?"

"Give me another week and I might be just getting started."

She didn't say anything.

"I thought I'd buy something," I said. "I guess I wanted to show off. But I've got to tell you, I don't know where to begin."

"It has that effect on people. It can be overwhelming."

"I hope when you go away for months at a time you have some way of protecting it."

"I do lock the gate."

"Don't you even have a burglar alarm?"

She shook her head. "You think I should?"

"Yes, and an armed guard, and spotlights, a siren, and killer dogs. I'd also put a moat around the house and fill it with crocodiles. That's for starters."

"Oh, it's no fun having something if you've got to lock it up . . . if it makes you paranoid."

"There's a difference between paranoia and common sense. You'd hate to come home someday and find all these books gone."

"Yes, but they're only books. I'd just go get some more."

I didn't know what to say to that.

She said, "I love what I do but I'm not very materialistic. If I don't have them, somebody else will. As long as they're not destroyed, the world's no worse off."

"I don't believe you said that. I could spend a week in that room without water, food, or air."

"Speaking of food and water, I'm fixing us something to eat. Hope you don't mind fruit and veggies. I'm trying to stop eating meat."

It was an Eastern dish, very tasty, with nuts and shoots and broccoli under a golden baked crust. She had a good bottle of wine and a little chocolate cake for dessert.

We talked over dinner. She was giving up meat for both main reasons, health and politics. She was an environmentalist, but I had already guessed that. I didn't think the individual could make much difference. She bristled at that and said, "As long as you think that way, you are the enemy. The individual is the only one who can make a difference." I didn't believe that but I didn't want to ruffle her. She was a woman who mattered to me, very suddenly, very keenly, and I wished we could talk without having our conversation sprinkled with land mines. I said, and meant it, that I probably agreed with most of her political views, I just didn't believe some of them could be won that way.

She looked at me with a blank expression. "I can't figure you out, Janeway."

"That makes us even. I can't figure you out."

"I don't know whether you're a poet or a thug."

I laughed at that: couldn't help myself. She shook her head and didn't seem amused.

"What do you do in the summer?" I asked.

"Travel. What do you do?"

"What I do all the time anymore. I look for books. Do you look for books in the summer, in exotic and faraway places?"

"I don't have anything to do with books in the summer. I am, for all practical purposes, closed down between May and September. I don't even read books in the summer."

"What do you do if you get a call on the first of May from some guy in New Mexico who says he's got ten thousand perfect books and he's selling them all cheap?"

"I tell him he'll have to call someone else. I might refer him to you, if I like you."

"You give me the impression that none of this matters."

"It matters. This collection was put together with tender loving care, so it does matter. It's just not the most important thing."

"What is?"

"I don't think I'll answer that question yet. Maybe I will, if I ever get to know you better. For now, it's none of your business."

We ate in silence for a moment. Then she said, "Tact is not one of my strong points. If you were still a policeman, I guess I'd have to tell you, wouldn't I? You can find out if you want: your friend Mr. Hennessey knows."

"I won't do that."

"Good. And really, it's no big deal. I'm just very . . . very . . . private. I value my privacy more than anything but my freedom."

"Hey." I held up both hands in a gesture of mock surrender.

The phone rang: the recorder kicked on. It was another dealer, in San Francisco, asking if she still had the first edition *Phantom of the Opera*. I knew she had it: I had seen it on my tour of the short wall.

"You've got your phone amplified all over the house?" I said.

She nodded. "That way I can weed out the pests. The answering machine puts a buffer between me and the world; the amplifier lets me know if it's someone I want to talk to now. But I never get calls that can't wait."

"Not even George Butler the Third," I said with false awe.

"George is a very large pain. I don't know why I fool with him."

"You know what I'd like to have?" I said suddenly. "Your Steinbeck, with the penis doodle."

She laughed, the first time I'd seen her do that. "'Tom Joad on the road.' It's one of my favorite books. Very expensive for that title."

I felt my throat tighten. "How expensive?"

"If you've got to ask, you probably can't afford it. Seriously, you don't have to buy anything. I don't charge admission up here."

I took out my checkbook and tapped it lightly on the table.

Her eyes narrowed and got hard. "Fifteen hundred," she said.

The knot in my throat swelled, but I began to write the check.

"Make it twelve," she said. "I usually don't give or ask for discounts, but I will this time. Make it payable to Greenpeace."

I blinked at her. "Greenpeace?"

"Do you want me to spell it for you?"

"Greenpeace," I said dumbly.

"Greenpeace gives me a reason to get up in the morning."

I handed her the check. "Oh, I'll bet you have at least a thousand very good reasons for getting up in the morning, Miss McKinley."

She blushed when I said that. She really did. I felt a flush in my own cheeks. It had been a long time since I'd tried playing the gallant.

"So," she said, going for more coffee, "you've just bought your first really nice book and paid retail for it. What are you going to do with it?"

"Gonna sell it."

"Good for you. You think there's any margin?"

"For something like this, there's always margin."

"You know, Mr. Janeway, I really do think you're going to turn out to be a good bookman. You already know what sometimes takes people years to learn."

"Which is . . . ?"

"When you buy something unique, and pay twice what it's worth, it's a great bargain. It took me a long time to learn that. Some people never learn it. George Butler never has. Now it's the only way I operate."

"That's fine if your pockets are deep enough."

"That does help. It's hard making it from scratch in the book business."

"Tell me about it."

Please tell me about it, I thought. We were going nowhere fast, on an endless merry-go-round of polite tea talk. I needed a break-through, something to batter down the walls she had built around herself. I had a hunch that if I walked out of there without finding that key, she'd never let me come back. There was something at work between us, and it was good but it wasn't all good. I couldn't get a handle on any of it. I knew she was curious about me but she'd never ask: by refusing to talk about herself, she had given up that right. I could see that if there was any opening up to do, I'd be the one to do it. Slowly I turned the talk to my childhood. She listened intently and I was encouraged to go on. It became very personal. Suddenly I was telling her things I had never told anyone.

In the first place, my birth was an accident. My father is a lawyer whose name heads a five-pronged Denver partnership on Seventeenth Street. He makes half a million in a good year and can't remember when his last bad year was. There's no way I'll inherit any of that— my old man and I haven't spoken to each other in fifteen years, and we weren't close even before that. Larry Janeway isn't a man people get close to. He is, however, dignified. He's famous in court for his dignity and composure. Once, as the song went, that composure sorta slipped, and a dalliance with a truly gorgeous woman thirty-seven years ago produced . . . me. Here I sit, brokenhearted. I look at my parents and on one hand I see chilly arrogance and deceit; on the other, frivolous insanity. All the Libertys were crazy, and Jeannie, my mother, was probably certifiable. It was Jeannie, I think, who caused me to distrust beautiful women. I'll take brains, heart, and wit over beauty every time out. What's amazing is how well I survived their best efforts to tear me apart, how, in spite of them, I turned out so well-adjusted and sane. So completely goddamned normal.

"Well, sort of goddamned normal," she said without a smile.

"Oh yeah? How goddamned normal do you think you are?"

"Pretty goddamned normal."

Suddenly she laughed, a schoolgirl giggle that lit her up and made her young again. "Now there's my intelligent conversation of the week," she said, and we both laughed. I wondered if that was the break I was looking for, but it didn't seem to be. She would listen, interested, to anything I wanted to tell her, but still she wouldn't ask. I've never been brilliant at monologue, but I did my best. I told her about life at North High, about growing up in a pool of sharks. "If there's a thug in me, I guess that's where it comes from." Where the poet came from, if there was such a thing, was anybody's guess.

"It's getting late," she said.

Was that strike three? Her tone gave away nothing.

A bold frontal attack, then, seemed to be the last weapon in the old Janeway arsenal.

"Look, give me a break. Why don't you open that door, just a little, and see what's on the other side?"

"I know what's on the other side. I haven't exactly led a monastic life."

"C'mon, let's cut to the chase, Rita. Dinner Friday night and a tour of Denver's hottest hot spots."

"Nope. Not my cup of tea, Mr. Janeway."

"Then I'll rent a tux and we'll go to the Normandy. I don't care."

"I don't think so."

"Oh, take the full thirty seconds and think it over."

She shook her head.

"I know a great restaurant that serves nothing but broccoli. I'll take you there for breakfast. Broccoli pancakes, the best in town. We'll take a ride on the Platte River bus. Race stickboats down the stream. Walk down Seventeenth Street and stick our tongues out at my old man's law office. Forget about books and crime and everything else for a few hours. Come on, what do you say?"

"No," she said firmly.

"I knew you'd see it my way."

She gave me the long cool stare. "You're pushing, Mr. Janeway. I don't want to be blunt."

"Go ahead, be blunt. I've got a thick skin, I can take it. I'm not gonna fall on my sword. Since we're being blunt, let me ask you something. Are you worried that I'll eat my fish with the salad fork? Or do you big-time book dealers have a rule about not playing with the little guys."

"Don't be nasty, sir."

"I'm just trying to figure you out."

"Then stop trying. It's very simple. I don't want to get involved."

"And you think knowing me will involve you in something?"

"That's exactly what I think."

"How, for God's sake?"

"How do you think? How do men and women always get involved?"

I sat back and looked from afar. "Well, now, that's quite a thing to say."

"A good deal more than I wanted to say."

"So what's wrong with that? It's what makes the world go 'round. If it happens, it happens."

"It's not going to happen, Mr. Janeway, I promise you that."

She had been sitting rigidly in her chair: now she relaxed; sat back and let her breath out slowly. "I didn't want to let you come up here at all. You know that."

"Don't give me that. You called me back, remember?"

"I don't know why I did that."

"You know, all right, you just don't want to say it."

"Doesn't need to be said. You're here, aren't you? Don't be so damned analytical. You're here, I must've wanted to see you again. That doesn't mean I'm going to let you into my life. I'm sorry if that's too blunt, Mr. Janeway, but you can't say you didn't ask for it."

Then a curious thing happened: her hands began to tremble. She groped for words, reached down into a stack of newspapers and came up with the newspaper. "I never stop my papers when I go away. There's a boy I hire who brings all my mail and newspapers in every day. I guess I should have them stopped but I don't. I like to see what's been happening while I've been gone. Look what I came across this morning."

The story was a little different than the one I had seen. The headline said COP NAMED IN BRUTALITY CHARGE. They had moved my picture out to page 1 for the late edition. It lay on the table, staring up at me, glaring angrily at the angry old world.

"Is this my dessert?"

She just looked at me.

"Miss McKinley, I'm wasting a helluva lot of great one-liners on you. I'm starting to think you've got no sense of humor at all."

She still said nothing. Her eyes burned into my face like tiny suns.

"You want maybe I should comment on this? Is that what you want?"

"I don't know what I want."

"My comment is this. Don't believe everything you read."

"That's it?"

"Tell me what you want and I'll do my best to give it to you. I mean, look, you read that this morning, right? Plenty of time for you to call to cancel. You didn't do that, did you?"

Her eyes never left my face. She gave a shake of her head that was barely a movement.

"Even after I got here, you could've shuffled me in and out. But you didn't do that, either. You gave me a good stiff drink and free run of the place, then you gave me dinner. What am I supposed to make of that?"

She said nothing, did nothing.

"I'm going home," I said.

I stood and paused for just a moment, my hands clasping the back of my chair. We looked at each other. Her face was a solid wall. She said nothing. I went to the door and looked back. What a great exit, I thought: I'll just fade away like some damnfool hero in a bad cowboy movie. In the yard I looked back. She had come to the doorway, a silhouette in the yellow light. I gave her a cheery wave. The hell with you, I thought. Then I thought, Don't walk away, it's too important; don't do this. What you say and do this minute will set the course of your life from this day on, I thought.

I had opened the car door, propped my foot inside, and leaned over the window. When I spoke, my voice carried strong and clear over the mountaintop. "What's in the newspaper is his side of it. Here's my side, in case you're interested. That guy is a killer. I've tried to pin him for more than two years. I guess I finally got sick of it. He raped a woman and beat her silly and was coming back for an encore. He found me there instead. As far as brutality is concerned, forget it—he's plenty big enough to take care of himself. When he says I cuffed him and beat him, he's lying. I took the cuffs off and it was a fair fight. That's the end of it. I'm going home."

I drove down the mountain feeling depressed. But under it was a strange feeling of elation, of joy, making a mix that's almost impossible to describe. I didn't know what was happening but it was big. Oh, was it big! Could I have lived thirty-six years and never once felt this? I stopped at the side of the road about five miles from her house and fought the urge to go back. I won that fight . . . one mark for good judgment.

I'd call her in the morning.

She'd call me.

Somehow we'd get past all the problems of her money and her expertise and my brutal nature.

One way or another, it wasn't over. That was the one sure thing in an unsure world.

29

I got to the store about quarter past midnight. The street was deserted except for an ambulance far away: the overture of another long night on East Colfax. I tucked the Steinbeck under my arm and let myself in. The place had a stale, slightly sour smell at midnight. I locked the door and put the book on the counter, then sat on my stool looking at it. I opened it and looked at the doodle Steinbeck had drawn all those years ago, when fame and glory and money were his, when his talent was at its peak. "May 12, 1940: Tom Joad on the road." A prize, yes, one might even say a small victory, but a hollow one. You can have it back, Miss Rita, you hear that? You can *have* the damn thing. All you've got to do is ask.

I cut a piece of plastic and wrapped the jacket anew. With a light pencil I wrote in the new price, $2,000, and looked in the glass case for the perfect centerpiece spot.

The phone rang.

It can't be, I thought. I watched it ring three times, then I picked it up and said hello.

"I knew you'd be there," she said.

"You're getting pretty smart in your old age."

"It's what I'd've done not so long ago. When you buy your first big piece, you can't wait to see how it looks in its new home. Even if it's midnight."

"For the record, it looks great."

"You're allowed an hour to gloat. After that, it's unbecoming."

There was a long pause, what I was starting to think of as a Rita-like white space. Then she said, "I called to tell you something but I don't know how."

"We could play twenty questions. Is it animal, vegetable, or mineral?"

"Animal," she said. Her voice sounded thick, lusty.

"I kind of thought it would be."

Another pause. I didn't know what to do but fill it with more comic relief.

"Does it walk on two legs, four, or slide on its belly like a reptile?"

"This is difficult," she said. "I know you think I've been manipulating you, but I haven't. I'm just not very consistent sometimes."

"Hey, if I want consistency I'll buy a robot. So you give off mixed signals. That's all part of the human comedy."

"You're angry."

"Just confused, Miss McKinley. First you tell me, in barely couched terms, to break a leg and go blind. Then you call and invite me up. You fix me a dinner but act like I'm the butcher of Auschwitz when I ask you for a date. You'd already read that newspaper, you knew full well that I stomp puppies to death for a hobby, but do I worry? Nah! I'm just glad I got to see your books."

There was white space, of course: a ten-second pause. I thought of whistling "Time on My Hands," but I didn't do it.

"You are one strange bird, Janeway," she said.

"I'm fascinating as hell, though, you've got to admit that."

"Yes," she said, and I felt that buildup in my throat again, and I hoped I'd be able to get through this conversation without croaking like Henry Aldrich.

"I have a dark secret," she said. "If I tell you what it is, will you promise not to try to see me again?"

"I never bet on a blind. Only fools and bad poker players do that."

"I guess I'll tell you anyway. I don't want you going away thinking I've been playing with you."

"What difference does it make, if I'm going away?"

"I told you before, don't be so goddamned analytical. Take a few things on faith."

"You haven't said anything yet."

"It's very simple. I hate violence, but all my life I've been attracted to violent men."

"That's very interesting," I said, struggling past a pear-sized obstruction in my throat.

"So the reason I didn't want you to come up here today is the same reason I finally did ask you up. The same reason I didn't cancel when I read the paper. The same reason I wouldn't go out with you. Does that make any sense?"

"No, but keep going. I like the sound of it."

"You wear your violence on your sleeve. It goes where you go. You carry it around like other men carry briefcases. It's like a third person in the room. I can't help being appalled by that."

I listened to her breathe. My pear had grown into a grapefruit.

"And yet, I'm always a sucker for a man who can make me believe he'll do anything, if the stakes are big enough."

I gave a wicked laugh.

Gotcha, I thought.

"I don't want to see you again," she said. "I just wanted you to know why."

"I've got a hunch we'll see each other."

"I'm engaged, Mr. Janeway. I'm getting married next month."

"Then it's a good thing I came along when I did."

"Good-bye," she said, and hung up.

God damn it, I thought.

Whoopie! I thought. Yaahoo!

Elation and despair were sisters after all.

I called her back: got the recording. When the beep came, I pictured her sitting in the kitchen listening to my voice. Insanity, the third sister, took over. I got real close and crooned into the phone. "Oh, Riiiiii-ta! This is the mystery voice calling! Guess my name and win a truckload of Judith Krantz first editions. Ooooh, I'm sorry, I'm not George Butler the Third! But that was a fine guess, and wait'll you hear about the grand consolation prize we have in store for you! *Two* truckloads of Judith Krantz first editions! Your home will certainly be a bright one with all those colorful best-sellers lying around. Your friends will gaze in awe—" The tape beeped again, and a good thing, else I might've gone on till dawn. I replaced the phone in the cradle and stared at it for a long moment. Ring, you sonofabitch, I thought, but the bastard just sat there.

Convulsed with laughter, I was sure.

Too weak to call.

Savoring my wit in her solitude.

Damn her.

I worked it off. In a bookstore there's always something to do. I had a small stack of low-end first editions that needed to be priced, so I did that. I watered Miss Pride's plant again, and studied the *AB*. I read for an hour. Sometime after two o'clock I fell asleep in the big deep chair near the front counter.

I opened my eyes to a feeling more desolate than despair. This was not the aching loneliness of new love, it was something far more desperate and immediate. The street was still dark: the world outside was hollow and empty and nothing moved anywhere. The store was like a tomb: still, silent, eerie.

Maybe I'd been dreaming. I hadn't had the Jackie Newton dream in months. Maybe that had come back and I just couldn't remember.

Then it came to me.

It was that sourness I had noticed when I'd first opened the door. It was stronger now, ripe and distinct, almost sweet in a sickening kind of way. When you've been in Homicide as long as I was, that's one thing you never forget.

The smell of death.

I got up and went toward the back. The smell got stronger.

Oh boy, I thought.

I opened the door to the office. I turned on the light. Nothing looked wrong. It was just as Ruby had said: everything shipshape.

But the smell was stronger.

There was one place Ruby couldn't have seen—the bathroom across the hall. That room had no windows, nothing but a skylight, no way for anyone to look in.

I opened the door. Miss Pride stared up at me with glassy eyes. Peter sprawled across her, facedown.

Each had been shot once through the head.

30

The killer had come in just after closing time. Miss Pride had not yet locked the front door.

He had come for a single purpose. No money was missing. No books were missing. He had come to kill. By the time I tried returning Miss Pride's call, at five twenty-five, she and Peter had probably been dead ten minutes.

He had come through the front door. We keep the back door locked. He had forced Miss Pride to lock up—her keys were still clutched tight in her fingers—and afterward he had used the back door to escape. Unlike the front door, which must be locked with a key, the back door had a latch lock that could be slam-locked from the outside.

The weapon was probably a .38. Ballistics would tell us more.

Miss Pride had been shot first. The shot had hit her in the front of the head, exactly between the eyes: she had fallen over on her back, her head twisted grotesquely against the wall.

Peter had been a more difficult target. In his panic he had done a great deal of scrambling. One slug had missed and gone through the wall. The second one got him.

The killer, of course, had taken the gun away with him.

He had probably worn gloves. There were no fingerprints on the back door latch or on the door itself. There were many prints on the front door, from customers who had come and gone all day long. Most of these would never be identified.

He had come, done his job, and left. The whole thing had probably taken no more than two minutes.

Everything else was speculation. My guess was that Peter had known who killed Bobby Westfall. He had come to the store to tell me about it but the killer got there first. Miss Pride had simply been unlucky, in the wrong place at the wrong time.

As always, there were more questions than answers. If this tied back into the Westfall case, why had Peter waited all these months to tell me about it? How had the killer suddenly learned that Peter was a threat? Why had it happened now, and what had caused it to suddenly come on? Had there been something in the Ballard library so valuable that someone would kill for it, then kill twice more? Was it in the Ballard library at all, and if so, how could Rita have overlooked it? Something small—so small that no one could see it, yet Bobby Westfall had had to take the entire library to be sure of getting it. *Look at the little things, Dr. J.* I heard Ruby's voice telling me that. It's the one lesson that even a good bookman finds hardest to learn. Look at the little stuff—pamphlets, broadsides, tiny books with no lettering on their spines—and remember that one little weatherworn piece could bring more money than an entire library done up in glamour leather.

Something small. Something you know is there but you're not sure where. If you're Bobby Westfall, you have to take every book: tear them apart if necessary, go page by page if necessary, slit the cloth and strip away the bindings if necessary, rip the hinges asunder and shred the pieces through a sieve if necessary. Kill or be killed if necessary. Something small and hidden, it had to be, had to, because if it were small and unhidden it would be too easy to steal. Rita McKinley could easily drop it down her dress while old man Ballard went for coffee; Bobby Westfall could've dropped it in his pocket, the Lord be damned, while he wandered among the stacks and ostensibly tried to make up his mind.

It all came back to money. That's what fueled Bobby and Peter and all the guys like them. Money was the one thing they never had enough of: it was the driving force in their lives. Bobby wanted to be respected as a book dealer, not joked about as a bookscout. It took money to do that. It took other things—knowledge, taste, a keen eye, good juice, a gambler's blood, and a hustler's imagination—but without money you just couldn't get started.

The scene at my place was like a hundred murder scenes I'd been to. Cops. Photographers. Sketchmen. The coroner.

It was the same, only different. This was me on the receiving end. That dead girl was one of mine.

From the moment I found her, I was a cop again.

A cop without a badge.

Hennessey had arrived with his new partner before dawn. Teaming Neal with Lester Cameron had been the final ironic fallout of the Jackie Newton affair, but Boone Steed worked in mysterious ways. Cameron and I had never liked each other: he was too trigger-happy and hot-collared for my taste, though I'd heard it said more than once that Cameron in action reminded people of me. I didn't like that much, though I did respect Cameron in a professional way. I thought he was a good cop, I just didn't like him as a man. He had a head on his shoulders and a block of ice where his heart was supposed to be. He had a take-charge demeanor that was a turnoff, but his record with DPD was a good one. He and I had been in the same class at the police academy, long ago. We had never been bosom buddies, even then. For most of an hour, Hennessey, Cameron, and I sat in the front room talking. We were three old pros: I knew what they needed and gave them what I could. Cameron sat on one of my stools like a grand high inquisitor and fired off the inevitable questions, and I answered them like clockwork. I knew the questions before they were asked. I told him about Miss Pride, where she'd come from, when and why. I told him about Peter, and his friendship with Bobby Westfall, who had also been murdered. Hennessey stood apart as I related this. He looked out into the dark street, and even when he looked at me, he avoided my eyes. I guess he knew what I was thinking, that you can't ever drag your feet on a murder case, can't ever assume that the victim isn't important enough to warrant the balls-out effort. You never know when a killer might come back for an encore.

We talked about Miss Pride. She had no enemies on this earth, I said, unless she had a dark side that I simply couldn't imagine. I told them what I thought: that it tied into Westfall, and Miss Pride was the innocent victim. I told them how skittish Peter had been the last two days, how frantic he'd been when he tried to reach me at Rita McKinley's. I told them about Rita, too, all the facts, all the rumors. As an afterthought, I told them that Jackie Newton had been hanging around.

"I don't know," I said. "This doesn't smell like Jackie."

"You sure thought it was before," Hennessey said, looking out the window.

"That was then, this is now."

"What's so different?" Cameron said. "You boys kiss and make up?"

"It doesn't fit Jackie. The first one did: go look up the M.O. yourself if you want to see what I'm talking about. There's a random nature to all of Jackie's old business. This wasn't random. Jackie doesn't come advertising before he kills somebody. That's my opinion."

"Opinions are like assholes," Cameron said. "Everybody's got one."

"That's cute, Lester," I said. "I'll have to remember that one."

By then it was daylight: it was seven-thirty and word of the tragedy had spread up and down the block. People were gathering on the walk and peering in the windows.

"What's the name of the guy who was dating her?" Cameron said.

"You mean Jerry Harkness?"

"If that's the guy who was dating her, that's who I mean."

"I wouldn't say he was dating her. He took her to dinner a couple of nights ago."

"We need to see him. And we need to go up in the hills and see this McKinley woman. See if she's still got that tape, for one thing. Maybe the lab can separate those voices and we can hear what they were saying when they were talking over each other. That should be the first priority. How do I get there?"

"You don't unless you call first. That's the way the lady operates."

"Well, here's the way I operate. You give me her address and let me worry about getting in."

"You could save yourself some grief if you call her. I don't think she did this, do you?"

"I don't know who the hell did it."

"Lester, she was with me at the time."

"Wrong, sport. She was with you when she played you a tape that she said had just been made. Besides, you don't have to pull the trigger to be involved in something."

I nodded slowly. "It's a calculated risk. If she's still got the tape, a phone call might make sure she keeps it."

"Or burns it."

"Or uses it over," Hennessey said. "That's the most likely thing.

She'll slip it back in the machine and just use it again. Shucks, even by calling her, we might be erasing it."

"Oh, hell," I said, remembering. "I think I may've already done that."

"What'd you do?" Cameron said meanly.

"I got back here about midnight. She called me almost as soon as I came in the door. We talked for a few minutes, then I called her back. God damn it, she had the recording on. I talked on it for a long time."

"How long?"

"Long enough."

"What'd you talk about?"

"Just stupid bullshit. Dumb, stupid stuff."

"Love talk?" Cameron asked.

"What do you mean by that?"

"I don't think that question requires a translation. Are you involved with this woman, Janeway?"

"Yeah," I said after a moment. "I believe I am."

"Shit," Cameron said.

"Next time I decide to have an affair with a woman, Lester, I'll be sure and come ask your permission first."

"We've got to go get that tape now," Hennessey said, "before she uses it anymore."

"You can't get in there without a warrant," I said.

"You still can't stop playing cop, can you, Janeway?" Cameron said. "I think maybe it's time you remembered who the police are."

"I'm trying to tell you something that might do you some good if you'll just shut up and listen. You don't just walk up to this lady's house and knock on the door. She's got a ten-foot fence and a gate that locks. If you go over that fence without a warrant, anything that comes from that tape is out the window, even if the killer confesses in verse and leaves you his telephone number."

"That's only true if she's involved," Hennessey said. "We couldn't make a case against her with the tape, but we sure as hell could if the killer's somebody else."

"Why not cover your ass?" I said.

"You've always been good at that, haven't you, Janeway?" Cameron said. "Except once."

31

They carried the bodies out in rubber bags strapped to stretchers. The crowd gave a soft collective sigh and moved back from the door. It all seemed to take forever, as if people were trapped in some slow-motion twilight zone. The lab men combed the place, and this is not a hurry-up process. I waited them out. I sat by the door and tried not to think, and when I could see that it was winding down I started working on a new sign for the window. I wrote it on chipboard with a heavy black marking pen. It said, CLOSED UNTIL FURTHER NOTICE.

I began to see familiar faces in the crowd. Clyde Fix. A couple of bookscouts I knew. I saw Ruby standing alone, and Neff a few feet away, also alone. I'd seen it before, how death both repels and attracts, leaving even best friends alone with their darkest fascinations, fears. Jerry Harkness peeked in and asked what had happened. When I told him, he looked sick. He drifted down the street without another word.

Any violent death is bad, but this one was worse than bad. I felt like I'd just been mauled by a tiger.

Then, suddenly, they were all gone. The lab boys rolled up their tents and packed away their gear and the crowd outside began to dissolve. Fifteen minutes later the place was empty. A wave of loneliness washed over me, deep and cutting, almost unbearable. How little we know about people, I thought. Can you ever really know anyone? Already I saw Pinky Pride as a one-dimensional figure. I liked her but I knew in years to come I'd have trouble remembering her face. How little time I had actually spent with her. Never mind, Pinky, I'll spend the time now. I'll spend it now.

I went from room to room turning off the lights. The bathroom was the worst. The blood was still there and the room was puffed with fingerprint dust and there was still the smell of death, but fading now. I'm not much of a crier: I hate to admit that these days, when *macho* is a dirty word and people use it to trap and unmask insensitive bastards like myself, but I did shed a few quiet, private tears for Pinky Pride. Then I dropped my new sign into the front window, locked the front door, and started on the trail of her killer.

32

"I can't believe this," Ruby said. "God damn, that poor kid. That poor sweet kid."

Neff looked truly shaken. He sat in his usual spot behind the counter, but his usually busy hands were idle.

"What were you boys doing last night?" I asked.

"We were right here, Dr. J. You called me here, you know where we were."

"Did you see anything, hear anything, or see anybody unusual?"

I was looking at Neff, who had gone pale. His hands had begun to tremble. "I . . . I think I . . . may've seen him," he said.

"We been sittin' here waiting for the cops to come down, but they never did," Ruby said. "We didn't know what to do."

"They had to chase down something urgent, but they'll be back," I said. "What did you see, Neff?"

But Neff couldn't speak. He put his hand over his face and sat there shivering.

"Give 'im a minute," Ruby said. "This's been one helluva shock."

"For all of us, Ruby," I said. "What were you doing between five and six?"

"Lookin' at books."

"What books?"

"We'd just gotten in some wonderful stuff. I was humped over here at the door, lookin' at the books. I didn't see a thing."

"That's what you were doing when I called?"

"Yeah. Em was here with me, sittin' right where he is now. He didn't feel good. . . ."

"I've had a touch of stomach flu," Neff said. "Had the runs all day long. I thought maybe if I got out awhile, if I went on a buy, I'd stop thinking about how lousy I felt. I shoulda gone home and went to bed. But I went out and bought these books instead. I'd just gotten back. I had to hit the can so bad I thought I'd bust. You know how we're set up back there, real cramped, with the toilet right on the alley. I sat down and did my duty, then opened the back door to air the place out. There was a guy . . . coming up from your way . . . Christ, I looked right in his face."

"What'd he look like?"

"Like a man I wouldn't want to run into, in a dark alley at night."

"Give me some color, Neff. Give me a size, a shape. How old was this dude?"

"I don't know. Forty . . . maybe older. I wasn't paying that much attention then. I know he was white, and big."

"How big? Two hundred? Six feet? You tell me, Neff, I'm a lousy mind reader."

"Yeah . . . big. Two hundred . . . at least that. Six feet . . . I don't know. But heavy through here. God, he saw me watching him."

"What did he do when he saw you watching him?"

"Turned his head away . . . like this . . . then went on by."

"Did that strike you as suspicious?"

"Why should it? I didn't know anybody'd been killed. I'm used to seeing weird characters around here; why should I think anything about it? Jesus, the guy looked straight at me. What am I gonna do?"

"Tell the cops what happened, just like you're telling me."

"Well, where the hell are they? And what if that guy comes back before they do?"

"I'm not telling you not to worry about it: somebody's killed three book people in this town and maybe we all better worry a little. If I were you I'd leave the store closed today. Stay together. Go downtown and wait for Hennessey, then tell him what you told me. Could you describe this guy for a police artist?"

"Maybe . . . I'm not sure. I didn't stare at him. When he looked away, so did I."

"How was he dressed?"

"Black. Black slacks, black sport coat open at the neck, pale gray shirt . . . no tie. Jesus, he might've had the gun right there under his coat. He could've shot me."

"Or he could've been some neighborhood bum who had nothing to do with it. I take it you've never seen him around here."

"Never seen him anywhere. He didn't look like a bum to me."

"Did you watch him at all after he went on by?"

"No. I came . . . right back up front."

I let out a long breath. "Okay, let me get a feel for the time frame. You say you went out on a buy and got back here when . . . about quarter to five?"

"It wasn't much later than that. I didn't look at the clock, but I'm sure I was here by five."

"It was right at closing time, Dr. J," Ruby said. "I remember I was thinking I'd be closing up in a minute, then Em came back."

"Then it was closer to five than quarter to," I said.

"I don't know," Neff said. "I thought it was earlier than that, but you may be right."

"It was a few minutes before five," Ruby said.

"What'd you drive?" I asked.

"My car, same's I always drive. Same one's out back."

"And you came up Colfax, right past all the stores?"

"Yeah."

"When you passed my place, did you happen to look in?"

"I gave it a glance, I always do. I like to see if there's any business on the block. I look in all the stores when I come by."

"Was the store open or closed?"

"I don't remember, I didn't look at the sign. There was nobody in the front, though, I do know that."

"Did you look in at Harkness and Fix?"

"Yeah, sure. Fix was sitting in that chair by his window like he always does. Harkness was gone somewhere—he had that clock on the door that said, you know, be back at such-and-such a time. I didn't notice what time it said. I need some water. This shit's got me shook."

I waited for him to come back. Then I started in again. "So you drove past the stores and pulled up here and unloaded the books. How long did that take?"

"No more'n a minute," Ruby said. "There wasn't all that much, quantity-wise. Just three boxes. Didn't take but a second to bring it all in."

I kept looking at Neff. "Then what did you do?"

"Like I told you, headed straight for the can. I thought I'd bust before I got back there."

"How long were you on the pot?"

"No more than a minute. You know how it is when you've got the runs, it's all water."

"Then you opened the back door and saw the guy."

He took a shivery breath, nodded, and let it out.

"So you were back there what . . . two minutes? And this would all have taken place by a few minutes after five? And you didn't see the guy get in any car and drive away, either of you?"

"I didn't see anything," Ruby said.

Neff looked ill. We were all silent for a moment.

"I don't mind telling you, Mr. Janeway, this thing's made a mess of my nerves. I'm not gonna sleep till they catch this bastard."

I gave him an encouraging little nod. "Tell me anything else that comes to you. Hair . . . scars . . ."

"I didn't notice any scars. He had thick black hair with deep recesses. It went way back, made the front of his head look like a big letter M, but the hair was still real thick where it did grow. He had a face like a . . . turtle . . . just a flat line for a mouth. I can't tell you about his eyes: he turned away before I got a look, and I probably wouldn't remember anyway."

"And he didn't say anything?"

"Hell no. The whole thing didn't take more than a few seconds. But that was enough."

"All right," I said. "Stay away from here today. Get downtown and tell Hennessey what you've told me. Get the artist involved. Do the best you can."

"Sure . . . you bet."

"A couple more questions, then I've got to go," I said. "I talked to Miss Pride in the middle of the day. Told her to call and tell you she'd be there alone at closing. . . ." I looked searchingly at both faces.

Ruby shook his head. "She never called me."

"No," Neff said.

Damn you, Pinky, I thought. Next time do what I tell you.

I felt the shivers in my own spine, and hoped I wasn't coming down with Neff's flu.

"What about Peter?" I said. "I asked you before if you knew where he lived."

"Didn't know then, don't know now," Ruby said.

"What was Peter's last name?"

"Uh, wait a minute . . . yeah, I know it, I just can't call it. Hell, Em, help me out, you know what it is."

"I don't remember."

"Come on, we've written enough hot checks to the old fart. I don't mean that the way it sounds, Dr. J . . . don't want to speak ill of the dead . . . I'm just . . . tryin' to . . . call the damn thing up for you and I can't get a handle on it. Haven't you ever written him a check?"

"I always paid him cash," I said.

"Must be nice. It's on the tip of my tongue, that's how close it is. It's Peter, uh . . . uh . . . God damn it! Peter, uh . . . I know the damn thing as well as I know my own."

"Think about something else for a minute," I said. I looked at three boxes of books stacked against the glass case. "Is this the stuff you bought yesterday?"

"Yeah. Damn lovely stuff it is, too. Go ahead, take a look."

I peeked over the edge and saw a fine copy of Ellison's *Invisible Man.* Under it was *A Clockwork Orange,* a beaut. Under that was a nice double stack, about fifteen books. The three boxes would hold forty, maybe fifty pieces.

"It was a hurry-up deal," Ruby said. "Woman was going out of town, she calls us and needs the cash right now. I tell you, Samson, we had to scrounge to get it up. Fifteen hundred we had to pool, and two hours to do it. But we did it."

I didn't go through the box. For once I didn't feel like looking at books.

I started to leave, stopped at the door and said:

"Hey, Rube! What's Peter's name?"

"Bonnema," he said. "Two *n*'s, and one *m*. Peter Bonnema. By God, Dr. J, that's a good trick. That's a damn good trick."

"Sometimes it works, sometimes it doesn't," I said, and left.

33

Harkness too had been out on a major buy late yesterday. His place reeked of fresh Stephen King. There were King books scattered across the counter and stacked on the floor. He had gotten the call two days ago and had closed early yesterday to go look at the stuff. The buy was in Boulder, thirty miles away. He had closed the store around one-thirty. He had walked up to my place and had stood talking with Miss Pride for about ten minutes. She had mentioned in passing that she would be closing alone—Mr. Janeway had made her tell him that, she explained with a frown—but he had told her he'd be gone at closing time so she should call Seals & Neff and let them know. She had rolled her eyes and said, "You men!" and that was the last time he had seen her. He looked to be on the verge of tears.

I asked what time he had come in last night. "It was almost eight," he said. "By the time I got to Boulder it was quarter to three. The buy didn't take long. King stuff never does. You know what it goes for and so do they: the only question is, can you get it from them for any kind of a decent price, or do they want to make all the money? Usually they want full pop, but this one was reasonable. I only had to pay sixty-five percent."

"Man, that sounds high," I said.

Harkness didn't react at all. He said, "It is, for anything but King. I'll put it away and in a year it'll look cheap, what I paid for it. What the hell difference does it make? What difference does anything make?"

"Yeah," I said.

The Kings had been owned by a woman. Her husband was the collector but he had died and she was trying to figure out the rest of her life. King didn't figure in it, but she could get a fair start with the money he would bring her. "It cost me plenty," Harkness said, "every damn dime I had in the bank, but look at what I got." It was all there, the entire King output: the five major Doubleday firsts, variant jackets on the two *Salem's Lot*s, all the signed limiteds. Harkness didn't seem to care.

"I was done with it by four o'clock," he said. "I should've come back. If I had, maybe she'd still be alive. I'd've got back here before five and taken her to dinner and she'd still be here."

"What did you do instead?"

"Went out to eat alone. Some burger joint near the campus. I sat there for an hour thinking about it."

"Thinking about what?"

"Her."

He looked at me with sad eyes that had aged immeasurably since the last time I had seen him. He said, "I know what you think, Janeway, but you're wrong. She was a kid. I knew that. But there was something about her that got me down deep. I couldn't shake her. You know what that feels like?"

I thought of Rita McKinley, but I didn't say anything.

"I knew it was all wrong . . . man my age, screwing around with a girl her age. But what can you do? When they get you they get you. So I ate a cheap supper and walked around killing time, just thinking about it. Then I came back here. Unloaded my stuff. Worked till ten o'clock. Went home."

"You didn't see anything?"

"What was to see by then?"

Clyde Fix, as usual, was no help. He had not seen Peter in months. He didn't like the son of a bitch. Peter wasn't welcome in his store. I asked Fix if he'd seen anyone resembling the man Emery Neff had described. He hadn't seen anyone and wouldn't tell me if he had. I wasn't a cop anymore: he knew that. He didn't have to tell me anything.

34

I sat in my store and called Motor Vehicles: told them I was Detective Cameron and needed a rundown on a murder victim. Impersonating a cop is against the law and, strictly speaking, it wasn't necessary. Motor Vehicle records are open to everybody, but being a cop speeds the process. Current driver's licenses had been issued to two Peter Bonnemas in Denver. One lived in Cherry Hills Village, a posh country club neighborhood, the other in a rooming house on the fringe of Five Points. It wasn't hard to choose: ten minutes later I pulled up at a rambling old brick tenement near Twenty-second and Arapahoe. I took a small pouch of tools out of my trunk, slipped it into my coat, and went inside. It wasn't the Brown Palace: there was no security door and some of the mailboxes in the stale-smelling foyer looked like they had never borne a name. Peter's name had been scrawled in pencil on a small white card and Scotch-taped to the mailbox for apartment 310. There was a letter inside. I took out my pouch and got a tool and picked open the box. It was really no lock at all, just a simple latch. I lifted the slim envelope out and closed the mailbox. It was handwritten and postmarked Portland, Oregon. The return address said "Mrs. Peter Bonnema, 12335 SW 123rd, Portland." I took it without a second thought, slipped it into my coat, and went upstairs.

The lock on Peter's door was almost as simple as the one on the mailbox. It's a real wonder more of these guys don't get murdered, I thought as I went in. I let out a long breath. Bobby Westfall's so-called apartment had been a cradle of luxury compared with this. There was a dank smell about it, like curdled milk. The bed was a rollaway, layered with old dirt that had worn itself slick: there was no sign that the bed had ever worn a sheet. I saw empty cans on the floor, rat droppings in the corner, and everywhere, of course, the inevitable books.

There were two small rooms and a toilet, and books were piled in
every crack and corner. There were books on the sills of both windows and piled high in the middle of the floor. I knew I had little time;
Cameron and Hennessey would be here before the day was done. I
pulled on a pair of gloves and went to work. I handled the books carefully, so as not to destroy any prints, and it was the same as before—
almost one hundred percent junk. It was so much like Westfall that I
wasn't surprised when I found, pushed away in the back of a closet, a
two-foot stack of good books.

Very good books.

It was about the equivalent of the stack I had found at Bobby's:
great titles, all modern lit, first editions, perfect condition, a healthy
mix of mainstream and genre. I didn't bother making a list this
time—I knew at once that when I walked out, these were going with
me. I looked at the mysteries and actually felt my mouth water, like
one of Pavlov's dogs. Early Rex Stout . . . Ross Macdonald . . . Cor-
nell Woolrich in his real name and both pseudonyms: a nice little
stack adding up to at least four grand retail. I didn't know yet how to
assess it, didn't know what to do with it, but I wasn't leaving it here.
Rats eat books, you know.

There was nothing else of any possible value: I was finished here
as a bookman and now I went through the place with the eyes of a
cop. The main room was depressingly bare, a bleak testament to the
way some people live today. There was no desk where papers might
be stored, no cabinet, no table with drawers. There were some trin-
kets, some Indian turquoise, probably mid-twenties Navajo that
Peter had scouted at a flea market. I pushed it aside and left it there.
Under the bed I found a bundle of letters held together by a rubber
band. They looked like the same cheap stationery as the letter from
the mailbox. I thumbed through them and noticed the obvious common denominators. All were signed "Mumsy." Each began with the
same line: "Your big box of books arrived today." There had been
one letter every two weeks for the last three months. Mumsy was a
lean, sparse writer: she got right to the point and didn't linger over
flowery sunsets. There was no return address inside because Peter
would undoubtedly know it. She had put a return address on the
envelope in case the letter, for some reason, had to be returned.

Mumsy was a practical soul who didn't write extra words and Peter didn't save envelopes. I had probably fished the only Mumsy envelope in existence out of the mailbox. It had probably been delivered only this morning.

I didn't open it till I got home. It was just like all the others. "Your big box of books arrived today and I put it with all the others." Not much chitchat. "Went over to Dadsy's grave today . . . Your friend Junie Sykes is expecting again, this makes six she's had with five different men. I said at the time and I say again, you are well out of that. You can't eat your heart out forever. . . . Why don't you come home?" A sudden image of Peter wafted up, a vision of the bleak and solitary road he had chosen becoming so clear in the half-dark room. A young man then with little verbal ability, crushed by love. Junie Sykes had eaten him alive and sent him on his way, banished to this. Getting by on fifty-cent books and bummed cigarettes, still carrying the faint hope of the Big Score, the $10 million map found in a Salvation Army store for six bucks. In his mind, Peter Bonnema drove home to Portland in a solid gold Cadillac and snatched Junie Sykes from all that. He would come on like Gary Cooper, tall and lean and silent, infinitely ready to forgive. Life was sooooo good, in that dream, and it was only one . . . god . . . damn . . . score . . . away! Just that moment in time when something wonderful was put out by someone stupid, and he was there. He'd go home vindicated, *king* of the bookscouts!

I opened the drapes and read again through all the letters. It never varied. Mumsy acknowledged the books, wrote a line or two about Dadsy or Dadsy's grave or what Dadsy would think of the world today, and slipped in a stinger about Junie Sykes. It was always "your friend Junie Sykes," slapped on the page like an indictment. Mumsy's apron strings snaked across the country, dooming her son to the life he led, sealing him in squalor.

Mumsy probably hadn't been informed yet. The cops would still be in the early stages of investigating Peter's next of kin, and without the Mumsy letters it might be days before they found her. I picked up the phone and called United Air Lines, got the next flight to Portland charged to my credit card. I called Hertz and had a rental car arranged on the other end.

If Jackie Newton wanted my money, he'd have to hurry. If I kept on this way, there wouldn't be much left.

I had five hours to kill and I killed them well.

I had never stopped believing in that U-Haul lead. A two-ton truck doesn't just materialize on Madison Street: someone somewhere rents it, buys it, or builds it from scratch in a backyard. I sat at my telephone with an open Yellow Pages and dialed one number after another. It didn't take nearly as long when you had a name. Peter Bonnema had rented a truck from an East Colfax gas station on the night of June 10. I had found the place on the sixth or seventh try; told the man I was Cameron of DPD and said I'd be over in a while to look at his records. Then I took a shower and lay down to rest. It was the first sleep I'd had in thirty-six hours.

Eighty minutes later my alarm went off. I got up feeling worse than ever, dressed, threw enough clothes together for a short weekend, locked up, and left. I didn't take any dress clothes or neckties— I wasn't flying to Portland to keynote a national conference of Disgraced Ex-Cops of America.

I pulled into the gas station with an hour to spare. The guy who had actually rented the truck to Peter didn't work there anymore. He wouldn't've remembered anyway, the manager assured me. I thought it was also too much to expect that the same truck would still be on the lot, and it was. "That baby's long gone," the man said. "That went out on a one-way to Florida back in early August." The truck had been rented out of this same station no less than eighteen times between Peter Bonnema and Tampa-St. Pete: any physical evidence, unlikely under the best circumstances, would've disappeared a dozen times over, but I had to ask. "Do you people keep stuff that's left in the trucks—papers, notes, anything like that?" The guy said yeah, sure, if it looked valuable or important. He showed me a box of junk. That's all it was, junk: I combed through it and found nothing. I asked to see the original contract that Peter had signed. The original had been turned in to the U-Haul people, but the gas station kept a file of duplicates going back a year. "See, this-un went out without the proper paperwork," the guy said. "That's one of the reasons Jerry don't work here no more, the bastard wouldn't do what I told him. All these trucks are supposed to be backed up with credit cards. I don't care if it's Jesus Christ straight from the cross, if he wants to drive one of these babies out of here he's got to have a card. I tell Jerry this fifteen times, and what's he do? He rents the goddamn thing for cash and we got nothing but the guy's driver's license number on file. What good does that do us if he cracks it up?"

I looked at the pink contract dupe. Peter had signed out at 4:18 on the afternoon of June 10. He had returned the truck in good shape at 2:56 P.M. the following day—at least, someone had returned it: there was no mention made as to whether the same guy had brought it in, but even if old Jerry had been on duty, he wouldn't've noticed. Old Jer wasn't real quick on the uptake. The truck had been out twenty-two hours and change. A few blocks from here, Peter had pulled over and stopped. Bobby Westfall had taken the wheel and Peter had faded into the night. These were the things that weren't noted on the dupe. Bobby had taken over and driven the truck into eternity. By five o'clock he had been at Buckley's store, cocky and alone: by seven he had been at Ballard's, again alone. He had worked alone all night and left in the morning. The obvious thing to do would've been to have Peter come along and help, but Bobby hadn't done that. Bobby would far rather do all the work himself than let Peter in on his secret.

Here was another important thing. On the contract dupe was a space for mileage. The truck had checked out with 39,523 miles on the odometer. It had come back with 39,597. Seventy-four miles. A guy could play with that in many ways, and none of it was certain. Bobby might've gone to Buckley's and then straight to his real destination. Or he might've spent the entire early evening just cruising, full of restless energy. The whole seventy miles might be accounted for in drifting, waiting for the allotted hour for his appointment. Somehow I didn't think so. Bobby had no driver's license, and that meant that every minute he spent driving was a risk. If a cop pulled him for anything, he'd be in the soup. So he went to Buckley's and killed time, and when Buckley closed the store he went to a café and sat over coffee to wait it out. That was my guess, and that meant he had taken Stanley Ballard's books to some point that could be roughly calculated. Twenty-five to thirty-five miles, fifty to seventy there and back.

Rita McKinley's place, for instance, was just about thirty miles from where I stood.

35

My flight into Portland arrived at seven forty-six, Pacific time. I slept the whole way. Hertz didn't tie me up too badly, and by eight-thirty I was driving south on Interstate 5 through subdivisions called Raleigh Hills, Metzger, and so on. Mumsy Bonnema wasn't easy to find, even with an address. I had to backtrack a couple of times through sprawling suburbs, and it was nine o'clock before I found her. She lived on a rural stretch, far away from neighbors. A mailbox on a post said BONNEMA in faded, worn letters. One of the *n*'s had peeled away, leaving its outline.

I pulled into the driveway. Brace yourself, Mumsy. It wouldn't be the first time I had broken bad news.

The place was weedy and rough, full of untrimmed trees. In a sad way it reminded me of the Liberty place, where I had lived with my crazy mother for the first six years of my life. There were huge piles of junk about, and the house was in pretty shabby shape. I killed the lights, killed the engine, took a deep breath, and got out. A pale yellow light shone through the drawn shades. Somewhere deep in the house, a dog barked. I knocked and the dog went into a frenzy. I heard a voice, a woman shouting at the dog, which, amazingly, shut up. Steps came and the door opened a crack. An eye peeped out.

"Mrs. Bonnema?"

She just watched me: didn't say a thing.

"My name is Janeway. I'm a sergeant with the Denver Police Department. I have some bad news for you."

The door opened wider. I got a glimpse of cheek, of brittle hair and a wrinkled cheek. Her face was old and haggard, as pale as a vampire's. She had deep red lipstick on. It smeared on her teeth and reminded me of Gloria Swanson in *Sunset Boulevard*.

My hopes for a safe and sane trip tottered precariously.

"Where're you from?" The voice was brittle, like the hair.

"Denver."

"A policeman."

I didn't deny it and she didn't ask for ID. In a small brassy voice that had begun to quake, she said, "Is this about Petesey?"

"Yes ma'am."

"Has Petesey been hurt?"

"He's dead, ma'am."

For almost a full minute she stood there, motionless and silent. Then a wail came up, a hideous inhuman cry that finally found its true pitch, somewhere around the scale of an air raid siren. The dog started howling and they blended flawlessly into two-part harmony. She disappeared from the doorway and the door creaked open. I could see her, collapsed in a chair. The wailing never stopped: she had unbelievable lung capacity and that dog, wherever he was, was pretty amazing too. It might have been comical if it hadn't been about death.

Eventually she had to stop. What she did then was equally enchanting: she began to destroy the room. She had done this on a regular basis, if the state of the house was any evidence. She began by hurling a heavy cut-glass ashtray through the front window. She ripped down the curtains and stomped them into the floor. She smashed and ripped and tore, and all the while the dog howled and howled and occasionally barked when Mumsy got winded and had to rest. She smashed a lamp and finished off a table that looked like it had somehow survived an earlier attack. This too had to pass. She sat on the floor, breathing heavily, muttering what sounded like medieval curses.

I stepped in, but without much enthusiasm. The hospitality of crazy people has always left me cold.

"That selfish little monster," Mumsy said. "That ungrateful, spiteful, rotten child!"

I didn't know whether to sit down, help her up, or stand still and wait for Act Three. She looked up at me and in a voice that had no emotion whatever said, "Did you know Petesey?"

"Yes ma'am."

"He was a selfish child, all his life. Didn't you think so?"

"I didn't know him that well."

"A selfish child. Cared for no one but himself. I knew someday he'd go away and leave me alone. What am I supposed to do now? Who's going to care for me? *You,* young man?"

She leveled her eyes on me and I thought, I'd rather be with Peter. I managed to hold her gaze till she looked away. She grunted and got to her feet. Lit a long black cigarette: filled the place with smoke. Bustled around, picking things up, putting them down, muttering, talking to herself.

"Hope he burns in hell for what he's done to me," she said. "Hope he burns, the selfish boy. It's Dadsy he'll have to answer to now, and we'll see how he likes that. Dadsy knows how to handle errant little boys."

Yes, I had broken a lot of bad news as a cop, but it had never happened quite this way.

You go to the scene, you break the news, you wait through the initial shock waves, the absolute heartbreak, and if you're lucky and the survivors don't collapse you might get to ask a few questions. Usually they had questions too: *Did he suffer? Did he go easily?* I realized suddenly that I was waiting for those questions that would never come. Mumsy Bonnema had no thoughts for Peter. Her world was herself. She was the center of the universe, and even her son was a prop for her amusement, convenience, or comfort. All I wanted at that moment was to put distance between myself and this clutching old bat.

But there was business to do.

"He sent you some books." I said this as a matter of fact, my voice heavy with authority.

"Books!" she shouted. "I'm going to burn those books!"

"I'm afraid not."

"Like to see you stop me. Just you try it. Those books are the reason I'm alone here. *They* took him away from me. If it hadn't been for *books,* Petesey would still be here."

"Let me try to explain something to you, Mrs. Bonnema—"

"Get a job, I said. Go out and find work and take care of your mother like any self-respecting boy should do. But no, would he do that? All his life, all he cared about was books!"

"Where are the books, Mrs. Bonnema?"

She gave a wicked little smile. "That's for me to know."

"You can't destroy them. They're not your property."

"Who says they're not? Didn't Petesey send them to me?"

"They weren't Petesey's to send. Those books are evidence in a murder case. If you try to keep them, or if you destroy them, you can be prosecuted."

"I don't care," she said, but she did care. The key to Mumsy was simple: hit her where she lives.

"You could go to jail, Mrs. Bonnema."

"I don't care. My life is over anyway. Everyone I loved has left me. I hope Dadsy punishes that boy."

I walked around and looked in her face. What the hell, I thought.

"Mrs. Bonnema," I said. "I'd hate to have to arrest you."

"You *dare* talk to me like that. Take them. Take the dirty things and get them out of my house. I never wanted them anyway."

"Where are the books?"

"In the garage, where do you think?"

I started through the house toward the back door.

"It's all junk," she cried. "I'm telling you that right now, there's nothing there but junk." I heard her footsteps: she was following me through the dark house. "Petesey was always off chasing silly dreams," she said. "Always scavenging, pawing through what other people threw out. It was shameful, my son picking through people's trash. I cringe when I think of it, how that must've reflected on *me*! He looked all his life and never found anything but junk. The world called it junk, but—oh no!—not him! He knew it all! Everybody else was wrong and he was right, that's the way he saw it. Everything he found was worth its weight in gold. Hah! He goes all the way to Denver, and what does he send me back? More junk! Can you beat that, Mr. Policeman? Can you beat that? Are you listening to me?"

I groped through the kitchen. The dog growled, very near, and I skirted the sound and felt for the door. I could still hear her yelling: her voice followed me through the yard and into the underbrush. She had turned into a book expert. "A book's gotta be old to be worth anything, everybody knows that. Gotta be old, but does he find *old* books? No, he picks up junk that anyone could find and then tries to tell *me* it's valuable. Same silly thing he's said all his life. . . ." At last she faded: her screeching blended with the crickets and the breeze and maybe she finally gave up. I saw the garage: it was forty yards from the house along a dark path. I pushed open the door and blundered along the wall in search of a light. The light I found was dim, but it was enough. Stacked against the far wall were eight cartons of books, most unopened, all with Denver postmarks. I cut open the tops and looked inside. There were twenty books, give or take, in each box. I took a quick inventory.

One hundred sixty-four titles. Flawless first editions from the period 1927 to 1955.

Retail value? My guess was as good as any.

I called it twenty grand, and started putting the boxes together again.

36

The earliest flight I could get back to Denver was the 6:47. I checked in an hour early and fought the ticket people at the Portland airport. There was a luggage limit and I was over it: even by paying excess freight charges, I couldn't get more than five boxes on board without special permission. I battled my way up the bureaucratic chain, telling them I was a Denver detective working undercover on a case involving a major book theft ring. I didn't have any identification, I said, because undercover cops never carry any, but my story could be verified by Detective Hennessey at DPD. Of course, before they could reach Hennessey, my plane would be gone, I said with the proper degree of helplessness. The man in charge at five-thirty in the morning was a suspicious bird: damned if he didn't call Denver.

"They do verify that a Detective Hennessey is employed with the Denver police," he said to the ticket people. He looked at me severely. "What did you say your name was?"

"Cameron."

He looked at my ticket. "It says Janeway here."

I rolled my eyes. "I'm traveling undercover," I said with just the right edge of strained patience.

"Is there a Detective Cameron on the Denver police force?" he asked the telephone. He nodded and hung up. "Let him through," he said to the ticket people.

God bless United Air Lines.

I slept all the way home.

At Stapleton, the chores of the day arranged themselves in my mind. The first order of business was to secure the books.

I drove to a storage locker I knew, rented a small unit, stacked the boxes two high on pallets off the floor, locked the unit, and went home.

I took a shower, shaved, and ate breakfast. A pot of coffee, double strength, brought me almost back to life, and I sat at the phone and lined up the day's work.

Hennessey. The Ballards. Rita McKinley.

I wanted to know what the cops had found when they had gone into Rita's place yesterday. I wanted to see the artist's sketch, if they had made one, from the description Neff had supplied. Hennessey was the best avenue to that information. But then I looked at the calendar and saw that my entire afternoon was blocked out: today I was scheduled to give my deposition on the Jackie Newton lawsuit. "Son of a bitch," I said. I said a few other things, fought back a temptation to throw my coffee cup through the wall, then settled down and called my lawyer.

Robert Moses wasn't handling my case gratis, but he might as well've been. A long time ago, when I was in uniform, I saved his child from a pervert—strictly my good luck, and the little girl's, that I was four blocks away when the stupid ass snatched the kid in broad daylight. A neighbor had seen it all, had called the cops, and a vehicle description was on the radio in less than two minutes. The dispatcher was still reading it when the car came speeding past the little greasy spoon where I sometimes stopped for coffee. I nailed the guy, and though I was only doing my job, Mose had been in my debt ever since. So he thought, and those are the only kinds of debts that matter. You couldn't put the man off: he owed me a big one, and when Jackie Newton went after my hide, Mose offered his legal services free. We argued over money and finally resolved it this way: he would give me his best shot and I would pay him what I could, when I could pay it. I wondered how he liked making janitor's wages.

"Where the hell've you been?" he said. "I've been trying to get you ever since I saw the paper this morning."

"Been up in Oregon communing with nature. What's the story this afternoon?"

"I dunno, what do you want it to be? I can get it put off, given what happened in your store yesterday. What the hell was that all about?"

"That's what I'm trying to find out. I could sure use the time this afternoon. How long is this likely to take?"

"They're gonna try to sweat you. Levin's a mean little prick; if he thinks you're in a hurry, you'd better pack your supper and bring your toothbrush. That's all this is, you know: he's just trying to run up your legal fees."

"Little does he know," I said.

"This is just the opening salvo, my friend. My guess is they'll try to bring you in again in a few weeks. Levin'll conveniently forget to ask a fairly crucial question, and he'll ask the court for a new deposition. Then there'll be a flood of interrogatories and if we're lucky we might get to trial sometime in 1994. My advice is this. Give 'em a stiff upper lip. Don't let the bastards rattle you. Be there today, right on time if you can. Let him take all night if he wants to. I'll be with you, pal."

"I know you will."

"Our turn comes next week. I can't wait to get that Crowell dame up here. I'm gonna nip this baby right in the bud. See, she's never been deposed before, she don't know what it's all about. If she thinks Jackie Newton frightens her, I'm gonna scare what's left of her into an early grave."

I gave a dry little laugh. "That poor kid."

"Save your sympathy. That poor kid is gonna put you under, if I let her. Which, given the handsome fee you're paying me, I don't intend to do."

"I can't help feeling sorry for her. None of this is her fault."

"It's all her fault. Don't even think of asking me to go easy on her."

"No," I said. "Do what you have to."

"I always do, Clifford. Now, what do you want to do about this afternoon?"

"You've probably rearranged your whole life for this."

"I have made a few minor adjustments, yes. But don't let that worry you; I can always take off and go fishing with my kids."

"No, let's do it. I'd sure like to be out of there by three o'clock if I can. It'd be nice to have some of the day left."

"Don't count on it," Mose said.

I called the mortuary and made arrangements for Miss Pride. I called the cemetery and arranged for a burial plot.

I called Hennessey downtown.

"Where the hell have you been?" It was starting to sound like a catchphrase, something people automatically said when they heard my voice.

We decided to meet for lunch in a place not far from City Hall: from there I could walk over to Levin's office and be there in plenty of time. It was already eleven-fifteen, so I went right over. All I wanted was a beer and a raw egg: Hennessey ate half a horse, with french fries. "Jesus, Neal, you'll be lucky if you live another year," I said, and knocked wood. I hoped he'd live forever, the sweet old son of a bitch. Hennessey had his stern look on. "Let's get down to cases, buddy," he said, and though I somehow guessed that he didn't mean it, I managed to give him my rapt attention.

"I been trying to get you for twelve hours," he said.

"I went for a walk in the mountains."

"What'd ya do there?"

"Walk. Think. Look at butterflies."

"It snowed in the mountains last night. There ain't no butterflies."

"The pretty kind, Neal, that ski and walk on two legs."

There was a long silence. Hennessey had been my partner forever, it seemed: he had deliberately taken a more or less subordinate role because we did our best work that way. But he knew me inside out: he knew when I began to bend the rules because he had seen me do it often enough. He said, "Y'know, my bullshit detector's going crazy here. The needle's knocking the roof off."

I ignored that. "What did you get from McKinley?"

He ignored that. "Cliff, what the hell are you up to?"

I said, "Actually, that elephant sandwich you're eating doesn't look half bad. Maybe I'll have one."

"C'mon, Cliff, stop screwing around. Look, I'll ask you point-blank: are you messing around in this case? If you are, Cameron's got a big package of trouble all wrapped and ready to dump right on your ass."

"When I came back from the hills this morning, I sat down and made up a list of all the things that bother me. My psychiatrist told me to do that. It's better than scream therapy, Neal, but you know what? I couldn't find Cameron's name anywhere on it."

"God damn it, he'd better be on it."

"Are you gonna eat that pickle?"

"Sure I am. Listen, do you want to talk to me or not?"

"I might, if you'll pull the cork out of your ass and stop being a cop for thirty seconds."

He took a long breath and held it. As he let it out, he said, "I'd just hate to see you take a fall."

I gave a little shrug. "Are we all finished with the dance now? If we are, I'll tell you something: the real truth, forty-carat, government-inspected stuff. You can take it to the bank, Neal. You ready? Here it is. This boy is dead meat. I don't know who he is or where he's hiding, but his ass is mine. He can't go far enough and he can't dig himself a deep enough hole. That's on the record, and frankly I don't give a fuck what Lester thinks."

I picked up his pickle and bit the end off. "Does that answer your question?"

"Yeah," he said grimly. "It's also what I was afraid of."

He ate the rest of the pickle fast.

"This is now my full-time job," I said. "You want to talk turkey, fine. How much time do you have in a day? Did you guys ever get through checking out that U-Haul lead? Well, I did, because I've got nothing else going with my time. My business is closed for the duration and I'm on this guy full-time. I can't wait for you guys, Neal, because you've probably got ten other cases on your desk right this minute. Hey, I know how it goes. I also know you've got to get on something like this right now, because evidence tends to dry up. I've already found something that would be ashes now if I'd waited for you. No offense."

"What evidence? What the hell've you found?"

"Only something that puts a whole new slant on things. Don't ask for specifics if you're not willing to punt the football. It's a two-way street. That's simple manners, and I know Mrs. Hennessey didn't raise anything but polite little walruses."

"You're out of your mind. Cameron'd have a hematoma of the left nut if he thought I was sharing information with you."

"It'll give him something to play with. Look, I've got to go, I can't sit here and bullshit all day. You've gotta make up your mind."

He sat perfectly still, struggling with the forces of good and evil.

"Don't hurry on my account," I said. I looked at my watch. "I'm due at an appointment, where I'm getting my ass sued off, in thirty minutes."

"One time and one time only," Hennessey said. "What do you want to know?"

"All the good poop. What happened at McKinley's. You can put in a lot of color. Tell me if her cheeks were rosy or pale when Lester broke her door open and wrestled her down just as she was about to throw the tape into the fire."

"You should do stand-up comedy." He fished in his pocket for a small notebook and leafed through the pages. "At eleven forty-eight yesterday morning, your police department, accompanied by officers from Jefferson County and acting on a warrant signed by District Court Judge Harlan Blakeley, scaled the fence at the mountaintop residence at the end of Road Twelve, otherwise known as Crestview Street. . . ."

"I think I've seen this one. In a minute it snows and turns into *Bambi*. I really don't have time for this much color."

He put his notebook away and looked at me long and hard. He was a cop who went by the book, and it broke his heart when he had to go the other way.

"She gave us the tape."

"No kidding. Was it all there?"

"Seemed to be."

"How about the part I erased?"

"Entirely different tape. You remember she had taken the tape out so she could play it for you when you arrived. She had already put another one in the recorder. The tape we wanted was still in the player when we got there."

"Did you listen to it? Stupid question. What was on it?"

"Same thing you heard."

"What'd you make of it?"

"We think it was the killer who came in at the end. Almost had to be, the way it goes. The time's about perfect, and the guy—Peter, right?—seems to fall apart right at that moment."

"Could you make anything out of the section where they're talking together?"

"It was pretty much of a mess. I've listened to one of the copies maybe two dozen times and I can't get it. The lab boys have the original; maybe they'll do some good with it. They've got the equipment: they can do some amazing stuff, separating voices. They might have something for me later today."

"Would it be too much to ask . . . you know, for old time's sake . . . could you tell me what they say?"

"I'm already a dead man. What's one more shot in the head?"

"What was McKinley like while all this was going on?"

"Couldn't've been more cooperative. Went right to the tape player and handed over the tape and we were out of there in ten minutes. Even Lester liked her."

I sat quietly, lost in thought.

"Your turn," Hennessey said.

I started with the U-Haul rental: told him how Peter had rented the truck and gave him the gas station's address. I told him about Portland, and the lovely Mumsy Bonnema. I told him about Peter's books: where I had found them, what I thought they were worth, where I had put them. He kept his eyes closed, a suffering man, all the time I was telling it. At the end, he said, "I don't wanna know how you found out all this, do I?"

"Probably not."

"So what the hell d'you expect me to do with it?"

"I'll try to find a way to get it to you. For now, let's say there's a gray point of law involved."

"Let's say your ass is gray. Come on, Cliff, what am I supposed to do? Just how the hell am I supposed to have gotten those books from Oregon to Denver, let alone found out where they were in the first place?"

"I guess you'll have to follow the evidence, like a good cop always does."

"Right through you. I'll send you postcards in Canon City."

"Yeah, I thought of that. Maybe I will have to do some jail time before it's over. I just know I couldn't leave those books in Portland. By now they'd be ashes in Mumsy's backyard."

"You wouldn't be so particular if the evidence was pornography or dope."

"You may be right."

"You know I'm right." He finished off his beer. "You're crazy, Cliff, you really are." He got up and put on his coat. "You're crazy," he said again. "God dang, you were a good cop, though. You sure were a good cop."

37

"This is getting us nowhere," Levin said. "You admit you hated Mr. Newton. You admit you harassed and persecuted him for more than two years prior to the incident in question. You admit you kidnapped—threatened and beat and illegally handcuffed and detained—Mr. Newton, not in the legal performance of your duty as a Denver police officer, but out of sheer malicious hatred. Then you took Mr. Newton, against his will, for a little ride. Sounds like something out of *The Untouchables,* Mr. Janeway, but this is what, by your own admission, seems to have happened that night. All these things you have admitted for the record, and now, when we come to that little clearing by the river, you would expect us to believe that you removed the handcuffs from Mr. Newton's wrists and not only allowed him an even break but actually let him strike the first blow?"

Mose leaned across the table and in a very weary voice said, "Counselor, if you keep asking questions like that, we'll all be old men before this thing ends. The golden age of oratory is over."

"Mr. Moses, this is a deposition, not a trial. I believe the rules allow me to obtain information in my own way."

"As long as you don't actually expect him to answer that."

Levin puffed on his cigar. He was a little man with a New York accent, a tough Jewish lawyer as someone, I forget who, had said. He turned and looked at me down the length of the table. "Let me ask you this. Are you seriously asking us to believe that you removed those handcuffs and inflicted the severe body and facial damage"— he opened the package of photographs and threw them across the table—"to Mr. Newton that we see in this evidence?"

"That's what happened."

"Now Mr. Newton is a big man, would you agree with that?"

"No."

"Nevertheless, he's bigger than you are, by quite a bit."

"He's got more beef, if that's what you mean."

"How would you describe Mr. Newton, Mr. Janeway? Just his physical appearance, please."

"He's a white male, approximately six feet four inches, two hundred thirty pounds, muscular, brown hair, blue eyes, sometimes wears a mustache."

"And yourself? Describe yourself in the same terms."

"White male, five-eleven, one ninety, dark hair, dark eyes . . ."

"Mr. Newton outweighs you by some forty pounds, by your own description."

"About that."

"His reach is longer. . . ."

"Yeah."

"And would you say that Mr. Newton carries much fat on him?"

"Not much."

"How much?"

"None that's evident."

"In fact, Mr. Newton is a bodybuilder, isn't that right?"

"That's what I hear."

"He boxes, lifts weights . . . all in all, for his age, a prime specimen of manhood, wouldn't you say?"

"Look," I said, "if you want to ask me questions, go ahead and ask. Don't make statements and try to get me to agree with them."

"Here's a question for you, then. Do you expect us to believe that you took on this man on equal footing—*in spite of the fact that his wrists still bore chafe marks from the shackles that you bound him with*—that you released him and defeated him so overwhelmingly in a fair fight?"

"Is that the end of it?"

"Answer the question, please."

"The answer is yes."

"How did you do it, Mr. Janeway? Frankly, I find it a little hard to believe. How did you conduct this fight and bring it to such a successful conclusion, from your viewpoint?"

"I beat the hell out of him. He tried to beat the hell out of me, but he lost."

"And you expect me to believe that."

"I don't particularly expect anything from you, sir."

"I should apologize for belaboring the point, but I find it very hard to believe—"

"You've said that," Mose said. "Get on with it."

"I'm trying to find out how he managed it," Levin said.

"It wasn't by the Marquis of Queensberry rules," Mose said. "They were two guys brawling in the country. You ever been involved in a fight like that, Levin? One guy throws a punch, then the other. The guy with the most heart usually wins."

"I don't know anything about this so-called heart, Mr. Moses. What I do know is what I see in evidence before me. This is a small man, compared with my client. My client is a man supremely conditioned to such physical combat, yet he was the only one who was physically battered. I'm trying to find out, if the handcuffs really were off, how that happened."

"It's simple," I said.

"If it's so simple, please explain it to me."

"Bring your client in here, clear away the furniture, and I'll show you how it happened."

38

"I don't think he'll ask that question again," Mose said. "I might have to do it for him."

"Why would you do that?" I said.

"Are you kidding? You couldn't have a more perfect answer to the most damaging question we'll get in the whole trial."

"How can it hurt us if nobody asks it?"

"Because it's there, Clifford, whether anybody asks it or not. They'll look at you, they'll look at him; then they'll look at those pictures and they'll ask it themselves. So I'll bring it out. You'll say the same thing all over again. Clear the court, bring him on down here, I'll show you how I did it. Jesus, I love it. You don't say it in any flip or arrogant way. Whatever you do, you don't act disrespectful to the court. You just say it, like you have no doubt whatsoever that it'll turn out the same way again. I'm even flirting with the idea of asking the court's permission to stage a fight between the two of you just for the benefit of the jury. That kinda shit's a little risky and it smacks of an old Perry Mason rerun. The court would never allow it, but it sure makes points. Once you say it, and mean it, the jury never forgets, no matter what that old man on the bench tells them."

We were sitting in a little café across from Levin's office, doing the postmortem on my deposition. Levin had eaten up the afternoon: it was four-thirty and already the streetlights were on. Hard to believe I had been in Oregon just this morning. I felt depressed, as if I had lost a week instead of one afternoon.

"Next time don't look so fierce," Mose said. "Lighten up a little. Think of this as a popularity contest, which it often turns out to be. I know that's distasteful to a purist like you, but a smile at the right time—if it's not forced—can sometimes pay big dividends."

I gave a big stupid grin.

"There you go," Mose said. "Now you've got it. Nobody'll find against a retard." He signaled for more coffee. "Come home with me for dinner."

It sounded good. They were all good people, Mose and his wife, Patty, and their two kids. The daughter I had saved was now nineteen. She was a forest ranger, a child of the earth, a lovely young woman. I hadn't seen her in a long time.

But not tonight. "Think I'm gonna work awhile," I said. "I've gotta make something out of this day."

"You're a real type A, Clifford," Mose said over his coffee. "You better learn to relax, pal, or what happens to you won't be so funny."

I was looking through the front window when the Lamborghini pulled up and stopped in front of Levin's office. Jackie Newton and Barbara Crowell got out just as Levin began to close shop for the day. It was cold in Denver. They huddled for a moment at the front door, then Levin pointed at the café and they started across the street. Mose must've seen me tighten up. He looked where I was looking, but we didn't say anything. A little bell rang when they came in. The place was crowded: the only open tables were against the far wall, and they had to walk past us to get there. Levin saw me and hesitated. He said something to Jackie and they all looked. Jackie smiled and said something: he pointed to one of the tables and they came toward us. Barbara passed two feet from where I sat. I hadn't seen her in all these weeks: she looked haggard, worn out, drained of life.

"Hello, Barbara," I said.

She couldn't look at me. Her mouth quivered, and Jackie took her arm and propelled her past our table. They sat in a far corner, as far away as possible.

Mose was looking at me over the sugar bowl. "That was Crowell?"

"That was the lady."

"She looks like a nervous breakdown waiting to happen."

"When Jackie gets his hooks in you, he doesn't leave much."

"He'll need more than a hook when I get hold of her. I really think you can stop worrying about this, Clifford. They are in very deep doodoo if that's their main witness."

This was good to hear even if I didn't quite believe it. Mose didn't know how strong Barbara's fear of Jackie Newton could be. I knew it was stronger than any threat of perjury or the risk of public ridicule: I thought it might even be running neck-and-neck with the will to survive. If the fear is intense enough, if it goes on forever and there's still no end in sight, death might begin to look almost appealing.

"You don't look convinced," Mose said. "I promise you, Cliff, I know how to get to people like her."

"Yeah, but what happens to her afterward?"

"Not your concern."

"That's where you're wrong. Her only crime, you know, is being too scared to think."

"Her real crime is that she's a self-centered lying bitch. She'll destroy you or anybody else to get the pressure off herself. I can't work up much sympathy for people like her."

Poor Barbara, I thought, and I looked at her across the room.

"Want some more coffee?" Mose said. "I was gonna go home, but I hate to have those bastards think they ran us off. Let's have another cup."

I took a piece of apple pie with mine. We lingered over small talk far removed from our case. Mose had taken up fishing in his middle age: he was engaged in a herculean effort to master the fly rod. He asked, out of politeness, how the book business was, and I told him it was a lot like urban fishing. On any weekend morning, the fisherman and the bookscout went through the same motions and emotions. A nice catch for both was a dozen good ones. The hunt was the main thing, the chase was its own reward.

I glanced at the table where Levin and Newton sat hunched over papers and briefs. Barbara was wedged between them, her eyes cast into the bottomless gulf of her coffee cup. Any minute now, if she looked deep enough and hard enough, the Loch Ness monster might surface and show her its face. Jackie said something to her and she nodded: he said something else and she looked at him, looked into the face of the monster. Then she looked at me. I could feel her pain half a room away. I tried to smile and then—I couldn't help myself— I winked at her.

She excused herself and went back to the narrow hallway where the restrooms were.

All I could think in that moment was that line from Shakespeare, how cowards die a dozen times before their deaths.

Death was on my mind.

And I was suddenly very uneasy.

Mose was talking about the summer's best fishing trip. I should take up fishing, he was saying: it was good therapy for us type A's. Scouting for books might bear some superficial resemblances to fishing, if you had a good imagination and wanted to stretch a point, but it was too intense. I needed something to help me relax, Mose said.

Jackie Newton gave me a long look from the far wall. I stared back at him. Levin was talking and shuffling papers. Mose was rattling on about a new lure he had found: fish were supposed to be able to smell it. A waitress brought Mr. Newton's order, putting plates in front of each gentleman and another in front of the empty space where, a few minutes earlier, Barbara Crowell had been sitting.

"She sure is taking her time in there," I said.

"Who?"

"Crowell."

I got up and started back toward the restrooms. Behind me, Mose called my name. "Hey, Clifford, what the hell do you think you're doing?" There was a note of worry in his voice that almost matched what I suddenly felt in my heart. I went past Jackie's table. Both Jackie and Levin looked at me as I went into the dark hall.

I called Barbara's name.

Doors on opposite sides were designated by gender: pants and skirts. I knocked on the skirts and listened. I pushed the door open and peeped in.

"Barbara?"

I was staring at the outer wall of a toilet stall. I called her name again and got nothing. "Hey, I'm coming in," I said, and did. I looked around the row of johns and there she was, sitting on the floor. She held a small gun in her hand, and she was staring at it the way you imagine a medical student might look at a scalpel before his first operation. Tears were running down her face. She lifted the gun and looked at it, business end first.

"Hey," I said, holding out my hands. "Don't do that."

It was a little .22 revolver. You can buy them cheap all over Denver without permits or hassles: a little gun, made for ladies and kids, but more than enough to do what she had in mind.

"Hey, Barb," I said. I tried to smile and wondered if it looked real. It was real: a smile of fear. Softly, I said, "You know what they say about suicide, honey. Permanent solution to temporary problem. This gets you nothing."

It gets me peace, she seemed to say. I came a little closer and tried to figure my chances. If I rushed her suddenly, without warning, I had about a dead-even chance of getting to her before she could cock the pistol and pull the trigger. She probably didn't know much about guns—a point for my side. But I was still ten feet away—a big point for her.

"Listen, I've got a great idea," I said. "You put that back in your purse and let me take you out of here. We'll go to a place I know and we'll talk it over. Okay? Okay, Barb? We'll talk it over, and if I can't give you at least ten reasons for living we'll both kill ourselves. Now what could be fairer than that? C'mon, Barb. I'll buy you a great dinner and we'll work it out. I know you don't want to do this."

I stopped talking. She had cocked the pistol, taking away my only real chance. I felt a tightness in my chest, almost like hyperventilation.

"Barb, please . . . listen to me . . . Here, look at me."

She did. Again, her misery was like a beacon, filling the room.

"I swear to God there's a way out of this," I said. "I swear there is. I promise you, but only if you do the smart thing."

I could see it in her eyes: she was on the brink, right at the edge. I've seen three people commit suicide, and at the end there's no doubt that it's coming. They all look the same, drained of all hope.

I was going to lose her.

She spoke. Her voice was raw, the words ragged and broken. "I've left a note . . . It clears you . . . backs up everything you said . . ."

"It won't mean anything if you do this. Are you hearing me? Barbara, are you listening to what I'm saying?"

"No."

"Just give me one chance. One chance, Barbara, to prove what I'm telling you. I won't even take the gun away from you, that's how sure I am that you'll see things different. Let me tell you something. Newton can't do anything to me, and I won't let him do anything more to you, either. I've got ways of fixing that bastard that he can't even imagine yet. Just put the gun away and I'll tell you about it."

It was pointing at her right temple: her finger was on the trigger. She was going to do it. I couldn't stop her. Janeway, if you've got any good quotes, you'd better get 'em up now, because there isn't going to be any tomorrow.

"I know a guy who can make Newton hate the day he first saw you. I'm not kidding. I wasn't just yanking your chain that day when I told you that. Just put the gun down a little and let me say this. Just let me say this much, Barbara. Newton's a master at playing the system for his own advantage. He's got it all going his way—money, a sharp lawyer—he knows his rights, old Jackie does. The system's all greased up for scumbags like Jackie Newton. So we'll go outside the system. I couldn't do that when I was a cop, but I damn sure can now. We'll play Jackie's game Jackie's way, and I promise you we'll make him hate it. And he'll never be able to lay a hand on you again. That's the main thing. When we get through with Jackie, he'll never want to see your face again."

"You don't know him," she said. "Don't know what he's capable of."

"Oh yes I do. But I also know what he's not capable of."

She opened her mouth. Nothing came out. I heard a woman come in behind me, stopping suddenly at the end of the toilet partition.

"What's going on?" the woman said.

"Get out of here," I said.

She didn't move: I could feel her behind me; I could hear her breathing.

"Lady, you better do what I tell you. Just turn around and walk out of here."

She went, quickly now. I heard the door swish shut.

"People will be coming now," Barbara said.

"Don't worry about it. I'll keep them away from you."

"Cops . . . cops'll come."

"I'll walk you through that, too. The way it stands now, it's no big deal."

We looked at each other. I hoped to hell I looked sincere. In the distance I heard noises: a woman shouting; someone running; sharp, excited voices. In the dimmer distance, somewhere far outside, a siren.

"They come fast," Barbara said.

"They're just a phone call away, hon. They've got cars all over town."

"Janeway . . ." Her voice broke.

"I'm right here."

"I don't want to live anymore."

"Sure you do. You can't make that decision now . . . you don't know what the alternative is . . . you haven't given me a chance yet."

Now her voice was bitter. "You had plenty of chances. You couldn't do anything. . . ."

The siren got louder. I knew if the cops came in, she would do it. I had maybe two minutes to talk her out of it.

She put the gun in her mouth and my time was up.

One last plea. Desperately, I shouted: "Barbara, for Christ's sake, don't do this to me!"

She blinked.

"Don't do it," I said. "Please."

And I watched her . . . slowly . . . come back from the brink.

She wavered. The gun came out of her mouth.

I reached out my hands. She didn't do anything. The gun was still cocked but she held it limply in her lap.

I touched her: ruffled her hair with my knuckles, touched her cheeks where the tears still ran. Kneeled and looked in her eyes.

Outside, the sirens were very close.

I put an arm around her shoulder and helped her up. "We'll go meet them together," I said. "Give me the gun now and I'll take you outside."

Then the door opened. Jackie Newton was standing in front of us, blocking the way.

"Get out of the way, Newton," I said.

He just stood and looked. His face was full of contempt.

"Move," I said.

He gave a little laugh. "Stupid bitch."

And before I could stop her, Barbara brought up the gun and shot him.

39

They put her in a police car and segregated the witnesses: mainly me. It was getting to be habit-forming. For the second time in two days I told a uniform the bare facts and was told to wait over here, away from the crowd, until a coat-and-tie arrived from downtown. Barbara sat in the car, huddled into herself while a cop leaned across the seat and tried to talk to her. Reading her rights, I imagined: it was amazing how fast your sympathies passed from the cops to the accused, once you knew something about it and were no longer part of that world where the gathering of information must be just so. A plainclothes cop arrived and took charge. He was a burly guy named O'Hara: I had known him for years, though not well. I thought he was probably pretty good. I heard him tell the uniforms not to ask her anything until she could comprehend what she was being asked and what she was saying. She seemed to be in shock, one of the uniforms said. "Okay, let's get her downtown right away and have a doctor check her out," O'Hara said.

All this happened in a few minutes, while the medics were still working on Jackie Newton on the women's room floor.

"Good grief," O'Hara said when he saw me. "Can't you stay out of trouble?"

He went back into the women's room and came out again a few seconds later.

"Well, I guess you finally got the bastard."

"Hey, all I was was the cheering section, O'Hara. If I'd had anything to do with this, she'd've used a real gun."

"Lucky for her she didn't."

The shot had hit Newton in the throat and had gone through his neck. The exit wound was at the base of the skull. It was messy, O'Hara said, but probably not fatal.

Whatever it was, the medics were taking their time.

"You wanna tell me about it?"

I told him the story, omitting nothing about why and how long Newton had been asking for it. Even at that it didn't take long: my main statement would come later, downtown, in a smoky room with a stenographer.

"What do you think my chances are of seeing her?" I said.

O'Hara gave a loud laugh. "What a guy. You know better than to ask a question like that, Janeway."

"I told her I'd help her through it, if I could."

"Well, you shouldn't've told her that."

"I believe she is entitled to see a lawyer. That's the way it works, isn't it, O'Hara? Or have they changed the rules since I went away?"

"Where's your law degree?"

"Standing over there with its thumb in its ear."

I called Mose and he came over.

"How about going down and talking to Crowell?" I said.

He blinked and looked at me as if I had suddenly started talking Arabic.

"I'm serious," I said.

"You're out of your mind, Clifford. You want me to represent that dame?"

"I want you to go talk to her, let her know she's not alone. Come on, Mose, nobody does that better than you. Tell her about your last fishing trip. While you're at it, you might slip in some free advice."

"Cliff, listen to me. There's no way I could properly do something like that. You understand what I'm saying? You know what conflict of interest is, I believe."

"Look, I don't want her facing these dinosaurs alone."

O'Hara let out a bellow. "What a guy!"

They were bringing Newton out now. He lay on a stretcher, his head immobilized by a brace, tubes dangling from his nose and arm. His eyes were open, lovely blue eyes, wet and terrified. He saw me and his terror doubled.

"Merry Christmas, Jackie," I said.

They packed him into the ambulance and slammed the doors. The siren came up and they drove away.

"She's damn lucky she didn't kill him," O'Hara said.

"Oh yeah, she's real lucky. Two months from now she'll have all her old problems back and a whole shopping cart full of legal problems as well. When she finally does get out of jail she'll probably find Jackie Newton waiting at the gate."

If she does, I thought, I'll be there too.

40

It was still on the right side of seven o'clock when I finished up at headquarters. I was wired to the gills and ready to make something happen. I drove out to Stan Ballard's house, more on a whim than anything else. A sign on the door said OFFERED BY JOHN BAILEY ASSOC., and under that was a phone number for an agent named Douglas Barton. There was a lockbox on the door: the place had a sad look about it, as if it had just lost its best friend. It was one of those fine old houses, vintage World War I, that still had a lot of life in it. They built houses to last then, not the prefab cardboard they use today. There was a time in Denver, not so long ago, when a house like this wouldn't last a day on the open market. The oil business was booming and shale was the coming thing, and there was an economic excitement in the Rocky Mountains that hasn't been here since. But the bottom fell out of the oil bucket, they never did figure how to suck the shale dry, and then HUD got into the real estate business and started giving houses away. The Ballard place lay fallow. There were simply more houses than people.

I walked up the steps and peeped through the window. Light fell in from old Mr. Greenwald's place next door and I could see most of the front room. It looked different with everything stripped away. The Ballards had left nothing but the walls and the carpet and, yes, the bookshelves. It was a house made to order for a bookscout, big and solid and already shelved. I wondered what they were asking for it. I went around back and tried to peep in, but visibility was poor: I could see just enough to know that the shelves back there were still intact. I walked across the lawn and tried the garage. It was locked, but I could see that it was a big one, made for two cars and a small workshop. A man could park his car and still have room for five thousand books out here.

I saw a shadow pass the window next door: Mr. Greenwald was watching. There wasn't anything to watch, but old habits die hard. I gave him a wave and walked into his yard. His porch light came on and he stood for a moment watching me through the door glass. He didn't seem to recognize me, but he opened the door anyway.

"I'm surprised it's still available," I said, gesturing to the house.

"If they don't sell it soon it'll start falling apart," he said.

"Are they not taking care of it?"

He made a sour face and waved me away with his hand. "They take care of nothing. They care about nothing. All they want is money. And to play their silly games."

"What games?"

"The game of hating each other. Of beating each other. You never saw anything like it. They act like a pair of dogs with a scrap of meat thrown between them. It's the worst case of jealousy I've ever seen. They don't care anything about the house: they just want to make sure that if there's one dollar left over, the other one doesn't get it."

"Do you know what they're asking for it?"

"Are you interested?"

"I don't know, I might be."

"Come on inside; it's too cold to stand talking like this."

Inside, he offered me coffee, which I was happy to accept. We sat in friendly territory—in his kitchen, surrounded by books—and talked.

"They started at eighty," he said. "That's very reasonable for this place, even in these times, don't you think?"

I did think, and I said so.

"When it didn't sell, they came way down. I hear it's sixty-five now and still no takers. I can't understand that. I'd buy it myself if I had money to burn. I don't know real estate but I know sixty-five for a place like this is nothing. Ten years ago Stan turned down an offer of a hundred and ten. But those were better times."

"There are people who think better times are coming back."

"Then those people could find worse things to do with their money. It's what I'd do, if I were a young man like yourself. I'd buy it strictly as an investment. I'd make them an offer of forty-eight five."

"They'd never take it."

"They'll take it. They just want to get rid of it. They've sold everything but the house and it's hanging around their necks like a millstone. Those two never want to lay eyes on each other again, and this house is the only thing that ties them together. They'll take it, Mr. Janeway. In fact, I think they'll take less than that."

"I didn't think you remembered me."

"I've got a good set of eyes and a good memory for a face."

"If they'd take fifty I'd buy it in a heartbeat."

"Try it on them. They'll fall all over themselves taking it. You see if I'm not right. I've never seen anything like it. Such hate . . . such pure venom. So much energy wasted, just burnt up, on hate."

"Where'd it get started?"

We looked at each other and I knew what I had begun to suspect: this old man had secrets that he hadn't yet told anyone.

"Where'd it get started, Mr. Greenwald?"

"There are things I can't talk about . . . matters of honor."

"There are also three dead people. I understand about honor, sir, but somebody out there is killing people and I'm trying to stop them. It's pretty hard if I'm only playing with half a deck."

He seemed lost in thought. Then his eyes locked on mine and he said, "They are not actually brother and sister." He got up, poured us more coffee, and returned the pot to the stove.

"How do you figure that?"

"It's not something I figured; Stan told me. Val Ballard was an adopted child."

"Well, that explains a few things."

He nodded. "Stan's brother Charles married a delicate woman. Physically delicate . . . you know, frail. It was thought she couldn't have children, so they adopted the boy. Years later she became pregnant with Judith . . . a midlife baby, a great surprise."

"I'll bet."

"There didn't have to be any great conflict with that. Sometimes those things work out fine, and Stan told me they really did try. Charles and his wife did everything possible to raise them equally, to play no favorites. But from the beginning there was anger, resentment, extreme jealousy."

"A modern-day Cathy and Heathcliff," I said.

"Except that love was at the bottom of it all in that story, and here you have just hate."

"I thought something was out of whack when I questioned them.

Judith said something—it didn't make sense at the time and I let it get past me. Something like, 'If you're looking for all the living Ballards, I'm it.'"

"Yes. I don't know what good it'll do you. . . ."

"It could be a motive for murder."

"If they were going to murder anyone, it would be each other."

"Maybe. Or maybe they enjoy the hate."

"Now you're talking in riddles."

"You've got to allow for the quirks of human nature," I said. "Maybe they like what's going on between them. You know what I mean. The sweet sorrow, the hate that's really love, the pull of opposites in a single emotion. Maybe they'd be lost without each other. This is the stuff Shakespeare wrote about, isn't it? If you kill off a hate object, it's over. So much better to do him in in other ways . . . to get the better of him in business, to rook him out of his eyeteeth. . . . That you can savor all your life."

"I don't believe it," he said, but I had a feeling he might believe it, deep in his gut.

"You still know something you're not telling me," I said.

"It's nothing . . . harmless."

"I think I'll have to ask you to let me be the judge of that."

He shook his head. "It's just something Stan told me. It couldn't have any bearing on this."

"I think if Mr. Ballard were here, from what I know of him, he'd want you to tell me."

"That may be, but he's not here, and I can't go back on him."

"There are things that make no sense at all about this deal. The man had ten thousand books. I know he got them from the clubs; I've been through every statement going back almost fifty years. They're legitimate, they're in his name, they're annotated in his hand. He writes in the margin when he received a book and when he read it. The books were appraised and the appraiser, who is a helluva respected authority, found nothing of value. And yet, in the last two days, two hundred books have turned up. They did not come from the clubs. They were fine first editions . . . very desirable, very valuable, worth maybe twenty-five thousand dollars. I don't know where they could've come from but here in this house."

"Unbelievable," he said. "People really pay that much, just to own a first edition?"

"Sometimes more than that. Are you telling me, Mr. Greenwald, that neither you nor Mr. Ballard knew what first editions can be worth?"

"We never discussed money. In our generation money was a man's private business. Besides, it's so uninteresting. We didn't care about money."

"Somebody did. Were you here when the woman came to look at the books?"

"I was minding my own business. Stan told me how it had gone, after it was over."

"He told you the woman had appraised the library as worthless."

"That's what he said, yes."

"You never met the lady?"

"No."

"Is there any way I can persuade you to talk to me?"

"That's what I've been doing."

"You have nothing else to say to me?"

"Not at this time."

I got up to leave.

He rose with me, his eyes linked to mine. He won't let me walk out of here, I thought: it's bothering him too much. But when he spoke, it was only about the house. "I think you should buy Stan's house, Mr. Janeway. I really do."

"I'm thinking about it."

"A man would be foolish if he could get a house like that for fifty thousand and he didn't snap it up. You could rent it for more than the payments. In a few years . . . who knows?"

I tried to penetrate that wall. A vast enigmatic gulf lay open between us.

"Sometimes, I've heard, houses talk," he said. "Sometimes they give up secrets. This one may be like that. Sometimes I feel Stan's presence . . . sometimes it seems like he's still there, sitting in the library reading. That's a solid house, Mr. Janeway: more than that, a kind house. I'd buy it myself, if I were younger and had the money."

41

It was just a matter of geography. Val Ballard lived in Littleton, south of town; Judith Ballard Davis was in Park Hill, a few minutes' drive from Madison Street. I went there first.

She peered at me through the screen door and struggled to put a name with my face.

"Detective Janeway," I said. "Remember?"

"Ah," she said, and let me in.

If she knew anything about my recent history, she didn't let on. To her my life began and ended and began again when I walked into, out of, and now back into hers. "You ever catch that guy?" she asked, leading me to the living room. I said no, I was still working on it. She motioned me to the big stuffed chair and asked if I wanted a drink. I said you betcha and she made me a double. She watched me take off the top third in one gulp. She never stopped watching me. I knew I didn't look much like a cop anymore, and I sure didn't feel like one, but she never asked any of the obvious questions—where was my tie, why weren't my shoes shined, how come I was drinking on the job. She just looked at me and waited.

"I went by your house a while ago," I said.

She looked momentarily confused. "Oh, you mean Stan's house."

"It's a nice place. I'm surprised you haven't sold it yet."

"It's a white elephant. You couldn't give it away, the way the Denver market is."

"Maybe you've got the wrong Realtor. I think that house should sell."

"Put your money where your mouth is, Detective. You could have my part of it damned cheap. I mean *damned* cheap."

"I'm listening."

"Is this why you came here?"

"No, but I'm listening anyway."

"Make me an offer."

"I'm not really in the market. I wouldn't want to insult you with what I could pay."

"Insult me, please. I've got thick skin and I want to get out of this."

"I'm almost embarrassed to offer it . . . fifty?"

"Give me twenty-five and you could walk out of here with my part right now."

"What do you think your brother would say?"

"Do you mind if we don't call him that? Just hearing it makes my stomach turn."

"What do you want to call him, then?"

"What I call him wouldn't be allowed on the radio. Let's keep it on a high plane. Let's not call him anything. That matches his personality."

"Okay. What do you think *he* would say?"

"He needs the dough worse than I do." She grinned maliciously. "Alimony. I hope she takes the little pissant for everything he's got or ever will have."

"Well, let's put it this way," I said. "At that price, I'd definitely buy it."

"Detective, you've made my day. Let me freshen up that drink for you."

I put my hand over the top. "I'd better not. I've got a lot to do yet tonight."

"Going to see him?"

"I'll have to, won't I?"

"Call me later, let me know what he says. I know he'll say yes. He'll cough and sputter and blow smoke out of his ass, but in the end he'll be as delighted to be out of it as I am. We can have the papers drawn up over the weekend and I'll never have to see that idiot again." She lit a cigarette. "So what's the real reason you came over here?"

"I've been thinking about those books. I even found some of them."

"So?"

"They weren't exactly the kind of books everyone thought."

"I don't mean to be short, but why should I care? They're gone now. Ancient history. None of my business anymore."

"You might decide to change your mind about that."

"You're talking in riddles, Detective."

"I think you people screwed up. Or maybe just one of you screwed up."

"You'll have to make it plainer than that."

I watched her eyes particularly. Liars usually look away unless they're very accomplished. She was meeting me head-on.

"I think somebody pulled a scam," I said. "I think those books were worth a helluva lot more than anybody ever knew."

"Who pulled a scam? Are you talking about that little man that got killed?"

"He was just a tool. Somebody else was the main guy."

"And you think it was one of us?"

"Coulda been. The question is, which one?"

"I don't even know what was supposed to've been done."

"I think you're brighter than that, Mrs. Davis."

"Ms. Davis, please. There is no Mr. Davis: never was, never will be. It's my mother's maiden name."

I didn't say anything. I could see by the color in her cheeks that she was getting a glimmer.

"That son of a bitch," she said in a voice that was almost a whisper.

"Somebody's a son of a bitch," I said.

She got up, walked to the window, and came back.

"Let me get this straight. You think one of us found out what the books were really worth, hired somebody to buy them, and . . . is that what's going through your head? Is that what he did to me?"

I shrugged.

"So tell me, how much did the bastard take me for?"

I wasn't sure I wanted to tell her that yet.

"How much?" she pressed.

I finished off my drink.

She lit another cigarette. "Can we get a straight answer here? Christ, you men are all alike."

"If I had a straight answer I'd give it to you. Like I told you, I've only seen two hundred books."

"Then let's start with that. How much would those two hundred books be worth?"

"There's no guarantee they even came from here. It's just my hunch."

"*What's* your hunch? Talk straight, please. How much are those two hundred books worth?"

"In a bookstore, at retail . . . twenty grand. Maybe as much as thirty."

Her nostrils flared, blowing smoke. She looked ready to erupt.

Then she did erupt.

"Thirty thousand dollars! *Thirty thousand dollars for two hundred books!*" She leaped up and spilled her drink. "Son of a fucking bitch!" she screamed. "Do you have any idea how many books there were in that goddamn house?"

"Books are funny things," I said calmly. "Just because one's worth a lot, that doesn't necessarily mean anything as far as the others are concerned."

She was trembling now as she faced me. "What it means, Detective, is that old Stan wasn't quite the klutz that everybody thought. What it means is that Stan knew exactly what he was doing. And what that means, Mr. Janeway, is that there's an excellent possibility that all those books were worth money. Christ, we could be talking a million dollars here! Even the house is nothing compared with that!"

I didn't say anything.

"I will kill that bastard with my own bare hands," she said.

"I wouldn't try that."

"Get away from me! Don't you dare try to stop me."

"I will stop you if you take another step."

"Don't you threaten me. . . ."

"I'm trying to reason with you. Do you want to listen or do you want to fly off half-cocked and screw everything up?"

She sat and folded her hands primly. She made no effort to blot her spilled drink, which was seeping into the carpet at her feet.

"First of all," I said, "we still don't know for a fact that it happened that way. Two, I still don't know if it was him: it could be you. Three, whoever it is has killed three people. I'm not talking metaphorically here, Ms. Davis. Have you ever seen anyone who's been shot in the face?"

She looked at her hands, which were trembling uncontrollably.

"It's one thing to say you're gonna kill somebody. This boy, whoever he is, is the one with the track record. He bashed the bookscout's brains out and shot two people in the head not two days ago. Do you think you want to get involved in something like that?"

She spoke through clenched teeth. "What do you want?"

"I want you to do nothing . . . understand? Don't make any phone calls, don't go ripping over there. Just sit tight and wait for me."

"God!" she cried. "How can I sit back and let that flaming asshole get away with this!"

"Nobody's getting away with anything. You can't hide eight thousand books in your hip pocket. I'm gonna find them, if I can get you to stay out of the way."

She didn't say anything. I said, "Can I get a couple of straight answers out of you?"

"About what?"

"You and him."

"There is no me and him. Never was. He has nothing to do with me."

"You were raised together."

"That's not my fault."

"Come on, Ms. Davis, what happened between you two?"

"Nothing. It was just a case of hate at first sight."

"Were you jealous of each other?"

"He always was." She lit another smoke, didn't realize that she had one going in the ashtray. "He was an adopted child. He always hated that. Hated me. I never had a chance with him, not from the first."

"Did he ever show any signs of violence, either as a child or later?"

"He never had the guts. He was always sneaky."

"Sneaky how?"

"I caught him looking in the window once . . . I was thirteen . . . that kinda stuff."

"Do you think he's capable of murder?"

She seemed to melt suddenly, and for a long, strange moment, I thought she might cry. She pulled herself out of it just as quickly.

"No," she said.

"That took a lot of effort."

"Damn right. I'd like to say yes, but I just don't think he could ever find the nerve to shoot someone. No, he'd be more the type to hire it done."

I thought of Neff's turtle-faced man.

"A hit man," I said.

"Sure. He'd do that, all right. I wouldn't put that past him at all."

42

I drove south, into the coming snowstorm. I thought about the U-Haul truck and the mileage that Bobby Westfall had racked up. I thought about Greenwald and the screwed-up Ballards and the turtle-faced man. Snow began to crust around the edges of my windshield. The road was getting slick. I had an odd feeling of some omniscient demon riding with me, a malignant force waiting to spring. The strange thing was, I couldn't remember Val Ballard's face: I could hear his voice and see his hands working as he sifted through his uncle's stuff; I could see his red tongue flicking as he licked and stuck labels on this item and that, but his face remained a blank. I could see Bobby Westfall easily enough, and we had only met a few times, months ago. I could see Peter and Pinky: silent passengers with the demon curled up between them. *C'mon, people, talk to me.* "Talk," I said out loud. Tell me something I don't already know. Who's the turtle-faced man, and where are the books, and how-oh-how had Rita McKinley's appraisal been so far off the mark?

In the old days, Littleton was a prime horse-racing town. Centennial was never a big-time track, but it wasn't the bush league either. Carol and I used to come down two or three times a summer to watch the horses run and lose a little of our hard-earned dough. Now when I come, all I feel is loneliness, and an aching sense of my own mortality. They're tearing everything down, and someday soon they'll come up behind me and tear me down too. Something as big as a racetrack ought to have a little bit of immortality attached to it. But they tore old Centennial down and plowed her under. Right out there where the grandstand stood are high-rise offices and apartment buildings. Oh, sacrilege. All that's left of the old days is the ever-flowing Platte: it snakes its way down from the mountains and winds past expensive subdivisions and subdivided farms and modern shopping centers built on the land of old ranches. In one of those houses, just south of the racetrack, Val Ballard lived.

I checked the address. The house sat back from the street in a grove of trees. It was very dark: the trees blotted out all light from the road. A wind had risen and the snow had blown in drifts over the driveway. I came in boldly, with my lights on, and sat for a moment with my lights playing across the front of the house. Nobody home, it looked to me. I turned off the lights, then the motor. The darkness was oppressive. I got out and followed my penlight up the walk to the front door. I rang the bell, then knocked. Nothing. I walked around the house, into the teeth of the gale, and fought my way across the yard to the garage. He had gone somewhere and he had gone in a hurry. He had left the door up and there were rubber marks on the cement. I could still see the ruts he had left in the yard, only half buried under the snow.

I went back to the car and got my tools. I knew I was a sitting duck for anyone who drove up—my car was there in the open yard, so there'd be no running away from it. When I decide to commit suicide, I don't brood over it. I did think once of consequences. I could get three to five for this. Then I held the penlight in my teeth and picked open the front door lock.

The first thing to do was find an escape hatch. The back door. I crossed the main room and went through a dark corridor and found it. I checked it to make sure it could be opened easily. Fine. Well, not fine, but it wouldn't get any finer. This was it. I had come looking for Ballard, I would tell my executioners. The house was dark but I had noticed the garage door up and had gone around to check. That's how they happened to catch me walking around from the backyard. I would slip out the back way and walk nonchalantly around the house, and this was what I would tell them. I had stopped behind the house to take a leak, a nice touch, I thought, that gave some credibility to a shaggy-dog tale like that.

With that settled, I went through the house, looking for . . . what? I had a half-baked hunch I might even find Stan Ballard's books. The place to start was in the basement. I found it with no trouble, a set of dark stairs that led down from the kitchen. If he came home now, I was sunk. Forget the back door, I'd never make it. I took a long breath and started down. The little light led me to a finished room. There were no books: just a water bed, a chest of drawers, a big-screen TV, a VCR, and a wall of pornographic tapes. I could see at a glance the kind of entertainment he liked, with titles like *Love in Chains* and *Ginger's Fantasy* throbbing on the shelf. It didn't mean anything. There was a room off the main room and I went there and opened the door. No books: not much of anything. The room was unfinished, and there were a few boxes inside, but a peek in them revealed nothing but junk.

I left it all as I had found it. The next likely place was an attic. Ballard didn't have a walk-up attic, but I found a tiny trapdoor in the ceiling. I pushed it open with a broom, which I found in the kitchen. I gripped the rim and chinned myself up into the hole. With my little light in my teeth, I turned my head from one direction to another, dropped, chinned, and did it again from the other side. Nothing. It looked like he had never been up there: the place was two inches deep in dust and had never been disturbed.

I went through his living room. There wasn't even a Reader's Digest condensed book for the criminally brainless. In fact, Ballard didn't have a single book in his entire house that I could see. I looked through the kitchen cupboards, remembering that twice before I had found in closets and cupboards small stacks of very good books. No luck this time. So . . . the hell with the books: maybe I could find a gun. A lot of cases are broken that way, through the almost unbelievable incompetence and stupidity of the killer. I went into the bedroom and looked in all the normal places where a man might keep a gun, and found nothing.

I came at last to his den. He didn't even have a law book. I had never been in a lawyer's house that had not even one book around, and it felt almost empty. He had a filing cabinet and a rolltop desk, neither of which was locked. I opened the cabinet and found his dead files, duplicates of old cases long disposed. I flipped through the folders double-time, looking for high spots. There weren't any.

The bottom drawer was full of pornography. Another waste of time.

The desk had pigeonholes and compartments and many sliding drawers. The pigeonholes were empty, the compartments were full of dust, and the drawers were stuffed with pornography. I didn't go through the whole boring inventory: it just didn't look like the den of a guy who practiced much law.

I found what I found in the last possible place. On top of the desk, pushed far back where it lay in dark shadow, was a yellow pad. The top sheet was filled with doodles and notes. There was a name at the top—Rubicoff—and under it a figure, $1,235. There was a phone number. I recognized the exchange as east Denver, not far from my store. Rubicoff. It sounded familiar, but I couldn't remember from where. At the bottom of the paper he had done some multiplying: the figure 8,500 multiplied by various numbers from 10 to 150. Each time the writing got darker, more slashing, angrier. I didn't know what it meant but I had some guesses. The figure 8,500 might correspond roughly to the number of books in old Stan Ballard's library. The figures were guesswork—somebody's idea of what the library might be worth if the books averaged $10, $50, $75, and so on. He didn't know books very well: it's unheard of to get a high average on that big a library. On the other hand, I hadn't seen a book yet that was worth less than $100.

And what about Rubicoff? I'd lay odds he was the turtle-faced man. I was getting close to cracking it, I thought.

I wrote the number in my notebook. I put everything back exactly as it was. Then I got the hell out of there.

43

I sat in the car and listened to the wind. A cold fear was blowing across the Platte.

At a gas station about half a mile from Val Ballard's, I called Hennessey at home.

"Me, sweetheart," I said when he answered.

"Oh, lucky day."

"What'd you find out on that McKinley tape?"

"I don't want to talk about this on the phone."

"What's Lester doing, running a tap on you now?"

"You're puttin' my ass in one big crack, Cliffie."

"Hey, one big crack deserves another. Come on, Neal, give."

I let the line hiss for a moment.

"What do you expect me to say?" he said.

"I expect you to say yes, Virginia, there is a Santa Claus. I imagine you'll break into song, with the chorus of 'Over the River and Through the Woods.' I'm hoping somewhere along the line you'll tell me something about the McKinley tape."

He sighed. "Why don't you come on over here?"

"'Cause I'm two thousand miles away and heading in the opposite direction."

"Then I guess I can't help you. I can't talk about it on the phone."

"They separated the voices, didn't they?"

"I don't want to talk about this. . . ."

"They separated the voices."

"I told you before, they can do wonders with modern equipment. You want to talk about that, fine, I can talk all night. I've become a regular scientist since I saw you at lunch, a real electronics wizard. Did you know they can take fifteen people and put 'em to talking all at once, then take machines and separate every voice? Did you know that, Cliffie? Got something to do with timbre and pitch. And all I always thought timbre was, was something loggers yell when they're chopping trees down."

"What did Peter say?"

"I think he yelled timber. Maybe he was an old logger up in Oregon."

"You're a pain in the ass, Hennessey," I said, and meant it.

"Oh yeah? Fine. Someday I'll sit down with you and compare notes and we'll see who the real pain in the ass is."

"It's you, Neal. You're becoming one of them."

"I got news for you. I always was."

"Hang up, then, if that's how it is."

We listened to each other's silence for ten seconds. Then, with an anger in his voice that I'd never heard, he said, "Cliff, you're abusing our friendship. It's bad enough when you put your own neck in a noose, but you want me to stick mine in too and call it for old times' sake. Dammit, you're gonna cost me my badge before this is over."

"I'm sorry you feel that way," I said, but I hung in there, knowing that my silence was working on him.

"God damn it," he said. "This isn't right, Cliff."

I didn't say anything.

"The bastard said nothing, all right? Not one damn thing you or anybody else can use. You want his exact words? I ought to know 'em, I been sitting here listening to the damn thing all afternoon. He said, 'Get away, get away.' He said that twice. Then he said, 'There's nothing you can do to me, people already know.'"

"What people?" I said—aloud, but to myself.

"I should've asked him that," Hennessey said.

"What people?" I said again.

The line was quiet for a moment.

"What about Miss Pride? Did she say anything?"

"She said, 'Oh, hi, everything's fine.'"

I blinked. "She said what?"

"She said, 'Everything's fine, I'll call you back.'"

The silence stretched.

"If you're waiting for an encore, there isn't any," Hennessey said.

"That was it, short and sweet: we busted our humps over nothing. I hope you're satisfied."

"Yeah, Neal, I'm satisfied."

"I want you to be happy, old pal. If you're not happy, I'm not happy. Is there anything else I can do for you, buddy?"

"I don't think so."

"Good. Don't ever do that to me again."

"Look, I'm sorry about—"

But he had already hung up.

44

I called Rita McKinley, a futile gesture, I knew.

But, wonder of wonders, she answered the phone. Scooped it up on the first ring.

"Rita McKinley," she said. I love women who answer the phone that way, crisp and cool and professional. "Go to hell, you slob" might have been okay too, when the best I expected was a monotone from the damned answering machine.

"Not the real McKinley! Not the genuine article, in the flesh?"

"Janeway!"

"Was that sound I heard you falling off your chair with pleasure at hearing my voice?"

"Where the hell have you been?"

"So far today, everybody I've called has asked me that. I was hoping to get some variation on the main theme from you."

"I've been trying to call you all day. What happened?"

"It's all in the newspaper, Miss Sunshine. I know how you like the crime news, so I assume you've read all about it."

"I want to see you."

"Now this is a definite step in the right direction. After you banished me to the National Leprosarium in Carville, Louisiana, I thought the only way I'd get back up there was to practice pole-vaulting."

"Can you come up? It's snowing pretty hard."

"Be just as hard for you to come down. You got anything to eat up there?"

"Two steaks in the fridge."

"What happened to the diet?"

"Don't ask."

"I'll be up in a while. Better give me at least an hour and a half."

"I'll leave the gate open."

It came again, that chill. "Don't do that," I said. "Look, it's nine-thirty now, I'll meet you at the gate at eleven. Drive your car down. If I'm not there, come back at half past."

"Why don't you want me to leave it open? What's the problem?"

"Tell you when I get there."

I headed west, into the stormy mountains.

45

It was truly a miserable drive. I sloshed along the deserted freeway and slipped into the canyon. By eleven o'clock I still hadn't reached Evergreen. I stopped at another gas station and called her, but she had the recording on. I left a cheery message and pressed on. The canyon too was deserted, leading to the inescapable conclusion that I was the only damn-fool in the state on the highways tonight. The headlights threw up a glare that was blinding, and I couldn't use my brights. Back and forth went the car, left and right in the twisted contour of the canyon road: it reminded me of a pendulum, or a hypnotist's watch. Visions floated on the periphery of my sight. I saw Peter walking beside the car: nervous, furtive. He turned slightly and opened a door and there, yawning back into the dark, was my bookstore. It was empty, except for Miss Pride. Peter was upset. He was so upset that Miss Pride was trying to call me at Rita's house. Then I lost the picture. I knew it was still playing out there but I couldn't see anything. It was like a TV show with the picture turned off. I could hear voices but I couldn't see them.

Miss Pride: *Let me talk to him, Peter. Give me the phone.*

Extrapolate, Janeway, figure it out. Figure it out and maybe the lights will come on again.

Someone had come to the front street window. Peter Bonnema locked eyes with death through a quarter inch of clear plate glass.

Miss Pride: *There's nobody on the line.*

Peter, his voice rising to a panic pitch: *It's a fucking tape recorder!*

And death walked in.

Miss Pride: *Someone's come in, I'll have to call you back.*

That's what I had heard. Hennessey had heard something else.

Peter knew. He knew exactly what was happening.

Get away! Get away! There's nothing you can do to me! People already know!

What people?

There was the source of that cold fear I had felt.

If Peter had bartered names for a few final seconds, those people were in trouble. Whether they knew anything or not, he had signed their death warrants.

My lights picked out her road. It looked like a tunnel, slick and steep and dangerous.

I shoved the car into four-wheel drive and started up.

I wasn't sure how far it was: a couple of miles, I thought, to the gate, maybe another hundred yards after that. I passed a car that had slipped off the road: clattered past it, kept going. You don't stop on a drive like that: you keep the wheels turning, keep the traction, try to slug your way up the hill. I had reached the steepest part of the incline, a place that shot up suddenly and gained hundreds of feet in no time—simple enough in dry weather with the sun shining, not so simple now. I bumped over ruts and kept going. The canyon yawned mistily to my right. The wind was just vicious.

I passed the last of the side roads. There were no lights anywhere, or perhaps it was just that I couldn't see them in the storm. The snow got deeper as I went higher. Not gonna make it, I thought: I could feel the car losing ground with every foot. The road had taken a hairpin curve and now the canyon lay off to my left. I couldn't see anything but snow. I began to look for a place to park and found it a few minutes later: a simple widening of the road at a place where it curved again and began climbing. I pushed my front wheels into a snowbank and stopped.

This was dangerous stuff. I had no coat—only the jacket I had worn to Levin's office. It was adequate for a late-autumn Denver afternoon but wouldn't do for a trek to the Pole. The only hat I had was a silly knitted thing in the trunk. This is how people die in Denver: they start out thinking they're going for a walk; one thing leads to another and it turns into something else. I shimmied the gun around on my belt and zipped the jacket. I got the hat from the trunk and got some bullets for the gun; put the hat on my head and the bullets in my pockets and away I went. The snow was deep, but I was fit and I made good time. I slipped and fell a couple of times but did no harm. I wasn't yet cold—that's another deceptive thing about Rocky Mountain weather, how it sneaks up on you. On the coast, when it gets down to freezing, you freeze: here, I've gone out in short sleeves when the temperature was in the thirties and never felt the need for even a sweater. Then, half an hour later, you notice your fingers are turning blue. Oh, well, it couldn't be much farther. The road was leveling off now: I remembered that from the other day. I'd be there in no time at all, a piece of cake. McKinley and I would spend Christmas together and live happily ever after. Trees were on both sides now: it was very dark. I kept my little light in my teeth and kept my head down, tried to keep my spirits up, and most of all I kept going.

At last I saw the gate, a silvery vision wavering like a mirage. I didn't see her, though, and that bothered me. I looked at my watch: it was quarter to midnight. Could she be sitting up there in the trees with her lights off? My own light was so puny it barely reached to the gate, yet it must seem like a beacon from the 1939 New York World's Fair in this dark. Suddenly the whole world lit up. Flash! She turned on her headlights and it was like a nuclear bomb going off: it froze me stiff and actually drove me back a step. She had her brights on. She flicked them down and I heard the car start. I could see it now, a gaunt outline behind the fence. I saw her pass in front of the headlights and heard the jingle of keys. A moment later the gate swung open.

"Are you crazy?" Her voice was disembodied, floating on the storm.

"Good evening to you, too. How've you been?"

"Don't you know you can die in this weather dressed like that?"

"I was just thinking the same thing. Don't scold me, now, it's been a hard day."

I walked through the gate and got in her car. The heater felt great.

She was certainly dressed for it: she wore heavy pants and a coat that buttoned under her chin. Her hat was pulled down over the coat and only a small square of her face could be seen: eyes, nose, and mouth. Enough.

God, I loved her then.

We went up the hill. The house looked mellow and warm. It

was. I stood in the hall watching her take off her gloves, and I thought it again. Jeez, I love her. Never thought that before, about anybody.

What a shock.

"You believe in love at first sight?" I asked.

She turned and looked at me directly. "What a silly question."

"What's your silly answer?"

She took a long time answering, of course . . . a long, endearing moment.

"I think I do," she said. "Yeah."

She blushed.

"I am so tired of being alone," she said.

"Don't be, then."

"Damn you," she said. "Damn you, damn you, Janeway. Of all the things I didn't need in my life, the list begins and ends with you."

"I bet you've been thinking about me constantly."

"You're a thug. My God, a policeman! Me with a cop."

"I'm a refined, wizened dealer in rare books."

"You wouldn't know a rare book if it fell on your head."

"But I learn fast. I soak up knowledge like mere mortals eat soup. I'm witty, I'm bright; I'm a bundle of goddamn laughs in case you hadn't noticed." I stopped, realizing suddenly, sadly, that I had lifted the pitch somewhere. It was almost the same half-joking plea that Miss Pride had used the night she'd come begging for a job.

Rita was looking at me intently.

"Here's the best part," I said. "I don't mind taking orders from a woman."

"How kind of you. How generous."

"Can't you just see it, lighting up the night sky? Janeway and McKinley. What a wow, huh?"

"Six days ago I'd never heard of you. I was five thousand miles away, lying in the sun. Now you're not only taking me over, you're getting top billing."

"That doesn't mean anything. It's like in vaudeville: the straight man always gets top billing."

"Shut up," she said, coming close. She took off her coat and threw it somewhere. The air seemed electric between us: the fine hair was standing up on her arms and neck. I knew if we touched, the static would fry us both.

She threw her arms around me and kissed me hard. The world went pop.

"This is insane," she breathed into my neck.

I kissed her too. Her hand was on my gun. I could feel her heart; I could hear it, like a distant drumbeat.

"You never cared about books," she said. "It's all just a ruse to get in my pants."

"I can't keep anything from you."

"Well," she said. "I guess it worked."

I remembered something Ruby had said: *It's the most hypnotic business a man can do.* He was talking about the book business, equating it to making love. I still had the gun in my hand: I don't even remember now how that happened, but somehow the three of us wound up in bed together. I clutched the gun and held on for dear life. That piece of cold blue steel was my last link with sanity. I shuddered my way inside her and she jerked, pulling me all the way down. I held on to the gun and went all the way. This was so right. I closed my eyes and lost it. Oh, I lost it all. Anyone could've come through the front door and killed us both: I wouldn't've known, much less cared. They could've come through with a battering ram and six regiments of cavalry. I think maybe they did. They ripped the door out of the frame and stormed through on the way to the Little Bighorn, and the last man through picked up the door, gave it a paint job, hung it back, closed and locked it good as new. Brushed himself off, saluted, and called me sir: then left us there, before I knew they had come.

"Janeway," she said.

"Mmmm."

"Tell me that isn't your gun mashed against my head."

I took the gun in my other hand and propped myself up.

She began to laugh. "Now that's one for the books. I've just been screwed by a man with a gun and it wasn't even rape."

"That's what you think," I said. "I never had a chance."

47

It was two o'clock in the morning and we were just getting around to the steaks. "This is my day for decadence," Rita said. "Lose my virginity. Go back on meat. I seem to be a wanton, savage creature at heart."

"Jeez, were *you* a virgin too?" I said.

She tousled my hair. I liked that. It showed affection, not just lust. I opened two beers. The steaks were almost done.

We ate. The food was wonderful, the company superb. We didn't talk at all.

It wasn't till much later, sitting by the fire, when she started to unwind. "I called Paul right after I talked to you the other night," she said. "The night . . . it happened."

"Paul is . . . ?"

"The guy I was gonna marry."

"I love the past tense. Go on."

"It was three o'clock in the morning back there. I got him out of bed. Guess I could've waited, but somehow it seemed too important. God, it seemed earthshaking. I felt like my whole world had tilted off its axis."

I kissed the side of her head.

"I called him to say good-bye," she said.

Suddenly there was no more white space, no eternity between the lines. "I met him in Greenpeace a couple of years ago. That's where I go every summer, to work in the field. I saved a whale this year, can you imagine that? Got in a wet suit, put myself between him and the killers, and harassed them till they went away. I didn't know I'd have the courage to do it till the time came: then there was no thought of not doing it, it was what I'd come for. We lost a volunteer this year, did you know that? We had a young man killed in a protest over a nuclear test. I knew him slightly, but his death made everything very suddenly real. I knew I could die too, and I didn't want to. I expected to be blown into nothing every minute. Have you ever seen what a modern harpoon gun can do? It's frightening, and here you are, taunting them, daring them to shoot you with it, knowing they'd like to do just that if they could find a way to call it an accident. They had me on NBC that night. Paul got me a video-tape of the broadcast and I never looked at it: it diminishes the real experience too much. It's what Hemingway meant when he wrote about hunting and war. Everything's ruined when you talk too much. I used to read that and think, What macho garbage, but god damn it, he's right. They show a twenty-second clip on Tom Brokaw and what it really was was a two-hour test of wills. Hemingway was right, the old fool. You do something that people call heroic and you can't talk about it, you can't sit in front of a tube and gloat over a tape, all you can do is carry it in your heart. Even talking about it this much fucks it up."

She pointed to the picture on the wall: the guy in the wet suit.

"That's Paul. I'll take his picture down if you want."

"Leave it," I said. I could afford to be generous. I knew Paul would be glad to let me be the picture on the wall and him be here on the sofa.

"He's a good man. I don't know why things never really . . . what's the word?"

"Ignited."

"Yeah, that's the word. He really is a fine man. Doesn't deserve a bitch like me. You, on the other hand . . ."

"I think I can handle you."

"I'm sure you do. So handle me, Janeway: tell me what you want to know."

"Anything you want to tell."

"Oh, please. Don't go soft on me now. You've been pushing me since the moment I first saw you. Long before that, if you count that snotty phone message."

"Then tell me all of it."

It took her a while to get started. We loosened up with brandy and put some logs on the fire.

"I was working in a bookstore in Dallas. We had a customer named William J. Malone. You know the name?"

"Uh-uh."

"You would if you'd been in the business longer. William J. Malone was a collector of books. You didn't see his name much in the *AB*. He was one of those guys who didn't like the limelight. A lot like me that way. Very private. No friends. Distant. I guess to people who didn't know him, full of mystery. But all the so-called big boys of the book world knew him. He had no credit limit with anyone. A thug from your side of the tracks would say he had deep pockets. And the ruling passion of his life was books. Modern lit, that was his thing. He was the last of his line and he never married, but God—what a bookman! Malone knew everything. He had a wall of reference books but he didn't need them. He had it all in his head. The joy of his life was to go into a bookstore and find wonderful things. He didn't care about the money, it was all a game. He paid what they asked and never wanted a discount, didn't matter whether he spent ten dollars or ten thousand. If he wanted something, he got it.

"Malone knew more about books than any ten dealers I ever met. In Dallas, where he lived then, he was a major celebrity in the bookstores, though he tried not to be. I don't know what first attracted him to me—maybe the fact that I didn't scrape and bow whenever he walked in the door. All I know is, suddenly he was in my life. What kept drawing him back to that one bookstore turned out to be—am I vain enough to say it?—me. We had something going from the start, long before we ever talked of such things. It's like something in the air that only the two of you can see. You know how that can be, Janeway, I know you know."

"I know now."

"Yes. That's exactly right. And when it happens, you don't care who the other person is, how old he is, how much money he's got. People who let stuff like that matter to them are fools. Things like race, religion, politics—none of it matters. So one day Malone came in and asked if I wanted to be his assistant. I quit my job on the spot. The guy I was working for was a jerk: I'd've quit in another week anyway. I didn't even ask Malone what kind of assistant I would be. I didn't care. I had been bouncing around the book business for a few years—libraries, bookstores—and I was tired of it. I was ready for something different. Well, I got it.

"For the next four years we went everywhere. We went all over the world looking for books. Everything I know that's worth knowing I learned in that time. We lived in Paris for six months, went to England every summer. One of the most interesting Jack London collections—part of it's still here, in the big room—we bought in Tokyo, of all places. You get the idea: there isn't much more to tell. Malone never went back to Texas and neither did I. He bought this place. He liked the solitude. He liked the fact that it came with that big fence already up. You can't put up a fence like that anymore—too many zoning restrictions—but they won't let you tear it down either. Malone had always liked Colorado, not in the summer when tourists come swarming in, but in the dead of winter. He liked being snowed in. He was always different than everybody else. I'd still be with him, if he'd lived. I don't think of it as a mad love affair, it wasn't like that. But I know I'd still be with him."

"He died, though."

"You don't have to ask that. I'm sure you've heard the stories. What's the version you heard? Was I supposed to've killed him for his money or his books?"

"It was just talk."

"Yeah, right. Well, I did kill him in a way. He was fifty years old. He smoked too much and couldn't quit, he had always smoked and he was dying from it. I guess there comes a time when it doesn't matter anymore. One day he said to me, 'Rita, I'm not going to die in a hospital.' I knew then what I was in for. During the next couple of days he tended to business. Had a lawyer come up, dictated what amounted to his last will. I knew he was leaving it all to me. It was never discussed between us, but I knew him so well, and you might not believe this . . . I didn't care. We were so businesslike. That's even how he wanted to die, according to a schedule of his own making. He'd had a lethal injection made up—I knew where it was and what it was there for, and when the time came I went to the cabinet and got the stuff and helped him as best I could. God, I was such a coward. I couldn't keep from crying and trembling. . . . I had never seen anyone actually die, and I know he wanted to go with me keeping a stiff upper lip but I just couldn't. I held his head on my lap while he gave himself the shot. That should've been all there was to it, only . . . he wouldn't die. People tell you that stuff always works: it's supposed to be painless and you're gone like the snap of a finger, only it didn't work that way. The man would . . . not . . . die. I thought he just didn't get enough. It knocked him out before . . . you know. And he was in such pain! He writhed and twitched . . . and still he wouldn't die! So I loaded that needle and I gave him another shot, enough to kill a dinosaur . . . and still he lived. It was like some nightmare. Then I remembered his gun.

"I knew it was in the bedroom, but it took me a while to find the shells. I don't know much about guns but I thought I could figure it out. I came into the room and sat beside him. His breathing was heavy and labored. He was struggling, fighting, and I took the gun and put it to his head and cocked it. I remember thinking, 'How can I do this, how can I possibly find the strength?' Then he seemed to relax and I knew he was gone. He just . . . slipped away . . . just in time. Another ten seconds and I might've been in real trouble. I didn't even know how to uncock the stupid gun. I pulled the trigger and blew a hole in the wall. You can still see the mark. I think the sheriff suspects me of something even to this day. When they read the will, I just sat there and didn't say anything, but it was an absolutely grand motive for murder. I knew Malone was well off, but I was shocked at how much there really was. He never told me how much he had: it was his business and I never particularly wanted to know. I guess I was lucky: I might've had some real explaining to do if Malone hadn't had the foresight to tell his lawyer what he intended. Even now there's a lot of suspicion. To the people on this mountain, and to some in the book trade, I'm the woman who killed her boyfriend and got away with it. So I keep to myself, don't have much to do with anyone, and that's the story. That's how I became rich and famous. It's also why I've been giving it away in buckets. It never really felt like mine."

The day dawned cold and wet and miserable, one of those days in the Rockies when it's too warm to snow and too cold to rain. We had slept for a few hours, and I came awake with her head nestled under my chin and my hand cradling her breast. I lay still, reluctant to wake her. But there was a killer to catch, and today was the day, and the day wasn't getting any younger. I thought I had narrowed it down to an either/or. Everything about it had begun to make sense, except her part in it, and that made no sense at all.

She turned over and opened her eyes. She touched my face and said, "Love me again," and I couldn't, couldn't, say no. Then, spent, we lay under the covers and locked eyes and touched. At some point I said we had to get up. She said, "We don't have to do anything, not ever again." She did get up, though, and for a moment she stood by the bed, naked and lovely. She walked away and I heard the shower start. I stared up at the darkest part of the house and thought about it. And I thought: God bless America, I hope you're not mixed up in this. I tell you it'll break my heart if you are.

48

Either/or: six of one, half a dozen of the other. We came down from the mountain and I did a mental crapshoot. It came up Littleton. We rolled in on Hampden and turned south on Santa Fe Drive. The streets were still slick but it was daylight now and I had made the drive down in less than forty minutes.

I pulled into a Denny's and stopped.

"This's where you get out."

"I told you before, Janeway, I have a constitutional problem with fast food."

"You'll live through it. Have a cup of coffee. Read the paper. And just wait here for me."

"How long am I supposed to wait?"

"Till I come back."

She gave me her long-suffering look. "I hope this isn't the kind of treatment I can expect from you."

She got out and came around to my side. I rolled down the window and she stood for a moment looking at me, her coppery hair wafting around her head. This is how I'll remember her twenty years from now, I thought: her priceless face framed in the car window on a lousy gray day. She leaned in and kissed me. "Don't get killed," she said in a tiny voice. "You too," I said. She had already turned away and was walking toward the restaurant. "Be back before you know it," I called, but she didn't do anything at that. Strange girl, I thought: strange woman, still full of secrets.

Our discussion that morning had been brief and to the point.

"I'd like you to stay with me today," I had said.

"Sounds lovely. What'll we do? Wanna fly to New York?"

"I'm going out to get the guy who killed those three people."

"And for this you need me?"

"I need to know you're safe," I had said. "I think there's a possibility he may try to kill you next."

A few minutes later I pulled up at Val Ballard's house. I could see the house in the misty morning. If I walked along the road, as I now did, I could soon see the garage. It was closed: the doctor was in. The road told me nothing: it was so full of puddles and melting snow that there was just no reading it. But the furrow he had plowed across the backyard was gone, washed away completely in the night, and there were no fresh tracks to take its place.

He had been home, then, for some time.

I didn't know what to expect: I just hoped I was ready for it. I had my gun in my hand with my jacket folded over it. Now I had to walk across thirty yards of open space to reach the house. The windows were dark: any of them was a perfect hiding place for a sniper. I took a breath and went: walked up to the front door just like the Fuller brush man. There, I flattened against the wall and listened. The house sounded exactly like it had the last time I had been here, nine hours ago: in other words, there was no sound at all. I started around it, stopping at every window. I peered down the hall and saw nothing. Moved on to the next window. Kitchen. No help. A ray of sunshine was starting to peek through the clouds. It cast a beam almost like a rainbow through the kitchen window. I eased my way to the back of the house. Turned the corner. The next window looked into his den, and there he was, sitting at the desk, his back to the window. He wasn't doing anything. I thought maybe he was asleep: that's how still he was. But suddenly he moved: dropped his feet, fumbled, lit a cigarette. He sat there smoking and I stood outside, not two feet from the back of his head, wondering what to do next.

There were really only two choices. I decided to play it straight. I walked around the house, went to the front door, and rang the bell.

I heard him coming immediately.

He jerked open the door and started to say, "It's about fuckin' time." He got most of it out before he realized that it wasn't about time at all.

"Who the hell're you?"

"Detective Janeway. I talked to you at your uncle's house, remember?"

"Yeah, sure. What're you doing here? Hell, it's only eight o'clock."

"Let me in and I'll tell you."

"Look, I'm expecting somebody. I don't have much time."

"That's okay, I won't take much."

Reluctantly he moved away from the door. I went in, keeping the gun handy under the jacket. You never knew what might happen with people.

We went into the living room. It looked vaguely like a place I'd seen before. He asked if I wanted some coffee. I wanted some badly, but I said no. One of my rules is never to eat or drink with people who might want to kill me.

He didn't look the part somehow: he was dressed well, in dry clothes: his hair was combed, and in fact he looked bushy-brained and sharp, like a lawyer about to go into court for a big case. He must've been sizing me up too. "You look like you've been through a war," he said.

"I have."

"I'll bet it's interesting as hell, but like I said, I'm expecting company. What can I do for you?"

"You can tell me what you know about your uncle's books."

He was a lousy liar. He looked away and tried to shrug it off. "What's there to tell? We went all through this."

"We went through something but it wasn't this. Look, you've got things to do and so do I. D'you want to tell me about it, or shall we wait till Mr. Rubicoff gets here and we can all go through it together?"

It was a sucker punch and he almost fell off his chair from the force of it.

"Why don't you get the hell outta here right now?"

"Fine. It's your house. But I'll be back, and I'll tell you something, Ballard. You're gonna have to be a lot better lawyer than I think you are to get yourself out of this mess."

I got up to leave.

"What mess? What're you talking about?"

"Oh, I think you know. Let's not waste time with this."

"Wait a minute. There's no sense being mean about it. We can get along. I mean, can't we get along?"

"I can."

"Sit down."

I eased myself down into the chair.

"How'd you know about Rubicoff?" he said.

"I've got ways. Sometimes they're slow and ponderous but I usually find out in the end. For instance, I know about Rubicoff but I don't know everything. Why don't you tell me?"

"Tell you what?"

We were fencing. This could go on forever. I groped for the words to break us out of it.

"Let's pretend I don't know anything; I'll like it better that way. You tell me who Rubicoff is and how you got mixed up with him."

"He's a dick I hired."

"Keep going. What's it got to do with the books?"

"I hired him to help me find the sons of bitches."

"Let me get this straight. First you all but give the books away. Now you hire a guy to help you get 'em back."

"I didn't know then what I know now."

"Which is what?"

"They're worth a fortune, that's what. And they're still mine, pal, make no mistake about that."

"You sold 'em. You signed a bill of sale."

"Doesn't matter what the hell I signed: that deal was done on a fraudulent premise. The guy knew something I couldn't be expected to know. You just let me find those babies, we'll see who winds up owning them in a court of law."

"How'd you find out about them?"

"About three weeks ago, a guy came and told me."

"Uh-huh. A guy named Peter Bonnema."

"I didn't know his name then; didn't know anything about him. I got a call out of the blue. The guy said I'd given away a fortune and he knew where the stuff was. He had some of it himself, and if I wanted it all back I'd meet him in a café on East Colfax at nine that night."

"Then what happened?"

"He didn't show up. I waited till ten. I don't know what there was about it . . . something told me it was for real. Then when he didn't show I said screw it, some silly bastard wasting my time. But he called me back the next day. I started to hang up on him, but there was something about it . . . I don't know which end is up when it comes to books, and I couldn't care less, but I knew there was something to it. Sometimes you just have a hunch."

I nodded.

"So at nine o'clock that night I'm in the same scuzzy café, and this time the guy comes in and sits down at my table. He was a goddamn bum, a tramp, for Christ's sake. I almost got up and walked out. Then he opens this box and takes out a book. It looks like any other book to me. Who gives a damn about a stupid book? But the guy says, 'Look at this,' and he takes out a little booklet, a catalog from some book dealer in Boston. 'Look at this,' he says, and he shows me in the catalog what the asking price is for a copy of the book he's holding. Six hundred mazumas, buddy! I damn near lost my supper. One fuckin' book, six hundred big ones. Then he takes out another book and another catalog. Three-fifty. Do I need to tell you that by now he's got my attention?"

"What did you do?"

"Asked what he wanted. He wanted one-third, a three-way split. I guess he'd done his homework. Anyway, he knew there was that third party involved."

"Your sister."

He waved that off with an impatient grimace. "Let's just say that the guy knew what was involved. Before he'd tell me what happened to the books, I'd have to draw up an agreement and have it signed by . . . you know. Then I'd have to sign it myself and we'd have to have it notarized. I didn't care. The damn thing wouldn't be worth the paper it's written on. Anybody could break a document like that when it's based on blackmail or fraud. So I said sure, I'd have it all drawn up, nice and goddamn legal. He's playing in my ballpark now. You don't sheist the shysters, Janeway, and I'm not nearly as bad a lawyer as you think I am. You bet I'd sign it. We'd see what happened later, in court."

"But then the guy got killed."

"Yeah. I knew I was onto something then."

"So you hired the gumshoe."

"That's right, and a lot of good it's done me so far."

"What's he been doing?"

"Nothing exciting, you can bet on that. He can't find his ass with both hands, if you want my opinion."

"Where'd you go last night, Ballard?" I said suddenly.

"How'd you know I went anywhere?"

"Tried calling you a couple of times."

"I went driving around. I couldn't get ahold of Rubicoff. I called his office, called his house—I did everything but go through City Hall, and I couldn't get anything but that friggin' answering service. I'm paying this guy more money than a lawyer makes, and I can't get him on the phone. Then I finally did get him and he couldn't see me. I couldn't believe it. He's got another case he's working on, and that pissed me off. He's gonna be out of town all day today, can you beat that? A whole goddamn day I'm losing while this keyhole-peeper is chasing down another guy's wife in Santa Fe. He says all he can do for me is see me for a few minutes this morning on his way to the airport. Can you believe that? Eight hundred dollars I've paid that clown, and maybe he can squeeze me in at eight o'clock on his way to catch a plane for somebody else."

"So you went driving around . . ."

"Yeah. No place special, just workin' off steam. What's the big deal?"

"Maybe nothing. I wanted to talk to you about your uncle's house."

"What about it?"

"I may be interested in buying it."

"You're kidding." Suddenly he was a pussycat.

"I'm not kidding, but I don't have a helluva lot of money to throw around."

"You won't need a lot for my half."

"That's what Ms. Davis said. It may be the only thing you two have ever agreed on."

"What's your offer?"

I shrugged an apology. "Fifty."

"I'll get the papers drawn up this weekend. I want to be done with it."

"That's fine," I said pleasantly. I asked if the house had had a recent appraisal done, if it had been inspected for termites, if there'd been any plumbing problems. I chatted and blabbed, went through all the stalling tactics I could muster, and a few minutes later Rubicoff arrived. We heard his car pull into the yard and the door slam. Ballard's kettle boiled over again. "Just watch what the son of a bitch says!" he shouted. "He won't have time to talk, he'll be in a hurry now 'cause he's late for his flight. Eight hundred I pay this jerk and this is what I get."

He went to the door and threw it open. Footsteps came up the walk. I moved slowly forward, the gun still under my jacket. I saw a shadow pass the window.

Their voices blended. Rubicoff was saying he was sorry, he'd get back on the case in a day or two but right now all he had was a few minutes. Ballard shouted him down. "As far as I'm concerned, pal, you can fuckin' stay in Santa Fe! Gimme my money back, you goddamn crook!"

There was a scuffle: Ballard had thrown a punch. It couldn't have been much of one because two seconds later he was flat on the floor. The guy had decked him without breaking stride. I walked around Ballard, who was struggling to sit up, and I stared into the face of the dick known as Rubicoff.

No turtle face. No flaring nostrils. He was short and bald. He looked like anything but a private detective who had just put his client down for the count.

"You want some too?"

"Not me, bud," I said. "I'm just the lady from the welcome wagon."

I eased my way past, went down the road, and got in my car.

49

Rita came out of the restaurant carrying a newspaper and a steaming bag of goodies. "Well," she said, "I don't see any murderer shackled in the backseat."

"Don't push me, McKinley. Get in."

I headed north toward Denver, up Santa Fe Drive into the heart of the rush hour. She had brought me a king-size cup of coffee and a sweet roll loaded with cinnamon and sugar. She fed it to me while I drove, in tiny morsels between sips of coffee.

"This stuff will kill you," she said. "It's probably half-and-half, cholesterol, and cancer-causing preservatives. You can have mine too if you want it."

"Thanks but no thanks. One dose of death's enough for a morning."

She ate the second roll herself.

We were in heavy traffic, halfway to Denver, when she opened the newspaper. "Interesting item this morning. Your friend Mr. Newton got himself chopped up. I see you were the main witness, as usual. How come you don't tell me the interesting stuff in your life?"

"You get too excited. Read it to me while I drive."

"Sure." She folded the paper over and read.

Nothing I didn't know, except that Crowell still hadn't talked to the police and Newton was listed as serious but expected to make it. Jackie's altercations with police, including his continuing troubles with me, were summarized at the end.

I thought of Barbara with a flash of guilt.

"I guess it proves something," I said. "You can drive anybody to murder."

"It proves something else," Rita said. "Murphy's law."

"Which one?"

"Time wounds all heels."

*   *   *

Ruby lived on Capitol Hill, in the 1300 block of Humboldt. I parked out front on the street, and told Rita to stay put.

The apartment was on the third floor. Ruby's face was still full of sleep as he opened the door. "Who the hell's this? Dr. J?" He was in that early-morning fog common to nighthawks, trying valiantly to jump-start his heart with a third cup of coffee. He waved me to a chair, handed me a coffee cup, nodded to the pot simmering on the stove, and disappeared into the john. I heard water splashing and a moment later the toilet flushed. I poured myself a cup, looked around, and sat in the chair. It was a neat place, which surprised me. I could see back into the bedroom, which was also neat except for the unmade bed. It was a plain apartment, almost stark, with high ceilings and old-fashioned radiator steam heating. There were framed nudes on the walls, four lovely Weston prints that added to the bare landscape. I liked it: could've lived there myself.

Ruby came out, fastening his shirt. He still looked foggy, disjointed. He sat and sipped his coffee and only gradually seemed to remember that he had company.

"What's goin' on? What're you doin' out here this time o' day?"

"How long's it take you to wake up?"

"Hour . . . two. I don't get started till the day's half gone. Gotta open the damn store this week. Neff's supposed to be opening, but he still don't feel good. I think he wants to stay away from there, if you ask me. This thing's got him scared plenty. Want some coffee?"

"Got some."

"Oh."

I leaned toward him, the cup clasped in my hands, warming them. "I want to ask you a few more questions."

At that point I had only one essential question. But an idea had begun forming in my mind.

"Tell me about those books again, Ruby."

"What books?"

"The ones Neff bought in Broomfield the day Peter and Pinky were killed."

"Like what more do you want to know?"

"It was a woman, wasn't it?"

"Yeah. Lady moving out of town."

"Did you talk to this woman?"

"On the phone, sure."

"Recognize her voice?"

"Why should I? I never met the lady."

"Did her voice sound like anybody you might know?"

"Jeez, I can't remember. I wasn't thinking in that context. She was just a voice on the phone."

"How much did the buy cost you?"

"Fifteen hundred. And if you think that wasn't a bitch to get up on the spur of the moment . . ."

"How did you get it up?"

"Well, there's still a guy or two who'll loan me money. We wholesaled a few items. Neff borrowed the rest."

"How much did each of you borrow?"

"All's I could get was a couple of bills. We wholesaled a couple of books for three. Neff had to come up with a grand."

"Where'd he get the grand?"

"Hell, he's got his friends, I've got mine."

"How'd you hear about this woman in the first place?"

"She called us cold. Saw our name in the phone book."

"When was this?"

"That same morning."

"So you must've put the deal together in an hour or two."

"We had to, else the books be gone. You know how it is when you get a crack at this kinda stuff. You gotta move now."

"How'd you know the stuff was good?"

"Sometimes you can just tell, Dr. J. What do we have to lose driving up there? The lady seemed to know her books. I mean, she knew 'em inside, outside, six ways from Sunday. None of this chickenshit 'what'll you give me' stuff. She reads off the titles and says what she wants, and she gives us plenty of room to make out on the deal. She knew exactly what she was doing. When you get somebody who talks to you like that, you've got to assume she's got what she says. If she don't, you bring your money back home."

"So you had the deal done by when?"

"We had the money together by, oh . . . two o'clock."

"Then what happened? Did you call her back?"

"She wouldn't give us a number: said she'd already turned off her phone and she'd have to call us."

"Which she did."

"Yeah, just a few minutes after we got the dough together. She calls up and says she'll meet us in Broomfield at three."

"That's when she talked to you?"

"Yeah, just for a minute. I answered the phone. But most of her dealing was with Neff."

"When you answered the phone, she asked to speak to him?"

"Yeah."

"And they agreed to meet . . . and Neff went right after that."

"That's right."

"He left around what . . . two-thirty?"

"I guess it was around then."

"And got back around five."

"Yeah. The deal took no time at all. The woman had just what she said, and it was all top-grade primo stuff. All Neff had to do was look at the stuff and hand her the dough, then drive back here."

"Then he went to the can and you started going through the books."

"Yeah. What's all this about, Dr. J?"

"This woman you talked to. You sure you never heard her voice before?"

"Hell, that's a tough question, Dr. J. I only talked to her a couple of seconds."

I picked up his telephone and dialed Rita's number. When her recording came on, I held it to Ruby's ear.

"I guess that *could* be her. Come to think of it, she did sound like somebody . . ." He squinted, listening. "Who the hell is that—Rita McKinley?"

I didn't say anything.

"That could be her, I guess," Ruby said.

"Did Neff and Rita McKinley ever meet before that day?"

"Well, I told you she's been in our store a couple of times. He might've seen her. I do remember when she was in last year, Neff wasn't here. He had taken off and gone back east, if I remember right. Bookscouting trip. I do remember that the whole time McKinley was in the store there was nobody else but her and me. I felt funny, like a kid just getting started. Nobody's been able to make me feel like that in a long time."

"But Neff wasn't there then."

He shook his head. "What're you gettin' at, Dr. J?"

"I don't know, Ruby." I looked at my watch: it was eight forty-two. "Tell me about the books again. I only saw a couple of titles when I peeked in the box."

Now he came to life. He was fully awake, his motor running on something much stronger than coffee.

"Best batch of stuff we've gotten in years. You sometimes get these kinda books onesy-twosy, never fifty at once. Never three boxes and every one an absolute cherry. Let me see, there was a fine run of Tony Hillerman stuff. All the early ones. *Blessing Way. Dance Hall of the Dead. Fly on the Wall.* All in the two, three-hundred range. It's like pickin' hundred-dollar bills out of the box when those babies come up. You just sit there and add it up, like money in the bank. Hell, it's *better* than money in the bank, 'cause this stuff just keeps gettin' better and better. Hillerman's the hottest writer going, especially in these parts. There were a couple of Rex Stouts from the forties, just *so* salable, so damn good. And Ellery Queen's first book . . . I know you hear me say this all the time, Dr. J, but this was truly the world's best copy by far. Bunch of early Micheners that you don't see much anymore. *Bridges at Toko Ri,* and his first book, *South Pacific.* And some other stuff . . . uh . . ."

"*Clockwork Orange,*" I prompted. "I saw that one myself."

"Yeah, and that lovely Eastlake thing, *Go in Beauty.* What a god-damn book, Dr. J, what a total and complete killer. You ever read that?"

I shook my head.

"A killer book. And let's see, there was some black stuff, a Richard Wright, a Ralph Ellison, and half a dozen horror titles. Just a super *Hell House,* by Matheson . . . that's two and a half now for one this nice . . . and a couple of Lovecrafts, and, oh yeah, another great Matheson title, *I Am Legend.* Now there's a real vampire book, scared the living bejesus out of me one night when I had nothing else to do. So much better than *Salem's Lot,* even King says so, but King's such a nice guy he always puffs everybody else's books and pooh-poohs his own. He's right this time, though. And listen, speaking of black stuff, we got Toni Morrison's first book, *The Bluest Eye* . . . hell, even I never saw that book before. Killer copy, I bet we get five bills for it. Let's see what else . . . great *Crazy in Berlin,* a couple of bills on that, and some Van Guliks with that chink detective, you can get two-fifty easy for those, and a great Chesterton Father Brown with a jacket that'll knock your damn eye out . . ."

I looked at my watch. I had stopped listening. I knew he was lost, drifting through that vast and wonderful world that all true book-men know. The most hypnotic business a man can do, like making love to a beautiful woman.

"You ever read that novel, Dr. J?"

I shook my head. I didn't know what novel he was talking about.

"My kinda stuff, baby. Just makes my blood go all tingly when I take it out of the box and it looks like it came off the press an hour ago. Yeah, we'll do great on this buy, even if we have to wholesale a few items to keep the wolf at bay. It's like a shot of new blood, you know what I mean? It puts joy back in your heart, makes the world right again for a little while. Wait a minute, there was more. . . ."

"That's enough, Ruby."

"Oh wait, I haven't given you much more than half of it, yet."

"It's enough anyway. I think I've got what I need."

"I don't understand you. What the hell're you lookin' for?"

I looked at my watch. "How's your sense of time, Ruby?"

"I don't understand."

"How long do you think we've been sitting here talking—just since I asked you what was in those boxes? How long do you think it's been?"

"Couldn't be much more than a minute. Two minutes at the outside. Couldn't be any longer than that."

"How about seven minutes and twenty seconds."

Surprise flicked across his face.

Then a flash of horror.

50

I juggled the pieces on the drive north. It gave me a sick, hollow feeling that deepened as we drove.

Rita knew that something had changed between us. She was very sharp that way.

"What's the matter?"

I shook my head and shrugged it off.

"What's wrong with you?" she insisted.

"Nothing." I looked at her and raised my voice to emphasize the point.

I saw her back stiffen. You couldn't bully her or force your will. You could mandate silence by being silent, but you couldn't make the mistake of believing that her own silence meant she was putting up with it.

We went at least ten miles before she spoke again.

"Where're we going? You mind telling me that?"

"Going to see a fella."

"What fella?"

I looked at her again. "You ever hear of Emery Neff?"

"I don't know . . . I guess I've heard that name. He owns one of the bookstores, doesn't he?"

"You never met him?"

"I don't think so."

"You never had occasion to sell him any books?"

"How do I know? Do you remember everybody you ever sold books to? I'll tell you something, I don't much like the way you're acting."

"I'm not acting."

She watched me for a moment, then turned away and lapsed into a curious wooden silence that matched my own. We couldn't talk and we couldn't be quiet: it was so deadly I had to turn on the radio, something I never do when I have people in the car. A couple of educated idiots were screaming at each other on KOA, giving a bad impression of what passes today for talk radio. I couldn't stand it. Eventually I found KEZW, a nostalgia station. They were playing "Sam's Song," a vocal banter by Bing and Gary Crosby that I had heard four thousand times by actual count. At least I could stand that.

Ruby had answered my one essential question by drawing me a map. He had only been here once, almost a year ago, but he remembered it well enough to get me here. I spread the map on the seat as we rolled up the back highway, the mountains sprawling whitely to the left. I caught Rita glancing at the map. Our eyes met again. I stopped at a light and we just looked at each other for a moment. On the radio they were playing "I Hadn't Anyone Till You." Tommy Dorsey. Jack Leonard was singing the vocal refrain.

"Light's green," she said, and I started off again.

Then, without looking my way, she began to take me apart. She did it like a surgeon, without a tremor in her voice to betray her.

"It would seem that I've become a suspect again. I don't like that, not from you."

I didn't say anything.

"Trust is a precious thing to me," she said. "If I didn't think you understood that, I promise you last night wouldn't've happened."

"I know that."

"Then talk to me, you bastard."

Even when the words were loaded, her voice remained calm, icy.

"There may be a woman involved in it," I said. "I don't know what she did or why."

"But you think it was me."

"I don't think anything."

"Wrong answer, Janeway, and a lie to boot."

I nodded.

"This is turning ugly," she said.

"It's always been ugly."

"That's funny, I thought it was something else. What happened to love at first sight?"

"Alive and well. It's got nothing to do with this."

"Then it can't be much good."

"Not true," I said. "I'm just doing what a cop always does. Following my nose."

"Is that what you were doing last night? You may've been following something, but it sure wasn't your nose. You know what I think?"

"I'm afraid to ask."

"You should be. It doesn't put you in a good light."

We were getting close to Longmont. My eyes scanned the road for the turnoff.

I knew the question was coming before she asked it: knew and dreaded.

"How long have you been thinking these things?"

I took a deep breath. "You want an honest answer?"

"You bet."

"It's always been there. I push it back in my head and try to smother it, but it won't ever go away."

"Then it was in bed with us last night."

"It's that goddamn appraisal. I just can't square it."

She gave a dry little laugh. "You're pretty good, though, I'll have to say that. You have a way of saying I love you that makes a girl believe it."

"It's true," I said. "It is, Rita."

"Ah," she said in a small voice.

I thought that might be the end of it, but she said, "What I can't figure out is why I'm supposed to have done this. It couldn't be for money. You want to see my bankbook?" She flipped open her checkbook from First Federal Savings. It made me dizzy, trying to drive and look. What really made me dizzy were all those digits, and not a decimal anywhere in sight. It was like standing on the edge of a deep cliff, looking straight down.

"This is my traveling money. My book account is about four times this big. I have another account that I use for business not related to books. I have another account for investments: my accountant talked me into doing that last year. I seem to take in more money than I can decently spend now; I can't even give it away fast enough. I make money while I'm lying in bed. Would you like to know how much I made last night while you were, ah, following your nose? I can calculate it, give or take a little. I'm making money this minute, for Christ's sake. I don't ever have to lift another finger. What work I do, I do because I've got to do something or go out of my mind. I was never made to be gracefully rich; I'm too restless to be idle. I don't want any more money, don't even want what I've got. So please tell me why I would lie and steal and kill for more stupid money."

I shrugged sadly. Maybe for kicks, I thought: maybe for love. Who can ever know what people will do, or why?

"I've got one other account," she said. "You could call it my fuck-you account."

I knew what she meant. I know all about fuck-you money, mainly because I've never had any.

In that same flat voice, she said, "You are the most exciting man. All I have to do is think of you and I just tingle. Even that first night. I walked out of your bookstore and it was so powerful I had to stop and lean against something. I thought, there's my guy. It was absolutely terrifying, the most thrilling moment of my life. Couldn't wait to see you again. But you've got no faith, Janeway. I don't think we're going to make it."

"I need to know. You've got to understand that."

"You need to believe. I know it's not quite fair. A just God wouldn't try us like this, before we even know each other. I'm not blaming you, but don't blame me either. This is what I am. At this particular point in my life, I need faith more than love. An equal moment of each would be nice."

"I guess I was a cop too long."

She sighed. "And there isn't any God, and life's not fair."

51

The road snaked away to the left, a narrow blacktop five miles south of Longmont. Houses were sprinkled on both sides. The pavement ended with a bump and the houses fell away and we clattered along a dusty washboard road. Trees appeared on the rolling edge of the prairie.

There was a rutted side road, just where Ruby's map showed it: then the house, peeping through the seams of a wooded arroyo. I turned in and stopped. My odometer showed that we had come twenty-six miles from downtown Denver.

"Looks like nobody's home," Rita said.

"We'll see."

I left her there with the motor running and walked the hundred yards to the house. It was an old country house, American gothic. The windows were dark and in the midmorning light it looked deserted. A rambling front porch flitted in and out of view through a blowing hedge. The wind was strong, whipping down the front range. Some of the windows had been boarded up: the front railing was down in places and the steps looked rickety and dangerous. On the east end some scaffolding had been erected and there was evidence of recent work. There were no cars in the yard. I watched for a while but saw nothing that mattered.

I moved to the edge of the house, then around to the front. The place was like a crypt: not even a bird to break the monotony, only that steady beating wind. I eased up the steps to the porch, flattened myself beside the door and listened.

Nothing.

How many times have I done this, I thought: how many times when I was a cop did I jack up my courage and walk into trouble with this same gun pointing the way? It never loses its charm: the prospect of sudden death, maybe your own, always comes with a clutching at the throat and a rush of adrenaline. I tried the door. It creaked open and I looked in at a picture of frontier America. Broken old furniture. Antique pictures. Farm relics from another time. A kerosene lamp stood on a table, its glass charred black. An old wooden yoke had been thrown in a corner.

I took one step inside. The floor creaked and in the silence it sounded like a gunshot. I flattened against the door and caught my breath. I waited, listening. I waited so long a mouse scurried across the room.

It didn't look promising. The dust in the parlor was half an inch deep. No one had been through here in at least six months.

Doesn't seem to be Janeway's year for hunches.

If it didn't pan out I was back to zero. Square one. Lookin' for a turtle-faced man and a whole new gambit.

I left deep black prints in the dust. I crossed the scurry marks left by the mouse. It's going to be a wash, I thought, another dead end. I had reached a long dark hallway and still nothing had happened. A thick ribbon of dust, undisturbed since time began, stretched out toward the back of the house.

I lowered the gun. My forces were still on alert, but the condition was downgraded from red to yellow.

There were two rooms on each side of the hall. At the end was another hall that went into the east wing. There was a door, which was closed.

But it opened without creaking when I tried it.

On the other side was a different world. A world of paint and glass and fresh-hung wallboard. A bright world where music played and people lived.

I went back on red alert, following my gun to whatever lay ahead.

A skeleton key was stuck in the door. The radio was playing so softly it could barely be heard a room away. The floor was shiny and new. I saw a kitchen off to the left: well lit, papered yellow, with shiny new appliances. There was a half-finished den and, across from that, a bedroom. A radio sent soft tones down the hall from the kitchen: elevator music from KOSI. The scaffold's shadow leaped across the room.

I peeped into the bedroom.

He was on the bed, fully dressed, lying on top of a bright blue bedspread. He seemed to be sleeping, but his face was to the wall so I couldn't be sure. I had a vision of him lying there, eyes wide, waiting. I went in cautiously and he didn't stir. His breathing was deep and rhythmic, as if he'd been asleep for some time. I eased my way to the side of the bed. I still couldn't see his face. He lay with one arm under him, his hand out of sight. I didn't like that, but I was as ready as a guy ever gets. I leaned over and shook him lightly.

"Get up, Neff," I said, "and bring that hand out very slowly."

He was awake at once: too quickly, I thought, but a man standing over your bed with a gun will bring you up fast. He drew himself up till he was sitting. It was when he tried to look surprised that I knew I had him. He wasn't enough of an actor to pull it off.

"Stand up real easy," I said. "Just like that. Good boy. Now. I want you to go to that wall and put your hands against it, just like you see on TV."

I patted him down. He didn't have anything.

"Sit down over there," I said. "Not there . . . over in the plain wooden chair. Just sit there and face me."

He sat and watched while I did what a good cop always does: checked the obvious, easy places for weapons and found none.

He moved.

"Sit still," I said.

"I was gonna scratch my leg."

"Don't scratch anything. Don't even look at me funny. This gun of mine gets nervous."

"You wouldn't shoot me."

"I sure as hell would."

"So what's going on?"

That was his total and token attempt at denial. He knew he couldn't act and now I knew it too. Ruby had said he had been a magician and maybe that was true, but he'd never win an Oscar for bluffing his way out of a tight one. I had known a few others like that, guys who could lie as long as you didn't suspect them. Look them in the eye, though, and accuse, and they'd fall apart.

Neff was trying to avoid my eyes. He looked at the ceiling, at the window—anywhere but at me. "You like my place, Mr. Janeway? My uncle left it to me; I've been working on it a year. Sealed off this part and I just do a little at a time. Eventually I'll do it all. This isn't really my thing . . . carpentry . . . painting . . . but I do like the way it's coming together. I just do a little here and there. I don't like to sweat much."

"That's what Ruby tells me."

He gave a little laugh: wry, affectionate, almost tender. "Ruby," he said. "What a swell guy. Do anything for anybody. Great guy."

"Would you like to tell me where you put the books?"

He shrugged. Jerked his head to one side. Couldn't seem to find the words.

He looked through the window. He had a clear view of the road from here. "I saw you coming. I knew the way you were coming, cautiously like that . . . well, I just knew. I could've shot you."

"Why didn't you?"

"Gun's in the barn. You'd've seen me run for it. And wasn't sure how much you really knew. I thought maybe I could . . . talk you out of it. Shoulda known better. How'd you find out? What'd I do wrong?"

You were born, I thought.

"Tell me," he said. "I need to know."

"Maybe I'll make you a deal. I might tell you if you tell me where the books are."

"Sure . . . I'll tell you. . . . What've I got to lose?"

I thought about it, and wavered. The evidence was slippery, fragmentary. I feared for its life in a court of law. I had proceeded without regard for its welfare and now I had a strange, almost chilly reaction, talking about it calmly with the killer. Neff gave a little smile and the chill settled in. I didn't need him, I thought: I'd find the books anyway, sooner or later.

But I was a bookman, not a cop, and I wanted to see them now. I had the fever, the bookseller's madness, and I wanted to see what had driven an otherwise sane man to murder.

How do you figure it out? You think about it all the time. How does a sculptor carve an elephant out of a block of wood? Takes a block of wood and carves away everything that doesn't look like an elephant. When you're sleeping your mind's working on it. When you drive through a snowstorm, dead people whisper in your ear. You even think about it when you're making love and it's then, in fact, that the first glimmer comes working through the haze. Writers and sculptors work that way, why can't cops? Books have been written about the creative process: tens of thousands of words from dusty academics about the writer's vision. The funny thing is, I've always worked that way as a cop, but nobody writes books about that.

You get a vision—not necessarily what is, but what might be.

I was making love with Rita and suddenly I heard Ruby's voice. *It's the most hypnotic business,* he said, and just like that I had broken Neff's alibi. Try to use that in a courtroom. You couldn't, but baby, I saw the vision. At last I put it into words. "I just kept digging, kept after it. It's a process of elimination as much as anything. Judith didn't do it. Ballard didn't do it. There wasn't any turtle-faced man, Neff: it was just a cover you made up on the spot. Once I saw that it might've happened that way, I started remembering things. They all added up to you.

"Here's what happened. Stop me if I go wrong. You walked in a minute or two before five. You threw a bunch of cream puffs down in front of Ruby, knowing he'd go into an instant trance. Then you went back to the crapper, only you didn't stop there. You went on out into the backyard, around the building, and up the street. Your timing had to be perfect. Any little thing could've messed you up: any glitch between one place and the other. A customer who lingered past closing time . . . somebody who saw you go into my store just after five . . . any one of a dozen things, and all of them broke your way. You must've been desperate, Neff, to've tried something like that, and it damn near worked."

He shook his head. "You don't know what desperation is . . ."

"But it all worked. It was already dark: there was nobody on the street; luck was riding on your wagon all the way. It took you what . . . thirty seconds to cover the ground from your back door to my place. You forced Miss Pride to lock the door, then you herded them into the back room and shot them. You were back in your own place in no time, surely less than five minutes. You came through the back and stashed the gun—it was probably still there, somewhere behind the shelves, when I talked to you the next day—and when you came up front, Ruby was right where you'd left him, thinking no time at all had passed. You couldn't've done a better job on him if you'd hypnotized him. In a way it was better than hypnosis.

"The flu was also a fake, a cover for the shakes you had after killing three people. Once I realized that, I started seeing other pieces everywhere. I remembered Ruby once telling me how you protect your privacy. I remembered him talking about the farm you'd inherited. Longmont's just thirty miles from Denver: the truck Bobby used had seventy-four miles on the odometer when he brought it back. I thought how strange it was that you gave your phone number to no one. Even your partner didn't have it. Ruby had laughed about that one night when we were working late in my store—how you didn't want to be called at home no matter what. There was something wrong with that, Neff; it bothered me and I couldn't figure out why. Then I remembered. Hell, *I* had seen your phone number: I'd seen it written down somewhere. Then I remembered where. It was in Bobby Westfall's little address book."

He laughed sadly and shook his head. He looked like he wanted to say something, but he didn't.

"It's there in his book," I said. "We can dig it out of the evidence room and I can show it to you. I'm surprised it took me so long to remember it. So why would you give your number to a bookscout, Neff? There is no bigger pest on this earth than a hungry bookscout, yet you give him your private number when even your partner can't get it. That doesn't make sense . . . unless you and Bobby have something going together. Then it makes all the sense in the world. And that's what happened. You had something going with Bobby. Something more important than your partner or your business or anything else in your life.

"Then there was the matter of the driver's license. Bobby didn't have one but you didn't know that. Ruby knew it, but not you. You still didn't know it, even after you killed Bobby. You never understood how Peter Bonnema got involved in it, because you always assumed that you and Bobby were in it alone. The one thing I never could figure was how you found out about old man Ballard and his books."

"I've known about them for years. Known about . . . thought about them . . ."

"How'd you know?"

"I had a little bookstore on Eighth Avenue. This was long ago, before Ruby and I even knew each other. It was on Eighth near Ogden. That's not far, you know, from where Mr. Ballard lived. One day he came in. We got to talking. He said he had a lot of books. One thing led to another, and I said I'd like to come see them. He was very cordial. So I went to his house . . . I went to his house. The man was . . . simply incredible. He had the best eye for books . . . I can't imagine how he so consistently managed to pick up these things and save them . . . things that appreciated—I don't know how else to say it—beyond belief. And he'd been doing this for forty years. In some cases he had two or three copies of a single title, untouched copies pushed back behind the ones you could see on the shelf. They were all first editions, every one . . . the most immaculate collection I have ever seen, and, Mr. Janeway, I have looked at a lot of books. And the damnedest thing . . . the rarest thing . . . he didn't care about them at all for that purpose. It was like he had no idea or interest in how much they might be worth. Here was the big score everybody dreams about, and there was no way I could buy them, I could just never get the money together. But the old man . . . God, he was so naive. I thought maybe if I threw some money at him—not too much but enough, I could get them away from him. If I was lucky, he wouldn't check any further and for a few grand I'd pull off the heist of a lifetime. I was actually . . . trembling . . . as I tried to assess it. Started to throw out a figure and called it back. Didn't know what to do. Couldn't make it too high or low. You know how it is—go too low and he figures, hell, he might as well keep them; go too high and he begins to suspect what they're really worth. You know how it goes—you play people in this business as much as books. I looked around. He didn't live in luxury, didn't look rich. Five thousand dollars, I thought: that'd really make a difference to this old man. So that's what I said, and he smiled like a gentleman and said that was most generous but he wasn't interested in selling them at that point. Maybe someday, he said. That was ten, twelve years ago, and I want to tell you something, there hasn't been a day that I haven't thought about that stuff. I've dreamed about it . . . it comes to me a dozen times a day, when I look out the window or see the shit the scouts bring in . . . when I realize how hopelessly I've mired myself in the workaday crap."

"And then he died."

"Yeah. The first thing I thought was, now it'll get out. Somebody'll go in there and find it and it'll make a major story. The *AB*'ll carry it, it's that big. Imagine my surprise when nothing happened. I couldn't believe it when those two idiots started to put it in an estate sale. I actually stood outside in the rain one night and watched them through the window. And I went wild with hope. My God, I went crazy. I had to get it, but it had to be done in such a way that it would never be tied to me. I knew there'd be trouble if it became known later that I had bought it. The courts are very consistent on this. They always return valuables to an original owner if someone with specialized knowledge buys it too cheap. And Christ, we were talking less than pennies on the dollar. We were talking nothing!"

"So you hired Bobby to do it."

"The books needed to simply disappear. I needed for them to be swallowed up by someone anonymous. I thought he could keep his mouth shut . . . he seemed perfect."

"Except for one thing. He had no driver's license."

"Two things," Neff said. "I didn't count on him getting so bitter about it. I thought he'd be happy with a few hundred for a hard night's work. But right from the beginning we were bickering, and after a while there was a threat implied in everything he said to me. That one night he just pushed it too far. I picked up the crowbar and before I knew it he was on the floor at my feet. I couldn't believe what I'd done. I wrapped him in an old blanket and dumped him downtown. Then I burned the blanket. And of course, you're right, the son of a bitch never did tell me he had no license."

"Of course not. Why would he want to screw things for himself? By then Bobby smelled a big score too. He went to a friend of his, Peter, and got him to rent the truck. By then Peter smelled a score. He followed Bobby to Ballard's house and waited up the block while Bobby carried out the books. In the morning he followed Bobby again, and Bobby led him straight here. Then Bobby was killed and Peter put two and two together and started bleeding you for the books. He sucked your blood out, first book by book, then by the box."

"It took me months to find out who he was. He was so careful—made me box them up and leave them at a place in the country, and he'd go pick them up later, when he knew I wasn't watching. I might never've found out, but he got too cocky. He sold you a book from Ballard's and I saw it in your store and knew where it had come from . . ."

". . . and you started following him."

"I was in the gas station across from the DAV. Didn't think he could see me there but the bastard had eyes like a hawk. I thought then it was all over; I thought he'd tell you right there on the street."

"He was too scared—too scared to think."

"Yeah, but that wouldn't last. Once he had time to think, I knew he'd be back. I had to get him before that happened."

"He tried to call me that night, in fact, but luck was still breaking your way. He got my recording. He tried the next day too, but I was up in the mountains, at McKinley's place. Finally he had to make a choice: hole up, leave town, or come to me. He knew I was always there at closing time. If he arrived exactly at five, got off the bus right at the store and came straight inside, he'd be fine. He figured I'd protect him. So he called Pinky and told her he was coming in. A few minutes later I called Pinky and told her I wouldn't be there. At that point we didn't know what he wanted or how to reach him: I just assumed he needed money, and I told Pinky to give it to him. I also told her to let you boys know she'd be closing alone, so you could watch out for her. She followed my orders after all, and got herself killed for it. She told you, didn't she? Didn't she, Neff?"

He stared at his hands and said nothing.

"She told you her silly boss was worried about her, but it would probably be okay because Peter was coming in. Peter would be there at five. That's when you knew you had to do it: that's when the whole bloody mess got planned. Peter got there at five, and instead of finding me waiting for him, he found you. You came in right on his heels. What you didn't know was that Pinky was talking to Rita McKinley's recorder. And what she said puts it all on you, as clearly as if she'd told us your name. She said, 'Hi, everything's okay.' I thought about that for a long time after the lab boys got it out of the recording. Why would she say that? It didn't make any sense. She was in the middle of saying good-bye: she was telling me someone had just come in and she'd have to call me back. Why would she suddenly say, 'Hi, everything's okay,' in the middle of hanging up? The only thing that makes sense is that she was talking to the guy who had just walked in. Couldn't be anybody but Harkness, Ruby, or you. Pinky still thought she was talking to a friend, the nice man from the store up the street who had come in to check on her at closing. It's okay, she was saying, Peter's here, I'm not alone. But Peter was already screaming. He knew what was happening. A minute later, so did she."

There didn't seem to be anything else to say: nothing except, for me, the most important thing.

"I've actually come to hate those books," Neff said.

"Don't worry, I'll take 'em off your hands."

"Yeah."

I held my breath, afraid to ask, scared silly of what the answer would bring.

"Who was the woman, Neff?"

He looked at me and didn't answer.

"I need to know that. Was it Rita?"

His lip curled up in a sneer. "Rita," he said. "The big-time book dealer. The biggest thief of all."

"What're you talking about? What's that supposed to mean?"

He smiled and reached into his shirt pocket. I cocked the gun but he only laughed in that faint, sad way. When he opened his fist, he had two tiny capsules in his hand.

"What's that stuff?"

"Guess."

We looked at each other: a long, searching moment. Barbara Crowell flitted through my mind, along with a hundred suicides and suicide attempts I had known over the years.

"Don't do that," I said.

But he popped them into his mouth and swallowed.

"I knew you'd get me," he said. "Knew it that first day, when they put you on Bobby's case. So I had these ready. . . ."

He doubled up and fell out of the chair.

"Neff," I said weakly.

I looked for the phone, but you can't do much with cyanide. It works in a minute.

He went into the shakes and groaned, a long cry of agony.

His pulse slowed, and I could almost see his heart giving up.

I got down beside him and opened his shirt.

Biggest mistake I ever made.

He moved like a snake. I didn't know what had hit me. Suddenly I was down and he was up and through the haze I knew he had kicked me in the head. He had caught me in the temple with the point of his shoe: the hardest kick he could muster. I spun around and he was on my back. He had a rope: I don't know where it came from, but he was a magician and there it was, twisted around my neck. He cut my windpipe, and the next twenty seconds were so desperate that I couldn't think of anything but my heaving lungs. I know the gun fell: it skittered across the floor and slammed into the wall. I was up on one knee with this thing on my back, and I couldn't shake it and if I didn't shake it I was going to die.

I tried to buck him and couldn't. We slammed into the wall. He held on, stuck to me like we'd been born that way, grotesque Siamese twins bent on killing each other. The world turned red. I was losing consciousness. . . .

I heard a scream, then a shot, and the rope went slack.

God, I could breathe again!

But I still had to struggle for it, and for at least a minute I had the heaves.

When the world cleared, I saw Rita standing over Neff's body. She was staring at the mess she'd made, clutching my gun with both hands.

52

I found the key to the storage locker in Neff's hip pocket. It was the only lock-it-yourself place in Longmont.

We drove the four miles from Neff's house in what seemed like total silence. Only when we reached the storage yard did I realize that the radio was still playing.

Benny Goodman. "It Had to Be You."

I drove to unit 254, opened the door, and walked in. It was like walking into King Solomon's Mines.

He had shelved the locker and some of the books were out on open display. Yes, they were wonderful things.

But I was tired of looking. If you get too much new blood, you begin to drown in it.

Rita had lingered but now she came in. She didn't touch anything, just walked along and looked at the spines.

"Well, this is it," I said wearily. "This is what people kill for."

She was just standing, staring at nothing. She looked older in the dim light.

On a worktable in a corner, I found some papers. The name Rita McKinley caught my eye and I leafed through them.

"Looks like a copy of your appraisal," I said. "You want to tell me about this?"

She shook her head and said, "I have no idea."

And that's how the case ended: with a stalemate, a standoff between someone I loved and everything I believed in. With a dead man and a treasure, a lack of faith, a beautiful girl, and the big question still unanswered.

53

But no:

It really ended on another day six weeks later. Emery Neff was in his grave and the Ballard heirs were embroiled in a battle of books that seemed certain to end up in court. Ruby was in business alone. Rita McKinley had been set free by the Boulder County DA, who had pronounced the shooting justified: she had gone somewhere and had left nothing, not even the damned recording, to tell people where she'd gone or when she might come home.

I saw Barbara Crowell every couple of weeks. Mose had found a way to handle her case, as a favor to me. They had me billed as her star witness, and things weren't looking too bad for her when all the mitigating factors were taken into account.

Jackie, after all, hadn't died. He couldn't feed himself or talk quite right: he'd have to be carried to the potty from now on, but he was alive. Doctors think he might live that way for another thirty years. It doesn't sound like much, but the alternative is nothing at all.

As for me, I was going through the old familiar symptoms of acute burnout. The book business, which had been so fresh and exciting just three months ago, was suddenly old, and I was growing old with it. I dreaded opening the store: I let it slide as long as I could; then I went in and painted the bathroom and opened for business. I had been off for a month: I had spent a lot of money and my rent was due, and it was time to get going again.

But in the end I was back where I'd been in the police department. The days were long and uneventful: the nights were worse. I didn't know where I was going, but I've never been one to languish. I knew I was in some vast personal transition, but only the past was spread out, clear and ugly. The future was still a void.

I closed on the Ballard house. The paperwork was done by the

first of December and I was ready to move in. I had planned to be out
of the store for three days during the move, and Ruby had promised
to bring me someone reliable to run it. That morning, when he came
in, the woman with him looked vaguely like someone I had once
known. It took me a long moment to recognize her.

I pointed to her face and snapped my fingers. "Millie Farmer, the
teaching bookscout."

"Just bookscout, Dad. I'm out of teaching forever. If I'm not going
to make any money anyway, I might as well have fun doing it."

"You've come to the right place," I said.

I broke her in: walked her through the store and showed her what
was what and how to find it. I gave her Miss Pride's key to the front
door and said I'd be in each day at four o'clock to be with her when
she closed. There seemed to be nothing more to discuss, yet we all
knew better. Painful, unfinished business lay between us. There had
been a strain between Ruby and me, and now it extended to her. We
had never talked about Neff. It made Ruby squirm, as if somehow he
shared the blame for what had happened. Emery Neff had touched us
all in some basic, primal way, and none of us had been able to throw
off his ghost.

Even now, getting into it wasn't easy.

"Wonder what's gonna happen to those books," I said.

Ruby gave a fidgety shrug and looked out into the street.

"We'll never see another collection like that."

"Probably not," he said.

I looked from one to the other. They said nothing.

"Hey, you want a job full-time?" I said to Millie.

"Hell yes."

"You're hired. Doesn't pay much. Six an hour and all your books
at twenty percent off."

"Dad, I just died and went to heaven," she said to Ruby.

I made another try at knocking down some walls. "The thing that
beats me is how those books changed from club books to firsts. If I
could get the answer to that, I'd die a happy man."

"They never were club books," Ruby said.

"It's not that easy, Ruby. If it were just McKinley's appraisal it
would be simple. But I saw all the invoices, all the club flyers. On

most of them he had written what he'd ordered and the date. Those damn books are there, the same books he ordered, only they're first editions, not club copies. He was the most compulsive record-keeper you ever saw. When the books came in from the club, he wrote down the dates. Then he wrote what he thought of them after he'd read them. It's all there, in Ballard's own handwriting. Only somehow between now and then a genie got in his house and waved a wand and turned those books into gold."

I could see Ruby wanted to leave but he couldn't find an exit cue.

"What's your answer?" I asked.

"Ain't got no answer. Hell, Dr. J, I don't know. I don't even think it's very interesting. Where the old man got his eye for books—that's where the real mystery is. If we knew that we'd all be rich in no time. How do guys like old man Ballard start from scratch and build a library that just knocks people for a loop? I don't know. Somehow they're plugged into the universe in this queer kinda way. They know what'll be valued, not just now but years from now."

"And they don't even think of value in terms of money," I said. "They have a totally different agenda. And I guess it was a lot easier to build a library then, when the average cost of a book was two bucks."

"It's all relative. You of all people ought to know that. A book has always cost about what a meal in a good restaurant costs. Did then, still does. I get sick of hearing how expensive books are. Which would you rather have, a good book or a tender steak? I know what I'd take, seven days a week."

He moved to the door: he was about to leave.

"That was a good move, hiring this lady," he said. "She'll be good for your business, just like the other one. She's got a sassy mouth but you can handle her. Just give her the back of your hand two or three times a day."

Millie stuck out her tongue.

"You need to unshackle your legs, get free again," Ruby said. "You're going through something, I can see it written all over you. It's a growth spurt. All of a sudden you're tired of retail. You're starting to see where the real fun is in the book business. Usually it takes five years: you've gone through it all in three months. You came into this business almost whole, and now you're ready to move on. The Zen Buddhists have a word for it. *Satori*. It means sudden enlightenment."

"I don't feel suddenly enlightened. I feel as dense as ever. I don't think I'll be able to rest till I know the answers to those two questions."

"What questions?" Millie said.

"How did those books change into fine firsts . . . and who was the woman?"

"What woman?"

"The day Peter and Miss Pride were killed, a woman called and asked for Neff. Ruby talked to her."

Millie Farmer blinked.

"Hell," she said, "I believe that was me."

54

I was out of my apartment in two hours.

I was surprised at how little I had. I wanted few things from that old life: my furniture, such as it was, was old and worn; the Salvation Army had been glad to come for it, and I was having new stuff delivered that afternoon. There had been some doubt about the bed arriving today, and I was prepared to bag it tonight on the floor. I arrived on Madison Street before noon. It was a warm day for December, but Denver is like that: it can have rain, snow, and a heat wave all in the same week.

Greenwald was sitting in a rocker reading a book when I drove up. He greeted me with a wave. I began to move my things in, arranging as I went. I gloried in the bookshelves: how many book dealers have room for nine thousand books at home? I looked through the front window and saw that Greenwald had fallen asleep with the book spread open across his chest. When I looked again, some minutes later, he was gone. But he was back again, wearing a sweater, when I made my last trip to the trailer.

"It's going to snow tonight," he said. "I just saw it on the weather. You can feel it coming already; there's a chill in the air."

He had made us some lunch. "Just come over when you're ready," he said. I went into my bathroom to wash. The floor had two small smooth spots where Stanley Ballard had stood every morning. Untold numbers of shaves he had had, standing at this same glass. Scraping his face with an old-fashioned straight razor (the hook for the strop was still there, fastened to the wall). Looking in his own eyes and seeing no mystery there. Knowing himself thoroughly.

Satori, I thought.

Maybe I'll become a Buddhist.

I knew things I hadn't known before. I could see Emery Neff sitting in his store that day. Ruby had walked up the street for a cup of coffee. Pinky had just called to say that she'd be closing up alone. But Peter was coming in, so everything would be fine.

He knew then what he was going to do. He picked up the phone and dialed a number he had called often in the past few months.

I want to see you . . . today, this afternoon . . . I need you.

And Millie, who thought she'd come to love him, could never say no.

The problem is, I've been gone from the store a lot. Ruby's start-ing to think I'm not pulling my weight. So here's what we'll do. You call back in ten minutes. I'll see that he answers the phone. Don't tell him who you are, just ask for me. Be formal . . . cool and distant. Call me Mr. Neff. He'll think I'm coming over on a buy, and we'll spend the afternoon together.

But he never came. Millie sat by the phone and it rang an hour later.

Sorry, hon, it's not gonna work . . . not feeling well . . . think I've got the flu. Going home to lie down . . . no, don't come up, you'll just get what I've got. I'll make it up to you. . . .

An illusion, like one of his old magic tricks. Now you see him, now you don't.

Like that illusion of death he had performed for me alone: two cold capsules popped into his mouth, and you were ready to believe anything.

So simple, so easy, once you knew how it was done.

I tried to call Rita, without much hope. There had been no answer up there for weeks, and there was none now.

Then I remembered that other number. Bobby Westfall had writ-ten it down and dropped the paper when he'd been in talking to Harkness. It took me a few minutes to find it, and another few min-utes to figure it out.

An out-of-state exchange.

I tried it with a Los Angeles area code and got the intercept operator.

San Francisco.

Intercept.

It rang through to New York. A woman answered.

"Greenpeace Action."

"Is this Greenpeace . . . International?"

"We're part of it."

"Uh . . . is Rita McKinley there?"

"She was here yesterday."

Now what the hell was this about? What had Bobby been doing with a number for Greenpeace?

"Do you know if she's coming back?"

"I don't know, sir. I believe she was going to Europe."

He had been trying to reach Rita, just before he was killed. About the time she was off saving whales.

She had been on NBC. Was it not possible that he had seen her Brokaw interview?

Which would mean . . . what?

Could it be Bobby's Christian conscience at work? He and Neff had just pulled off the literary heist of the decade, and you could bet that something was at work.

The woman on the phone was talking.

"Is there a message, sir . . . in case we do hear from her?"

"Just tell her Janeway called."

And please, please call back.

Now I sit with old Mr. Greenwald and I know the end is coming. I think I may even know what it is. *Satori* is working overtime, and my enlightenment is both sudden and overwhelming. It comes in waves, like a tide pushed up by a hurricane.

"So the house is finally yours—the deal, as they say these days, is truly finished."

"It's truly finished, Mr. Greenwald."

"Have some more coffee."

This is how it is in Greenwald's world: civilized society comes first and business is done in its own good time.

Being among the newly enlightened, I don't push him.

And eventually he does get to it. "Things have been preying on my mind since Stan died. I only wanted to do right by him, to do what he wanted done."

"I think you've done that, sir."

He gives me a little smile, gratitude and appreciation, but laced with doubt. Four people, after all, have died. It's hard to know what to do when you don't come equipped with a crystal ball.

"Oscar Wilde once said that a cynic is a man who knows the price of everything and the value of nothing. Judith and Val have become cynics in just that definition of the word."

"I'd agree with that."

"They have not turned out to be good people."

"No one's responsible for that but them."

"Stan felt responsible. He was also horrified. He had a dream one night, not long before he died. They were fighting over his books, tearing them apart. The next morning he told me about it. He said, 'I don't care about the house, don't care about any of it . . . I just don't want them to have my books. Give them away, throw them away, I don't care, but I won't rest easy unless I know they won't get them.'"

"He had no idea what they were worth, did he?"

"I think he knew, toward the end, that they were worth some money. Enough, at least, that there would be a squabble over them. But you're right—he had no real idea. He'd be mortified if he knew."

"He could've saved a lot of trouble and just left them to you."

"Where would I put them? I have my own books, my house is full of books, most of them the same titles he had. Where would I put them?"

"So he figured it the way he always figured—that his library would do the most good by being broken up and given away."

"Sure: give them to the people. Stan gave away books by the carload. He used the book club as his first line of reading, and gave those books away. Gave them to nursing homes, hospitals, people he knew and people he barely knew. He was especially interested in helping young people discover the world of books. So he gave them away, but the ones he liked he kept for himself. Gave away the club books and bought his own copies in the stores downtown."

"And the easiest way to break up the library . . ."

". . . was to leave a document proving that the books had no money value. Done by an expert no one would challenge. Only Stan and I knew, and he asked me to keep that secret until the last of his estate was disposed of. The house was the last of it."

And now we all know. Ballard left the appraisal among his papers but tucked a copy for good measure among his books. Emery Neff found that appraisal, scanned it, and jumped to the logical conclusion: that McKinley was a crook, lowballing so she could buy the books for a song. But Bobby had taken the time to actually read the appraisal. He alone knew the truth, that McKinley had been duped. That's why he was trying to reach McKinley when the deal between Neff and himself had begun to go sour. Maybe a better deal could be struck with McKinley.

Greenwald offers more coffee, served with a sad little smile.

"Stan got the appraisal he wanted. We traded houses the night the appraiser came out. The books she looked at were mine."

THE BOOKMAN'S WAKE

To Jack Kisling of Hairline Press,
who navigates with a steady hand the eddies and
shoals of the printshop.

Again, prices on actual books discussed by characters in the story may be a year or two out-of-date. In a time of madness, when a new novel can bring ten times its cover price a year after publication, prices become obsolete almost as they're published. Janeway remains a cynic when people pay too much too soon and glorify the trendy. But he is an equal-opportunity cynic who saves his deepest skepticism for me, when he and I are alone at four-thirty in the morning.

Another tip of the hat to Warwick Downing, who bullied me for three years. To George Fowler for turning me left and right in the Seattle rain. To Pat McGuire for long friendship and a kick in the duff when I needed it. And a kind word for the small-press publishers of today. Some still struggle valiantly in the great lost cause.

The man in St. Louis died sometime during the afternoon, as near as the coroner could figure it. It happened long ago, and today it is only half-remembered even by old-timers who follow crime news. The victim was eccentric and rich: that, combined with the inability of the police to identify either a motive or a suspect, kept it on front pages for a week. Then the press lost interest. Reporters had been charmed by the puzzle, and by the colorful background of the deceased, but they could only sell that for a few days and then something new had to happen. It didn't—the case slipped off the front pages and became history, perhaps to be resurrected periodically in anniversary pieces or in magazine accounts of unsolved mysteries. On the news desk at the *St. Louis Post-Dispatch,* an editor ripped and read an AP squib about a triple murder in Phoenix, fifteen hundred miles to the southwest and thought—not for the first time—that the world was getting dangerously crowded with crazy people. He considered using it as a two-graph filler on page eight: then he thought, Christ, we've got enough crazy people of our own, and the Phoenix murders got bumped by a UPI account of a squabble along the Chinese-Russian border. In Phoenix, that day and for the rest of the week, the case was front-page news. The cops didn't have a clue. If murder had to happen, said the cop in charge of the Phoenix case, it should at least be logical. It's not the garden-variety passion killer we find scary, the cop said, it's the guy who kills for no good reason and then disappears into the night. The police hardly ever catch him because he strikes without reason and has no motive. The trouble with random murder is that all the common denominators are superficial. The killer may break in the same way, he may use the same weapon, but there is never anything that hints of a motive because there isn't any. Give me a motive, other than craziness, said the cop, and I'll clear this case.

That cop didn't know, because it didn't make the papers in Phoenix and was one among many brutal homicides on the national teletype as the long weekend began, that a Baltimore man had just been killed in much the same way. This time there was a survivor—his wife, blind from birth and left babbling madly in the killer's wake. She was useless as a witness and was soon committed to a state institution, but perhaps even then she might have had something to tell an investigator with knowledge of Phoenix and St. Louis and the perspective to see them all as a single case. But computers weren't yet in broad general use: communities separated by vast distances weren't linked as they are today; murders weren't grouped electronically by such factors as weaponry, forensic matching, and killer profiles. There was the teletype, with its all-points bulletins advising that murders had been committed, but what else was new? The term *serial killer* had not yet entered the common lexicon, and to most people it was inconceivable that a killer might strike in St. Louis on Monday, Phoenix on Wednesday, and in a Baltimore suburb on Friday night. On Sunday there was a double murder in Idaho—a rancher and his wife killed just as they were sitting down to dinner. This was big news in Boise, but it made hardly a ripple in St. Louis, Phoenix, or Baltimore. On the ninth day the killer struck for the last time—an elderly woman living alone in New Orleans. This time he set fire to the house, hoping, police theorized, to cover up his crime. In each of the five cities teams of detectives worked their local angles and found nothing. They sifted false clues, chased down rumors, and slowly over the weeks watched their final leads disappear into the big blank wall. The one common denominator remained hidden by the vast expanse of geography and by the often cryptic methods of police teletyping.

No one knew it then, but in each of the death houses lived a book collector.

That's how I got into it, more than twenty years later.

BOOK I ELEANOR

Slater wasn't my kind of cop. Even in the old days, when we were both working the right side of the good-and-evil beat, I had been well able to take Mr. Slater or leave him alone. He had played such a small part in my life that, for a moment, I didn't know who he was. I was working in my office, a small room in the rear of the used-and-rare bookstore I owned in Denver, writing up books for my first catalog, when Millie buzzed me from the front. "There's a Mr. Slater here to see you," she said, and the last person I would've thought about—did think about— was Clydell. This was annoying. My work was going slowly: I was an absolute novice at bibliography, and even with modern books there are pitfalls everywhere. Open on the table before me was a copy of *Nickel Mountain*, by John Gardner, as fresh and crisp as the day it was born in 1973. Gardner had signed it on the half title, a nice little touch, since he won't be signing any more, that almost doubled its value. It's not yet an expensive book—about $25 to $40 unsigned, in fine first edition—the kind of book that should be a snap to describe and price. The publisher was Alfred A. Knopf, who not only puts out fine books but also gives you the straight bibliographical poop. He's not like Lippincott, who states *first edition* most of the time, or McGraw-Hill, who states it when the guy in the back shop feels like putting it on: if Knopf says it's a first edition, you can take it to the bank and cash it . . . although I do remember one or two Willa Cathers that might or might not follow tradition. Let's face it, all these houses are dotted with land mines. William Morrow was a model of consistency, but on one pricey little Harry Crews title, instead of noting *second printing* as always before, he put two tiny dots at the bottom of the copyright page. Cute, Morrow. That little piece of camouflage cost me $40 for a spectacular non-first last year. Doubleday always, and I mean *always,* puts the words *first edition* on his copyright page and takes it off for later printings.

But on one John Barth he didn't: he put no designation whatever, instead hiding a code in the gutter of the last two pages. The code must say H-18—not H-38 or H-Is-for-Homicide or H-anything-else—or it's not a first. Harper and Row was as reliable as Knopf over the years, except in one five-year period, circa 1968-73, when for reasons known only to Messrs. Harper and Row in that great bookstore in the sky, they started putting a chain of numbers on the *last* page, for Christ's sake, in addition to saying *first edition* up front. Figure that out. The only way I can figure it out is that people who publish books must hate and plot against people who cherish them, make collectibles of them, and sell them. I can just see old Harper and Row, rubbing their translucent hands together and cackling wildly as some poor slob shells out his rent money, $700, for a *One Hundred Years of Solitude,* only to discover that he's got a later state, worth $40 tops. Harper really outdid himself on this title: in addition to hiding the chain of numbers (the first printing of which begins with "1"), he also published a state that has no numbers at all. This is widely believed to be the true first, though there can still be found a few keen and knowledgeable dealers who would beg to differ. The one certainty is that on any Harper title for that era, the back pages must be checked. Thus concealed are points on early Tony Hillermans in the $750-and-up range, some Dick Francis American firsts (the numbers on one of which seems to begin with "2," as no "1" has ever been seen), a good Gardner title, and, of course, *Solitude,* a fall-on-your-sword blunder if you make it, the rent's due, and the guy who sold it to you has gone south for the winter.

So I was stuck on *Nickel Mountain,* with a guy I didn't want to see storming my gates up front. I was stuck because I seemed to remember that there were two states to this particular book, A. A. Knopf notwithstanding. I had read somewhere that they had stopped the presses in the middle of the first printing and changed the color on the title page. God or the old man or someone high in the scheme of things didn't like the hue, so they changed it from a deep orange to a paler one. Technically they are both first editions, but the orange one is a first-first, thus more desirable. It's no big deal, but this was my first catalog and I wanted it to be right. The title page looked pretty damn orange to me, but hot is hot only when you have cold to compare it with. Go away, Slater, I thought.

I took an index card out of my desk, wrote *check the color,* and stuck it in the book. I told Millie to send the bastard back, and I got ready to blow him off fast if he turned out to be a dealer in snake oil or a pitchman for a lightbulb company. Even when he came in, for a moment I didn't know him. He was wearing a toupee and he'd had his front teeth pulled. The dentures were perfect: you couldn't tell the hairpiece from the real thing, unless you'd known him in the days when the tide was going out. His clothes were casual but expensive. He wore alligator shoes and the briefcase he carried looked like the hide of some equally endangered animal. His shirt was open and of course he wore a neck chain. The only missing effect was the diamond in the pierced ear, but I knew it was only a matter of time before he'd get to that too.

"You fuckhead," he said. "Lookitcha, sittin' there on your damn dead ass with no time to talk to an old comrade-in-arms."

"Hello, Clydell," I said without warmth. "I almost didn't know you."

He put his thumbs in his lapels and did the strut. On him it was no joke. "Not bad, huh? My gal Tina says I look twenty years younger."

Tina, yet. An instant picture formed in my mind—young, achingly beautiful, and so totally without brains that she just missed being classified as a new species in the animal kingdom.

"You're the last guy I'd ever expect to see in a bookstore, Clydell," I said, trying to keep it friendly.

"I am a doer, not a reader. It's good of you to remember."

"Oh, I remember," I said, sidestepping the gentle dig.

"My deeds of daring have become legends among the boys in blue. I'm still one of their favorite topics of conversation, I hear. So are you, Janeway."

"I guess I can die now, then. Everything from now on will just be downhill."

He pretended to browse my shelves. "So how's the book biz?"

I really didn't want to talk books with a guy who—you could bet the farm on it—couldn't care less. "Have a seat," I said reluctantly, "and tell me what's on your mind."

"Listen to 'im," he said to some attendant god. "Same old fuckin' Janeway. No time for bullshit, eh, Cliffie? One of these days they'll make a movie about your life, old buddy, and that's what they'll call it: *No Time for Bullshit.*"

It was all coming back now, all the stuff I'd always found tedious about Slater. His habit of calling people old buddy. The swagger, the arrogance, the tough-guy front. The false hair on the chest, as some critic—probably Max Eastman—had once said about Hemingway. The glitz, the shoes, the bad taste of wearing animal hides and buying them for his wife. Then bragging about it, as if going deep in hock on a cop's salary for a $4,000 mink was right up there on a scale with winning the Medal of Honor for bravery. Some of us thought it was poetic justice when the missus took the mink and a fair piece of Slater's hide and dumped him for a doctor. But there was still light in the world: now there was Tina.

"It's just that I'm pretty sure you didn't come in here for a book," I said. "We sold our last issue of *Whips and Chains* an hour ago."

"You kill me, Janeway. Jesus, a guy can't even stop by for old times' sake without getting the sarcasm jacked up his ass."

"To be brutally honest, you and I never ran with the same crowd."

"I always admired you, though. I really did, Janeway. You were the toughest damn cop I ever knew."

"I still am," I said, keeping him at bay.

He made dead-on eye contact. "Present company excepted."

I just looked at him and let it pass for the moment.

"Hey, you know what we should do?—go a coupla rounds sometime. Go over to my gym, I'll give you a few pointers and kick your ass around the ring a little."

"You wouldn't last thirty seconds," I said, finally unable to resist the truth.

"You prick," Slater said in that universal tone of male camaraderie that allows insults up to a point. "Keep talking and one day you'll really believe that shit." He decided to take my offer of a chair. "Hey, just between us old warriors, don'tcha ever get a hankering to get back to it?"

"You must be out of your mind. No way on this earth, Clydell."

He looked unconvinced. "Tell the truth. You'd still be there if it wasn't for that Jackie Newton mess. You'd go back in a heartbeat if you could."

"The truth? . . . Well, what I really miss are the Saturday nights. I hardly ever got through a whole shift without having to wade through guts and pick up the pieces of dead children. It's pretty hard for something like this"—I made the big gesture with my arms, taking in the whole infinite and unfathomable range of my present world—"to take the place of something like that."

We looked at each other with no trace of humor or affection. Here, I thought: this's the first honest moment in this whole bullshit conversation—we've got nothing to say to each other. But the fact remained: Slater hadn't come waltzing in here to show off his togs and tell me about Tina.

He lit a cigarette and looked at the bookshelves critically, the way a scientist might look at a bug under a microscope.

"Is there any money in this racket?"

I shook my head. "But it's so much fun we don't care."

"Yeah, I'll bet," he said dryly.

I felt my temperature rising. Slater had about twenty seconds left on his ticket and he must've known it. Abruptly, he switched directions.

"Y'know, there are some jobs where you can have fun and still make a buck or two. Maybe you've heard."

I think I knew what he was going to say in that half second before he said it. It was crazy, but I was almost ready for him when he said, "I could use a good man if you're ever inclined to get back in the real world."

I let the full impact of what he was saying settle between us. He raised his eyebrows and turned up his palms, pushing the sincere look. It probably worked like a charm on children and widows and one-celled organisms like Tina.

"Let me get this straight, Clydell . . . you're offering me a job?"

"More than a job, Cliffie . . . a lot more than that."

"I don't think so."

"Don't jump too fast, old buddy, till you hear me out." He took a long drag and blew smoke into the air. "Last year I paid tax on a quarter of a million dollars."

"Somebody's gotta pay for those two-hundred-dollar toilet seats the Pentagon keeps buying."

"Listen, you asshole, just shut up and listen. The best thing I ever

did was take early retirement and go out on my own. Right now I'm
the hottest thing Denver's ever seen. I may branch out into radio. I was
on two shows last week and the program director at KOA says I took
to it like nobody she ever saw. Are you listening to me, Janeway? I
could make a second career out of this if I wanted to. It's so easy it
oughta be against the law. None of those guys work more than two or
three hours a day, and I'm just gettin' warmed up then. It's all bullshit.
I can bullshit my way out of anything, and that's all you need in radio.
I found that out after the first five minutes. It ain't what you know, it's
what you got between your legs. You hear what I'm saying?"

"Clydell, what's this got to do with me?"

"Keep your pants on, I'm getting to it. This is all by way of saying
that your old buddy is leading a very full life. They invite me on to
talk about the detective business and find out I can hold my own on
anything. I'm filling in for the morning drive-time host next week.
Denver Magazine is doing a piece on me, a full-blown profile.
They're picking me as one of Denver's ten sexiest men over fifty. Can
you dig that?"

I could dig it. Any magazine that would come up with a horse's-
ass idea like that deserved Slater and would leave no stone unturned
in the big effort to find him. I hoped they'd shoot their pictures in the
morning, before the town's sexiest man got his hair off the hat rack
and his teeth out of the water glass.

Slater said, "On radio they're thinking of billing me as the talking
dick."

"This also figures."

"I can talk about any damn thing. Politics? . . . Hell, I'm a walking statistical abstract. Ask me something. Go ahead, ask me a question . . . about anything, I don't care."

"Oh, hell," I said wearily.

"*I've* got an answer for everything and *you* can't even come up
with a fuckin' question."

I looked at him numbly.

"Here's something you didn't know. They skew those micro-
phones in my favor. If I get any shit from a caller, all I've gotta do is
lean a little closer and raise my voice and he just goes away." He gave
me a grin and a palms-up gesture, like a magician who'd just made

the rabbit disappear. "I'll tell you, Cliff, I'm really hot as a pistol right
now. I'm at the top of my game. There's even talk about them doing
one of my cases on the network, on *Unsolved Mysteries.*"

"If you're such a ball of fire, how come you didn't solve it?"

"I *did* solve the goddamn thing, that's why they want to do it, you
goddamn moron, as a follow-up to a story they did last year about
all the meatheads who *couldn't* solve the damn thing. Get this
straight, Janeway—there is no case I can't solve. That's why I'm cutting Denver a new rear end, because I guarantee everything. I get
results or I don't cash the check. You got a missing person? . . . I'll find
the son of a bitch. If he owes you money, I'll drag his ass back here,
and before we're through with him, he'll wish he'd never laid eyes on
you, this town, and most of all me. I can find anybody in a day or
two—it's just a matter of knowing your guy and using the old noggin.
We've got a computer database with access to seventy million names
in every state in the union. If the bastard's got a MasterCard, works
for a living, or has ever subscribed to a magazine, I've got his ass in
my computer. I can tell you his home address, phone number, the size
of his jockstrap, and how many X-rated videos he watched last week.
I can tell you stuff about yourself that you didn't even know."

"Clydell . . ."

"Okay, the point is, I can't keep up with it. I've got three legmen
and three tracers on my payroll full-time, and I still can't keep up
with all the work. I could put on three more people right now and
we'd still be a month behind in our billings. I turn down more jobs
now than I take on: I take on any more, I won't be able to do the sexy
ones myself. I'll just be a paper man, shoveling shit and passing out
assignments. Not the life for your old buddy, if you know what I
mean. This is where you come in."

"Uh-uh," I said, shaking my head.

"You'd be second-in-command. Write your own ticket. I guarantee you'd make fifty grand, rock bottom, your first year. You'd have
your pick of all the interesting cases, you'd be the go-between
between me and the staff. You'd get a staff car and all expenses paid.
I'm telling you, old buddy, my people go first-cabin all the way. My
liquor cabinet opens at four and the staff has all the privileges. And
if you're lonely at night, we've got three secretaries with world-class

t-and-a, and they do a helluva lot more for a guy than take his dictation. I know you're not crazy about me, Janeway, I got eyes in my
head. But you ask anybody who works for me, they'll all tell you
what a pussycat I am. A guy does it my way, he's got no problems.
You're gonna love this, and you'll love me too before it's over. Even
if you don't, nobody says we've gotta sleep together."

With that sorry premise, I excused myself and went to the bathroom.

He was still there, though, when I came back.

"Think about it," he said.

"I already have."

"*Think* about it, you dumb schmuck." He looked around critically. "You're like me, Janeway, a man of action. What the hell are
you doing here?"

I'll give it one try, I thought, see if I can make him understand the
tiniest truth about the world he's blundered into. But I couldn't find
the words even for that. You'll never convince a doorknob that
there's anything more to life than getting pushed, pulled, and turned.

"I appreciate the thought," I said, "but I've got to pass."

"This job's tailor-made for you, it's got your name stamped all over
it. You want proof? . . . I'll toss you a plum. Two days' work, you pick
up five grand. There's even a book angle, if you're interested."

I stared at him.

"Do I finally have your attention?" he said, grinning. "Did I just
say a magic word or something?"

"You might've started with that, saved yourself a lot of time."

"Shut up and listen. I need somebody to go pick up a skip. My
staff's booked solid for the next two weeks; I'm so tight right now I
can't even send the janitor out there. This lady needs to be delivered
back to the district court in Taos, New Mexico, ten days from tomorrow, absolute latest. The bondsman's out fifty grand and he's willing
to grease our cut to fifteen percent for dragging her back. I've already
done the arithmetic: that's seventy-five big ones, just for taking a
couple of plane rides. I pay your freight out there, you go first-class
all the way, *plus* I give you the big cut."

"Where's out there?"

"She's in Seattle."

"How do you know that?"

"I went to Madame Houdini and looked in a crystal ball, you fuckin' schlemiel. I play the odds, that's how. This gal comes from there, she's still got people there, where else is she gonna go? I called a guy I know and put him on her case. Just sit and watch, you know the routine. Yesterday, around four o'clock, there she comes, bingo, we got her. My guy just gives her plenty of rope, and after a while she leads him to the Y, where she's staying."

"Where's your guy now?"

"Still on her tail. He called me from a phone booth an hour ago, while she was getting her breakfast at the bus station lunch counter."

"Why not just have him pick her up? Seems to me that'd be the easy way."

"It's not him I'm trying to impress, meatball. Let me level with you, Janeway: I don't give a rat's ass about this case, it's just a way for you to make some quick and easy dough and see how much fun workin' for your old buddy really is. I swear to God, when I thought of you last night, it was like the answer to some prayer. I've been needing somebody like you as a ramrod in my office for at least a year now, but nobody I talked to seemed right for the job. Then this Eleanor Rigby thing popped and it came to me in one fell swoop. Cliff Janeway! What a natural."

"What Eleanor Rigby thing?"

"That's the skip's name."

I blinked. "Eleanor *Rigby?*"

"Just like the song," Slater said in the same tone of voice. But his eyes had suddenly narrowed and I sensed him watching me keenly, as if, perhaps, I might know Eleanor Rigby as something other than a song of my youth.

"Eleanor Rigby," I said, staring back at him.

"Yeah, but this little baby's not wasting away to a fast old age."

I blinked again, this time at the picture he showed me.

"Not bad, huh? You make five big ones and you get to ride all the way home handcuffed to *that*. I'd do this one myself, old buddy, if it wasn't for a radio date and *Denver Magazine*."

Then, very much against all my better judgment, I said, "Tell me about it."

Eleanor Rigby had gone to Taos to steal a book: that, at least, was how the betting line was running. On the night of September 14, four weeks ago, she had by her own account arrived in New Mexico. Five nights later she had burglarized the country home of Charles and Jonelle Jeffords. While tossing the house, she was surprised by the Jeffordses' sudden return; a struggle ensued and shots were fired. According to a statement by Mrs. Jeffords, the Rigby woman had shot up the place in a panic and escaped the house. The law came quickly and Rigby was flushed out of the surrounding woods. She had initially been charged with aggravated burglary, a violation of New Mexico statute 30-16-4: then, after further interviews with the victims, the DA had added the more serious business—aggravated assault, assault with a deadly weapon, and attempted murder. I didn't know what the penalties were in New Mexico, but they probably weren't much different from Colorado's. The whole package could get her ten years in the state penitentiary. The judge had set a standard bail: the DA had probably argued that Rigby had no ties to the community and was not a good risk, but judges, even in the punitive era we seem to be heading into, are reluctant to throw away the key before a defendant has had her day in court. Bail was $50,000: Rigby had put up as collateral a property she owned, a wooded tract near Atlanta that had been left her by her grandfather. The bondsman had posted the cash bond and had taken title to the property as a guarantee that she'd appear for her court date.

But Rigby did not appear. She returned to the Jeffordses' house, broke in again, stole some papers and a book, and this time got away.

"That's where we come in," Slater said. "The Jeffords woman wants her book back; it's one of those things, you know how people get over their stuff. A few days later she heard from the cops that Rigby had been seen in Denver; Jeffords got pipelined to me. It didn't take us long to figure out that Rigby had been here for one night only, just passing through on her way to Seattle. The rest is history. My guy's got a bead on her and she's sittin' in the bus station, waiting for one of us to come pick her up. That's when I thought of you, old buddy. I'm sittin' at my desk thinking about this crazy dame and her book, and all of a sudden it hits me like a bolt of lightning right in the ass. *Janeway!* And I wonder where the hell my head's been the last two years. I didn't give a damn about the case anymore, I've got bigger problems than that on my mind, and you, my good old buddy, are the answer to all of 'em."

I looked at him, wondering how much of this bullshit I was expected to swallow at one time.

"Think of it this way, Cliffie. You got nothing to lose, and you can buy a helluva lot of books for five grand."

It was almost uncanny: that's exactly what I was thinking, almost to the word. It was as if Slater had drilled a hole in my head and it had come spilling out.

"And while you're up there, you can double your money if you happen to stumble over that little book that Jeffords wants back so bad. Best deal you've had in a month of Sundays. You get five grand guaranteed, just for getting on the airplane. Get lucky and make yourself another five."

"What's the name of this book you're looking for?"

He got out his wallet and unfolded a paper. "You familiar with a thing called *The Raven?*"

"Seems like I've heard of it once or twice. It's a poem. Written by Edgar Allan Poe."

"This one was by some guy named Grayson. Does that make any sense to you?"

"Not so far."

"All I can tell you is what the client told me. I wrote it down real careful, went back over it half a dozen times, and it's still Greek."

"Can I see the paper?"

He gave it up reluctantly, like a father giving away a daughter at a wedding. The paper was fragile: it was already beginning to wear thin at the creases. I didn't say anything about that, just unfolded it gingerly and looked at what he had written. "Actually, I do know the book," I said. "It's a special edition of *The Raven*, published by the Grayson Press."

I sensed a sudden tension in the room, as if I had caught him stealing something. Our eyes met, but he looked away. "I don't understand this stuff," he said.

"What about it don't you understand?"

"What makes these things valuable . . . why one's worth more than the others. You're the expert, you tell me."

"Supply and demand," I said in a masterpiece of simplicity.

Slater was probably a lifelong Republican who was born knowing the law of supply and demand. It's the American way. If you want something I've got, the price will be everything the traffic will bear. If I've got the only known copy, you'd better get ready to mortgage the homestead, especially if a lot of other people want it too. What he didn't understand was the quirk of modern life that has inflated ordinary objects and hack talents into a class with Shakespeare, *Don Quixote*, and the Bible. But that was okay, because I didn't understand it either.

But I told him what I did know, what almost any good bookman would know. And felt, strangely, even as I was telling it, that Slater knew it too.

"The Grayson Press was a small publishing house that dealt in limited editions. I've heard they made some fabulous books, though I've never had one myself. Grayson was a master book designer who handmade everything, including his own type. He'd take a classic, something in the public domain like *The Raven*, and commission a great artist to illustrate it. Then he'd publish it in a limited run, usually just a few hundred copies, numbered and signed by himself and the artist. In the trade these books are called instant rarities. They can be pretty nice collector's items, though purists have mixed feelings about them."

"Mixed feelings how?"

"Well, it's obvious they'll never take the place of the first edition. Poe's work becomes incidental to this whole modern process. The books become entities of their own: they're bought mainly by people who collect that publisher, or by people who just love owning elegant things."

He gave me a nod, as if waiting for elaboration.

"It's not an impossible book to find, Clydell, that's what I'm telling you. I think I could find your client one fairly easily. It might take a month or two, but I could find it, assuming the client's willing to spend the money."

"The client's willing to spend ten grand . . . which I'd be inclined to split with you fifty-fifty."

"The client's crazy. I could find her half a dozen copies for that and still give her half her money back."

"Don't bullshit me, Janeway. How do you find half a dozen copies of a rare book like that?"

"People call them instant rarities: that doesn't mean they're truly rare. My guess is that this Grayson *Raven* is becoming a fairly scarce piece, but I still think it can be smoked out."

"You guys talk in riddles. Rare, scarce . . . what the hell's the difference?"

"A scarce book is one that a dealer might see across his counter once every five or ten years. A rare book—well, you might spend your life in books and never see it. None of the Grayson books are really rare in that sense. They're scarce just by the fact that they were all limited to begin with. But they're all recent books, all done within the last forty years, so it's probably safe to say that most of them are still out there. We haven't lost them to fire, flood, war, and pestilence. As a matter of fact, I can tell you exactly how many copies there were—I've got a Grayson bibliography in my reference section."

I got the book and opened it, thumbing until I found what I wanted.

"'*The Raven and Other Poems,* by Edgar Allen Poe,'" I read: "'published by Darryl Grayson in North Bend, Washington, October 1949. Four hundred copies printed.' It was one of Grayson's first books. The last time I saw one in a catalog . . . I'm trying to think . . . it seems like the dealer was asking around five hundred dollars. That's pretty steep, actually, for a book like that, but I guess this Grayson was a pretty special bookman."

"And you really think you could get your mitts on half a dozen of these?"

"Well," I hedged, "I could find her one, I'm sure enough of that."

"How do you go about it? I mean, you just said you'd only get to see one of these every five or ten years."

"Across my counter. But I won't wait for that, I'll run an ad in the *AB*. That's a booksellers' magazine that goes to bookstores all over the country. Somebody's bound to have the damn thing: if they do, they'll drop me a postcard with a quote. I might get one quote or half a dozen: the quotes might range from two hundred up. I take the best deal, figure in a fair profit for myself, your client pays me, she's got her book."

"What if I decide to run this ad myself and cut you out of the action? Not that I would, you know, I'm just wondering what's to prevent it."

"Not a damn thing, except that *AB* doesn't take ads from individuals, just book dealers. So you're stuck with me. *Old buddy,*" I added, a fairly nice jab.

It was lost on him: his head was in another world somewhere and he was plodding toward some distant goal line that he could only half see and I couldn't imagine.

"My client wants the book, only the one she wants ain't the one you're talking about."

"I'm not following you."

"This Grayson dude was supposed to've done another one in 1969."

"Another what?"

"*Raven.*"

"Another edition of the same book? That doesn't sound right to me."

I thumbed through the bibliography, searching it out.

"There's no such book," I said after a while.

"How do you know that?"

"It would be in the bibliography."

"Maybe they missed it."

"They don't miss things like that. The guy who put this together was probably the top expert in the world on the Grayson Press. He spent years studying it: he collected everything they published. There's no way Grayson could've published a second *Raven* without this guy knowing about it."

"My client says he did."

"Your client's wrong, Clydell, what else can I tell you? This kind of stuff happens in the book world . . . somebody transposes a digit taking notes, 1949 becomes 1969, and suddenly people think they've got something that never existed in the first place."

"Maybe," he said, lighting another smoke.

A long moment passed. "So go get Rigby," he said at the end of it. "Pick her up and cash your chips. At least we know that's real."

"Jesus. I can't believe I'm about to do this."

"Easiest money you ever made."

"You better understand one thing, Slater, and I'm tempted to put it in writing so there won't be any pissing and moaning later on. I'm gonna take your money and run. You remember I said that. I'm happier than I've been in years. I wouldn't go back to DPD for the chief's job and ten times the dough, and listen, don't take this personally, but I'd rather be a sex slave for Saddam Hussein than come to work for you. Can I make it any clearer than that?"

"Janeway, we're gonna love each other. This could be the start of something great."

For an hour after Slater left I browsed through the Grayson bibliography, trying to get the lay of the land. I had owned the book for about a year and had never had a reason to look at it. This is not unusual in the book business—probably 90 percent of the books you buy for your reference section are like that. Years pass and you never need it: then one day a big-money book comes your way and you really need it. There's a point involved and you can't guess, you've got to be sure, and the only way to be really sure is to have a bibliography on the book in question. In that shining moment the bibliography pays for itself five times over. Bibliographies are not for casual browsing or for bathroom reading. They are filled with all the technical jargon, symbols, and shorthand of the trade. The good ones are written by people with demons on their backs. Accuracy and detail are the twin gods, and the bibliographer is the slave. A bibliography will tell you if a book is supposed to contain maps or illustrations, and on what pages these may be found. It will describe the binding, will often contain photographs of the book and its title page, will even on occasion—when this is a telling point—give a page count in each gathering as the book was sewn together. If a printer makes an infinitesimal mistake—say the type is battered on a *d* on page 212, say the stem is fractured ever so slightly, like a hairline crack in a skier's fibula—it becomes the bibliographer's duty to point this out. It matters little unless the printer stopped the run and fixed it: then you have what is called in the trade a point. The bibliographer researches relentlessly: he gets into the printer's records if possible, trying to determine how many of these flawed copies were published and shipped before the flaw was discovered. Those copies then become true firsts, hotly sought (in the case of hot books) by collectors everywhere.

Bibliographies are among the most expensive books in the business.

A struggling book dealer on East Colfax Avenue in Denver, Colorado, can't possibly buy them all when the asking price is often in three figures, so you pick and choose. I remembered when the Grayson book was published: it was announced with a half-page spread in the *AB,* an ad that promised everything you ever wanted to know about the Grayson Press. I had torn out the ad and stuck it in the book when it arrived. The title was *The Grayson Press, 1947–1969: A Comprehensive Bibliography,* by Allan Huggins. The blurb on Huggins identified him as the world's top Grayson scholar and a collector of Grayson material for more than twenty years. The book looked substantial, one for the ages. It was thick, almost eight hundred pages, and it contained descriptions of every known book, paper, pamphlet, or poem ever issued by the Graysons. It had come in a signed limited edition at $195 and a trade edition at $85. To me it was a working book. I took the trade edition, and now, as was so often the case, I was damn glad I had it.

It was divided into four main sections. First there was a narrative biography of Darryl and Richard Grayson. This, combined with a history of their Grayson Press, took sixty pages. The second section was by far the biggest. It attempted the impossible, the author conceded, to catalog and annotate every scrap of Grayson ephemera, all the broadsides that the brothers had printed over a twenty-two-year career. This consumed more than four hundred pages of incredibly dense copy. The third section was called "Grayson Miscellany": this contained the oddball stuff—personal scraps, Christmas cards (the Graysons had for years printed their own cards, charming pieces that, today, are eagerly sought), special announcements, trivia. Even the commercial jobs they had taken on—posters, menus for restaurants, brochures for the Oregon Fish and Wildlife Department—all the unexciting ventures done purely for cash flow, are now avidly collected by Grayson people. There would never be a complete accounting: a fire had destroyed the printshop and all its records in 1969, and it's probably safe to say that previously unknown Grayson fragments will be turning up for a hundred years.

It was the final section, "Grayson Press Books," that was the highlight of the bibliography. Grayson had made his reputation as a publisher of fine books, producing twenty-three titles in his twenty-two

years. The books were what made collecting the scraps worthwhile
and fun: without the books, the Grayson Press might have been just
another obscure printshop. But Darryl Grayson was a genius, early in
life choosing the limited edition as his most effective means of self-
expression. When Grayson began, a limited edition usually meant
something. It meant that the writer had done a work to be proud of,
or that a printing wizard like Darryl Grayson had produced something aesthetically exquisite. Scribners gave Ernest Hemingway a
limited of *A Farewell to Arms,* 510 copies, signed by Hemingway in
1929 and issued in a slipcase. But in those days publishers were pru-
dent, and it was Hemingway's only limited. Covici-Friede published
The Red Pony in a small, signed edition in 1937, with the tiny Steinbeck signature on the back page. Perhaps the nearest thing to what
Grayson would be doing two decades later was published by a noted
printer and book designer, Bruce Rogers, in 1932: a limited edition of
Homer's *Odyssey,* the translation by T. E. Lawrence. People can
never get enough of a good thing, and around that time the Limited
Editions Club was getting into high gear, producing some classy
books and a few that would become masterpieces. The Henri Matisse
Ulysses, published in the midthirties, would sell for eight or ten grand
today, signed by Matisse and Joyce. Slater would find that interesting, but I didn't tell him. It would be too painful to watch him scratch
his head and say, *Joyce who? . . . What did she do?*

Like almost everything else that was once fine and elegant, the
limited edition has fallen on hard times. Too often now it's a tool, like
a burglar's jimmy, used by commercial writers who are already
zillionaires to pry another $200 out of the wallets of their faithful.
There are usually five hundred or so numbered copies and a tiny
lettered series that costs half again to twice as much. The books are
slapped together as if on an assembly line, with synthetic leather the
key ingredient. As often as not, the author signs loose sheets, which
are later bound into the book: you can sometimes catch these literary
icons sitting in airports between flights, filling the dead time signing
their sheets. Two hundred, four hundred, six hundred . . . the rich get
richer and God knows what the poor get. The whole process has a
dank and ugly smell that would've horrified the likes of Bruce Rogers,
Frederic Goudy, and Darryl Grayson. According to Huggins, Grayson

was the last of the old-time print men, the printer who was also an artist, designer, and personal baby-sitter for everything that came off his press. Look for him no more, for his art has finally been snuffed by the goddamned computer. Grayson was the last giant: each of his books was a unique effort, a burst of creativity and tender loving care that real book people have always found so precious. The Thomas Hart Benton *Christmas Carol* had been Grayson's turning point: he had worked for a year on a new typeface that combined the most intriguing Gothic and modern touches and had engaged Benton to illustrate it. The book was sensational: old Charles Dickens was covered with new glory, said a *New York Times* critic (quoted in Huggins), the day the first copy was inspected by the master and found fit to ship. The *Times* piece was a moot point: the book was sold out, even at $700, before the article appeared, and it mainly served to make the growing Grayson mystique known to a wider audience. People now scrambled to get on Grayson's subscription list, but few dropped off and Grayson refused to increase the size of his printings. The *Christmas Carol* was limited to five hundred, each signed in pencil by Benton and in that pale ink that would later become his trademark by Grayson. There were no lettered copies and the plates were destroyed after the run.

I skimmed through the history and learned that Darryl and Richard Grayson were brothers who had come to Seattle from Atlanta in 1936. Their first trip had been on vacation with their father. The old man had their lives well planned, but even then Darryl Grayson knew that someday he would live there. He had fallen in love with it—the mountains, the sea, the lush rain forests—for him the Northwest had everything. After the war they came again. They were the last of their family, two boys then in their twenties, full of hell and ready for life. From the beginning Darryl Grayson had dabbled in art: he was a prodigy who could paint, by the age of eight, realistic, anatomically correct portraits of his friends. It was in Atlanta, in high school, that he began dabbling in print as well. He drew sketches and set type for the school newspaper, and for an off-campus magazine that later failed. He came to believe that what he did was ultimately the most important part of the process. A simple alphabet, in her infinite variety, could be the loveliest thing, and the deadliest. Set a newspaper in a classic typeface and no one would read it: use a common newspaper type for a fine book and even its author would not take it seriously. The printer, he discovered, had the final say on how a piece of writing would be perceived. Those cold letters, forged in heat, sway the reading public in ways that even the most astute among them will never understand. Grayson understood, and he knew something else: that a printer need not be bound to the types offered by a foundry. A letter Q could be drawn a million ways, and he could create his own. The possibilities in those twenty-six letters were unlimited, as long as there were men of talent and vision coming along to draw them.

Personally, the Grayson brothers were the stuff of a Tennessee Williams play. They had left a multitude of broken hearts (and some said not a few bastard offspring) scattered across the Southern landscape. Both were eager and energetic womanizers: even today Atlanta remembers them as in a misty dream, their exploits prized as local myth. Darryl was rugged and sometimes fierce: Richard was fair and good-looking, giving the opposite sex (to its everlasting regret) a sense of fragile vulnerability. In the North the personal carnage would continue: each would marry twice, but the marriages were little more than the love affairs—short, sweet, sad, stormy. The early days in Seattle were something of a career shakedown. Darryl got a job in a local printshop and considered the possibilities; Richard was hired by a suburban newspaper to write about sports and cover social events— the latter an ideal assignment for a young man bent on proving that ladies of blue blood had the same hot passions as the wide-eyed cotton-pickers he had left in Atlanta. Having proved it, he lost the job. Huggins covered this thinly: an academic will always find new ways to make the sex act seem dull, but I could read between the lines, enough to know that Richard Grayson had been a rake and a damned interesting fellow.

A year of this was enough. They moved out of town and settled in North Bend, a hamlet in the mountains twenty-five miles east of Seattle. With family money they bought twenty acres of land, a lovely site a few miles from town with woods and a brook and a long sloping meadow that butted a spectacular mountain. Thus was the Grayson Press founded in the wilderness: they built a house and a printshop, and Darryl Grayson opened for business on June 6, 1947.

From the beginning the Grayson Press was Darryl Grayson's baby. Richard was there because he was Darryl's brother and he had to do something. But it was clear that Huggins considered Darryl the major figure: his frequent references to "Grayson," without the qualifying first name, invariably meant Darryl, while Richard was always cited by both names. Richard's talent lay in writing. His first book was published by Grayson in late 1947. It was called *Gone to Glory,* an epic poem of the Civil War in Georgia. Energetic, lovely, and intensely Southern, it told in nine hundred fewer pages and without the romantic balderdash the same tragedy that Margaret Mitchell had spun out a dozen years earlier. Richard's work was said to have some of the qualities of a young Stephen Crane's. Grayson had bound it in a frail teakwoodlike leather and published it in a severely limited edition, sixty-five copies. It had taken the book four years to sell out its run at $25. Today it is Grayson's toughest piece: it is seldom seen and the price is high (I thumbed through the auction records until I found one—it had sold, in 1983, for $1,500, and another copy that same year, hand-numbered as the first book out of the Grayson Press, had gone for $3,500). Huggins described it as a pretty book, crude by Grayson's later standards, but intriguing. Grayson was clearly a designer with a future, and Richard might go places in his own right. Richard's problems were obvious—he boozed and chased skirts and had sporadic, lazy work habits. He produced two more poems, published by Grayson in a single volume in 1949, then lapsed into a long silence. During the years 1950-54, he did what amounted to the donkey work at the Grayson Press: he shipped and helped with binding, he ran errands, took what his brother paid him, and filled his spare time in the hunt for new women. He freelanced an occasional article or short story, writing for the male pulp market under the pseudonyms Louis Ricketts, Paul Jacks, Phil Ricks, and half a dozen others. In 1954 he settled down long enough to write a novel, *Salt of the Earth,* which he decided to market in New York. E. P. Dutton brought it out in 1956. It failed to sell out its modest run but was praised to the rafters by such august journals as *Time* magazine and *The New Yorker.* Amazing they could find it in the sea of books when the publisher had done what they usually did then with first novels—nothing at all. The *New York Times* did a belated piece, two columns on page fifteen of the *Book Review,* just about the time the remainders were turning up on sale tables for forty-nine cents. But that was a good year, 1956: Grayson's *Christmas Carol* rolled off the press and Richard had found something to do. He wrote a second novel, *On a Day Like This,* published by Dutton in 1957 to rave reviews and continued apathy from the public. One critic was beside himself. A major literary career was under way and America was out to lunch. For shame, America! Both novels together had sold fewer than four thousand copies.

His next novel, though, was something else. Richard had taken a page from Harold Robbins and had produced a thing called *Warriors of Love.* He had abandoned Dutton and signed with Doubleday, the sprawling giant of the publishing world. The book was a lurid mix of sex and violence, a roaring success in the marketplace with eighty thousand copies sold in the first three weeks. The critics who had loved him were dismayed: the man at the *Times* drew the inevitable comparison with Robbins, recalling how in his first two books Robbins had seemed like a writer of some worth and how later he had callously sold out his talent for money. The only critic in Richard's eyes was his brother, though he'd never admit it or ask for Grayson's judgment. It was clear, from a few surviving pieces of correspondence, that Grayson had had nothing to say beyond a general observation that whoring—a noble and worthy calling in itself—ought to be confined to the bed and never practiced at the typewriter.

Richard never wrote another book. His big book continued making money throughout his life. It was filmed in 1960, and a new paperback release again sold in vast numbers, making an encore visit up the best-seller charts. Huggins viewed Richard as a tragic literary figure, lonely and sensitive and often mean, ever seeking and never finding some distant personal El Dorado. He continued to live in North Bend: had a house built on the property for his wife, who soon left him for another man. But there were long periods when he disappeared, absorbed into the decadent life of Seattle and Los Angeles and New York. In North Bend he filled his nights with classical music, so loud it rocked the timbers. Often he would drift down to the printshop, where he sat up all night composing poems and bits of odd prose for nothing more than his own amusement. Sometimes he would set these pieces in type, striking off one or two or half a dozen copies before dismantling the layout and staggering to bed at dawn. Old acquaintances might receive these in the mail, lyrical reminders of a time long past. One poem, containing four stanzas and lovingly printed on separate folio sheets in Grayson's newest typeface, was fished out of the garbage by a neighbor. It remains, today, the only known copy. An occasional piece might be sent to a childhood friend in Atlanta, a girl he once knew in Hollywood, an old enemy in Reno who, inexplicably, kept it, only to learn later that it was worth real money. These would arrive out of the blue, the North Bend postmark the only hint of a return address. In an apologia, Huggins described the bibliographer's nightmare of trying to include it all—there was simply no telling how many had been done and completely destroyed, and new scraps were turning up all the time. At least one Grayson collector had assembled more than two hundred unpublished poems and bits of prose, set in type by Richard in his odd moments. There had been talk of getting these writings published, if rights could be determined and the heirs could ever agree. A dual biography had been published three years ago: titled *Crossfire* with the subtitle *The Tragedies and Triumphs of Darryl and Richard Grayson,* it had been written by a woman named Trish Aandahl and brought out by the Viking Press. The Graysons died together in a fire that destroyed the printshop on October 14, 1969. Both had been drinking and apparently never knew what happened to them. Aandahl was cited by Huggins as the chief source of information on Grayson's final project, which had been destroyed in the fire. It had engaged him for years, off and on around other work. Reportedly he had designed two intricate, separate-though-compatible alphabets for the two parts, English and French. Based on a few surviving letters and the recollections of people who knew Grayson, Huggins was able to pinpoint the French volume as Baudelaire's *Flowers of Evil.*

I remembered that Baudelaire had been one of Poe's biggest fans in his lifetime. In fact, Baudelaire had translated Poe's works into French.

I flew to Seattle the same afternoon. The job was a piece of cake, Slater said at the airport. The kid had no priors and had offered no resistance to the deputy who arrested her in the woods. No weapon had been found, either in Rigby's possession or in a search of the vicinity. The shooting was believed to be an act of panic, and Rigby had ditched the gun immediately afterward. At the bond hearing her lip had described her as a sweet kid committed to nonviolence. She was either Mother Teresa or Belle Starr, take your pick. I took my gun along for the ride. I wasn't about to shoot the kid, but when you've been a cop as long as I was, you don't leave home without it. I cleared it through the airline and tucked it in my bag, which I checked through luggage. I was also carrying a certified copy of the bench warrant and an affidavit describing in detail the Rigby woman's crime. I read it all through again on a bumpy two-hour flight.

Slater had arranged everything. I had a car waiting and a room at the Hilton downtown. My plan was short and sweet: I would bust the Rigby woman, park her for safekeeping in the Seattle jail, cut a swath through the Seattle bookstores tomorrow, and deliver her to New Mexico tomorrow night. The ghosts of Poe and Baudelaire were my companions, but I shook them off. I was not going to get into that, I promised myself. Poe sat beside me as the plane circled Seattle: the gaunt little son of a bitch just wouldn't go away. The hell with you, I thought: I'm taking this woman back to New Mexico. Poe gave a crooked little smile and fastened his seat belt, and the plane dropped into the dense cloud cover and rumbled its way downward.

My contact was a guy named Ruel Pruitt. Slater had used him on several cases with Seattle angles and found him to be "a good guy at what he does. He hates the world," Slater said, "but he's like the damn invisible man, and there's nobody better at this cloak-and-dagger shit."

I was to check into my hotel and wait in my room until Pruitt called, then go pick up the girl. After that I was on my own. I had never done any bounty-hunter work, but I knew the routine because I had cooperated with enough of them when I was a Denver cop. Some were okay, highly professional: then there were the goofballs right out of a Chuck Norris movie. All I needed for this job, Slater assured me, was a sturdy pair of handcuffs, and he had given me a set of good ones from the trunk of his car.

I got into Seattle at three-thirty Pacific time. Of course it was raining. Perry Como might think the bluest skies you ever saw were in Seattle, but all I've ever seen there is rain. I almost missed the hotel—the Seattle Hilton has its check-in lobby on the ninth floor, and only a garage entrance and elevator at street level. By four-thirty I was settled in my room, on the seventeenth floor with a window onto rain-swept Sixth Avenue. At 5:05 the telephone rang. A velvety voice said, "Janeway?" and I said, "Yeah," and he said, "I'm in a bar near the Kingdome." He gave me an address and said he'd be outside in a blue Pontiac. He read off his plate number and I got it down the first time. "Don't let the door hit you in the ass on the way out," he said. "I got no idea how long this little dyke's gonna sit still."

Wonderful, I thought, listening to the dead connection—just the kind of charmer I'd expect to find working for Slater. I slipped the cuffs into my jacket pocket and ten minutes later I pulled up behind the Pontiac on First Avenue. The plate matched the number he'd given me, and I could see two people sitting inside. One of them, I thought, was a woman. The bar nestled at the foot of an elevated double-decker viaduct, looking like a cliff dwelling at Mesa Verde. It was triangular, squeezed in where the street slashed through on a kitty-corner layout. The rain was heavy now. I sat waiting for a break, but the rain in Seattle isn't like the rain in Denver: a guy could grow a long white beard waiting for it to slack off here. At 5:45 by the digital in my car, I decided to run for it. I flicked up my parking lights, got his attention, hopped out, and ran to his car. The doors were locked. Pruitt and his ladyfriend sat smoking, chatting as if I weren't there. I rapped on the backseat doorglass and Pruitt looked around, annoyed, and pointed to his custom seatcovers. I stood with water running down my nose and looked at them through the glass, said, "Son of a bitch," and hoped they could read my lips. Eventually he got the message: he leaned over the seat, found an old blanket, and spread it over his seat covers. By the time he was ready to open the door, I was drenched.

I pushed the blanket roughly out of the way and flopped down on the backseat.

"Hey, cowboy," Pruitt said, "are you trying to piss me off?"

The woman giggled and we all looked at each other. Pruitt was an ugly pockmarked man. His face had been badly pitted long ago, the way you used to see on smallpox victims, and it gave him a look of rank decay. He smelled of cedarwood aftershave and peppermint, which on him had a faintly sickening effect. He was in his late forties: his girlfriend was younger, a brassy-looking blonde. But it was Pruitt who commanded the attention. His coat was open so I could see the gun he wore. He was an intimidator, I knew the type well, it had crossed my path often enough when I was a cop in Denver. Give him an inch and he'll walk all over you. He'll bully and embarrass you and make life miserable. I never give guys like him an inch, not even when I could see, like now, the eyes of a killer.

"Where the hell did Slater dig you up?" he said.

"He used to date my mother. I hear he found you the same way."

The blonde gave a small gasp: one didn't, I was supposed to believe, talk to the man in that tone of voice. Pruitt's eyes burned holes in my head. "We've got a real smart-ass here, Olga. Ten thousand guys in Denver and Slater sends me a smart-ass."

"Tell you what," I said evenly. "Let's start over. I'll go back to my hotel and dry out, have a drink, get a good dinner, maybe find myself a friend of the opposite sex to help me pass the time. You sit here in the rain, follow Slater's girl, and call me when you want to pass the torch. How does two weeks from tomorrow sound?"

"A real smart-ass. You're getting water all over my car, for Christ's sake, didn't your fucking mother teach you anything? Where were you raised, in a back alley behind some Denver whorehouse?"

"As a matter of fact, yeah. I seem to've missed all the advantages Mrs. Hitler gave you."

He burned me with his killer eyes. The blonde seemed to be holding her breath, waiting for him to crawl over the seat and kill me.

"Just for the record," I said pleasantly, "I'm about this close to pushing what's left of your face right through that windshield. Do we understand each other yet, Gertrude? . . . or do I have to take that gun away from you and empty it up your ass?"

We sat and stared. I was ready for him if he came, and I thought he might. The rage simmered in the car and fogged up the windshield. In the end, he had a higher priority than teaching a cowboy from Denver who was boss.

"You want to tell me about this woman?" I said.

"You've got her picture. She's in there, it's your job now."

"I'll tell you when it's my job. If I have any more trouble with you, I'm out of here, and you and Slater can figure it out by yourselves."

"Shit."

I couldn't improve on that, so I let it ride. We sat in the car for a few minutes without talking. "Go inside," he said to Olga as if I weren't there. "See if our pigeon's getting lonely." She got out and ran through the rain, disappearing into the bar. Pruitt sat in silence, his collar turned up to his ears, his eyes riveted on the neon lights in the window. He lit a cigarette but put it out without comment when I cracked the window and the rain came in on his seats.

"Let's get this over with," he said. He got out in the rain and walked to the bar. I trailed along behind him. He tapped the hood of an old roadster parked at the front door—Rigby's, I was left to conclude. It was a true jalopy, with current Washington plates and bad tires. We went inside. Pruitt didn't want to go past the dark aisle that led into the barroom. We stood there a moment in the pitch, trying to adjust our eyes. It was still early, but already the bar was crowded with happy-hour zombies and refugees from various wars. Music was playing loudly on the jukebox: "Sea of Love." Maybe thirty people were at the bar and at tables scattered around it. The bartender was a fat man who looked like Jackie Gleason. Olga sat on a stool at the far end. Two stools away was Eleanor Rigby.

"There she is," Pruitt said.

We stood for another moment.

"Is it your job yet, or am I supposed to stand here all night?"

"Go on, blow."

He motioned to Olga, who left an untouched beer and came

toward us. "I'll probably meet you again sometime," he said to me. "The circumstances will be different."

"I'm in the Denver phone book, if you ever get out that way."

"Maybe I'll make a point of it."

Asshole, I said, not entirely under my breath.

I ambled to the bar and sat on the only empty stool, directly across from Rigby. The bartender came; I ordered a beer and sucked the foam off. Ten yards away, Eleanor Rigby had another of whatever she was drinking. I watched her without looking. I looked at two guys having a Seahawks argument and I watched her with peripheral vision. I watched the bartender polishing glasses and I looked at her. She looked bone weary, as if she might fall asleep at the bar. I stole a frontal look. There wasn't much danger in it, she was just another good-looking girl in a bar and I was a lonely, horny guy. She'd be used to gawkers, she must get them all the time. She was twenty-one, I guessed, with thick hair pinned back and up. "Eleanor Rigby." I shook my head and tried to clear away the Victorian spinster the song conjured up. I wondered what it does to people, being named after something like that and having to carry that baggage all your life.

I was in it now, committed to the deed. I told myself she was nothing more than a cool five grand, waiting to be picked up. I wasn't sure yet how to take her—probably later, on the street. I didn't like the smell of the crowd in the bar. It was a blue-collar crowd, a sports crowd, and there's always some ditz ready to rise up out of a crowd like that and defend a pretty woman's honor no matter what. Never mind my court papers, never mind the cheap-looking ID Slater had given me as I left. The ID identified me as an operative of CS Investigations of Denver, but there was no picture of me on it and it gave me no authority beyond what Slater had, what anybody has. What I could use right now was a state-issued license with my kisser plastered all over it. But the state of Colorado doesn't require its private detectives or its psychotherapists to have special licenses: all a bozo needs is an eight-by-twelve office, the gift of gab, and the power of positive thinking. I was making what amounted to a citizen's arrest, and I had the law on my side because she had jumped bail and was now a fugitive. But if you have to explain that to a crowd in a bar, you're already in trouble.

I nursed my beer and waited. She sat across the waterhole, a gazelle unaware of the lion's approach. The stool had opened to her immediate left. I was tempted, but a shark moved in and filled it. Story of my damn life: the studs make the moves while I sit still and consider the universe, and I go home to a cold and lonely bed. I thought about Rita McKinley and wondered where she was and what she was doing with herself. In a way that was difficult to explain, Eleanor Rigby looked a little like Rita, like a younger model. Actually, she looked nothing like Rita at all. The stud to her left was already hitting on her. In happier times she might've been thrilled, but now she just looked tired and bored. The bartender drifted down and asked if I wanted another brew. I said I was okay, I'd send up a flare when the need became great. At the front table the Seahawks flap was still raging, a real-life commercial for Miller Lite. Across the way, Mr. America said something and gestured to her drink. She shook her head and tried to go on with her life, but he remained doggedly in her face. She swished her ice and sipped the watery remains while her hero worked his way through the first twelve chapters of his life story. He was one of those loud farts, the kind you can't insult: he probably couldn't be killed, except with a silver bullet. He was halfway to his first million and nobody to share it with. I couldn't imagine any interesting woman falling for that line, but interesting probably wasn't what he was after. The guy was a moron, either that or I was. I didn't have time to dwell on it because just then Eleanor Rigby got up and left him flat, halfway between the big deal he had just pulled off and all the bigger ones coming down the pike.

I liked her for that. In a way it was a shame I was going to have to bust her. I left two bills on the bar and followed her down the hall to the johns. She disappeared into the ladies'. I checked to make sure there was no other way out, then I drifted back into the bar and took up a position where I couldn't miss her. I was standing near the only window, which looked out into the street. Heavy black drapes were closed over it, but I parted them slightly so I could see out. I was staring at her car, my hand suspended between the curtains. Someone was sitting behind the wheel. I saw a light, very faint: he was looking for something, rummaging through the glove compartment. He put on his hat and got out in the rain. Pruitt. He stood for a moment, oblivious to the rain that had bothered him so much before. He gave her door a vicious kick, leaving a dent six inches across. I saw the snap of a blade, a wicked stiletto, and he bent over and poked a hole in her tire. Then he walked away and I watched the car go flat.

Just then she came out of the hallway. She walked past, so close I could've touched her. I let her go, following her out through the narrow foyer. By the time I got to the door she had run to her car. I stood watching her through the tiny pane of glass. Yes, she had seen the flat tire: she was sitting in her car doing nothing. I could imagine her disgust. Time for Lochinvar to appear, as if by magic: a knight with a bouquet in one hand and a set of shackles in the other. Bust her now, I thought, walking out into the rain: bust her, Janeway, don't be an idiot. But there was Poe, grim and pasty-faced, lurking in the dark places under the viaduct.

I stopped at the curb and pointed to her tire. She cracked the window ever so slightly.

"You got a flat."

"No kidding."

"Hey," I said in my kindest, gentlest voice. "I can't get any wetter than this. Gimme your keys, I'll get out your jack and change it for you."

5

She sat in the car while I changed her tire. I jiggled her up, took off her lugs, and hummed a few bars of "Singin' in the Rain." Her spare tire was like the others: it had been badly used in at least three wars, the alleged tread frequently disappearing into snarls of frayed steel. I hauled it out of the trunk and put it gently on the curb. The street was as deserted as a scene from some midfifties end-of-the-world flick, but it fooled me not. Pruitt, I thought, was still out there some-where, I just couldn't see him. If this were *Singin' in the Rain*, he'd come on down and we'd do a little soft-shoe routine. I'd be Gene Kelly and we'd get Eleanor Rigby out of the car to play Debbie Reynolds. Pruitt would be Donald O'Connor, tap-dancing his way up the side of the viaduct and out onto the highway, where he'd get flattened by a semi. Suddenly I knew, and I didn't know how, that there was a joker in the deck: Slater hadn't hired me for my good looks after all. A far greater purpose was hidden under the surface: what had been presented as an interesting side dish was in fact the main course, and the big question was *why the camouflage?* I was told to play lead in *Singin' in the Rain,* and now, well into the open-ing number, I learned it was really *West Side Story* we were doing. In a minute Pruitt would come down and we'd do one of those crazy numbers where the good guys sing and dance with the hoods, just before they all yank out their zip guns and start zipping each other into hoodlum heaven. I scanned the street again, searching for some sign of life, but even Poe had disappeared into the murky shadows from whence he'd come.

I tossed Rigby's flat tire into her trunk and contemplated the spare. I resisted the inclination to laugh, but it was a close call: she must've searched the world to've found five tires that bad. *I'll take your four worst tires and save the best of my old ones for a spare.* You gotta be kidding, lady, there ain't no best one. *Oh. Then throw away the three worst and give me whatever's left.* You know the routine, Jack Nicholson did it in a restaurant in *Five Easy Pieces:* four over well, cooked to a frazzle, and hold the tread. Pruitt didn't need a knife, a hairpin would've done it for him. I hummed "I Feel Pretty" in a grotesque falsetto as I fitted the tire onto the wheel, but it didn't seem to brighten the moment. Crunch time was coming, and I still didn't know what I was going to do. It was that goddamned Poe, the wily little bastard: he had cast his lot with Slater and was waxing me good. That one line about Baudelaire in the Huggins bibliography had been the hook, and I was too much the bookman to shake it free.

Was it possible that Darryl Grayson had been working on a two-book set, Poe and Baudelaire, English and French, at the time of his death, and that one copy of the Poe had been completed and had survived? If you read "Dear Abby" faithfully, as I do, you know that anything is possible. What would such a book be worth, quote-unquote, in today's marketplace? . . . A unique piece with a direct link to the deaths of two famous bookmen, snatched from the blaze just as the burning roof caved in. Was it truly the best and the brightest that Darryl Grayson could make? If so, it was worth a fair piece of change. Ten thousand, I thought, Slater even had that right: it was worth just about ten grand on the high end. But with one-of-a-kind pieces, you never know. I could envision an auction with all the half-mad Grayson freaks in attendance. If two or three of them had deep pockets, there was no telling how high such a book might go.

I tightened the last of the lugs with my fingers. Not much time left now, and it wasn't going to end with the whole company out in the street singing "Maria." I needed some quick inspiration and got it—the thin point of my filing-cabinet key shoved into her air valve brought the spare hissing down flat. She didn't hear a thing: the rain was drumming on her roof and her window was up. I got up and walked around the car, looking at her through the glass. She cracked the window and gave me a hopeful smile.

"The news is not good. Your spare's flat too."

She didn't say anything: just took a deep breath and stared at her knuckles as she gripped the wheel. I fished for a legitimate opening, any bit of business that might make her trust a half-drowned stranger on a dark and rainy night. "I could call you a cab," I said, and my luck was holding—she shook her head and said, "I don't have enough money left for a cab." That was a cue, but I didn't leap at it like a sex-starved schoolboy, I let it play out in a long moment of silence. "I could loan you the money," I said cheerfully, and I thought I saw her doubts begin to vanish in the rain. "Hey, you can mail it back to me when you're flush again." She gave a dry little laugh and said, "That'll probably be never." I shrugged and said, "You're on a bad roll, that's all. Look, I don't want you to get any wrong ideas, but I've got a car right across the street. I could drive you home . . . as long as you don't live in Portland or someplace."

She seemed to be considering it. I knew I didn't look like anything out of the Seattle social register, so sincerity was probably the best I could hope for. I leaned in close, crossed my arms against her window, and talked to her through the crack. "Look, miss, you can't stay out here all night. If you're broke, I'll loan you the money for a place . . . a cheap place, okay? . . . no strings attached. Call it my good deed for the year, chalk it up to my Eagle Scout days. If you're worried about me, I can understand that; I'll slip you the money through the window and give you an address where you can send it back to me when your ship comes in. What do you say?"

"I thought Good Samaritans were extinct."

"Actually, I'm your guardian angel," I said, trying for a kidding tone to put her at ease.

"Well, you've sure been a long time coming."

"We never show up until the darkest possible moment."

"Then you're right on time."

"I could spare thirty dollars. You won't get much of a room for that, but it's better than sitting in your car all night."

She leaned close to the crack and studied my face. "Why would you do something like that?"

"Because you look like you've just lost your last friend. Because I know you'll pay me back. Because once or twice in my life, I've been so far down it looked like up to me."

"Richard Farina."

I didn't say anything, but I was surprised she had made that connection.

"That's the title of a book by Richard Farina. *Been Down So Long It Looks Like Up to Me.*"

I said, "Oh," and pretended not to know it. I'd have to watch that, keep the literary metaphors out of my talk until I saw where we were heading.

"So what do you say?" I asked.

"I won't take your money . . . but, yeah, maybe a ride. . . . I could use a ride if you're going my way."

"I'm sure I am."

I told her to stay put and I'd drive up close so she wouldn't get wet. Then I had her, snuggled in the seat beside me. No wonder monsters like Ted Bundy had it so easy. That thought crossed her mind too and she said, "I guess I'm a sitting duck if you're some wacko from a funny farm." She shrugged as if even that wouldn't matter much. I gave her the big effort, a smile I hoped was reassuring. "Ma'am, I don't blame you at all for thinking that, I'd be thinking it myself if I were in your shoes. All I can tell you is, you're as safe with me as you'd be in a police station."

I hoped this wasn't laying it on too thick, but it didn't seem to bother her. "My name's Janeway."

Her hand was warm and dry as it disappeared into mine. "Eleanor Rigby."

I was surprised that she'd use her real name: she probably hadn't had time yet to get used to being a fugitive.

"Eleanor Rigby," I repeated. "You mean like . . ." and I hummed the staccato counterpoint.

She tensed visibly at the melody. For a moment I was sure she was going to get out and walk away in the rain. "You've probably heard that a million times," I said, trying to make light of it. "I imagine you're sick of it by now." Still she said nothing: she seemed to be trying to decide about me all over again. "Look, I didn't mean anything by that. I grew up on Beatles music, it was just a natural connection I made. I sure wasn't relating you to the woman in the song."

Her eyes never left my face. Again I was certain I was going to lose her, she seemed that ready to break and run. "We can start all over if you want. My name's Janeway, and I'll still loan you the thirty if you'd rather do it that way."

She let out a long breath and said, "No, I'm fine."

"And your name is Eleanor Rigby, I understand. It's a great name, by the way. Really. How'd you come to get it?"

"The same way you got yours, I imagine. I come from a family of Rigbys and my father liked the name Eleanor."

"That's as good a way as any."

Now she looked away, into the rainy night. "This is going to be a lot of trouble for you."

"Trouble's my middle name. Which way do you want to go?"

"Get on the freeway and go south. Stay in the left lane. When you see I-90, branch off to the east, take that."

I turned the corner and saw Interstate 5, the cars swirling past in the mist. I banked into the freeway, glancing in my mirror. No one was there . . . only Poe, interred in the backseat.

"You'd better turn that heater on," she said. "God, you're so wet."

"I will, soon's the car warms up."

She gave me a look across the vast expanse of my front seat. "I guess you're wondering what I was doing in a bar if I was so broke."

"I try not to wonder about stuff like that."

"This is the end of a long day, in a very long week, in a year from hell. I was down to my last five dollars. The only thing I could think of that I could buy with that was a margarita. I had two and killed the five. Sometimes I do crazy things like that."

"So now what do you do? Do you have a job?"

She shook her head.

"At least you're not stranded here. I couldn't help noticing the Washington plates on your car."

"No, I'm not stranded. Just lost on planet Earth."

"Aren't we all. I'm not so old that I don't remember what that feels like."

"You're not so old," she said, looking me over. "You must be all of thirty."

I laughed. "I'm not doing you that big a favor. I'll be forty years old before you know it."

"Almost ready for the nursing home."

"You got it. Where're we going, by the way?"

"Little town called North Bend."

Ah, I thought: Grayson country.

She sensed something and said, "Do you know North Bend?"

"Never been there."

"I'm not surprised. It's just a wide place in the road, but it happens to be where my family lives. You know what they say about families. When you come home broken and defeated, they've got to take you in."

She was still tense and I didn't know how to breach that. Food might do it: I'd seen that happen more than once.

"Have you had dinner?"

She looked at me. "Now you're going to buy me dinner? Jeez, you must really be my guardian angel."

"So what do you say?"

"I feel like the last survivor of the Donner party. That means yes, I'm starving."

I saw an intersection coming up, filled with neon promise.

"That's Issaquah," she said. "There's a Denny's there. It was one of my hangouts when I was in high school. Can you stand it?"

I banked into the ramp.

"You look terrible," she said. "I don't suppose you have a change of clothes. Maybe they'll let you in if you comb your hair."

"If I get thrown out of a Denny's, it'll be a bad day at Black Rock."

Inside, we settled into a window booth. I ordered steaks for both of us, getting her blessing with a rapturous look. I got my first look at her in good light. She was not beautiful, merely a sensational young woman with world-class hair. Her hair sloped up in a solid wall, rising like Vesuvius from the front of her head. It was the color of burnt auburn, thick and lush: if she took it down, I thought, it would reach far down her back. Her nose was slightly crooked, which had the strange effect of adding to her appeal. She could stand out in a crowd without ever being a pinup. Her looks and ready wit probably made job-hunting easy, if she ever got around to such things.

"So what do you do for a living?" I asked.

"Little of this, little of that. Mostly I've been a professional student. I'll probably still be going to college when I'm thirty. I graduated from high school at sixteen and I've been in and out of one college or another ever since. I go for a while, drop out, drift around, go somewhere else, drop out again. I transfer across state lines and lose half my credits, then I have to start up again, learning the whole boring curriculum that I learned last year and already knew anyway, just to get even again. Schools shouldn't be allowed to do that—you know, arbitrarily dismiss half your credits just so they can pick your pocket for more tuition. But that's life, isn't it, and I'm sure it's nobody's fault but my own. It drives my family nuts, the way I live, but we are what we are. My trouble is, I've never quite figured out what I am. This is a mighty lonely planet, way off in space."

It was the second time she had said something like that. I was beginning to wonder if she had been star-crossed by her name, doomed to play out the destiny of a lonely woman whose entire life could be told in two short stanzas.

"I do what I can, but then I get restless," she said. "My mom and dad help out when they can, but they don't have any money either. For the most part it's on my shoulders."

"So what do you do?" I asked again.

"I'm versatile as hell. I know a lot of things, some of them quite well—just survival skills, but enough to buy something to eat and a room at the Y. I can work in a printshop. I wait a dynamite table. I mix a good drink—once I got fired for making 'em too good. I type like a tornado and I don't make mistakes. I'm a great temporary. I've probably worked in more offices as a Kelly girl than all the other Kellys put together. I could get in the *Guinness Book of World Records*. Do they pay for that?"

"I don't think so."

"Probably not. They make a fortune off us freaks and pay us nothing."

"You could probably get on full-time in one of those offices if you wanted. Law office maybe. Become a paralegal. Then go to law school."

"I'd rather lie down in a pit of snakes. I find the nine-to-five routine like slow poison. It poisons the spirit, if you know what I mean. About three days of that's about all I can stand. But that's most likely what I'll do tomorrow—get my dad to take me into town, go on a temporary, fill in somewhere till I've got enough money for a few tires and some gas, then drift away and do it all over again."

There was a pause, not long, while she seemed to consider something. "If I feel lucky, I might look for books tomorrow."

I tried not to react too quickly, but I didn't want to let it get past me. "What do books have to do with working in an office?"

"Nothing: that's the point. The books keep me out of the office."

I stared at her.

"I'm a bookscout." She said this the way a woman in Georgia might say *I'm a Baptist,* daring you to do something about it. Then she said, "I look for books that are underpriced. If they're drastically underpriced, I buy them. Then I sell them to a book dealer I know in Seattle."

I milked the dumb role. "And you make money at this?"

"Sometimes I make a lot of money. Like I said, it depends on how my luck's running."

"Where do you find these books?"

"God, everywhere! Books turn up in the craziest places . . . junk stores, flea markets . . . I've even found them in Dumpsters. Mostly I look in bookstores themselves."

"You look for books in bookstores . . . then sell 'em to other bookstores. I wouldn't imagine you could do that."

"Why not? At least sixty percent of the used-book dealers in this world are too lazy, ignorant, and cheap to know what they've got on their own shelves. They wouldn't invest in a reference book if their lives depended on it. They might as well be selling spare parts for lawn mowers, that's all books mean to them. Don't get me wrong: I love these people, they have saved my life more times than you would believe. I take their books from them and sell them to one of the other book dealers—"

"One of the forty percent."

"One of the *ten* percent; one of the guys who wants the best of the best and isn't afraid to pay for it. You bet. Take from the dumb and sell to the smart."

"That's gonna be hard to do tomorrow, though, if you've got no money."

She opened her purse. "Actually, I've got a little over three dollars in change. Pennies, nickels, and dimes."

"I don't think you could buy much of a book with that."

She finished her soup and thought it over. "I'll tell you a story, and you see what you think about it. I was down and out in L.A. I was broke, just about like this, down to my last bit of pocket change. So I hit the bookstores. The first one I went to had a copy of *Let Us Now Praise Famous Men*. You ever hear of that book?"

I shook my head, lying outrageously.

"A guy named James Agee wrote it and another guy named Walker Evans illustrated it with photographs. This was a beautiful first edition, worth maybe three or four hundred dollars. The dealer was one of those borderline cases—he knows just enough to be dangerous, and he had marked it ninety-five. He knew he had *something,* he just wasn't sure what. I figured my friend in Seattle might pay me one-fifty for it, but of course I didn't have the wherewithal to break it out of there. I also knew it wouldn't last another day at that price—the first real bookman who came through the door would pick it off. I drifted around the store and looked at his other stuff." She sipped her water. "You ever hear of Wendell Berry?"

The poet, I wanted to say. But I shook my head.

"The poet," she said. "His early books are worth some money, and there was one in this same store, tucked in with the belles lettres and marked three dollars. I counted out my last pennies and took it: went around the corner and sold it to another dealer for twenty dollars. Went back to the first store and asked the guy if he'd hold the Agee for me till the end of the day. The guy was a hardass: he said he'd hold it if I put down a deposit, nonreturnable if I didn't show up by closing time. I gave him the twenty and hit the streets. My problem was time. It was already late afternoon, I had only about an hour left. What I usually do in a case like that is sell some blood, but they'll only take a pint at a time and I was still seventy dollars short. So I worked up a poor-little-girl-far-from-home hustle. It was the first time I'd ever done that, but you know what? . . . it's easy. You guys are the easiest touches; I guess if you're a young woman and not particularly hideous, you really can make men do anything. I just walked in cold off the street and asked twenty shopkeepers in a row if they could let me have two dollars for something to eat. One or two of them snarled and said, 'Get out of my life, you effing little deadbeat,' but you get a thick skin after the first two or three and then it all rolls off. One guy gave me a ten.

In a café on the corner I got money not only from the owner but from half the guys at the counter. I could probably make a living doing that, but it has a kind of self-demeaning effect, except in emergencies. You don't learn anything, and one day you wake up and you've lost your looks and can't do it anymore. So I made a pact with myself, I would never do it again unless I had to. I got back to the store right on the button and bought my book. And my luck was running like a charm, I didn't even have to call Seattle, I found a guy in east L.A. who gave me more than I'd counted on—one seventy-five. He specialized in photo books and I thought he might be good for this one."

"That's amazing."

"Yeah, but that's not the end of the story. Even while he was paying me, I noticed a box of books on his counter, new stuff he'd just gotten in. On top of the stack was a first edition that damn near stopped my heart. I finally worked up my courage and asked him, 'Hey, mister, whatcha gonna want for this?' He got a stern, fatherly look on his face and said, 'I think that's a pretty nice book, sweetie, I'm gonna want twenty to thirty bucks for it.' And I almost died trying to pay him with a straight face. The next day I called my friend in Seattle and he sent me a good wholesale price, four hundred dollars. And there I was, back in the chips."

"Incredible," I said, and I meant it. I didn't know many bookscouts who could pull off something like that.

"Oh, yeah! . . . yeah! And *so* much more fun than working in some accountant's office or typing dictation for a lawyer. I mean, how can you compare *typing* all day with bookscouting? The only trouble with it is, it's not reliable. You can go weeks without making a real score, and the rest of the time you're picking up small change. So it all depends on how I'm feeling. If I think I'm gonna be lucky, I'll hit the stores: if not, I'll go to work for Ms. Kelly again."

I knew I shouldn't ask, shouldn't be that interested in the specifics. But I had to.

"What was that book, that was worth so much?"

She grinned, still delighted at the memory and savoring each of the title's four words. "*To . . . Kill . . . a . . . Mock-ing-bird!*"

I tried for a look that said, *It means nothing to me,* but what I wanted to do was close my eyes and suffer. Jesus, I thought . . . *oh, man!* That book is simply not to be found. Stories like that are what make up the business. A dealer in photography hands a pretty raga-muffin a thousand-dollar book, so desirable it's almost like cash, and all because he hasn't taken the time to learn the high spots of modern fiction.

The waitress brought our food. Eleanor reached for the salt and I saw the scar on her wrist. It was a straight slash, too even to have been done by accident.

At some time in her past, Eleanor Rigby had tried to kill herself, with a razor blade.

"So," she said, in that tone people use when they're changing the subject, "where were you heading when I shanghaied you in the rain?"

"Wherever the wind blows."

"Hey, that's where I'm going! Are you married?"

"I don't think so."

"Ever been?"

"Not that I can remember. Who'd put up with me?"

"Probably one or two girls I know. D'you have any bad habits?"

"Well, I don't smoke."

"Beat your women?"

"Not if they do what I tell them."

She laughed. "God, a nonsmoker with a boss complex. I may marry you myself. Don't laugh, Mr. Janeway, I've lived my whole life on one whim after another. Have you ever been at loose ends?"

"Once, I think, about twenty years ago."

"Well, I live that way. My whole life's a big loose end. I go where the wind blows. If the natives are friendly, I stay awhile and warm myself in the sun. So where's the wind blowing you?"

"Phoenix," I said—the first place that popped into my mind.

"Oh, lovely. Lots of sun there—not many books, though, from what I've heard. I'd probably have to work for a living, which doesn't thrill me, but nothing's perfect. How would you like some company?"

"You've decided to go to Phoenix?"

"Why not, I've never been there. Why couldn't I go if I wanted to?"

She was looking right down my throat. She really is like Rita, I thought: she had that same hard nut in her heart that made it so difficult to lie to her.

"What do you suppose would happen," she said, "if we just turned around and headed south? Strangers in the night, never laid eyes on each other till an hour ago. Just go, roll the dice, see how long we could put up with each other."

"Would you do that?"

"I might." She thought about it, then shook her head. "But I can't."

"Ah."

"I've been known to do crazier things. I've just got something else on my agenda right now."

"What's that?"

"Can't talk about it. Besides, it's too long a story. My whole life gets messed up in it and I don't think you've got time for that."

"I've got nothing but time."

"None of us has that much time."

She was feeling better now, I could see it in her face. Food, one of the most intimate things after the one most intimate thing, had worked its spell again. "Oh, I needed that," she said. "Yeah, I was hungry."

"I'm glad you decided to stick around."

"Sorry about that. I just have a bad reaction to that song."

"I think it's a great song."

"I'm sure it is. But it gives me the willies."

"Why would it do that?"

"Who's to say? Some things you can't explain."

Then, as if she hadn't been listening to her own words, she said, "I've got a stalker in my life."

She shook her head. "Forget I said that. I'm tired . . . at the end of my rope. Sometimes I say things . . ."

I stared at her, waiting.

"Sometimes he calls me and plays that song."

"Do you know who he is?"

"I know him by sight, I don't know his name. Obviously he knows mine." She shivered deeply. "I don't talk about this. But you've been such a dear . . . I can't have you thinking I'm crazy."

"Have you called the cops?"

She shook her head. "Cops don't seem to be able to do much with people like that."

"If he's harassing you on the phone, they can catch him. The time it takes to trace a call these days is pretty short; damn near no time at all."

"So they'd catch him. They'd bring him in and charge him with something minor, some nothing charge that would only stir him up."

"How long has he been doing this?"

She took a deep breath, let it out slowly, and said, "Not long, a few weeks. But it seems like years."

"You can't put up with that. You've got to protect yourself."

"Like . . . get a gun, you mean?"

I let that thought speak for itself.

She sighed. "I've never fired a gun in my life."

The strange thing was, I believed her.

"Do you have any idea what he wants?"

"I think I know what he wants. But just now I would like to please change the subject. Let's get back to happy talk." She cocked her head as if to say, *Enough, already.* "Those wet clothes must feel awful."

"I've been wet so long it feels like dry to me. What was that guy's name?"

"That's more like it. His name was Richard Farina."

"Is his book worth anything?"

"Mmmm, yeah," she said in a singsong voice. "Hundred dollars maybe. I wouldn't kick it out in the rain."

The waitress came and left the check.

Eleanor looked at me hard. "So tell me who you really are and what you're doing. I mean, you appear out of the night, kindness personified, you walk into my life when I've never been lonelier, you're going where the wind blows but you don't have a change of clothes. What are you running away from?"

"Who said I'm running away?"

"We're all running away. Some of us just don't get very far. Yours must be some tragic love affair for you to run with only the clothes on your back. What was her name?"

"Rita," I said, suddenly inspired. "It's funny, she was a book person, a lot like you."

"No kidding!"

"The same only different." I fiddled with the check. "She'd love that story you told me."

"The book world is full of stories like that. Books are everywhere, and some of them are valuable for the craziest reasons. A man gets put on an Iranian hit list. His books go up in value. A guy writes a good book, a guy writes a bad book. Both are worth the same money on the collector's market. A third guy writes a great book and nobody cares at all. The president of the United States mentions in passing that he's a Tom Clancy fan and suddenly this guy's book shoots into the Hemingway class as a collectible. And that president is Ronald *Reagan,* for God's sake. Does that make any sense?"

"Not to me it doesn't."

"It defies logic, but that's the way it is today. People latch on to some new thing and gorge themselves on it, and the first guy out of the gate becomes a millionaire. Maybe Clancy *is* a master of techno-babble. Do you care? To me he couldn't create a character if his damn life depended on it. You watch what I say, though, people will be paying a thousand dollars for that book before you know it. Then the techno-babble rage will pass. It'll fade faster than yesterday's sunset and the focus will move on to something else, probably the female private detective. And that'll last a few years, till people begin to gag on it. Meanwhile, it takes a real writer like Anne Tyler half a career to catch on, and James Lee Burke can't even find a publisher for ten years."

"How do you learn so much so young?"

"I was born in it. I've been around books all my life. When I was fourteen, I'd ditch class and thumb my way into Seattle and just lose myself in the bookstores. So I've had six or seven years of good hard experience. It's like anything else—eventually you meet someone who's willing to show you the ropes. Then one day you realize you know more about it than your teacher does—you started out a pupil, like Hemingway with Gertrude Stein, and now you've taken it past anything the teacher can do with it. And it comes easier if you've had a head start."

"Starting young, you mean."

She nodded. "At sixteen I had read more than a thousand books. I knew all the big names in American lit, so it was just a matter of putting them together with prices and keeping up with the new hot-shots. But it's also in my blood. I got it from my father: it was in his blood. It took off in a different direction with him, but it's the same stuff when you get to the heart of it. Books . . . the wonder and magic of the printed word. It grabbed my dad when he was sixteen, so he knows where I'm coming from."

"Does your father deal in books?"

"He wouldn't be caught dead. No, I told you his interest went in another direction. My dad is a printer."

She finished her coffee and said, "I'd give a million dollars if I had it for his experience. My father was present at the creation."

I looked at her, lost.

"He was an apprentice at the Grayson Press, in this same little town we're going to. I'm sure you've never heard of the Grayson Press, not many people have. But you can take it from me, Mr. Janeway, Grayson was the most incredible book genius of our time."

6

There wasn't much to see of North Bend, especially on a dark and rainy night. I got off at Exit 31 and Eleanor directed me through the town, which had long since rolled up its awnings for the night. The so-called business district was confined to a single block, the café, bar, and gas station the only places still open. But it was deceptive: beyond the town were narrow roads where the people lived, where the Graysons had once lived, where Eleanor Rigby had grown from a little girl into a young woman. We went out on a road called Ballarat and soon began picking up numbered streets and avenues, most of them in the high hundreds. It was rural by nature, but the streets seemed linked to Seattle, as if some long-ago urban planner had plotted inevitable annexations well into the next century. We came to the intersection of Southeast 106th Place and 428th Avenue Southeast: I still couldn't see much, but I knew we were in the country. There was a fenced pasture, and occasionally I could see the lights of houses far back from the road. "Here we are," Eleanor said abruptly. "Just pull over here and stop." I pulled off the road across from a gate, which was open. My headlights shone on a mailbox with the name RIGBY painted boldly across it, and under that—in smaller letters—THE NORTH BEND PRESS. We sat idling. I could hear her breathing heavily in the dark beside me. The air in the car was tense.

"What's happening?" I asked her.

"What do you mean?"

"Is there a problem?"

"Not the kind of problem you'd imagine. I just hate to face them."

"Why would you feel like that?"

"I've disappointed them badly. I've done some things . . . stuff I can't talk about . . . I've let them down and suddenly it's almost impossible for me to walk in there and face them. I can't explain it.

The two people I love best in the world are in there and I don't know what to say to them."

"How about 'hi'?"

She gave a sad little laugh.

"Seriously. If people love each other, the words don't matter much."

"You're very wise, Janeway. And you're right. I know they're not going to judge me. They'll just offer me comfort and shelter and love."

"And you shudder at the thought."

"I sure do."

We sat for another minute. I let the car idle and the heater run and I didn't push her either way. At last she said, "Let's go see if Thomas Wolfe was right when he said you can't go home again."

I turned into the driveway. It was a long dirt road that wound through the trees. The rain was beating down steadily, a ruthless drumbeat. In a moment I saw lights appear through the trees. A house rose up out of the mist, an old frame building with a wide front porch. It looked homey and warm, like home is supposed to look to a tired and heartsick traveler. But Eleanor had begun to shiver as we approached. "Th-there," she said through chattering teeth. "Just pull around the house and park in front." But as I did this, she gripped my arm: my headlights had fallen on a car. "Somebody's here! Turn around, don't stop, for God's sake keep going!" Then we saw the lettering on the car door—THE VISTA PRINTING COMPANY—and I could almost feel the relief flooding over her. "It's okay, it's just Uncle Archie," she said breathlessly. "It's Mamma's uncle," she said, as if I had been the worried one. A light came on, illuminating the porch and casting a beam down the stairs into the yard: someone inside had heard us coming. I pulled up in front of the other car at the foot of the porch steps. A face peered through cupped hands at the door. "Mamma," Eleanor said, "oh, God, Mamma." She wrenched open the door and leaped out into the rain. The woman met her on the porch with a shriek and they fell into each other's arms, hugging as if they hadn't seen each other for a lifetime and probably wouldn't again, after tonight. I heard the woman yell, "Gaston! . . . Get out here!" and then a man appeared and engulfed them both with bearlike arms. I had a sinking feeling as I watched them, like Brutus might've felt just before he stabbed Caesar.

Now Eleanor was waving to me. I got out and walked through the rain and climbed the steps to the porch. "This is the man who saved my life," Eleanor said dramatically, and I was hooked by the woman and pulled in among them. The man gripped my arm and the woman herded us all inside. "This place is a shambles," she said, picking up a magazine and shooing us on. I was swept through a hallway to a well-lit kitchen where a tall, thin man sat at the table. He got to his feet as we came in, and we all got our first real look at each other. The woman was young: she might easily have passed for Eleanor's older sister, though I knew she had to be at least my age. But there wasn't a wrinkle on her face nor a strand of gray: her only concession to age was a pair of small-framed granny glasses. The man was burly: my height and heavier, about the size of an NFL lineman. His hair was curly and amber and he had a beard to match. The man at the table was in his sixties, with slate-gray hair and leathery skin. Eleanor introduced them. "This is my father, Gaston Rigby . . . my mother, Crystal . . . my uncle, Archie Moon. Guys, this is Mr. Janeway." We all shook hands. Rigby's hand was tentative but his eyes were steady. Archie Moon gripped my hand firmly and said he was glad to meet me. Crystal said that, whatever I had done for their daughter, they were in my debt—doubly so for bringing her home to them.

There was more fussing, those first awkward moments among strangers. Rigby seemed shy and reserved: he hung back and observed while Crystal and Eleanor did the talking. Hospitality was the order of the moment: Crystal wanted us to eat, but Eleanor told her we had stopped on the road. "Well, damn your eyes, you oughta be spanked," Crystal said. She asked if we'd like coffee at least: I said that sounded wonderful. Eleanor said, "I think what Mr. Janeway would like better than anything is some dry clothes," and Crystal took my measure with her eyes. "I think some of your old things would fit him close enough, Gaston," she said. "Get him a pair of those old jeans and a flannel shirt and I'll get the coffee on."

Rigby disappeared and Crystal bustled about. "Get down that good china for me, will you, Archie?" she said, and Moon reached high over her head and began to take down the cups. Eleanor and I sat at the kitchen table, lulled by the sudden warmth. Impulsively she reached across and took my hand, squeezing it and smiling into my eyes. I thought she was probably on the verge of tears. Then the moment passed and she drew back into herself as Moon came with the cups and saucers and began setting them around the table.

"None for me, honey," he said. "I been coffeed-out since noon, won't sleep a wink if I drink another drop."

"I got some decaf," Crystal said.

"Nah; I gotta get goin'."

"What've you gotta do?" Crystal said mockingly. "You ain't goin' a damn place but back to that old shack."

"Never mind what I'm gonna do. You don't know everything that's goin' on in my life, even if you think you do."

They laughed at this with good humor. They spoke a rich Southern dialect, which Crystal was able to modify when she talked to us. "This old man is impossible," she said. "Would you please talk to him while I get the coffee on?—otherwise he'll run off and get in trouble."

Moon allowed himself to be bullied for the moment. He sat beside Eleanor and said, "Well, Mr. Janeway, what do people call you in casual conversation?"

"Cliff sometimes brings my head up."

"What line of work are you in?"

"Why is that always the first thing men ask?" Crystal said.

"It defines them," Eleanor said.

"So, Mr. Janeway," Moon said loudly. "What line of work are you in?"

"Right now I'm between things."

"An old and honorable calling. I've been in that line once or twice myself. Sometimes it can be pretty good."

"As long as you come up smiling."

"Just for the record," Crystal said in her Southern voice, "we don't care what you do for a living. I'm just glad you were in the right place at the right time, and I'm grateful to you and we're so glad you're here with us."

"That was gonna be my next comment," Moon said, "in more or less that same choice of words."

"Where're you staying, Mr. Janeway?" Crystal asked.

"He's going where the wind blows, Mamma," Eleanor said, as if that explained everything.

"Tonight the wind dies here," Crystal said. "I won't hear any argument about it, we've got a fine room in the loft over the shop. It's warm and dry and there's a good hard bed. Best of all, it's private."

"You'll love it," Eleanor said.

"In fact," Crystal said as Rigby came in carrying some clothes, "why don't we get that done right now?—get you into some dry duds and checked into your room. We're putting Mr. Janeway in the loft," she said to Rigby, who nodded. To me she said, "The only thing I need to ask is that you not smoke over there. Gaston doesn't allow any smoking in the shop. I hope that's not a problem."

"Not for me."

"Good. I'll whip us up some cinnamon rolls to go along with the coffee. You get yourself thawed out and come back over in half an hour so we can all get acquainted."

"Me, I gotta go," Moon said.

"You ornery old cuss," Crystal said. "Damn if you're not the unsociablest one man I ever met."

"I'll take Mr. Janeway over to the loft while I'm goin' out," Moon said to Rigby. "No sense you gettin' wet too."

I followed him back through the house. We popped open two umbrellas and went down into the yard. Moon pointed out the path with a flashlight he carried, leading the way to an outbuilding about twenty yards behind the house. The first thing I noticed, even before he turned on the light, was the smell . . . the heavy odor of ink mixed with something else. The light revealed a long room, cluttered with machinery and steel cabinets. Two large ancient-looking presses stood against the far wall, a smaller handpress on a table near the door, and nearer the door was a vast, complicated machine from another century, which I thought was probably a Linotype. It was. "That smell shouldn't bother you any," Moon said. "It's just the smell of hot type. Gaston must've been working out here till just before you showed up. You shouldn't even notice it upstairs."

He flipped on the lights. Our eyes touched for less than a second, then he looked away. "I'll leave you a slicker here by the door, and the flashlight and the umbrella too. If you need anything else, there's a phone upstairs, you can just call over to the house."

The first thing I saw was a NO SMOKING sign. Moon moved me past it, onto the circular staircase in the corner opposite the presses, then up to the loft, a spacious gabled room with a skylight and a window facing the house. In the middle of the room was a potbellied stove, which looked to be at least a hundred years old. Moon stoked it and soon had a fire going: "This old bastard'll really dry out your duds. And it's safe, Gaston has it checked every so often. It'll run you right out of here if you let it get too hot on you." He walked around the room looking in corners. Opened a door, peeped into an adjacent room. "Bathroom. There's no tub, but you've got a shower if you want it."

He made the full circle and stood before me. He radiated power, though his was wiry, a leaner brand than Rigby's. His voice was the prime ingredient in the picture of hard male strength that he presented to the world. It was a deep, resonant baritone, bristling with Southern intelligence. He'd be great on talk radio, I thought, and I was just as sure that he'd have nothing to do with it. "The phone's here beside the bed," he said. "It's on a separate line, so you just call over to the house just like any other phone call." He bent over the end table and wrote a number on a pad. Then he stood up tall and looked at me. "I can't think of anything else."

"Everything's great."

He turned to leave and stopped at the door. "Crystal kids around a lot, but I really do have to go. There's a waitress in Issaquah who's got dibs on my time. You look like a man who understands that."

"I do have a faint recollection of such a situation, yes."

He gave a little half-laugh and asked if I'd be around tomorrow. "If you are, come see me. I run the newspaper, my shop's over in Snoqualmie, just a few minutes from here. Anybody in either town can tell you where I'm at. If the sun comes out tomorrow, I'll show you some of the best country in the world. I've got a cabin up in the hills about an hour's drive from here. Built it forty years ago and it's been swallowed up by national-forest lands, about a million acres of it. That'll keep the Holiday Inn bastards at bay, at least for the rest of my life. It's yours if you'd like to unwind in solitude for a few days."

Again he paused. "I can't quite put my finger on it, Janeway. I've got the feeling we owe you more than we know. Does that make any sense?"

"I can't imagine why."

"I don't know either, it's just a feeling I've got. Like maybe you came along in the nick of time, not just to keep our little girl from getting herself wet."

"If I did, I don't know about it. But I'm glad I could help her."

He looked at me hard. "The kid doesn't tell us much anymore. She's all grown-up, got a life of her own. She never had a lick of sense when it came to strangers. Hitchhiked home from L.A. when she was eighteen, damn near drove her mamma crazy when she told us about it that night at dinner. Today she got lucky and found you. Don't ask me how or why, but I know we're in your debt."

I made a little motion of dismissal.

"All of us. Me too. Hell, I've known that kid since she was born, she used to hang around my printshop for hours after school, asking questions, pestering. 'What's this for, what's that do?' She's such a sweetheart, I couldn't think any more of her if she was my own daughter. And I know that anybody who helped her out of a tough spot could walk in here and the Rigbys would give him damn near anything they owned. So rest easy, I guess that's what I wanted to say, just rest easy. These people aren't kidding when they say they're glad to see you."

Then he was gone, clumping down the stairs, leaving me with one of the strangest feelings of my life.

I sat at the stove in Gaston Rigby's clothes, goldbricking.

What the hell do I do now? I thought.

A few minutes later I climbed down the stairs to the printshop and stood there in the quiet, aware of that primal link between Gaston Rigby's world and my own. It was there, huge and fundamental—amazing that I could live a life among books and be so unaware of the craftsmen who made them. Darryl Grayson had worked in a shop much like this one, and not far from this spot. Here he had practiced his voodoo, making wonderful things on quaint-looking equipment, just like this. I felt a strange sense of loss, knowing that someday we would attain technological perfection at the expense of individualism. This magnificent bond between man and machine was passing into history. I was born a member of the use-it-and-throw-it-away generation, and all I knew of Grayson's world was enough to figure out the basics. The big press was power driven. The plate identified it as CHANDLER AND PRICE, and it was run by a thick leather strap that connected a large wheel to a smaller one near the power source. On a table was a stack of leaflets that Rigby had been printing for an east Seattle car wash. I looked at the handpress. It had been made long before the age of electricity, but it was still, I guessed, what Rigby would use for fine work. It had a handle that the printer pulled to bring the paper up against the inked plate. The table beside it contained a few artistic experiments—poems set in typefaces so exotic and disparate that they seemed to rise up on the paper and battle for attention. It's like beer, I thought foolishly. I had once been asked to help judge a beer-tasting, and I had gone, thinking, *This is so damn silly.* Beer was beer, wasn't it? No, it was not. I learned that day that there are more beers in heaven and earth than mankind ever dreamed of. And so it is with type.

Rigby seemed to have them all, yet instinctively I knew that this was far from true. Still, his collection was formidable. They were stacked in tiny compartments of those deep steel cabinets: there were at least fifty cabinets set around the perimeter of the room, and each had at least twenty drawers and each drawer held a complete and different face. I pulled open a drawer marked COOPER BLACK and saw a hundred tiny compartments, each containing twenty to fifty pieces of type. I looked in another drawer farther along: it was called CASLON OLD STYLE. I did know a few of the names: recognized them as pioneers of type development, but the names conjured nothing in my mind as to what their work would look like. I didn't know Caslon from a Cadillac, and most of the names were as foreign to me as a typeface of old China. There were DEEPDENE and BODONI, CENTURY and DEVINNE, KENNERLEY, FUTURA, BASKERVILLE, and GRANJON. Each took up several drawers, with compartments for various point sizes. There were some that Rigby himself didn't know—entire cabinets labeled UNKNOWN in all point sizes. UNKNOWN ANTIQUE FACE, C. 1700, FOUND NEAR WHEELING, WEST VIRGINIA, 1972. WHEELING, Rigby called it, and it seemed to have come, or survived, in only one size. At the far end, nearest the presses, was a cabinet marked GRAYSON TYPES, each row subtitled with a name—GEORGIAN, PACIFIC, SNO-QUALMIE. On the other side were cabinets marked DINGBATS and WOODCUTS. I opened the first drawer and took out a dingbat. It was a small ornament that, when I looked closely, became a fleur-de-lis that could perhaps be the distinguishing mark of a letterhead. In the far corner was a paper cutter: next to it, coming down the far wall, a long row of paper racks. Then the Linotype, an intricate but sturdy machine the size of a small truck. This was the world of Gaston Rigby. Enter it and step back to the nineteenth century, where—forgetting its sweatshops and cruelties and injustices—man's spirit of true adventure, at least in this world, made its last stand.

And there was more. I came to a door halfway down the far wall and opened it to find a room almost as large as the first. I flipped on a light and saw what looked at first glance to be another workshop. But there was a difference—this had neither the clutter nor the workaday feel of the other. It looked like the workplace of a gunsmith I had once known, who also happened to be the world's most vigorous neat-freak. There was a long workbench with rows of fine cutting tools—chisels, hammers, and files of all sizes. There were several large anvils, a row of powerful jewelerlike eyepieces, two strong and strategically placed lamps. This is where he does it, I thought: does it all by hand. I realized then that I was thinking of Grayson, not Rigby, as if I had indeed slipped back in time and somehow managed to saunter into Grayson's shop. I saw the sketches on the wall—an entire alphabet, each letter a foot square and individually framed, upper and lower case. The drawings ringed the entire room. I looked closely and decided that they were probably originals. Each was signed *Grayson,* in pink ink, in the lower-right corner. At the end of the workbench I found a large steel plate. It was a die or matrix, a foot square, containing the letter *G* in upper case. It corresponded exactly to the *G* framed on the wall. Just beyond the matrix was a long device that looked like a draftsman's instrument: it had a swinging arm that could trace the *G* and, I guessed after examining it, scale it down. Suddenly I could see the process. Grayson would first sketch his letters on paper. Then he would cast a die in metal. Then, using his one-armed machine, he could scale it down to any point size, down to the type on an agate typewriter if he so chose. He was the Compleat Printer, with no need of a type foundry because he was his own typemaking factory. Rigby had saved a set of his sketches and some of his equipment: he had maintained the working environment of Darryl Grayson, almost like a museum.

When I looked around again the world had changed. My calling had shifted at the foundation, and I knew I would never again look at a book in quite the same way. I lingered, hoping for some blazing enlightenment. At the far end of the room, half-hidden in shadows, was a door I hadn't noticed before. Perhaps it was in there, the answer to everything. But the door was locked, so I had to forgo the pleasure.

I heard a bump up front: someone, I imagined, coming to fetch me. I turned out the light and went back through the shop to the front door. But when I opened it, whoever had been there was gone.

At the end of my universe is a door, which opens into Rigby's universe. Either side must seem endless to a wayward traveler, who can only guess which is the spin-off of the other. We sat at the kitchen table, talking our way through their high country and along my riverbeds, and if much of what I told them was fiction, it was true in spirit and gave them little cause to ponder. I discovered that I could tell them who I was without giving up the bigger truth of why I was there. Occupation, in fact, is such a small part of a man that I was able to frame myself in old adventures and bring them as near as yesterday. Crystal served sweet rolls steaming with lethal goodness, the butter homemade, the sugar flakes bubbly and irresistible. Rigby sat across from me at the kitchen table, his face ruddy and mellow, cautiously friendly. Eleanor had excused herself and gone to the bathroom. Crystal pushed another roll toward me with the sage comment that nobody lives forever. That was one way of looking at it, so I took the roll while Rigby considered going for a third. "Ah, temptation," he said in that soft, kind voice, and he and Crystal looked at each other and laughed gently as if sharing some deeply personal joke. I reached for the butter and said, "I'll have to run for a week." Crystal told me about a bumper sticker she had seen that said: DON'T SMOKE . . . EXERCISE . . . EAT FIBER . . . DIE ANYWAY. And we laughed.

In twenty minutes my dilemma had been honed to a razor-thin edge. Something had to give, for deception is not my strong point. There was a time when I could lie to anyone: the world I went around in was black-and-white, I was on the side of truth and justice, and the other side was overflowing with scum-sucking assholes. Those days ended forever when I turned in my badge. I could like these people a lot: I could open a mail-order book business in a house up the road and be their neighbor. Every morning at eight I'd wander into Rigby's shop and learn another secret about the universe beyond the door, and sometimes in the evenings Crystal would invite me for dinner, where I'd give them the true gen about my rivers and deserts. Shave about eight years off my age and you could almost see me married to their daughter, raising a new generation of little bookpeople in the shadows of the rain forest. They were the real stuff, the Rigbys, the salt of the earth. Suddenly I liked them infinitely better than the guys I was working for, and that included all the judges and cops of the great state of New Mexico.

They were not rich by any means. The microwave was the only touch of modern life in the house. The refrigerator was the oldest one I'd ever seen still working in a kitchen. The stove was gas, one step up from a wood burner. The radio on the shelf was an Admiral, circa 1946; the furniture was old and plain, giving the house that rustic, well-lived look. Whatever Darryl Grayson had taught Gaston Rigby all those years ago, the art of making money was not part of the mix. Grayson's name had come up just once, in passing. Fishing, I had cast my line into that pond with the offhand remark that Eleanor had told me of a man named Grayson, who had taught Rigby the business. His hand trembled and his lip quivered, and I knew I had touched something so intrinsic to his existence that its loss was still, twenty years later, a raw and open wound. Crystal came around the table and leaned over him, hugging his head. "Darryl was a great man," she said, "a great man." And Rigby fought back the tears and tried to agree but could not find the words. Crystal winked at me, encouraging me to drop the subject, and I did.

"What's all this?" Eleanor said, coming in from the hall. "What're we talking about?"

"I was just asking about the Linotype," I said, making as graceful a verbal leap as a working klutz can expect to achieve.

"There hangs a tale," Eleanor said. "Tell him about it, Daddy."

Rigby tried to smile and shook his head.

"You tell 'im, honey," Crystal said.

Eleanor looked at her father, then at me. "It's just that we had a kind of an adventure getting it here."

"It was a damned ordeal was what it was," Crystal said. "What do you think, Mr. Janeway, how does ten days without heat in weather that got down to twenty below zero sound to you?"

"It sounds like kind of an adventure," I said, and they laughed.

"It was our finest moment," Eleanor said, ignoring her mother, who rolled her eyes. "Daddy heard from a friend in Minnesota that a newspaper there had gone broke and they had a Linotype in the basement."

"It had been sitting there for twenty years," Crystal said, "ever since the paper converted to cold type. Hardly anyone there remembered what the silly thing had been used for, let alone how to use it."

"It was ours for the taking," Eleanor said.

"Craziest damn thing we ever did," Crystal said.

"Who's telling this, Mamma? Anyway, it was the middle of winter, they were gonna tear down the building and everything had to be out within two weeks."

"It was one of those instant demolition jobs," Crystal said. "You know, where they plant explosives and bring it all down in a minute."

"So we drove to Minneapolis," Eleanor said.

"Nonstop," said Crystal.

"The heater in the truck went out in Spokane . . ."

"Didn't even have time to stop and get it fixed. We took turns driving, sleeping when we could."

"Hush, Mamma, you're spoiling the story. So we get to Minnesota and it's so cold my toenails are frozen. The snow was piled four feet deep, the streets were like white tunnels. You couldn't even see in the shops at street level."

"They had this thing stored in a basement room that was just a little bigger than it was," Crystal said. "They must've taken it apart and rebuilt it in that room, because right away we could see that we'd never get it out unless we took it apart and carried it piece by piece."

I looked at Rigby. "Had you ever done anything like that?"

He shook his head.

"He had to figure it out as he went along," Eleanor said.

"Gaston can do anything, once he sets his mind to it," said Crystal.

"Anybody can, with a little time and patience," Rigby said.

"We spent two days in that basement," Eleanor said, "tearing down this machine, packing the parts, and putting them on the truck.

It was so cold your hands would stick to the steel when you touched it, and all around us the wreckers were stringing explosives."

"But we got the damn thing," Crystal said, "and sang Christmas carols all the way home . . . in February."

"We thought of getting the heater fixed in Montana," Eleanor said, "but by then, hey, it was up to ten degrees—a major heat wave."

"And we could smell home," Rigby said.

I could almost feel the satisfaction and joy of getting it set up here in working order, and I said something to the effect.

"Yeah," Crystal said, "even I can't deny that."

"You can't put a label on it," Rigby said.

"Somehow you mean more to each other," Eleanor said, "after you've done something like that."

A sudden silence fell over the table. The evening was over, and I knew that, once again, I was not going to bust her. I didn't know why—it certainly wasn't Poe anymore—but I was ready to live with it, whatever happened.

"You'll find a lot of books over there if you'd like to read," Crystal said. "Sorry there's no TV."

I made a so-who-needs-it gesture with my hands.

"Breakfast at six-thirty," she said. "That's if you want to eat with us. I'll rustle you up something whenever you come over."

She walked me to the door, leaving Eleanor and her father alone at the kitchen table. On the porch she took my hand. "Thank you," she whispered. Then she hugged me tight and disappeared back into the house. I stood on the porch listening to the rain. The night was as dark as it ever gets, but I felt as if a huge weight had been lifted from my back. There would be no bust, no handcuffs, no force. I watched my five grand grow wings and fly away into the night. Half the puzzle was finished.

Now that I knew what I was not going to do, I thought I could sleep.

9

I opened my eyes to the ringing of the telephone. It was five after three by the luminous clock on the table beside me: I had been asleep almost five hours. Par for the course, I thought, staring into the dark where the phone was. I let it ring, knowing it couldn't be for me, but it kept on until I had to do something about it. When I picked it up, Eleanor was there in my ear.

"I'm coming over. Is that okay?"

"I don't know . . . what'll your parents say?"

But she had hung up. I rolled over and sat on the bed. When five minutes had passed and she hadn't arrived, I groped my way to the window and looked across at the house. It was dark except for a faint light on the side facing away from me. Soon that too went out— someone in a bathroom, I thought—but then another light came on in the opposite corner. Something moved in the yard: I couldn't tell what as I tried to see through the rain-streaked glass, but it looked like some critter standing under the window had moved quickly back into the darkness. A deer maybe, or just a mirage thrown out by a brain still groggy from too little sleep. But I hadn't forgotten about Eleanor's stalker and I sat on the sill and watched the yard. The light went out and again I swam in an all-black world. I sat for a long time looking at nothing.

At ten to four I decided that she wasn't coming and I went back to bed.

I heard a sharp click somewhere, then a bump. *There she is,* I thought. But nothing happened. The drumming of the rain was the only reminder that I could still think and I could still hear. The minutes stretched toward the dawn. There was not yet a hint of light, which, given the clouds covering the state, was at least ninety minutes away. Again a light flashed. This one brought me up with a start—it was here in my room, inches away. As my eyes focused, I saw that it was the extension button on the telephone—someone had picked up the phone downstairs in the printshop and was having a conversation at four o'clock in the morning. This went on for some time, at least two minutes, then the line went dark. I rolled out of bed and went to the door, opened it, and listened down the circular staircase. *Nothing.* No sound, no light, not a hint of movement anywhere.

I lay on the bed staring up into the dark. Eventually, though I wouldn't have believed it possible, I began to doze off.

It was almost as if she had stepped out of a dream. I was drifting, somewhere between worlds, when my eyes flicked open and I knew she was there. "Hey," I said, and I felt her sit beside me on the floor. I reached out and touched her head: she had laid it across her folded arms on the bed. "Thought you'd never get here." She still didn't speak: for several minutes she just lay there under my arm, her breathing barely audible above the rain. Then she said, "I didn't come because I felt stupid. I am stupid, waking you up in the middle of the night."

"It's okay, I was awake anyway," I lied.

"The truth of the matter is, I've just been through the loneliest night of my life. It got so desolate I thought I'd die from it."

There was a long pause. She said, "I keep thinking that maybe my mom and dad can help me when I get like this, but they can't. I know they love me, but somehow knowing it just makes the loneliness all the stronger. Does that make any sense?"

"You're not their little girl anymore. You've lost something you can't ever get back, but you haven't yet found what's gonna take the place of it in the next part of your life."

"The next part of my life," she said with a sigh.

I could hear the pain in her voice. "I'll help you," I said, "if you'll let me."

She seemed to consider it. "Just talk to me, help me get through the night. I know you want to sleep and I'm being a thundering pain in the ass. But you have no idea how much it would help, Mr. Man from Nowhere, if you'd just talk to me for a little while."

"Listen and believe it. There's nothing I'd rather do, right this minute, than talk to you."

"Oh, Janeway." Her voice got thick, and broke. "I hurt so bad. I hurt so bad and I can't talk to anyone."

"Talk to me."

"I don't know, maybe somebody like you, who's just passing through and doesn't know me. I can't talk to Mamma and Daddy, there's just too much in the way. I don't know what it is, we can't get past the facts of the matter and get down where the real trouble is."

"What are the facts of the matter?"

"How completely and beyond redemption I've fucked up my life."

"Maybe it just seems that way."

"I've done a stupid thing. Don't ask me why, it was just insane. I felt compelled, like I had no choice. Then they said I'd done something worse, and one thing led to another and I did do something worse . . . only it wasn't what they said I'd done. But they locked me up for it, and now they want to lock me up again, maybe for years. If they do that, I will kill myself, I swear I will. I couldn't live in a cage."

"None of us can. That's not really living."

"But some people survive. I couldn't even do that, not if we're talking about years." She shook her head: I felt the movement. "No way."

Gently, I prodded her. "What did you do?"

She was a long time answering, and at first the answer was no answer at all. "I can't tell you either."

"I won't judge you."

"It's not that. There are pieces of the story missing. Without them I just look like a fool."

"Take the chance. Maybe I can help you find the pieces."

"No one can. None of it makes sense. I'm like that guy in *The Man Without a Country,* I've got no roots, nothing solid to hold on to. I love my parents but I have an awful time talking to them."

"Everybody does. It means you're one hundred percent normal."

She chuckled, a sad little noise. "And all the time I thought I was crazy. I have the worst time trying to talk to them. And I know I've got to, I don't think I can let another day pass without doing that. But how can I?"

"Try it out on me first."

She didn't say anything. I let her alone for a few minutes, then I nudged her arm. "What happened to you?"

"I was in New Mexico," she said at once, as if she'd been waiting for me to ask it one more time. "I got in trouble. . . . I can't tell you about that. But I've been carrying it around for weeks now. If I don't tell somebody . . ."

I gave her a little squeeze: nothing sexual, just friendly encouragement.

"That's where I picked up my stalker, in Taos." Again she tried to lapse into silence. But then she said, "I had a room there. I'd come home and things would be moved."

"Ransacked?"

"No . . . but yeah, maybe. I had the feeling he'd done that, been through all my stuff and then put it all back, just so. But he'd always leave one little thing out of place, something obvious like he'd wanted me to see it. Once he left a cigarette, still burning in a Styrofoam cup. He wanted me to know he'd just left. Then he started with the phone. It would ring late at night and I'd hear him breathing . . . or humming that song."

"You told me before: you knew what he wanted."

"He told me. But I can't explain it now, so don't ask me."

"Explain what you can."

"I felt like something evil had come into my life. I'd turn a corner and he'd be there, right in my path. He looked like a cadaver, his eyes were all sunken and he had holes in his face, deep pits across both cheeks. Scared me deaf and dumb. I can't tell you what it was like. I'd walk down to the phone booth and call home and he'd come up behind me, rip open the door, and stand there staring. He said he could kill me, right there at the telephone—*kill you and go up to North Bend and kill your mother too.* God, I just freaked. Then one night he got into my room when I was sleeping. When I woke up the next morning there was a dead . . . rat . . . on the bed beside me. And I really freaked."

I was listening to her words, trying to figure how and when this had all happened. It had to be sometime after the first Jeffords breakin, but before the second. Whatever else her stalker had done, he'd pushed her to that next level of desperation. She had failed to get what she'd gone after at the Jeffords place—what the stalker also wanted—and had gone back for another run at it. Then what?

Then she took it on the lam: jumped bail, struck out for home. "So how'd you get back here?" I asked. She had driven her car, she said in that flat tone of voice that people use when you ask a stupid question. But I was trying to get at something else, something she couldn't yet know about. "What roads did you take?" I asked, and she laughed and wondered what possible difference it could make. "I came across the Sangres, up the Million-Dollar Highway to Grand Junction, then took the freeway home."

Slater had lied about her coming through Denver. He had probably lied about other things as well. The pockmarked man sounded like someone I had met quite recently, and my whole involvement felt suddenly dirty.

I couldn't get her to say any more. "I've already said too much," she said. "If I keep on, I'll feel worse than ever. Maybe I should just take poison and save us all the grief."

"That, of course, would be the worst thing you could do." I calculated my next line and said it anyway. "I hope you're not one of those people who turn suicidal on me."

"Have you known people like that?"

"One or two. It's always tragic, especially when they're young."

"I saw you looking at the scar on my arm. Back in the restaurant."

"No use lying about it. I couldn't help noticing."

"Well, you're right. I did that to myself."

"Why?"

"Loneliness," she said without missing a heartbeat. "Desolation, the undertow, the barren landscape. I can't explain it. The loneliest times come when I'm adrift in a big city, or here with people who love me. When I'm really alone, up on a mountaintop somewhere, I'm fine. I go up to Archie's cabin and I can go for a week without seeing another living soul. The feeling of peace is just incredible. Too bad we can't live our lives on mountaintops. I really like being with people until I actually am, then I can't stand them. Maybe I should try to find Jesus; people say that works, though I can't imagine it working for me. I'm just not spiritually oriented. So I drift. Sometimes I don't even know where the road's gonna take me."

"Talk to me, Eleanor. You got in trouble in New Mexico, then you came back here. What happened then?"

"Nothing. That's the stupid part of it. I came fifteen hundred miles and I couldn't go the last mile home. Instead I drove out to see Amy. But she wasn't home and I couldn't find her."

"Who's Amy?"

"Amy Harper. She was my best friend till she married Coleman Willis. The cock that walks like a man. Our relationship got a bit strained after that. It's hard to stay friends with someone when her husband hates you."

"How could anyone hate you?"

"I wouldn't go to bed with him. To a guy who wears his brain between his legs, that's the last word in insults."

In a while I said, "So you went to see Amy but Amy wasn't there. You wouldn't want to kill yourself over that. Amy'll be back."

"How do you know?"

"People always come back."

"Maybe so, but I won't be here."

No, I thought: you probably won't be.

"What did you do then?" I said.

"Drove out to my parents' place. Stood in the rain watching the house, afraid to come up and talk to them. God, I've never been so alone in my life. Then I saw them come out and drive off—going to town, I figured, for the week's groceries. I went over to the house and sat on the porch. I wanted to die but I didn't know how. I thought if I could just lie down and close my eyes and not wake up, I'd do it. But it's not that easy. It's impossible, in fact; I don't want to *die*, for God's sake, I never wanted to die. I thought maybe I could find some peace in the printshop. I used to do that when I was a little girl. When I'd get blue, I'd go back in the shop and put my cheek against that cold press and I could feel the warmth come flooding into me, especially if there were books back there and if they were books I loved. I could take a book and hold it to my heart and the world was somehow less hostile, less lonely."

"Did that work?"

"It always works, for a while. But it's like anything else that has fantasy at its roots. Eventually you've got to come back to earth.

Now I'm running out of time. Something will happen, today, tomorrow . . . something'll happen and I'll be history."

She pulled herself up on the bed. I heard her shoes hit the floor.

"Would you do something for me, Mr. Janeway?"

"If I can."

"Hold me."

"I don't think that'll be any great hardship."

"That's all I want . . . just . . . just . . ."

"Sure," I said, taking her into the cradle of my arm.

She was shivering. I drew the blanket up under my chin and the body heat spread around us. Her hair smelled sweet, as if she had just washed it. I knew I had no business smelling her hair. She snuggled tight against me and I had no right to that either. Maybe she'd go to sleep now. Maybe I could forget she was there, just like the people at Lakehurst forgot the *Hindenburg* when it was blowing up in front of them. Somewhere in the night Helen Reddy was singing "I Am Woman" and I was thinking *you sure are,* to the same driving melody. I had been what seemed like a very long time without a woman, and this one was forbidden, for more reasons than I could count.

We lay still on the bed, and slowly the dark gave way to a pale and ghostly gray. Saved by the dawn. It was five-thirty: the Rigbys would be getting up for the new day. I patted her shoulder and rolled out of bed, moving to the window for a look at the house. It was peaceful and ordinary in the rainy morning, nothing like the den of tears I had blundered into last night. I turned and looked at Eleanor. Her face was a white blur in the half-light: her eyes, I thought, were open. We didn't say anything. I hit the john, and when I came out, she had not moved from her spot on the bed. I looked out the window. Someone in the house had turned on a light, the same one I had seen earlier. I knew then what I was going to do.

"Listen," I said, still looking out the window. "I've got to tell you something." But I never got the words out. A car came out of the misty woods and up the road toward the house. I felt heartsick watching it come. Only when it had pulled in behind my rental and stopped did the cop behind the wheel turn on his flasher.

It filled the room and colored us a flickery red and blue. Eleanor lay still as death. Down in the yard, two county cops had stepped out in the rain. One walked up the steps, meeting the Rigbys as they came out on the porch. The other came up the path to the printshop.

"Judgment day," Eleanor said. "I had a feeling it would be today."

10

"Next case."

"The matter of Eleanor Jane Rigby, Your Honor. Filing number one three seven five nine six."

"Is this the prisoner? . . . are you Eleanor Jane Rigby?"

"Yes, ma'am."

"Do you understand the nature of this proceeding?"

"I think so."

"Let's be sure. This is an extradition hearing, to determine whether you will be returned to the state of New Mexico to face criminal charges outstanding there. Do you understand that?"

"Yes, ma'am."

"You may contest the extradition or waive that right. Do you have an attorney?"

"A public defender, in Taos."

"But here, in Seattle?"

"No, ma'am."

"Would you like to consult with an attorney here?"

"I don't see any point in it."

"You wish to waive that right?"

"Sure . . . might as well."

"Do you understand, Miss Rigby, that commencing any legal proceeding without an attorney is a risky and unwise decision?"

"It won't matter."

"So you wish to go ahead."

"Sure. I just want to get it over with."

"Very well. Mr. Wallace?"

"Yes, Your Honor. All we want to do is get her out of here."

"I can understand that. Do you have the extradition waiver form?"

"Yes, Your Honor."

"Thank you. For the record, I am now handing to the prisoner, Eleanor Jane Rigby, the consent form as required by Revised Code of Washington, title ten dash . . . uh, eighty-nine dash . . ."

"Uh, oh three oh, Your Honor."

"Thank you, Mr. Wallace. Will the prisoner please sign where the bailiff indicates?"

"What happens if I don't sign this?"

"We will hold you here for up to sixty days, New Mexico will make a formal filing of its demand, and there will be a full hearing."

"And in the end I'll go back anyway."

"The court cannot advise you of that, Miss Rigby. That's what an attorney would do."

"Where do I sign? . . . Here?"

"Let the record show that the prisoner is signing the waiver consent form in the presence of the court."

"And at this time I am tending the document to the court for your signature, Your Honor."

"Thank you, Mr. Wallace. The prisoner will be remanded to the King County jail, until such time as the New Mexico authorities send someone to escort her back."

"Your Honor?"

"Was there something else, Mr. Wallace?"

"We'd like to get her out of here tomorrow. We've been informed by New Mexico that they can't send a deputy until at least Tuesday of next week."

"Is that a particular problem?"

"It's a potential problem. Today is what? . . . Thursday. That means she'll be in our custody five days and nights. I know I don't have to remind Your Honor about potential problems with young female prisoners. We don't want another Bender case on our hands."

"Is there a special reason to think we might have such an incident?"

"I understand this prisoner has a history of suicide attempts."

"Is that true, Miss Rigby?"

"I wouldn't call it a history . . . I cut my wrist once."

"Your Honor—"

"I understand, Mr. Wallace. Nobody wants a replay of Bender. What do you suggest?"

"We have a man here to take her back."

"It's New Mexico's responsibility. Will Washington be reimbursed for the costs of such a trip?"

"It won't cost us anything."

"Tell me about it . . . gently, please."

"Shortly after the arrest of the prisoner and her transfer here from East King County, our office was contacted by a Mr. Cliff Janeway of Denver, Colorado, who was sent here to arrest the suspect and escort her back."

"Sent by whom?"

"An agent of the bail bondsman."

The judge closed her eyes. "Mr. Wallace, are you seriously asking me to release this young woman in the care of a bounty hunter?"

"He's not a bounty hunter, Your Honor."

"Please, then . . . what is he?"

"He's a rare-book dealer in Denver. More to the point, he's a former officer of the Denver Police Department with more than fifteen years' experience."

"Is Mr. Janeway in this court?"

"Yes, ma'am."

She motioned with her hand. "Come."

I walked down into the arena.

"You are Mr. Cliff Janeway?"

"Yes, I am."

"And you were engaged, as Mr. Wallace said, to arrest the defendant and return her to New Mexico."

"Yes."

"Do you have papers? . . . Let me see them, please."

"We've checked him out thoroughly, Your Honor. We've talked with a Detective Hennessey at the Denver Police, who was his partner for several years, and to a Mr. Steed, who is chief of detectives. Both gentlemen spoke uncompromisingly of his dedication and character."

"All right, Mr. Wallace, I get the picture. Be quiet a minute and let me read this stuff, will you?"

Silence.

The judge cleared her throat. "Mr. Janeway?"

"Yes, ma'am."

"You were hired by a Mr. Slater of Denver, who was representing the Martin Bailbondsmen of Taos, is that correct?"

"Yes, it is."

She blinked and looked at me through her glasses. "I can't help wondering, sir, how a police detective becomes a dealer in rare books."

"He gets very lucky, Your Honor."

She smiled. "Have you ever done any bounty-hunter work?"

"No, ma'am."

"This is not something you do for a living?"

"Not at all."

"How did you come to accept this case?"

"It was offered to me. Mr. Slater didn't have time to come out of town, and he asked me to come in his place."

"How did you propose to escort Miss Rigby back to New Mexico?"

"By air."

She nodded her approval. Just to be sure, she said, "No three-day trips by automobile?"

"No, ma'am."

"What does New Mexico have to say, Mr. Wallace?"

"Well, naturally they'd love to come get her—you know how those sheriff's boys love to travel. But they understand our problem too."

"They have no objection to Mr. Janeway?"

"They're comfortable with him. One or two of them know him, as a matter of fact."

"What about you, Miss Rigby? Do you have any objection to being escorted by Mr. Janeway?"

"I don't care who takes me."

"We sure don't want to keep her any longer than we have to, Your Honor."

"All right. The prisoner is remanded to the custody of the jailer, who will release her to Mr. Janeway upon presentation of the papers *and* the airline tickets. I hope I'm making myself clear, Mr. Janeway. I'm holding you personally responsible for this prisoner's safe pas-

sage. I'm not interested in any deal you may have made with this . . .
what's his name? . . . Slater, in Denver. You baby-sit this one all the
way into Taos. Are we clear on that?"

"Yes, ma'am."

"Good. Next case."

11

The Rigbys sat in stony silence in the first row of Judge Marla McCoy's court. Archie Moon sat beside Crystal, directly behind the defendant's table. The room was nearly empty beyond the second row: there were a couple of legal eagles—people who drift from court to court, endlessly fascinated by the process—and across the aisle sat a young blond woman with a steno pad. I was surprised to find even that much Seattle interest in the plight of a defendant in a legal action thirteen hundred miles removed.

"I shouldn't even talk to you, you son of a bitch," Crystal said.

I had found them in the cafeteria, eating sandwiches out of a vending machine, and I sat with them and tried to explain how the deceit had begun, how the lie kept growing until the appearance of the cops put an end to it. We got past it quickly. It was my intent they now embraced, and they gripped my hand with the desperation of shipwreck survivors who come upon a lifeboat in choppy, hostile waters. I told them what was going to happen and what I was going to try to do. I would ferry Eleanor into Taos, meet with her lawyer, and see if any mitigating circumstances might be uncovered that would sway the court toward leniency. There had been a time, not too long ago, when I had done such work for a living, and I had been good at it. But I hadn't even heard Eleanor's side of things yet, so I didn't know what was possible.

"I've got to tell you," Crystal said, "we don't have any money to pay you. None at all."

"Call it one I owe you. If I can help in any way, it'll be my pleasure."

Crystal asked if she should try to come to New Mexico. I told her not yet: let me get my feet on the ground and see how the wind was blowing. Gaston Rigby watched us talk, his sad and weary eyes moving from her face to mine. "If it does become a question of money," he said, "you let us know, we'll get it somehow." Archie Moon said he had a little money put aside, enough to get him to Taos if I thought he could do any good. I told him to keep that thought on the back burner and I'd let him know.

Then there was nothing more for them to do but take the long ride home, face a house that would never again seem so empty, and wait out the days and weeks and months for the justice system to do what it would.

For me the case had taken on a kind of inevitable flow. Everything about it felt orchestrated, as if my part in it had been preordained. A woman named Joy Bender had killed herself in the Seattle jailhouse and had named me her chief beneficiary. The Bender case was an ugly one, full of posthumous rape-and-abuse charges. A letter had been left with Bender's mother, who had released it to the press with a raging broadside at the system. In time the Bender letter had been discredited as the work of a sick and angry mind. The mother had written it herself, but the headlines were a cop's worst nightmare for a month. Even now there was widespread public belief that the true facts had been covered up and the mother was being framed to clear the real villains, the jailers and the cops. Things like that do happen, often enough that people retain their disbelief when a case against the cops collapses like a house of cards. So the DA was primed and ready when I walked in and made a case that sounded halfway legit. When I mentioned in passing my real concern that Rigby might harm herself, he was all ears. When I told him she had already tried it once, this hardened man who had seen everything shivered and drew in his wagons. And the overworked and bludgeoned system in Seattle had bent a rule or two and sent New Mexico's problem packing with the fastest reliable messenger—me.

I was still sitting at the table in the cafeteria when a shadow passed over my left shoulder, too close to be moving on by. I looked up and into the face of the young blond woman I had seen taking notes in the courtroom earlier.

"Mr. Janeway."

"Yes, ma'am."

"Trish Aandahl, *Seattle Times*."

I gave her a long, wary look. "This must be a slow news day. I didn't think major metropolitan dailies bothered with simple extradition hearings."

"Nothing about this case is simple, and everything about it interests me. May I sit down?"

She did, without waiting for the invitation. The steno pad was still clutched tight in her left hand.

"Listen," I said. "Before you draw that Bic out of the holster, I don't want to be interviewed, I've got nothing to say."

"May I just ask a couple of questions?"

"You can ask anything you want, but I'm not going to let you put me in print saying something dumb. The fact is, I don't know anything about this case that could possibly be worth your time. And I learned a long time ago that when you don't know anything, the last guy, or gal, you want to see is a reporter."

"You've been burned."

"Basted, baked, and broiled. There was a time when Blackened Janeway was the main lunch course at the Denver Press Club."

She smiled, with just the right touch of regret. She was good, I thought, and that made her dangerous. She made you want to apologize for not being her sacrificial lamb.

"I'm not a hard-ass," I said by way of apology. "I like the press. Most of the reporters I know are fine people, great drinking buddies. I even read newspapers once in a while. But I've lived long enough to know how your game works."

"How does it work?"

"If you quote me accurately, your obligation ends right there, even if I don't know what the hell I'm talking about. My viewpoint gets run through your filter system and I wind up holding the bag."

She flashed a bitter little smile and I took a second, deeper look at her. She was one of those not-quite-rare but uncommon women, a brown-eyed blonde, like the wonderful Irene in Galsworthy's sadly neglected *Forsyte Saga*. Her hair was the color of wheat in September. Her face was pleasantly round without being cherubic: her mouth was full. She was in her thirties, about Rita's age, not beautiful but striking, a face carved by a craftsman who had his own ideas of what beauty was.

Belatedly I recognized her name. "You wrote the book: the Grayson biography."

"I wrote the book," she confessed.

"I should be asking you the questions. You probably know more than I do."

"That may be. That's what I'm trying to find out."

"I keep telling you, I don't know anything. I'm just a friend of the court, delivering a prisoner back to the bar."

"Right," she said with a tweak of sarcastic skepticism. She opened her purse and dropped the steno pad inside it. "Off the record."

"Everything I've got to say I said on the record in open court."

"You didn't say why you're really here and what you're doing."

"It's irrelevant. I'm irrelevant, that's what you need to understand."

"Who is Slater?"

"You're not listening to me."

"There's someone else involved in this. Slater's not just working for a Taos bonding company."

I shrugged and looked at a crack in the ceiling.

"I made some calls after the hearing. You left deep footprints in Denver."

"That's what they said about King Kong. On him it was a compliment. As a gorilla he was hard to beat."

I waited but she missed her cue.

"You were supposed to say, 'That gives you a goal to shoot for.' If we're going to play Wits, the new Parker Brothers game, you've got to be sharp."

She gave me a look of interested amusement.

"We'll put it down to midafternoon sag," I said.

"You are a handful, aren't you? My sources in Denver didn't exaggerate much."

"So who are these people and what are they saying about me?"

"Who they are isn't important. They told me what anybody could get with a few phone calls and a friend or two where it counts."

"Read it back to me. Let's see how good you are."

"You were with DPD almost fifteen years. Exemplary record, actually outstanding until that caper a while back. You have a fine-tuned but romantic sense of justice. It should always work, the good guys should always win. Then the end would never have to justify the means, a cop could always work within the rules and evil would always take the big fall. How am I doing so far?"

"You must be on the right track, you're starting to annoy me."

"You asked for it. Shall I go on?"

"You mean there's more?"

"You have an intense dislike of oppressive procedure. It galled you when the courts let creeps and thugs walk on technicalities. You nailed a guy one time on an end run that cops in Denver still talk about . . . probably illegal but they never stuck you with it. So the guy went up."

"He was a serial rapist, for Christ's sake. He got what he needed."

"You're getting annoyed all over again, aren't you? They told me you would. That case still bothers you, it's the one time you really stepped over the line and let the end justify the means. Your fellow cops remember it with a good deal of admiration, but it rankles you to this day, the way you had to get that guy."

"I sleep just fine. My only regret is that I didn't get the son of a bitch a year earlier, before he started using the knife."

"You're a guy out of time, Janeway. You were a good cop, but you'd've been great fifty years ago, when there weren't any rules."

"There's probably a lot I'd appreciate about life fifty years ago."

"You don't like telephones, televisions, or computers. I'll bet Call Waiting drives you crazy."

"People who load up their lives with crap like that have an inflated sense of their own importance. You might not believe this, but I've never missed an important phone call."

"I do believe it. It's all in the eye of the beholder."

"If it's that important, they always call back." I looked at her hard. "You really are getting on my nerves."

"Good. If I can't get you to talk to me, at least I can ruin your day. If I tell you enough about yourself, maybe you'll understand something."

"And what is that?"

"If you don't talk to me, somebody else will."

"I can't help what other people tell you."

"They tell me you've got this code you live by and you've got it down pat. You see a lot of things in black and white: if you give your word, people can take it to the bank. The problem is, you expect the same thing out of others. You tend to be hard and unforgiving when someone breaks the code. When you come up against a brick wall, your tendency is to go right on through it. You had little finesse when it came to official policy and no patience with politics."

"I can't think of anything offhand that's as evil as politics. It turns good men into bad all the time."

"You spend a lot of your time alone. You trust no one in a pinch as much as you do your own self. You've got such self-confidence that sometimes it strikes others as arrogance. Your reputation as a smart-ass is as high as the Rockies. Richly deserved would be my guess."

"I work on it every day. I hire four people to sit on a panel, test me once a week, and tell me how I'm doing. Lately I've been unable to afford the sex therapist, but you could probably tell that. I don't feel that my day's properly under way unless I've run three miles and verbally abused someone of far less mental dexterity than myself—preferably in public, where the scars of their humiliation will be shattering and damn near impossible to shake off."

She gave a little smile. "Actually, you're a champion of the underdog. The strong never abuse the weak in your presence."

"Now I'm a regular Robin Hood. You'll have to make up your mind."

"You've got quite a name as a fighter. People don't mess with you much."

"Some have."

"But they didn't come back for seconds."

"Not since I killed that blind crippled boy last summer."

She laughed. "You're an American original, aren't you? Listen to me, Janeway. I mean you no harm. I come in friendship and peace."

"That's what Custer said to the Indians."

"You and I are probably a lot alike."

"That's what Sitting Bull said back to Custer."

"And like the Indians and the cavalry, we'd probably end up killing each other. But I'll tell you this, it'll all be up front. I never break my word." She leaned forward and looked me straight in the eyes. Our faces were closer than strangers' ought to be. "Who is Slater?"

I looked at her hard and gave her nothing.

"Maybe it would make a difference if I told you what else I know."

"What's that?"

"That Darryl and Richard Grayson were murdered."

Her sense of timing couldn't have been better: I felt the tingle of her words all the way to my toes. Without taking her eyes from mine, she reached into her bag and took out a card. "Both my numbers are here if you decide you'd like to talk. Anytime, all off the record. If not, have a nice flight to Taos."

She got up and walked out.

12

Who was Slater? The question lingered through the night.

Why was I here?

In my mind I saw him working his scam, dancing his way into my life with that cock-and-bull story about him and me and our brilliant future together. I watched again as he spread open that paper, where someone had written the particulars of Grayson's *Raven* so long ago that it was beginning to fall apart. It wasn't about me, it wasn't about a bounty fee on a skip, it might not even be about Eleanor except in an incidental way. The real stuff had happened long ago, probably before she was born.

But it didn't matter now, did it? I was under a court order, and I had to play according to Hoyle.

I sat up late reading a bad novel. I watched some bad TV. At three o'clock in the morning I sat at my window and looked down into the rainy Seattle street.

But I couldn't forget Trish Aandahl, or that parting shot she had given me.

I called the first travel agency that opened at seven-thirty and told them to get me to Taos with a fellow traveler ASAP. It was a heavy travel day. United had two flights that would put us in Albuquerque early and late that afternoon. From there I could rent a car or hook up with a local airline that would jump us into Taos. But both flights were packed. The agent could squeeze us in, but our seats would be separated by the length of the plane. The next viable flight was a red-eye special, leaving Sea-Tac at 11:18 P.M., arriving in Albuquerque at 2:51 A.M., mountain time. I took the red-eye, told the agent to deliver the tickets to the Hilton, and put the tariff on my charge card. The tickets were $800 each, typical airline piracy for last-minute bookings. I sucked it up and hoped to God I could get some of it back from the good people of New Mexico.

Then I called Slater and got my first surprise of a long and surprising day.

"Mr. Slater's not available," said his woman in Denver.

"When will he be available?"

"I'm not sure. He will be calling in. Who is this, please?"

"My name's Janeway. I've been working a case for him. Something's come up and I need to talk to him."

I heard her shuffling through some papers. "I'm afraid I don't know you."

"Then I must not exist. I'll bet if you tell him I'm here, though, he'll talk to me anyway."

I heard a spinning sound, like a roulette wheel in Vegas. "Everyone who works for us is in this Rolodex. Your name's not here."

"Then it's Slater's loss. Give him a message, tell him I tried."

"Wait a minute."

I heard her talking to someone, but her hand had covered the phone and I couldn't make out the words.

"I could maybe have him call you back."

"Won't work. I'm heading out in about five minutes."

"Hold, please." She punched the hold button: elevator music filled my ear.

There was a click. Another woman said, "Mr. Janeway? . . . I'm sorry for the hassle. It's just that we don't know you and Mr. Slater's out of town."

"How could he be out of town? He hired me because he didn't have time to go out of town. Where's he gone?"

"I'm not at liberty to discuss that. I guess I'll have to take a message."

"Tell him Janeway called, I've got the girl, and I'm taking her on to Taos myself."

"Is that what he wanted you to do?"

"It doesn't matter what he wanted me to do. Tell him I'm not working for him anymore."

* * *

I sat on my bed feeling the first faint gnawing of a mighty hunch.

I placed another call to Denver.

"U.S. West."

"Howard Farrell, please."

I listened to the click of a connection, then a woman's voice said, "Mr. Farrell's office."

"Mr. Farrell, please."

"May I say who's calling?"

"Cliff Janeway."

Another click, followed by the familiar resonance of an old and confidential source.

"Hey, Cliff! Where the hell've you been?"

"Cruising down the river, you old son of a bitch."

"Jesus, I haven't heard your voice for what? . . . seems like a year now."

"More like two. So how're things at the good old phone company?"

"Same old shit."

"Howard, you need to start breaking in a new act. But then what would guys like me do when they need a favor out of old Ma Bell?"

"Uh-oh. You're not official anymore, are you?"

"Is that a problem?"

"Damn right it is. Just for old times' sake, what do you want?"

"Clydell Slater."

"My favorite cop. He still playing smashmouth with Denver's finest?"

"He does it on his own now."

"What an asshole. Look, Cliff . . . this isn't likely to cause Mr. Slater any grief, is it?"

"It might pinch his balls a little."

"Then I'll do it. Same ground rules as always. Give me a number, I'll call you right back."

Five minutes later Farrell called and, for my ears only, gave me Slater's home number.

I placed the call.

It was answered by a recording, a woman's voice. "Hi, this's Tina. Me 'n' Clyde are out now. We'll call ya back."

I hung up on the beep.

*   *   *

I lingered over breakfast in a downtown café. Read the high points in last night's *Times*. Looked for her byline but it wasn't there. Drank my third cup of coffee over the local homicide page.

Went back to the hotel. Took a shower and went upstairs to the lobby. My tickets had arrived. I slipped them into my inside jacket pocket with my court papers and went to the jail to see Eleanor.

It was still early, well before ten. They led her in and we sat with glass between us, talking through a bitch box.

"How're you doing?" I said.

"Just wonderful."

"I wanted to see you and say a few things."

"You don't have to."

"What are you now, a mind reader?"

"I know what you're gonna say, I can see it in your eyes. I know you're bothered by all this. Don't be . . . you don't owe me a thing."

"In a cold-blooded, dog-eat-dog world, that would be one way to look at it."

"Well, isn't that what it is?"

"Only sometimes."

"I'll bet this was your big failing as a cop. People can look in your face and see what's in your heart."

"Would you believe nobody's ever said that to me? . . . Not once. In some circles I'm known as a helluva poker player, impossible to read."

"Amazing."

We looked at each other.

"If you're waiting for absolution, you already have it," she said. "You were doing a job. You've got a strange way of doing it, but I've got no kick coming. If it makes you feel better, you've got my unqualified permission to deliver me up and get on with your life, forget I ever existed."

"That's not going to happen, Eleanor. That's one promise I'm making you."

"What can you do, tell me that . . .what can you do?"

"I don't know. Did you do the burglary?"

"Yes, I did. So there you are."

"Why did you do it?"

"Personal reasons."

"Did you take a gun into the house?"

"Does it matter?"

"Does it matter? Hell, yes, it matters. It can be the difference between a first-time offender asking for probation and a gun moll doing heavy time."

She didn't say anything.

"You said something back in the restaurant when we were talking about your stalker. The subject of a gun came up. Do you remember what you said?"

She looked at me through the glass. "I've never fired a gun in my life."

"Did the cops do a gunshot residue test?"

"I don't even know what that is."

"So I'll ask you again. Did you take a gun into that house?"

"No. Believe it or not."

"Okay, I believe it. Did you get a gun while you were in the house, maybe from the guy's gun rack? Was it you that did the shooting?"

"I never shot at anyone. I was the one shot at. I'm lucky to be alive."

"If we can prove that, you've got a fighting chance. You were still wrong to be there. You broke in, they had every right to shoot at you. But almost any judge would wonder why they'd lie about it."

"I guess they want me to go to jail."

"For a long time, apparently." I leaned closer to the glass. "I'd still like to know why you broke in, what you were looking for."

"Maybe I'll tell you sometime. But not today; I don't think I know you well enough to get into the wired-up hell of my life with you. When do we leave?"

"Late tonight. I'll come for you around seven-thirty."

"Lots of dead time for you to fill. What'll you do, hit the bookstores?"

"Maybe."

"That's the only part of this that really surprises me. I never had a hint you were a book dealer. You played that card very well."

I tried to smile at her. "I'd better go." But something powerful held me there. Then, so quickly that I didn't know how it happened, I stepped off the straight and narrow for the first time that day. I stepped all the way off and said something that could never be unsaid.

"How'd you like to get out of here? . . . go with me? . . . be my guide through the Seattle book jungle?"

She looked like a person half-drowned who had suddenly been brought back to life. "Can you do that?"

"Probably not. The jailer will look at my tickets and wonder what the hell I'm doing taking you out ten hours early. The judge'll schedule a new hearing, I'll get drawn and quartered, and you'll end up riding back to Taos handcuffed to a deputy."

I shrugged. "We could try."

She reached out as if to touch my face. Her fingertips flattened against the glass.

"You've got to promise to behave." I felt a sudden desperation, as if I'd taken a long step into the dark. "I'm taking a big chance, Eleanor. It's my responsibility now. I'll take the chance because I like you. I owe you one for the big lie. And it just occurs to me that you'd probably rather spend the day in bookstores than chained by your neck to the wall of some crummy jail cell. But you've got to behave."

"Absolutely. Who wouldn't love a deal like that?"

The jailer gave our tickets a cursory glance. He looked at my papers, read the judge's order, and at half past ten Eleanor Rigby and I walked out into a drippy Seattle day.

13

It was a day of magic. The two of us were charmed: Seattle was our oyster and every stop coughed up a pearl. She took me to a place called Gregor Books on Southwest California Avenue. The books were crisp and fine and there were lots of high-end goodies. You don't steal books out of a store like that—the owner is far too savvy ever to get caught sleeping on a live one, but Rita McKinley's words echoed in my ear. *You can double the price on anything if it's fine enough.* Gregor had the finest copy of *Smoky* I had ever seen. Signed Will James material is becoming scarce, and James had not only signed it but had drawn an original sketch on the half title. Gregor was asking $600, $480 after my dealer's discount. I took it, figuring I could push it to $800 or more on the sketch and the world's-best-copy assertion. I figured James was a hotter property in the real West, Colorado, than here in Seattle, and when the day came for me to go in the ground, I could rest just fine if they threw this book in the hole with me. Speaking of dying, Gregor had a dandy copy of *If I Die in a Combat Zone*, Tim O'Brien's 1973 novel of the Vietnam War. He had marked it $450, but I was making his day and he bumped my discount to 25 percent for both items. I took it: the O'Brien is so damn scarce that I thought it was overdue for another price jump, and I left the store poorer but happier. Eleanor directed me downtown. We stopped at the Seattle Book Center, a lovely store on Second Avenue with half a dozen rooms on two floors. I bought a Zane Grey *Thundering Herd* in an immaculate 1919 dust jacket for $160. I was flying high now. There were books everywhere we looked, and even if the Seattle boys weren't giving them away, I saw decent margin in almost everything I touched. "This is one of those days, isn't it?" Eleanor said. "I'll bet if you went back there and flushed the toilet, books would come pouring out." We went to a mystery specialist called Spade and Archer. It was in a bank building downtown, in a fifth-floor office that old Sam Spade himself might have occupied in the thirties. The owner was a young blond woman whose credo seemed to be "keep 'em moving." She had two of the three Edgar Box mysteries at a hundred apiece, cost to me, and I took them, figuring they'd be good $200 items in the catalog I was planning. As mysteries they're just fair. But Gore Vidal had written them, hiding behind the Edgar Box moniker when he was starting out in the early fifties, and there's always somebody for a curiosity like that.

In another store I fingered a sharp copy of *White Fang,* amazed that the asking price was just $75. Eleanor warned me off with a look. In the car she said, "It was a second state, that's why it was so cheap." I felt like amateur night in Harlem, but I asked her anyway, what was the point of it, and this kid, this child, gave me another lesson in fly-by-your-pants bookscouting.

"There was a mistake on the title page. Macmillan just sliced it out and glued a new one on the cancel stub. . . . You look perplexed, Mr. Janeway, like a man who's never heard the terminology. You don't know what a cancel stub is. . . . How long have you been in the business?"

"Long enough to know a lot about a few things and damn little about most of it."

"Well, this kind of thing happened a lot in the old days. The publisher would make a mistake in a line or word, but by the time they noticed it, ten thousand copies had been printed and maybe five thousand had been distributed. If it was an important author, like Jack London, they didn't want to release any more with the mistake, but they didn't want to redo all those books either. So Macmillan printed a new title page, in the case of *White Fang,* then they sliced out the old ones on all those flawed copies and just glued the new one right onto the stub."

"They just tipped it in."

"Sure. Labor was cheap then, and even those factory grunts could do a decent job of it. The average book collector won't even see it, but a bookman can't miss it unless it's done with real finesse. Just look down in the gutter and there it is, like a man who had an arm cut off and sewn back on again. Doran did the same thing with one of Winston Churchill's early books, *My African Journey*. They bought the remainder from the British publisher and just slashed out the title page and put in their own on the cancel stub. That's why the first American edition comes in a British casing, with Hodder and Stoughton on the spine and a tipped-in Doran title page. It was one of Doran's first books, and he was lowballing to save money."

"Oh," I said lamely.

We stopped for lunch. I wanted to talk about her case but she wouldn't get into it: it would only screw up an otherwise pleasant day, she said. We drifted back toward the Kingdome. Her car was gone: her father had picked it up for her and had it towed to a gas station a few blocks away. We drove past and saw it there in the lot. We were in the neighborhood anyway, so we stopped in the big Goodwill store on Dearborn. I don't do thrift stores much anymore—usually they are run by idiots who think they are book dealers, without a lick of experience or a grain of knowledge to back them up. In Denver the Goodwills have become laughingstocks among dealers and scouts. They have their silly little antique rooms where they put everything that looks old—every ratty, worn-out never-was that ever came out of the publishing industry. They mark their prices in ink, destroying any value the thing might have, and when you try to tell them that, they stare at you with dull eyes and say they've got to do it that way. The store in Seattle didn't ink its books to death, but it didn't matter—they had the same mentality when it came to pricing. The shelves were clogged with common, crummy books, some still available on Walden remainder tables for two dollars, marked six and seven in this so-called thrift store. Naturally, they missed the one good book. Eleanor found it as she browsed one side while I worked the other. She peeked around the corner with that sad-little-girl-oh-so-lost look on her face. "'Scuse me, sir, could you loan me a dollar? . . . My family's destitute, my daddy broke his leg, my little brother's got muscular dystrophy, and my mamma's about to sell her virtue on First Avenue." I made a convulsive grab at my wallet. "Damn, you *are* good!" I said with forced admiration. "You're breaking my damn heart." She grinned with all her teeth and held up a fine first of Robert Traver's wonderful *Anatomy of a Murder*. It was a nice scarce little piece, worth at least $100, I guessed: a good sleeper because the Book of the Month edition is exactly the same size and shape and so prolific that even real bookpeople won't bother to pick it up and look. Goodwill wanted $4 for it. She paid with my dollar and her nickels and dimes, then haggled with me in the parking lot: "Gregor would give me at least forty for this, and I'm waiting breathlessly to see if you're inclined to do the honorable thing." I gave her forty-five, but made a point of getting my dollar back, and we both enjoyed my good-natured grumbling for the next half hour.

After wading through the dreck, it was good to be back in a real bookstore again. In a place downtown, she spent most of her money on a miniature book, a suede-leather copy of Shakespeare no larger than the tip of her thumb. "I'm really a sucker for these things," she said. "I'll buy them if there's the least bit of margin." I knew almost nothing about the miniature-book trade, only that, like every other specialty, it has its high spots that are coveted and cherished. Eleanor filled me in as we drove. "This was published by David Bryce in Glasgow around the turn of the century. Bryce did lots of miniatures, some of them quite special. I once had a Bryce's dictionary, which they called the smallest dictionary in the world. It was only about an inch square and it had about four hundred pages, with a little metal slipcase and a foldout magnifying glass. You could carry it on a key ring."

I held the Shakespeare between my thumb and forefinger. "You think there's any margin in this?"

"I don't care, I didn't buy it to get rich. Maybe I could double up wholesale, but I think I'll keep it for a while as a memento of this day. It'll be my good-luck piece. I think I'll need one, don't you?"

Bookscouting gives you the same kind of thrills as gambling. You flirt with the Lady in much the same way. You get hot and the books won't stop coming: you get cold and you might as well be playing pinochle with your mother-in-law. I was hot, and when Luck is running, she flaunts all the odds of circumstance and coincidence. I found two early-fifties Hopalong Cassidy books by a guy Eleanor had never heard of, some cowboy named Tex Burns. I savored the pleasure of telling her that Tex Burns was like Edgar Box, a moniker . . . in another lifetime he had been a young man named Louis L'Amour. Amazing to find two such in a single day, but I take Luck where I find her. These cost me $4 each and were worth around $250. I razzed Eleanor for not knowing. We headed north and I said, for at least the fifth time, "I thought *everybody* knew about Tex Burns." She crossed her eyes and looked down her nose at me, a perfect picture of rank stupidity.

It was the damnedest day, full of sorrow and joy and undercut with that sweet slice of tension. I'll blink and she'll be gone, I thought at least a dozen times: I'll turn my head for a second and when I look up, she'll be two blocks away, running like hell. But I had set my course and the day was waning, and still there had been nothing between us but the most cheerful camaraderie. Out of the blue, in midafternoon, she said, "I guess it's a good thing you turned into an asshole when you did: I may've been on the verge of falling in love with you and then where would we be?" Coming from nowhere like that, it put me on the floor. It also brought to a critical point a problem I had failed to consider—I had to pee in the worst possible way. I told her to stay put, disappeared into the rest room, and found her still there, working the shelves, when I came hustling out a minute later. I didn't worry much about her after that.

She took me to a place near the university called Half Price Books. It nestled modestly on a street named Roosevelt Way, a cornucopia of books on two floors. There were no real high spots, but I could've spent two hundred on stock, it was that kind of place. I bought only what I couldn't leave and got out for less than eighty. We were going out the door when Eleanor spied a copy of Trish Aandahl's book on the Graysons. "You oughta buy this," she said. "It's a helluva read."

She was a little curious at how fast I did buy it. I still hadn't told her about my interest in Grayson and probably wouldn't now until we were on the airplane and well away from here. "You drive," I said, throwing her the keys. "I want to fondle my stuff." But all I did as she wove through the crowded, narrow streets was browse through Aandahl. The jacket was an art deco design, with elegant curlicues and old-style fringe decorations. It was dominated by black-and-white photographs of the Grayson brothers, a little out of focus and solving none of the mystery of the men. The art director had overlapped the pictures and then pulled them apart, leaving parts of each infringed upon the other, the ragged gulf between them suggesting disruption and conflict. The title, *Crossfire,* stood out in red: under it, in black, the subtitle, *The Tragedies and Triumphs of Darryl and Richard Grayson.* Richard's resemblance to Leslie Howard was more real than imagined: Darryl Grayson's image was darker, fuzzier, barely distinguishable. His was the face on the barroom floor, and not because it had been painted there. The jacket blurb on Trish Aandahl consisted of one line, that the author was a reporter for the *Seattle Times,* and there was no photograph. If the lady wasn't interested in personal glory, she'd be the first reporter I had ever known who felt that way. I thumbed the index: my eye caught the name of Allan Huggins, the Grayson bibliographer, mentioned half a dozen times in the text. Gaston Rigby made his appearance on page 535, and there were three mentions of Crystal Moon Rigby. Archie Moon was prominent, entering the Grayson saga on page 15 and appearing prolifically thereafter. A section of photographs showed some of Grayson's books, but, strangely, the only photographs of the subjects themselves were the same two of poor quality that had been used on the jacket. It was 735 pages thick, almost as big as the Huggins bibliography, and packed with what looked to be anecdotal writing at its best.

The only negative was that it was a remainder copy, savagely slashed across the top pages with a felt-tip marker. I hated that: it's a terrible way to remainder books, and Viking is the worst offender in the publishing industry. "Look at this," I griped. "These bastards must hire morons right off the street with a spray can. I can't believe they'd do that to a book."

"It's just merchandise to them," she said. "Nobody cares, only freaks like you and me. It is a fine-looking book, except for the remainder mark."

"I saw a woman once who would've been a beauty queen, if you could just forget the fact that somebody had shot her in the face with a forty-five."

We were stopped at a red light about a block from the freeway. She was looking at me in a different way now, as if I had suddenly revealed a facet of my character that she had been unable to guess before. "Are you interested in the Graysons? If you are, I know a guy who used to have the best collection of Grayson books in the universe. Maybe he's still got a few of them. His store's not far from here."

"I think we've got time for that. Lead on."

Otto Murdock was an old-time Seattle book dealer who had seen better days. Twenty years of hard drinking had reduced him to this— a shabby-looking storefront in a ramshackle building in a run-down section on the north side. "This man used to be Seattle's finest," Eleanor said, "till bad habits did him in. For a long time he was part-ners with Gregory Morrice. You ever hear of Morrice and Murdock?"

"Should I have?"

"If Seattle ever had an answer to Pepper and Stern, they were it. Only the best of the best, you know what I mean? But they had a falling-out years ago over Otto's drinking. Morrice does it alone now—he's got a book showplace down in Pioneer Square, and Otto wound up here. I hear he ekes out a living, but it can't be much . . . he wholesales all his good stuff. They call him In-and-Out Murdock now. A good book means nothing but another bottle to him."

She pulled to the curb at the door of the grimiest bookstore I had seen in a long time. The windows were caked with dirt. Inside, I could see the ghostly outlines of hundreds of books, stacked ends-out against the glass. The lettering on the hand-painted sign had begun to flake, leaving what had once said BOOKS now reading BOO. The interior was dark and getting darker by the moment. It was a quarter to five, and already night was coming. A block away, a streetlight flicked on.

"He looks closed for the night," I said.

"He's still got his OPEN sign out."

I knew that didn't mean much, especially with an alcoholic who might not know at any given time what year it was. We sat at the curb and the rain was a steady hum.

"I'll check him out," Eleanor said. "No sense both of us getting wet."

She jumped out and ran to the door. It pushed open at her touch and she waved to me as she went inside. I came along behind her, walking into a veritable cave of books. There were no lights: it was even darker inside than it had looked from the street, and for a moment I couldn't see Eleanor at all. Then I heard her voice: "Mr. Murdock . . . Mr. Murdock . . . hey, Otto, you've got customers out here." She opened a door and a dim beam of light fell out of a back room. "Mr. Murdock?" she said softly.

I saw her in silhouette, moving toward me. "That's funny," she said. "Looks like he went away and left the store wide open."

I groped along the wall and found a switch. It was dim even with the lights on. I took my first long look at how the mighty could fall. Murdock had tumbled all the way down, hitting rock bottom in a rat's nest of cheap, worn, and tattered books. His bookshelves had long since filled to overflowing, and the floor was his catchall. Books were piled everywhere. The piles grew until they collapsed, leaving the books scattered where they fell, with new piles to grow from the rubble like a forest after a fire. I walked along the back wall, looking for anything of value. It was tough work—the fiction section was almost uniformly book-club editions of authors who aren't collected anyway: Sidney Sheldon, Robert Wilder, Arthur Hailey. A sign thumbtacked to the wall said BOOKS FOR A BUCK. Cheap at half the price, I thought.

"You see anything?" Eleanor asked from the far corner.

"Four computer books, two copies of *The Joy of Sex,* and five million Stephen King derivatives."

She sighed. "Put 'em all together and what've you got?"

"Desktop breeding by vampires."

She gave a sharp laugh, tinged with sadness. "This place gets worse every time I come here. I'm afraid I'm wasting your time; it looks like Otto hasn't had a good book in at least a year."

You never knew, though. This was the great thing about books, that in any pile of dreck a rose might hide, and we were drawn on through the junk in the search for the one good piece. I had worked my way around the edge of the front room and had reached the door to the back when I heard Eleanor say, "Good grief, look at this." She had dropped to her hands and knees, out of sight from where I stood. I asked what she had and she said, "You'll have to come look, you'll never believe it." I found her near the door, holding a near-perfect copy of *The Fountainhead.*

"It's a whole bag of stuff," she said. "All Ayn Rand, all in this condition."

There were two *Fountainhead* firsts, both binding states, red and green, in those lovely crisp red jackets. There was an *Atlas Shrugged,* signed *Ayn* in old ink and inscribed with endearment as if to an old friend. Finally there was the freshest copy of *We the Living* that I ever hoped to see in this lifetime. A Rand specialist had once told me that there were probably only a few hundred jacketed copies of *We the Living* in existence.

Six, seven grand retail, I thought. Sitting by the door in an open bag, in an unattended store.

"It doesn't make much sense, does it?" Eleanor said.

I shook my head.

"If the door blew open, they'd get screwed by the rain in a minute," she said. "Jesus, Otto must've really lost it."

"Look, you know this guy—do you think he's so far gone that he wouldn't know what he could get for these?"

"I doubt that. Otto might not know about the new guys—the Graftons, Paretskys, Burkes—but he'd sure as hell know about Ayn Rand."

We stood there for a minute and touched them.

"What're you gonna do?" Eleanor said.

"Damned if I know. I'm dying to buy these from him."

"What would you offer him?"

I pondered it. "Three grand. Thirty-five hundred if I had to."

"You could get them for less than that. There are some guys in this town who'd pay him that kind of money, but Otto's burned his bridges here. I'll bet you could get 'em for two."

"I'd give him three in a heartbeat."

"Take 'em, then. Leave him a note, make him an offer like that, and you'll be doing him the biggest favor of the year. Tell him you'll send the books back if he doesn't like it. I guarantee you you're doing him a favor, because nine out of ten people would come in here and see those books and take 'em and run like hell. You know that's true. Take 'em and leave him a note."

"That's probably against the law," I said, but I knew it probably wasn't. In most states, theft requires evil intent.

I put the books back in the bag, folded the top over carefully, and tucked it under my arm. "What's in the back room?"

"Just more of the same," she said.

We went on back. The room was cluttered with books and trash. In a corner was an ancient rolltop desk half-buried in junk books and old magazines.

"I see he still reads the *AB*," I said.

"That's probably how he sells most of his books." Eleanor looked along the shelves behind the desk. She held up a thin canvas bag. "Here's his briefcase. He never goes anywhere without this. In the old days, when he and Morrice were top dogs, you'd see him at book fairs and stuff, and he'd always have his two or three best pieces in this book bag. It was his trademark: if he liked you, you'd get to look in the bag; if he didn't, you wouldn't."

She fiddled with the straps. "Wanna look?"

"I wouldn't do that."

Reluctantly, she pushed the bag back to the corner of the desk. "He probably hasn't used it in ten years, except to carry a bottle around." She sighed. "Not a Grayson book in sight. So much for my good intentions."

"That looks like another door over there." I walked across the room and opened it.

A set of steps disappeared into the dark upper floor.

"Try calling him again," Eleanor said.

I cupped my hands to my mouth and shouted Murdock's name up the stairwell.

"He's just not here," she said.

"I don't know. Something's not right." I moved into the stairwell.

"Don't go up there. That's how people get blown away."

I turned and looked at her.

"Otto's got a gun. I saw it once when I was here last year."

"Good argument." I backed away from the stairs.

"He's gotta be up there sleeping one off. He'll wake up in a panic over those books, come running down the stairs, and when he finds your note, he'll be so relieved he'll drop dead right there on the spot."

I wavered.

"Goddammit, take the books," she said. "Don't be a fool."

She's right, I thought. I went back and sat at Otto's desk, pulled out a sheet of paper, and wrote out my offer. I made it three thousand and signed it with both my Denver phone numbers, then taped it to his canvas bag where he'd be sure to find it.

In the car we sat fondling the merchandise, lost in that rapture that comes too seldom these days, even in the book business.

It was just six o'clock when I happened to glance in the mirror and saw Pruitt watching from the far corner.

14

He appeared like a single frame in a set of flash cards. You blink and he's gone, and you're not quite sure he was ever there at all. I was as sure as I needed to be: I was suddenly tense, keyed up, and ready to fight. We headed down to the Hilton. I was driving now, handling the freeway traffic with one eye on my mirror. If he was on my tail as I swung into town, I didn't see him. He was a magician, good enough to make you doubt your eyes. The invisible man, Slater had called him, the best tail in the business, and he wasn't keeping after me because he liked my looks. *Who is Slater?* The voice of Trish Aandahl played in my head. I had a hunch I was about to find out who Slater was and what he wanted. He had just five hours to break the stalemate: if Pruitt didn't play Slater's hand by then, we'd be in the air and it would all be academic.

I parked in the hotel garage and took Eleanor to my room. I poured us drinks, cutting hers slightly with water. She asked if she could use the shower and I said sure. I sat on the bed at the telephone, happy for a few minutes alone.

I punched up Slater's number in Denver.

A woman answered. "Yeah?"

The lovely Tina, no doubt.

I tried to sound like someone from their social set, a cross between George Foreman and Bugs Moran: "I need Slater."

"So who're you?"

"I'm the man with the money."

"I'm not followin' ya, Jack."

"Just put Slater on the phone, he'll be glad you did. Tell him it's the man with the money."

"Clyde's not here."

"So where's he at?"

"What's it about?"

"It's about a bagful of money, sweetheart, and I'll tell ya what, if I don't get to give it to him pretty damn quick, I'm out of here. Slater can fly to Jacksonville and pick it up himself."

"I don't know anything about this."

"That's how you want to keep it, hon. Let's just say Slater did a little job for me and this is the bonus I promised him."

"Well, damn."

"Oh, let's not agonize over it. If you don't wanna tell me where the man is, it's no skin off my nose."

She was breathing in my ear. "Is it . . ."

I waited.

". . . is it a *lot* of money?"

I couldn't help laughing: I had played her just right. "Let's say there's a good reason he wanted it in cash."

"Wait a minute, I'll give ya a number."

I could hear her fumbling around. "Call him at area code two oh six. It's six two four, oh five hundred. Ask for seventeen twelve."

I sat staring at the phone. Slowly I straightened up and looked at the far wall.

Slater was in the room next door.

And I knew I might as well have him in my lap.

Eleanor came out of the bathroom in a swirl of steam. She sat at the mirror sipping her drink and combing out her incredible hair. I thought she was lovely, alive with the sparkle of youth in spite of her trouble. She wanted to talk. Our short mutual history was the topic of the moment, to which was added her general assessment that we were a damned exceptional book-hunting team. "Today was special," she said, "a real toot." I looked at the far wall, where Slater was, and told her the pleasure was all mine. To her way of thinking, it was the perfect day, one she'd remember: "This is how I'd live my life, every day of the year, if I had my way. A loaf of bread, a jug of wine, some good books . . ."

She looked at me with open affection in the glass. "And you."

She tugged at a place where her hair had knotted up. "We

wouldn't even need much money," she said. "Money just takes the edge off. You need to be a little hungry to get that rush that comes with finding a really good one."

Again she amazed me, this kid barely out of her teens.

"It's not having money that keeps you on your toes," she said, meeting my eyes in the mirror.

I told her we were probably the most on-our-toes pair since Ginger Rogers and Fred Astaire, and she laughed. "Why couldn't I've found you a year ago," she mused. "Why-o-why-o-why?"

"It wouldn't've done much good," I said absently, "since we've already got it well established that I'm old enough to be your father."

She scoffed at this. "Yeah, if you'd started hiking up skirts when you were thirteen, maybe." She looked at me in the mirror and said, blushing fiercely, "You're probably not up to a little seduction right now, I'll bet."

I thought long and hard about how to respond, the words to use. The ones I picked were clumsy and inadequate. "Under the circumstances, you know, this is not the best idea you've had all day."

"Well, it was just a thought."

I told her it was a lovely thought, I was flattered. In another time, maybe . . . in another place . . .

"In another life," she said, closing the book on it.

I decided to hang out here until just before our flight left. The certainty of Slater's listening in on us I accepted as the lesser of two evils: here I could keep my back to the wall until the last possible moment. I looked at the wall but it told me nothing. I knew what I needed to know. Detectives today can punch a hole the size of a pin through a concrete wall, run a wire into a bed with a cheating housewife, record her ecstasy with the other guy in eight-track stereo, and add a Michael Jackson sound track for the entertainment of the office staff. I told Eleanor none of this: no sense waving a red flag just yet. I called out and ordered a pizza delivered. She kept up a running chatter while we ate—her way, I guessed, of relieving her own building tension. She talked about all the great books she had found that had been screwed up by one anal-obsessive chucklehead or another. I laughed as only a fellow traveler can: I too knew that peculiar heartache. You find a grand copy of an old Ross Macdonald and open it to see that some fool has written all over it, destroying half its value and all of its factory-fresh desirability. Why is a book the only gift that the giver feels free and often compelled to deface before giving? Who would give a shirt or a blouse and write, in ink, *Happy birthday from Bozo* all over the front of it? Even worse than the scribblers, Eleanor said, were the name embossers. "When I become the queen of hell, I'm going to parade all those embosser freaks past me in a long naked line. I'll have an embosser with the word IDIOT on it, smothered in hot coals, and I'll emboss *them,* sir, in the tenderest place that *you* can imagine." That punishment sounded pretty sexist to me, which was exactly her point. "Have you ever seen an embosser mark with a woman's name on it . . . ever?" I had, but only once and it probably didn't count—a sadistic dominatrix whose murder I had investigated long ago. "Women write in the spirit of giving," Eleanor said. "Men emboss like they're branding cattle, to possess." For the books, we sadly agreed, the result was the same.

I hoped Slater was getting an earful. I looked at the clock: the plane took off in three hours, I was almost home free. The day was ending on a wave of nickel-and-dime book stuff. I asked her to define anal-obsessive chucklehead, please, and tell me how that particular characteristic expresses itself. She laughed and slapped my hand and said, "Get out of here, you damn fool," and the night wound down. We drank a toast to the defilers of good books—scribblers, embossers, and the remainder goons at the Viking Press—may their conversion to the cause be swift and permanent. At eight-thirty she asked if she could mail a letter. She sat at the table and scratched out a few lines on hotel stationery: then she turned away, shielding the letter with her body so I couldn't see it. I knew she had taken something out of her purse and dropped it in the envelope with the letter. I was riddled with second thoughts, but there wasn't anything to be done about it: I could either be her jailer or her friend. She licked the envelope, sealed it, and called for a bellhop to mail it. And I sat mute, her friend, and watched it disappear.

I was a bit curt with her after that. She asked when we should leave and I told her not to worry about it, I'd let her know. I had decided to linger here until exactly seventy minutes before takeoff, then haul ass for Sea-Tac in a cloud of smoke. I hoped the TV would cover our sud-

den retreat. I'd let Slater listen to the *Tonight Show* until reality began
to dawn: if I was lucky, we'd be halfway to the airport before he knew
it. Out on the street I'd have only Pruitt to deal with.

Duck soup, I thought, an even-money standoff.

I always bet on me with odds like that. I had forgotten that line
from Burns about the best-laid schemes of mice and men. I should
read more poetry.

15

At 9:35 the telephone rang. We looked at each other and neither of us moved. I let it ring and after a while it stopped. Now we'd see, I thought: if it had been a test, somebody would be over to see if we were still here.

At 9:43 it rang again. By then I had rethought the strategy of silence, and I picked it up.

"It's me." Slater's voice sounded puffy, distant.

"So it is," I said flatly, with a faint W. C. Fields undertone.

"We need to talk."

"Send me a telegram."

"Don't get cute, Janeway, your time's running out."

I gave a doubtful grunt.

"We need to talk now. I'm doing you a favor if you've got the sense to listen."

I listened.

"Come out in the hall."

"Yeah, right."

"I'm in the room next door." His voice was raspy, urgent. "I need you to come out in the hall so we can talk."

Then I got a break I couldn't have bought. Eleanor got up and went to the bathroom.

"You must think I was born yesterday," I said as soon as she closed the door.

"This is on the level. I know you're on the eleven-eighteen. I'm giving you fair warning, you're never gonna make it."

"Try and stop me and you're a dead man, Slater. That's fair warning for both of you."

"It's not me that's gonna stop you, stupid. Goddammit, are you coming out or not?"

I thought about it for five seconds. "Yeah." I hung up.

I opened my bag and got out my gun. Strapped it on under my coat and waited till Eleanor came out of the bathroom.

"Just a little problem with my bill, no big deal," I told her. "I've got to go upstairs and straighten it out. You sit right there, we'll leave as soon as I get back."

She didn't say anything but I could see she wasn't buying it. She sat where I told her and clasped her hands primly in her lap, her face a mask of sudden tension.

I opened the door and eased my way out into the hall. I had my thumb hooked over my belt, two inches from the gun.

Slater was down at the end of the hall, looking at the wall. I pulled the door shut and he turned. I think I was ready for anything but what I saw. His face had been beaten into watermelon. His left eye was battered shut, his nose pounded flat against his face. His right eye was open wide, a grotesque effect like something from an old Lon Chaney film.

"What happened to you?"

I had flattened against the wall so I could see both ways. Slater came toward me, shuffling in pain. His leg was stiff and he held his arm in a frozen crook, suspended as if by an invisible sling.

"Pruitt," he rasped, livid. "Fucking bastard Pruitt."

I just looked at him, unable to imagine what might have gone down between them. He came closer and I saw what had caused that puffiness in his voice. His dentures were gone—smashed, I guessed, along with the rest of him—and he talked like a toothless old man.

"Goddammit, I'll rip that fucker's guts out."

"What happened?" I said again.

"Bastard son of a bitch sapped me, damn near took my head off. I went down and he did the rest of it with his feet."

He did it well, I thought.

"He'll pay, though, he'll pay for this in ways I haven't even thought up yet. Even if he doesn't know it was me, I'll know, and that'll be enough." He took a little step to the side and held on to the wall for support. "And it starts today. I'm gonna tell you something, Janeway, and then it's your baby. Pruitt will kill you if he has to."

"He should play the lottery, his odds are better."

"Don't you underestimate that fucker, that's what I'm telling you."

"I'm reading that. Now why don't you tell me what he wants."

"The book, stupid, haven't you figured that out yet? He's been after it for years."

"Tell me something real. Grayson couldn't make a book worth this much trouble if he used uncut sheets of thousand-dollar bills for endpapers."

"That's what you think. Forget what you thought you knew and maybe you'll learn something. Your little friend in there's got the answer, and Pruitt's gonna take her away from you and get it out of her if he's got to tear out her fingernails."

"Say something that makes sense. Pruitt had her and you two handed her to me. Now he's ready to kill me to get her back?"

He started to say something but a click in the hall brought him up short. We both tensed. I gripped the gun under my coat.

The door swung in and Eleanor peeped into the hall.

She didn't say anything. She was looking past me, at Slater, and he was looking at her. Her face was ashen, her eyes wide with fright.

"Eleanor," I said, "go back in the room and sit down."

She backed away and closed the door.

"She knows you," I said to Slater. "She recognized you just then."

He tried to move past me. I stepped out and blocked his way.

"What do you want from me, Janeway? I'm doing you a favor here, maybe you should remember that. I didn't have to tell you anything."

"You haven't told me anything yet. Pick up where you left off. Make it make sense."

"Goddammit, I'm hurting, I need to lie down."

"Talk to me. Give me the short version, then you can lie down."

He grimaced and held his side. But I wasn't going to let him pass until he told me what I wanted to know.

"Me and Pruitt grew up together. Southside Chicago, early fifties. You want my life story?"

"The short version, Slater. We haven't got all night here, I've got a plane to catch."

They were kids together, birds of a feather. Nobody could stand either of them, I thought, so they hung together.

"He called me for a few favors when I was a cop. We'd have a beer or two whenever he passed through Denver. Four years ago, on one of his trips through, he told me about this book."

He coughed. "He'd been chasing it for a long time even then. He was trying to track down a woman he was sure had taken it, but he never could find her. He'd run every lead up a blind alley."

"What's the big attraction?"

"Pruitt knows where he can sell it. For more money than any of us ever saw."

"I don't believe it."

"Then fuck you. Do you want to hear this or not? . . . I can't stand up in this hall forever. I'll tell you this, he convinced the hell out of me. That night I wrote out the stuff he told me on that paper you read, but nothing ever came of it . . . until last month. Then I get a call from Seattle and it's Pruitt. It's all hitting the fan over this book he's after. There's a woman named Rigby in the Taos jail and Pruitt thinks she's got it."

"Why didn't he go down himself?"

"Later on he did: he had some Seattle angles to work out first. He thought the girl's parents might know about it, might even know where she'd hidden it; maybe she'd even mailed it to 'em. So he sent me to Taos to nose around, see what was what. I'd barely got there when she came up for bail. Pruitt came in the next day."

"And did what?"

"Made her wish she'd never been born. That was just the beginning of what he had up his sleeve for her. The book's been like a monkey on his back, I could see it driving him closer to the edge every day. I started thinking he might even kill her for it. But she wouldn't give it up."

"Probably because she didn't have it."

"But she went back to get it, didn't she?"

"She went back for something. Weren't you boys on her tail?"

"You're not gonna believe this, Janeway. She slipped us."

I just stared at him.

"She's cute, all right, a little too cute for her own damn good. The next thing we knew she'd skipped the state. Pruitt went nuclear."

"This must be when you got the bright idea of dragging me into it."

"Our time was running out. She could be picked up by the cops anywhere and we'd be up the creek. Pruitt thought she'd head for Seattle: he put out some people he knew to watch her haunts. And it didn't take long to spot her: she turned up in North Bend a few days later. I didn't know what to do. I sure didn't want to let it go. Pruitt had promised me a piece of it, if I helped him reel it in. I'm talking about more money than you'll believe, so don't even ask."

"I thought money didn't matter to you, Clydell. What about the radio job? What about *Denver Magazine?*"

"All bullshit. I owe more federal income tax than I've got coming in. I do a weekend gig on radio, not enough to pay my water bill. The magazine piece'll be lining birdcages before the ink's even dry. Business sucks; I'm almost broke. What more do you need to know? And besides all that, I really was afraid of what he'd do to that kid."

He took a long, painful breath. "So if you're looking for a good guy in this, it's probably me. That same night I told Pruitt about you. I thought I could tempt you with the bail money, it was easy to get the papers from the bondsman; hell, he doesn't care who brings her in. But the bail was just bait. I knew you'd never bust Rigby for that bail money, not once you had that book in your mind."

He touched his face. "I really thought you might get the book from her. You might have, too, if the cops hadn't busted her and messed everything up. I sold you to Pruitt as a bookhunter. He didn't like it but I talked hard and late that night he decided to try it."

"And that's what finally got your face kicked in. Pruitt didn't like the way it turned out."

"I had to try something. She knows us both on sight, and Pruitt's her worst nightmare. She's right to be scared of him: he's over the edge now. He's your problem, you and that poor kid in there. Me, I'm out of it, I've had enough. I'm goin' back to Denver."

He pushed his way past. Stopped at his door; looked back at me. "I'll give you two free pieces of advice. Pruitt didn't get to be called the Invisible Man for nothing. He can fade into a crowd and you can't see him even when you know he's there. He's great with makeup—wigs, beards, glasses—he can make himself over while you're scratching your ass wondering where he went. And he's always got people around him, scumbags who owe him favors. One of 'em's a fat man, but there may be others. Don't trust anybody. Don't let 'em get close and sucker punch you."

He opened his door. "You didn't hear any of this from me, okay? I'll figure out my own ways of paying Pruitt back, and I don't want him sticking a knife in my ass before I've got it worked out. So here's your second hot tip. Pruitt fucked up your car. If you're counting on that to get you to the airport, think again."

He looked at his watch. "You cut it pretty short, old buddy. You got one hour to get her there. Stay clear of old ladies and fat men, Janeway. If you ever get back to Denver, call me, we'll have lunch. Maybe I'll have a job for you."

16

My brain kicked up in the cop mode. From then on I was running on overdrive.

My goals had narrowed to one. Nothing else mattered—not money or pain, not even the books I had foolishly taken from Otto Murdock.

We were going on the run. That meant travel light, travel fast: leave the books, leave the clothes, call the Rigbys from New Mexico, hope Crystal could come pick up my stuff. Not a perfect answer, but when you've got a woman to guard, six or seven grand worth of books in a cardboard box, and a man on your tail who might be seriously unhinged, perfection is a little too much to ask for.

We were going to Taos, over Pruitt's dead body if that's how he had to have it.

No time for cops: no help there. By the time Seattle checked me out, my flight would be somewhere over Wyoming.

Move.

Move now and move fast.

I called out for a cab. The dispatcher said she had drivers in the neighborhood. The wait would be five minutes, ten tops.

Cover your ass.

I called the desk. Yes, the Hilton ran a shuttle service to the airport. It ran twice each hour, at seven minutes past the half hour.

It was now 9:55.

The key.

Crystal would need my room key to get in here and take out my stuff. Had to hide it somewhere so she could find it.

In the car.

Out there in the garage, all logic dictated, Pruitt would be waiting.

Good. Face the bastard head-on.

Eleanor sat rigidly in the chair. She looked terrified, her knuckles white as she gripped the armrests.

"Wh-why're you . . . d-do-ing this?"

I reached out to her but she recoiled. "I'm on your side, kid," I told her, but it didn't help.

"Th-at m-man in the hall . . ."

"His name is Slater. He's gone now."

"He's with the d-darkman."

"He's nothing. He's out of here."

"Darkm-man."

I squeezed her shoulder. "Cheer up now, you're in good hands."

I turned off the light, flipped off the TV. Nobody was fooling anybody anymore.

"Let's go," I said.

We went with the clothes on our backs. I hung a DO NOT DISTURB sign on the door.

"Stay close," I said as we came into the garage.

She was shivering so violently she could barely walk. Our footsteps echoed as we crossed to the far wall, where I had left my car.

He was with us all the way, I could feel him out there in the dark. "Oh, please." Eleanor's voice quaked with fear. She too had sensed him there, and Slater had it right, he was her bogeyman: just the thought of him made her incoherent and numb.

"Darkman," she whispered. "D-d . . . kman."

I put an arm over her shoulder. "Everything's cool. We'll laugh about it on the plane."

"Darkm-m-an's s-here."

"Hush now. We're heading for the land of sunshine."

I jerked open the door and hustled her into the car. I looked over the roof, my eyes sweeping down the ramp and across the garage to the door. Just for show, I moved around the car, opened the driver's door, and slid under the wheel.

I kept watching through the mirrors. I put the key in the ignition and turned it. It did nothing but click.

Eleanor whimpered faintly in the seat beside me.

"It's okay, I expected that," I said calmly. "Just sit tight, we'll be out of here in a minute."

I got out of the car, locking the doors.

Went through some motions, with peripheral vision working like sonar.

Raised the hood.

Scanned the garage.

Looked at my watch while pretending to look at the engine.

Ten oh one. The shuttle took off in six minutes.

Got down on the garage floor. Pretended to look under the car. Palmed the key to my room and slipped it behind the front bumper.

Scanned the garage from there. With my back to the wall, I could see everything under the wheels of fifty automobiles.

Two pairs of feet . . . two men, coming my way.

I came up slowly, an Oscar-winning performance. It was a fat man with dark hair, flanked by a young, muscular guy in jeans. The fat man wore a business suit and waddled my way with an air of sweet benevolence.

I slammed the hood and wondered why I wasn't surprised when they came to the car in the slot next to mine.

"Hey, buddy," the fat man said. "You know how to get to Queen Anne Hill?"

"I think it's on the west side, just north of town. I'm a stranger here myself."

He looked at me over the roof of his car. "Got trouble?"

"Yeah. Damn thing won't start."

"I'll have the guy downstairs call you a tow truck if you want."

"Won't do much good. I'm in kind of a hurry."

"Might be something simple. Bobby here's good with cars. Why don't you just let him take a peek under your hood?"

"That can't cost me much."

I raised the hood and the three of us crowded into the space between the car and the wall. Here they were, close enough to kiss. I could see a fresh scrape on the fat man's neck where he'd cut himself shaving. The meat quivered around his ears like vanilla pudding. The kid was carrying his right hand in a fetal position, curled inward toward his belt. He was cradling a roll of quarters, I thought—

almost as effective as a set of brass knucks if he got his weight behind it.

Here I am, I thought, take your best shot. When the kid moved, I took a fast step to one side. His closed fist smacked against the car, the roll broke open, and the coins clattered across the floor. I hit him a hard right to the jaw and he went down like a sack of laundry. I could sense the fat man groping for something under his coat, but I was faster and I had the same thing under mine. I whirled around and kneed him in the groin. I punched his wind out, and the next time he blinked I had my gun in his jowls, half-buried in fat.

He was breathing hard through his nose, his eyes wide with fear and surprise. I slapped him across the mouth and spun him around, slamming him against the wall. I took a .38 snub-nose out of his belt and put it in mine. The kid was still cold. I knelt down, frisked him, and got another gun for my arsenal.

I manhandled the fat man back around the car. "Where's Pruitt?"

"I don't know any Pruitt."

I grabbed his necktie and jerked him silly. He tried to roll away: I hammered him under the ribs and he doubled over, wheezing at the floor. I grabbed his hair and smashed his head hard against the car, got down there with him between the cars, and said, through gritted teeth, "You wanna die in this garage, fat man? You wanna die right now, here on this floor?" I had the gun jammed between his jawbone and his eardrum, and I had his attention.

He rolled his eyes down the ramp, into the spiraling darkness.

"That's better. Lie to me again and you're dog food. Tell me now, are there any more rats down there with him?"

He shook his head none.

"Gimme your keys."

He fished them out of his pocket.

"Which one's for the trunk?"

He held it up. I took the ring and opened the trunk.

"Get in and lie down."

He looked at me with pleading eyes. I grabbed him by the scruff of the neck and spun him around and sat him down hard in the trunk. I motioned with the gun and he swung his legs over the rim, curling his butterball body around the spare tire.

I slammed the trunk. It was 10:08, and the enemy himself had delivered us from evil.

I got Eleanor moved over and threw the guns on the seat between us. We careened down the ramp in the fat man's car. Eleanor sat frozen, gripping her knees like a kid on her first roller-coaster ride. I reached the street just as the shuttle pulled out. I pealed rubber turning north into Sixth Avenue. I was soaring, I was high enough to hit the moon. I had to rein myself in, force myself to stop for a red light. The last thing I needed, now that I had the game all but won, was to get stopped by a traffic cop, and me with a car full of guns.

I was trolling the side streets looking for an on-ramp. I stopped for another light. "Darkman," Eleanor said, but I looked and the street was empty.

"He's gone. We kicked his ass, Rigby. It's time to start thinking about what you'll do when you get to New Mexico."

I leaned over the wheel and looked at her. She looked like a stranger, mind-fried with fear.

"We won," I said.

She looked like anything but a winner. She looked like the thousand and one women a cop meets in a long and violent career. A victim.

"Darkman . . ."

"Is he your stalker?"

She looked at me. "He's everywhere. I can't turn around . . ."

"He's a wrong number, honey, a guy in a gorilla suit. He's only scary if you let him be."

"He was in New Mexico." She closed her eyes and quaked at some private demon. "No matter where I go he finds me. I pick up the phone and he's there, playing that song."

The guy behind us blew his horn. The light was green. I moved out, giving her shoulder a little rub, but she seemed not to notice.

"He's there," she said. "I saw him."

I scanned the street in my mirrors and saw nothing.

"Oh, God," she said. "Oh God oh God oh God . . ."

"We beat him. We're gettin' out of here."

"Take me back to jail."

"We're going to New Mexico."

"No! . . . No . . . take me back to jail . . ."

"I want you to listen to me."

"Take me back to jail . . . take me . . . take me . . ."

No more talk, I thought: the less said at this point the better. I thought if I could get her on the plane, I could win her back: then we'd have the whole ride into Albuquerque to calm down and start digging the truth out. I gave her a long sad look. She had covered her face with her hands, but I could see her eyes looking at me through her fingers.

I gunned the car and banked south onto the freeway. I was almost up to thirty when she wrenched open the door and, with a shriek of madness, jumped.

I hit the brakes and the car spun across the wet pavement and slammed into the guardrail. I leaped out on the rim, running along the edge of a dark gulf. She was somewhere down in the street: I couldn't see her, but I heard her scream as I skidded down the slope. I had a long clear look at the street running back downtown: she hadn't gone that way, so she had to have ducked under the freeway to the east. This led me into a dreary neighborhood of shabby storefronts and dark flophouses. The rain had kept people off the street and the hour was late . . . the block was as dead as an old graveyard. The wet clop of my feet punctured the steady hiss of the rain, but I was chasing a ghost. She was gone.

I reached a cross street still clinging to a shred of hope. She could be blocks away by now, going in any direction. Guess wrong and kiss her good-bye: the next time she stuck her head up, she'd be scouting books in Florida. She could make a pauper's living forever in that anonymous subculture, never pay taxes, never have her name recorded on any official docket, never be seen again by friend or foe. I pushed on into the rain, as if she had suddenly materialized in the block ahead. But the street was as empty as ever. I came to another intersection and stopped to look. No use running anymore, I could just as likely be running away from her. I walked along a dim wet block looking in cracks and crevices. Gone with the goddamn wind, son of a bitch. I passed the flickering light of a neighborhood bar and looked at my watch: 10:23. It was still possible to make the plane, if she came to her senses this very minute, if we stumbled into each other in the murk, if the car was still on the ramp where I'd left it, if I was all paid up with the man upstairs, if pigs could fly and I could break every speed limit going to Sea-Tac and get away with it. I stopped and leaned against a mailbox and longed for a break, but Luck had gone her fickle way.

I looked into the bar on a hunch. Nobody there but the neighborhood drunk, who'd been holding up his end of the bar since Prohibition ended. I walked up the street in the rain, unwilling to admit that the fat lady had sung her song. Something could still happen. Something can still happen, I thought again, but my watch was pushing ten-thirty, and it had to happen now.

What happened wasn't quite what I had in mind. A car turned into the street and I knew it was Pruitt half a block away; I had the color and shape of that Pontiac cut into my heart forever. I stepped into the shadows and watched him roll past me. Apparently he hadn't seen me: he cruised by slowly; I stood still and watched him go the length of the block. He was hunting, same as me: he would drive a bit, slow, occasionally stop and look something over. It seemed she had given us all the royal slip. Pruitt stopped at the corner and turned. I broke into a full run, reaching the cross street well before he had turned out of the next block. He was taking it easy, trying to miss nothing as he worked around one block and into another. The block was dark: a streetlight was out, and I thought I could run along the edge of the buildings without being seen. Something might still be salvaged from this rotten night, if I could get close enough to pull that door open and jerk Pruitt's ass out of that car.

A pair of headlights swung toward me two blocks away. I flattened into a doorway as the two cars flicked their brights on and off. It was the fat man's car—I could see the crushed fender where it had hit the guardrail. I patted my pocket and knew I had left them the keys, a stupid mistake, and I'd left their guns there on the seat as well. The two cars pulled abreast for a confab. Then Pruitt turned right, went on around the block, and the fat man was coming my way. He passed and I could see there were two of them in the car—the kid, riding shotgun, was slumped in the seat as if he hadn't yet come back to the living. Lacking Pruitt, I'd be thrilled with another shot at these two. I wanted to put somebody in the hospital, and any of the three was okay with me.

I let the fat man go on into the next block. I moved out in the rain and ran after Pruitt. He was still the grand prize in this clambake, but by the time I reached the next corner he was gone. Again, I could go off in any direction and be right or wrong, or wait right here while the wheel took another spin. When nothing happened, I crossed to the dark side of the street and walked along slowly, hoping they'd all catch up. For a time it seemed that the action had moved on to another stage. No one came or went. I worried about it, and I was worrying three blocks later when Eleanor turned a corner far ahead and walked briskly up the street toward me.

She was two blocks away but coming steadily. I stood flat in a shallow doorway and egged her on in my mind. I peeped out and she was still there. She passed a light in the next block and I could see her clearly now, looking none the worse for her tumble down the slope. Her hair had come down but that was good: I could get a grip on it and hold her that way if I had to. She was close enough now that I could catch her, but I let her keep coming, each step a little added insurance. If she kept on, she'd pass so close I could grab her without a chase. I had pushed myself as far back in the doorway as I could get: I didn't dare even a peep as she came closer. I thought sure I'd have her, then everything seemed to stop. I had lost the sense of her, I had to look. She was still a block away, stopped there as if warned off by intuition. I waited some more. With a long head start and terror in her heart, she could still make it, though.

She crossed the street. Something about the terrain was bothering her: an alarm had gone off in her head and she was like a quail about to be flushed. I buried my face in the crack and held myself still as death. But when I looked again, she was walking in the opposite direction, back up the street the way she had come.

I leaped out of the doorway and ran on the balls of my feet. I stretched myself out and ate up the block, trying to make up lost ground before she turned and saw me. She ducked into an alley. I clopped up and looked down a dark, narrow place. Something moved a block away, a fluttery blur in the rain. She was spooked now, going at a full run: I gave up stealth and chased her through the dark. I hit a row of garbage cans and went down in a hellish clatter, rolled with the momentum, came up running. But I didn't see her anymore, didn't see anything in the murk ahead.

I came out into a street lit only by a distant lamp. It was high noon on Pluto, a world bristling with evil. She screamed, a shriek of such ungodly terror that it smacked me back in my tracks and damn

near stopped the rain. Far down the block I saw Pruitt's kid man-
handling her into the car. The fat man stood by the driver's door,
smoking a cigarette down to his knuckles. I had no chance to catch
them. The fat man gave me the long look as I ran up the block. He
flipped his smoke, flipped me off, got in the car, and drove away in
a swirl of mist.

18

I walked under the freeway and up toward Sixth Avenue. I no longer felt the rain. The specter of Pruitt dogged my steps, spurring me along the deserted street. I saw his face on storefront mannequins and felt his eyes watching me from doorways. I heard his voice coming up from the drains where the water ran down off the street. Then the heat passed and I felt curiously calm. I had remembered something that might be his undoing: I had a sense of urgency but none of defeat. The night was young, the game wasn't over yet, I was more focused with each passing block. I wasn't going to sit in my room all night knitting an afghan.

I had a pretty good idea what Pruitt would be thinking. In the morning I would call the court, file a complaint, and put the cops after him. This meant he'd be on the move tomorrow but perhaps holed up tonight. As far as they knew, I was a Denver knuckle-dragger who couldn't find my way around Seattle at midnight if the mayor suddenly showed up and gave me his chauffeured limo. This was good: this was what I wanted them to think.

By the time I was halfway up Sixth my juice was pumping. I stopped at the Hilton, fetched my key, and let myself into my room. I didn't bother changing clothes—this was just a pit stop, I'd be going out again, I'd be on foot, and I was going to get wet. I sat on the bed with the Seattle phone book and did the obvious stuff first. There was no listing for a Ruel Pruitt or an R. Pruitt in the White Pages: nothing under his name under *Detective Agencies* or *Investigators* in the Yellow. In a strange way, this too was good: it contributed to that sense of security that I hoped Pruitt was counting on for tonight.

Now to find him.

I dug through my dirty clothes, and in the pocket of the shirt I'd worn that first day, I found the scrap of paper I had used to jot down his license number.

I called Denver.

A sleepy voice answered the phone. "'Lo?"

"Neal?"

"Yeah . . . who's this?"

"Cliff Janeway."

"Cliff . . . Jesus, what time is it?"

I looked at my watch. It was exactly 11:18. My plane for Albuquerque was taking off even as we spoke.

"It's after midnight back there. Listen, I'm sorry, I know how hard you sleep. But I'm lost in Seattle and I need one helluva big favor from an old pal."

I heard him stirring on the bed thirteen hundred miles away. His wife asked who it was and he told her. She gave a long-suffering sigh and I told him to give her my regrets.

"Lemme move to the other phone," he said.

I waited, hoping that loyalty between old partners was still alive and well in Denver.

"Yeah, Cliff? . . . What the hell's goin' on?"

"I need a big one, Neal." I slipped into the lie with a little dig from my conscience. Hennessey was too straitlaced to hear the truth, and I'd make sure that none of it ever came back to bite him. "I'm supposed to meet a guy and we missed each other in the night. All I've got is his plate number and I need an address."

There was silence on the line.

"This is important, Neal . . . I can't tell you how badly I need this. I thought there might be something on NCIC . . . you could tap into that in twenty seconds."

"You got reason to suspect the guy's car is hot?"

"No, but those goddamn computers tell you everything. If the guy's even been late paying his traffic tickets . . ."

"Cliff," Hennessey said in that measured tone I knew so well, "sometimes you're a hard guy to be friends with."

"I'll be singing your praises with my dying breath."

"Dammit, this information is not intended for this kind of use."

We both knew that. As always, I waited him out.

"I'll make a call, but I'm promising you nothing. Call me back in half an hour, forty minutes."

I knew it wouldn't take that long: Hennessey would have the information almost instantly, such was the power of a cop in the age of computers. He would get the dope through the DPD dispatcher, who would tap into the national system, and then he'd brood for half an hour before he decided to let me have it.

Meanwhile, I had some time on my hands.

I was walking again, on through the rain into the night. I needed wheels, so I went to the gas station where Rigby had had Eleanor's car towed. It was still there, in a fenced yard behind the rest rooms. I told the attendant I was her brother and they had sent me over to fetch it for her. He didn't worry much: we weren't exactly dealing with a Lexus here, and he was anxious to get it off his lot. "I rustled up four pretty fair used tires with another eight, ten thousand in 'em. Tab comes to eighty-six dollars and ten cents. You wanna pay that now?"

I said sure: I was well past the point of brooding over money, so I handed him my sagging MasterCard. "She's all yours," he said, slotting my card through his machine. "Keys're over the visor." I went back to the yard and opened the car door. It squeaked on rusty hinges. The seats had worn through, the windshield was cracked and a cold draft wafted up from below. The odometer was playing it for laughs—it showed 34,512, which could only be serious if the meter was on its third trip around. I opened the glove compartment. A small light came on, a pleasant surprise. I saw some papers—registration, proof of insurance, and a sheath of notes that looked to be tables of current book valuations, handwritten on ledger paper in ink. They were all Grayson Press books.

There were separate pages for each title. They were fully described, with many variants noted, with prices and the names of dealers who had sold them. These had been taken from *Bookman's Price Index*, with the volume numbers in the margins. She had sifted the material as professionally as any book dealer, noting the year of sale and the condition, along with her own impression of whether the dealers tended to be high or low. It was a ready reference on Grayson's entire output. The final sheet was marked *Poe/The Raven, 1949 edition.* Only three copies were listed for the past ten years. In pencil she had noted that Russ Todd down in Arizona had sold an uncataloged copy for $600. I knew Russ well enough to call and ask if I needed to. Most interesting, I thought, was the word *edition,* which appeared for this book only. It seemed to indicate what I already knew—that some people believed there had been another edition and Eleanor may have been one of them.

I tucked everything back as it was. In a slipcase at the side of the glove compartment I found her address book. It fell open to the letter *G,* so often had that page been used. She had written some names under the general heading *Grayson.* There were book dealers from coast to coast, several of them known to me as specialists in fine-press books. There was a local number for Allan Huggins, the Grayson bibliographer, and at the bottom of the page were three names in bold, fresh-looking ink.

Nola Jean Ryder.

Jonelle Jeffords.

Rodney Scofield.

Jonelle Jeffords I remembered as the name of the woman in Taos whose house Eleanor had burglarized. There was a phone number beginning with a 505 area code. The number for Rodney Scofield was a 213 exchange, which I recognized as Los Angeles. The space beside Nola Jean Ryder was blank.

I sat behind the wheel, crossed my fingers, and turned the ignition.

Yea, verily, it started.

I was back in business. I had wheels.

I stopped at the Hilton and called Hennessey. I knew by the cautious sound of his voice that he had what I wanted.

"I've got bad vibes about this."

"Neal, it's your nature to have bad vibes. The time for you to really start worrying is when you don't have bad vibes."

"Very funny. Someday you'll get me fired, I've got no doubt of that at all. No, don't tell me about it, please . . . you're not gonna kill this guy, are you?"

"Now why would you ask a thing like that?"

"I don't know. I just had a vision of the beaches up there littered with cadavers, all of 'em named Pruitt. It doesn't sit well at one o'clock in the morning."

"I'm just gonna pay him a friendly little visit."

"Like the Godfather, huh? You've got that edge in your voice."

There was nothing else to say: he'd either give or he wouldn't.

"Your plate's registered to a Kelvin Ruel Pruitt. He's got half a dozen old unresolved legal problems, all in Illinois. Careless driving, failure to appear, a bad check never made good, stuff like that. They're not about to go after him in another state, but if he ever gets stopped in Chicago, it'll be an expensive trip."

He sighed and gave me Pruitt's address.

"Bless you, Mr. Hennessey, you lovely old man. Now go back to bed and make your wife happy."

"She should be so lucky."

I sat at the table and unfolded a Seattle street map. Pruitt lived in a place called Lake City, north of town. I marked the map, but I already had the routes memorized. As a courtesy I called Taos and told them Rigby had escaped. The lonely-sounding dispatcher took my message and managed to convey his contempt across the vast expanse of mountains and plains. I didn't bother telling him that I was going to find Rigby and bring her back to him. I didn't think he'd believe that anyway.

19

It was a fifteen-minute drive at that time of night. The draft from the floorboards became a freezing gale, numbing me in my wet clothes. The heater was only partly effective, just beginning to get warm as I reached the Lake City turnoff. I went east on 125th Street, zigzagging through dark and narrow residential lanes until I found the street where Pruitt lived. It was wrapped in wet murk, the sparse streetlights as ineffective as candles. The rain kept coming, beating down like a draconian water cure. The first thing I saw as I turned into the block was the fat man's car, parked under a tree at Pruitt's address. I whipped around and pulled in behind him, then sat for a few minutes with the heater running, recovering from the cold drive. The house was draped by trees and flanked by thick underbrush. None of it could be seen from the street. There was also no sign of Pruitt's Pontiac, which was troubling but might be explained by a garage out back. It was now 1:18 by my watch: almost three hours since they'd snatched her off the street. I had to assume the worst and go from here. Assume all three men were in the house. Figure one of them would be posted as a lookout. The fat man and the kid didn't scare me much: I had dealt with goons many times, and they always fold when the game gets rough. Pruitt was the X-factor, the unknown. You never know what a psycho will do, or what you'll have to do if you get him started.

I pulled my gun around to the front of my belt. Still I sat, bothered by something I couldn't pin down. Then I saw that the fat man's car door was open in the rain, cracked about six inches. The interior light had come on: this had run the battery down and cast the car in a dim, unnatural glow. He took her in the house, I thought: he had to carry her and never got his door closed, then he forgot to come back out and shut it. I thought of Otto Murdock's store, pulling that connection out of the rain, from God knew where. Things were left empty, open, unattended. People went away and didn't come back. Nothing sinister about that, except my own nagging feeling that somehow it shouldn't be that way.

I'd have to move Eleanor's car, I knew that. Pruitt would know it on sight, and if he happened to drive up, I'd lose my biggest advantage, surprise. I drove around the block and parked in the dark behind a pickup truck. Again I was walking in the rain. I approached the fat man's car cautiously. Walked around to the driver's side and looked in. His wallet lay open on the seat. It was stuffed with money . . . five, six hundred dollars. I fished out his driver's license and stared at his picture. William James Carmichael, it said. I wrote down his name and address. I looked in the glove compartment and found several letters addressed to Willie Carmichael. I put them back, got out of the car, and walked to the driveway that led back to the house.

It was heavily draped with trees. I could see lights off in the distance, and a walk that skirted the drive. The walk was shrubbed but too visible, I thought, from the house. I came up the drive, dark as a load of coal, planting each step firmly. It converged with the walk near a flagstone approach to the front door. The only light came from the front windows, dimmed by curtains and reflecting off the slick stones of the walkway.

Three long strides brought me flat against the house. I moved to the door, looking and listening. There was nothing doing anywhere. The door was locked, hardly a surprise. I put my head against it, listening for footsteps, movement, anything that betrayed some living presence. There was nothing.

Just . . . a faint strain of music.

I took my head away and the music stopped. I listened again. The beat sounded tauntingly familiar, like something I knew but couldn't quite call up. The steady hiss of the rain all but drowned it out. It quivered just outside my senses, one of those half-remembered bits of business that drives you crazy at two o'clock in the morning. Other than that, the house was still, so quiet it gave me a queasy feeling. I eased back into the brush and around to the side. I saw a light in a window, dim and distant, escaping from another room well back in the house. I pushed through the undergrowth and looked through a small crack in the curtain. I could see a piece of a drawing room, neat and well furnished with what looked to be antique chairs. Somehow it didn't fit what I knew about Pruitt, but you never can tell about people: I really didn't know the man. I squinted through the crack and saw a doorway that led off to a hall. The light came through from the front, and nothing was going on back here.

I touched the glass and there it was again, that rhythmic vibration, as much feeling as sound. I put my ear against it, and on came that far-away melody, that staccato tune that was right on the tip of my . . .

I froze, unable to believe what had just gone through my head.

"Eleanor Rigby."

Somewhere inside, someone was playing that song.

Over and over.

Loud enough to shake the walls.

At two o'clock in the morning.

I kept moving. Everything was the color of ink. I came into the backyard, taking a step at a time. Around the edge of a porch, groping, groping. I touched a screened door and saw a long, dim, narrow crack of light. I pulled open the door and moved toward it. It was the back door of the house itself, cracked open like the fat man's car. The music seeped through it like some dammed-up thing that couldn't get through the crack fast enough. I had my gun in my hand as I nudged the door with my shoulder. It swung open and the music gushed out.

I was in a black kitchen, lit only by the glow from another room. I could see the dim outlines of a range and refrigerator, nothing more . . . then, straight ahead, a table with chairs around it. I crossed the room, feeling my way. The music was loud now: I had come into a hallway that led to the front. I walked to the end, to the edge of the parlor. It looked like some proper sitting room from Victorian days. The light came down from above, where the music was playing. I reached the stairs and started up. There was a blip that sounded like a bomb, and the music started again, a shock wave of sound.

I saw a smudge on the stair, a red smear ground into the carpet . . .

Another one . . .

. . . and another one.

More at the top.

I heard a soft sigh. It was my own. The overhead light at the top revealed a dark hallway. I could see a room at the end of it, dimly lit as if by a night-light. I saw more red marks on the carpet coming out of the hall. I moved that way, the hall closing me in like a tunnel. There was a door on each side halfway down, the one on the left open, the room there dark. I kept flat against the wall, breathing deeply, aware of the sudden silence again as the record ended. The room smelled strongly of ashes. My mind caught the smell but it didn't hold: there was too much going on. I reached inside and felt along the wall with the palm of my hand, found the light, flipped it up, and the flash turned the room the color of white gold. I could see my reflection in a mirror across the room: I was standing in a half-crouch with the gun in my hand, moving it slowly from side to side. It was some kind of office. There was a desk and a filing cabinet, with one drawer hanging open and several files strewn across the floor. The walls were painted a cream color: the only window was covered by a dark curtain.

I turned and faced the room across the way. I could see the thin line of light at the bottom of the door, and in the light cast out from the office, more crusty red smears on the floor. There, I thought: that's where all the blood's coming from. I pivoted back on my heel and flattened against the wall. Turned the knob, pushing the door wide. And there he was, Fat Willie Carmichael, and I didn't need a medical degree to know he had done Pruitt his last favor. The room looked like a slaughterhouse, with blood on the bed and the floor and the walls: splotches of it spewed as if by a high-pressure pump. The fat man had fallen on his back and died there. His head was wrenched back and I could see that his throat had been cut. His fingers were rigid and clawlike, clutching at nothing. I stood in the doorway, heartsick with fear for Eleanor. My hand was trembling, I felt like a rookie cop at his first bad murder scene. I had looked upon more rooms like this one, streaked with red violence, than I could ever add up and count, and now I shook like a kid. There was still one room to check—the open door at the end of the hall.

I reached the dim circle of light and the music came up full as I peeped in. I almost laughed with relief—nobody there! The record player squatted on a table near the window, one of those old portables from the days before stereo. A 45-rpm disc spun wildly. The set was fixed to the automatic mode: the record would play like that for-ever, till the power failed or the needle wore the grooves off. It was starting again now, a concert from hell.

It was so loud I felt shattered by it. I had an urge, almost a need, to rip out the plug. The night-light flickered precariously, the bulb on its last legs. I found the switch and turned on the overhead, washing the room in light. It looked like a guest room: there was a single bed in a corner facing a portable TV set, a telephone on a table near the record player, a digital alarm clock. The bed had been rumpled but not slept in. Someone had lain or sat on top of the covering.

Handcuffed to the bed.

The cuffs were still there, one bracelet snapped tight to the bed-post, the other lying open on the pillow. The key had been left in the slot where it had been used to release the prisoner from the bed. The cuffs were the same make and style as the set Slater had given me. I came closer and examined the bed, turning back the rumpled folds of the blanket. There I found the book, no larger than a thumb joint, Eleanor's miniature Shakespeare, her good-luck piece.

I fingered the soft suede leather, opened the cover, and looked at the publisher's name. *David Bryce and Son/Glasgow.*

I put it in my pocket and came back up the hall. Last chance at the death scene, I thought. I was thinking like a cop, and I was not a cop, this was not my town. In an hour the room would be full of real cops. I stepped inside, giving the body a wide berth. I looked at Fat Willie Carmichael and thought, *Talk to me, baby,* but the fat man was keeping his last awful secret to himself. He had been taken from the front, stuck in the sternum with a weapon that was wicked and sharp, then slashed deep across the neck. Either wound was proba-bly fatal, but the killer had hacked him up in other ways, as if vent-ing some raging fury or settling an old score. His clothes were ripped apart: pocket change was scattered around, and his keys were thrown against the wall. The killer had been looking for the one key, I guessed, to unshackle his prisoner in the next room. I looked around the edges of the body: I could see his gun—he had retrieved it from the car and it lay under his hip, still in its holster. This indi-cated an attack of surprise: taken from the front, but too quickly to react. Or done unexpectedly, by someone he knew.

Time to call the cops, I thought. Out in the hallway, I smelled again that faint whiff of ashes. The office across the hall was thick with it. I looked into the room and saw where it came from—a wastebasket, half-filled with some burned thing, a bucket of ashes. I got down on the floor and touched the can with the back of my hand. It was still warm. I probed into it with my knife, carefully . . . carefully, lifting one layer away from another. Whatever it was, it had been thoroughly burned, with only a few solid remnants left to show that it had once been sheets of paper. Maybe a police lab could make something out of it; I couldn't. Then I saw a flash of white—two pages fused together in heat, with small fragments unburned. And as I leaned over it, I smelled another odor, half-hidden under the ash but unmistakable if you knew it. Ronsonol. The can and its contents had been doused with lighter fluid to make sure the papers would burn. Some of the fluid had soaked into the carpet but had not burned because the fire had been confined to the inside of the can. Lighter fluid was a smell I knew well. It is one of the bookscout's major tools, used for removing stickers from book jackets safely and without a trace. Paper can be soaked in it without getting stained, wrinkled, or otherwise damaged, unless someone remembers what lighter fluid's really for and sets it on fire.

I sniffed around the can and again probed it with the knife. I worked the point between the two pages and jiggled them apart. The words *still* and *whisp* stood out on the unburned fragment, the two words arranged one over the other, at a slight angle, with the paper charred close around them. The lettering was striking and quaint: the typeface lovely. Here was the *Raven*, I thought. It might not make sense, but it looked as if Pruitt had it all along, lost his mind, whacked Willie Carmichael, and burned the damn thing. It didn't make sense, I thought again. I parted the ashes and went deeper. There was only one other scrap with unburned letters: *ange,* it said. I took this piece, to have a sample of the typeface, and left the other segment for the cops.

I nudged off the light with my elbow and left the room as I'd found it. I stood for a moment in the hall, listening. But the record had numbed my senses, and now I had to concentrate just to hear the song.

I moved through the hall to the stairs. Looked down into the drawing room.

Something was different. I waited and listened and waited some more, but I saw and heard nothing.

It was my life that had changed. My dilemma. The universe.

I took a solid grip on the gun and went down quickly. Everything was turned around, like a house of mirrors at a carnival. There were two doors: I looked through the other rooms with that same sense of dread and found nothing: then went back through the hall the way I had come. I didn't know what was eating me until I got to the kitchen. There's more, I thought: I've missed something, I haven't seen it all yet. I nudged open the swinging door, groped for a light, found it, flipped it, and saw what it was that I had missed.

The woman was sprawled in a lake of blood by the table. I had walked past her in the dark, so close I might've stepped on her hand. Like Fat Willie Carmichael, she had died by the knife—throat cut, body ripped and torn. I moved closer and looked at her platinum blond hair. I didn't want to look at her face, but I did. It was Pruitt's girlfriend, Olga.

Then I saw the footprints, my own, and, oh, Christ, I had walked through her blood coming in. It was like looking down and seeing your crotch covered with leeches: your skin shimmies up your tailbone and your gut knots up and you just want them gone. I didn't even stop to think about it—the whole fifteen years I'd spent with DPD was so much jackshit, and I went to the roll of paper towels near the range and ripped some off, wet them in hot water at the tap, and washed out the prints. And in that moment, while I played footsie with the killer, I became part of his crime.

Call the cops, I thought: call them now, before you're in this any deeper.

I rolled the bloody wet towels into a tight ball, wrapped it in two fresh ones, and stuffed it in my pocket. Everything till then had been blind reflex. Again I thought about the cops, but even then I was smearing the water tap with my handkerchief, where I'd touched it wetting the towels.

Stupid, stupid . . .

I left the record playing: give the cops that much, I owed it to Eleanor, even if I had to pay the price.

I was lucky on one count—the heavy underbrush made it unlikely that neighbors would see me coming or going. Almost too late, I remembered that I had gone through Fat Willie's wallet: I went back to his car and smeared it with my handkerchief. I walked around the block and sat in Eleanor's car with my feet dangling in the rain. I took off my shoes, knowing that human blood can linger in cracks longer than most killers could imagine, and I turned them bottoms-up on the floor.

I drifted downtown, my conscience heavy and troubled.

I was at least five miles away when I called them. I stood in a door-less phone booth outside an all-night gas station and talked to a dispatcher through my handkerchief. Told her there were two dead people, gave her the address.

I knew I was being taped, that police calls today can be traced almost instantly. When the dispatcher asked my name, I hung up.

I stopped at Denny's, put on my shoes, and went inside for a shot of coffee. It was 3:05 A.M. I sat at the fountain and had a second cup. I thought of Eleanor and that record blaring, of Slater and Pruitt, of Crystal and Rigby and the Grayson boys. I wished for two things—a shot of bourbon and the wisdom to have done it differently. But I was in the wrong place for the one and it was too late for the other.

BOOK II TRISH

20

I found what I needed over my third coffee. It always happens, I don't know how. When life goes in the tank, I bottom out in the ruins and come up with purpose, direction, strength.

I knew what I had to do. It was too late now to do it the right way, so the same thing had to happen from a different starting point.

I sat at the counter looking at her card.

I made the call.

She caught it on the first ring, as if she'd been sitting there all night waiting for me.

"Hello."

"Trish?"

"Yup."

"Janeway."

"Hi."

She didn't sound surprised: she didn't sound thrilled. She sounded wide-awake at four o'clock in the morning.

"You said if I'd like to talk . . . well, I'd like to talk."

"When and where?"

"As soon as possible. You say where."

"My office, half an hour. Do you know where the *Seattle Times* is?"

"I'll find it."

"I'll tell you, it'll save time. Go to the corner of Fairview and John. You'll see a big square building that looks like all newspaper buildings everywhere. You'll know you're there by the clock on the Fairview side—the time on it's always wrong. Turn into John, park in the fenced lot on the left, come across the street and in through the John Street door. The guard will call me and I'll come down and get you."

The clock on the building said 11:23, but it was an hour before dawn when I got there. The rain was coming down in sheets. I parked in a visitor's slot and made the sixty-yard dash in eight seconds, still not fast enough to keep from getting soaked again. I pushed into the little vestibule and faced a middle-aged man in a guard's uniform. I asked for Miss Aandahl: he didn't think Miss Aandahl was in. He made a call, shook his head, and I sat on a bench to wait. Water trickled down my crotch and I felt the first raw tingle of what would probably be a raging case of red-ass. I squirmed in my wet pants and thought, I *hate* this goddamn town.

She came in about ten minutes later. She was wearing a red rain-coat and hood. She was brisk, getting me quickly past the formalities with the guard. He looked at me suspiciously as I disappeared with her into the building. We went past a receptionist's booth, empty now, then through a door to the right and up a set of stairs. We came out on the second floor, in a corridor that led past a string of offices. There was a bookcase filled with review copies, overflow from the book editor, with a sign to the effect that the staff could buy them (the money to go to charity) at $3 a copy. In a quick flyby, I saw some hot young authors—David Brin, Dan Simmons, Sharyn McCrumb— whose newest books, with author photos and publicity pap laid in, could already command cover price plus 50 percent in a catalog. That's the trouble with review books; they tend to be wasted on book editors. I wanted to clear out the case, buy them all.

She was standing about thirty feet away, waiting. I joined her at the edge of the newsroom, a huge chamber quiet in the off-hours. It gave the impression that news happened on its timetable, at its com-mand. *Let there be news,* the keeper of the key would shout at eight o'clock, and fifty reporters would materialize at their computers, clicking furiously. On the far wall was a full-length mural of the world, with clocks showing times in various places. The world looked as peaceful as the newsroom, which only proved how little the world knew.

She hung up her raincoat, then led me into a narrow place defined on both sides by tall filing cabinets. It was crowded with desks, maybe a dozen of them packed into a space the size of a medium-sized living room. It was like walking into a canyon: it was part of the newsroom yet it wasn't, because an editor couldn't see in there with-out getting up and making the grand effort. I didn't have to be a reporter to know what a coveted spot it was . . . out of sight, out of mind. Her desk was far back in the corner, as secluded as you could get without moving up in management, getting yourself glassed in and becoming a different breed of cat.

She sat and motioned me to a chair. She looked different somehow from the image I had retained from our one meeting in the court-house cafeteria. She looked harder and tougher, more of the world. Then she smiled, like the child looking up at Frankenstein's monster, and I felt good again.

"Nice racket you've got," I said. "You people must get some great poker games going back here."

"We call it the Dead Zone. They'll have to kill me to get this desk."

"Are they trying?"

"So they say."

She didn't push me. If I wanted to small-talk and break the ice, she could do that. She was looking straight in my eyes.

"You look miserable . . . tired, wet, and hungry."

I nodded. "Your city has not treated me well."

"I'm sorry," she said, and managed to look it. "You've come in the rainy season."

"Oh. How long does that last?"

"Almost all year."

She offered coffee but I had had enough. We looked at each other across her desk.

"I came here from Miami," she said. "My first month was a killer. It rained twenty-eight out of thirty days. I was a basket case. I was ready to go anywhere. If the newspaper in Grand Island, Nebraska, had offered me a job covering the grasshopper beat, I'd've been on the next bus out of here. Then it cleared up and I learned what a sensational place this is."

"I guess I'll have to take your word for that."

"There're two secrets to living here. You've got to dress for weather and you can't let it get you down."

"That's two for two I missed."

"Now the only thing that bothers me is the traffic. This town has got to be the worst bottleneck in the United States. It's great as long as you don't need to drive, or if you do need to drive, you don't need to park."

"It sounds better by the minute."

"I guess I'm here for the long haul. I can't imagine going anywhere else. What's Denver like?"

"I had forgotten what rain looks like till I came here."

"Sun city, huh?"

"Somebody once said that Denver has more sun and sons of bitches than any other city in the country."

She smiled and said, "I'll stay with the rain. I bought a boat last year, I'm a pretty fair sailor now. Sometimes I just take off on Friday and drift up the coast. I put in at some warm-looking marina and spend the weekend exploring. If I've got a difficult piece to write, I do it there, out on deck if the weather's nice."

"Is that where you wrote your book?"

"Would have, if I'd had it then. Have you read it?"

"Not yet, but it's high on my list. I just picked up a copy."

"Yeah, well, don't believe everything you read."

I thought that was the strangest thing I had ever heard a reporter say. She shrugged and said, "It's a good book, I'm not apologizing for it; if I had it to do over again, I'm sure it'd come out mostly the same. A little better, maybe. That's the curse of being a writer, you never want to look back at what you did last year because the trip's too painful. You see stuff you should've done better, but now it's set in stone."

"What would you change?"

"A thousand little things . . . and of course I'd write a new ending."

"Of course?"

"The ending leaves the impression that the Graysons died in an accident. Just some tragic twist of fate."

"Which is . . . ?"

"Not true."

"They were murdered, you said."

"Read the book, then talk to me again. Just keep in mind that the last chapter wasn't what I would've done, then or now."

"If you didn't do it, who did?"

"It was sanitized by an editor in New York. The problem was, I had produced this monster-sized book and it was ending with more questions than it answered. They didn't like that, they felt it would not be satisfying for a reader to go through seven hundred and fifty pages and come out with the kind of questions I was asking. Especially when the experts seemed to agree that it was an accident and I couldn't prove it wasn't. The book really didn't need to end with any unanswered questions at all. They died. That was the end of it."

"But not for you."

"I still keep my finger in it. As you can see."

"You must have something in mind."

She smiled into the sudden pause that stretched between us. "I've been doing some fiction lately. I'm finding a voice, as the literati say. I've had three or four pieces in the literary reviews and I'm working on a novel. Maybe that's how I'll finally get rid of the Graysons. I read somewhere that fiction's the only way you can really tell the truth. I never even understood that when I was learning the ropes, but I sure believe it now."

She gave me a look that said, *Hey, I'm not pushing you, but why the hell are we here?*

I said, "I've got a deal for you."

"I already own the Space Needle, I bought it last year. I never could resist a deal." She got up and came around the desk, patting me on the shoulder. "Let's go get some breakfast. I don't think I want to hear this on an empty stomach."

21

It was a lick and a promise, all I had time for. My reading on her would have to be the abridged version, once over lightly. This is your life, Trish Aandahl, a tour of the high spots. From that I'd decide: move on alone or bring her to the party.

Conventions and courtesies, five minutes. She had grown up in Ohio, her parents simple people who lived for the moment. Life was what it was: you worked at it every day and got up the next day and did it again. Her father had worked for wages in Cincinnati; her mom found jobs in restaurants, dime stores, car washes, wherever there was women's work that demanded no special skills. They had produced a child unlike either of them, a daughter who didn't believe in women's work and grew up thinking she could do most anything. At least the parents had had the wisdom to indulge her differences.

She beat the clock with a minute to spare. She knew I was fishing, but she had tapped into my growing sense of urgency and was willing to give me some rope.

Personal color, three minutes. Trish was her real name, listed that way on her birth certificate. Her mother had named her after a best friend and had never known that the name was a diminutive of Patricia.

She was alone in the world. Her parents were dead and there were no other children. If there was a man in her life, it wasn't readily apparent. She wore no rings, but that doesn't mean as much as it once did.

She was amused now, wondering how far I'd go into this Dick-and-Jane style personal Baedeker. I wondered about her gripes and dislikes and gave her one minute for that.

She didn't need it. Phonies, stuffed shirts, chiselers, and liars. Her code was much like mine, her hate list virtually identical.

Extra bit of business, thirty seconds. She was a chronic insomniac, able to sleep undisturbed only about one night in four. That's why she had been sitting there by the telephone, reading a novel, when I called.

I knew everything about her by the time the waitress brought our breakfasts. What more do you need to know about anyone, until the chips are down and you discover that you never knew anything at all?

"I'm ready to tell you about Slater," I said.

"Why the change of heart?"

"Because the circumstances have changed and I want something back from you. Isn't that how life works?"

"If it's an even trade, sure. Is the Slater story worth anything?"

"I think you'll find it interesting. The entertaining part is trying to figure out where it's heading. It's still unfolding, as you newsies might put it."

"The terminology is *breaking*. I don't do breaking stories anymore."

"I think you'll do this one."

"So what do you want for it?"

"A lot less than you paid for the Space Needle. Are we off the record yet?"

"If that's how you want it."

I threw in a zinger, to test her dedication to the code. "Don't take offense at this, but how do I know your word is good?"

She did take offense: she bristled in her chair, and for a moment I thought she might pick up and walk out. "I'll tell you the answer to that, but you're only allowed to ask it once. You can check me out with a phone call. I worked in Miami for four years. I went to jail down there over just this kind of stuff."

"Really?" I said in my most interested voice. "How long were you in?"

"It was only ten days. My paper made it a front-page embarrassment for them and they were glad enough to see me go. I might still be there, though, if they hadn't gotten their information from someone else."

"That's okay, ten days is long enough. At least you know the taste of it."

"The taste, the smell, the color. It colors your whole life. But I'll go back again before I let them make me betray . . . even you."

"Hey, I believe you. In a funny way, though, it makes what I'm trying to do more difficult."

"I don't understand."

"I'm not quite ready to go on the record yet. But I can't even explain the situation to you off the record without handing you a piece of my legal jam."

"What kind of legal jam?"

"There was a crime done tonight. A bad one."

"Did you do it?"

"No, ma'am, I did not."

"Then . . ."

"I did some other stuff, stupid stuff that will not make them love me. If the cops don't love you, you need something in your corner besides a motive, the means, and no alibi. You'd look good in my corner. But you need to know the risks."

Warily, she said, "Can you tell me in general terms what happened?"

"Generally speaking, two people got killed. I've been busy all night destroying evidence and obstructing justice. They'll almost certainly charge me with that, but at least I can bail out on it. That's my magic word right now, *bail*. I have this compelling need to be out. I've got to be out." I let a long pause emphasize that point for me, then I said, "But over the last two hours I've come to realize that the magnitude of my fuckup may make that impossible. I've got a growing hunch they might start taking my measurement for the murder rap."

She let out her breath slowly, through her nose. I saw a slight shiver work its way across her shoulders.

"That's it in a nutshell," I said. "I'm still trying to figure out how to handle it. I need to do that before I can get into the story or tell you what I want from you."

"I don't think it's a problem. I'm not legally obligated to tell the police what you tell me."

"I can see a situation, though, where they'd call you in and ask some questions you'd rather not answer."

"I'll claim privilege."

"And end up in jail again."

"Maybe I'll take that chance, if the story's worth it."

"The story's worth it. But between the two of us, we may still have to dig for the end of it."

She looked out into the rainy street, just now awash with the palest light of morning. I floated a hint of what I hoped she could do for me.

"I'm hoping you know a great cop in this town, or a DA with a real head on his shoulders. The closer you'd be to such an animal the better."

"I'm not sleeping with anybody right now," she snapped. "If I was, I sure wouldn't use him that way."

"You're touchy as hell at five o'clock in the morning, aren't you? You should learn to sleep better."

"Janeway, listen to me. You and I may become the best of pals, but we won't get to first base if you keep dropping insults on my head."

"And we'll never get anywhere if you're one of those politically correct types who takes offense at everything. I'm no good at walking on eggs. Do you want to hear what I meant or sit there and be pissed off?"

"Tell me what you meant, maybe I'll apologize later."

"I may need to turn myself in. If I do, all this is a moot point, you can do anything you want with it. But I'd at least like to be talking to my kind of cop, not one of those tight-asses who thinks the first mistake I made happened way back in Denver, when I quit the brotherhood."

She didn't say anything.

"The Rigby girl's gone. I have good reason to believe that the killer may have taken her. I want to be out looking for her: I *need* to be looking, I really can't overstate that. I will come totally unzipped sitting in a jail cell. All humility aside, I'm still the best cop I know. I'm not saying Seattle will give her a fast shuffle, but I know how it is in these big departments, I know how many cases those boys have to clear. I'm here, I'm focused, I'm looking for Eleanor, and I'll open all the doors."

I took a deep breath, which became a sigh. "But I'm far from home, I'm being slowly driven crazy by this rain, and I know nobody here but you. The cop in me wants to tear up this town looking for her, but I'm not even sure yet where the doors are. And if that kid winds up dead and the real cops could've prevented it while I'm out playing policeman . . ."

We looked at each other.

"I'll tell ya, Trish, I'd find that damn near impossible to live with."

She answered my sigh with one of her own, but it was a long time coming. "You want it both ways. It can't be done."

"If it can't be done, I go in—no arguments, no questions. Her welfare is the first priority."

"Maybe you should go in. Can you really do her any good out here by yourself?"

"I might surprise you. I really was a decent cop. With me looking too, her chances would have to go up. I don't know, I've got to try. But there isn't much time."

I droned on, summarizing the immediate problem. The cops had to be told about Rigby now, this morning, before they closed down the scene. In a homicide investigation, every minute wasted on the front end is critical. I looked at my watch: I had already blown three hours.

"Let's make it very clear, then, what you want from me and what kind of restraints I'm under," she said. "As it stands now, I can't even ask the cops an intelligent question."

"That's why I was hoping you knew somebody."

"That I was sleeping with the chief of police, you mean. Sorry, Janeway, no such luck. I don't drink with them or eat lunch with them, I don't backslap or schmooze or let them tell me dirty jokes. My relationship with these guys is respectable but distant. It's extremely professional and I've taken some pains to keep it that way."

"Do you know anybody on the paper who does schmooze with them?"

"Nobody I'd trust, and I'd be wary of any cop such a guy might bring me. I don't like reporters who party with people they write about."

We thought it through another stretch of quiet.

She said, "I feel like I'm playing pin the tail on the donkey, or a card game with half a deck."

"You want to hear the story, I'll tell you the story."

"Sure I want to hear it, isn't that why we're here? I'll take it any way you want to tell it, on the record or off."

I told it to her with no more clarification than that. I took her from Slater's arrival in my bookstore through my hasty retreat from

Pruitt's house three hours ago. She asked nothing and made no judg-
ments until it was finished. Her eyes darted back and forth as if she'd
been replaying parts of it in her head.

"God, I've got more questions now than I had at the beginning. I
know who Slater is, but who is Pruitt? Is this really about a Grayson
book or is something else at the bottom of it? What happened to the
kid who was tagging along with the fat man? And you . . . oh,
Janeway, what on earth possessed you and what're you thinking
now? Do you think Pruitt lost his mind, killed his friends, and took
off with Rigby? Does that make sense to you?"

"All I know for sure is there were five people, counting Eleanor.
Only two are accounted for and they're dead."

"And what about that record playing? What do you make of
that?"

"She was being stalked and harassed on the phone. It had to've
been Pruitt, that's obvious now. He was her darkman, her worst
nightmare."

"But why leave the record playing, at home, with a dead man
there?"

The check came. I made a stab at it but she was quicker. She
looked through her purse and fished out a twenty.

"I'm going on up to the scene," she said. "At least then we'll know
what cops are working it. Maybe I can take them off the record and
get them to tell me something."

We walked out in the rain. I stood beside her car, getting wet
again, and talked to her through the narrow crack at the top of her
window.

"I'll be holed up in my room at the Hilton. You call me."

"As soon as I can."

"Sooner than that. Remember, I am not calm, I'm not taking this
in my stride. I am very nervous."

"I hear you."

"You call me, Trish. The minute you can get the smell of it and
break away, you get on that phone."

"I'll call, but don't get your hopes up. I think you're gonna have
to go in to get what you want. And the cops won't be naming you
citizen of the year."

22

I stood under a hot shower, put on dry clothes, lay on the bed with the TV low, and waited uneasily.

She called just before eight.

"The cops on the case, Quintana and Mallory . . . I know them both, not well, but maybe enough to give you a reading. It's not good news."

"Of course not," I said, sitting up on the bed.

"You might be able to talk to Mallory if you could get him alone. But it wouldn't do much good, he'd take it all to Quintana anyway."

"It's pretty hard to hold out on your partner."

"And then Quintana would be running it, and your troubles would just begin. Mallory's the weak sister in this Mutt-and-Jeff show: you can't ask him about the weather with Quintana in the same room—you ask him a question and Quintana answers it. Quintana's an overriding presence, extremely inhibiting. He is tough, intelligent to the point of being cunning, and damned condescending to women and other small animals. I don't think he'd look at a former cop with much sympathy. People call him supercop, and not all of them mean it the way he'd like to think."

There's one in every department, I thought. I'd had one for a partner myself, before Hennessey. It didn't last long. Steed had had to split us up to keep us from killing each other.

The prognosis was obvious. Grimly I moved on to the next round of questions. Had the cops been able to make the Rigby connection from the "Rigby" record?

"I haven't been able to get into that with them. They're just not open with stuff like that, and everybody's wondering what I'm doing here anyway. I told you I don't do breaking stories. We've got other people covering this, and I'm bumping into them every time I turn around."

"What's your best guess?"

"About the record? . . . I can't see them linking it."

I lost my temper, probably because I couldn't see them linking it either. "Goddammit, who does Seattle put on these homicide jobs, Peter Sellers? What's the matter with these fucking cops, what does it take to get their attention?"

"You asked me what I think and I told you. I could be wrong. But I think they'll figure the record as noise, to cover up what was happening in that house. The music will go right past them. A million people in this town like Beatles music—it might as well have been the Judds on that deck, or the Boston Pops. Why would the police think twice about 'Eleanor Rigby'?"

"Because a woman by that name just went through their stupid nitwit court system!"

"You're assuming the right hand knows what the left hand's doing. In a system this big, you should know better. Anything's possible: I just think it would take one brilliant cop or a stroke of luck for that to happen."

I heard an emergency vehicle pass in her background, the siren fading as it went by on the way somewhere else.

"They'll be putting a wrap on it soon," she said. "Are you coming in?"

I thought of supercop. It was almost more than I could bear.

"Janeway . . ."

"I hear you. I'm just having a lot of trouble with it."

"It's the right thing to do."

"What if I didn't come in?"

"I think that would be a mistake."

"What have I got to lose at this point, supercop's gonna have my ass for breakfast anyway. They don't need me, they've got you."

"I think I'm still off the record. Did we ever get that straight?"

"If we did, consider it inoperative."

"What do you want me to tell them?"

"Everything. Anything that helps them find Rigby. Tell them if they waste manpower looking for me, they're a bunch of losers."

"What are you going to do?"

"Start from ground zero, go till I drop."

"Listen," she said as if she had just made up her mind about something. "We need to talk some more. Don't just disappear on me. Call me tonight."

"I'll see where I am then."

"I know some stuff I didn't tell you yet . . . things you need to hear. Will you call me?"

"I'll try."

"It's important."

We seemed to have reached the end. But she was reluctant to let me go.

"Cliff, is this really what you want?"

"No. But it's what I'm going to do."

23

How do you disappear in the other man's town? I went about it step by step, covering my tracks, playing the odds, counting on what I knew of the supercop mentality to help me along. Aandahl would be getting back to the scene right about now, just as I was packing my stuff out of the Hilton and loading up in Eleanor's trunk. She'd be starting to tell them now, as I turned into University and hit the freeway. She'd probably start out talking to the quiet one, Mallory: that was her nature, avoid the supercops of the world as long as possible. It wouldn't be possible for long: Mallory would call in supercop as soon as he realized what he had . . . just about now, I thought. She'd be segregated in one of the rooms away from the investigation and they'd start on her slowly and work their way up to heat. She'd have to repeat it all, everything she'd told Mallory: supercop never settled for hearsay, even from a partner. Again Mallory would ask the questions and she would answer, and when it was time for the heat to come down, supercop would take over and see if she scared. Maybe she'd tell him where to shove it. I thought about her and decided she just might. It would take an hour off the clock for them to get to that point.

I found a bank that was open on Saturday, half-day walkup-window service. My paper trail would end here, it was cash-and-carry from now on. The paper I had already left would soon take them through Slater to the Hilton. Supercop would also know that I'd been driving an Alamo rental, but he'd be annoyed to find it disabled in the Hilton garage. How long a leap would it be until he had me driving Rigby's car? It could be half a day or it might be done with two two-minute phone calls. A lot depended on luck—his and mine—and on how super the asshole really was.

I drew a $3,000 cash advance on my MasterCard. There was more where that came from, an untapped balance maybe half again as much. In the other pocket of my wallet I had a Visa, which I seldom used: the line of credit on that was $2,000. I never maxed out on these cards: I always paid it off and the jackals kept bumping my line upward, hoping I'd have a stroke of bad luck and they could suck me into slavery at 18 percent along with the rest of the world's chumps. It was a good strategy, finally about to pay off for them.

I took the cash in hundreds, two hundred in twenties. It made a fat wad in my wallet.

I stopped in a store and bought some hair dye, senior-citizen variety, guaranteed to turn me into a silver panther. I'd have to do it in two stages, bleach my dark hair white and then dye it gray with an ash toner. I'd be an old man till I dyed it back or it grew out. I bought a good grease pencil with a fine point and a hat that came down to my ears. I bought some sealing tape, shipping cartons, a marking pen, and a roll of bubblewrap. I doubled back toward town. In the Goodwill on Dearborn I bought a cane and an old raincoat. For once in my life I left a thrift store without looking at the books.

I sat in the car with the windows frosting up and did my face. I gave myself a skin blemish under my right eye, added some dirty-looking crow's-feet to the real ones I was getting through hard living, and headed out again. I looked at myself in the glass. It wasn't very good, but maybe it didn't have to be. All I needed now was to pass in a rush for an old duffer with the hurts, when I talked to the man at the check-in counter.

I chose a motel not far from the Hilton, the Ramada on Fifth just off Bell Street. I pulled my hat down and leaned into the cane as I walked into the lobby. For now I would be Mr. Raymond Hodges, a name I pulled out of thin air. I also pulled off a pretty good limp, painful without overdoing it. I gave a half-sigh, just audible with each step down on my right foot. The guy behind the desk didn't seem to notice me beyond the bare fact of my presence, a sure sign that he had taken me at face value. *There's nobody in that room but an old guy who can barely walk,* he'd tell anybody who wanted to know. It wouldn't fool supercop if he got this far, but if they were checking around by phone, it might discourage them from coming out for the personal look.

It was still only midmorning: registration for the night wouldn't be opening for another four or five hours, but the man let me in when I told him I was tired. The only thing that seemed to throw him momentarily was the sight of cash. In the age of plastic, a man with cash is almost as suspicious as a man with a gun.

For my own peace of mind, I had to get rid of Otto Murdock's books, and it was Saturday and the post office was on a banker's schedule. In my room I sealed the books in the bubblewrap and packed them tight, with the other books I'd bought all around them. I sealed the boxes and addressed them to myself in Denver. I called the desk for directions and he sent me to the main post office at Third and Union. I insured the boxes to the limit—not nearly enough—and felt a thousand pounds lighter when they disappeared into the postal system.

The library was just a few blocks away, and I stopped there to look at a copy of *The Raven*. The most accessible Poe was the Modern Library edition, on an open shelf in the fiction section. I sat at a table and browsed it, looking for the words *still* and *whisp*, printed diagonally one above the other. I found them in the fifth stanza, partial words but strong as a fingerprint.

> *Deep into that darkness peering, long I stood there,*
> *wondering, fearing,*
> *Doubting, dreaming dreams no mortal ever dared to dream*
> *before;*
> *But the silence was unbroken, and the stillness gave no token,*
> *And the only word there spoken was the whispered word,*
> *"Lenore?"*
> *This I whispered, and an echo murmured back the word,*
> *"Lenore!"*
>   *Merely this and nothing more.*

I took the charred scrap from my wallet and looked for the letters *ange*. It was there, twice, in the sixteenth stanza, reference to the sainted, radiant maiden Lenore, who had been named by the angels.

I made photocopies of the three pages and headed back to the Ramada.

*   *   *

In my room I did my hair, watching with some amazement as the black became white and then gray and by degrees I took on the appearance of my father. I quit when it seemed right. When it dried, I hit it with the grease pencil, giving myself a slightly speckled look.

I redid my face and made a better job of it.

There was a kind of fatalistic rhythm to my movements. I was doing what I had to do and time no longer mattered. Eleanor was either dead or alive: if she still lived, I rather liked her chances for the immediate future. He wasn't about to kill her, not after all this grief, till he had what he wanted. Never mind the ashes: appearances could be deceiving, and the feeling persisted that what I wanted was still out there somewhere, alive and well. If I could find it first, I'd have a strong bargaining chip, and there was a fair chance we'd even converge in the hunt. I didn't know Seattle, I had no idea where Pruitt or the fat man's kid might do their drinking, but I did know books. I'd let the cops do the legwork—the job I'd set them on at no small personal risk to myself, the work they had the manpower and the skill to pull off—and I'd go after the book.

It was now after ten-thirty. Supercop would be finished with Trish, at least for the moment, and he'd be on the phone to Denver, going after my mug shot and stats. I pictured the looks on Hennessey and Steed and almost laughed at the thought. It would go against Steed's grain, but he'd have to honor supercop's request and wonder to himself if I had finally popped my buttons and started cutting out paper dolls. As for Hennessey, I'd have some serious fences to mend there, but what else was new?

I knew I was tired—the last real sleep I could remember was the Rigby loft, more than forty-eight hours ago—but I didn't want to stop. I sat on the bed and began working the phone. I opened Eleanor's little address book to the Grayson page and decided to start with Allan Huggins, the man who knew more about the Graysons than they had known about each other. I punched in the number, but there was no answer.

I kept going. I called Jonelle Jeffords in Taos. A machine answered. "Hi, this's where Charlie and Jo live. If you've got something to say that I might want to hear, leave a number, maybe I'll call you back."

No bullshit there: old Charlie cut right to the short strokes. I hung up on the beep.

I sat for a while looking at the name Rodney Scofield. It seemed vaguely familiar, like something I'd heard once and should've remembered. Finally I called his number cold, a Los Angeles exchange.

A recording came on. I wondered if it's possible in this day and age to punch out a phone number and actually speak to a living human being.

I hung on through the entire recording, hoping for some hint of what Scofield was about. A female voice began by telling me I had reached the business offices of Scofield Plastics on Melrose Avenue. Their hours were nine A.M. to five P.M., Monday through Friday. At the end was a menu of punch codes: if I wanted to reach the voice mail of various department heads, I should punch one, two, three, and so on. Finally, there was this:

"If you have business pertaining to the Grayson Press, please press number eight now."

I punched it.

The phone rang.

A recording began on the other end.

"This is Leith Kenney. I'm not here but I do want to talk to you. If you have Grayson books for sale, or information about single books or collections, please call me back or leave a number where you may be reached. You may also reach me at home, at any hour of the day or night. We are interested in any primary Grayson material, including letters, photographs, business records, broadsides, and even incomplete projects and partial layouts. We pay top cash money, well above auction rates. We will match any offer for important material, and we pay equally well for information that results in major acquisitions."

He gave a home number and I called it. Again came that scratchy, unmistakable sound of a recording machine. There again was Kenney's voice, apologizing. He had stepped out but would return soon. Would I please leave a number?

No, I would not.

I had a hunch I had found Pruitt's moneyman, and I wanted to catch him cold.

*   *   *

I slept five hours. No apologies, no bouts with conscience. My tank was empty: I needed it.

I awoke at four o'clock in a state of anxiety. I had heard a bump somewhere and had come to life thinking of supercop. Dark shadows passed outside, beyond my window, probably a SWAT team getting ready to crash the door.

But when I parted the curtains, it was just a family checking in. The rain had stopped for the moment, but a heavy cloud cover hung over the city, and the streets were wet from a recent drenching. I took a hot shower and dressed, thinking of my immediate future in terms of moves.

My first move had to be to ditch Eleanor's car. I walked over to the lobby, giving the clerk a good look at me in my old-man role. I used the cane well and was satisfied when he gave me nothing more than a smile and a passing glance.

I bought a *Seattle Times* from a box and sat in my room browsing the classifieds. I found the car I wanted in less than a minute, but when I called, the party had sold it. I tried again: there were plenty more like that. All I wanted was something cheap that would run for a week.

The one I found was twenty minutes away, in a ramshackle garage behind a tenement house. It was a Nash from the fifties, the oldest car I would ever own. The body was consumed by rust but the engine sounded decent, rebuilt, said the young man selling it, just three or four years ago. He wanted four hundred: it was a classic, he said, selling hard. I told him everything today was a classic and offered him three. "This is a great make-out car," he said. "The seats fold back into a full bed, with five different positions." I gave him a long gray stare and asked if I looked like a guy who needed five different positions. He grinned and said, "Just need wheels to get you to the VA, huh, pops?" We settled on three-fifty with no further commentary.

The whole business took less than half an hour. He brought out some papers and signed them over to my Raymond Hodges alias and had one last-minute doubt about the license plates. "I think you're supposed to pull those plates and go down to Motor Vehicles and get

a temporary." I told him I'd take care of it and he accepted this cheerfully. I left Eleanor's car on the street a block away, noting the
address so I could call the Rigbys to come pick it up. It was a quiet
residential neighborhood and I thought the car would be safe there
for a few days before somebody called in and reported it to the city
as abandoned.

Back in the motel, I made my phone checks again. Neither Leith
Kenney in L.A. or Charles and Jonelle Jeffords in Taos were yet
answering the telephone, but I reached Allan Huggins on the sixth
ring.

"Mr. Huggins?"

"Speaking." He sounded out of breath, as if he'd run some distance to catch the phone.

"My name's Hodges, you don't know me, I'm a book dealer from
Philadelphia. I've been hired by a private investigator to track down
a book and I'm hoping it's something you might be able to help me
with."

His laughter was sudden and booming. "You're a card, aren't you,
sir? . . . A book dealer who's also a detective, you say? What'll they
think of next?"

"I guess it's that combination of skills that makes me as good a bet
as anybody to find a book that nobody thinks is real."

"Aha, you must be looking for the Grayson *Raven* . . . Darryl
Grayson's lost masterpiece."

"How'd you know that?"

"It's what everyone's looking for. I must get half a dozen calls a
year on it, maybe more. It's one of those urban myths that got started
just after the Graysons died. It just won't go away, and it's all pre-
posterous, just total nonsense. Read my bibliography."

"I've done that."

"Well, then . . ."

"It's a great piece of work, but it won't answer the one question
that keeps coming up."

"Which is . . . ?"

"If there's nothing to it, why do so many people keep chasing it?"

"Now you're asking me to be a psychologist, and all I ever was,
was a poor bibliographer. This is the reason I stick to books. No mat-

ter how complicated they become, bibliographically, their mysteries can always be solved. With people, who knows? Have you ever solved the mystery of anyone, sir—your brother, your son, the woman you love?"

"Probably not. Maybe I could come see you, we could put our heads together and solve the riddle of the Graysons."

"Not very damned likely."

"I won't take much of your time."

"If you think it'll help, come ahead. But I can tell you right now, you won't get any encouragement from me in this Grayson *Raven* business. If you ask me was Grayson planning another *Raven,* my answer would have to be yes. I've alluded to that much in my bibliography. But there've been no major changes in the Grayson Press bibliography since my book was published. Some poems by Richard have turned up, and maybe fifty significant broadsides. But in my humble opinion, the *Raven* project never got off the ground. If you want to ask me why foolish people keep chasing that myth, I have no idea."

"Maybe you could show me some of their books. I've heard you have the biggest collection in the world."

My compliment fell strangely flat: he didn't seem unusually proud of the fact, if it was a fact. But he said, "When will you come? I'm not doing anything wonderful right now."

"Now is fine."

I took down his address. He lived on the sound, in Richmond Beach. Five minutes later, I banked the Nash into I-5, heading north.

24

Huggins lived in a two-story brick house on a large wooded lot facing the water. It was well back from the street, hidden from the world. In the last light of the day I could see the water gleaming off in the distance as I drove into his yard. I saw a curtain flutter: a door opened and he came out on an upper deck.

He had a shock of white hair and a curly white beard, a big belly, and burly, powerful arms. Santa Claus in coveralls and a flannel shirt, I thought as I came toward him. His sleeves were rolled up to the elbows: he looked like a workingman waiting for some wood to chop. We shook hands and he welcomed me to his home. There was a spate of polite talk as we went inside. I asked if he'd been here long and he said yes, twenty-six years in this house this coming November. His wife had died a few years ago and for a while he had considered selling it—lots of old memories, you know, lots of ghosts—but he had kept it and now he was glad he had. It was home, after all: everything he had was here, and the thought of moving it all, of winnowing down, was . . . well, it was just too much. Then about a year ago all the pain had begun melting away. He had begun taking comfort in these nooks and crannies and in all the thousands of days and nights he had lived here.

We went through the living area and into his kitchen, where he had just brewed a pot of coffee. The window looked down a rocky hillside to Puget Sound, which stretched away like an ocean into a wall of coming darkness.

"You'll have to forgive me," he said, "I'm terrible with names."

I fed him my alias again and he repeated it in an effort to remember. The coffeepot gushed its last orgasmic perks and he poured two huge mugs without waiting for it to end. "I like it strong," he said, and I nodded agreeably, waving off the sugar and cream. "So," he said, getting down to cases, "you want to know about the Graysons. Where do you want to start? I'm afraid you must be the guide here, sir—I don't mean to brag, but my knowledge of the Grayson Press is so extensive that we could be here for days." He gave a helpless-looking shrug.

"I'm not sure where to start either. I said I wouldn't take up much of your time, but I'm just beginning to realize what a deep subject this is."

"Oh, my dear," he said, rolling his eyes.

"Even the Aandahl biography is a monster. It'll take me a week to read it."

He made a derisive motion with his hand. Santa was suddenly cross. "The woman's a maniac."

"Who, Aandahl?"

"Journalists," he sneered. "All they ever want is the garbage in a man's life. Gossip. Bedroom stories. Lurid sex. But what can you expect from a newspaper reporter?"

"I guess I won't know that till I've read it."

"Don't waste your time, you won't learn anything about the books, Mr. Hodges, and isn't that what we're here to discuss? Listen, if Darryl Grayson himself were sitting with us at this table, he'd tell you the same thing. A man is nothing. All that matters is his work."

I had never been able to swallow that notion, but I didn't want to push him on it. It seemed to be a sore spot that he had nurtured for a long time.

"I don't mean to be harsh," he said in a kinder tone. "It's easy to like Trish: she's witty and quick and God knows she does turn a phrase. I'm sure she can be delightful when she's not chasing off to Venus or obsessing over the Grayson brothers. But get her on that subject and she's crazy. I don't know how else to put it."

He gulped his coffee hot. "I'll tell you how crazy Trish Aandahl is. She thinks Darryl and Richard Grayson were murdered."

I stared at him as if I had not heard the same words from Trish herself. "Is she serious?"

"Damn right she is. She gets her teeth into something and never lets go of it. She's like a bulldog."

"I guess I'm at a disadvantage here. I just got her book and I've barely had time to look at it."

"You won't find any of this in there. The publisher made her take it out."

"Why?"

"The obvious reason—she couldn't prove any of it. It was all conjecture. As a reporter you'd think she'd know better. But I hear she fought with her editor tooth and nail, really took it to the wall. It almost jeopardized the book's publication. If she hadn't listened to her agent's advice, the whole deal might've fallen through."

"What advice?"

"To take what she could get now—publish the biography without all the trumped-up mystery. To keep working the other angle if she believed it that strongly. If she could ever prove it, it might make a book in itself, but as it was, it just undercut the credibility of the book she'd written."

"That sounds reasonable."

"Of course it's reasonable. But a reasonable person also knows when to stop. What's it been now, three or four years since her book was published? Four years, and I don't think she knows anything more today than she did then. But she's still out there digging. Or so I hear."

"I take it you and she are not bosom buddies."

He smiled, struggling to mellow. "We're certainly not enemies. It's just her book I don't like: I don't like it even without the epilogue, or whatever she called the murder chapter. Who *cares* how many prostitutes Richard Grayson knew in Seattle, or that even poor Darryl never could keep his own pants zipped? I just don't like that kind of business. I'm not a prude, I'm just suspicious of it. Trish will tell you she did more than three hundred interviews for her book. I say so what. How can we be certain that even Archie Moon, who was Darryl Grayson's friend for life, was telling her the truth?"

"People usually tell the truth when they know they're being quoted in a published record of their best friend's life."

"That's what you think. You'll pardon me if I remain a skeptic. I'm not saying Moon would lie—I just know that people do put their own spin on things. It's human nature. How can anyone know what really went on between Grayson and Moon over a forty-year friendship, when one of them's dead and the other might have an ax to grind? Moon's agenda might be nothing more devious than to have Grayson viewed well by posterity. So he might not tell you something that would undercut that, even though it might well contribute to a better understanding of Grayson's genius and how he made his books."

"It sounds like you're saying that Grayson's genius had a dark side."

"Can you imagine any genius that doesn't? It comes with the territory, as people say these days. You'll hardly ever find a truly brilliant man who isn't a little sick in some way. But what difference does it make? The Graysons are of general interest only because of the books they produced. If they hadn't done the books, they'd be nothing but a pair of swaggering cocksmen, forgotten by everybody including Ms. Trish Aandahl. Anyone can lie down with whores, but only one man could have done the Thomas Hart Benton *Christmas Carol*. Only one. That book was a *creation,* you see, and that's what I choose to focus on. I don't do interviews for my work, I'm not interested in what people *say* about the Graysons, all I want to know is what really happened. My disciplines are rigid, precise, verifiable, true. If that sounds like bragging, so be it. I don't report rumors or pillow talk."

He held my eyes for a long moment, then said, "You look like you disagree with everything I've just said."

"I'm absorbing it."

He poured me another cup, got a third for himself, and sat down again. "Very diplomatic, sir. But look, tell the truth—as a bookman, do you actually *like* biography?"

"It's like anything else, a lot of it's slipshod and crummy. I don't like the *Mommie Dearest* crap. But I guess I believe there's a need for biographies of people like the Graysons, done by a writer who's a real writer, if you know what I mean. No offense to you—what you do is indispensable, but . . ."

"But I'm not a writer and Trish is. You won't get any argument from me on that point. The woman is just a sorceress when it comes to words. There's a seductive quality to her writing that hooks you by the neck and just drags you through it. Just wait till you get started reading her book—you won't be able to leave it alone. You'll wake up in the night thinking about Darryl and Richard Grayson, their times and the lives they led. Trish is just brilliant when it comes to conveying emotions with images and words. She could've been a great fiction writer, done the world a favor and left the Graysons alone."

"What about you? Did Aandahl interview you?"

"Several times. I had to overcome a good deal of reluctance to sit still for it. In the end, I'm no better than anyone else, which only proves my point all the more. I'm a ham, Mr. Hodges. I was fascinated with her subject, with the things she was finding out, and I was flattered that she considered me an indispensable source. There's no getting around it, I did want to know what she was doing."

"Did she quote you accurately?"

"I didn't give her much choice. I insisted on reviewing her material—at least the parts where I was mentioned."

"Did you find any errors when you read it?"

"No."

I raised an eyebrow and cocked my head slightly.

"She had a *tape* recorder, sir, how can you misquote someone when you record every syllable and grunt? Look, I'm not saying she isn't a good reporter—she may very well be the greatest newspaperwoman since Nellie Bly. And if she keeps digging at it, who knows what she might uncover? Maybe she'll prove that Richard Grayson was in league with Lee Harvey Oswald and her work will go down in history. Pardon me in the meantime if I doubt it. We're going around in circles—I have my opinion, Trish has hers, and I'm sure you have yours. Where do you want to start?"

I didn't know. "It's a little like jumping into a sea. All I know about the Graysons so far is what I got from that capsule biography in your book."

He fidgeted. "I hated to do even that much. But the requirements of the book . . . the publisher demanded it, it was felt that readers would want at least the essentials of their lives. So I did it, but I kept it short—only what could be absolutely verified. It's still the part of the book that I'm least proud of."

"That doesn't mean you didn't know the lurid details."

"I know *all* the lurid details. I've read everything that's ever been published on the Graysons. I can touch the paper a Grayson book is printed on and tell you whether it's the regular run or one of his variants. In a sense, every book he made was a variant. Did you know that?"

I shook my head no.

"It was one of his trademarks, one of his eccentricities. That's what makes the man so endlessly interesting. Try to get a grip on him by looking at his work—you'll end up in a rubber room talking to men in white coats. I can spend days with his books, and I'm talking about different copies of the same title, and I'll find some little variation in every one of them. Every time I look! *I'm* supposed to be the Grayson expert, I'm supposed to know everything there is to know about these things, and I can still sit down with five copies of his *Christmas Carol* and find new things in every one of them. Sometimes they're subtle little things in the inks or the spacing of words. Can you imagine such a thing in this day of mass production?—Grayson made every copy in some way unique. It was a trademark, like Alfred Hitchcock appearing somewhere in all his films. Only what Grayson did was far more difficult than anything Hitchcock ever dreamed of. Try to imagine it—the chore of producing an exquisite book in a run of five hundred copies, and making many copies different from the others without messing anything up. It would drive a normal man nuts. He must've worked around the clock when he had a book coming out. The binding alone would've taken anyone else six months to a year, full-time. Grayson did it in a gush."

"He had Rigby to help him."

"But not until 1963."

"Before that there was Richard."

"Who was a pretty fair binder, as it turned out. I'm sure these people helped out, but I don't think anything ever went out of that shop that Grayson himself didn't do. This is partly where the mystique comes from. Grayson did things that to other printers look superhuman, and once he decided *what* he was going to do, he did it with a speed that defies belief. He'd fiddle and change things in the process: then, for reasons no one understands, he'd toss in a real variant. It's as if he suddenly got a notion in the middle of the night, and he'd change the paper or the binding, for that one book only. If the book passed muster when he'd finished it, he'd go ahead and ship it. People on his subscription list were always thrilled when they discovered they had a variant—though it was sometimes years later that they found out."

"Some of them probably never found out."

"That's an excellent assumption. You can bet there are still many Grayson books sitting on the shelves of people who have no idea what they've got."

"The original owner dies, leaves them to his children . . ."

"Who don't understand or care."

"Is there any way of tracing these books?"

"Don't think that hasn't occurred to me . . . and to one or two other people. You'd think it would be simple—Grayson must've kept a master list of his subscribers, but it's never been found. Some of the books have come to light on their own. They'll pop up in the damnedest places . . . last year I got a card from a woman in Mexico City. Her husband had been a subscriber. He had just died and she had all the books, still in their shipping boxes."

"What did you do?"

"I flew down and bought them. On the first available plane. That's one of the perks that comes with being an expert. Everything gets funneled your way."

"I wonder if Aandahl gets any of that."

"I wouldn't be surprised. When you've published a book on something, people do tend to think you know what you're talking about, whether you do or not. And they'll call you when they think they've got something you'd buy for a price. Trish has a certain advantage in that her book will be read by many thousands more people; mine is so narrow and specialized. But I really doubt if she'd know the differences between the Benton standard issue and the Broder variant"—he grinned widely—"without consulting my book first."

I didn't say it, but it seemed to me that Huggins had been reading Aandahl at least as much as Aandahl had been reading Huggins. He caught my drift at once.

"I've read that goddamn book cover to cover ten times. That doesn't count endless browsings. Sometimes I dip into it when I'm at loose ends. I've got two copies back there, one for the shelf and the other for the workroom. The working copy's so marked up you can barely read it anymore. I argue with her in the margins, I rail at the liberties she takes. The book is bashed and battered where I threw it against the wall when I first read it. So, yes, I do know it well. I can quote passages from it the way some people quote Shakespeare. And if we're going to be totally honest, I've got to tell you this: the goddamn thing can move me to tears in places. It has a brilliance that I . . . I don't know how to describe it. At its best it rings so true that you just *know* . . . you find yourself pulling for Trish to be right. But her book is fatally flawed because there are many other places where you know she's stretching it. I can tell the minute she starts that horseshit, sometimes right in the middle of a sentence. And in the end the whole book's meaningless: it's a fascinating piece of pop culture. Trish can talk to a million people, and even if they all slept with Grayson, they still won't be able to tell her what she really wants to know."

"Which is what?"

"For starters, *what* drove the man, *what* made him do things, *why* he did them the way no one before or since has come close to doing, and *where* did the genius come from. I can't remember who said this, but it's got the stamp of truth all over it. James Joyce could spend a lifetime trying to teach his son to write, but the son could never write a page of *Ulysses*."

"Grayson sounds like a pure romantic."

"Trish seems to think they both were—that's one of the many flaws in her book. Take the term *romance* strictly in its sexual context and you'll see right away how silly her thinking is. Darryl Grayson couldn't have been more his brother's opposite in his relations with the opposite sex, even if encounters with women invariably ended up in the same place. In bed, I'm saying—they both had enormous sexual appetites. But women to Richard were just objects. Richard sometimes said that he had slept with more than twelve *hundred* women, Mr. Hodges, can you even begin to imagine such a thing? Trish Aandahl must've been in hog heaven when she uncovered that juicy little tidbit. But the point is this—Richard hated women; Darryl loved them. That's the difference. Darryl Grayson never met a woman he couldn't just love to death. And it didn't matter what they looked like: he loved the homely ones the same as the beauties. I've known a few of Grayson's ladies and they all say the same thing. He had a way of making them feel cherished, even when they knew he'd be with someone else tomorrow."

"The most difficult kind of man there is, from a woman's viewpoint."

"Absolutely. Richard had the reputation of being the ladies' man, because he conquered so many and they fell so fast. But it was Grayson who broke their hearts. His printshop fascinated them—they'd go in there and it was like stepping into a world they'd never dreamed of. Then they'd see what he was *doing,* and what he had *done,* with all those Grayson Press books lined up on a shelf above his matrix, and even a whore would know that something great had touched her life."

"Did he ever show them work in progress?"

"All the time. Grayson was completely secure in himself. I don't think the notion that anybody might steal his work ever crossed his mind. How could you steal it?—he created it all, from the alphabets to the designs. He took special delight in seeing the uninitiated light up at their first encounter with his art. In the last five years of his life, Darryl Grayson enjoyed his celebrity, as restricted as it was. He loved his uniqueness. He didn't brag, but he'd spend hours talking to you, explaining the process, if you were interested."

"Would you mind telling me a little about his process?"

"He was like great artists in every field, from literature to grand opera. Ninety percent of his time on a given project was spent in development, in planning, in trial and error. He created and threw away a lot of books. Sometimes he made a dozen copies, using various papers and inks, before he decided what was what. On the *Christmas Carol,* for example, he spent a year comparing the color reproductions on various papers. It wasn't every day you got Thomas Hart Benton to illustrate one of your books, and it was damn well going to be perfect. And it was! What he finally chose was a fifty-year-old stock that he bought from a bank, which had taken over a publishing house and was disposing of the assets. The paper had been in a warehouse, sealed in boxes since 1905. It was very good stuff, intended for the fine-press books of that day but never used. It took the colors perfectly, the registers are just gorgeous."

"What did he do with the dummy books?"

"Destroyed them. They were just for experimental purposes, and the last thing he wanted was for some flawed copy to turn up later, in the event of his unexpected death. Grayson was extremely aware of his place in publishing history. Rightly so, I might add. A hundred years from now his books will be as prized as anything you can name."

"And he knew that."

"Oh, yes. Oooooh, yes, my friend, no doubt of that at all. Grayson gave the impression of being a humble man, and in some ways he was. But don't let anyone tell you that he ever sold his art short, or that he wasn't acutely aware of his own importance."

A thought crossed my mind and I shivered slightly. Huggins asked if I was cold and I said no, I was just thinking of Grayson's dummy books. "Imagine turning one of those up. What do you suppose it would bring if a thing like that just turned up suddenly at auction?"

He rolled his eyes.

"What if a whole set survived?"

He was too much a gentleman to say it, but the look he gave me said it well. *You've been out in the rain too long, mister, it's starting to make your brain soggy.*

"So what about *The Raven*?" I said.

He gave a laugh and rolled his eyes, a vision of Looney Tunes.

"You did know he was working on it—that much is in your book."

"Obviously he died before the project was finished."

"Do you know how long he'd been working on it when he died?"

"In a sense you could say he'd been working on it since 1949. That's where it started, you know, that obsession with Poe. It began in Grayson's nagging dissatisfaction with his first *Raven*. Personally, I love the book. I'll show it to you when we're through here, you can see for yourself. It's simple and lean, but what's wrong with that? It was done on a shoestring budget, that's all. It wasn't the lack of money that kept *The Raven* from being a great Grayson—Grayson would never let money stand in his way. If the money wasn't there to commission an artist like Benton, he'd get someone else to do the art. That someone might be a total unknown, but he'd be good, you could bet on it, and the book would still be a Grayson. The trouble with *The Raven* was with Grayson himself. He was just too young, he didn't know enough yet. His alphabet was wrong: he was trying for an effect he couldn't yet achieve—letters that combined the modern and the Gothic in a way that had never been done, that would draw out Poe in the context of *his* time and still keep him relevant to a modern reader. It was too ambitious for a boy, even a genius, not yet out of his twenties. His vowels in particular were too modern for the rest of it—the *A*'s and the *O*'s, but even the bowls of the *D*'s and *B*'s too sleek-looking to give him the effect that the other letters were working for."

"Damn, it sounds complicated."

"You can't begin to imagine. At Grayson's level it can't even be adequately explained to a layman. But look, let's try. You have twenty-six letters. Your goal is to have them mesh perfectly, each with the others in every possible sequence, and in absolute harmony. So you tinker around with your *E*. At last it seems perfect, it looks great, until you discover—*after* the goddamn book has been bound and shipped—that when you put it between an uppercase *L* and a lower-case *n*, as in the name *Lenore*, it looks just like dogshit. You can't do this mathematically and you can't do it with computers: you just have to slug it out in the trenches and hope you don't overlook some silly thing that makes your work look to all the other printers in the world like it was done by a kid in kindergarten. Sure, the average guy won't know the difference—even a collector or a bookman like yourself wouldn't know. Any of you would look at the Grayson dummies and think they were perfect. But a printer like Frederic Goudy could tell right away, because he was also a master designer. Goudy was dead by then, but Bruce Rogers was asked about Grayson and he said what Goudy probably would've said—'This is very good, but it was done by a young man who will get nothing but better.' The remark got into print and Grayson read it. Rogers meant it as a compliment, but it stung him, and the book always haunted him. He wouldn't discuss it, and he went through a time when he considered denying that he'd ever done it. Good sense prevailed and he soon got off that silly kick. Grayson in the end was like most great artists, he could never reach his idea of perfection, and he was always too hard on himself. He didn't understand that the charm of his *Raven* lay in the very flaws that always tormented him. They show the budding genius at work. The flaws illuminate the brilliance of the other parts, and they do what none of Grayson's other works can begin to do. They show him as human after all. Especially the mistake."

"What mistake?"

"There was a spelling error in the poem 'Annabel Lee.' He never forgave himself for that."

"What did he do?"

"He spelled the word *sepulchre* wrong—with an *re* in one place, and an *er* in the other."

"That's an easy mistake to make."

"Of course it is. But gods don't make mistakes."

"Actually, I think you can spell it both ways."

"It had to be spelled the way Poe spelled it. To've messed that up was to a man like Grayson the height of incompetence. But it proves what old-time printers all knew—there's no such thing as a perfect book."

"Damn. Then what did he do?"

"After the denial stage, he went through another silly time—he decided to round up all the surviving copies and destroy them. Trish has this wonderful scene in her book, and who knows, maybe it even happened that way. Grayson had retrieved five copies and was about to set them on fire in the dump behind his house. But he couldn't do it—thank *God* he couldn't light that fire. I think it was then, that night, when he decided he'd do another *Raven* someday, in the distant future, when he had the money and the skills to do it right. He saw his career enclosed by those two *Raven*s, like definitive parenthetical statements."

Huggins let a long, dramatic moment pass. Then he said, "Isn't it too bad he never got a chance to do that second one?"

The clock ticked and the question hung in the air. A long silence fell over the room. I knew we were thinking the same thing, but Huggins would never admit it. Once or twice he looked to be on the verge of something: then he'd look away and hold his peace. I still had a million questions and the sinking hunch that even then it would come to nothing.

A simple question could tie us up for an hour. Huggins was expansive: a gesturing, conjecturing, extrapolating encyclopedia on the Graysons, and I didn't know enough to be able to decide what of all he was telling me was relevant. Then I thought of the one thing that might boot us up to another level—that scrap of charred paper in my wallet.

"Could I ask you something . . . in confidence?"

"Certainly."

I took the paper out and put it on the counter between us.

"What's your opinion of that?"

He squinted at it, then got out his glasses. I heard him take in his breath as if an old lover, still young and beautiful, had just walked into the room. He looked up: our eyes met over the tops of his glasses, and I could see that my hunch was right. I had shaken him up.

"Where'd you get this?"

"I can't say. That's part of what has to be kept confidential."

"What do *you* think it is?" he said, suddenly coy.

"You're the expert."

He gave a mirthless grin. "You're trying to tell me that this little fragment is part of something that I'm an expert in. But what can you expect from me, with such a small piece? There are only four letters. How can I tell?"

"The word *angel* appears in *The Raven*."

"I know that. But what's it prove? You think this is part of Grayson's *Raven*? It isn't."

"How can you tell?"

He picked up the fragment and held it up to the light. He looked at it through a jeweler's eyepiece, then put it back on the counter.

"The paper, for one thing. Grayson would've used a much finer stock than this. Probably an old stock. And he'd have printed it damp. You follow what I'm saying—he'd dampen the paper slightly, so the press could get a real bite into it, so the ink would go deep and become part of the page. Look at this and you'll see the ink's sitting right on top of the paper, which is a common and I'll bet cheap brand of copy paper."

I felt a surge of relief. It was a photocopy, my hunch was right, the real book was still out there, somewhere.

I picked up the paper chip and put it in my wallet. Huggins followed it with his eyes. He seemed irritated when I put the wallet away in my pocket.

He looked at the clock. "It's getting late."

I apologized for eating up his evening.

"A few more questions?"

He nodded. "Make it quick, though. I've got a headache coming on."

I took Eleanor's address book out of my pocket and opened it to the Grayson page.

"Does the name Nola Jean Ryder mean anything to you?"

He took off his glasses and squinted at the book, then at me.

"Where'd you hear that?"

"It just came up," I said, not wanting to tell him. "It's probably not important."

"She was one of Richard's . . . girls."

"Is she still around?"

He gave a faint smile. "Thinking of talking to her?"

"Sure, if I can."

"What could you possibly hope to gain by talking to one of Richard's old whores?"

"Is that what she was?"

He shrugged.

"It's like you said yourself," I said. "With a man like Richard Grayson, who knows where the answers are?"

He grunted. "You think she's got your *Raven*?"

Before I could answer, he said, "You'll find everything that's known about Nola Jean Ryder in Trish's book."

"You sure make her sound mysterious."

"Do I? I don't mean to, though she's certainly mysterious enough. She disappeared after the fire and she hasn't been seen since."

We looked at each other and the questions rose in my throat. He cut them off unasked. "Look, I don't know a damn thing about that. I told you before, this is not my thing. If you want to talk about Grayson's *books*, then I'm your man. But if you're interested in people, especially the whores in their lives, then you'll have to ask Trish. Or read her book."

I started to put the address book away.

"What other names do you have in there?" He was suspicious now, his tone accusing.

I looked at the page. "Jonelle Jeffords."

He shrugged.

"Rodney Scofield."

He sat up with a start. "What about Scofield?"

"That's what I was going to ask you."

"Did Scofield send you here?"

"I don't even know the man."

He looked dubious.

"Really."

"Then where'd you get his name?"

"It's just something I picked up."

"Of course it is." His tone was suddenly mocking, almost hostile. "Really, sir, I think you've been taking advantage of me."

"I can't imagine how."

"Can't you really? Do you think I'm a complete idiot? You come in here and I don't know you from Solomon Grundy. How do I know who you are or what you really want? You'll have to leave now. I'm tired."

Just that quickly, I was hustled to the door.

I took a chance, told him to call me at the Ramada if he had second thoughts, but I probably wouldn't be there beyond tonight. I sat in the car and looked at his house. The questions had only begun. I still didn't know why Trish Aandahl thought the Graysons had been murdered, and I never did get to see Huggins's books.

On the way downtown I stopped at a Chinese joint. I ate some great moo-shoo and arrived back at the Ramada at eight o'clock. I sat on the bed and made my phone checks. Leith Kenney was still incommunicado: in Taos, the recorded welcome mat continued on the Jeffordses' phone. By nine o'clock I was tight in the grip of cabin fever. I tried Trish Aandahl, but there was no answer. Outside, the rain had resumed its hellish patter.

Nothing to do at this time of night but wait it out. At quarter after nine a knock at the door made me jerk to my feet, knocking the phone to the floor. I stood for a moment, that line from Poe running through my head . . .

> " 'Tis some visitor," I muttered, "tapping at my chamber
> door—
>
> > Only this and nothing more."

. . . and slowly I moved to the window and parted the curtains. I could see the dark outline of a man, his shoulders and legs and the back of his head. He knocked again: he meant business. He had probably heard the phone falling and knew I was here, and he didn't seem interested in helping me by moving back out in the light so I could see his face. I bit the bullet: went to the door and opened it.

It was the deskman. "Sorry to disturb you, I just wanted to check and see if that's your car. I didn't recognize it from anybody who checked in today."

I assured him it was mine: the other car had belonged to a friend. He apologized and went away. But he stopped in the courtyard and looked back at the Nash, just long enough to give me the jitters. He didn't write the plate number down, and I watched him through the curtain until he disappeared into the office.

If I had any thought about staying here past tonight, that ended it. I'd be gone with the dawn, looking for a new place and a new name. I sat on the bed and tried the phone again, but the world was still away from its desk. Kenney and Jeffords I could understand, but Trish had asked me to call, you'd think she'd be there. I would try her each half hour until she came in. I was reaching over to make the ten-o'clock call when it rang almost under my hand. It caught me in that same tense expectancy, and again I knocked it clattering down the table to the floor. I gripped the coiled wire and the receiver bumped its way back up the nightstand into my hands.

"Hello."

"Mr. Hodges?"

"Yes . . . yeah, sorry about the racket."

"It's okay, I've done that a few times myself." There was an awkward pause. "It's Allan Huggins."

"Ah."

"I've been thinking about that chip of paper you showed me."

I waited, letting him get to it in his own way.

"Actually, I haven't thought about anything else since you left."

"Have you changed your mind about it?"

"No . . . no." I heard him breathe . . . in, out . . . in, out. "No, I feel sure it's a photocopy. The question I can't get out of my mind is, what's it a photocopy of? . . . And where's the original? . . . And how and when was it made?"

"Interesting questions."

"I'm wondering if I could see it again. I know I wasn't too hospitable when you were over earlier. I apologize for that."

"It's no problem."

"Would it be asking too much . . . Could I perhaps make my own photocopy from your sample? I'd like to study it at greater length."

"I don't think I want to do that just now. You can see it again, if you'd like."

"I would like, yes . . . very much. The lettering's what's getting to me. The more I think of it . . . I've never seen that exact typeface, and yet . . ."

He didn't have to elaborate: I knew what was going through his head.

"Tomorrow, perhaps," he suggested hopefully.

"I'll give you a call if I can."

"Please do . . . please."

"You could do something for me while we're at it. Call it a trade-off."

"Surely," he said, but his voice was wary.

"Tell me why the name Rodney Scofield set you off like a fire."

"Don't you really know?"

"No," I said with a little laugh. "I keep telling you, I never heard of the guy."

He grunted a kind of reluctant acceptance. "Tomorrow, then. We'll talk about it then."

He hung up. I made my phone checks yet again, to no avail. Outside, the rain fell harder, bringing my spirits down with it.

In this mood of desolate pessimism, having exhausted for the moment my last best hopes by telephone, I lay back on the bed and started reading Trish Aandahl's book on Darryl and Richard Grayson.

26

The earliest Grayson alphabets were etched in the cool, hard sand of Hilton Head Island in the fall of 1937. It was a wild beach then: there were no luxury hotels or golf courses, and the beach was fringed by strips of jungle. On Sunday mornings Grayson would crank up his '29 International pickup and clatter out on the oyster-shell road from Beaufort. *Never again have I known such a sense of freedom and raw potential,* he wrote, years later, to a friend in Atlanta. *Never have I had such a clear vision of the road ahead.* He was seventeen and on fire with life. He walked the beach alone, glorying in the solitude and in the wonder of his emerging wisdom. His cutting tool was a mason's trowel. He covered the beach with alphabet, running with the sunrise and racing the tide. He knew all the classic typefaces: he could freehand a Roman face that was startling, and when the tide came up and washed it all away, it left him with a feeling of accomplishment, never loss. It was all temporary, but so necessary—the sweet bewilderment, the sudden clarity, the furious bursts of energy that sometimes produced nothing more than a sense that in his failure he had taken another vital step. It would come, oh, it would come! He could do things at seventeen that he could not have dreamt at sixteen. His youth was his greatest ally, as fine an asset as experience would be when he was forty. A photograph exists—two photographs, reproduced back-to-back in Trish's book. The young Richard Grayson stands on the beach, his face in shadow, the sand behind him etched with letters. The same scene on the verso, a young woman standing where Grayson had been. The capsule identifies her as Cecile Thomas, the day, September 15, 1937. *He was my first love, the dearest, most desperate, most painful. I was eighteen, a year older than he was, but he was in all ways my teacher.* On that moonlit night, warm for early autumn, they had become lovers on the sand, obliterating the writing he had done by firelight. *Never mind,* he said, *I'll make you another one,* and he did, running blind in the dark with the tide going out, and when they came back in the morning, the incoming tide had not yet reached it. *Oh, it's perfect,* she had said: *when the tide finally did come up and wash it away, I cried, and he laughed and said it was nothing.* Someday, Grayson told her, he would create something that couldn't be washed away, so why cry now for trifles such as this? *God, I loved him . . . still do in a way. I couldn't believe how it affected me when I read of his death, and I hadn't seen him in more than twenty-five years.* The world was a poorer place when he died. He cared nothing for money or roles or the things that drove others. He learned his art the only way an artist ever learns, by probing the secrets of his own vast heart. He always took the road less traveled, always: he rose up on the page and strode across it, an unspent force even in death. Here he comes now, walking up Hilton Head alone. He carves up the sand with his trowel, running an alphabet of his own creation, knocked off on the spot. The tide licks away the *A* even as he touches off the small *z*, and he stands ankle-deep in the surf, breathing the pure Carolina air and tasting his coming victories. Only the spirit of Trish Aandahl is there to keep him company, this woman yet unborn, a kindred essence wafting in the wind. Somewhere in the cosmos they connect, inspiring her to better prose, perhaps, than she can ever do. And slowly as she writes of Grayson, a dim picture emerges of herself. She's there beside him, coaxing him along the sandy shore. She tells me things about Grayson that would leave a photographer baffled. The camera would miss it all. A magnificent picture is never worth a thousand perfect words. Ansel Adams can be a great artist, but he can never be Shakespeare. His tools are too literal.

27

I finally reached Leith Kenney at midnight. The conversation was short but potent.

"Mr. Kenney?"

"Yes."

"I'm calling from Seattle." I didn't tell him who I was. I was more interested at this stage in finding out who he was. I played my trump card right out of the gate. "I'm calling about Grayson's *Raven*. The 1969 edition."

I heard him catch his breath, as Lewis and Clark might've done at their first glimpse of the Pacific Ocean. I knew one thing right away: I had dealt myself a strong hand, even if I couldn't see all the cards.

I let his pause become my own. Then I said, "Are you interested in talking about it?"

"Oh, yes." His voice quivered at the prospect. "Yes, sir," he said, underlining the *sir* part.

His eagerness was so palpable that I knew I could run the show. "Tell me about Rodney Scofield."

"What do you want to know?"

"Look, I'm just a guy who's stumbled into something. I was tipped to you people by somebody who might know a lot more than I do. But right now I don't know you boys from far left field."

"Mr. Scofield is a businessman . . ."

"And?"

"He collects books."

"Grayson books."

"Yes."

"And it's fair to say that Mr. Scofield is a pretty substantial man."

"You can check him out. You'll find him in most of the financial reports that are available in the library."

"And who are you?"

"Well," he said as if it should be obvious, "I work for Mr. Scofield."

"Doing what, besides taking questions about Grayson?"

"That's my full-time job."

I thought my way through a stretch of silence. "Would it be fair to say that Scofield would pay a small fortune if a Grayson *Raven* were to fall into his hands?"

The silence was eloquent. Mr. Scofield would pay more than that. Mr. Scofield was that most dangerous of book animals, the man with the unquenchable passion and the inexhaustible bank account.

"I'll get back to you," I said.

I hung up before he could protest. I wouldn't worry anymore about Leith Kenney or Rodney Scofield. I had their number, I knew where they were, and they'd be there when I wanted them.

Trish was another matter. I let her phone ring ten times before giving her up. I tried her desk at the *Times,* but she wasn't there either.

Jonelle Jeffords continued keeping the world at bay with her husband's answering machine.

At half past midnight, I shut down for the night.

I would sleep six hours. If supercop didn't come in the night, I'd be well out of here in the morning.

I had a plan now, a destination that I hoped would take care of the lodging problem. It was a gamble, gutsy as hell. For that reason alone I thought it was probably the safest hotel in town.

In the morning I would become Mr. Malcolm Roberts of Birmingham. I was going back to the Hilton.

I let Trish put me to sleep with her lovely prose.

In the first hour of the new day, I walked in Grayson's shoes.

28

The Grayson odyssey twisted its way through Georgia half a century ago. The forces that shaped them were already centuries old when they were born. Their grandfather was still alive and whoring when they were boys in grade school, the gnarled old buzzard a whorehouse regular well into his eighties. The old man never stopped fighting the Civil War. The big regret of his life was not being born in time to be killed at Fredericksburg, where his father had died in 1862.

A plantation mentality ran the house of Grayson. The father ruled and allowed no dissent. His politics were boll-weevil Democrat and his neck was the color of the clay hills that stretched around Atlanta. Women were placed on pedestals and worshiped, but they quickly lost their sex appeal if they wanted anything more out of life than that. It was Darryl Senior's profound misfortune to marry Claudette Reller, a free spirit who could never quite see the charm of life in a cage. She abandoned her family on a sunny day in 1932, walking off in the middle of her garden-club luncheon without notice or fanfare. Her sons, ages eight and twelve, never saw her again. She was said to have died three years later in Paris. The old man announced it at supper one night and forbade her name to be uttered again under his roof.

The younger, fair-haired son obeyed his father well. A psychologist would say, years later, that he never forgave his mother and that every experience with sex was a slap at her memory.

The older son remembered her less harshly. He knew why she'd done what she'd done, and he wished she would write him from wherever she'd gone so that he might answer her and tell her he understood. He and his father were locked in their own battle of wills, and when he thought of his mother, there was sympathy in his heart.

In the summer of his seventeenth year, young Grayson escaped to the Carolina coast. There he lived on a sea island, thinking about life and supporting himself by working in a Beaufort garage. But in the fall he was back in Georgia, doing battle with his father in the determined effort to become his own man. Women became an ever-larger part of his life. Cecile Thomas had been lovely but temporary: now there was Laura Warner, older and more experienced, twice married, widowed and divorced, cerebral, moneyed, and addicted to genius. She saw herself as Mrs. von Meck to Grayson's Tchaikovsky, one of their literary friends suggested, but Grayson was having none of that. They parted amicably after a short but intense friendship. She moved to Birmingham and, in 1939, sailed from Miami to London, where her trail petered out.

But Grayson's life was rich with women like that. A biographer trying to dig up his footprints forty years later could still find some of them eager to talk and have their memories mined. Others had been swallowed by time. A line had to be drawn on the hunt for old girlfriends and the book brought back to its dual focus. So Trish Aandahl let Laura Warner slip away into wartime London while she worked her narrative around and brought Richard again into the picture.

There are people in Atlanta today who remember Darryl and Richard Grayson and believe that a strong streak of real hatred existed between them. But there are others who tell a different story. They remember the hazing Richard took from a pack of bullies when he first started high school. The leader of the gang was one Jock Wheeler, a mean little bastard as remembered by the Marietta shipping clerk who had known them all. Today Jock Wheeler is an elderly mechanic in an Atlanta garage. He's a quiet man who lives alone and bothers no one. Ask Jock Wheeler about the Grayson boys, said the shipping clerk to Trish Aandahl. Ask him about that night in the midthirties, when he was ambushed on a dark country road by two men he couldn't, or wouldn't, identify and beaten so badly he almost died. Wheeler had nothing to say, but the rumor mill persisted that one of the assailants was little more than a boy, twelve or fourteen years old. The sheriff floated the Grayson boys as the leading candidates, but Wheeler said no, twasn't them. The rumor mill churned. The more thoughtful of their contemporaries pointed to it as a strange quirk of human nature. Probably on some level the Graysons truly did hate each other, but blood is thicker than water. That's the thing about clichés, you know. They are usually true.

29

I woke to a gray dawn, certain I'd heard a noise off to my left elbow. It went click-click, like the sound a lockpick makes when someone is trying to open a door. But I had been dreaming about a raven, its talons clicking as it walked across the table to peck my eyes out.

Both sounds stopped as I came awake and sat up in the bed.

It was Sunday, the day of rest.

Television promised more rain, followed by bad weather. The weather clown played with his million-dollar toys, swirling clouds over a map and grinning with all thirty-two as he did his dance. But this was a floor show next to the competition. Evil, two-faced evangelists pranced about, talked of Jesus and money in the same foul breath, and sheared their glass-eyed flock. Praise the Lord, suckers.

The radio was fixed to an oldies station, with something called a salute to the British Invasion already in progress. I got "Eleanor Rigby" as a curtain call to my shave-and-shower, and I stood in the buff anticipating every beat and lyric, for all the good it did me.

The clock was pushing nine, and my departure seemed somehow less urgent than it had at midnight. Nothing was open yet. Check-in at the Hilton wasn't till three o'clock. The library, another of my scheduled stops, informed by recorded message that its Sunday hours were one to five P.M. I had time on my hands.

I sat on the bed and started my phone checks. It was ten o'clock in Taos.

I punched out the number and heard it ring.

"Hello?"

"Jonelle Jeffords?"

"Who are you?"

It didn't seem to matter so I told her my real name, then began to improvise. "I'm a friend of the court. The judge in Seattle gave me the job of getting Miss Rigby back to New Mexico in the burglary of your house. I need to ask you a few questions."

She expelled her breath like a hot radiator. "Goddammit, can't you people leave us alone?"

This was a strange attitude for a victim, but I already knew she was not the run-of-the-mill victim. I put an official tone in my voice and said, "Most people who've been burglarized cooperate. I find your attitude a little unusual. Is there a reason for that?"

She hung there a moment, surprised, then said, "My husband is very upset by all this. It's going to be bad enough having to go to court when they finally do bring that crazy girl back here. What can I tell you that hasn't already been asked and answered fifty times?"

"I'm sure you're tired of answering questions. But I'm in Seattle, I don't have access to the files they've built in Taos, and I need to know more about what she stole from you. Otherwise I don't know how you expect to get your property back."

"I don't want it back. I should've burned it years ago."

"Burned what?"

"That book."

"It was mainly a book, then, that she took from you?"

"If I'd just given it to her when she first came here, maybe she'd've just gone away. Then none of this would've happened."

"Where did you get the book?"

"I don't see what that has to do with anything. It's personal business, very old business. It doesn't have any bearing on this."

"It might, if we have to determine who owns it."

"What are you saying, that *I* stole the book?"

"I'm just asking a few questions, Mrs. Jeffords. If I seem to be going in a way you don't like, it's your attitude that's leading me there. You're going to have to answer these questions, you know, sooner or later."

"Listen to me, sir, and understand what I'm telling you. My husband is extremely upset by all this. He's outside now on the deck, he'll be in here any minute, and the last thing I need is for him to find me talking to you about that crazy girl. It hasn't been easy coping with this. She could've killed us. Charlie gets a little crazy himself just thinking about it. If you call here again, you'll cause me a lot of trouble."

"Can you describe the book?"

"No! Can't I make you understand English? I haven't even looked at it in twenty years."

"Are you familiar with the names Slater or Pruitt?"

"No. Should I be?"

"Slater says you hired him to find your book."

"He's lying. I never heard of the man."

"What about Pruitt?"

Her voice dropped off to a whisper. "Charlie's coming. Charlie's here. Go away, don't call me again."

She banged the phone down.

What a strange woman. I could just see her, scurrying across the room to distance herself from the telephone. Smoothing her dress, sitting primly, trying to look like a poster from *Fascinating Womanhood* as her big old bear came home from the hill.

Trying her damnedest to give away a book others would kill for.

I hadn't gotten to the hard questions yet. Who really fired that gun, Mrs. Jeffords? What's the link between you and the Rigby girl, and why do I get the feeling that it's personal?

I knew, though, that I'd had my one shot at her. She was far away and she wouldn't be picking up the telephone again without letting that recording screen it first.

I tried Trish and got nothing.

Decided to put Allan Huggins on hold for the moment.

Checked out of the motel and went looking for breakfast.

At eleven o'clock, I parked on the street outside the library and passed the time reading.

30

Suddenly it's 1963. Gaston Rigby stands in North Bend at the dawn of his life, ready and waiting to be molded by the genius Darryl Grayson. Who would think that Grayson might hire him, even to sweep out the shop? Now there are days when every green kid with a yen to publish turns up on Grayson's doorstep, hat in hand, begging for a chance to work for nothing. The mystique is in full bloom, and Grayson is still well on the sunny side of fifty. What is it that separates Rigby from the others? . . . How does he get to Grayson on that primal level, that place where the genius lives? Grayson leaves no clue. He is not one to talk of such things. The hunt for verbal profundity makes him uneasy and, if he's pushed too hard, cross. Speaking of Rigby, Grayson will say only that he's a good one. He's willing to let it go at that, as if trying to isolate and define everything that goes into making a good one is beyond him. And this is Archie he's talking to, and Archie knows a good one as well as he does.

Moon looks back at it many years later. At times he thinks Rigby took the place of the younger brother—almost but not quite. He thinks Grayson and Rigby were, almost but not quite, like father and son. That spiritual bond can be difficult to understand when you stand outside it: it goes deeper than anything Moon has ever seen between men of solidly heterosexual persuasion. He insists he felt no jealousy: he is secure in his own importance to Grayson, and if Rigby mattered as much on another level, why should it worry him? He was still Grayson's best friend in life. They grew up together, they swam buck naked as kids, tramped woods and fields, hunted deer and birds, chased women as young hell-raisers, drank, dreamed and shared the same calling. When Grayson left the South after the war and wrote that he had found a promised land, Moon came along to see for himself. Moon still remembers the first words he spoke as he got off the train in Snoqualmie. *What the hell is this little burg gonna do with two goddamn printers, for Christ's sake?*

But Moon is a mechanic and Grayson is an artist. They coexist perfectly, perhaps the only friends in history—to hear Moon tell it—who never had a disparaging word between them. Moon does worry, especially in the beginning, that Grayson is chasing an impossible dream. Nobody ever made money doing small-press books. Put that in caps and say it again. NO-body. If you can do it for twenty-five years and not lose your pants, you can call yourself blessed. Grayson never made a dime. His entire operation was bankrolled with family money. Eventually the boys came into hundreds of acres of prime Georgia planting land—peaches, corn, just about anything a man wanted to grow. But Darryl and Richard Grayson were not farmers. They sold the land and Grayson took his half and did what he did with it. His books made enough to keep most of his principal intact, and that's all they ever made in his lifetime.

What is it about the book business anyway? Moon wonders. Sometimes it seems like nobody on any level of it makes any money. Maybe if you're Random House and you can figure out how to publish nobody but James A. Michener, you can make a little money. Everybody else picks up peanuts.

Why do they do it? he wonders. But he knows why.

Now it's 1963 and Rigby arrives, joining Grayson in the quest for the perfect book. *Look at you, Darryl,* Moon says over beer in the town bar, *you're launching a life.* Grayson just nods in his cups. What has never been said—what Moon tells Trish Aandahl years after Grayson's death—is how much influence Rigby had on Grayson. Rigby was truly remarkable for a kid: *Damn, he had the greatest hands,* Moon says, *he'da been a great doctor, delivering babies, coaxing 'em into the world . . . he could coax butter out of a witch's heart* and his instincts for binding and design were almost as fine and fully formed as Grayson's. Rigby offers his opinions timidly at first— a kid does not come in and tell a genius how to run his business—but he soon learns that Grayson has no ego in the heat of the work. Grayson will listen to the man in the moon if the guy can give him an idea, and Gaston Rigby is a fountain of ideas. *Do you think, Darryl, that the center of the page is too dense? . . . Not by much, maybe, but listen to what the words are saying and look at it again.* Grayson studies it. He walks away and looks from afar. More often than not, he decides that Rigby is right. Their talk runs nonstop through the day, every word germane to the work at hand. There is never a joke between them or a comment on the outside world or a reflection on womanhood. There are no calendar-girl pinups, no radios or newspapers, nothing that would take away Grayson's concentration even for a moment. There are no clocks. Grayson comes down to the shop in the morning and Rigby is already there. They work until some inner clock tells Grayson that the day is done. In Grayson's shop, time stands still. He alone knows when the work is through and he walks away, leaving Rigby to wash the press and tidy up the workbench and put everything back where it goes.

Rigby's responsibilities grow along with his salary. By his second year he seems indispensable. His eye is uncanny: he catches things that might even escape the master in various stages of trial and error. Broken serifs, hairline cracks, typos: he spots them instantly. He checks each impression for indentation, uniformity of punch, blackness of ink ("needs a little more color here, Darryl"). His eye is so good that Grayson comes to depend on him in those final stages when the books are inspected and shipped. This gives him a sense of family, something he's never known. Rigby lives upstairs, in the loft over the shop. He stands in darkness now, staring off through the black woods at the lights of the big house. He knows that sometimes the brother brings whores over from Seattle, but this too he sees as part of the process. If Grayson can be relaxed and made ready for tomorrow by the services of a whore, let him do it. They come and go, harmless fluff. Only near the end does the one called Nola Jean take on a major negative importance. She screws with Grayson's head and is not good.

It is now 1968. Rigby is twenty-two. He has been with Grayson five years and life is sweet. He has a woman of his own, a relationship nurtured slowly like a courtship from another time. This is Crystal, Moon's teenage niece, who ran away from her home in Georgia and now finds work in the North Bend bakery. Crystal loves Rigby's shyness, his brilliance, his teddy-bear presence. He is the first solid man in her life, always the young gentleman. Rigby has none of the stormy impatience that runs rampant through his generation. Politics bores him: even the Kennedy assassination, he tells her, struck him as little more than another TV show. Crystal marvels at this. She is seventeen, and in love.

31

I reread the last chapter, which told of the fire. The facts rolled out like an epilogue. On the night of October 14, 1969, the shop had caught fire and gone up like a torch. A fire investigator had come out from Seattle, poking through the ashes for days before calling it, officially, an accident. But I knew from my own experience that these things are often vague. At least one hundred thousand fires a year are written off to unknown causes, Aandahl pointed out, and the presumption in law is that these are accidents. Arson must be proved beyond a reasonable doubt: a fireman's suspicion, however strong, doesn't cut it. An old-fashioned printshop like Grayson's was a firebomb waiting to go off.

In the first place, there is paper everywhere. There are rags, often soaked with solvents or ink. The printer must work with fine papers and keep them in pristine condition, but he also works with ink, which gets on his hands, under his fingernails, and on his tools. Everything must be washed, many times a day. A working printer might go through 150 gallons of solvents a year. Kerosene was the stuff of choice for many shops. Grayson liked gasoline because it was harder and faster. He kept it in a fifty-gallon drum behind the shop. The drum sat upright in a wooden frame, with a spigot at the bottom where the squirt guns could be filled.

The fire broke out in the main part of the shop—the fire investigator was able to figure that out by the pattern of the wood charring. It had quickly consumed that room, spread up to the loft, then to the little storeroom in back. By the time it was seen from the road, flames had broken through the ceiling and back wall. The gas drum caught on fire and exploded, sending a fireball a hundred feet in the air. The remains of Richard Grayson were found in the shop: he had been drinking and had apparently passed out in a chair. His brother was in the back room. He too was drunk, and the fireman theorized that he had gone back to lie down on a cot that was kept there for just that purpose, when he'd had too much booze to walk himself back up the dark path to the main house.

Gaston Rigby had gone to town. It was for him a rare night out. He had taken his girl, Crystal, to dinner in Seattle and arrived home at midnight to find his world in ruins.

I was standing at the door when the library opened. It didn't take long to dope out Rodney Scofield. I looked through periodical and newspaper indexes, and in half an hour I had come up with all the applicable buzzwords.

Oilman . . . manufacturer . . . eccentric . . .

Billionaire, with a *b*.

Recluse. Twenty years ago, when Scofield was in his late forties, he had taken a page from Howard Hughes and disappeared from the public eye. He had been written about but seldom seen since 1970. His business deals were conducted and closed by the battalion of toadies and grunts who worked for him. Nowhere in the general press was his hobby, books, given a line.

I went to *AB/Bookman's Weekly,* which publishes its own yearly index.

I found nothing on Scofield, but Leith Kenney was prominent in the magazine's index of advertisers. He had been a bookseller, with a store in San Francisco.

He had been a notable bookseller, with membership in the Antiquarian Booksellers Association of America. This is not an easy group for flakes and fly-by-nights to get into. They nose around in your credit, they check your bank references and take a long look at your stock before admitting you to the club. People who bounce checks and cheat little old ladies get a quick brush-off from ABAA.

Kenney was a past president. His field was fine-press books.

But he had not run an ad in the magazine since 1986. I found out why in that year's December issue, in a news column headlined "Kenney to Close S.F. Bookstore." No, he laughed, he was not going broke. He had been offered a job that was simply too lucrative and challenging to pass up. He was going to create a world-class library on the career of Darryl Grayson. He would be looking for anything that pertained to the man's life or work—ephemera, photographs, correspondence, business records, and, of course, the books, in any quantity. Multiple copies were eagerly sought. The work of Richard Grayson was also of interest, Kenney said, but it was clear from the tone that he was considered an association figure. As far as posterity was concerned, there was only one Grayson.

I didn't want to park in the Hilton garage: my rust bucket was a little too prominent for a class hotel like that. I put on my raincoat and carried my bag, leaving the car parked on the street.

I rode up the elevator to the lobby on the ninth floor. Paid cash for two nights and told them I might be longer. I asked for a quiet room on a high floor, where I could see the city.

The clerk had rooms on fifteen, seventeen, and twenty.

Seventeen would be fine, I said. I was given a key to 1715.

I rode the elevator up and walked along the hall. The door to my old room was open. I walked past and looked in.

Two men were there, going through the wastebasket. The big one with the pale olive skin stood up and turned as I came by. I turned as he did, letting him see the back of my tired gray head.

I opened the door and went into my new room. Couldn't help gloating just a little as my door clicked shut.

Score one for old dad in the game of guts football.

Up yours, supercop.

32

I sat on the bed and called Leith Kenney in Los Angeles. This time I had no trouble getting through to him.

He had had a dozen hours to think about it and decide how he wanted to handle it. He gave me the direct frontal approach, which I liked. We were two bookmen talking the same language, even if only one of us knew it.

If the material was genuine, he wanted it. If there were questions of ownership or provenance, he would still pay top money for possession and would hash out the legality when the thing went to court. This to him was a foregone conclusion. We were talking about a substantial sum of money, and people tend to bicker when money arises. At the same time, Kenney had no doubt where *The Raven* would end up, where it *should* end up. He was prepared to top any offer, many times over. He was prepared to fly to Seattle at a moment's notice or fly me to Los Angeles in Scofield's private jet. He was prepared for just about anything.

"Let's put it this way," he said. "If you've got something you even *think* might be the genuine article, we want to see it and we'll pay you for that privilege no matter how it turns out. We've been looking for this item for a very long time."

"That's pretty good, for a book the bibliographer swears was never made."

"We know it was made. Mr. Scofield has seen it. He's held it in his hands. Maybe Allan Huggins wouldn't be quite so smug if he had done that."

Before I could ask, he said, "It was a long time ago, and that's all I want to say about it until I know more about you. You've got to appreciate my position, sir. I don't even know your name. Mr. Scofield may be the only man alive who has actually touched this book, and we don't want to be put in the position of giving away what we know about it."

That was fair enough. I didn't like it, but I had to live with it.

"Remember one thing," Kenney said. "If you do turn it up, people like Huggins will be all over you. Don't make any deals on it without giving us a chance to top their bids. We *will* top them, you'll be shocked at how much. And you'll be doing yourself or your client a terrible disservice if you sell it anywhere else."

At last we were down to bedrock. The big question.

"How much money are we really talking about here, Mr. Kenney?"

"Whatever you'd like."

33

I didn't move for a while: just sat on the bed listening to my inner voice. It drew my mind back across the hall to the room where Eleanor and I had spent our last few hours together.

Homework's finished, said the muse. One more phone call, maybe two, and you can hit the street.

In the room across the hall, Eleanor had mailed a letter. Against my better judgment, I had watched her write it and then I had let her send it off.

What was it, who got it, where had it gone?

Questions with no answers, but sometimes the muse will give you a hint. Her nearest and dearest was one obvious call, a risky one I'd rather not make on this telephone. Still the letter had to be chased—if it dead-ended, at least it would lead up an alley that had to be checked anyway.

And then there was Trish, a source of growing discontent. I seemed to have lost her in the heat of the moment. She faded to black while I scrambled around covering my tracks, and now, suddenly, my need to hear her voice was urgent.

The muse played it back to me.

Call me, she said. Don't disappear, I have some things to tell you.

Having said that, she herself had dropped off the earth.

So the night work was there. Chase the letter, track down Aandahl.

I called her home, wherever that was, but the telephone still played to an empty house. I tried her desk at the paper, without much hope. At the end of three rings there was a half-ring, indicating a shift to another line.

A recording came on, a woman's voice.

"Hi, this's Judy Maples, I'll be running interference for Trish Aandahl for a few days. If it's vital, you can reach me through the main switchboard, four six four, two one one one."

I called it. The operator wouldn't give me a number for Maples, but did offer to patch me through to her at home. The phone rang in some other place.

"Hello."

"Judy, please."

"This is she."

"I'm a friend of Trish."

"Aha. What friend would you be?"

"One who's a little worried about her."

"She's fine. Something came up suddenly and she had to go out of town."

"When will she be back?"

"Not sure, couple of days maybe." There was a kind of groping pause. "Trish left a package for a friend, if you happen to be the one."

"What's in it?"

"Can't tell, it's sealed up in a little Jiffy bag. Do you think it's for you?"

"Is there a name on it?"

"Initials."

I took a long breath. "How about C.J.?"

"You got it. Trish didn't know if you'd get this far or not. For the record, I have no idea what this is about. I'm just the messenger gal. She told me to say that. It's true. I left your package with the guard at the paper. If you want to go pick it up, I'll call him and tell him to release it to you."

I said okay, though nothing about it felt okay.

I walked out past my old room. The cops were gone and the place was closed tight. I rode the elevator down, drew my raincoat tight, pulled my hat down to my eyebrows. The day was going fast as I went out into the timeless, endless rain. Everything in the world was gray, black, or dark green.

I fetched my car, went to the *Times,* and got my package.

It was a cassette tape, wrapped in a single piece of copy paper. A cryptic four-line note was handwritten on the paper.

If you'd like to stay at my house, consider it yours. I have no
reason to believe you'd be unsafe there. The key's in the
flowerpot. Don't mind the dogs, they're both big babies.

                                                                    Trish

A postscript told her address, on Ninetieth Avenue Southeast,
Mercer Island.

I put it back in the bag and slipped it under my seat, then moved
on to the main business of the evening.

I wanted to be well out of the downtown area when I made this
call. I drove south, got off the freeway near Boeing, and looked for a
telephone. Phones are like cops: there's never one when you need it.

At last I stood at a little lean-in booth and made the call. It was a
hard quarter to drop.

I heard it ring three times in North Bend.

"Hello."

"Crystal?"

"Yeah, who's this?"

"Janeway."

You could eat the silence, it was that heavy. I didn't know how to
begin, so I began by telling her that. But she already knew.

"The police were here. They've been here off and on since noon."

Good for the cops, I thought: good for them, not so hot for me.

I was getting nervous. It already seemed I'd been on that telephone
a long time.

"Are the police there now?"

"No. They may come back tonight."

The funny thing was, she never once stated the obvious: she never
said, "They're looking for you, you know," or anything like that.
Still, she wasn't going to give me what I needed unless I could move
her that way.

"I'm going to ask you for something. I wouldn't blame you if you
told me to go to hell. I haven't done much right so far."

She was listening.

"I guess I'm asking you to trust me. I'd like you to believe that everything I've done, at least after that first night, I've done for Eleanor."

She punished me with silence. I endured it till I couldn't anymore.

"Crystal."

"Yeah, I hear you."

"I'm trying to find your daughter."

"I guess I knew that. And I don't know why, but I do believe it."

The wall between us crumbled. Whatever she'd been telling herself with the logical part of her brain gave way to instinct.

"Even when we were talking to the police, I kept thinking of you," she said. "Kind of like an ace in the hole."

"That's what I am. It may not be much . . ."

"I get feelings from people. Not psychic, nothing like that, but people hit me either warm or cold. When I hugged your neck on the porch that first night, I felt the warm between us. Sometimes people just connect, you know what I mean? I could see that between you and Ellie right from the start. It was warm, but not the kinda thing a mother needs to worry about . . . except maybe on her side."

She gave a little laugh. "That's why I never really gave up on it, even when it came out why you were really here."

"I'm going to find her if I can. I don't know how and I'm starting pretty far back. I need your help."

"Tell me what you want."

"Are the cops taping this call?"

"They talked about doing that. There was some doubt about whether it'd be productive. Just a minute." She put the phone down and blew her nose. Then she said, "They're not exactly expecting a ransom demand."

"When will you know?"

"They may come back tonight and put it on. Or they may not."

"If they do and I call back, could you let me know?"

"How?"

"Clear your throat when you answer the phone. I'll try to find a way to let you know if I've got anything new."

"Or you could call Archie. He wants what we all want."

"A couple of questions. Do you know a guy named Pruitt?"

"He's the one the cops are looking for. They think he took Ellie with him."

"Had you ever had any contact or dealing with Pruitt before this came up?"

She paused as if groping for words. "I knew who he was."

"Tell me about it."

"A crazy man. He seemed to think we had something . . ."

"A book."

"Yeah, but I didn't know what he was talking about. He wouldn't go away, though, wouldn't leave me alone. I'd go to town and see him watching from a car. Then he started bothering us on the telephone. At night he'd call, play music. Just a few notes, but we knew it was him."

"He was stalking Eleanor too."

She expelled a shivery breath.

"Listen, did you get a letter from Eleanor in yesterday's mail? It would've probably been on Hilton Hotel stationery."

"It never came here."

"It may come tomorrow. What time is your mail delivered?"

"Whenever he gets here. Early afternoon as often as any."

"I'll try to call then."

"What's in the letter?"

"That's what I need to find out. It might be her laundry bill. For our purposes, think of it as some dark secret she'd rather not tell the world. Is there anybody else she might send something like that to?"

"Amy Harper," she said immediately. "Nobody but Amy."

I remembered the name. "Eleanor mentioned her once. Said she'd gone to see Amy but Amy wasn't there."

"Amy moved into Seattle, I coulda told her that. Her life out here'd turned to hell the last six months, especially after her mom died. I worry about that child, don't know what's gonna become of her. She's made some wrong choices in the last few years. But really a sweet kid. She and Ellie were like sisters all through school."

"I seem to remember there was some kind of rift between them."

"They had a falling-out over Coleman Willis. That's the fool Amy let knock her up when she was still at Mt. Si High. Then she made it worse: married the fool and quit school and had a second kid the next year. The trouble between them was simple. Ellie had no use for Coleman Willis, couldn't be in the same room with the man. Amy was still trying to make it work. You can see what happened."

"Sure."

"But Amy's no fool. There came a time when even she'd had enough of Coleman and his bullshit, and she took her kids and left him. She and Ellie got together once or twice after that. I really think they'd fixed things up between 'em, I think they were good as new."

"Is there a phone number for Amy?"

"God, Amy can't afford a telephone, she's lucky she's got a roof over her head. I've got an address if you want it . . . it's a rooming house on Wall Street. Are you familiar with the section they call Belltown?"

I wasn't.

"It's easy, right off downtown. Just a minute, I'll get it for you."

34

It was just fifteen blocks from the Hilton, about as far as Oz is from Kansas. It made me remember myself as a kid, bouncing around for a year of my life in places not much better than this. Now I go through these neighborhoods and the memory of rank and scummy beds hits me like a shot of bad whiskey. It's a chilly reminder of what life hands out to those who slip and can't climb up again. The young seem unbothered by the lack of elegance: time, they believe, will see them through it, and time when you're twenty is a thing you'll never run out of. You can sleep anywhere when you're running on your rims, and you don't give too much thought to the dripping tap or the cracked and faded walls or the mice that come tearing across your landscape. The young endure and hope, until suddenly they're forty and time isn't what it once was. The old suffer and save their hopes for the real things in life—a high, dry present and a quiet place to die.

On the second floor of this environment, at the end of a long, dim corridor, lived Amy Harper. The floor creaked with every step and the walls were thin. I could hear people talking—in one room shouting—as I walked past the doors and stopped at 218.

Be there, I thought, and I knocked.

She was: I could hear her move inside. Soft footsteps came at me and a soft voice asked who I was. I said I was a friend of Eleanor's.

She opened the door and looked at me through a narrow crack. I could see a chain looped across the crack, a little piece of false security she had probably bought and installed herself. A man like me could break it with one kick, long before she had time to get the door closed.

"I'm sorry, who are you?"

"My name's Janeway, I'm a friend of Eleanor's."

For a moment she didn't know what to do. I got the feeling she'd have opened the door if she'd been there alone. But I could hear a baby crying and I knew she was thinking about her children.

"Crystal gave me your address," I said, and at that she decided to let me in.

It was just what I'd expected—a one-room crib with a battered couch that pulled out and became a bed; a table so scarred by old wars and sweating bottles that you couldn't tell what color it had been; two pallets for the children; a kitchenette with a gas stove and an old refrigerator; a bathroom the size of a telephone booth. There was one good chair: she had been sitting in it, reading a paperback. Stephen King, the grand entertainer of his time. God bless Stephen King when you couldn't afford a TV.

She had been nursing the baby: she still held it in the crook of her arm. Her left breast had soaked through the faded blouse she wore. She covered it, draping a towel over her shoulder, excusing herself to put the child on the pallet next to the other one. "So, hi," she said with a cheery smile as she stood and brushed back a wisp of red hair. Crystal had called her a sweet kid and the adjective seemed just right. Amy Harper had the sweetest face I'd ever seen on a girl. You looked at her and saw a young woman who wanted to love you.

She couldn't offer much—a cup of instant decaf or a Diet Coke maybe—but her manners were alive and well. I let her fix me some coffee, mainly because she seemed to want to. She went into the kitchenette, stand-up room for only one, and turned on the gas. "So how is Eleanor?" she called back across the room. Apparently they had not been in touch.

"Actually she's not so good," I said, sitting on the chair where she had been. "She seems to've disappeared on us."

She looked out of the kitchen, her face drawn and suddenly pale.

"I'm trying to find her."

"What're you, some kind of detective?"

"Some kind of one. Crystal hoped you could help us."

"If I could, God, you know I would. I haven't got a clue where she might be. Just a minute, this water's boiling."

I heard the sounds of water pouring and the tinkle of a spoon stirring in the coffee crystals. She came out with two steaming cups, insisting that I stay in the chair. She sat on the floor against the wall and looked at me through the steam rising from her cup.

"I haven't got a clue," she said again.

"When was the last time you saw her, or heard from her?"

"Haven't seen her in . . . must be more than a month ago."

"Any mail from her . . . cards, letters . . . anything?"

"No, nothing."

"I'm looking for one letter in particular. I'm not sure if it's had time to be delivered yet. She may've mailed it Friday night."

"To me, you mean?"

"We don't know. Crystal thinks that's a possibility."

"Probably come tomorrow then."

"If it does, would you let me see it?"

"Yeah, sure, if it'll help; I'll do anything I can."

We sipped our coffee: I could see her running it all through her mind.

"If she mailed something to me, it probably wouldn't come here. I haven't seen her since I moved into town. She'd send it out to my mamma's place in Snoqualmie."

"Could we ride out there and see?"

"Yeah, sure. I'll have to take off from work . . . my boss is a little touchy about that. . . . I'll just tell him I'm taking off. If he fires me, he fires me."

"I don't want you to get fired. Maybe I could go check the mail for you."

She shook her head. "No, I want to go too. You've got me worried. Jesus, I hope she didn't hurt herself again."

"Crystal said you were special friends."

I saw a tremor of feeling ripple through her. "Oh, yeah. She's like my soul mate. I don't mean . . ."

I knew what she didn't mean. She said, "We were just great together, all through grade school, then high school. We were inseparable. If I wasn't sleeping over there, she was over with my mamma and me. We'd sit in our rooms and talk about boys, and the drudgery of life at Mount Success."

She gave a sad little laugh. "That's what we used to call Mt. Si High—Mount Success—because so many of the people who went there seemed to go nowhere afterward. They just stayed in that little town forever. I never understood that, but now I do. Here I am in the big city and all I want is to get back home."

"Why don't you? It's only twenty-five miles."

"It's a lot farther than that." She shrugged. "I had to get out of there. My ex lives there and he's bad news. If I went back, he'd just hassle me."

"Crystal said you and Eleanor had drifted apart, then got together again."

"The drifting was my fault. I married a guy who was a jerk. Want some more coffee?"

"Sure."

She got up, poured, came back, sat. "That's the first time I ever said that. My husband was a jerk. There, maybe now I can get rid of it. He was a grade-A heel." She laughed. "Hey, it feels better all the time. Maybe if I call him what he really was, I'll be good as new. Wouldn't be very ladylike, though."

I let her talk.

"Ellie tried to tell me what he was like, that's why we almost lost it. I didn't want to hear that. But the whole time I was married to this fella, and carrying his children, he was trying to make it with my best friend. What do you do with a guy like that?"

"You leave him."

"Yeah. And here I am, bringing up my children in this palace. Working in a bar and giving most of my money to the day-care people. Wonderful, huh? But I'll get through it."

I leaned forward, the coffee cup clasped between my hands, warming them. "Amy, I don't have any doubt of that at all."

She smiled that sweet smile. I thought of Rosie Driffield, the light-hearted heroine of *Cakes and Ale*. Maugham would've loved this one.

"The great thing about Ellie, though," she said, "is, she never let it bother her. The hard feelings were all on my side."

"But you got over it."

"Yes, thank God. Even an ignoramus sees the light if it's shined right in her face."

"And Crystal said you two got together again and patched it up."

"My mamma died. Ellie came to the funeral and we cried and

hugged and it was all over, just like that. Then I found that stuff of hers . . ."

She looked away, as if she'd touched on something she shouldn't be talking about.

"What stuff?"

"Just some things my mamma had."

"Things . . . of Eleanor's?"

"Not exactly. Just . . . stuff. Papers in Mamma's stuff . . . it really isn't anything."

I felt a tingle along my backbone. "Tell me about it."

"I can't. I promised."

I looked straight into her eyes. "Amy, whatever you tell me, I'll try not to let it out. That's all I can promise you, but this may be important."

Her eyes were green: her face radiated hope, her eyes searched for trust. But she was also a child of this planet who had begun to learn that you can't trust everyone.

"I don't even know you."

"Sure you do."

She laughed at that and I laughed with her.

"You don't know, do you," I said, "about the trouble she got in, down in New Mexico."

Her eyes opened wide. No, she didn't know.

I told her.

Tears rolled down her cheeks. "I knew it, I knew it, I just knew something bad was gonna come of this. This is my fault, I should've burned it, I never should've shown it to her."

"Shown her what?"

"When Mamma died she left me some stuff. God, you never saw so much stuff. My mother was a pack rat, that house of hers is just full of stuff, it's packed to the rafters. You won't believe it when we go out there. I know I'm gonna have to start going through it, it's got to be done, but I just can't face it yet. I've got to soon, though . . . that house just has to be cleared out."

It seemed she had lost her drift in the maze of problems she had to deal with. She got it back, looked at me, and said, "There were some papers in Mamma's stuff . . . things I thought Ellie should see."

I nodded, urging her with body language.

She got up and went to a little end table half-hidden by the couch. I heard a drawer squeak open and saw her leafing through some papers. She pulled out a manila envelope, came over, and got down on one knee beside my chair. She opened the flap and handed me a photograph.

It was an eight-by-ten black-and-white. It was Eleanor in jeans and a sleeveless blouse, taken in the summertime in good light. She was leaning against the door of an old frame building, smoking a cigarette and smiling in a sly, sexy way. "Nice picture," I said.

But I looked again and in fact it wasn't a nice picture. It was her eyes, I thought, and that killer smile. She looked almost predatory.

"It's not her," Amy said.

I turned the picture over. On the bottom, handwritten in fading ink, was an inscription.

Darryl's printshop, May 1969.

35

"Isn't that a kick in the head," Amy said, looking around my shoulder. "Imagine looking at a mirror image of yourself, in a picture taken the year you were born. I thought about it for weeks, you know, whether I should show it to her or not. I knew the minute I saw it that nothing good would come of it. I felt all along that I should've burned it."

"Why didn't you?"

"It didn't seem like I had the right. It wasn't my call to make."

"What did you do?"

"One day I just showed it to her. She had come out to Mamma's to help me get started on going through things. We putzed around all morning on the first floor—I didn't even want to go upstairs where all this stuff was—and we were sitting in the kitchen having lunch. It had been on my mind all morning, and I still didn't know what to do. Then she looked across the table at me and said, 'You're like the sister I never had, you're just so special, and I'm happier than you'll ever know that we're okay again.' I felt tears in my eyes and I knew then that I had to tell her, there was no stopping it, and the best I could do was put a happy face on it."

"How did she take it?"

"I couldn't tell at first. I was hoping she'd look up and shrug it off, say something like, 'Yeah, I never told you, I was adopted,' and that would be the end of it. Then we could laugh about it and let it blow away and I could rest in peace knowing I'd done right by her. But the longer she sat there, the worse it got, and I came around the table and took her hands, and I knew for sure then that it had just knocked her props out. Her whole world was scrambled, it was like she couldn't think straight for a long time, like she couldn't get a grip on what she was seeing. I put my hand on her shoulder and said something stupid about what a coincidence it was, but we both knew better. There's no way."

"Then what happened?"

"She said she had to go home, she wasn't feeling well. And she left."

"Did you see her again after that?"

"Yeah, she called the next day and asked if she could come out to the house again and look through the stuff in the attic. So we did that. I worked downstairs and she sat all day in that hot attic, going through papers and old letters."

"Did she tell you if she found anything?"

"All I know is, she didn't *take* anything . . . just the one picture of this woman. I think she made some notes, though."

"Were there other pictures?"

"There was a whole roll taken at this same place. I think Mamma took them; it's her handwriting on the back and I know she was doing some photography then. There were maybe twenty shots of different people."

"Do you have the other pictures?"

"They'd still be out at the house, up in the attic."

"Were they people you knew?"

"Mostly, yeah: there were pictures of Gaston and Crystal and Archie. God, were they young!"

"What about Darryl and Richard Grayson?"

"I don't think so. But I wouldn't know them if I saw them. I think they were just friends of Mamma's, way back then."

"Do you know if Eleanor ever told Crystal about this?"

"No, and I wasn't going to. I felt like I'd done enough harm."

"Then it's possible they still don't know."

"Yeah, sure it is. But we can't tell them. The last thing Ellie said to me was not to tell anybody, especially not Crystal and Gaston. She made me promise I wouldn't."

"It takes courage to break a promise like that. Sometimes you have to, if the person's welfare is at stake."

"Is that what you think?"

"I don't know what I think. Has anybody else been up in that attic since your mother died?"

"There was a man who came, just after it happened."

"What man?"

"Just a minute, I'm trying to think, he gave me his name. He said he was an old friend of Mamma's who saw the item about her funeral in the newspaper."

"What'd he look like?"

"Old . . . older than Mamma, even. Kinda frail."

"What did he want?"

"He said she had promised to help him on something he was writing . . . some magazine article. She had some information he needed to make it work."

"Why didn't he get it from her while she was still alive?"

"He was going to. Her death was pretty sudden. She was in the kitchen, peeling potatoes for supper, when her heart gave out."

"So what did you do?"

"About this man, you mean? . . . I let him look through the attic. I didn't think there was anything special or valuable up there."

"This was even before Eleanor got up there, then?"

"Yes, at least two, three weeks before."

"And you don't remember this man's name?"

"It's right on my tongue, I'll think of it in a minute."

"Did he take anything out of there?"

"Not that I remember. He did have a big canvas briefcase with him. I suppose he could've put something in that. I don't know, maybe I shouldn't trust people so much. Do you think he took something?"

"If you remember his name, I'll see if I can find him and ask him."

She shrugged.

"You said your mother may have shot the picture herself. Did you ever ask her about her life when she was young—who her friends were, what they did, stuff like that?"

"I was a kid. You know how it is, all I ever thought about then was kid stuff. Now I wish I'd taken more time with her, but then we were all into boys and music and makeup. When you're a kid, your parents are probably the least exciting people in the universe. And you never want to learn too much about them, you're always afraid they'll just be human, have the same failings and hang-ups you've got."

"You said there was other stuff in the attic . . . besides the pictures?"

"Tons of stuff . . . boxes and boxes of records and papers and letters. It just fills up that attic."

"What was the purpose of it? Did she ever tell you?"

"She always said she was going to write a book about Mr. Grayson, who had been her friend for years."

"Did she tell you how they met?"

"No."

"What about your father?"

Her brow furrowed: dark clouds gathered behind her eyes. "What about him?"

"Who was he?"

"Just a man Mamma knew. He wasn't around long."

"Was his name Harper?"

"What's that got to do with Eleanor? My father's been nothing in my life."

"It's probably got nothing to do with anything. It's just a question a cop asks."

"My father's name was Paul Ricketts. I don't know whether he's dead or alive."

"Was he there then?"

"When?"

"The year we're talking about . . . 1969."

"He must've been, at least for twenty minutes." She blushed a little. "I was born that year."

"Where'd the name Harper come from?"

"It was Mamma's family name. She never married this man. I really don't see why you're asking me this."

I backed off. I didn't want to lose her. "I'm just trying to find out who was there, who's still around, and what they might know. What about this book your mother was writing?"

"She never wrote a word, never had the time. It was always tomorrow. 'Tomorrow I'll get started.' But tomorrow came and guess what? . . . She didn't have the time. She always had to work two jobs to keep me in shoes and have good food for us to eat. And then that other Grayson book came out, you know, by that woman at the *Times,* and that put the kibosh on it. Mamma knew she'd never write anything after that."

"But she did keep the material?"

"She never threw away anything in her life."

The thought that had been building in my mind now occurred to her. "Are you thinking maybe Eleanor found something up there in Mamma's stuff that caused her to go to New Mexico and break into that house?"

"There's a fair chance of it. That does seem to be where everything started coming apart for her."

"Damn. Makes you want to go out there now and start looking through it, doesn't it?"

"If that's an invitation, I'd love it."

She shook her head. "The house is dark, there's no power, they turned off the lights three weeks ago. And I'll feel a lot better tomorrow without the kids. I can drop 'em in day care at seven-thirty and we can head out then."

"If that's what you want."

"I'm as anxious as you are. I'm just not crazy about having my kids spend the night in a dark house in the country . . . you know what I mean?"

"In the morning then."

But she was my one real link to the past and I hated to leave her there.

Then I realized I didn't have to.

36

I talked her into my room at the Hilton with little effort. I explained it away as a room I had rented but couldn't use, and she wasn't inclined to ask questions. To her it was a *Wheel of Fortune* vacation: two nights in Oz, with a color TV, a king-size bed, and room service. I told her to order whatever she wanted, it was already paid for; then I left another hundred on deposit at the desk to cover it. It was after nine when I got over to Mercer Island, a wooded, hilly residential neighborhood just across the bridge from the city. Mercer dominates the lower half of Lake Washington: you come off Interstate 90 and swing along a spectacular bluff that overlooks the highway; then you curl back inland on a street called Mercerwood Drive and up past some expensive-looking real estate. It was not a place I'd imagine a working reporter to live in. So she had a boat, pricey digs, and a job that let her write her own ticket: I still couldn't imagine the *Times* paying her more than fifty grand. As I backtracked west, the houses seemed more ordinary. I turned left, dead-ended into a high school, and eventually found my way around it and came into her block.

It was an older house with a well-lived look to it. It sat on a large lot surrounded by trees. I pulled into her driveway and fished out the package she had left me from under the seat. She had left the night-light on as well as two lights inside the house. I got out and walked up like I owned the place.

The key was in the flowerpot, just where she'd said.

I came into a dark hallway. A brief memory of Pruitt's house flashed through my mind before the place burst into life—two golden retrievers charged from the rear in joyous welcome. I got down with them and roughed them the way big dogs seem to like it. Mitzi and Pal, the tags on their collars said. Mitzi was especially affectionate and I felt welcome, less like a stranger in this town of endless rain.

The hall opened into a large living area. There was a TV, VCR, and disc player, all the comforts. Just off the big room was a dining room, with a mahogany table that seated eight, and beyond that was the kitchen.

In the middle of the table was a cassette tape player, with the door flipped open.

Near the tape player was a note, telling her friend Judy Maples how much to feed the dogs and where things were. The dogs came and went, I saw, through a doggie door that opened off the kitchen onto a ground-level deck, and from there into a backyard.

I opened the refrigerator, which was well stocked with beer; I fetched myself one and sat at the counter sipping the foam. I took the tape out of the bag and snapped it into place in the machine.

"Hi," she said. "Isn't this cozy?"

She paused as if we were there together and it were my turn to talk. I said, "Yes, ma'am, and I thank you very large."

"You'll find beer in the fridge," she said, "but knowing you, you already have. Seriously, make yourself at home. The dogs will want to sleep with you, but they won't pester: if you close your door, they'll whine for about five minutes, then they'll shut up and go about their business. They're well behaved; I'm sure you'll get along famously.

"There's plenty of food. The freezer's well stocked, and if you don't see anything there you want, there's a big freezer in the garage. You can defrost just about anything in the microwave. Again I'm anticipating your little idiosyncrasies and impatiences, and assuming that you've never read an instruction booklet in your life. Do yourself a favor and read the two paragraphs I've left open and marked on the table. It's impossible to defrost food without knowing the codes. You could spend years of your life trying to figure it out on your own. I imagine you'll try anyway.

"I thought you'd be most comfortable in the big room on the right at the top of the stairs. It's a man's room—I rented this house from an FBI agent who's now doing a tour of duty in Texas. So that's where you should go—the room upstairs, not Texas—when you're ready to call it a night."

There was another pause. I stopped the tape, looked through the freezer, found a pizza, and put it in the real oven on a piece of tinfoil. The hell with instructional booklets written by committee in Japan.

I pushed the ON button on the tapedeck.

"So," she said, "on to business."

Yes, ma'am.

"The cops picked up that kid who was with Pruitt and Carmichael. His name is Bobby John Dalton, date of birth"—I could hear her shuffling through notes—"one nine . . . umm . . . sixty-six. He's got a record, nothing major: one or two fights, one assault charge, a drunk and disorderly, carrying an unlicensed weapon, having an open can in a moving vehicle. He thinks of himself as a tough guy, a muscleman. Maybe he is—I mention it so you'll know . . . he'll figure he owes you for what you did to him in the garage. He was a bouncer in a nightclub, a bodyguard . . . Quintana wouldn't tell me much more than that. I'm recording this on Saturday night. My plane leaves in two hours and I don't know at this moment whether they've actually booked this Dalton kid or are just holding him for questioning. He was still downtown the last time I checked, about an hour ago. I don't know if the cops have any new leads on Pruitt after talking to the kid."

Again she leafed through her notes. "Here's a little more personal information on the Dalton kid . . . just a minute."

She read off a home address, on Pine Street east of I-5. "It's a boardinghouse owned by his mother. She seems to be a character in her own right, in fact as mean as he thinks he is. His father's been dead for years, though probably not long enough. The old man was a gambler and a drunk and was probably abusive. It's no wonder Bobby's on a fast track to nowhere.

"This should make you feel pretty good. At least the cops are doing their part. They're looking at Rigby as a serious abduction, so you've accomplished what you wanted without coming in. However, comma, be advised that Quintana is still on your case."

I heard a click, then another, as if she had turned the machine off then on again. "As you would imagine, the cops are playing it close to the vest on the particulars at the murder scene. I did find out, from a source inside the department, one strange bit of information. At this point they think the woman in the house was killed sometime earlier than Carmichael . . . maybe as much as two hours. They'll know more when the lab gets through and, hopefully, so will I. But assuming that holds up, don't you find it strange?"

Yes, ma'am.

"That's all I have on it. I guess you should burn this tape. I've set a fire for you in the living room: all you've got to do is light it and toss this in. In fact, I don't know if you'll get in touch with Judy, or if you'll hear this tape, or if you do hear it, when that might be."

She took a deep breath. "I should be back in Seattle by Tuesday night . . . earlier if I get lucky."

I could hear doubt in her voice now, as if she had come to a new bit of business and wasn't sure how much if any of it she wanted to tell me.

"Have you read my book yet? Did you like it?"

Yes, ma'am.

"I guess you could say I'm rewriting the final chapter."

I heard her breathe: she had moved the microphone closer to her mouth and was fiddling with it, trying to set it up straight.

"Help me, Janeway, I'm not having an easy time here. Send me some vibes, give me a clue. I'm trying to tell you some things you should probably hear, but I'm still a reporter and this is the big story of my life. I've lived with it a long time and I don't share these things easily."

I waited. The tape was hot and running.

"I'll tell you some things I put in my original draft and later had to take out. But I won't name names or places here, and I don't want to tell you yet where I've gone. We'll talk about it next week, when I get home, and we'll see where we are then.

"There was a man I wanted to interview, back when I was doing my research. He lived in the city I'm going to tonight. He probably wasn't important. His connection to Grayson was slender—all he did was collect and love Grayson's books. I don't think they ever met, and to tell the truth I'm not sure what my original intent was in seeking him out . . . to see his books, maybe, or get some insight into the quintessential Grayson collector. I didn't think he'd contribute more than a line to my book, but I was in his town, I had his name and a few hours to kill. So I tried to look him up.

"Turned out he was dead . . . he'd been murdered years before, in

1969 as a matter of fact, a few days after the Graysons died. This in itself might mean nothing, but it put an uneasy edge on my trip. I decided to stay over an extra day and ask around. The investigating officer had since retired from the police. I found him running security for a department store. He didn't mind talking about it—it was an old case then, nothing had been done on it for years, and the old cop told me things about the scene that he might not've said a few years earlier. One thing in particular stood out, and I thought of it this morning when you were telling me about the scene at Pruitt's. This Grayson collector was found dead in a room full of books twenty years ago. Right beside his body was a pile of ashes."

I opened my eyes to a blinding sunrise. It was six forty-five, the clock radio had just gone off, and the sun was shining.

I shooed the dogs off the bed and hit the shower. Wrapped in steam, I considered Trish and the tape she'd left me. The fire had eaten the tape, but the chimney had gagged on the words. They hung in the air and chilled the morning.

Traffic was reaching its rush-hour peak, a freeway horror show that made I-25 in Denver seem like a solo flight. But the sun was shining: the city sparkled like a crown jewel in a setting of lakes and mountains, and there wasn't a speck of pollution in the air. I felt better than I had in days, better by far than a confirmed fuckup had any right to feel. Damned if this wasn't the first day of the rest of my life. Good things lay off in the distance, waiting to be discovered; I could feel the potential as I crawled off the exchange at Interstates 90 and 5. It was so strong that even having to fight traffic all the way downtown and back again couldn't sour the moment.

By the time I picked up Amy and we got her kids dropped off at day care, it was after eight o'clock. She caught my upbeat mood and we crept back along the freeway with hopeful hearts. She had been enchanted by her night in the hotel: when you're young and poor and the best thing you've ever slept in was a $20 room by the railroad tracks, the Hilton must seem like Buckingham Palace. We chatted our way into Issaquah, ate breakfast in the same Denny's where Eleanor and I had eaten a lifetime ago, and made the final run into North Bend a few minutes shy of nine o'clock.

It was the first time I'd had a good look at the town: I had only been here at night, in a misty rain, or on the fly. Now I saw what Grayson had seen when he'd first stepped off here in 1947: a land of swirling mists and magnificent vistas and above it all that incredible mountain, looming like a sleeping giant. As a rule mountains do not impress me much: I grew up in Colorado, and I had seen many that were higher, deeper, bigger in every way. But I'd never seen one that so dominated its landscape, that commanded without being majestic. It pulled at you like a vast black whirlpool: it stood alone over the town and defined it. "Impressive, isn't it?" Amy said. "Mamma came here as a child in 1942 and never wanted to go anywhere else. She told me once that she got here when they were tearing up the streets for the new highway and the town was nothing but mud. But right from the start, she wanted to live her life here."

"It's the mountain. It gets a grip on you."

"People say there's an Indian in the mountain. If you look on a clear day, like today, you're supposed to be able to see his face. The knee's about halfway down. I never could do that, though. Can't see diddly."

The sister towns, North Bend and Snoqualmie, were connected by narrow back roads. We came into Snoqualmie past the high school, Mount Success, which Amy followed with her eyes as we circled around it.

"My whole history's tied up in that stupid building," she said sadly.

"Amy, you haven't lived long enough to make a statement like that. Your history's hiding out there somewhere, in the next century."

She smiled. "You're a good guy, aren't you, Mr. Janeway?"

"Just one who's lived a fair piece of his own history . . . enough to wish for a little of it back."

She gave the high school a last lingering look. "In the ninth grade they gave us an IQ test. I got one twenty-eight, which surprised a few people. For a week or so I thought I was hot stuff. I asked Eleanor how she'd done, but she kinda blew it off and said not very good. I found out about a year later, when Crystal let it slip one day."

She directed me along a road to the left.

"Her score," she said, emphasizing each digit, "was one . . . eighty . . . six."

She laughed. "She's a genius, sealed and certified."

Somehow I wasn't surprised.

Amy, suddenly moved to tears, said, "God, I love her."

* * *

Snoqualmie was just a few blocks of businesses, two bars, stores, a laundry, a Realtor, and a bowling alley. Many of the shops were named for the mountain: There was Mt. Si Hardware, Mt. Si Video, and the Mt. Si Country Store, which had a sign in the window that said THIS FAMILY SUPPORTED BY TIMBER DOLLARS. Begone, spotted owl: never mind what your habits are, you'll have to find another place to have your habits. We were on the town's main drag, looking for a gas station. The street was called Railroad Avenue: it skirted the train tracks, with an old-time railroad station (was this where Moon had stepped out all those years ago and been drawn by Grayson into his new life?) and a historic log pavilion that boasted a log the size of a house perched on a flatbed. As if on cue, Amy said, "There's Archie's place," and I saw a dark shop with the letters THE VISTA PRINTING COMPANY painted on glass and under it, in smaller letters, THE SNOQUALMIE WEEKLY MAIL. He put out a newspaper, I remembered. I got a glimpse of him through the glass, talking to someone I couldn't see. Again I thought of a timber wolf, lean and wiry, and I had the feeling he'd be a good man to know, if I ever had the time.

I stopped at the Mt. Si 66. Amy filled the tank while I checked in with Denver from a pay phone.

Millie answered at my store. She had been worried, she said: the Seattle police had been calling. Business was lousy, she said. On the other hand, there was an appraisal job in the works, almost twenty thousand books, a job that could run weeks at $50 an hour. But they needed me to start next week.

I told her to give them my regrets and refer the job to Don at Willow Creek Books. If the cops called back, ask for Quintana and tell him I'd buy him a pitcher at his favorite watering hole when this was all over.

We backtracked through town. If Quintana doesn't get me, the poorhouse will, I thought.

Selena Harper had lived just outside town. "There's a helluva waterfall a few miles that way," Amy said. "Supposed to be half again higher than Niagara." But we weren't on a sight-seeing trip and she turned me off on one of those narrow blacktops running west. I saw a marker that said SE 80TH: we hung a left, then another, and doubled back into SE 82nd. There was a mailbox at the end, but the lettering had long ago worn away and had never been replaced. "Mamma never believed in doing any unnecessary work," Amy said. "Everybody in both towns knew her, so why bother putting a name on the box?" The mailbox was empty.

A dirt road wound back into the trees. The woods were thick and undisturbed here; the road was rutted and muddy from last week's rain. I didn't see a house anywhere, but soon it appeared as we bumped our way through the brush. A clearing opened and a ramshackle building shimmered in the distance like a mirage. There had once been a fence, but it had long ago crumbled, falling section by section until now only a few rotting posts and an occasional tangle of wire marked where it had been.

"Welcome to my castle," Amy said. "The only real home I've ever known."

I pulled into a dirt yard, slick with mud and ringed by weeds. The house was indeed in a sorry state. "I just don't know what to do with it," Amy said: "it's become a white elephant. I've been told the land's worth something, but not as much as Mamma owed. I doubt if I'll break even when I sell it, if I can sell it. I'm having a real problem with that, you know. How do you cut your losses on a piece of your heart?"

She got out of the car and stood looking at it. "The last big thing she went into debt for was a roof. Right up to the end, she wanted to protect all that stuff in the attic, make sure it didn't get ruined by a leak. So about five years ago she borrowed the money and had a guy come out and fix it. She's been paying the interest on the loan ever since, but hasn't made a dent in the principal. So what we have here, ladies and gentlemen, is a ten-dollar tablecloth for a two-dollar table. Let's go inside."

We picked our way up to the porch, where she found two notes taped to the door. On one was scrawled the word *BITCH;* on the other, which had been there longer, *Amy you whore you better stop this shit.* She tore them down and crumpled them in her fist: "Well, I see my ex has been here. Now my day is complete."

I heard the jingle of keys. She opened a door, which creaked on rusty hinges, and I followed her into the most jumbled, crowded, disorganized room I had ever seen. "Don't say you weren't warned," Amy said over her shoulder. "My mother was constitutionally unable to throw out anything. This is just the beginning." She turned and leaned against a doorjamb, watching me as I beheld it. The first problem was the magazines—years of such extinct publications as *Coronet, Collier's, Look, Radio Mirror* . . . they were piled in every corner, on the chairs, at both ends of the sofa. As a book dealer I had made house calls on people who had survived their family pack rats, but I'd never seen anything quite like this.

"The funny thing is, she really did write for some of these magazines," Amy said. "She really was a good writer, she just had trouble deciding what to write, and then making the time to do it. She got five hundred dollars once from one of these jobs. I think that's when she began to talk to Grayson about doing his life in a book. She had worked for him, you know, she was the first person he hired when his shop began doing so well back in the fifties. She answered his phone, wrote his letters, kept his business records. And at work she was neat as a pin . . . or so she said. She never left work without putting everything where it belonged, then she'd get home and throw her own stuff on the nearest pile."

She led me through the hall to the kitchen. The cupboards too were clogged with papers, magazines, clippings.

"Happy New Year," she said.

She pointed to a stair that led down into darkness: "Cellar. More of the same down there. Whatever's there is pretty well ruined by the moisture . . . the whole place has got a mildewy smell. I never go down there without getting depressed and wanting to douse the whole thing with gasoline and burn it to the ground."

The kitchen opened on the other side into a back bedroom. There was another short hall, with steps to the upper floor.

"What you want's up there. You won't even need a flashlight on a sunny day like this. There's a big window in the attic that faces east, and the sun'll light you up like the Fourth of July. Do you need me for anything?"

"Let me go on up and see what I find."

"I'll putz around down here. Stomp on the floor if you want me."

* * *

Sunlight beamed down the stair like a beacon. The air was heavy and filled with floating dust. I went up past the second floor, up a narrower stair to the top. Light from the east flooded the room, giving you the notion of being a sample on a slide under a microscope. It wasn't an unpleasant feeling—after the days of rain, you were willing to be a bug if it bought you a little sunshine—and I stood there for a moment with my head poking up into the attic before going the last few steps. The attic felt crowded, like the rest of the house, but the room was small and an immediate difference was apparent up here. There was order . . . there was purpose . . . there was care. The boxes were all of one size, fitted together in one large block. They were neatly stacked on pallets in the center of the room, far away from the walls. Each had been wrapped in polyethylene and sealed with clear tape; then the whole bundle was covered by a sheet of the same plastic, making it as nearly waterproof as possible.

It was one of those moments that only a bookman can appreciate, that instant of discovery when you know without opening that first box that you've just walked into something wonderful. Your mouth dries up and your heart beats faster, and the fact that none of it belongs to you or ever will is strangely irrelevant. I walked around the stuff, taking its measure. It was a perfect cube—four high, four deep, four across: sixty-four cartons of Grayson lore.

I stripped back the plastic cover and leaned down for a closer look. I could read the words she had written on the cardboard with a heavy black marker.

Richard/Letters, Poems, Miscellany
Sketches for Christmas Carol/Correspondence with Benton
Tape Recordings/Darryl Grayson and Selena Harper
Worksheets/Logs of Days
Correspondence/1950–55
Ideas for Phase Two

I took down the box marked *Richard/Letters* and broke open the seal. It was packed tight with original notes, all of them handwritten on legal pads. Selena Harper had probably done his typing and kept the originals, maybe without the author's permission or knowledge. I put the box off to one side and opened the one marked *Correspondence*. It was full of carbon copies, letters Grayson had written and typed himself during the formative years of the Grayson Press. Here was the man's life and philosophy . . . you could plunge in almost anywhere and be caught up in whatever had engaged his mind at the time. He wrote impressions of history to old friends in Georgia; he had long discussions on art with a teacher he'd had in high school and wrote rambling letters on almost any topic to people he'd never met. He was a faithful and generous writer. If you wrote to him praising one of his books, he would answer you, even if he'd never heard of you till that moment. He had a Southerner's sense of chivalry and honor: women would get more consideration than men, warm, chatty greetings to ladies who loved his work. He had a lengthy correspondence of more than five years with a woman in Knoxville: it was a romance of the mind, as they had apparently never met. I picked up a handful of pages, several hundred, and came upon a correspondence with Bruce Rogers that ran through much of 1953. It was hard-core typography, incredible stuff. Grayson had saved all of Rogers's originals along with copies of his own replies. At one time they had sent drawings through the mail, the old master illustrating his points to the prodigy in that language that only they and others like them could read. This will be published someday, I thought— some university press will bring it out in two volumes, *The Letters of Darryl Grayson,* with scholarly footnotes and an index, and some expert—maybe Huggins—would write a long introduction setting Grayson in his proper significance. Grayson was an average speller, and the editor would probably apologize for that and leave it alone. In the final analysis, writing and spelling don't have much to do with each other.

Behind this box was another, *Correspondence/1956–58,* and behind that was another covering the next year. Grayson liked to write. He seemed to have written at least one letter a day, sometimes more. I thumbed through the year 1957 and saw many letters headed *Dear Laura.* It was his old friend Laura Warner, who had not, it seemed, been lost in the Blitz after all. She had moved to New

Orleans after the war and was following his career from afar. In one letter she teasingly called him *My Pyotr,* to which he angrily replied that, goddammit, he was not Tchaikovsky and she was not his god-damn patron saint, and she laughed in her next letter and called him *my darling boy* and said one of the characteristics of genius was tem-per. Huggins would die to get into this, I thought. So would Trish. How different their books would've been.

The box labeled *Tape Recordings* was just what it said—a dozen reels of fragile-looking recording tape, sandwiched between sheaths of notes. *Selena Harper and Darryl Grayson: October 4, 5, 6, 1958.* The master's voice, if it could be retrieved, was apparently preserved right here. The oldest recordings seemed to be from mid-1953, brown on white, oxide on a paper backing, and the oxide was begin-ning to flake. I kept digging. It didn't take long to figure out what *Ideas for Phase Two* was. The material dated from 1968 and 1969—notes, letters, and lists of possible projects, along with rough sketches of new alphabets. There was a list of artists whose work Grayson had admired, who might have been invited to collaborate on future projects. I remembered something Huggins had said, that Grayson had seen his career enclosed by those two *Raven*s, like definitive parenthetical statements, but Huggins had only been half-right. Grayson in no way considered his career finished. He was still a young man with much great work to do: a successful *Raven* would simply write an end to his youth and launch him into his major phase.

I found a box of letter sketches, hundreds of freehand drawings on thin paper. He couldn't be sitting still, I thought—if he had dead time on his hands, he'd draw letters. Some were signed, some were not. All were originals.

There was too much. I began to skim.

I tore down the block and scattered the center cartons around the room. In the exact middle was the box with the photographs. There were pictures of Grayson's childhood home, of the high school, of the parents, . . . but again, nothing of the brothers themselves. There were copies of the newspaper that Grayson had worked on in school and pictures of old girlfriends. In a separate folder was the North Bend stuff—Grayson's shop under construction, his house, the finished shop, the ancient-looking Columbian press with its cast-iron ornamentation—eagle, sea serpent, snakes—alive in the hard light that poured in through the window. Then there was a run of people shots. Rigby and Crystal: she convulsed over some long-forgotten joke, he slightly uncomfortable in coat and tie, politely amused. Moon in his element, hiking in the high country. Moon again, standing at the edge of a mountain cabin with the alpine scenery stretching out behind him. And there she was, the woman who looked like Eleanor Rigby, posed in the woods with a man I had never seen. She had her arm around him and both of them were laughing into the camera, exuding sexuality. In the background was another woman, obviously unhappy. If looks could kill, the woman in the background would kill them both. There were no names, just that faint inscription in Selena's hand, giving the location and date, always May 1969. But there was something about the two women that drew them together and kept them that way in your mind.

Then there was the snapshot, shoved deep in the file between papers and obviously taken by a much less sophisticated camera. The Eleanor-woman, fat with child, standing on the mountain at Moon's cabin: Grayson's handwriting on the back (I could recognize it now at a glance) giving a date, September 28, 1968, and a short caption, *Queen of the world.* She had that same seductive smile, a wanton, sexual animal even in the last days of pregnancy. She pointed at the picture-taker with her left hand, at her swollen tummy with the other. I could almost hear her teasing voice in the room: *Oh, you nasty man, you naughty boy, you.*

Eleanor's voice.

I heard Amy bumping up the stairs. "Hey," she called. "You gonna die up here? . . . It's almost two o'clock."

She came through the trap and sat on one of the boxes. "Now maybe you've got some idea what I'm up against." She got up, paced, and sighed. "What am I gonna do with all this stuff?"

I broke it to her softly. "You're gonna get rich with it."

38

She couldn't imagine such a thing. "I'd probably feel pretty rich if somebody wanted to walk in here and give me a hundred dollars for all of it," she said. When I didn't bite, she let it go. Just as well, I thought: there was no use speculating, she'd probably faint if I told her half of what I was thinking. But she looked at me across the room and a sense of it began filling up the space between us. The air seemed brighter: the sun had a different aura as it beamed through the window on the west side and lit up a million floating particles of dust. Amy moved out to the middle of the room and flipped up one of the flaps.

"Mamma never told me anything," she said, fingering the papers in the box. "Not once did she ever say she thought this stuff might even be worth the paper it's printed on."

Maybe she didn't know, I thought. Maybe value to her had nothing to do with money. Maybe she figured she'd talk about it someday and just ran out of time. You can't plan a heart attack.

"I guess I should've figured there was something to it," Amy said. "The way she never wanted me to let on it was here, not even to Archie or the Rigbys. I think she was always afraid somebody would come and take it away from her."

"Yeah, but where'd it come from? How'd she get it?"

"Just like she got everything else. Piece by piece, starting way back when she first went to work at Grayson's. I think that's when they started talking about her doing his book someday. And he read some of the things she'd published, and he liked what she'd written, and he said okay, but it's too early. He hadn't done enough yet. But he gave her this stuff, sometimes just a few pages a day, to read and think about. She'd bring 'em home with her—a few letters, some sketches he'd thrown aside—just stuff, you know. I never paid any attention when she told me about it."

"And over the years it became this."

Amy was reading. Whatever was on top was working its way through her brain as she tried to understand its larger significance. "This looks like a plain old letter. He's talking about fishing . . . what's so special about that?"

"It's something other people will have to decide."

"And these other people will want this stuff?"

"You can count on that. They'll want this stuff."

"And you know who they are?"

"I do now."

She picked up the pages and read it all—the three-page letter that Grayson had written on January 4, 1954, I saw as I crossed the room and looked over her shoulder. I moved on to the window and stood staring down at the muddy yard, letting her read in peace. When I turned again, her eyes were fixed on mine. She gave a little smile, naive and worldly all at once. Do what you want, she seemed to say: I won't fuss, I'll go along.

The only thing in my mind was that it all had to be moved. It had been here twenty years and I couldn't leave it even one more night. "The real question is, how does this help us find Ellie?" Amy said. I didn't know, it was too vast, like standing at the edge of a forest on a hunt for one tree. But it had to be moved and then maybe we could start asking questions like that.

Now a funny thing happened—Amy lit into the work with a kind of driving impatience, as if she could clear the house all at once. She had put it off forever, but moving that first box had a galvanizing effect. "You go on," she said, "I'll keep working on it." We had filled up the car. It would take six loads and a full backseat when we made our last run out of here. It was three o'clock, her children had to be picked up by seven, and I still had no idea where I'd make the stash or how long it would take us to get it all moved.

"Go," she said, insistent now. "Go, dammit, you're wasting time."

I drove through Snoqualmie and out along the road to North Bend. Clouds moved in from the west and the air grew ripe with the promise of rain. It came, hard and furious, washing away the hope of the morning. I didn't know how I felt anymore, I wasn't sure of anything. I had made a colossal discovery, but I was no closer to Eleanor than I'd been yesterday. Overriding everything was the depressing thought that I could be saving one life and losing another. Amy Harper wouldn't ever be going back to Belltown, but where was Eleanor?

I settled for the North Bend Motel, one of those older places with the rooms laid out in a long single-story row. I rented a room at the far end, where it might not be so evident to the guy in the office that I was using it for a storage locker. I paid two days in advance. The room was small—piled four high around the table and bed, the boxes would fill it up. I unloaded fast and started back. The rain had come and gone, but the clouds hung low and you could see there was more on the way. I turned into the Harper place at quarter to four. Amy had moved a dozen boxes and was still running hard. She was slightly giddy, confirming what I'd thought earlier, that the act of moving things had given her some badly needed emotional release. Her shirt was dark with sweat, soaked across the shoulders and under the arms, and her face was streaked with dirt. "Don't forget to check the mail," she called as I was going out with the second load.

But again the mailbox was empty.

At the end of the fifth load I ran into trouble. I stopped at the road and knew something was different.

The mailbox was open. I knew I had closed it.

I got out and crossed the road. The box was empty, but a cigarette had been thrown down and was still smoking on top of the damp grass. A beer bottle had been dropped in the mud. Beside it was the print of a man's shoe, an impression that hadn't yet begun to fill with water.

I felt the fear. Night was coming fast, fingers of fog wafted across the land, and Amy was alone in the house.

I splashed along the road with my lights off. I could see a flickering light in the trees ahead. It took on bulk and form and became a car, idling in the clearing.

I stopped and reached under the seat where my gun was. I clipped it to the front of my belt near the buckle. I got out of the car and walked up through the trees.

Headlights cut through the mist at the edge of the porch. Two men sat there in the dark.

I started across the clearing. A voice came at me from somewhere.

"Hey! . . . Where you going?"

I looked at them across the gap. "Going to see Ms. Harper."

"Ms. Harper's dead."

"Ms. Amy Harper wasn't dead, when I left her here half an hour ago."

"That's *Mrs.* Amy *Willis* to you, dum-dum. You can't see her now. She's busy."

"She's having a re-yoon-yun with her old man," the other one said, and they both laughed.

I started toward the house. They got out of the car. They were punks, I had seen their kind many times, I had sweated them in precinct rooms when I was a young cop working burglary. When they were fifty, they'd still be seventeen.

The one riding shotgun had the James Dean look, dark, wavy hair over a fuck-you pout. They thought they were badasses and I was an old fart. That made two surprises they had coming.

"This asshole don't hear so good," the James Dean act said.

His partner said, "What'll it be, Gomer? . . . You wanna walk out of here or be carried out strapped over the hood of this car."

"I'll take the hood, stupid, if you two think you can put me there."

I veered and came down on them fast. I caught little Jimmy a wicked shot to the sternum that whipped him around and juked him across the yard like Bojangles of Harlem, sucking air till he dropped kicking in the mud. His partner jumped back out of range. My coat was open and he'd seen the gun, but he'd already seen enough of what went with it. I stepped over Little Jimmy as the ex loomed up on the porch.

"Who the hell're you?" he growled.

"I'm Rush Limbaugh. Who the hell're you?"

"I don't know you."

"I'm taking a poll to see who's listening to the Asshole Radio Network. Maybe you'd better get out of my way."

"Maybe what I'll do is come down there and kick your ass."

"Maybe what you'll do is shit, if you eat enough."

He started to launch himself off the porch. He balked, almost slipped, and stood tottering at the top.

Then he came, with too little too late. His pal yelled, "Look out, Coleman, he's got a gun!" and he balked again, missed his step, and splashed face-first in the mud.

I went around him in a wide circle. "So far you boys are terrifying as hell," I said. He struggled to one knee. I asked if he could sing "April Showers." I hate to waste a line like that, but I know he didn't get it. I walked past him, close enough for him to grab my leg, but he didn't. I knew he wouldn't. By the time I got Amy to open the door, they were gone.

Amy stood at the window and watched them go. It was the last vestige of her childhood, the beginning of a long and wonderful and fearsome journey.

"*C'est la vie*," she said to the fading day.

I thought about the woman in Irwin Shaw's great story of the eighty-yard run. I told Amy to read it sometime and take heart.

She had never heard of Shaw. I felt a twinge of sadness, not only for the fleeting nature of fame but of life itself. I told her what a powerhouse Shaw had been when he was young, and how the critics had come to hate him and had made him the most underrated writer of his day. She didn't understand why people would do that, so I explained it to her. Shaw made a lot of money and they never forgive you for that. She asked what the story was about and I said, "It's about you and the damn fool you married, when you were too young to know better." I didn't want to diminish it by telling her any more than that.

We gathered ourselves for the trip to town. I'd be leaving fourteen boxes under Selena Harper's roof for one more night.

"I don't think we made much headway," Amy said.

"We didn't find Eleanor. Maybe we found you, though."

She didn't say anything. She gave me the key and I locked the house. She sank back in the car and closed her eyes, a picture of sudden weariness.

I told her what I had in mind as we drove. "I'm going to call a man who knows all there is to know about this stuff. If I'm right, he'll want to fly up from Los Angeles and look at it."

"It's in your hands. I trust your judgment and I won't go back on you, whatever you decide to do."

I pointed out the motel where I'd made the stash. She gave it a polite look and we swung west with the night, into the freeway, into the driving rain.

39

The night was full of surprises. The first came when I called Leith Kenney from Amy's room at the Hilton. She sat behind me, discreetly nursing her child while I punched in the call.

It rang three times in L.A. and a woman answered.

"Mr. Kenney, please."

"I'm sorry, he's not here."

"Do you know when he'll be back?"

"I really can't say." There was an awkward pause. "He's gone in to a meeting tonight and it'll probably run late. Then he's going out of town."

I blinked at the phone but recovered quickly. "I'm calling from Seattle."

"That's where he's going. Is this Mr. Pruitt?"

I felt my heart trip. I looked at Amy in the mirror, but she was busy changing breasts and didn't notice anything.

"Yes," I said, thinking on my feet. "Yes, it is."

"Has there been a change of plan? This is Mrs. Kenney. Lee will be calling me when he gets there. I could give him a message."

"I don't know . . . I might have to change things."

There was a brief silence. It would really help, I thought, if I had the slightest idea what the hell I was talking about.

"Well," she said, "would you like to leave a message with me?"

"I'll catch him here. Is he staying at the same hotel?"

"Yes, the Four Seasons. They should get in early tomorrow morning."

"Is Scofield coming with him?"

"I don't think you could keep him away, Mr. Pruitt."

"I'll see them then. Thanks."

I hung up and stared at the floor. Pruitt stared back at me.

Amy was looking at me in the glass.

"Something wrong?"

"No," I said. "Everything's fine."

She went across the room and put her children down. I headed for the door and got the second surprise of the night.

"I remembered something today," she said. "I thought of the man who came and looked in the attic just after Mamma died. His name popped right into my head. I knew I'd forget it again, so I wrote it down."

She fished in her jeans and came up with a paper. "His name was Otto."

Again I walked through that cluttered bookstore. I held a bag of Ayn Rand and wondered why the man wasn't there. I looked up a dark stairwell leading to . . . what?

"Otto Murdock."

She looked at me hard. "How'd you know that?"

40

I headed north on the freeway and hoped I'd remember where Murdock's was. I found it after twenty minutes of trial and error. I arrived on a wave of déjà vu. It looked exactly as I'd last seen it—the same dim light shone from deep in the building, the same OPEN sign was propped in the window and tilted at the same slight angle—even the rain was the same, as if the world had turned back on its axis and erased the last seventy-two hours. I pushed open the door and called his name. There was no sound. If any customers had come in since last Friday night, they had left no evidence of their presence. They had come, looked, and left as we had, perhaps with a slight sense of unease. Those who knew Murdock would figure it as another bout with demon rum: the others would mind their own business.

I crossed the store and looked in the back room. Everything was the same . . . the dim light in the corner . . . the rolltop desk with its piles of magazines and papers . . . the canvas briefcase pushed off to one side with my note still taped to the handle . . . the rickety stacks of books and the thick carpet of dust, undisturbed where we hadn't walked and already filming over where we had. I followed our three-day trail across the room and into the stairwell. I looked up into the black hole and called him, but I knew he wasn't going to be inviting me up. My voice felt heavy, like that of a man shouting into a pillow.

I touched the bottom of the stair with my foot. I leaned into it, took a deep breath, got a firm hold on my gun, and started up. The light faded quickly: there was none at all after the fifth step and I had to go by feel, knowing only that the next step would be onward and upward. I had a sense of movement coming from somewhere . . . *music!* . . . and now the feeling that it had all happened before was as sharp as a scream. I planted each foot, letting my fingers slip along the inner edge of the wooden banister and guide me up. *Don't screw up again,* I was thinking: *don't make the same mistake twice.*

Now I could hear the melody, some classical piece on a radio. I saw a thin line of light . . . the crack at the bottom of a door. It dropped below eye level as I climbed higher, and a kind of sour dampness lay over the top. And I knew that smell, better than the people of Seattle knew the rain. In my old world it came with the smell of Vicks, the stuff homicide cops use to help them get through the bad ones.

I was standing at the top with an old memory playing in color and sound. My partner was a skinny guy named Willie Mott, who was giving me the lowdown on Vicks VapoRub. *This one's ripe . . . put a little glop of Vicks up each nostril and you won't notice it so much.*

I stood at the door of hell and nobody had brought the Vicks.

I touched the wood with my knuckles. Found the knob. Gripped it carefully by the edge, with the joints of my fingers and thumb.

The latch clicked: the door creaked open and the warm moist air sucked me in.

I retched.

I backtracked and stumbled and almost fell down the stairs.

On the third try, I made it into the room. I cupped my hand over my nose and got past the threshold to the edge of a ratty old sofa.

A single lamp near the window was the only source of light . . . a forty-watter, I figured by the dim interior. Dark curtains covered the window. I couldn't see the body yet, but the room was full of flies. The music poured out of an old radio. It wasn't "Rigby," just something he'd been listening to when he finally ran out of time. I moved toward it, still fighting my gut. I hadn't seen much of anything yet.

There was the one window.

A closed door across the room.

A pile of books on the table.

A typewriter . . . a pile of magazines . . . a roll of clear sealing tape . . . and a bottle of lighter fluid.

I moved around the table, watching where I walked. A wave of rotten air wafted up in a cloud of flies.

I tasted the bile. What I didn't need now, after compromising the first scene, was to throw up all over this one.

The lighter fluid might help. I know it's an evil solvent; I've heard it can get in your blood through the skin and raise hell with your liver. But it's stronger by far than Vicks, and even the smell of a cancer-causing poison was like honeysuckle after what I'd been smelling.

I put my handkerchief on the table, then turned the plastic bottle on its side and pried open the squirt nozzle. Liquid flowed into the rag. I touched only the ribbed blue cap, so I wouldn't mess up any prints on the bottle itself.

I made the wet rag into a bandanna. Found a roll of cord and cut off a piece, then tied it over my mouth and nose.

I was breathing pure naphtha. It was cold and bracing and it had an immediate calming effect on my stomach.

If it didn't kill me, I could function like a cop again.

I found him sprawled on the far side of the table. He had been there most of a week from the looks of him. His face was gone, but I could guess from the wispy white hair that he had probably been Otto Murdock.

I didn't know what had killed him: there wasn't enough left to decide. What there was was hidden under a carpet of flies.

Let the coroner figure it. Whatever they pay him, it's not enough, but let him earn it . . . and in the end tell supercop what I already knew.

Murdock hadn't keeled over and died of old age.

And Janeway hadn't done it. This would break his superheart, but when the reaper came calling, Janeway was still in Denver, doing what came naturally. Trying to fit John Gardner into his proper shade of orange, with murder the last thing on his mind.

I didn't see any weapon. Nothing on the table looked promising as a motive or a clue.

There were no ashes.

No sign of a struggle. Even the chair he had been sitting in was upright, pushed back slightly as if he'd been getting up to greet a visitor.

I went to the far door and opened it.

His bathroom. Nothing out of place there.

I was feeling lightheaded by then: the naphtha was doing its dirty work. The skin under my eyes felt like blisters on the rise.

I ripped off the rag and got out of there.

Downstairs, I looked through his rolltop.

Some of the notes in the pigeonholes were three years old.

I looked through the drawers.

Bottle of cheap bourbon, with not much in the bottom.

Letters . . . bills . . .

The sad debris of a life that didn't matter much to anybody, not even, finally, to the man who had lived it.

Pushed off to one side was the canvas bag. Eleanor had wanted to look inside, but I wouldn't let her.

I opened it now and hit the jackpot.

A thick notebook, old and edgeworn . . .

I seemed to be holding Darryl Grayson's original subscriber list. With it was a manuscript, a dozen pages of rough draft on yellow legal paper. I knew the handwriting, I had seen it on other papers in Amy's attic. The top sheet was a title page, aping Victoriana.

THE CRAVEN
A Tragic Tale of a God's Downfall
Told in Verse by Richard Grayson,
A Witness

I took it all and went back to Aandahl's and read it. I read it many times. I was reading it again at midnight when Trish came home.

41

She had returned almost a full day early. There was a click and the dogs swarmed her at the front door.

She looked at me across the room, as if she hadn't expected me to be there and didn't know whether to be disappointed or relieved. "You've changed," she said, and I gave her an old man's grin. She threw her raincoat over a wicker basket, came slowly around the couch, and sat facing me with an almost schoolmarmish primness.

"I've been thinking about it," she said. "Been running it through my head all the way home from Albuquerque, trying to figure out what I ought to do."

"What's the verdict?"

"I'm in it now."

"I thought you always were."

"It's different now. I'm in it with you."

This was happy news. I felt a warm glow at the sound of it.

She said, "Whatever happens, we go together."

We didn't need to hash out the ground rules. When you connect with someone, things like that are understood. Suddenly we were like police partners, comparing notes, poring over evidence. There was a lot to be done, and the first commandment was the test of fire. You never hold out on your partner.

We ate a late supper and talked into the morning. For the first time in a long time I broke bread with a good-looking woman without thinking of Rita.

42

She had covered a lot of ground in two days. She had flown out of Sea-Tac at nine-forty Pacific time on Saturday night. Her destination was St. Louis, where she arrived in light snow at two-twelve in the morning. She had a room reserved, but her old companion, insomnia, was along for the ride. She filled the dead time reading. At nine A.M. she was in the homicide room downtown, looking at photographs and evidence from an old murder case. Stuff that was once under tight wraps was shared with her, off the record, by the man on duty Sunday morning. It had been a long time, years, since anything exciting had been added to the file, and they didn't have much hope of cracking it now. She had flown two thousand miles and that impressed them. She had observed the proper protocol, speaking first by telephone with the chief, and they let her see the file.

The victim was Joseph Hockman, fifty-two, a bachelor. She looked at the pictures, including the close-ups. It didn't bother her: she had been a reporter for a long time and had seen it all many times.

The victim lay in a pool of blood in a library room. Pictures had been taken from every angle, so she could see the shelving and the arrangement of books on all four walls. The black-and-whites were vivid and sharp, clear enough that the titles could be read and the jacket formats identified. Her eyes traveled along one row and she saw some famous old books.

All the King's Men.

Elmer Gantry.

Miss Lonelyhearts.

Manhattan Transfer . . .

She began to make notes. Mr. Joseph Hockman collected so-called serious fiction—no mysteries, no fantasy, nothing that smacked of

genre. He liked his literature straight, no sugar, no cream. He did
have a weak spot for fine limiteds: a shot over the body toward the
window wall showed a good-sized section of books in slipcases. She
asked for a magnifying glass, and the detective, fascinated, got her
one from a desk drawer.

Grapes of Wrath in two volumes.

Anthony Adverse in three . . .

"Looks like Limited Editions Club," she said.

The detective said, "Oh," the way people do when they have no
idea what you're talking about.

Near the end of the shelf was a gap where some books had been
taken out but not returned.

"Looks like there's fifteen or twenty books missing here," she
said.

The detective, who had been reading the reports from the original
investigating officers, said, "There was some discussion at the time
about the possibility of theft being the motive. They thought that was
pretty weak, though. Who'd kill a man that way just to steal a bunch
of books?"

"Any indication in the file whether the books ever turned up?"

"Not that I can see."

"Or what they were?"

"Nope. One of the officers pursued that thought as far as he could
take it, but the guy didn't keep records like that. He kept it all up
here." He tapped his head.

"Somebody took those books and the officer knew that—that's
why he pursued it," she said. "Look in this shot, you can see a book
on the floor, right under that empty place in the bookshelf. When he
pulled the books out, this one came out with it. But he didn't bother
to pick it up."

"What does that tell you?"

"It tells me he didn't want that book, just the ones that filled about
this much shelf space." She held up her hands about two feet apart.
"He didn't care about any of the others."

She went book by book with the glass. Some of the titles were
unreadable, but there wasn't a Grayson book that could be identified
as such anywhere in the room.

"That's funny," she said. "I heard this guy had all the Grayson books."

The detective said, "Oh," again, as if he hadn't quite made up his mind whether he cared enough to ask her who Grayson was. "They tossed the book angle back and forth but it didn't excite them much. The feeling was, yeah, the perp might've taken a few books, but that wasn't the prime motive."

"But they never found a motive."

"Early in the investigation, the feeling was it might've been personal."

"Did Mr. Hockman have any enemies?"

"Looks like he'd had some words with people. He was becoming a crusty old bastard. But, no, they never got anything they could pin on anybody."

"Did their thinking change later?"

"Like it always does with crimes like this that you can't solve. Some nutcase." He flipped a page and went on reading. "Here's something about a book."

She looked up.

"They interviewed a woman named Carolyn Bondy, who did secretarial work for Hockman. Once a week she'd come over and take dictation, do his correspondence. The week of the murder he sent a letter to a book publisher. He'd gotten a book with a mistake in it and it seemed to ruin his week."

"Really?"

"Does that interest you?"

"Yeah, you bet."

"Too bad they didn't take it much further than that."

"They didn't ask her what the book was or who published it?"

"It just seemed to come up in the course of things."

"Or what the mistake might've been?"

"Just that he was annoyed. He'd been looking forward to this book . . . something special, I guess. Nobody thought it was much of a motive for murder. The woman did say Hockman was a good deal more annoyed than he let on in his letter. The letter he wrote was pretty soft and that surprised her. It was almost like Hockman was apologizing for telling the guy he'd screwed up."

"Anything else?"

"Just this. The reason Hockman was annoyed was because it was the same mistake the guy had made before."

"Is that what she said? . . . The same mistake . . ."

"That's what's in here."

"Is there an address or phone number for this woman—what's her name?"

"Carolyn Bondy." The detective read off an address and phone number. "Doubt if she still lives there. It's been twenty years."

She looked through more evidence. She picked up a clear plastic bag that was full of ashes.

"I'll have to ask you not to open that," the detective said. "I mean, we do want to cooperate, but, uh . . ."

"Hey, I appreciate anything you can do. May I just move it around a little?"

"I don't guess that'll hurt anything."

She took the bag with both hands and made a rotating motion like a miner panning gold. Slowly a fragment of white paper rose through the charred silt on the top.

She peered through the filmy plastic and saw two letters.

"Look at this . . . looks like a capital *F* . . . and a small *r* . . . part of the same word."

The detective leaned over her shoulder.

She looked up in his face. "Are you in the mood to do me a huge favor?"

"I won't kill ya for asking."

"Is that a Xerox machine over there? . . ."

She called Wilbur Simon, an assistant managing editor at the *St. Louis Post-Dispatch*. As a young reporter from Miami, she had won a National Endowment for the Humanities fellowship, a year of study and meditation at the University of Michigan at Ann Arbor. Simon had been one of her teachers. They had had good rapport and he had pursued her for his own paper ever since.

She sat in the empty newsroom on Sunday afternoon, reading the clip file on the Hockman case. She and Simon had coffee in a diner not far away and talked about old times, the rain in Seattle, and the Hockman case. Simon had vivid recollections of Hockman. He had been the paper's news editor then and had done the layout on the first-day story and on most of the follow pieces. It stuck in his mind as the beginning of the crazy age. He had said as much in a diary he had kept then and had dug out and reviewed just after she had called him this morning. He had written about life and work and his personal evolving philosophy. The thing about Hockman was, you never thought much about random killers before then and you were always aware of them since. Suddenly you couldn't pick up hitchhikers without taking your life in your hands. The day of the serial killer had come.

"I don't think this was a serial killer, Wilbur," she said.

At least not the kind of serial killer people meant when they used the term, she thought.

They parted with a hug and Simon offered her a job. She smiled and said she was flattered, but it would take more than rain to get her to give up Seattle for St. Louis.

She looked up Carolyn Bondy in the telephone book. There was a George Bondy at that address. The man who answered said Carolyn Bondy, his mother, had died just last month.

She ate dinner alone in the city and caught a ten o'clock flight to Albuquerque.

She slept on the plane, just enough to keep her awake the rest of the night. A rental car got her into Taos at three o'clock in the morning, mountain time, thankful that she had reserved a room and secured it with a credit card. She had made photocopies of the *Post-Dispatch* clips, but it was that single sheet from homicide with the shadowy image of the two connected letters shot through plastic that she looked at now as she faced the new day. She had done her homework: she knew that Charlie and Jonelle Jeffords lived in the hills fifteen miles from town. She had studied the maps and knew where to drive with only occasional stops to refresh her memory. She bumped off the highway and clattered along a washboard road, leaving a plume of dust in her wake. The road twisted up a ridge and skirted a valley. She saw patches of snow in the high country as the road U-turned and dipped back into the hills. There were washouts along the way, but each had been repaired and the drive was easy. She reached the gate at nine o'clock. A sign nailed to a post said KEEP OUT, and she thought that hospitality at Rancho Jeffords was like the weather, chilly with a chance of sudden clouds. She slipped the rope loop off the gate and drove in. The house was a hundred yards away, shaded by trees and hidden from the road by hilly terrain. It was a split-level mountain home with a deck that faced west. There was no sign of life. She pulled into the yard and decided to go ahead with caution, remembering the inclination of the cheerful Mr. Jeffords to greet trespassers with the business end of a gun.

She walked out in the yard and stood in the sun.

Called out to whoever might hear.

"Hello! . . . Is anybody here?"

The hills soaked up her voice.

She tried again but got nothing for it.

She went up the walk and knocked on the door. There wasn't a sound inside.

It had been a gamble coming here without an appointment, but she knew that when she booked the flight. She walked along a flagstone path to the edge of the house. The path led around to a garage, whose side door beckoned her on.

She knocked on the door. "Anybody in there?"

No one.

She touched the door and it swung open.

A workroom, long ago surrendered as the place for cars.

There was clutter, but also a staleness in the air. It was a shop set up for a workingman but unused for some time now. The walls gave off a feeling of dry rot and musk.

She saw some equipment she recognized and it drew her into the room. A heavy iron bookpress had been set up on the edge of the bench. A much older bookpress, made of wood, stood on a table behind it.

The tools of a bookbinder.

As she came deeper into the room, her impression of disuse deepened. The place was deep in dust and heavily cobwebbed. The chair at the bench was ringed with spiderwebs.

She was nervous now but she came all the way in, wanting to see it all with a quick look. Again she observed the bookbinder's tools: the rawhide hammer lying on the floor where he'd dropped it long ago, covered with dust; a steel hammer at the edge of the bench, a few feet from the bookpress; balls of wax thread; needles; paper. There was lots of paper, fine marbled stock for endsheets, standard stock for the pages, colored papers and white sheets and some with a light creamy peach tone. Against the wall was a paper rack. And there were leathers, very fine under the dust, and edging tools that looked like cookie cutters and were used, she knew, for laying in the gilt on a gold-trimmed leather book. There was a hot plate to heat the edging tool on, and behind the hot plate was a row of nasty-looking gluepots. She opened one and smelled PVA, the bookbinder's glue. A newspaper, open on the table, was a year old.

She went outside and closed the door. The wind whistled down from the hills. She walked back to her car, opened the door, and sat with her feet dangling out, hoping they'd come home soon.

An hour passed and the sun grew hot. The arroyo baked under the glare of it and the chill melted away. Slowly she became aware of a creepy sensation, like the feeling you get driving on the freeway when the man in the next car stares at you as he comes past.

She looked at the house and saw curtains flutter upstairs. This might be nothing more than the temperature control blowing air up the window, but her sense of apprehension grew as she looked at it.

She wanted to leave but she couldn't. She had come a long way, and though the chance of failure had always been strong, she had never failed at anything by default.

The curtain moved again. No heating flue did that, she thought.

She got out and walked across the yard. She went up the path to the door and gave it another loud knock.

There was a bump somewhere. Her unease was now acute.

She circled the house. Out back was a smaller deck with steps leading up to a door. She went up and knocked. Through a filmy curtain she saw movement, as if someone had crossed from one room to another.

"Hey, people," she called. "I've come a long way to talk to you. Why don't we hear each other out?"

Nothing.

Not a sound now, but the presence behind the door was as tangible as the purse slung over her shoulder. She had a vision of something sexless and faceless, holding its breath waiting for her to leave.

"It's about the Rigby girl and the burglary you had here."

She could feel her voice soaking through the old wood around the window sash. There wasn't a chance of them not hearing her.

"It's about Darryl and Richard Grayson, and the book Grayson was working on when he died."

Even the house seemed to sigh. But the moment passed and nothing happened, and in a while she wondered if the sound had been in her mind.

"It's about the Graysons and their friends . . . you and the Rigbys." She took a breath and added, "And Nola Jean Ryder."

As if she'd said a magic word, the door clicked and swung inward. Someone—a man, she thought—looked through a narrow crack.

"Mr. Jeffords? . . . Is that you? . . . I can't see you very well."

"Who are you?"

It was the same voice she had heard on the telephone recording—the same only different. The recording had rippled with macho arrogance: this man sounded tired and old and shaky.

"What do you want here?"

"I came down from Seattle to talk to you. I'm a reporter for the *Seattle Times.*"

She told him her name, but he seemed not to hear. Technically, ethically, it didn't matter. The rules only demanded that she give him fair warning. He was talking to a reporter and they were now on the record. She could use him if he said anything worth using.

But she had never played the game that way. "I'm a reporter, Mr. Jeffords." It still meant nothing to him. He heard but did not hear. He listened but his mind heard only words and blipped out meanings. She had done too many interviews with people like him, private souls who suddenly found themselves newsworthy without understanding how or why it had happened. They were always appalled when they opened their newspapers the next morning and learned what they had said.

"Trish Aandahl, *Seattle Times,*" she said, loud and clear.

She still couldn't see him. He stood just beyond the doorway, a shadow filling up the crack, his face reduced to an eye, a cheek, part of a nose.

"D'you think it would be possible for me to come in and talk to you for just a minute? I promise I won't take up much of your time."

He didn't seem to hear that either. He leaned closer to the door and in a voice barely louder than a whisper said, "Did you say something about Nola Jean?"

This was the key to him, the only reason he had opened his door to her. Blow this and you lose him, she thought.

"We can talk about Nola," she said as if she'd known the woman all her life.

He opened the door wide and let her in.

She had to squeeze past him in the narrow hall. In that second they shared the same space, close enough to bristle the hair on her neck. She brushed against his arm and felt the soft flannel of his long-sleeve shirt. She smelled the sun-baked male smell of him. She smelled tobacco, the kind her father used to smoke, that Edgeworth stuff with the hint of licorice.

She moved quickly past him, through the dim hall to the big room at the end. The door clicked shut behind her and she heard the lock snap in. His footsteps came along behind her, and for a strange moment she fought the urge to run on through and out the front door.

His house was orderly. The hardwood floor gleamed under a coat of varnish, and there were rugs with what looked to her like Navajo designs in the places where people walked the most. It was not a new house. The floor creaked under her weight and she could see faint ceiling stains where the roof had leaked. The room was steeped in ancient smoke. It had soaked into the drapes and walls and furniture, and in here it had no hint of flavor. They were both chain-smokers, she thought, remembering her parents and what her childhood had smelled like. They smoked what they liked when they had it, but if times were tough, they'd sweep the dust off the floor and roll a tobacco paper around that.

He had a homemade going in the ashtray and a coffee cup that still had almost a full head of steam. His living room was narrow and long. It opened out to the front deck and a secondary hall led away to the right, probably to a bedroom. She turned and looked at him. He was a rugged guy in his sixties. His hair was slate gray, his skin the leathery brown of a cowboy or a farmer. His demeanor was flat, the last thing she expected after hearing his forceful voice on the telephone recording. He had a curious habit of avoiding eye contact: he almost looked at you but not quite. He seemed to gaze past her left shoulder as she told him her name for the fourth time. He sat without offering her a chair and made no move to offer coffee as he leaned forward and sipped his own.

She grappled toward an opening. "I've heard a lot about Nola."

What a bad start, she thought, but it seemed to make no real difference to him. His eyes lit up at the mention of the name; then his mind lost its focus and he looked around the room. He flitted his eyes across her face, stopping on a spot somewhere behind her head. But he didn't say anything and she came toward him slowly and sat on a hard wooden chair facing him. His eyes followed her down, but he kept looking slightly behind her, always picking up something just behind her left ear. *There's nothing back there,* she wanted to say, but she didn't.

Then he spoke. "Who . . . did you say you are?"

"Trish Aandahl . . . I write for the *Seattle Times.*"

"Why did you come here? Did you bring Nola back with you?"

There's something wrong with this guy, she thought. He acted like the prototype for all the dumb jokes you heard kicking around. *One shovel short of a full load.* She didn't know how to talk to him, but she made the long reach and said, "I'm going to try to find her, Mr. Jeffords."

"Good." He gave what passed for a smile. "Real good."

He blinked at whatever held his attention behind her head and said, "I want to see her real bad."

"I want to see her too."

"She was here."

"Was she?"

"Yeah. Nola Jean."

"When was she here?"

"Soon."

This guy's from the twilight zone, she thought. She leaned back in her chair and smiled. "When will Mrs. Jeffords be home?"

"She's gone to the store."

"When will she be back?"

"Grocery shopping."

She would have to wait until Mrs. Jeffords returned and, hopefully, gave her something coherent. The thought of entertaining Jeffords until then was less than thrilling, but she had done heavier duty for smaller rewards than this story promised.

Then she looked in his face and knew what his problem was. She had seen it before, and the only mystery was why it had taken her so long to figure it out.

The recording on the telephone was an old one—a year, maybe two years or more.

Charlie Jeffords had Alzheimer's.

Her next thought chilled her even as she thought it.

She was thinking of the gunplay the night of the break-in, and what Eleanor had said. *I never fired a gun in my life . . .*

She thought of Mrs. Jeffords and the temperature in the room dropped another ten degrees. Goose bumps rose on her arms and she hugged herself and leaned forward in the chair.

"I don't think I'll be able to wait for your wife."

"Aren't you gonna bring Nola Jean back?"

"I'd like to. Would you like to help me?"

He didn't say anything. She took a big chance and reached for his hand.

He looked into her eyes, his lips trembling.

"Nola," he said.

She squeezed his hand and he burst into tears.

He sobbed out of control for a minute. She tried to comfort him, as much as a stranger could. She held his hand and gently patted his shoulder and desperately wanted to be somewhere else. This was the curse of Alzheimer's: even as it eats away your brain, you have times of terrible clarity. Charlie Jeffords knew exactly what was happening to him.

"Mr. Jeffords," she said.

He sniffed and sat up and released her hand.

"The night the trouble happened. Can you tell me about that?"

He didn't say anything. She pushed ahead. "That girl who broke in. Do you remember what she wanted?"

"Her book."

"What book?"

"Came for her book back."

"What book?"

"She wanted her book back."

"What was the book?"

"I been holding it for her."

"Whose book was it?"

"Nola's."

"Wasn't it Grayson's book? Wasn't that Darryl Grayson's book, Mr. Jeffords?"

"It's Nola's book. Gave it to me to hold."

She leaned forward. He tried to look away but she wouldn't let him.

"I'm tired," he said.

Damn, she thought: don't know what's real anymore.

She tried again. "Mr. Jeffords . . ."

But that was as far as she got. Through the front curtain she saw a pickup truck pull into the yard.

Mrs. Jeffords was home.

She left Charlie Jeffords there on the couch. She hurried down the hall and let herself out the back way.

There'd be time enough later to think back on it. She'd have a lifetime to wonder if she'd acted like a frightened fool.

Now all she wanted was to put some distance between herself and the woman in the truck.

She stood on the back porch, flat against the wall, listening for some hint of how and when to make her break.

She heard the woman yell.

"Charlie!"

Then, when he didn't answer, a shriek.

"Charlie!"

She heard the thumping sounds of someone racing up the front steps. At the same time she soft-toed down the back and doubled around the house.

She stopped at the corner and looked out into the yard. For reasons she only half understood, she was now thoroughly spooked.

There was no time to dwell on it. The truck sat empty beside her rental car: the woman had jumped out without closing the door or killing the engine.

Go, she thought.

Run, don't walk.

She sprinted across the yard, jumped in her car, and drove away fast.

43

She looked at me across the table and said, "It seems silly now, and yes, before you ask, I do feel like a fool. I've never done anything remotely like that. To break and run just isn't my nature. I can't explain it."

"You don't have to. I've done a few things that I can't explain either."

"Charlie Jeffords never shot at anybody, and I don't think the Rigby girl did either. Where does that leave us? All I can tell you is, the thought of being there when that woman came home was . . . I don't know. The only thing I can liken it to is having to walk past a graveyard at night when I was a kid."

"It's like me walking through the blood at Pruitt's house, and every dumb thing I've done since then. Sometimes you do things."

"I don't know, I had this feeling of absolute dread. My blood dropped to zero in half the time it takes to tell about it, and I was just . . . gone, you know?"

"So what did you think about it later, when you had time to think about it?"

"I kept thinking that one of the people who's missing in this story is a woman, this Nola Jean Ryder. She's always been the missing link."

"You didn't have much about her in your book."

"I didn't know much about her. She was just a girl Richard met and brought home. I couldn't find out where she came from and nobody knows where she went. It's like she dropped off the earth when the Graysons died."

"How much work did you actually do on her, trying to track her down?"

"Quite a bit. Probably not enough. By then it was obvious even to me that I wasn't going to get it in the book. I was still making more changes on the galleys than the publisher wanted to live with, and we were up against a horrendous deadline. The book was already scheduled and promoted as a March title and publishers want everything done yesterday."

She shrugged and poured herself more coffee. "I had to let her go. Then, after the book came out, I tried to keep up with it, but I had a living to make. I wasn't exactly Robert Ludlum, flush with royalties. It made me some money, but not enough to stop being a working gal."

I reached for the coffeepot. "So what do you think about it now? Are you thinking this missing woman is hiding out down there in Taos?"

"When I saw the truck pull up, I didn't think at all, I just wanted to get out of there. Halfway back to town I realized that, yeah, I had been thinking of them as one. In my head, Ryder had become Jeffords."

"Which is at least possible, I guess."

We looked at each other.

I said, "If you had to make book on it now, what do you think happened twenty years ago?"

"I think Nola Jean Ryder set fire to that shop and killed the Graysons. I've always thought that."

"Okay," I said in a semidoubting voice. "Make me believe it."

"I probably can't, unless you're willing to give me some veteran's points for intuition."

"I'll play with you up to a point. But you've got to have something concrete, you can't just pull this intuition act out of thin air."

"I've got three things and that's all, you can take it or leave it. First, I talked to the fire investigator who worked the Grayson fire. This man is extremely competent, and he's convinced it was arson. He's got my slant on life, if you know what I mean . . . we talk the same language, he gets the same vibes I do. You don't meet many people like that, and when you do, you listen to what they say. And he knows that fire was set, it just killed him not to be able to prove it. In a thirty-year career you get maybe half a dozen like that, so strong yet elusive. It sticks in your craw and you remember every bloody detail till the day you die. That's my first point.

"Here's the second. Nola Jean Ryder was very much in evidence at the Grayson place all through the last year of their lives and was never seen again afterward. She was there the day of the fire. Archie Moon saw her arguing with Grayson. Her relationship with Grayson was volatile, very stormy: he couldn't seem to live with or without her, and toward the end it got so bad it affected his work. One man I talked to saw Ryder in the North Bend pub that afternoon, drinking with some guys. She went off with one of them and was gone a couple of hours. Then she was seen walking back to Grayson's in the early evening, in a light rain. That's the last time anybody ever saw or to my knowledge heard of Nola Jean Ryder. A few hours later the Graysons died and she dropped off the edge of the earth.

"Last point. Nobody who knew her doubts that she was capable of doing it. She had a temper that went off like a firecracker and burned at a full rage for hours. Even today it makes people uneasy to talk about her. Archie Moon told me some stuff, then he clammed up and called it ancient history and said he didn't want to talk anymore. Rigby wouldn't talk at all. Crystal at least was willing to give her the benefit of the doubt, for a while anyway. Nobody could understand the hold she had on Grayson: it was as if, after a lifetime filled with women, he had met the one who brought him to his knees."

"This is Darryl Grayson we're talking about now."

"Absolutely. Richard's the one who first met her, but it was Darryl Grayson who wound up with her. I guess things like that can't be explained, how a woman can get under the skin of even a strong man and make him do just about anything."

"And vice versa."

"Yes. There isn't much that separates us when you get down to what counts."

I sat thinking about what she'd told me, then it was my turn to talk. I told her about Amy Harper and she listened like a bug-eyed kid, trying to imagine that treasure hidden all those years in the Harper woman's attic. "I never understood why she was so hostile when I tried to interview her. Now I know. She considered Grayson her own personal territory. She was going to write her own book."

Then I told her about Otto Murdock. I watched the sense of wonder drain out of her face, replaced by horror and dread.

"Did you call the police?"

"Sure. I seem to spend a lot of my time doing that."

"Where'd you call them from?"

"Phone booth not far from Murdock's."

"Did you talk to Quintana?"

"He didn't seem to be there. Supercops in this neck of the woods have a different work ethic than I used to have."

"Did you tell the dispatcher this was part of Quintana's case?"

"I had to. I've told you how important that is, for the main guy to know that stuff right out of the gate."

She took a deep breath. "Sounds to me like you did everything but give them your name."

"I did that too. I wanted to make sure it got to him right away. That part of it doesn't matter anymore, he'd know it was me anyway. They've got me on tape twice now and I've never been much of a ventriloquist. They'll also have the paper I left."

"What paper?"

"Last Friday when I went to Murdock's with Eleanor, I took some pricey books out of his store. I left an offer taped to the canvas bag."

She closed her eyes, then opened them wide. "Let's see if I've got this straight. You left him a note and signed your name to it. Then you went back there tonight and the note was still there but he was dead, and you left the note there for the police to find. Is that about it?"

"It's a bookseller's code, Trish—thou shalt not steal thy colleague's books. I owed the man three thousand dollars. Now I owe it to his estate, wherever that goes. Maybe he was one of those nuts who left everything to his pet cat, but that doesn't change my obligation to him. If I walked out with that note, I'd be stealing his books, in the eyes of the law and in my eyes too."

She looked at Grayson's notebook but did not touch it. "What about this?"

"I didn't steal that, Murdock did. When I'm finished with it, it goes back to Amy Harper."

She gave me a long, sad look.

"All right," I said, "what would you have done?"

"I can't even imagine. I'm not making light of it, it's just that I'm starting to worry about your chances of ever getting back to Denver as a free man."

"I'll worry too if you think that'll help. But I'm still going to pay off Murdock's cat, so I can own those books with a clear conscience and not add grand theft to all the other stuff I've got hanging."

She didn't say anything, but I knew what she had to be thinking.

"If this is getting too dicey for you, I can understand that. If you want to change your mind, I'll understand that."

"No," she said too quickly. Then, after a few seconds' thought: "No, I'm fine."

She gestured at Grayson's notebook. "But look what you've done, you've messed up another crime scene. Quintana will have your head on a stick."

"Maybe I'll get lucky and he won't have to find out."

"I hate to break this to you, Janeway, but luck is not the first word that crosses my mind when I think of you."

"Then you'll have to admit that I'm due for a break."

"You're hanging by a thread. You're walking a tightrope with deep trouble on both sides of you. It had to occur to you that this little notebook just might be the motive for that old man's murder."

"Then why didn't the killer take it?"

"How should I know? . . . Maybe he couldn't find it . . . you said yourself the place was a mess."

"He didn't even *look* for it, that's what I'm telling you. The place was a mess, but it was an accumulated mess. There weren't any drawers emptied, no papers thrown around. I didn't see any ashes on the floor. I don't think the killer even knew this notebook was there."

"Then why was Murdock killed?"

"I don't know that. All I can tell you is, it's different than the others."

"Different killers? . . . Is that what you're saying?"

"No, it's the same guy, and if you dig deep enough, you'll find one motive at the bottom of it. But he was drawn to these guys for different reasons. Carmichael was killed for what was in Pruitt's house. Same thing with Hockman, years ago: he was killed for what he had. Murdock was killed for what he knew."

She leaned over and looked at the notebook close up. But she avoided touching it, as if whatever lay beneath its cover had been hopelessly tainted. "It's still a wonderful motive for murder. Imagine what someone like Huggins would pay for it. He'd sell his house to get it. It's the map to Treasure Island, the only thing a Grayson freak would ever need for the scavenger hunt of his dreams."

I was thinking the same thing, with Scofield playing the Huggins role. A rich man could chase down the subscribers or their heirs and suck the market dry in no time. Each year fewer Graysons would appear at auction and no one would quite know why. Suddenly dealers would list them in catalogs as *rare* and mean it. In ten years the prices on the few odds and ends would be stratospheric.

I told her about Scofield and Kenney and about the interesting talk I'd had with Mrs. Kenney earlier in the evening. She listened with her fingers to her lips and came to the same conclusion I had reached a few hours before.

Kenney and Scofield were flying in to meet Pruitt.

That meant Pruitt had been in touch, sometime since I last spoke with Kenney, probably well within the last twenty-four hours.

"My God, he's found the book," Trish said breathlessly.

"That . . . would seem to be the case."

"What else could it mean?"

"I don't know what it means. Or might mean for Eleanor."

"What are you going to do?"

"I'm gonna be there when the deal goes down. After that it's up for grabs."

She said something under her breath that sounded like "Jesus."

I nudged Grayson's notebook in her general direction. "Maybe you should break down and give this a look. It tells us some things we never knew before."

"Such as what?"

"It turns out that Grayson did a tiny lettered run for each of his books. A superlimited series that went to a few select customers."

"I don't remember seeing that in Huggins."

"It wasn't in Huggins. I looked."

"Huggins would never leave something like that out."

"Unless he never knew about it. Or maybe he did know and

couldn't verify it, like the fact that Grayson was working on another *Raven.*"

"This is different than another *Raven.* The *Raven* might not even exist. But if there was a lettered series, Huggins would have to have it."

"But the limitation was so small it was next to nothing. None of the books has ever turned up to prove their existence, and until now it was assumed by everybody that Grayson's records all went up in the fire."

She still made no move to pick up the notebook. I picked it up for her and opened it to the first page.

"Each title had five hundred numbered copies. There were also five lettered copies. These were for customers who had been with Grayson from the beginning . . . the faithful. They loved his books way back when everybody else could care less."

I watched her eyes. It was beginning to come to her now, she was starting to see the dark road we were heading into.

"These lettered copies usually preceded the regular run by a month or so," I said.

Suddenly she knew where we were going. I could see it in her eyes.

"*A,*" I told her, "was a fellow named Joseph Hockman, of St. Louis, Missouri."

She didn't say anything. She reached across the table and took the notebook out of my hands. She read the name in Grayson's own hand, as if nothing less would make her believe it. She put it down on the table, looked across at me, picked it up, and read it again.

"*B,*" I said, "was Mr. Reggie Dressler of Phoenix, Arizona. *C* was Corey Allingham of Ellicott City, Maryland. *D* was Mike Hollingsworth, looks like a rural route somewhere in Idaho. *E* was Laura Warner of New Orleans. That's all there were. The faithful five."

She finally got past Joseph Hockman and let her eyes skim the page. "He knew Laura Warner from Atlanta."

"I know he did. I read your book."

"Jesus! . . . Have you checked these other names yet?"

"I've only had the damn thing a couple of hours. I didn't want to make any police checks from this telephone, even to departments a thousand miles from here. There are other offices I could check, but they won't be open at midnight."

"No, but the newspapers will be."

* * *

She sat at her telephone and made some calls: to night city editors at
the *Arizona Republic,* the *Baltimore Sun,* the *Idaho Statesman,* and
the *Times-Picayune* in New Orleans. While people in distant cities
chased down any clip files that might exist, we sat at the table drinking coffee.

Now that she had begun on Grayson's notebook she couldn't
leave it alone. "I've interviewed some of these people. Look, here's
Huggins . . . number twenty-three of the regular run. He got in
early."

A minute later she came to Otto Murdock, number 215.

"Let's look at what else we've got," I said. "I hear dawn cracking."

We had our physical evidence spread out on the table between us.
We had Richard's poem, which Trish had yet to read. We had the
paper chip from Pruitt's house, and the sheet she had brought back
from St. Louis with the two dim letters standing out in the soot. And
I had brought in from the car an envelope containing the photographs I had found in Amy Harper's attic.

Trish opened the envelope and looked at the first picture—the
Eleanor woman, shot at Grayson's printshop in May 1969.

"Imagine how the kid must've felt, finding this," she said. "You
grow up thinking you know where you come from. Your home and
family are the real constants in life. Then in one second you see that
nothing's what you thought it was."

She turned the picture down and looked at the one beneath it.
Three people walking in the woods: the Eleanor woman, another
woman, and a man.

"Look at this," she said. "There's Charlie Jeffords."

"Really?" I took the picture out of her hand. The guy was standing in a little clearing, smirking at the camera. The Eleanor woman
was posing with him in the same sleeveless blouse, her arm over his
shoulder. The other woman stood a few feet away, clearly unhappy.

"This is Jeffords?" I said. "You're sure of that?"

"Sure I'm sure. He's got dark hair here and that horny leer of his'll
never be there again, but yeah. Same guy I talked to in Taos."

"I wonder who the other woman is."

She shook her head. "This bothers me a lot. It's fairly obvious now that Jeffords was a player of some kind in Grayson's life and I missed it. Damn."

I wanted to move her past it, beyond her own shortcomings. I took the handle of my spoon and changed the subject, nudging the chip of paper until my words *still* and *whisp* lined up opposite her *Fr.*

"I'm no expert," I said. "But this typography looks the same to me."

"They seem to be the same point size. But the letters are different so it's hard to be sure."

I unfolded the library copy I had made of the original "Raven" and showed her the words *still* and *whisp* where I had circled them in the fifth stanza. "Here's where your *Fr* comes from. Fourth line, second stanza, first word. 'From my books surcease of sorrow—sorrow for the lost Lenore.'"

But I could see she had already accepted the inevitability of its being there. She picked up the yellow pages and read Richard's poem. I watched her face as she read it, but she went through the entire thing deadpan.

"What do you make of this?" she said, putting it down.

I told her what I thought, the obvious supplemented with guess-work. It was a rough draft of something, hand-dated July 1967, two years before the Graysons died. There were numerous strike-outs and places where lines had been rewritten between lines. In the margins were long columns of rhyme words, many keyed to the dominant suf-fix *ore*. Mixed among the common words—*core, store, door, lore*—were exotic and difficult possibilities such as *petit four, centaur,* and *esprit de corps*.

"Whore," she said, looking up from the page. "That's one Poe couldn't use."

In technique it was like "The Raven," written out in eighteen full stanzas with the Poe meter and cadence. The tone was allegorical, like the old Orson Welles version of *Julius Caesar* in a blue serge suit. You couldn't quite be sure what was real and what had been skewed for effect, or how much might just be the author's own grim fantasy.

The style was in part mythic. It told the story of two young gods, one fair, the other dark: brothers forced to choose between good and evil when they were too young to understand the consequences. The road to hell was an orgy without end, lit up with laughter and gay frolic. Salvation came at a higher price.

One took the path of least resistance and tumbled into hell. The other chose the high road, finding strength in purpose and contentment in his work. But temptation was a constant, and in the end the dark-haired god was his own undoing.

Rigby was the symbol of blind youth. His was the only proper name in the tale. Richard had chosen to write it that way, the entire eighteen stanzas a lecture to youth.

On paper he could do that. He could sit Rigby down and make him listen. He could turn whores into saints and make the dark-haired god bow at the devil's feet.

"There are a couple of lines crossed out," she said, "as if he had changed his mind about something and took off in another direction."

"He wanted to take his brother's name out. You can still read it, though: all he did was draw a squiggly line through it."

She read aloud.

Rigby was a fresh young boy when he arrived like Fauntleroy
And took his bashful place beyond the shadows of the
   Grayson door;
Little did he know that Grayson had a legendary place in
Bedrooms: everywhere he'd hasten, wives and daughters to
   explore.
Grayson had them everywhere; on the stair and on the floor,
                              Grayson lusted, evermore.

"Why take that out?" she said.

"It's too blunt. He wanted it to flow differently, he wanted that godlike flavor. He felt he could do that better by keeping himself and his brother nameless."

The telephone rang. She picked it up and said a few words, scribbled a few notes, asked a few questions about when, where, and how. "That's great, friend," she said. "Yeah, do send me copies of those clips, and listen, that's one I owe you if you ever need a Seattle angle."

She hung up and looked at me. She didn't say anything and I

didn't need to ask. She looked down at the poem and said, "I think you're right, if it matters. Richard had a well-honed sense of bitter satire. A frontal attack was never as much fun as a hit-and-run."

"The title was blatant enough."

" 'The Craven.' What an insult that would've been to a man like Darryl Grayson."

"It belittles his genius. It reduces Grayson's life to the level of his own. And yet it has moments of real . . . what?"

"Love."

"Read it again."

She read aloud from the top: the world according to Richard, first revised version.

> One night sitting with dear Gaston, as the night fell deep and
>   vast in
> All its blackened glory: such a night to chill him to the very
>   core;
> A colder wind I blew upon him, one I thought would shake
>   and stun him
> And might even break and run him far away from sorrow's
>   door.
> But the child remained undaunted: all his faith again he swore
>   Was in his god forevermore.

"I don't believe this," she said. "It doesn't square with what I know about Richard or Rigby."

"You can't take it literally, you'll end up doubting it all. I admit it strikes a false note at the top. We know Rigby wouldn't sit still for what comes later, but that doesn't mean other parts of it aren't true."

She read two flashback stanzas telling of the gods' humble origins.

"I had it right," she said. "If anything, I underwrote it."

The father was a mean drunk and drunk much of the time. The mother was dead and unforgiven. If she wanted understanding, she'd have to find it in the next world because the son she'd left on earth had none to give her.

Lines in the middle of the third stanza made short work of these two and the sorry life they'd given their sons.

Brute and whore together spawned 'em; then forsook 'em,
tossed and pawned 'em
To the devil who upon them did his vile and wicked powers
pour . . .

I joined her reading, quoting from memory.

One would join Old Scratch the devil, while he watched the
other revel
In himself, and gaze with level eyes upon the predator . . .

"I don't see that in here."

"He squiggled it out. But it's there, off to the side of the verse he kept. You can read it through the squiggle."

"Yeah, I see it now."

Up to this point Richard had worshiped his brother blindly, much as Rigby would do a generation later. "At that time, he was buying his own god scenario," I said. "Grayson was his protector, the only real constant in his life."

"Then it all changes. The god proves false."

"He has his first serious romance, and Richard rankles with fear and jealousy."

"Cecile Thomas," Trish said. "I talked to her. She had gone to grammar school with the Graysons, then her parents moved away to North Carolina and came back to Atlanta when she was a teenager. A classic coming-of-age romance. Grayson thought of her as a brat when they were kids. Then suddenly there she was again, eighteen and lovely."

"There's a squiggled-out verse, just partly finished, when Richard was still trying to do it in a half-modern idiom, with names and all." She read it.

Grayson had with him a harlot, who had come to him from
Charlotte,
Though Atlanta, Georgia, was her domicile of yore . . .

"There's another line I can't read," she said.

"It says, *Who, you ask me, could this pig be, who so got the goat of Rigby.* If you look at it under a glass, you can make it out."

"He's doing it again, mixing his own role with Rigby's."

"But he catches it before the stanza's done and squiggles it out."

Her telephone rang.

She took back-to-back calls, from Phoenix and Baltimore. She made her notes with a poker face, as if she were working a rewrite desk assembling facts for a weather report.

She looked up from the phone without a word, pushed her notes off to one side, and again took up Richard's poem.

"You can see the words changing as it goes along. The tone gets darker, angrier."

"He was a clingy kid," I said. "He was what? . . . thirteen, fourteen years old. His brother was four years older, the difference between a boy and a young man. Richard counted on his brother to be there when things in his life went wrong."

"Then it got to be too much." She flipped a page. "We can only guess how Darryl felt, when all we've got is Richard's side to go by."

"My guess is the same as yours. He was being suffocated by his father on one side and by Richard on the other. So he ran away with his girlfriend to the coast, only his friend Moon knew where."

"And Moon wasn't telling."

"And Richard settled into a cold rage. He had already lost his mother, and now the unthinkable was happening, he was losing his brother. To a kid that age, the feeling of abandonment was probably enormous."

"He hated Moon for obvious reasons."

"Moon was everything he could never be. Strong, independent . . . the kind of man Grayson would want for a brother."

"In South Carolina, Grayson found that sense of purpose that would carry him through life. He'd fought Old Scratch and won."

She read it.

*And when the young god chose to fight, he waged a battle
    that was mighty;*
*Purpose kept his honor far away from Satan's harsh and
    blust'ry roar.*

This was how he rose above it: did his work and learned to
  love it,
And his skills made others covet everything he made and
  more.
'Tis some deity, they marveled, living there beyond that door:
                    He'd joined the gods, forevermore.

For three stanzas the god walked on water, could do no wrong. All
he touched was blessed: he was on a spiral ever upward.
Then came *The Raven*.

And when it seemed that none could daunt him,
A sepulchre rose up to haunt him
Stuck in there as if to taunt him, all the more to underscore
That he who'd walked among the gods
Had tumbled down to hell's back door,
                    A-burning there, forevermore.

"The misspelled word," she said. "But it's all out of sequence.
He's giving his brother all that success before *The Raven*, when it
really didn't happen till five or six years later."

"Creative license again. He thought it worked better dramatically. But the real question is, what is this business of the misspelled word? What the cop in St. Louis told you, that Hockman
had just gotten a new book with a misspelled word . . . that's
damned interesting."

"And not just any word. The same word."

"How could Grayson make that mistake again?"

"If we knew that, we'd know something, wouldn't we?"

"Whatever happened, it was disastrous."

"The god begins to fail. He starts doubting himself, becomes
obsessed by a vision of his failure. He tries to put it right, but he can
never do it well enough."

"Nothing he does can satisfy him now."

"It can never be good enough."

"He sinks into despair."

"And takes refuge in alcohol and sex."

And Rigby heard in disbelief the Craven's method and motif
Of luring maidens into wretchedness behind his bedroom
    door.
One poor fool she filled herself with fantasy, then killed
    herself,
Unable to instill herself into his craven heart before
She turned up high the unlit gas and died upon her father's
    floor:

                         To irk the Craven nevermore.

"God, there was a girl who killed herself," Trish said. "I kissed her off with a paragraph. I didn't think it had that much to do with Grayson, it was months after their affair and she seemed despondent over everything, not just him."

She looked at me, riddled with doubt.

"Who knows what it had to do with," I said. "Maybe it's just Richard again, trying to blame some circumstantial tragedy on his brother."

"What about Laura Warner?"

"You did what you could with her. You chased her pretty hard."

"Not hard enough."

"Then that's what revised editions are for."

We were in the last lines now. The dark-haired god idolized in the early verse had suddenly been reduced to ridicule.

The time had come to resurrect the ancient failure that
    infected
Every facet of his life . . .

She looked at me and I gave her the next line from memory.

But his second task was tougher; it was Poe who made him
    suffer . . .

"Poe defeated him," she said. "He never did get it right."

"Then where'd the book come from?"

She shook her head.

"And the ashes . . ."

"I don't know."

"If Grayson was such a failure at the end of his life," I pressed, "why is his book still causing so damned much trouble?"

"I don't know. I just don't know."

We didn't speak again till the phone rang. The late man at the *Times-Picayune* in New Orleans.

She talked for a while and hung up.

"He burned her house," she said flatly. "Killed her, then set fire to her house."

"Laura Warner."

She nodded. "They're all dead. St. Louis, Phoenix, Idaho . . . all dead. All but a blind, crazy woman in the Maryland case."

BOOK III THE RAVEN

44

It was raining again. I heard two things, the steady drumming of the rain and the click of my bedroom door as Trish came in. I lay still for a moment, listening to her footsteps as she approached my bed. I had been in a deep sleep for all of ninety minutes: the digits on the clock beside the bed told me it was now 4:52. I blinked my eyes and gradually came awake, aware of her presence a foot or two away. She stood for a long minute, then leaned over and touched my shoulder, shaking me gently.

"It's time," she said.

"Yeah, I'm awake."

"We gotta get going."

She went away and I lay there for another minute, thinking about what we had discovered in the night. I thought about five old murder cases in five different cities, and about the blind woman the killer had left alive in Maryland.

I hit the shower. Thought about it some more as I stood in the steam.

I smelled bacon as I came downstairs. She stood in the half-dark kitchen, cooking by the light from the smoke hood over the range.

"Didn't we just eat?" I asked in a surprised tone of voice.

"Such as it was."

But my appetite is always good in the morning and I was hungry again. I sat at her kitchen table and let her pamper me.

"Scofield and Kenney are due in at six-thirty, more or less, according to the flight plan they filed in L.A.," she said. "We should play it safe and be there with time to spare."

I agreed with that. We were probably safe if we could leave in another ten minutes. We were already slightly south of town, and that would give us a full hour to make the few miles to Sea-Tac before the rush hour began.

I asked if she'd gotten any sleep. "Didn't even try," she said, hand-ing me a plate of food. She sat across from me with her own plate and said, "I can't sleep with stuff like this going on."

She had been thinking about the sequence of those five old murder cases and had come up with a point of logic that had escaped us at midnight. "The cases all followed the Grayson lettering sequence, in precise order. *A* came before *B,* then came *C, D,* and *E,* all within days of each other. Think about that a minute. Picture a map of the United States and ask yourself, if you were going to kill people in five differ-ent parts of the country, how would you go about it? I'd do the two in the West first because I'm out here already and it's closer. Do Idaho first, then fly to Phoenix. Then go east and do the others, St. Louis, then New Orleans and Baltimore, in either order. What the killer did, though, was St. Louis first . . . *A.* Then he went to Phoenix, *B;* then he flew clear back across the country to *C,* Baltimore. Then back across the country again to Idaho. Then back again to New Orleans. Does this make sense? Not unless you've got Grayson's list and can see the connections."

"It's like he couldn't see anything beyond the list."

"Just get there, do it, and move on to the next one."

"Whatever it was, the urgency was so great he didn't even think about geography."

She shivered. "This is a real crazy one we've got here."

"And he's still out there doing it."

Forty minutes later we were sitting in a maintenance truck at the end of a concourse where the smallest airline carriers and various private flights were routed. Our driver was a cheerful fellow named Mickey Bowman, who ran the airport's public relations office and didn't seem to mind being roused from bed when Trish had called him at three-thirty. I knew a little about the odd relationships that some-times develop between PR people and the press—the Denver cops had a public affairs specialist with the rank of division chief, and depending on who held the job, you could sometimes see the good and bad of what he did on the front pages of the Denver newspapers. If he stonewalls, they dig out the facts anyway, only they write them in such a way as to make his boss look stupid, silly, or devious. A good PR guy knows when to promote and when to back off and do the gal a favor. He is always in when the press calls: he never gives her the feeling that, all things considered, he'd rather be in Philadelphia than sitting in a maintenance truck at six o'clock on a rainy morning talking to her. He is an expert at damage control, and if the story is going to be critical, he sometimes earns his pay more for what's left out of a piece than what's put in.

Bowman had been a reporter himself in a previous life and he knew the routine. He knew what her deadlines were, just as he knew that she seldom did stories of that nature. "We'd like to meet a guy at the airport, Mickey," she had said, "and we're not sure yet whether we'll want to announce ourselves after he gets here." Bowman's dad had been in the Seabees in the big war, she told me later: he had passed along that can-do mentality to his son. Bowman was waiting when we arrived. He got us through security, verified when and where Scofield's plane would be coming in, and now we sat with Trish wedged tight in the seat between us, the airport VISITOR tags clipped to our lapels.

I sat quietly splitting my concentration. One side of my brain listened to the shoptalk between Aandahl and Bowman while I thought about our killer with the other half. I thought about a blind woman in Baltimore who had been left alive in the middle of a nine-day rampage, who had later gone mad and been committed. Trish was telling Mickey Bowman about a great public-relations man she knew by phone but had never met. The guy worked for United Air Lines in Miami, and he had all but written her first big story for her on deadline. A plane had been hijacked: FBI sharpshooters had gotten under the aircraft without the hijacker's knowledge, and one was trying to crawl up the plane's nose assembly before the gunman figured out where they were. The United man had an office window that looked down on the scene. Trish sat at a desk across town, her phone rigged through a headset, taking verbatim descriptions as the United guy talked the story out to her. "They killed the hijacker," she said, "but I've never forgotten that PR man. You're pretty good yourself, Mick."

This was high praise from someone who never dealt in bullshit, and Bowman knew it. "Mickey used to be a bureau chief for the AP in Indianapolis," Trish said for my benefit. I joined the small talk and learned a few things about wire-service reporters. But I was still thinking about the blind woman in Maryland.

At six-thirty sharp a burst of noise came through Bowman's radio. "Your bird's on the ground," he said. At almost the same instant a car materialized, a black Cadillac that came slowly up the runway and stopped, idling about thirty yards to our right. The two men sitting in the car would be Scofield bodyguards, I guessed. Bowman started his engine and cleared away the steam from our windows with his air blower. I had to hand it to him: he must be curious as hell about the story we were doing, but he never asked.

A sleek-looking jet nosed its way around the corner and came toward us. "Well, what do you think?" Trish asked. I told her I tried not to think, I just react, and Bowman laughed when she did not. She was letting me call the plays, at least for now. It had been my decision to get on Scofield's tail as soon as he touched down at Sea-Tac; I just wasn't comfortable waiting around for him to show up at the Four Seasons. When you're dealing with a fruitcake like Pruitt, a lot can happen in ten miles.

The plane taxied in and came to a stop. The ground crew rolled out a steel stairwell, a door opened, and a man got out and popped open an umbrella. Then Rodney Scofield stepped out in the rain. I didn't need a formal introduction: he was an old man whose snowy hair curled in tufts under the edges of his hat, whose ruddy face—as near as I could tell from that distance—was all business. This was his clambake, he was the boss. The grunt beside him held the umbrella over his head, and the two grunts in the Caddy got out and stood at attention. He was at the bottom of the stairs when Leith Kenney emerged from the aircraft. Kenney looked just as I'd pictured him, which doesn't happen often when all you have is a voice to go by. He had a neatly trimmed beard: he was slender and tall and had the word *bookman* stamped all over him. He was carrying a small suitcase, which he looked ready to defend with his life. He reminded me of a diplomatic courier in wartime, transporting top secrets with the valise chained to his wrist. But I was willing to bet that this suitcase contained nothing but money.

Here we go, I thought.

* * *

We went south, a surprise. I was happy to have done something right for a change and picked up Scofield at the airport. The Cadillac whipped onto I-5 and headed for Tacoma like a homing pigeon. Bowman followed without question: Trish would owe him a big-league debt when it was over. The Caddy cruised at the speed limit and Bowman kept our truck two or three cars behind it. We didn't talk: just sat rigid, tense in the seat. After eight or ten miles, the Cadillac turned off the highway and took a two-lane, state-numbered road. Bowman dropped back but kept him in sight, cruising along at forty.

The rain had stopped and the sky was breaking up into long streaks of blue. A stiff wind blew down from Rainier, buffeting the truck as we rocked along. I thought we must be due east of Tacoma now, skirting the city on Highway 161. It was small-town suburban, broken by stretches of open country. Snow blew off the mountain in the distance, a swirling gale driven by the same wind that rolled down the valley. We came to a river, crossed it, and arrived in the town of Puyallup.

The Cadillac stopped. Pulled off to the side of the road.

We drove on past and I got a glimpse of Scofield and Kenney conferring over something in the backseat.

"They're looking at directions," Trish said. "Double-checking."

"Then we're almost there."

Bowman hung a left, did a quick U-turn, and came cautiously to the corner. We could see the Cadillac still parked off the road in the distance. We sat at roadside and waited.

They came a minute later. Bowman allowed just the right gap to develop, then swung in behind them. I wasn't too worried: none of the guys in the Caddy looked like pros to me, meaning the only way they'd make us was by accident. The Caddy hung a right, into a road that ran along the river. The place they were going was about half a mile along, a small café well back from the road. There was a gas pump out front and a couple of junk autos at the east side of the building. The yard was unpaved, puddle-pocked from all the rain. "Pull in," I said, and Bowman did, taking a position between cars on the far end. Scofield and Kenney got out and went in, leaving the two grunts alone in the car.

"Well," I said. "Looks like we fish or cut bait."

"Let me go in," Trish said. "At least if Pruitt's in there he won't know me on sight."

"Okay, but do it quick. Get us three coffees to go, then get back out here and tell me what's going on."

She clutched her raincoat and struggled through the wind to the front door. I got back in the truck and waited. Bowman didn't say anything, and in a minute I forgot he was there. I thought about Pruitt and Grayson, and about the blind woman in Baltimore. And I was suddenly very nervous.

One of Scofield's grunts got out of the Caddy and tried valiantly to light a cigarette. No smoking allowed in the old man's car, I thought. But the wind was fierce and at last he had to give it up.

The café got busy. It was a workingman's joint, the customers coming and going in blue jeans and flannel. The slots in front of the building were now filled in with cars, and another row had begun out near the road behind us. A young couple brushed past, then two farmers, then a guy in coveralls who looked like the town grease monkey. They all converged at the front door, just as the door swung open and Trish came out.

She stepped aside, clutching a brown paper bag against her breast. I got out and let her into the truck and she gave me the news. Our friends had taken a booth at the far end of the dining room and were sitting there alone, waiting.

Trish gave out the coffees. "Hope you don't have to be any-where," she said by way of apology to Bowman. He just grinned, well aware of the points he was piling up with her, and said his time was her time. He'd need to call in at nine and make sure a few things got done: other than that, he was all hers. More people came and went, old men in twos and threes mixed with the occasional loner. They would fill up the tables in a corner, eat their soft-boiled eggs and gripe as old men in small towns have always done about the thieves and sons of bitches running things in Washington. I could fit right in if they'd let me: a helluva lot better that would be than sitting out here like three bumps on a log. This was a difficult place for a stake-out. But you'd be much too conspicuous out on the road, so you took what the situation gave you and hoped you blended in. I hunched down in the seat till my eyes were level with the dash. I could still see everything that went on at the front door.

Bowman and Trish were talking shop again. I listened but did not hear. Then we all settled into that quiet restlessness that always seems to come in the second hour. I replayed the case in my head, trying to remember everything from the top. Slater walked into my store and we did our little macho dance. I crossed swords with Pruitt, came to know Eleanor and the Rigbys, absorbed the legend of the Graysons, met Huggins and Amy Harper. But through it all I kept thinking about a woman I had never met and probably never would, a blind woman who had gone crazy in Baltimore.

I got my chance at her when Bowman went to make his phone call. "The guy in Baltimore," I said. "When he called you back, did he say anything about the particulars of that case?"

"He read me some stuff from the clips. I made some notes." She opened her purse and got out her steno pad. "I spent more time with him than the others because of the blind woman."

"Yeah, the blind woman."

"What're you thinking?"

"I don't know yet. Go on with what he told you."

"The victim's name was Allingham. He lived with his wife on the outskirts of Baltimore, a suburb called Ellicott City. Nice house, secluded neighborhood, well-to-do people in their midfifties."

"And the wife survived."

"Not only survived, she seemed to've been deliberately left alone. He came into the room with her. She could hear him breathing."

"*Him* . . . did she say it was a him?"

"That's how the clips had it. *He* came in . . . *he* stood there breathing hard. She knew what was happening, too: knew they had an intruder and he had just killed or seriously hurt her husband. Blind people see better than we think."

"What else?"

She flipped a page. I looked at her notes and saw a cryptic brand of shorthand, probably something of her own making that was unreadable to the rest of the world. "Her name was Elizabeth. She was never a credible witness. She just sank into darkness after that. But who could blame her?"

I closed my eyes and tried to see it. Trish said, "The cops thought it might've been her dog that saved her. She had this German shepherd Seeing Eye dog, very protective. They say the dog raised hell when the cops arrived. They had to bring in a dog man to muzzle him before they could interview the widow."

"I don't think the dog had anything to do with it."

"How so?"

"Dogs don't usually discourage that kind of killer, at least not for long. If he'd wanted her, he'd go through the dog to get her."

"Maybe the noise scared him off."

"Maybe. And I can't help wondering how she could hear the killer breathing if the dog was barking."

"Who knows what she really heard? But look, are you going somewhere with this?"

"I don't know yet. It's just nagging at me. Did any of your news guys mention ashes at the scene?"

"No, but that wouldn't be in the clips. The cops never—"

"But you did say the house in New Orleans was torched and burned."

"Yeah, the cops there thought it was done to cover up the murder."

"They may've told the press that, but I'll bet there were some cops down there who didn't believe it."

"What're you thinking?" she asked again.

"Might've been somebody burning a book. He left it burning and the fire spread and burned the house."

Bowman had come out of the restaurant, standing off to one side to grab a smoke. I looked at Trish and the question that had nagged at me all morning bubbled up and out.

"Why would he leave the blind woman alive?"

"You tell me."

"Because of her blindness. That's the one thing all the others had in common that made her different. They could see."

"He knew she couldn't see him. Couldn't identify him."

"That's the logical answer. But this bird wasn't thinking logically. And I can think of another possibility."

She shook her head. "I must be dense."

"There was something in the book. Something they could see and she couldn't. Something that had been put in or bound in by mistake. Something so awful in the killer's mind that it had to be retrieved, and anybody who had seen it killed."

"I don't know, Janeway."

"I don't know either. I'm just doing what cops always do in murder cases, I'm playing it through in my head. Maybe he never intended to kill anybody. But he went to St. Louis to get his book back, and Hockman wouldn't play. Now we get into the collector's mentality. Hockman suddenly knew he had something unique. He wasn't about to give it up, not for Jesus Christ, not for Darryl Grayson himself. The only way to get it from him was to kill him."

"Keep going," she said, but her voice was still laced with doubt.

"The killer was single-minded, you figured that out yourself. He flew from *A* to *B,* and so on. He had one thing on his mind, getting that book. There was a desperate urgency to it, the cause transcended geography, transcended everything: he couldn't think about anything else. So he gets to St. Louis and Hockman won't give it to him. He whacks Hockman, maybe in a fit of rage. Now he's a killer."

I let that thought settle on her for a few seconds.

"Let me tell you something about killers, Trish . . . something you might know but never thought about. There are people who never kill till they're forty, fifty, then they kill a dozen times. That first one pushes them over the edge, sets them on a dark path they never intended to travel. The first one's the catalyst: there's no question after that. He goes to Phoenix and this time he doesn't even ask. He wades in, kills the people, takes the book. And so it goes."

"Until he gets to Baltimore . . ."

"And he walks into the room and there's this woman, obviously blind, with a dog and all, maybe a cane leaning against a table. She's blind, she didn't see anything, she's not part of this. He leaves her alive."

"But who'd go to such a length? Who'd do something like that?"

"Only one guy I can think of. The guy who made it."

Her eyes opened wide. "Jesus, Janeway, what're you thinking?" she asked for the third time, her voice now an urgent whisper.

"Did you ever talk to the coroner who did the Graysons?"

"No," she said in a tiny voice. "There was never a reason."

"There was never any doubt that it was really Darryl and Richard Grayson who died in that fire?"

She never got to answer because Bowman came back and got in beside us. We sat in the car, still as death, thinking about it.

All this time we've had the wrong motive, I was thinking. We've been thinking money, but that was never it. All the specter of money had done was cloud it. Only after Scofield had begun to collect Grayson and the books had become so avidly sought and eagerly paid for did money become a credible possibility. But this case had begun long before that.

The clock pushed ten: the breakfast rush was over. Scofield and Kenney had been inside more than two hours.

"They must be getting discouraged by now," I said.

It was on that weary note that Pruitt arrived.

45

He was the invisible man, leaving footprints in the snow. *Watch out for old ladies,* Slater had said, but you still couldn't see him except that he was carrying Scofield's suitcase. The suitcase was like the snow in that old horror film: it lit him up, made his tracks visible so you could pop him as he ran across the yard. It danced of its own volition, as if the arm clutching it against the gingham dress had vanished. He had tried to cover it with a shawl, which was too small. I sat up straight in the seat, so suddenly that Trish jumped up with a jerk of her own. "What's going on?" she said, but I was already out of the truck, splashing after the hooded squaw who moved between cars and headed across the muddy yard twenty yards to our right. He looked like old Mother Bates in *Psycho,* walking with the sure and deadly gait of a man. I fell in behind him and we headed out toward the row of cars parked by the road. The wind whipped at his shawl and clutched the corners of his hood. I got a glimpse of cheek as he half-turned and tried to look back. But he didn't turn far enough: he was caught in the Satchel Paige syndrome, afraid to look, afraid to see how much trouble followed him. If he could make it to his car without having to look upon his enemy, he'd be home free.

He didn't make it.

"Pruitt," I said, and he spun on his heel and locked on my eyes from a distance of six feet.

His free hand slipped down into the folds of his dress. I danced in close and grabbed him. With the other hand I ripped away the suitcase and made him fumble it. It popped open on the ground and the wind sucked up the money, a fluttery gale of greenbacks that blew back across the yard toward the café. He cried out and tried to dive down and save it. I met him coming down with a knee to the jaw, flopping him back on his ass in the mud.

It was all fast motion and unreal after that. I stood over him and said, "Take out that gun and I'll kick your head off," but I knew that wouldn't stop him. He cleared the dress with a handful of iron and I drove my shoe under his armpit. He grabbed at the sky, fired a round in the air, and I nailed him hard with the other foot. He withered, twisting in agony like a deflating balloon, rolling under the wheels with a gaffing, hissing sound. I kicked his gun and it spun off into a puddle. I knew I had hurt him, maybe busted his ribs, but he wasn't finished yet. He still had the knife, and as I dragged him out, he rolled into me with the blade leading the way. I caught his wrist with a wet smack. For a few seconds we strained against each other while the point of the knife quivered like a seismograph that couldn't tell if an earthquake was coming. Then I knew I had him. I saw it first in his eyes, that chink in the hard shell that comes to all bullyboys when they play one hand too many. He didn't look mean anymore. He looked small and tired and astonished.

"Now you are going to tell me where the girl is." I said this with the knife at my throat but the tide turning fast. His arm collapsed and he let the knife fall away as if surrender could save him. I hit him hard with my fist so he'd know better, and I hit him again, then again, then I lost track as I battered his face back and forth. I could hear my voice pounding at him as well, "Where is she? . . . Where is she?" with every punch, and after a while he stopped saying he didn't know. I felt Trish on my back, heard her screaming at me to for Christ's sake stop it, but for that long minute stopping was just not possible. I had slipped over the edge and become every bad cop who ever took up a rubber hose or swung a billy club in anger.

Trish grabbed me around the neck. I shrugged her off and went at Pruitt again.

Then I did stop. I lunged at him one more time, a reflex, but I pulled back without letting that last fist fall. I looked at him, bloody and cold, and I knew he wouldn't be telling anybody anything for a while.

I got up and looked around. Trish was sitting in mud ten feet away. Bowman was standing far back, watching as if he couldn't quite believe what had just happened. Farther back, people were running out of the diner as word spread that hundred-dollar bills were falling out of the sky.

In the babble of the crowd I heard the word *police*. I had a few minutes on the long end to do what I had to do and get out of there.

I dragged Pruitt around the car, took out Slater's handcuffs, and locked him to the door handle. I didn't see Trish when I looked for her again: I didn't know where she'd gone, but Bowman was still there. I went over to him and said, "Gimme the truck keys, Mickey," and he looked at me as if I was not a guy to argue with and he gave me the keys. I handed him the keys to the cuffs and told him to give them to Trish.

I headed toward the café. The crowd at the door pushed back and gave me a wide berth.

I heard voices as I moved through. Again the word *police*. Somebody else said they were on the way. A woman asked what the hell was going on and a man said, "Some crazy guy beat up an old lady in the parking lot."

I pushed past the waiting area and saw Scofield and Kenney sitting at the booth in the corner. They were looking at something on the table between them, studying it so intently they couldn't even hear the commotion up front.

I walked right over and pulled up a chair. Scofield jerked back, as startled as if I'd attacked him. He grabbed a book off the table and put it out of sight on his lap. Kenney looked at me with unruffled eyes and I jumped into the breach as if we were all old friends.

"I'm glad to see you didn't come all this way for nothing."

"Do I know you?" Kenney was wary now, but in his manner I caught a glimmer of recognition.

"That's a good ear you've got. I'm the guy you've been talking to on the phone."

He didn't say anything. I could see he was with me but he tried to shrug it off. This was all a moot point: they had what they'd come for.

"Before you go flying back to Tinseltown," I said, "I should tell you there's a lot more where that came from."

"Lots more what?"

"I don't have time to draw you a picture. I'm talking sixty cartons of Grayson ephemera. I'm talking notes, diaries, letters, sketches, photographs. You name it, I got it."

Kenney took the news like a world-class poker player. But Scofield began to tremble.

"And, oh, yeah," I said as an afterthought: "I also happen to have picked up Grayson's original subscriber list along the way . . . if something like that could be of any interest to you."

Scofield fumbled in his pocket and got out a vial of pills. He took two with water. Kenney looked in my eyes and said, "What do you want?"

"Right now just listen. You boys go on up to Seattle and wait for me in your room at the Four Seasons. I'll either come to you or call you later today or tonight. Don't talk to anybody about this till I get back to you. Are we all on the same page?"

They looked at each other.

"Yes," Scofield said in a thin voice. "We'll be there."

I got up and left them, pushing my way through the crowd. Outside, the yard looked like a convention of lunatics. People ran back and forth, crawled under cars in the mud, screamed at each other. Two fistfights were in progress off to the side, and in the distance I heard a siren.

I didn't see Bowman or Trish and didn't have time to look. I got in the truck and drove away.

I was well up the highway when I realized that something was clinging to my windshield. It was a crisp C-note. Franklin flapped madly against the glass as I banked north into I-5. I didn't stop even for him. In a while he lost his hold and blew away.

46

I was waiting at a table in the Hilton coffee shop when Huggins came in. He glanced around nervously, scanning the room twice before he saw me. A flash of annoyance crossed his face, but he chased it away and put on a passive mask in its place. I didn't move except to raise my eyes slightly as he crossed the room in my direction.

"Mr. Hodges," he said, sitting down.

"My name isn't Hodges, it's Cliff Janeway. I'm a book dealer from Denver."

If this surprised him, he didn't show it. His eyes had found the bait that had lured him here, that charred paper chip that had been haunting his dreams since Saturday night. I had put it out on the table, on top of the sheet Trish had brought back from St. Louis.

He leaned over the table and looked at it. "May I?"

"Carefully."

He picked up the fragment and again gave it the long, hard look through the eyepiece. His breath flared out through his nostrils as he looked. When at last he put the paper down, his eyes looked tired, as if he'd just gone halfway round the world.

"What do you think?"

He grunted. "It's hard to say."

"Come on, Mr. Huggins, let's not play around. The day is going fast and I've got lots to do."

"I'm not sure what you want from me."

"Let's start with this." I shoved the paper from St. Louis across the table and under his nose. "That look like the same alphabet to you?"

It pained him to look: you could see it in his eyes, the sure knowledge that he had something here but he'd never be able to keep it.

"Mr. Huggins?"

"Yes . . . I guess I'd have to say it probably is."

We looked at each other.

"So," he said: "now you can go tell Scofield and that'll be that."

I was finding it hard to argue with him. A part of me knew where he was coming from and sympathized with his viewpoint. As a book-man I was offended at the prospect of Scofield buying up every remaining scrap of Grayson's work. But I had Amy Harper to con-sider. This stuff was her future.

Suddenly Huggins was talking, one of his now-familiar mono-logues. But the tone was different: his voice had taken on the soft weariness of the defeated. "Twenty years ago, Grayson was an incredibly fertile field for a collector. He had just died and his books could still be had at almost every auction of fine-press items. I built my own collection piece by piece, scrap by scrap. It was so satisfying. You carve out your expertise, you shape and define it, and because of your scholarship others come into it and find the same pleasures and satisfactions you have. But you remain the leader, the first one they think of when they've taken it as far as they want to go with it and they're ready to sell. Then a man like Scofield comes along and every-thing changes."

He sipped his water and gave me a hard look. "I haven't been able to buy anything now for more than seven years. Only isolated pieces here and there, things that fall into my lap. You can forget the auction houses . . . Scofield's man is always there, always. And you can't outbid him, you'd have to be Ross Perot . . . . I don't know, maybe it's time I donated what I've got to a library and got out of the Grayson business. The trouble is, I don't know what else there is in life. I've never known anything that can give me the thrill of finding a Grayson variant . . . the thought of not having that is almost more than I can bear. Now, with my wife gone, the notion of clearing out my Grayson room and giving it all away . . . and yet, I've always been a practical man. When something's over, it's over."

"You could try taking pleasure in what you have."

He gave me a bitter smile. "I think you know better than that. The thrill is in the hunt, sir."

"Of course it is. And I wish I could help you."

"But in the end you're just what I feared most . . . Scofield's man."

"Not quite that. I wasn't lying to you, I didn't know who Scofield was."

"But you do now, and that's where you'll go. I don't blame you, understand, but I can't help fretting over it and wishing money didn't rule the world."

We seemed to be finished. Then he said, "How did you find it? Was it Otto Murdock?"

I sat up straight. "What about Murdock?"

"That's what I'd like to know. Obviously you know the name."

"How does he figure into it?"

"The same way everyone else does. He's been chasing it."

"You mean the Grayson *Raven*?"

"That, or anything else that'll keep him in potato water for the rest of his life."

"I understand he was a pretty good Grayson man once."

"Second only to yours truly," he said with a sad little smile. "Otto really had the bug, fifteen, twenty years ago."

"And had a helluva collection to prove it, I've been led to believe."

"Until he started selling it off piece by bloody piece to pay the whiskey man."

"Where'd he sell it?"

He gave a little laugh. "That shouldn't be hard to guess."

"You bought it."

"As much of it as I could. Otto was going through periods of trying to straighten himself out. Then he'd fall off the wagon and have to sell something. He sold all the minor stuff first. Then, just about the time he was getting to the gold-star items, along came Scofield with all the money in the world to buy them from him. I was like a duck shot right out of the water. Scofield paid him fifteen thousand dollars for a Benton *Christmas Carol* that wouldn't get fifteen hundred at auction. How do you compete with somebody like that?"

I let a couple of heartbeats pass, then I said, "Have you seen Murdock recently?"

"Hadn't seen him for years, till about a month ago."

"What happened then?"

"He called me up one night and asked if I could get some money together."

"Was he trying to sell you something?"

"That's what it sounded like. I never could get him to be specific. All he'd say was that he was working on the Grayson deal of a lifetime. Stuff he'd known about for years but had never been able to get at. Whoever owned it was unapproachable. But that person had died and now somebody else had come into it, somebody who didn't know as much or care as much about it. He needed some money to approach her with."

"How much money?"

"He wasn't sure. He had seen this person once and he couldn't tell if she was as naive as she seemed or was just taking him for a ride. My impression was, she wasn't a heavyweight, but you only get one shot at something like that. Misjudge her and you lose it. Pay too little, lose it. Pay too much, you still lose it. What he asked for was five thousand."

"He was going to try to steal it."

"I figured as much. If he was going to pay five, it had to be worth fifty. God knows what a madman like Scofield would pay."

"Why wouldn't Murdock go to Scofield for the money in the first place?"

"Who knows what Otto was thinking? If this really was a once-in-a-lifetime Grayson score, you'd want to try to buy it yourself and *then* sell it to Scofield. That's how I'd do it, if I was Otto and had a little larceny in my heart."

"So when he came to you for the five, what'd you tell him?"

"What do you think I told him? I said I'd need to know exactly what I'd be getting for my money. You don't just hand over five thousand dollars to a man who's fully capable of drinking it up in a lost weekend."

Now he wavered. "I made a mistake. I can see it in your face."

"You both did. He could've bought it all for a hundred dollars. She might've given it to him just for hauling it out of there."

He looked ready to cry. He didn't want to ask, didn't dare ask, but in the end he had to.

"What the hell are we talking about?"

"You don't want to know."

"No," he said dryly. "I probably don't."

"So Murdock came and went. Was that the last time you saw him?"

"Saw him, yes."

"But you heard from him again."

"He called me about ten days ago. He had been drinking, I could tell that immediately. He was babbling."

"About what?"

"He was raving about some limited series of Grayson books that I had missed in my bibliography. He seemed to think Grayson had made a special set, just a few copies of each title, at least since the midfifties."

"What did you tell him?"

"To find a good hangover cure and go to bed."

"Did he say anything else?"

"They're all dead. That's what he said, they're all dead, all five of 'em."

"What did you make of that?"

"Nothing. He was hallucinating."

"Was that the end of it?"

"Just about. He rambled on for a while longer. Talked about getting himself together, becoming a real bookman again. Said he was going to write the real story of Darryl Grayson: said it had never been told but he was going to tell it, and when he did, the book world would sit up and take notice. It was all drunken balderdash."

He looked weary, suddenly older. "If you want to chase down a drunk's pink elephants, be my guest. Archie Moon and the Rigbys might know something. Otto said he'd gone out to North Bend and talked to them about it."

"What did he say?"

"I don't know. I couldn't take any more."

He was ready to leave now. As he pushed back his chair, I said, "By the way, did you know Murdock was dead?"

He blinked once and said, "No, I didn't know that."

"I'm sure it's been on the news by now."

"I don't read newspapers and I never watch anything but network news on television. I can't stand these local fools."

"Anyway, he's dead."

"How? . . . What happened?"

"Murder."

He blinked again. "What the hell's happening here?"

"Good question, Mr. Huggins. I don't know, but I'm gonna find out."

47

Amy Harper had brushed out her long red hair and put on her one good dress. She looked less all the time like the doe-eyed schoolgirl I had rescued from Belltown. She had found someone to stay with her children overnight: a good thing, because this was going to run late.

She wouldn't be doing any lifting and toting today. She was going to sit in a chair and supervise while a billionaire's handyman did the work for her.

We zipped along I-90 in the Nash and I told her what the game plan was. Somewhere on the road, ahead of us or just behind, Scofield and Kenney were heading for the same destination: I had called them from Amy's room and told them where to go. She listened to what I was telling her and demanded nothing. She had a Spartan nature, patient and gutsy and uncomplaining, and I liked her better every time I saw her.

A kind of muted excitement filled the car as we flew past Issaquah for the run into North Bend. I was anxious without being nervous. I knew what we had: I knew the power it would hold over Scofield, and even Amy felt the strength of it as the day gained momentum. I had taken on the role of Amy's guardian, her agent, in the talks to come. But a murder case was also on the fire: the fate of another woman I cared about greatly was still in doubt. *It's not about money,* I thought again. I believed that now more than ever. But money had become so mixed up in it that only the moneyman could help me untangle it, and I wasn't above using the Grayson papers as a wedge on him.

It seemed impossible but it was still only one o'clock. I thought about Trish and wondered how she was doing with Pruitt. I had left Bowman's truck at her house and changed over to the Nash before meeting Huggins at the Hilton.

Now I banked into the familiar North Bend off-ramp. The day was lovely, chilly like a mountain pool, and the wind swirled clouds behind the mountain in the distance. For a moment I thought I saw the Indian in the mountain, but when I blinked and looked again, he was gone. I headed down toward the main street and turned into the motel where I'd left the stash.

The black Cadillac was there in the yard.

"They're here," I said.

I got out, went to the office, and asked for Rodney Scofield. Room four, the man said, and I walked up the walk and knocked on the door.

Kenney opened it. He had a cocktail glass in his hand, ice bobbing in amber liquid.

We went in. I drew up a chair and Amy sat on the foot of the bed. "This is Miss Amy Harper. She's running this show. My name's Cliff Janeway, I'm a book dealer from Denver."

"Leith Kenney." He shook hands, first with Amy, then with me.

"Where's Scofield?" I asked.

"In the bathroom. He'll be out. Want a drink?"

"Sure. What're we having?"

"Can you drink scotch?"

"I'm a William Faulkner bourbon man. That means between scotch and nothing, I'll take scotch."

He smiled: he knew the quote. Suddenly we were two old bookmen, hunkering down to bullshit. He looked at Amy and said, "Miss Harper?"

"Got a Coke?"

"7-Up."

"That'll be cool."

Kenney and I smiled at each other. He took a 7-Up out of a bag, filled a glass with ice, and poured it for her. He asked how I wanted my drink and I told him just like they shipped it from Kentucky.

A door clicked open and Rodney Scofield came into the room.

He was thin, with a pale, anemic look. His white hair had held its ground up front, retreating into a half-moon bald spot at the back of his head. His eyes were gray, sharp, and alert: his handshake was firm. He sat at the table, his own 7-Up awaiting his pleasure. He had a way about him that drew everyone around to him, making wherever he chose to sit the head of the class. He was a tough old bird, accustomed to giving orders and having people jump to his side. Now he would sit and listen and take orders himself, from a girl barely out of her teens.

It was up to me to set the stage, which I did quickly. "Everything I told you in the restaurant is true. Gentlemen, this is the Grayson score of your lifetime. This young lady here owns it, and she's asked me to come and represent her interests."

"Whatever you pay me," Amy said to Scofield, "Mr. Janeway gets half."

I looked at her sharply and said, "No way."

"I won't even discuss any other arrangement." She looked at Kenney and said, "If it wasn't for this man, I'd've given it away, maybe burned it all in the dump."

"Amy, listen to me. I couldn't take your money, it'd be unethical as hell, and Mr. Kenney knows that."

"Lawyers do it. They take half all the time."

"So do booksellers, but this is different. And you've got two kids to think about."

"Maybe I can help you resolve this little dilemma," Kenney said smoothly. "Let's assume for the moment that you've really got what you think you've got. That remains to be seen, but if it's true, Mr. Janeway would have a legitimate claim for a finder's fee."

I felt my heart turn over at the implication. I had come here chasing five thousand dollars, and now that jackpot was beginning to look small.

"What does that mean?" Amy said.

"It's a principle in bookselling," I told her. "If one dealer steers another onto something good, the first dealer gets a finder's fee." I looked at Kenney and arched an eyebrow. "Usually that's ten percent of the purchase price."

"That doesn't sound like much," Amy said.

"In this case it could be a bit more than that," Kenney said.

I leaned forward and looked in Amy's face. "Trust me, it's fine."

"Let's move on," Kenney said. "Let's assume we're all dealing in good faith and everybody will be taken care of. Where's the material?"

"It's not far from here," I said. "Before we get into it, though, I need to ask you some questions. I'd like to see that book you bought back in the restaurant."

Kenney was immediately on guard. "Why?"

"If you humor me, we'll get through this faster."

"What you're asking goes beyond good faith," Kenney said. "You must know that. You've told us a fascinating story but you haven't shown us anything. I've got to protect our interests. You'd do the same thing if you were me."

I got up and moved around the bed. "Let's you and me take a little walk." I looked at Amy and said, "Sit tight, we'll be right back."

We went down the row to the room at the end. I opened the door and stood outside while he went in alone. When he came out, ten minutes later, his face was pale.

My first reaction to the Grayson *Raven* was disappointment. *It's been oversold as a great book,* I thought as Kenney unwrapped it and I got my first real look. It was half-leather with silk-covered pictorial boards. Grayson had done the front-board design himself: his initial stood out in gilt in the lower corner. The leather had a still-fresh, new look to it, but the fabric was much older and very fine, elegant to the touch. In the dim light of the motel room it gave off an appearance of antiquity. The boards were surprisingly thin: you could take it in your hands and flex it, it had a kind of whiplash suppleness, slender and tough like an old fly rod. The endpapers were marbled: the sheets again had the feel of another century. You don't buy paper like that at Woolworth's and you don't buy books like this on chain-store sale tables. The slipcase was cut from the same material that had been used for the boards: the covering that same old silk. A variation of the book's design, but simpler, serving only to suggest, was stamped into the front board of the slipcase. My first reaction passed and I felt the book's deeper excellence setting in. The effect was of something whisked here untouched from another time. Exactly what Grayson intended, I thought.

I opened it carefully while Kenney stood watch. Scofield hadn't moved from his chair, nor had Amy. I leafed to the title page where the date, *1969,* stood out boldly at the bottom. A plastic bag con-

taining some handwritten notes had been laid in there: I picked it up
and moved it aside so I could look at the type without breaking my
thought. The pertinent letters looked the same. Later they could be
blown up and compared microscopically and linked beyond any
doubt, if we had to do that. For my purpose now, I was convinced.

I flipped to the limitation page in the back of the book. It was a
lettered copy, *E,* and was signed by Grayson.

E was New Orleans. Laura Warner's book.

"Well," I said to Scofield. "How do you like your book?"

"I like it fine."

"Then you're satisfied with it?"

"I don't know what you mean." His eyes were steady, but there
was something about him . . . a wavering, a lingering discontent.

"Are you satisfied you got what you paid for? . . . That's what I'm
asking."

"It's the McCoy," Kenney said. "If it's not, I'll take up selling
shoes for a living."

"Oh, I don't think you'll have to do that, Mr. Kenney," I said.
"But something's wrong and I can't help wondering what."

They didn't say anything. Kenney moved away to the table and
poured himself another drink.

"On the phone you told me something," I said. "You said Scofield
had touched the book and held it in his hands."

I looked at Scofield. "What I seem to be hearing in all this silence
is that this is not the book."

"It's not the one I saw," Scofield said. "I don't know what this is.
It may be some early state or a variant, maybe some experiment that
Grayson meant to destroy and never did."

Kenney sipped his drink. "It's a little disturbing because we know
that Grayson didn't do lettered books."

"So the hunt goes on," I said with a sly grin.

Scofield's eyes lit up. This was what kept him alive as he headed
into his seventh decade. The hunt, the quest, that same hot greed that
sent Cortez packing through steamy jungles to plunder the Aztecs.

I fingered the plastic bag.

"That's just some ephemera we found between the pages," Kenney said.

I opened the bag and looked at the notes. One was from Laura Warner, an enigma unless you knew how to read it. *Pyotr,* she had written, *don't you dare scold me for teasing you when you yourself tease so. It does please me that you can laugh at yourself now. Was this a test to see if I'd notice? How could you doubt one who hangs on your every word? I'm returning your little trick, lovely though it is, and I await the real book with joyful anticipation.*

None of us rehashed the words, though the last line hung heavy in the room. I opened the second note, a single line scratched out on notebook paper. *Hang on to this for me, it'll probably be worth some money. Nola.*

"What do you make of it?" I said.

"Obviously it's passed through several hands," Kenney said. "People do leave things in books."

I turned the pages looking for the poem "Annabel Lee." I found it quickly, with the misspelled word again misspelled.

Kenney had noticed it too. "Strange, isn't it?"

I held the page between my fingers and felt the paper. I thought of something Huggins had said: there's no such thing as a perfect book. If you look with a keen eye, you can always find something. I pressed the page flat against the others and saw that the top edge trim was slightly uneven. There's always something.

"Just a few more things and we can get started," I said. "I know you boys are dying to get into this stuff, but you have to help me a little first."

"What do you want?" Scofield said.

"I want to know everything that happened when you saw that other *Raven* and held it in your hands. I want to know when it happened, how, where, who was involved, and what happened after that. And I want to know about Pruitt and where he came from."

"I don't understand what any of this has to do with you."

"I've got a hunt of my own going, Mr. Scofield. I'm hunting a killer and I've got a hunch you boys are sitting on the answers I've been looking for."

48

Twelve years ago, Pruitt had been a hired gun for Scofield Industries. He was a roving troubleshooter whose job took him regularly into fifteen states, the District of Columbia, Europe, South America, and the Far East. Within the company he was known as the Hoo-Man, an inside joke that had two cutting edges. *HOO* was short for his unofficial title, head of operations, but in private memos that floated between department heads it was often spelled *WHO*. Pruitt knew who to see, who to avoid, who would bend, who would bribe. In third-world countries, Scofield said without apology, bribery was a way of life. If you wanted to do business in Mexico, it was grease that got you through the doors. You could play the same game in the Philippines, as long as you played by the Filipino rule book.

The remarkable thing about Pruitt was his ability to function in foreign countries without a smattering of language. There were always translators, and Pruitt knew who to ask and how to ask it. He was fluent in a universal tongue, the whole of which derived from half a dozen root words.

Love and hate. Sex. Life and death. Fear. Money and politics.

The stuff that gets you where you want to go, in far-flung places that only seem different from the town you grew up in. A military junta has a familiar look to a guy who's gone before a mom-and-pop city council in Ohio, asking for a liquor license.

Grease rules the day, from Alabama to Argentina.

This was a big job and Pruitt was good at it. He was always at the top of his game when the specs called for double-dealing and mischief. He was a shadow man whose best work could never be preplanned or monitored. He was judged strictly on the big result, success, while the boss insulated himself in a glass tower high over Melrose Avenue, never to know the particulars of how a deal had been set up.

"I wasn't supposed to know these things," Scofield said. "But I didn't get where I am by not knowing what's going on. I have a remarkable set of ears and I learned sixty years ago how to split my concentration."

Pruitt had witnessed Scofield's Grayson fetish from the beginning. He watched it sprout like Jack's beanstalk, exploding in a passion that was almost sexual. Pruitt knew, without ever understanding that attraction himself, that this spelled money.

With cool eyes he saw Scofield's collection outstrip itself ten times during the first year. By the end of year two it resembled a small library, with the end nowhere in sight. Scofield was no green kid, to burn bright and burn out when his whim of the day withered and left him dry. Scofield knew what he wanted for the rest of his life. He was a serious player in the Grayson game. Pruitt may have been the first of the Scofield associates to understand the old man's real goal: to be not just a player but the only player.

By the middle of the third year, Scofield had acquired many of the choice, one-of-a-kind items that push their owners into paranoia. He had moved the collection from the office to his mansion in the Hollywood Hills, where it was given an entire room in a wing on the second floor. Scofield was nervous. He summoned his security people, discussed plans for a new system, impregnable, state-of-the-art. Pruitt, who was expert in such things, was brought in to consult and was there to help supervise the installation.

Thus sealed in artificial safety, Scofield breathed easier. But no system is better than the men who create it.

Pruitt waited and watched, biding his time.

"That year I began buying books from Morrice and Murdock in Seattle," Scofield said. "My dealings were all with Murdock, who was then considered the country's leading dealer in Grayson books."

It was the year of the Morrice and Murdock breakup, when Murdock stumbled out on his own in an alcoholic stupor. "He still had a lot of books," Scofield said, "things he had hoarded over the years. But he was cagey, difficult. He knew Grayson was on an upward spiral, but the books were his ace in the hole. He also knew that I was the market: if I happened to die or lose interest, it would stabilize and Grayson would settle into his natural level, still upward bound but at a much slower rate. Murdock wanted to make all he could on every book, but even then he was afraid of selling. No matter what I paid him, he seemed to go through it at an unbelievable clip.

"He was the kind of man who would promise the moon and give you just enough real moonbeams that you couldn't help believing him. He talked of fabulous things, hidden in places only he knew about, and all that time he dribbled out his books one or two at a time. I bought everything he showed me and paid what he asked. I knew the day was coming when he'd get down to brass tacks and I'd see what he really had. I've had experience with alcoholics. Eventually they lose everything."

In the fourth year the big break came. Murdock called, claiming to have a client who owned the only copy of Darryl Grayson's last book.

But the deal had to be handled with tenterhooks. The woman was extremely nervous. She would only meet with Scofield under mysterious conditions, in a place of her choosing, with her identity fully protected.

"Did you ever find out," I asked, "why this was?"

"It was fairly obvious to me," Scofield said, "but Murdock explained it later. His client knew Darryl Grayson personally. They had had an intimate relationship. She had been a married woman then, still was, and if any of this came out, her marriage might be jeopardized."

"Did you buy that?"

"Why not, it was perfectly feasible. Have you read the Aandahl biography on the Graysons?"

I nodded.

"Then you know how Grayson was with women. The fact that a pretty young woman was married to someone else wouldn't have slowed him up much. She wouldn't have been the first woman to have carried on with Grayson while she was married to someone else. And Grayson was known to have given his women presents—books, notes, charts . . . mementos of completed projects. It was part of the pleasure he took in his work, to give out valuable pieces of it after the main work was finished. Once a project was done, Grayson wasn't much for keeping the records or hanging on to his dummy copies. For years it's been assumed that these were all destroyed, but I've never been convinced of that."

"So what happened?"

"We flew to Seattle."

"Who is we?" I looked at Kenney. "You?"

Kenney shook his head. "I hadn't been hired yet."

"I took Mr. Pruitt," Scofield said.

"Surely not," I said in real dismay.

"There was no reason to doubt him then."

"But what purpose did he serve?"

"He was what he always was: a bodyguard. I learned long ago that it pays to have such men with you. When you've got money, and that fact is generally known, you get accosted by all kinds of people."

"But you had nobody with you to function as an expert . . . nobody like Kenney?"

"Murdock was my expert. He had already had one meeting with this woman and had examined the book himself. There was no doubt in his mind what it was."

I didn't point out that the ax Murdock was grinding would've given Paul Bunyan a hernia. It wouldn't help to beat that horse now.

"So you took Pruitt," I said. "What happened when you got there?"

"Murdock met us at the airport and took us straight to the meeting place. I wasn't at my best: I'm prone to colds and flu, and I felt I was coming down with something. The weather was bad: I remember it was raining."

"What else does it ever do in this town?"

"We went to the place she had picked out, a restaurant downtown. She wanted to meet in a public place, probably for her own protection. Murdock had reserved a table in a far corner, where she'd told him to go. It was dark back there, but that's how she wanted it. We did it her way . . . everything her way."

He sipped his drink, gave a little cough. "She was late. We waited half an hour, maybe more. Murdock and I had little to talk about. It seemed like a very long wait, and I was not feeling well."

"Where was Pruitt all this time?"

"Posted at the door, up front."

"So when she finally did get there . . ."

"She had to walk right past him."

"And he'd have seen her."

"But not to recognize. She wore a veil . . . black coat, black hat . . . and a deep red dress. The veil did a good job. I never saw her face and neither did Murdock. With the veil, and the darkness at that table, she could've been anyone."

"Did she bring the book?"

"Oh, yes." He trembled at the memory of it. "It was superb . . . magnificent . . . completely lovely. Beyond any doubt, Grayson's masterpiece."

"You could tell all this in the dark?"

"Murdock had come prepared. He had a small penlight and we examined the book with that. You can't be sure under conditions like that, but there we were. I still didn't know what she wanted. She didn't seem to know either. She seemed in dire financial need one moment and unconcerned the next, as if her two greatest fears were selling the book and losing the deal we had come there to make. The ball was in my court: I felt I had to do something or risk losing it. I had brought some cash—not much, about twenty thousand dollars in thousand-dollar bills. I offered her this for the opportunity to examine the book for one week. The money would be hers to keep regardless of what we finally decided to do. We would sign a paper to that effect, handwritten by me and witnessed by Murdock. In exactly one week we'd meet back at that same restaurant. If the book passed muster, she would be paid an additional fifty thousand. Her reaction was palpable: it was more than she'd dreamed . . . she took it, and I felt I was home free."

The room was quiet. Kenney stood back like a piece of furniture. Amy sat on the edge of her chair. I held fast to Scofield's pale eyes.

"So you had the book," I said. "Then what?"

"We flew back to Los Angeles with it. I wrote Murdock a check for his work, and at that point I decided to have some independent appraisers fly in and look at it. I called Harold Brenner in New York."

He looked at me expectantly. I had heard the name, had seen

Brenner's ads in *AB*, but I had never had any dealings with the man. Kenney said, "Brenner's one of the best men in the country on modern small-press books."

"But Brenner couldn't come out till the end of the week," said Scofield. "This would still leave us time to have the book examined and get back to Seattle for our meeting with the woman in red, early the following week. Then I got sick—whatever I had caught in Seattle got dangerously worse, and on my second day home I was hospitalized as a precaution. That night my house was burglarized. My choice Grayson pieces were taken."

"Including *The Raven*, I'm sure," I said. "How long did it take you to realize that Pruitt was behind it?"

"The police were surprisingly efficient. Pruitt had been out playing cards that night: four other men would swear that the game had gone on till dawn and he'd only left the room once or twice to use the facility. But from the start, one of the detectives knew it was an inside job. How could it be anything else? . . . Who else would know how to defeat the system and get in so easily? The big problem was proving it . . . they had to catch the perpetrator and make him talk. Within forty-eight hours they had questioned everyone remotely connected with the installation of the security system, including all of Pruitt's local cronies. Early on the third day they made an arrest, a petty hoodlum named Larson, who had known Pruitt for years. When he was picked up, he still had one of the break-in tools in his possession."

I gave a dry little laugh. Even after my long police career, the stupidity of some criminals amazes me. This is why the jails are full.

"It was a screwdriver," Scofield said. "One of those extra blades that comes on a utility knife, you know, a six-tools-in-one instrument. He had used it to break open the bookshelf locks. This was easy: once he'd gotten into the house, then into the library, breaking open the cabinets themselves was relatively simple—he just wedged his screwdriver into the metal lock and pried it open. But it left a scrape mark, which was identical to the sample police made later with the same tool. He also left a partial heel print in the garden outside the house. His heel fit it perfectly. We had just fertilized that flowerbed, and a chemical residue was found in the nail holes of his heels. I was getting that fertilizer from Germany, it wasn't yet widely available in the United States, so the odds of finding that precise mix of ingredients in any other garden would have been quite long. We didn't even have the analysis back from the crime lab yet, but Mr. Larson—and more to the point, Mr. Pruitt—must have known what it would show. Larson was a two-time loser who was looking at a long trip up the river. His incentive to deal was getting better by the hour."

"To give them Pruitt's head on a platter."

"You could put it that way."

"I can almost guess the rest."

He nodded. "Suddenly my attorney got a call from Larson's lawyer . . . Larson's *new* lawyer. We were told that full restitution might be made if the case could be discreetly dropped."

"I'll bet the cops loved you for that."

"The detective who had made this case was not thrilled, to say the least. He fumed and yelled and said this was not my call to make."

"But he soon learned better, didn't he? Grease runs the world in L.A. too."

"You've got to understand something. This was never said, but there was a strong implication that if I didn't agree right then, on the spot, my books might end up in the Pacific Ocean. What was I supposed to do? I agreed to have the case dropped, and on Monday morning a note was delivered to my office. If I showed up at a certain corner at a certain time, a taxi would arrive and the driver would have my books in two big boxes. And that's what I did. I never saw Pruitt again until just this morning. End of story."

"Not quite, Mr. Scofield. You left the woman in red hanging from a cliff."

"I flew back to Seattle that same night. There wasn't time to have the book examined by Brenner or anyone else. I went on my gut, as they say, not the first time I've done that in my life. I was still weak from my illness, and the stress of having lost the book for the better part of a week had also taken its toll. I went against my doctor's orders, had to be helped to my chair in the restaurant. She was already there when I arrived. She seemed quite nervous, unsure. But even then I had no idea anything was wrong. We chatted for perhaps three minutes. I had the money all ready for her, in a small valise, just as I brought it to Pruitt this morning. The book and the valise were there on the table between us. I felt so sure . . . and then . . ."

"What?"

"I remember I had a coughing attack . . . a bad one. And it was almost as if that was what finally made her balk and call the deal off. She reached out and picked up the book, not the money, and for a minute I still didn't realize what it meant. Then she apologized and said she just couldn't sell it after all. I tried to persuade her . . . if it was more money she needed . . . but no, it was more like . . ."

I waited, my eyes on his.

"I don't know how to put it exactly . . . an act of conscience maybe. I guess that's it, she was overcome by conscience and guilt. She reached in her purse and brought out the money I'd given her. I made her keep it. I thought maybe it would give me a claim on the book if the day ever came when she'd change her mind again."

He looked around from face to face. "Then she walked out. We never heard from her again."

No one said anything for a long moment.

"Just like Dillinger," I said.

None of them seemed to know what I was talking about.

"You and John Dillinger," I said. "Both laid low by a woman in red."

49

I left them there, Kenney and Scofield to their work and Amy watching them from a chair near the door. I drove into North Bend alone. I had fish to fry.

This is where it all happens, I thought: it doesn't have anything to do with Baltimore or Phoenix or even Seattle except that those cases all spun out of here. I was thinking of Grayson, doing the work he loved without having to compete with his own fame and glory. We do get older: sometimes we even get wiser. Fame and glory don't mean as much when we're fifty, when they're finally within reach, as they did when we could only dream about them at twenty.

The gate was locked at the Rigby place so I went on past to Snoqualmie. Fingers of sunlight led the way, beaming down through pockets of mist that wafted across both towns. The area bustled with commerce in the middle of the afternoon. Tourists drifted along the avenue, going or coming to or from the waterfall. A mailman moved along the block, stopping in each store. Near a corner a team of glaziers was busy replacing a broken storefront.

I drove past Smoky Joe's Tavern and turned a corner, pulling up at the curb. Archie Moon's printshop was dark and locked. I got out and went to the door, cupped my hands, and peeped through the glass. Somewhere back in the shop a faint light shone, but I rapped on the glass and no one came.

"I think she's gone for the day," a voice said.

I turned and said hello to the mailman.

"If you're looking for Carrie, she usually takes half a day off on Tuesdays," he said.

"Actually, I'm looking for Archie."

"Carrie can tell you where he's at: she rides herd on him like a mother hen. But you'll have to catch her tomorrow."

I thanked him and got back in the car. I watched him sort some mail and drop it through the front-door slot. Then he moved on down the street and I drove out of town, on to Selena Harper's house.

Things were soon looking up. Trish was sitting on the front porch steps when I turned into the yard.

"I figured you'd turn up here," she said. "The only hard part was finding this place. And psyching myself up for a long wait."

I wanted to hear all about the other theaters of war, about Pruitt and the cops and all that had happened since I'd seen her five hours ago. But her mood was cool, almost hostile as she watched me come toward her.

"Sorry I had to run out on you like that. Things got kinda hectic."

"Didn't they, though," she said, unforgiving. "You're quite an act, Janeway. But I can't say I wasn't warned."

She cocked her head to one side, showing a long bruise under her left eye. "Pretty, huh?"

"What happened to you?"

"Think about it a minute. You're a bright boy, you'll figure it out."

I thought about it and came up with nothing.

"You were trying to turn Pruitt into next week's dog food. I grabbed you around the neck. Next thing I knew I was flat on my back in the mud."

"Wait a minute, hold it. Play that back again."

"You slugged me, you son of a bitch."

I was, for once in my life, speechless.

"Wanna hear it again?"

"No . . . I really don't think I do."

"Do you know what I did to the last man who tried to raise a hand to me?"

"I've got a feeling I'm about to find out."

"Think of a hot-oil enema and maybe you can relate to it."

"Ayee." Beyond that I didn't dare laugh. I tried to reach out to her, but she looked at my hand the way you'd look at a spittoon.

"Come on, Trish."

She stared off at the graying sky.

"Come on."

She didn't move.

"Come on. Please."

"Please what?"

"Get up, tell me it's okay, and let's get on with it."

"Is that the full and complete text of your apology? Now I know why you're so successful with women."

"I am sorry. I really am."

She didn't respond, so I said it again. "I'm sorry."

"How sorry are you?"

"I don't know. How sorry do you want me to be?"

"I want you to do something for me."

I didn't say anything. I seemed to know what she wanted.

She gripped my wrist and I pulled her up. She smoothed her skirt with her free hand and said, "I want you to go in and talk to Quintana."

I moved on past her to the top of the porch.

"I'm serious about that," she said, losing no ground behind me.

I turned and she was right there, so close we bumped together.

"He's gonna treat you right. But you've got to do it now."

I unlocked the front door and stood aside so she could go in first. The house smelled musty and looked golden and gray. A light rain had begun, with the sun still shining off to the west, the dark places broken by splashes of streaky sunlight. She came in reluctantly, like an infidel desecrating a holy place, and I followed her on through the front room toward the kitchen. She stopped for a moment, seemed to be listening for something, then turned and looked at me across a shaft of watery yellow haze. "Am I imagining this," she said, "or is something happening between us?" The question was sudden and improbable, infusing the air with erotic tension. I thought of the midnight supper we had had and how easily she had done the impossible, taken Rita's place at the other end of the table. "It does seem to be," I said. But I didn't yet know the shape it might take or where it might go from here. She lived in Seattle and I lived in Denver, and neither of us had had time to give it much thought.

She looked away, into the clutter of the kitchen. I came up behind her, close enough to touch. But she was not a woman you did that to until you were very sure.

She sensed me there behind her, took a half-step back, and pressed herself lightly against me.

I put an arm around her, then the other. She leaned her head back and I hugged her a little tighter.

"Something's certainly happening," she said. "I know *that's* not my imagination."

"In Rome they had a term for it."

"*Lustus profundus,*" she said, stealing it.

"The next best thing to a chariot race."

She laughed and pulled herself away, moving across the room. "God, I don't know what to do with you. I wish I knew."

"Whatever you want. It's not that complicated. I don't come with a Japanese instructional booklet."

She took a long breath. "I've been celibate almost two years."

"I can't imagine why. It can only be by choice."

"I got hurt. I mean really burned. I swore off men. And meant it, too, until . . ."

She blushed. Her skin looked hot.

"I don't know what I want to do," she said.

"But, see, you don't have to know. You can figure it out in your own good time. Nobody's pushing you."

"Now that I'm over here," she said, and we both laughed.

She asked where the Grayson stuff was and I led her back to the stairs and up to the loft. I crawled up into the room and reached back for her. We clasped hands and I helped her up. It was all as I'd left it, the two remaining rows separated by a three-foot gap and draped by a sheet of clear polyethylene. I walked out on the plastic and held up my hands like Moses going through the Red Sea.

Behind me, she said, "Who the hell am I kidding?"

When I turned, she had pulled her blouse out of her skirt and had taken loose the top buttons.

"So what do you think?" she said brightly. "Is that plastic cold?"

I've always hated plastic, the symbol of everything phony in the world.

Not anymore.

It was hot and quick, intense. We were both long overdue.

I buried my face in her hair, loving her, and she clawed the plastic down and sealed us inside it. We slipped around like a pair of peeled avocados twisted together in Saran Wrap.

Then we lay on top and cooled off, and in a while, when she was ready, she told me about Pruitt. They had parked him in the Pierce County Jail on a hold order from Seattle. Quintana would be sending someone down, maybe as early as tonight, to pick him up. Trish was vague on the possible charges. What Quintana wanted now was to talk to him and see how his story compared with the version they had gotten out of the kid, Bobby John Dalton. "I had a long talk with Quintana on the telephone. He actually talked to me. I must be living right."

"Cops tend to do that when they think you know more than they do."

"He seemed almost human. I got some great background out of him, off the record."

"What did he tell you?"

"Off the record. That means you tell no one without my permission, under penalty of death."

Sure, I said: I could play her reporter game.

"Bobby's version of that night remained constant through two days of questioning. You broke his jaw, by the way—the cops had to take his statement through clenched teeth. He's eating through a straw, which is hard work for a meat eater."

"I'll send him a get-well card."

"Bobby and Carmichael took the Rigby girl to Carmichael's

house. That's just off Aurora Avenue, not far from downtown. By the time Pruitt got there Rigby had been trussed up, gagged, and stashed in a room off the kitchen. There was an argument over what to do with her. Carmichael was worried about Pruitt—he had this sudden fear that Pruitt might go too far and hurt her if she didn't come up with the book. I take it Pruitt doesn't always know when to stop once he gets started."

I thought of Slater's battered face and told her Carmichael had good reason to worry. "Where was Bobby in all of this?"

"By then he was hurting so bad he wasn't worrying about anybody but himself. Carmichael was the one sweating it. If Rigby was going to come to any real harm, Carmichael didn't want to know about it—and he sure didn't want it happening there in his house. But he couldn't stand up to Pruitt. At one point Pruitt lost his temper and knocked Carmichael back into the kitchen table and broke off one of the legs. Pruitt yelled at him and said he was worse than Slater. If it hadn't been for Slater, he'd have taken the girl last week and they'd have the book by now."

"Which is probably true."

"Pruitt went into the room with Rigby alone. There wasn't a sound, to hear Bobby tell it. He said it was spooky, the two of them standing in the dead silence looking at each other and not knowing what was happening in the other room. Then Pruitt came out and said he was going to get the book."

"He scared it out of her. He was her bogeyman, Slater said. I don't know why."

"Maybe why's not important. It was in the bus station, in a locker. She had put it there the first day she got to town."

I gave a little laugh and shook my head.

"That's about it. Pruitt told Carmichael to take Rigby on up to his house, he'd be along himself as soon as he could get downtown and get the book. Then he'd settle up with them and they could both go to hell. Bobby took off for the nearest emergency room, and that's the last he saw or heard of them till he read about Carmichael in the newspaper."

"We can finish the story ourselves from there. Carmichael took Eleanor on to Pruitt's alone. Olga was already dead in the house and the killer was still inside waiting. The only thing about it that I can't believe is that Quintana would tell it all to you."

"He wants you to come in."

"He's moved on in his thinking. He's past Pruitt now, same as I am. He knows it's not Pruitt and he knows it's not me. He told you this stuff to send me a message. This goddamn man is one pretty good cop."

"Go see him, Cliff. Do this for me, please, do it now, before it gets any worse. Who knows when the moon will turn and Quintana will start drinking blood again."

"I'll make you a deal. If I don't wrap this mother up by tomorrow, Quintana can have me. Solemn word of honor."

She lay there weighing it, clearly unhappy.

"I've got to follow this one out, Trish. If I'm wrong, Quintana can have everything I've got and you can come visit me every third Tuesday of the month in the crowbar hotel."

"You're chasing a ghost."

"I'm betting all those deaths were set off by something in those books. Something that humiliated him beyond any imaginable reason. It attacked him in his guts, in his heart, where he lived: it made his life unbearable to imagine them out there for someone else to see. It threatened to destroy the one thing that made life worth living. The Grayson mystique."

"But you're hanging all this on the blind woman."

"It's not just the blind woman, it's far more than that now. We've got the chronology, with the homicides following the Grayson lettering schemes to the point of making no geographic sense. We've got the ashes at Hockman's and Pruitt's, and what do you want to bet there weren't ashes at all the others too? The house in New Orleans caught fire, there were lots of ashes there. We know he didn't go there to burn old newspapers, we know exactly why he was there and what he'd come to burn. Why do I have to work so hard convincing you of this?—it's even in your book, that scene when he wanted to burn those 1949 *Raven*s because of the misspelled word. Now the injury was ten times worse. This was to've been his masterpiece, the book to put that old one to rest at long last. And somehow he messed it up again, and the masterpiece turned to dust. And that offended him so deeply that he couldn't even wait to get those books outside the murder scenes to destroy them. Who else would do that but Grayson himself?"

"He would kill people, you're saying, because of the mistake he'd made."

"No. He kills people because he's a killer. He just didn't know that till he'd done the first one."

This is how it works. You get an idea. Usually you're wrong. But sometimes you're right. In police work, you follow your idea till it pays off or craps out.

One thing leads to another . . .

And suddenly I knew where Eleanor was.

"There's a cabin in the mountains," I said. "She goes there when she wants to be alone."

I kicked into my pants, tore into my shirt, got up, sat on a box, and pulled on my shoes.

"What're you thinking now," Trish asked, "that she's free to come and go?"

"I don't know. But I'm betting that's where she'll be."

"Where is this cabin?"

I stopped short. I didn't know.

"So what do you know about it?"

"Moon's supposed to own it, but they all use it. It's an hour's drive from here."

"Maybe still in King County, though."

"Moon said he built it forty years ago and gradually it's been surrounded by national-forest lands."

"But he still owns it."

"That's the impression I had."

"If it's in his name, I can find it. There's a title company the paper uses when we're doing stories that deal with land. They can search out anything. If I can catch them before quitting time, we can plot it out on a topographical map."

We agreed to coordinate through Amy at the motel. Then we split up, Trish on a fast run back to Seattle, me to Snoqualmie, to stake out Archie Moon's printshop.

51

I waited but he didn't come. Eventually I headed on over toward North Bend. It was almost six o'clock, almost dark, and almost raining when I drove up to the Rigby place and found the gate open. The sun had gone and the night rolled in from the Cascades, pushing the last flakes of light on to the Pacific. The house looked smaller than I remembered it. Crystal had left the front porch light on, casting the yard in a self-contained kind of glow that was almost subterranean. You got the feeling that divers would come down from the hills, swim around the windows and eaves, and wonder what strange creatures might be living there.

Behind the house the printshop was dark. Beyond that, a stretch of meadow ran out to the woods. For a brief time, perhaps no more than these few moments on this night only, the field caught the last of the day's light in this particular way and spread a silver-blue blanket at the foot of the trees.

Crystal heard me coming and was standing at the door. I clumped up the stairs and she opened the door.

"Well, Janeway, I didn't expect to see you here. You look like an old man."

"I am an old man, and getting older by the minute. Have the cops been back?"

"Just once, that same night. They decided not to tap the phone. They don't seem as worried about you as they were at first."

"That's good to know. Can we talk?"

"Sure. Come on in."

The house was dark, like the first night I'd seen it, except for the one light coming out of the kitchen down the hall. I went on back like one of the family. She came in behind me and motioned to the table, and I pulled out the same chair I'd sat in earlier.

"Where's your husband?"

"Out in the shop working."

"I didn't see any lights out there, that's why I wondered."

"You can't see the lights when he's in the back room."

She poured coffee from a pot on the counter and offered second-day rolls. They microwaved instantly, she said, and were about as good the day after. I shook my head no and she sat across from me, her face etched with the sadness of the ages. She sipped her coffee, looked at me through her glasses, and said, "What's on your mind?"

"Nola Jean Ryder. We could start with that, go on from there."

Her face didn't change, but I could sense her heartbeat picking up to a pace something like a jackhammer.

"I haven't heard that name in twenty years."

"Really?"

"Well, that woman who wrote the book about Darryl and Richard did want to ask me about her. I couldn't help her much. That's something Gaston and Archie and I never talk about."

"Why not?"

"It wasn't what you'd call a pleasant association. It's something we'd all rather forget."

I waited her out.

"Nola Jean was Darryl's . . . I don't exactly know how to put it."

"Huggins called her his whore."

She stared off at the dark window. "So who the hell's Huggins and what does he know about it? Was he there? I only met the man once or twice, years ago, and he didn't seem much interested in Nola Jean then."

"Well, was she a whore?"

"If you mean did she walk the streets and hook for her supper, the answer's no."

"There are all kinds of whores, though."

"Are you talking from experience?"

"You seem to forget, I was a cop. I did my time in vice."

"Of course. You've probably seen whores in their infinite variety, and all in the line of duty. Somehow I don't think you ever met anyone quite like Nola Jean. She was the kind of dark-spirited gal people write books about."

She got up and went to the coffeepot but did not pour. Looking out across the meadow, she said, "She could get men to do anything. I never knew how she did it. The only one she couldn't touch that way was Gaston. She sure tried, but none of it worked. I guess that's why she hated him."

She rinsed out her cup and turned it bottom-up on the counter. Again she stared through the window, past the edge of the printshop to the meadow. She turned her head toward me and said, "This is all ancient history. I don't see what she's got to do with anything today."

"Do you have any idea where she went?"

"No idea at all. Just drifted away, seems to be what everybody thinks."

The room was heavy with the presence of this long-lost woman. Crystal hugged herself as if that would make her warm again.

"I don't think about her anymore." But she looked away. She was not a woman who lied easily.

"I can't even remember what she looked like," she said, trying to shore up one lie with another.

"It shouldn't be this hard. Just think of Eleanor."

She jerked around and smacked her coffee cup into the sink, breaking it. Surprise became anxiety, then dismay, finally despondence.

"How did you know?"

"Saw some old photographs. There's really not much doubt."

"Oh, God." She gave a mighty shiver. "Oh, Jesus Christ."

"Crystal," I said as kindly as I could. "We've got to stop the lies now. Get your husband in here so we can talk it out."

"No! . . . No. We don't talk about these things to Gaston."

"We're gonna have to start. It can't stay buried any longer."

"Oh, don't do that. Please don't do that. Ask me . . . whatever you want, ask me."

"Why would Gaston Rigby raise Nola Jean Ryder's daughter?"

She gave a little cough and took off her glasses. Dabbed at her eyes with trembly hands.

"Crystal . . ."

"Why do I get the feeling you already know these things? You ask the questions but you already know the answers."

"There's only one answer that makes sense. Grayson's her father."

She looked out at the shop and said nothing.

"What did Gaston think when she started to grow up? When every time you looked in her face you saw this evil woman you all hated?"

"It wasn't like that."

She turned and looked at me straight on, wanting me to believe her.

"Truly," she said, and I did believe her.

"Then tell me how it was."

"I don't know if I can. You'd have to've been part of it, watched them together when she was growing up. She didn't look anything like Nola then, all we could see was Darryl in her face. And Gaston thought the sun rose and set on that child, she just lit up his life. I've never heard that song 'You Light Up My Life' without thinking of Gaston and Ellie. He loved her to pieces. Read to her nights, took her over to Seattle to walk along the waterfront. He was so crazy about that child, I actually envied her sometimes. He'd take her walking and later tell me it was like Darryl himself was walking with them. So that's how it was. She's ours but she came from Darryl, the last living part of him. It was like he'd made her, like a book, without any help from any woman, and left her here for us. And what's in a face? I mean, really, who cares what someone looks like? Ellie's really nothing like Nola Jean in any way that counts. She didn't get her heart from her mamma, or her mind . . . we all know where that came from. And when she started to grow up and look like Nola, Gaston didn't seem to notice at all. To him she was Darryl's little girl, and I don't think he ever worried or even stopped to consider who her mother was."

"What about you, Crystal? Did you think about it?"

She didn't want to answer that. She had thought about it plenty. "She's got nothing to do with Nola Jean Ryder anymore. You can't raise a child from the cradle and not love her." She fidgeted with her hands. "Only two things have mattered in my life—first Gaston, then Eleanor. Anybody who thinks I didn't love that child is just full of it, and they'd better not say it to me. I had her almost from the day she was born. Nola never cared: as soon as Ellie was born, she was out of here, gone on the road with some bum she met down at the tavern. We started thinking of Ellie as ours, right from that first winter. Even when Nola came back here in the spring and took up with Darryl again, she couldn't care less about her daughter. And after Darryl died, she never came back."

We looked hard at each other. I leaned across the table so she couldn't escape my eyes. "I hate to break this to you, Crystal, but you're still lying to me."

Another shock wave rippled across her face. She touched her lips with her fingers and seemed to be holding her breath.

"You keep talking about Darryl Grayson as if he's really dead."

"Of course he's dead. Everybody knows that."

"I think he's alive and well."

"You're crazy."

"I think he's alive and still working after all these years."

She shook her head.

"And you and Rigby and maybe Moon have devoted your lives to his secret. You've created a safe haven where he can do his stuff in peace and seclusion, back there in that shop, in that back room where nobody ever goes."

"You are out of your mind."

"Then I might as well tell you the rest of it, since you feel that way anyway. I think Grayson is obsessed by the idea of his own genius. I think after a while it became all that mattered to him. The mystique, the Grayson legend, the almost religious following that's coming along behind him. I think that's what this case is all about. You tell a guy often enough that he's a god, after a while he starts to believe it. And it led him straight over the edge, till he became as cold-blooded a killer as I've ever seen."

"You must be mad."

"Let me ask you this. Have you ever heard of Otto Murdock?"

She tried to shake her head. I wouldn't let her.

"He's a book dealer, or was, but you know that. He's dead now. Murdered."

"I saw it . . . in the newspaper."

"Ever hear of Joseph Hockman?"

She made a little *no* movement with her head.

"What about Reggie Dressler? . . . Mike Hollingsworth?"

"I don't know what you're talking about."

"What about Laura Warner?"

Nothing from her now. Her face looked like stone.

"They were book collectors. Grayson killed them."

"I want you to leave now," she said numbly.

"You remember your stalker? . . . The guy named Pruitt?"

Her eyes came up and gripped mine. Oh, yes, she remembered Pruitt.

"He'd be dead now too if he hadn't been lucky. Somebody else took the knife that was meant for him."

"Will you leave now?" she said thickly.

"Yeah, I'm finished. And I'm sorry, Crystal, I really am. I liked you all."

I got up from the table. "I suppose you'll tell Grayson what's been said here tonight. I imagine he'll come after me next."

I gave her a last sad look. "Tell him I'm waiting for him."

I walked out.

Down in the yard, where the night was now full, I turned away from the car and went along the path to the printshop. I looked back once, but Crystal was nowhere in sight. I was confident now, strong with faith in my premise. The old bastard was out there somewhere, his return as inevitable as the rain. I remembered the night I'd spent here, squirreled away in the loft, and the constant feeling that some presence was close at hand. Someone downstairs. Someone a room away. Someone walking around the house in the rain at four o'clock in the morning. Bumps in the night. You feel him standing in the shadows behind you, but when you turn to look, he's gone. Cross him, though, and he will find you and cut your heart out.

I stood in the total dark of the printshop door. I put my hand in my pocket and took hold of the gun. Then I pushed open the door and went inside.

I crossed to the inner door. It made a sharp little click as I pushed it in.

"Crystal?"

It was Rigby's voice, somewhere ahead. I stepped into the doorway and saw him, perched on a high steel chair halfway down the long worktable. No one was in the room with him, but that meant nothing. People can be anywhere, for any reason.

"Who's there?"

I came all the way in, keeping both hands in my pockets. My eyes took in the length and breadth of it, from the far window to the locked door on this end that looked like nothing more than a storage room. Then, when I was sure he was alone, I came around the end of the workbench so he could see my face. I felt a chill at having my back to the door.

He took off his glasses and squinted.

"Janeway. Well, gosh."

He'd been doing something there at the table, working on a sketch of some kind. He pulled open a thin, flat drawer, dropped his work inside, closed and locked it. Then he put one foot down from the chair he sat on and leaned forward into his knee.

"You look different," he said.

"It's this case. It's aged me a lot."

"Case?"

"Yeah, you know. Your missing daughter."

He didn't say anything for a long moment. "These are hard days," he said after a while.

"I'm sure they are. Maybe it's almost over now. You could help . . . answer a few questions maybe?"

"Sure," he said, but he was instantly uneasy. He was not a great talker, I remembered. He was private and sensitive and reluctant to let a stranger see into his heart.

He smiled kindly through his beard and gave it a try. "What do you want to talk about?"

"Grayson."

His smile faded, replaced by that shadow of distress I had seen in him that first night. "That's a long time ago. I don't know what I could tell you that would make any difference today."

I waited, sensing him groping for words. Let him grope it out, I thought.

"I have a hard time with that."

"What about Nola Jean Ryder?"

His eyes narrowed to slits. I never found out what he might have said, because at that moment the outer door slammed open and Crystal screamed, "Gaston!" and I heard her charging through the dark front room.

She threw open the door and vaulted into the back shop.

"Don't say another word!" she yelled at Rigby.

"What's—"

"Shut up! . . . Just . . . *shut up!* Don't tell him anything."

She came toward me. I moved to one side.

"I told you to get out of here."

We circled each other like gladiators. By the time I reached the door, she and Rigby were side by side.

"Don't you come back," Crystal said. "Don't ever come back here."

"I'll be back, Crystal. You can count on it."

I went through the shop with that chill on my neck. The chill stayed with me as I doubled back toward Snoqualmie. I thought it was probably there for the duration.

52

Headlights cut the night as Archie Moon turned out of Railroad Avenue and came to a squeaking stop on the street outside his printshop. For a time he sat there as if lost in thought: then, wearily showing his age, he pulled himself out of the truck's cab and slowly made his way to the front of the building. A key ring dangled from his left hand: with the other hand he fished a pair of glasses out of his shirt pocket, putting them on long enough to fit the key in the lock, turn the knob, and push the door open. He took off the glasses and flipped on the inner light, stepping into the little reception room at the front of the shop. He stopped, bent down, and picked up the mail dropped through the slot by the mailman earlier in the day.

He rifled through his letters with absentminded detachment. Seeing nothing of immediate interest, he tossed the pile on the receptionist's desk and moved on into the back shop.

I got out of the car across the street, where I'd been waiting for more than an hour. I crossed over, opened the door without a noise, and came into the office.

I could hear him moving around beyond the open door. The back shop was dark with only a single light, somewhere, reflecting off black machinery. Shadows leaped up in every direction, like the figures in an antiquarian children's book where everything is drawn in silhouette.

I heard the beep of a telephone machine, then the whir of a tape being rewound. He was playing back his messages, just around the corner, a foot or two from where I stood.

"Archie, it's Ginny. Don't be such a stranger, stranger."

Another beep, another voice. "Bobbie, sweetheart. Call me."

And again. "Mr. Moon, this is Jewell Bledsoe. I've been thinking about that job we discussed. Let's do go ahead. And, yes, I would like to have dinner sometime. Very much. So call me. Tomorrow."

Moon gave a little laugh laced with triumph. "Ah, Jewell," he cried out to the empty room. "Ah, *yeah!*"

He was a busy man with a heavy social docket. He was much like his pal Darryl Grayson that way. In great demand by the ladies.

There was another message on the tape. She didn't identify herself, didn't need to. It was a voice he had heard every day for twenty years.

"Oh, Archie, where are you! Everything's gone crazy, I feel like I'm losing my mind. Call me, please . . . for God's sake, call me!"

He picked up the telephone and punched in a number. Hung up, tried again, hung up, replayed the message.

"Goddammit, honey," he said to the far wall. "How the hell am I supposed to call you if you're over there blabbin' on the goddamn phone?"

He tried again and hung up.

I heard him move. I stepped back to one side, leaning against the receptionist's desk with my left hand flat on some papers. I rolled my eyes around and looked out to the deserted street. My eyes made the full circle and ended up staring down at the desk where my hand was.

At the stack of mail he had thrown there.

At the letter Eleanor had mailed from the Hilton.

I touched the paper, felt the lump of something solid inside. A federal crime to take it: not much time to decide.

"Janeway." He was standing right there, three feet away. "Where'd you come from? You look like you been rode hard and put away wet."

"You got the wet part right." I leaned back from the desk, trying not to be too obvious. "And, yeah, I been rode pretty hard, too."

"How'd you get in here? I didn't hear the door."

"Just walked right in. Saw the light, came in, heard you back there on the phone . . . thought I'd sit on the desk and wait till you're done."

"Half-blind and now I can't hear either. What's on your mind?"

"I've been thinking some about that cabin of yours."

"I guess I told you I'd give you a tour of God's country, didn't I? Can't say I expected you tonight, though."

"Just thought I'd come by and see if the offer's still good."

"Yeah, sure it is. Why wouldn't it be? If you're still around in a few days . . ."

"You get up there much?"

"Not anymore, not like I used to. It's too hard to make a living these days; I gotta work Saturdays and sometimes Sundays and I'm gettin' too damn old and too slow. Two or three times a year is all."

He held his hand up to his eyes. "Let's step on back in the shop. That bright light's playing hell with me."

I followed him around and leaned against the doorjamb, keeping my hands in my pockets and letting my eyes work the room. It was a busy printer's printshop, cluttered with half-finished jobs and the residue of last week's newspaper. Long scraps of newsprint had been ripped out and thrown on the floor. Paper was piled in rolls in the corner, and in stacks on hand trucks and dollies. A fireman's nightmare, you'd have to think. He had a Chandler and Price like Rigby's, a Linotype, and an offset press that took a continuous feed of newsprint from a two-foot roll.

He stood in the shadows a few feet away. "Crystal said you're still trying to find Ellie. Havin' any luck?"

"As a matter of fact, I'm having a helluva time just getting people to talk to me."

"Maybe you're asking the wrong people."

"I don't know, Archie, you'd think the people who're supposed to love her would be knocking me down to help. But everybody seems more interested in pandering to the vanity of a dead man than finding that girl."

This bristled him good. I thought it might.

"Who's everybody? Who the hell are you talking about?"

"Crystal . . . and Rigby."

"Hell, that's easy enough to understand."

"Then make me understand it."

"Why do I smell an attitude here? It oughta be obvious what their problem is, if you came at them the way you just came at me."

"Rigby's relationship with Grayson, you mean."

"Yeah, sure. You don't walk in that house and say anything against Darryl . . . not if you want to come out with your head in one piece. And the same is true over here, by the way, so let's back off on the rhetoric and we'll all be a lot happier."

"And I still don't get my questions answered."

"You got questions, ask 'em. Let the sons of bitches rip."

"Let's start with this one. Do you think Nola Jean Ryder set the fire?"

He rocked back in his tracks. But he kept on moving, trying to cover his surprise by making the sudden movement seem intentional. He climbed up on a high steel chair at the table where the answering machine blinked its red light and looked at me from there, leaning in and out of the shadow.

I wasn't going to ask him again. Let him stew his way through it. Finally the silence got to him and he said, "The fire was an accident."

"Some people don't think so."

"Some people think the world is flat. What do you want me to do about that?"

Who's got an attitude now? I thought. But I said, "Give it a guess."

"Darryl died, that was the end of it. That's my guess. There wasn't any reason for Nola Jean to be here anymore. I doubt she ever stayed in one place more than six months in her life till she came here. Why would she stick around after Darryl died? Everybody here hated her."

"Did you hate her?"

"I never gave her that much thought."

I grunted, the kind of sound that carries a full load of doubt without the bite.

"Look," he said, annoyed that I'd caught him lying. "She was Darryl's woman. That made her off-limits to me, no matter what I might've thought from time to time or how willing she might've been to play around."

"Did she come on to you?"

"That woman would come on to a green banana. Look, I'm having a hard time understanding how any of this old shit's gonna help you find Ellie."

"This sounds like the stone wall going up again, Arch."

"Well, fuck, what do you expect? This stuff hurts to talk about."

"Who does it hurt? Grayson's dead, right? Can't hurt him."

He didn't say anything.

"Who does it hurt? . . . You? . . . Rigby? . . . Crystal?"

"Hurts us all. When you lose somebody like that, it hurts."

"But real people get over it. At least they move on past that raw hurt and get on with life. I'm not saying you forget the guy: maybe you love him till you die. But you don't carry that raw pain on your sleeve for twenty years."

He rocked back, his face in darkness.

"So what's the real story here? Why does Rigby get the shakes every time Grayson's name comes up? Why does Crystal go all protective and clam up like Big Brother's listening? You'd think the man just died yesterday."

"Gaston . . ."

I waited.

"Gaston thought Darryl walked on water. Damn near literally. Haven't you ever had somebody in your life like that, Janeway?"

I shook my head. "I've got enough trouble with the concept of a real god. Don't ask me to deal with men being gods."

"Then how can you expect to understand it?"

I reached into my jacket where I'd tucked the envelope under my arm. Took out the glossy photograph and held it up in the light so he could see it. "Can you identify the people in this picture?"

He made a show of it. Took the picture and grunted at it. Leaned way back in his steel chair. Put on his glasses, squinted, and finally said, "Well, that's Nola Jean Ryder there in the front with her arm around that fella."

"Are you telling me you don't know the others?"

"I don't seem to recall 'em."

"That's strange, Archie, it really is. Because here's another shot of all of you together. I believe that's you over there in the corner, talking to this fella you say you can't remember."

"I can't remember everybody I ever talked to. This has been a long time ago."

"Try the name Charlie Jeffords. Does it ring a bell now?"

"That's the fella down in New Mexico . . ."

"Whose house Eleanor burgled. Now you've got it. Maybe you see why it bothers me so much, the fact that all of you know exactly who Jeffords was right from the start. The minute she got arrested and the name Jeffords came up, you knew why she went down there and what she was trying to find out. You could've shared that information with me when it might've meant something, last week in court. But for reasons of your own, you all hung pat and let that kid take the fall."

The room simmered with rage. "I'll tell you, Janeway, you might be thirty years younger than me, but if you keep throwing shit like that around, you and me are gonna tear up this printshop."

"Who was Charlie Jeffords?"

He was still rocking slightly. The steel chair made a faint squeaking noise as he moved back and forth on it.

"Charlie Jeffords," I said.

"Leave it alone."

"Who's the other woman in this picture with Jeffords?—the one standing back there glaring at them from the trees?"

He shrugged.

"I seem to be doing all the work here. Maybe I can figure it out by myself; you can sit there and tell me if I go wrong." I gave the picture a long look. "The first time I saw this, something struck me about these two women. They look too much alike not to be related. They've got the same hairline. They've both got Eleanor's high cheekbones."

He leaned forward and looked at the picture as if such a thing had never occurred to him. "That damn Ryder blood must be some strong shit."

"Keep trying, Archie, maybe you can find somebody you can sell that to. Me, I'm not buying any more. When you've worked in the sausage factory, you try to be careful what brands you buy."

"What do you want?"

"The only thing that's left. Everything."

"I don't think I can help you with that."

"Then I'll tell you. Charlie Jeffords was Darryl Grayson's binder."

He took in a lungful of air through his nose.

"Grayson never wanted that known, did he? That's why you're all so tight about it, you're still protecting the legend, pushing the myth that every book was created from dust by one man only, start to finish. The mystique feeds on that. Even Huggins can't understand how Grayson could turn them out so fast and so perfect and with so many variants. Well, he had help. That's not a capital crime, the man was human after all. Most of us would be proud of that, being human. But not Grayson."

"I don't think we should talk about this anymore."

"I'm not guessing here, you know. A friend of mine went to Taos to see Jeffords. What do you think she found there? A garage full of binding equipment. Very fine leathers, a bookpress or two . . . do I need to go on? Charlie Jeffords was a bookbinder by trade, right up till last year when he got sick. Jeffords did the binding on every Grayson book that came out of here."

"That's not true."

"Then what is?"

"Darryl did a lot of it . . . a helluva lot. I did some. Gaston did. Richard did, before he started making so much money with his own books. But Charlie was the best . . . him and Gaston. Those two could bind a book you'd want to take home and eat." He leaned forward, slapped his knee, and said, "Ah, shit," with a sigh.

He shook his head, hating it. "You can't take anything away from Darryl just because he turned some of it over to other people at the end. He did *all* the conceptual stuff. The design, the lettering, the layout—that's where the real genius is. And he told all of us how he wanted 'em bound and we did 'em that way to the letter. And he looked 'em over with an eagle eye and tossed back any that weren't right. I'm not saying the binding's not important, it's damn vital, it's the first thing you see when you look at it. But it's a craft, it can be learned. What Darryl did came from some goddamn other place, who knows where. Ain't that what genius is?"

"I guess."

"You know damn well."

"Well, we'll leave it at that. You wanna tell me now who the other woman was?"

"Jonelle."

"And she was . . ."

"Nola Jean's sister."

He got off the bench and I tensed. But he sat back down again, pushed back and forth by restless energy.

"Richard played around with both of 'em at one time or another.

Then he brought 'em over here and the trouble started. I guess it
appealed to his sense of humor. Two screwed-up sisters and two
screwed-up brothers. I remember him saying that one time. Nola
thought it was funny as hell."

"Did anybody ever ask Jonelle what became of her sister?"

"She didn't know either. That's what she told the people that
investigated the fire. Me, I didn't give a damn. Good riddance, we all
thought. Then Jonelle moved away too."

"And she and Jeffords landed in Taos."

"Apparently so."

"And ended up together."

"I guess that proves some damn thing. Fairy tales come true or
something. Jonelle always had this crazy lust for Charlie Jeffords. But
Nola Jean always took Jonelle's men away from her. It came as
natural as breathing. She tortured Charlie Jeffords and drove that
poor bastard nuts. Diddled and teased him and never even gave him
a good look at it."

The telephone rang. He didn't want to answer it. But we both
knew who it was, and he picked it up just as the recording started to
kick in.

"Yeah," he said. "Yeah, he's here now."

Then Crystal told him something that made his mouth hang open.

He held the phone away from him, looked at me, and said, "I've
got to take this."

"Sure."

"Shut that door but don't go away. We're not done yet."

I stepped back into the front room and closed the door. I couldn't
hear anything. Crystal seemed to be doing all the talking.

I looked down at the desk, at Eleanor's letter. Picked it up and put
it in my pocket.

What's a little federal crime at this stage of the game, I thought,
and I walked out.

I crossed the street and stood in the dark place between buildings.
I watched his storefront and I waited. He seemed to be back there a
long time. When he did come out, he came slowly. He came to the
front door and out onto the sidewalk.

"Janeway," he called up the empty block.

I didn't move.

"Janeway!"

He jumped in his truck and drove away, leaving his door wide open. I let him get well ahead. I wasn't worried. I knew where he was going.

53

Archie, she wrote.

I've done it again. Took one of the books thinking I'd put it back in a day or so. Then got busted and the book's still in my car, wrapped in a towel under the front seat. I know, you've warned me about it, but he never seems to miss them and it brightens my life when I've got one with me. I love them so much. I wish I could love people that way but I can't. The books never disappoint me. They are eternally lovely and true, they've been at the core of my life for as long as I can remember. Even when I'm far away, just knowing they're there can lift me out of the gutter and make me fly again. Just the possibility that he might destroy them fills me with despair. I think I would die if that happened, especially if the cause was some stupid act of my own. So please get the book and put it back in the room, so he won't notice it's gone. Here are my keys so you can get in. Think good thoughts and smile for me. Love ya. Ellie.

There were three keys in the envelope—one for a car, two for more substantial locks. I put them in my pocket, got out of the car, and started across country through the woods.

It was easy going. The ground was damp but hard: the underbrush sparse. I followed my flashlight till the trees began to thin out and a clear beam of moonlight appeared to light the way. I saw the Rigby house in the distance as I approached from the east, moving along the edge of the silver glade. Dark clouds drifted across the moon in wisps, and the meadow seemed to flutter and undulate in the stillness around it. The light from the kitchen window stood out like a beacon, the darkened printshop squatting like a bunker behind it. I stayed at the edge of the trees, skirting the dark wall to blend in with the night. As I walked, the printshop seemed to drift until it slowly covered the light from the window like an eclipse.

When the blackout was full, I turned and walked straight across the meadow.

I came up to the back of the shop and eased along the outer wall. The clouds had covered the moon and again the night was full. The glow from the kitchen was a muted sheen at the corner of the shop, a suggestion of radiance from some black hole. I turned the other way, circled the building from the south, and came to the front door at the corner where there was plenty of dark cover.

I was looking into the front yard and, beyond it, down the side of the house. Rigby's truck was gone but Moon's was there at the front steps. The only light anywhere was the one cast out of the kitchen. I slipped along the front of the shop, keeping in shadow as much as I could. A clock had begun ticking in my head, a sense of urgency that drove me on.

I reached the door with the keys in my hand. Fished out the car key and dropped it in my other pocket. The heavy brass key slipped in easily on the first try and the lock snapped free. I put that key away too and stepped inside the shop. The smell of the lead pot, faint but unmistakable, was the evidence that Rigby had been here plying his trade. I flipped up the switch one notch on the flashlight, so it could be flicked on and off at a touch. I flicked it once, satisfied myself that nothing stood between me and the back room: then I locked the front door, crossed the room, and went into Grayson's workshop.

Funny to think of it that way, as Grayson's, though that had been my thought the first time I'd seen it. I knew the back-room lights could not be seen from the house, but it was not a chance I wanted to take. I flicked my light, three quick flashes around the room. Saw the high steel chair where Rigby had been sitting three hours ago and the open space where Crystal and I had squared off as if in battle. Across the room was the door I had noticed with the half-frivolous thought, *Perhaps it's in there, the answer to everything.*

The padlock was a heavy-duty Yale, the same color as the third key in my hand. I snapped it open, gave a soft push, and the door creaked inward.

It's a wine cellar, was my first thought.

A cool, windowless room, perfect for storing things away from heat and light. But something else, not wine, was aging on those shelves.

Books.

Dozens of books.

Scores . . .

Hundreds . . .

Hundreds!

And they were all *The Raven.*

A Disneyland of *Ravens,* row after row, elegantly bound and perfect-looking, all the same, all different. Some so different they seemed to mock the others for their sameness.

Funny thoughts race through your head.

Eureka!

Dr. Livingstone, I presume . . .

And Stewart Granger, buried alive in that African mountain, crawling into a treasure chamber with a torch over his head and the miracle of discovery on his lips.

King Solomon's Mines!

That's how it felt.

I took down a book and opened it to the title page.

1969.

I looked at another one.

1969.

Another one . . . and another one . . . and another one . . .

1969 . . .

 . . . 1969 . . .

 . . . 1969 . . .

A year frozen forever, with no misspelled words.

I try not to presume too much in this business. That's how mistakes are made.

But it was probably safe to say I had found the Grayson *Raven.*

54

I couldn't shake the thrill of it, or chase away the faceless man who had made it. I stood at the dark front door, watching the house and not knowing what to do next. Then the second impact hit and I had to go back for another look. The room was different now, transposed in a kind of shivery mystical brew. It was alive and growing, nowhere yet near whatever it was trying to become. Twenty years ago it had been empty. Then the first book came and life began.

But where was it going? When would it end?

I supposed it would end when the artist died and his quest for the perfect book had run its course. Maybe he had even achieved that perfection, reached it a hundred times over, without ever accepting what he'd done.

It would never be good enough. He was mad, crazier than Poe. He had locked himself in mortal self-combat, a war nobody ever wins.

Again I watched the house. A shadow passed the kitchen window, leaping out at the meadow.

A light rain began.

I stood very still but I wasn't alone. Grayson was there. In the air. In the dark. In the rain.

Across the yard I heard the door open. Two shadow figures came out on the porch and I moved over by the hedge, a few feet from where they stood.

"Archie." Her voice was low and full of pain. "How could this happen to us?"

He took her in his arms and hugged her tight.

"Were we so evil?" she said. "Was what we did that wrong?"

"I got no easy answers, honey. We did what seemed best at the time."

Now she cried. She had held it in forever and it came all at once.

She sobbed bitterly and Moon patted her shoulders and gave her what comfort he could: "We'll get past it. I'll go find Gaston and bring him back here so we can figure it out together." But she couldn't stop crying and Moon was not a man who could cope with that. Gently he pulled away and turned her around, sending her back to that desolate vigil inside the house. He hurried down the steps and got into the truck, and I stepped behind the hedge and stood there, still, until his headlights swung past and he was gone.

I hung around for a while: I didn't know why. Crystal was alone now but that wasn't it. She was shaken and vulnerable and I thought I could break her if I wanted to try again. But I didn't move except to step out from the hedge to the corner of the house. In a while the kitchen light went out and the house dropped into a void. Pictures began with color and sound and the case played out, whole and nearly finished, the way they say a drowning man sees his life at the end. A chorus of voices rose out of the past—Richard, Archie, Crystal, Grayson—battling to be heard. I couldn't hear them all, only one broke through. Eleanor the child, growing up as that room grew and the bookman worked in his solitude. She read *The Raven* and read *The Raven* and read *The Raven,* and with each reading her knowledge grew and her wisdom deepened. Her entire understanding of life came from that poem, but it was enough. She heard the bump at the door and looked up from the table where she read *The Raven* by candlelight. *'Tis some visitor,* she muttered, *tapping at my chamber door . . .*

The visitor was me.

She was six years old, what could she know? But her face bore the mark of the bookman: her mother had not yet returned to claim her. I hung there in the doorway, waiting for her statement, some tiny insight that had escaped us all. What she had for me was a sassy question.

Don't you know what a cancel stub is? . . . How long have you been in business?

I trudged across the meadow in a steady rain. I was wet again but I didn't care. I was locked in that book room with Eleanor, caught up in its wonder and mystery. I stopped near the edge of the trees and looked back at the house, invisible now in a darkness bleached white. I wished Crystal would turn on a lamp. A powerful army of ghosts had taken the woods and the rain bore the resonance of their voices. In a while I moved on into the trees. The light from the house never came, but I could follow the bookman's wake without it.

The cabin was fifty miles north, far across U.S. 2 near a place called Troublesome Lake. It was a wilderness, the access a graveled road and a dirt road beyond that. "There's no telling what the last five miles is like," Trish said, spreading the map across the front seat. "It shows up here as unimproved. That could be okay or it could be a jeep trail."

She asked about police and I told her what I thought. There might be a sheriff's substation at Skykomish, a hole-in-the-wall office staffed by one overworked deputy who wouldn't move an inch without probable cause. Unless we could lay out a case for him, we were on our own.

Trish was tense and trying too hard to fight it. We both knew I should take it from here alone, but somehow we couldn't get at it. She was my partner, she had earned her stripes, I wasn't about to insult her with macho-man bullshit. I had never had a female partner in my years with the Denver cops. I'd always thought I'd have no problem with it—if a woman was armed and trained and tough, I could put my life in her hands. Trish was not trained and she was unarmed. You never knew about the toughness till the time came, but that was just as true of a man.

It had to be said so I made it short and straight, well within the code. "If you have any doubts about going up there, this is the time to say so. It's your call. But you've got no gun, we don't know what's there . . . nobody would think any less of you."

She gave me a doleful smile. "I'll be fine. I get nervous before anything that might put me on the spot. That's all it is. If something starts, I'll be fine."

She had borrowed a press car equipped with a two-way radio to her city desk. She had left a copy of the map, sealed in an envelope, with her night city editor. At least her common sense was alive and kicking. The problem was, the radio might not work at that distance, she said: its effective range was about forty miles, but mountains played hell with the signal and could cause fading at any distance. Once she had called in from Bellingham, a hundred miles north: another time she had barely got through in a thunderstorm from Issaquah. You never knew.

She asked for some last-minute ground rules. "If we find your friend up there, we wrap her up and bring her down. No theatrics, no cowboy heroics, no waiting around for whoever might come. We bring her down. Period, end of story. You go see Quintana and we let the cops take it from there."

Life should be so simple. I said, "Deal," and I hugged her and I truly hoped it would work out that way. She held me tight for another moment. "I'm fine," she said, and that was the end of it. There would be no more said about nerves or rules, no more second-guessing.

She started the car and drove us north on Highway 203.

For about twenty miles we headed away from where we wanted to go. The map showed the cabin off to the northeast, but the road drifted northwest. The entire middle part of the county was mountainous backwoods with no main roads, so we had to go around. We stopped for coffee, took it with us, and pushed on. I wasn't tired: I was running on high octane as the case played out and I was drawn to the end of it. The night had been a revelation. I had broken the problem of the misspelled word after taking another long look at Scofield's Laura Warner book at the motel. One thing leads to another. Once you knew how that had happened, you could make a reach and begin to imagine the rest.

How the fire might have started.

The who and why of the woman in red.

What had happened to Nola Jean Ryder.

What the face of the bookman looked like.

I rode shotgun and let the case play in my head. I ran it like instant replay, freeze-framing, moving the single frames back and forth. I peered at the blurred images and wondered if what I thought I saw was how it had all happened.

The road dipped and wound. The rain beat down heavily.

Somewhere on the drive north, I began to play it for Trish.

"Richard sabotaged his brother's book. I should've seen that long ago. The bitterness between them was obvious in your own book, and there was plenty more in that 'Craven' poem he wrote. There's one line in 'The Craven' that even tells how he did it. 'And when it seemed that none could daunt him, a sepulchre rose up to haunt him.' The line after that is the one I mean. 'Stuck in there as if to taunt him.' That's exactly what he did—came down to the shop, unlocked the plate, scrambled the letters, printed up some pages on Grayson's book stock, then put the plate back the way it was, washed the press, took his jimmied pages, and left. This is a simple operation. A printer could do it in a few minutes.

"Remember how Grayson worked. He was an old-time print man who liked to lay out the whole book, make up all the plates before he printed any of it. This is how he got that fluidity, the ability to change things from one copy to another: he didn't print up five hundred sheets from the same plate, he tinkered and moved stuff throughout the process. And he cast his own type, so he always had plenty even for a big book job. So here they were, Grayson and Rigby, ready to print *The Raven*. They did the five lettered copies. You can imagine the back-and-forth checking and double-checking they went through. No nit was too small to pick—never in the history of the Grayson Press had pages been so thoroughly examined. There must be no flaws, no hairline cracks, not even the slightest ink inconsistency, and—you can be damn sure—no misspelled words. The finished books were examined again. Rigby probably did the final look-over and pronounced them sound. He was the one with the eagle eye—remember you wrote about that, how Grayson had come to count on him to catch any little thing. Boxing and wrapping them was the point of no return. Once those five books were shipped, *The Raven* was for all practical purposes published. This was it, there'd be no calling it back: he was telling the world that this was his best. And he knew he'd never get a third crack at it, he'd look like a fool.

"I don't know how Richard got to the books. I imagine they were right there on an open shelf in the printshop the night before they were shipped. The shop would've been locked, but Richard had a key. His big problem was that Rigby was living in the loft upstairs. Maybe Grayson took Rigby out to celebrate and that's when it was done. Maybe Richard waited till he was sure Rigby was asleep, then came quietly into the shop, lifted the books, took them to his house, and did the job there. It doesn't matter where he did it—the one thing I know now is what he did. He sliced that one page out of each book and bound in his own page. And the misspelled word was misspelled again."

"You make it sound simple."

"It is simple. It's like outpatient day surgery for a world-class doctor. It's even been done for commercial publishers by people a helluva lot less skilled than he was. You cut out the page with a razor, trim the stub back to almost nothing, give the new page a wide bead of glue so the gutter seals tight and the stub won't show at all. I think I could do it myself, now that I know how it was done, and I'm no bookbinder."

"When did you figure this out?"

"Eleanor saved me from buying a book that had been fixed like that. It wasn't uncommon for publishers in the old days to do it. And later, when I examined the book that Scofield had bought from Pruitt, I noticed that the top edge was just a hair crooked. It didn't impress me much at the time, but when I looked at the book again a while ago, it was just that one page that was off. When I looked down at it from the top, I could see the break in the page gathering where the single sheet had been slipped in past the stub. Even when you know it's there, it's not easy to see. He did a damn good job of it and the book is the proof. The whole story is wrapped up in that book—the only surviving copy of the five Grayson *Raven*s.

"Laura Warner's note tells us how the book got back to North Bend. She saw the misspelled word and thought Grayson was joshing her. She should've known better—Grayson didn't kid around, not about this stuff. In St. Louis, Hockman had already seen the mistake and had sent Grayson a letter about it. What would Grayson do when he got such a letter? Stare at it in disbelief for a minute, then get right on the phone to St. Louis. He wanted the book back, but Hockman had had time to think about it. He was a collector first of all, and it had crossed his mind that he might have something unique, maybe some preliminary piece never intended to be released. It was ironic—he had sent the letter wanting Grayson to take the book back, but he ended up refusing to part with it."

"At that point Grayson would go out to his shop. Look at his plate . . ."

"And see what?" I let her think about that for a few seconds. Then I said, "If you were Richard and you wanted to drive your brother crazy, what would you do? I'd wait till the books were shipped, then I'd go back in that shop and change the plate back to the mistake again. Talk about diabolical—you'd have Grayson doubting his sanity. He wouldn't be able to believe his eyes, but it would be right there in front of him. In trying so hard not to make a mistake, he'd made the same old one again. Such things do happen in printing. It's the stuff you think you know that comes back to bite you."

"So then Grayson did what? . . . Went to St. Louis? Killed Hockman?"

"I don't know. I'm not so sure of that anymore."

"Well, somebody did."

"Let's keep following the natural order of things. I think Richard set the fire. One thing leads to another. If Richard did the book, he also did the fire. Whether he knew his brother was passed out drunk in the back room is something we can argue till shrimps learn to whistle. Richard was a screwed-up, pathetic man and everybody knew it. Nobody knew it better than he did. No one has ever made a case that this guy had even one happy day in his whole lousy life. He hated his brother but he loved him too. What he'd done to him had him jumping for joy one minute and despising himself the next. But it was done and you can't undo something like that. He couldn't get it off his conscience—he'd never find the courage to confess. He had wrecked his brother's dream, destroyed his vision, and left his masterpiece in ruins. He'd been planning it for years, probably since Grayson had made the decision to do another *Raven*. We know he was thinking about it at least two years before the fact: his *Craven* notes are dated 1967, and he writes of it then as a fact accomplished. Now he'd done it and he was glad, but in the end he couldn't forgive himself. He cashed his chips, but he still had enough rage to take Grayson's printshop with him."

A small town sprung up on the wet road. I saw a sign for U.S. 2 and she turned right, heading east.

"The story should've ended there," I said, "but the dark parts of it were just beginning. Laura Warner's book had arrived back in North Bend. The sequence of events was tight—the book may've come a day or two either side of the fire, or maybe on the day itself. In any case, the scene at Grayson's was chaotic, and it all centered on this one book. The book arrived and Nola Jean Ryder lifted it and passed it on to her sister for safekeeping. My guess is that Nola got the book before anybody even knew it was there. Then something happened, I don't know what, that caused her to drop off the face of the earth. Hold that thought for a minute. Something happened, we don't know what. And it set our killer off on a chain reaction that's still going on."

"He killed her."

"That's what I think. She was the first victim. That's what made him snap, and he hasn't drawn a sane breath since."

"He killed her," Trish said again. Her voice was a strange mix of certainty and doubt. "Have you got any evidence?"

"Not much, not yet. Nothing you'd want to take into court without a body. But the argument still packs a lot of weight. Turn the question around. What evidence do we have for her being alive? There isn't any. She's been missing twenty years, three times what the law demands for a presumption of death. That seven-year-wait didn't get established in law by itself. When people go missing that long without a trace or a reason, they're almost always dead. Damn few of them ever turn up alive again. Add to this the fact that Nola was self-centered and greedy—you know she'd come back for that book if there was money in it. But her own sister hasn't seen her—Jonelle still had the book, after all, twenty years later. Charlie Jeffords told you Nola'd been there, but that wasn't Nola, it was Eleanor. That's what got him so upset. That's why Jonelle was so upset when Eleanor popped up without any warning on her doorstep. What a shock, huh? There stood Nola Jean in the flesh. The woman who'd always driven Charlie a little crazy, whose memory still does on the bad days. And damn, she hadn't changed a bit."

We stopped at the side of the road and I sat with my eyes closed while Trish looked at the map. I was thinking of the sequence again, probing it at the weak places. Laura Warner sent her book back, but by then the killer was on the road, coming her way. Hockman had mailed his letter from St. Louis, as much as a week earlier. Hockman was already dead and the killer was somewhere between St. Louis and New Orleans, taking the scenic route. The killer arrived in New Orleans after stopovers in Phoenix, Baltimore, and Idaho. He killed Laura Warner but couldn't find her book. So he burned the whole house down, figuring he'd get it that way.

We were moving again: I heard Trish give a nervous little sigh and the car regained its steady rhythm. "Not much further now," she said, and I answered her with a grunt so she'd know I was still among the living. I was thinking of the woman in red, nervous about selling her *Raven*, willing to consider it because of the money but finally backing out in a jittery scene that Scofield would remember as a sudden attack of conscience. And I thought of the Rigby place where all the *Raven*s were, and I thought again how one thing leads to another in this business of trying to figure out who the killers are.

We had stopped. I opened my eyes and saw that she had turned into a long, straight forest road, a mix of mud and gravel that stretched out like a ribbon and gradually faded to nothing. She was looking at me in the glow of the dash, and I had the feeling she was waiting for me to laugh and say the hell with this, let's go back to town and shack up where it's dry and warm. I reached over and squeezed her hand.

"Let's go get her," I said.

Her mouth trembled a little. She put the car in gear and we started into the woods.

56

It was desolate country, the road rutted and water-filled. We banged along at fifteen miles an hour and it seemed too fast, and still we got nowhere. I sat up straight, watching the odometer move by tenths of a mile. The road would run north by northeast for seven miles, I remembered from the map: then we'd come to a fork and the branch we wanted would run along the creek and climb gradually past the lake. The cabin would be in the woods at the top of the rise. Our chances of making it would depend on the condition of the road beyond the fork. Down here the gravel kept it hard, basic and boring, one mile-slice indistinguishable from the next. We would come to a bend, but always the ribbon rolled out again, winnowing into a black wall that kept running away from us. I had a vision of a vast mountain range off to my right, though nothing could be seen past the narrow yellow shaft thrown out by the headlights. We could be anywhere in the world, I thought.

I put an arm over Trish's shoulder and stroked her neck with my finger. She smiled faintly without taking her eyes off the road. I touched her under the left ear and stirred the hair on her neck. She made a kissing gesture and tried to smile again. Her skin felt cool and I noticed a chill in the air. She had started to shiver, perhaps to tremble—I had never thought about the difference until then—but she made no move to turn on the heater, and finally I reached over and did it for her. "Don't pick at me, Janeway, I'm fine." In the same instant she reached up and took my hand, pressed it tightly against her cheek, kissed my knuckles, and held me tight. "Don't mind me," she said. "I'm fine."

Incredibly, we had come just two miles. It seemed we had been on this road to nowhere half the night. The odometer stood still while the clock moved on, flicking its digit to 1:35 in the march toward a gray dawn four hours away. We had already debated the wisdom of coming in the dark, the most significant of the pros and cons being the possibility of getting in close before anyone could see us coming versus groping around in an alien landscape. Best to stay loose, I thought: see what we found when we got there. We could park and wait in the trees if that seemed best. Given my temperament, neither of us could see that happening.

The road had begun to rise gradually out of the valley and the rain was now little more than a fine mist. The headlights showed a wall of rock rising up from the right shoulder and a sudden drop-off on the left. We came to a short steep stretch, then it leveled off again and the climb went on at its steady upward drift. "I think the lake's over there," Trish said, nodding into the chasm. "The fork's got to be right here somewhere."

We reached it a few minutes later, as the clock turned over at 2:04. Now the tough part would begin. But it wasn't tough at all. The rain ceased to be a factor up here as the road faded into simple ruts on a grassy slope. The grass held the earth firm even in the rain. We could make it, but it was going to be slow going on a road well pocked with deep holes. The car rocked, sloshed through what seemed like a gully, and then began to climb again. This continued until we crested on a hill. "Probably lovely up here on a sunny day," Trish said. God's country, I thought. I hoped God was home to walk us through it.

"Let's do it," I heard myself say. "Let's get it on."

This was a stupid thing to say and she laughed a little. She said, "Jesus," under her breath, and the name seemed to come up from some ethereal force in the car between us. How did we get here, defying logic, with no viable alternatives in sight? I wanted to get it done now, pull out the stops and get on down the road. But we rocked along at a crawl. It was 2:30 A.M.

Then we were there. I knew it. She knew it. There were no signs posted and no cabins in sight, but something made her stop on the slope and let the car idle for a long moment. "I think we're very close," she said in a voice just above a whisper. The terrain had stiffened in the past hundred yards as if in a last-ditch effort to push us back. We were sitting on a sharp incline, her headlights pointing into the sky. "Careful when you go over the hill," I said. "Better cut your lights and go with the parking lights." She pushed the switch too far and the world plunged into a darkness so black I had nothing in my experience to compare it to. She pulled on the parking lights and the only relief from the oppressive night was that the dashboard light came on and lit up our faces. "Not gonna be able to see a damn thing with these parking lights," she said. But we didn't dare make our final approach any brighter.

"Let's see how the radio's doing," she said.

She lifted the little transmitter off its hook, pressed a button, and said, "Car six to desk, car six to desk."

Static flooded the car.

She sighed and tried again.

Nothing.

"No offense to you, sweetheart," she said, "but I can't remember ever feeling quite this alone."

"Let's get going."

She eased the car over the hump. The road made a severe dip to the right, and I braced against the door with my foot and leaned against her to keep her steady behind the wheel. We straightened out and went into another dip. The floor scraped against the rocks as we straddled deep holes at the bottom. Up we went again, Trish hunched tight over the wheel, fighting shadows and ghosts that hadn't been there before. The parking lights weren't much better than nothing. "God, I can't even see the road now," she said. "I don't know how much longer I can do this."

"Hold it a minute."

She stopped and I told her I was going to get out and lead her along on foot. She didn't like that, but she didn't like this either. I took my flashlight and opened the door and stepped out on a rocky hillside. Underbrush grew thick on the slope beneath me: I could see an almost impenetrable blanket of it in the faint glow of the parking lights. The rain was steady but light: it didn't bother me at all. I flicked my flashlight and motioned her on, walking slowly three feet ahead. The ground rose again and we took it easy and gradually worked our way to the top.

Something flashed off through the trees. She killed the lights and I felt my way back to the car.

We sat in the dark, listening to the rain drumming lightly on the roof.

"Looks like somebody's home."

It was my voice, rising out of nothing. I moved over next to her and we sat for a while just looking at the light from the cabin.

"Whoever's there keeps late hours," I said.

I put my gun on the seat beside my right leg, along with the flashlight. It was hard to know what to do, to do the wise and right thing. It would be a grope, going up there in the dark, and I couldn't take a chance on using the light. Slip on the rocks and maybe break a leg. But I knew I couldn't sit here till first light either.

Trish was trying the radio again. "Car six to desk."

A broken voice came at us from the dash. ". . . esk . . . ix . . . you . . . ish?"

"Stand by, please." She turned her face and spoke in my ear. "I don't know if he's really reading me. What should I tell him?"

"Whatever you want."

It doesn't matter, I thought grimly. It's up to us.

Correction. It was up to me.

I felt a little sick thinking about my predicament. Trish had no place in this action except to complicate it. Should've seen that, Janeway, and read her the rules accordingly. You see things differently at the bottom of the hill. You play by her rules, bending over to be politically correct, and you bend too far and put your tit in a wringer.

But it wasn't my call anymore because that's when the killer came for us.

57

These things happened in less time than it takes to tell it.

I felt his presence. I knew he was there, and then he was there.

The windshield smashed and shards burst in on us. I heard a clawing sound, someone tearing at the door on the driver's side. I brought up the light and saw a flash of steel, and I killed the light and fell across Trish as two slugs came ripping through the door glass.

The back glass blew out, crumbling into hundreds of little nuggets. I reached behind me and slammed down the lock—just in time, as he grabbed the handle and yanked it hard, rocking the car with his power. Something heavy came down on the roof: the car took a rapid-fire pounding as if some giant had begun battering it with a log. He was kicking at the door with his boots, as if he could smash it in and tear us apart with raw power. I heard the side window break: another kick and it came completely out of its frame, and I knew in seconds he'd have his hand inside grabbing for the lock. I couldn't find my gun—in the scramble on the seat it had fallen somewhere and I didn't have time to fish for it. What I did was instinct: I grabbed the gearshift, jerked it down, and hit the accelerator with my fist. The car bumped down the slope, driverless and blind, clattered off the road, hit a deep hole, and threw us together with a punishing jolt. Trish took the brunt of my weight: her breath went out like a blown tire, and the car careened again and she took another vicious hit. I thought we were going over, but no—there was a tottering sensation and a heavy thud as the wheels came down. I heard the sound of bushes tearing at us: we were plunging through the underbrush, spinning crazily on a quickening downward course. I was going after the brake when the crack-up came—a thud, a crunch, and a shattering stop, flinging me against the floor with Trish on top. I felt a tingle in my legs, and in that moment my great fear was that I had broken my back.

I kicked open the door and slipped out on a carpet of wet grass. I lay there breathing hard, listening for approaching footsteps. I heard Trish move inside the car, a few feet away. "Where are you?" she said thickly, and I shushed her and pulled myself close. I reached back into the car, felt along the seat and down to the floor. I felt her leg, her thigh, her breast, her arm . . . and under the arm, my gun.

"Hold tight," I whispered. "Don't move."

I pulled myself around to the end of the car, facing what I thought was the upslope. Now, you son of a bitch, I muttered. Come now.

Now that I can bite back.

But of course he didn't come, he was too cunning for that. I sat in the rain and waited, guessing he could be anywhere. He could be ten feet away and I'd never know it till too late. This worked two ways—he couldn't see in the dark any better than me, I could hope, and in any exchange of gunfire my odds would have to be pretty good. I had been in gunfights and left two thugs in cold storage: all he'd done was kill people.

I felt better now. The gun was warm in my hand, like the willing flesh of an old girlfriend. Sweetheart, I thought, Papa loves you. I looked back where I knew the open door was: wanted to say something that would cheer her up but didn't dare. I didn't know where he'd gone: couldn't risk even a slight bit of noise that might stand out in the steady drip of the forest. He'd have to assume I was now armed. He'd have missed his chance to overpower us and now he would know—if he knew anything about me—that I'd had time to get out my piece. If not, it was a big mark for our side. Maybe he'd even come after us in that same reckless, frenzied way. Come ahead, Fagan, I thought—come and get it. I willed him to come and I waited in the grass like a scorpion. But he wasn't there.

I felt a great sense of calm now. He had tried and missed—tough luck for him. He had taken his shot but I was still here, huddled in the cop mode with my gun in my hand. I heard something move behind me. Trish was out of the car, coming on her hands and knees. I shushed her again, took her in my arms, and pulled her down against me. I told her it was all right now, it was going to be fine. I was goddamned invincible and I wanted her to know it, to help quiet the desperate fear I thought must be eating her alive. Then she whispered, "What do you want me to do?" in a voice so wonderfully calm it pushed me up another notch, past the cop mode to a place I'd never been.

It wasn't just me anymore, protecting some helpless woman. She was my partner again and I drew on her strength.

"Janeway."

"I'm thinking."

"Well, knock it off."

I made a little laughing sound through my nose and hugged her tight.

Don't get too cocky, I was thinking: don't try to be Doc Savage or Conan the Barbarian. You don't need to be now, she's here with you.

Gotta plan, I thought. Gotta be more than strong, gotta be smart.

Draw him out. Use the environment, whatever the hell it is out there. Bloom where you're planted, in the country of the blind.

See him first and you've got him. Draw him to the place where he thinks you are, then be somewhere else.

H. G. Wells had it right when he lifted that proverb. *In the country of the blind, the one-eyed man is king.*

Light might do it.

Noise might.

I put my mouth against her ear and said, "I'm going back to the car. Keep alert."

I crawled to the door and up to the front seat. Static poured out of the radio, through the open door, and blended into the rain. I wasn't sure yet what I was doing: the first bit of business was to find out what was possible. I needed to see. I took off my jacket to make a shield against the light, then I reached over and turned the light switch back so the dash would light up. A voice came through the radio—"Desk to car six"—and I jumped back against the seat, startled. But the voice broke up and disappeared in the static. I opened the glove compartment. There wasn't much inside—a few papers, the registration, an ownership manual, a screwdriver, some road maps, and a roll of electrical tape. What could I make of that?

The radio said "six" and faded, and I had an idea. I leaned out and hissed. Trish crawled over and I told her what I was going to do. The static on the radio was now a jumble of voices, low enough that it couldn't be heard much beyond the open door, but the noise was constant. It wouldn't matter, I thought: he wouldn't hear it. I tore one of the road maps apart, wadded up a quarter section, added some spit, and made it into a gummy mass, a spitball about half the size of my fist. It would fit well enough into the slight recesses of the steering wheel spokes where the horn buttons were. I picked up the electrical tape and leaned out into the rain. "Here we go," I said.

I blew the horn. Twice . . . three times.

"Scream," I said, and she screamed my name at the black sky.

I mashed the wadded paper into the horn button and the steady wail began. I whipped the tape tight around it, three, four, five times, and left it dangling. The horn blared away: it would drive a sane man crazy and a crazy man wild. He'd have to come now, I thought: he'd have to.

I took her hand and we moved away from the car.

Carefully . . . one step at a time.

Eight steps . . . ten . . .

Underbrush rose up around us.

"Get down here," I said. "Lie flat under those bushes and don't move."

She dropped to the ground and was gone. I stood still and waited.

I tried to remember what little I had seen of the terrain. The car had tilted right as it clattered down the slope. We had gone a hundred yards, I guessed, which would put the cabin somewhere to the left and above us.

The horn filled the night with its brassy music. I felt as if I were standing on top of it, it was that loud.

Off in the distance a light flashed. It flicked on and off twice. I said, "Uh-huh," and waited. He was gambling, hoping he could find his way without tipping his hand. You lose, I thought. His flashlight came on again, swung in a quick semicircle, dropped briefly down the slope, and off again. I now knew that the road was about fifteen feet above me, that the ground was steeper than I'd thought, and he was forty to sixty yards away, moving along to my right. He wouldn't dare use the light again, I thought, but almost at once he gave it another tiny flick, as if he'd seen something he couldn't quite believe the first time. Yes, he had caught a piece of the car in that swing past it: he saw it now, and if he raised the beam by a few degrees, he'd see me too, standing by the trees waiting. If he moved the light at all, I'd go for him right from here. Knock him down and he's done for . . . give him a flesh wound, a broken arm, a ventilated liver. On the firing range I'd been a killer—shooting from the hip, in a stance, close up or distant, it didn't matter. I could empty a gun in three seconds and fill the red with holes. It's an instinct some cops have and sometimes it saves your life.

I should've taken him then, but the light was gone now and it didn't come back. Minutes passed and I battled my impatience. Think of the hundred and one stakeouts in a long career: waiting in a blowing snow for fifteen hours and not being bothered by it. I had learned how to wait: I'd learned the virtue of patience—and had unlearned it all in minutes. I saw the bookman's face pass before me in the dark.

Rigby.

Who else fit the Grayson pattern all up and down the line?

Who did Grayson count on? Who would be this destroyed by a misspelled word? Who would take that failure so personally and torture himself and take up the sword against those who'd tarnish Grayson's memory?

Who had the skills and the single-mindedness to spend the rest of his days trying to finish Grayson's book?

He had the greatest hands, Moon had said. He had the finest eye.

Rigby.

That's what happens when you make gods out of men, I thought.

And now he was here. I felt my hand tremble slightly, uncharacteristically. Chalk it up to the dark: I still couldn't see him and I strained against the night, trying not to make that big fatal mistake. We were a few feet apart, microorganisms, deadly enemies who would kill each other if we happened to bump while floating through the soupy ether that made up our world.

There wasn't a sound. The blaring horn had ceased to exist. It can happen that way when it's constant, no matter how loud it gets.

I was betting my life on a shot in the dark.

Be right with your own god, I thought, and I opened fire.

In the half-second before the gun went off I had a flash of crushing doubt. Too late, I wanted to call it back. Instead I pumped off another one, took his return fire, and the slope erupted in a godawful battle in the dark. I went down—didn't remember falling, didn't know if I'd been shot or had slipped on the wet slope. Something hard had hit my head. I rolled over on my back, only then realizing that my gun was gone and he was still on his feet. There was light now, bobbing above me. I saw his shoes, heard the snap of the gun as the pin fell on an empty chamber, saw the log he'd hit me with clutched in his other hand. He dropped the gun and got out the knife. I tried to roll to my feet but couldn't quite make it. Got to one knee and fell over, like a woozy fighter down for a nine count. He loomed over me, then something came out of the dark and hit him.

Trish.

It wasn't much of a fight. The light dropped in the grass and they struggled above it. He knifed her hard in the belly. She grabbed herself, spun away, and, incredibly, spun around and came at him again. He knifed her in the side and this time she went down.

She had bought me a long count, fifteen seconds.

I was up on one knee with the gun in my hand, and I blew his heart out.

58

I carried her to the car and put her down on the seat.

Don't die, I thought. Please don't die.

I worked her clothes off . . .

Gently.

Everything was blood-soaked. The frontal wound was the scary one. The knife had gone in to the hilt, just at the hairline above her crotch. Her navel was a pool of blood, like an eight-ounce can of tomato paste. The cut was raw and ugly. I dabbed at it and tried to push the blood back, but it welled up again like a pot flowing over. I covered it with my hand. The last thing I worried about, now, was infection.

Blood oozed between my fingers and kept coming. She was going to die, right here on this car seat, and there wasn't a thing on earth I could do to save her.

There wasn't anything to be done. Even if I could get the hole plugged, she'd be hemorrhaging inside. I was watching her die.

She smiled. Her face had a peaceful, dreamy look.

"Tam-pons," she said. "Almost that . . . time of month."

Tampons. Jesus Christ, tampons.

I got them out of her bag. The package looked small in my hand. It was what it was.

I tore the electrical tape off the steering wheel. There wasn't enough left to go around her. But I had my belt, my shirt . . .

I ripped off the shirt and rigged her up the best I could. I cut a hole in my belt so it would fit her tight, and I pulled the shirt up between her legs, tying it to the belt front and back. It would be like a crude chastity belt and would work about as well as that ancient device ever had.

I shoved the tampons in and it took the whole package to stop the flow in the front. The wound on the side had sliced through her flesh, but the entire layer was still hanging there. I laid it back and drew the shirt tighter so it would hold.

A work of art.

A waste of time and we both knew it.

Then I got on the radio. I called nonstop for two hours and had no idea if I was getting through.

I held her hand and told her to be brave. These were just words. Who the hell was I to tell her about bravery?

She slipped into a deep sleep.

I was losing her.

Dawn was breaking as the helicopter came over the trees.

Now the medics had it. I had to get away from there: my guts were in turmoil.

I climbed the hill. The cabin rose up suddenly, the lights still blazing. A woman stood in shadow at the window.

Eleanor.

I clumped up the steps and walked in. One look at my face and she knew. She cried and I held her and I looked down the slope with its aura of death and its red lights flashing.

In a while one of the medics came up the hill. "They're taking her off now," he said. "She's awake and she wants to see you."

I asked him to sit with Eleanor while I climbed back down the slope. Someone had covered Rigby with a blanket and I stepped around him on my way to the copter. I got inside and sat on the floor beside the cot where Trish lay pale as death.

She didn't say anything, just held my hand a moment. "We gotta get moving," the medic said, and his eyes met mine and I knew what he meant. It was touch-and-go.

"You boys ride her easy," I said. "She's got a bigger heart than all of us put together."

I met the second medic coming down the hill. I stood on the bluff and watched the copter rise slowly over the woods. In the distance I could see police cars coming.

I went into the cabin to look for Eleanor, but she was gone.

59

I was sitting in the precinct room on the perp's side of the table when I finally met Quintana. He came into the room with a steaming cup in his hand, sat across from me, and doled out the evil eye.

"You dumb fuck," he said after a while.

The coffee was for me. I drank it black, same as he did.

They interrogated me for two hours. His partner, Stan Mallory, brought in some Danish and we went till noon. Twice during the questioning Quintana let me phone the hospital, where nothing had changed.

At twelve-fifteen he said, "Let's get out of here."

He seemed to be talking to me, so I followed him out to the parking lot, where he shuffled me to the shotgun side of a late-model Ford.

"This is supposed to be my day off," he said as he drove the wet streets.

I waited a moment, and when he didn't follow his thought, I said, "There aren't any days off, Quintana. Don't you know that yet?"

He knew it. He was just about my age and going through the same brand of burnout that had made my last year on the job so restless.

"I hear you were a good cop," he said.

"I was okay."

"A damn good cop. That's what they all say. I made some calls."

"I put a few assholes away."

"I hate to see a cop take a fall. Especially a good cop."

He was up on the freeway now, heading north. But he dropped off on the John Street ramp. We drove past the *Times* building, where the clock on the Fairview side said quarter to three.

"We need to talk to Eleanor," he said.

"You'll never find her. She could be anywhere by now."

"You remember where you left her car?"

"I think so."

"Show me."

We went north, and after a bit of double-tracking I found it. He opened the door and looked under the seat and took out the *Raven* she had left there.

"What do you think, maybe she took this out to compare it with the other one?" he said.

"I think that's part of it. And some of it's just what she said. She just loved having them."

He touched the book with his fingertips. "Isn't that a lovely goddamn thing."

"Rigby was no slouch. They say Grayson was good, but there ain't no flies on this."

We drove back downtown. A voice came through his radio, telling us Miss Aandahl was out of surgery. Her condition was guarded.

"I got a guy at the hospital keeping tabs," Quintana said. "We'll know what he knows as soon as he knows it. If I were you, I'd get some sleep. Where've you been holed up?"

I looked at him deadpan. "At the Hilton."

"You son of a bitch," he said with a dry laugh.

Surprisingly, I did sleep. Six hard hours after a hard shower.

I came awake to a pounding on the door. It was Quintana.

"I didn't say die, Janeway, I said sleep. Get your ass dressed."

I asked what he'd heard from the hospital.

"She's been upgraded to serious. No visitors for at least three days, and she won't be climbing Mount Rainier for a while after that. But it's starting to look like she'll live to fight another day."

He took me to dinner in a seafood place on the waterfront. It was superb. He paid with a card.

We didn't talk about the case. We talked about him and me, two pretty good cops. He was going through burnout, all right, it was written all over him. At thirty-eight he was having serious second thoughts about decisions he had made in his twenties. He had been a boxer, a pretzel baker, a welder, a bodyguard, a bartender, and, finally, at twenty-three, a cop. He was solidly Roman Catholic, a believer but unfortunately a sinner. In his youth he had studied for the priesthood, but he had repeatedly failed the test of celibacy. A guy could go crazy trying to do a job like that. Now, after spending a few hours with me, he was charmed by something he'd never given a moment's thought. Quintana was the world's next killer bookscout.

"This stuff is *just* goddamn fascinating," he said.

"My world and welcome to it." I didn't know if he'd make the literary connection, so I helped him along. "That's a line from Thurber."

"I know what it's from. You think I'm some wetback just crawled over the border? *Walter Mitty*'s from that book."

"Good man."

He had a leg up on the game already.

I asked if he had a first name.

"Shane," he said, daring me not to like it.

But I couldn't play it straight. "Shane *Quintana?*"

"I see you come from the part of Anglo-town where all brown babies gotta be named Jose."

"Shane Quintana."

"I was named after Alan Ladd. Kids today don't even know who the hell Alan Ladd was." He deepened the Chicano in his voice and said, "Ey, man, Shane was one tough hombre, eh? He knock Jack Palance's dick down in the mud and stomp his gringo ass."

"I think it was the other way around. And Shane was a gringo too."

"Don't fuck with Shane, Janeway. I can still put you in jail."

"That's your big challenge in the book world, Quintana. *Shane.* Find that baby and it gets you almost two grand."

We went to a place he knew and shot pool. Neither of us would ever break a sweat on Minnesota Fats but we took a heavy toll on each other. He had a beeper on his belt but nobody called him. I could assume Trish was alive and holding her own.

Late that night we ended up back downtown in the precinct room. Mallory was still there, two-fingering some paperwork through an old typewriter.

We sat and talked. Eventually Mallory asked the big question.

"So what're you gonna do?"

About me, he meant.

Quintana shrugged. "Talk to the chief. I dunno, Stan, I don't see where we've got much evidence for a case against this man."

Mallory gave him a you've-got-to-be-kidding look.

"We'll see what the chief says tomorrow," Quintana said.

In a little while Mallory left. Quintana said, "If I get you out of this shit, it'll be a miracle. The Lady of Fatima couldn't do it."

I followed him into an adjacent room. He sat at a table with some video equipment. "I talked to Mrs. Rigby today. You interested?"

"Sure I am."

He popped a cassette into a machine and Crystal's haggard face came up on a screen. "Most of this's routine. Stuff you already know. The kicker's at the end."

He hit a fast button and looked in his notebook for the counter number where he wanted to stop it. "Her problem was, they never had any money," he said. "They owned the property they lived on, they'd bought it years ago before prices went out of sight. And she had a piece of land in Georgia that she'd inherited. I guess that's gone now. She'd given it to Eleanor and they put it up for the bail."

The machine whirred.

"Rigby wasn't interested in anything that generated their day-to-day income. He was always doing his *Raven* thing. But she loved him. So he sat out in that shop and made his books, and they just kept getting better and better. After a while she thought they were better than Grayson's. One day Rigby went down to Tacoma to look at some equipment in a printshop liquidation, and Crystal brought Moon over to see the books. Moon couldn't believe his eyes. He thought Grayson had come back to life, better than ever.

"The temptation to sell one was always with her after that. She started hearing what people were paying—all that money changing hands out there and they had none of it. If she could just sell one, for enough dough. She could hide the money and dribble it into their account and they wouldn't be so damn hard up all the time. Rigby didn't seem to notice things like that. As long as there was food on the table and a roof over their heads, he didn't spend a lot of time fretting. He didn't care much about the books either. He'd finish one and toss it back in that room and never look at it again. Sometimes he talked about destroying them, but he never did because Eleanor loved them and he couldn't stand to hurt her. But all of them knew—Crystal, Moon, Eleanor—they all knew that if he ever made one that satisfied him, the others were all history.

"The temptation killed her. But she was afraid, scared to death. If Rigby ever found out . . . well, he'd never forgive her, would he?"

"If she was lucky."

"Yeah, except she didn't think of it that way. She'd be betraying Grayson in his eyes and that scared her silly. It came to a head about seven years ago. They had a string of money problems all at once and she started making some calls. Eventually she got funneled to Murdock, who was then the leading Grayson dealer in the country. The rest of it's pretty much like Scofield told it to you. When he had that coughing attack, that's what scared her off. It dawned on her what an old man she was dealing with. If Scofield should die and the book get out . . . well, that would make news, wouldn't it?"

"It would in the book world."

"And there was a chance Rigby would hear about it and go look and see the book was missing from that back room."

"Eleanor might even tell him. She'd read it in *AB*, a new Grayson book found, and tear it out and show it to him."

He stopped the tape, ran it back slightly to the spot he wanted, and leaned back in his chair. "That's when Pruitt came into it. When he lost his job with Scofield, it was all downhill from there. He thought if he could find this woman in red, he could do two things—get back at Scofield and put himself on easy street. But he figured wrong. He thought it had to be one of Grayson's old girlfriends, and for most of a year he chased down that road, trying to track 'em all down."

"What a job."

"That's what he found out. This Nola Jean—he worked on her for months and came to the same dead end everybody else came to. He went out and interviewed the Rigbys one time, even went to Taos, tracked down her sister, tried to talk to her. None of it panned out. Finally he ran out of leads and had to give it up. But he never stopped thinking about it.

"In the last five years, Pruitt really descended to his natural level in the order of man. He was a cheap hood, dreaming of glory. Then Eleanor got busted in New Mexico. That was the catalyst, that's what started this new wave of stuff. There was a little article in one of the Seattle papers, not much, just police-blotter stuff. There wasn't any what they call byline on the story, it was just a long paragraph, Seattle woman arrested in Taos heist and murder attempt, but your friend Aandahl says she wrote it. Pruitt saw it. Suddenly Grayson was back on the front burner again. The Rigby girl had broken into the Jeffords woman's house. What could that mean? Maybe Jeffords had been Scofield's woman in red. The only thing Pruitt knew for sure at that point was that Jeffords had had something the Rigbys wanted, and he had a pretty fair idea what that thing was. He called Slater and sent him to New Mexico to watch Rigby. Then Pruitt went to North Bend to confront Crystal, but she wouldn't admit anything. He harrassed her for a day or two, but that didn't get him anywhere. So he flew down to New Mexico and turned up the heat on Eleanor. He stalked her, called her at night with threats. He'd call at midnight and hum that song. Anything to rattle her, to get her to give up the book."

"This was when she was out on bail."

"Yeah, there was a period of about a week there when Pruitt and Slater were hard on her case. She didn't have the book then but she knew where it was. Charlie Jeffords had told her it was Nola's book. So she went back and took it and made her run. The funny thing is, she might not've done any of that if the Jeffords woman had just talked to her."

"All she wanted was to find her mother."

"So they get back up here and Pruitt starts in on Crystal again. Stalking, calling. There were some death threats. He'd call her at night and play that song, just a snatch of it, just enough of it, just enough of it. But loud, menacing. Then he started on Rigby too, and that was his big mistake. He was messing with the wrong dude. Rigby wound up at Pruitt's house and you know what happened after that. He ransacked the joint and found the photocopies of Grayson's *Raven*—that's what you found burned in the wastebasket. I figure Pruitt made that copy when he stole Scofield's book, years ago.

"There wasn't even a misspelled word in that one."

"I'll bet he didn't even look."

He punched the tape. Crystal's voice filled the room.

"We stood around in shock," she said, faltering.

Quintana leaned back in his chair. "She's talking about the morning after the fire."

"We were over at Archie's shop, in Snoqualmie," she said. "We were like three dead people. Gaston and Archie were beside themselves. Gaston was inconsolable. It was the worst day of our lives . . . until this one. I don't think we said a word to each other the whole time. What could be said? Then we heard the door open . . . someone had come into the shop. And I remember Archie yelling out that he was closed . . . go away, just . . . go away. But the footsteps came on, and then she was there. Nola. I kept waiting for her to say something . . . maybe to cry. But she looked at Gaston across the room . . . she looked straight at him and said, mean as hell, 'Cry if you want to, suckers. I'm glad the son of a bitch is dead.'"

Crystal sniffed and dabbed her eyes. "I knew she didn't mean that, it was just spite. She'd had that awful fight with Darryl the day before . . . and she'd always hated Gaston because she could never move him the way she always got at other men. When she said it, I felt sick. I turned away from her, I couldn't look at her . . . and then . . . then there was this thump, or a kind of . . . crushing sound . . . and when I turned around, she was lying there with her brains . . . and Gaston stood over her with the bloody hammer and Archie . . . Archie'd kinda shrunk back to the wall and we all just . . . just . . ."

Her face was pale. She looked faint.

Quintana's voice came in. "Take your time, Mrs. Rigby. Would you like some water?"

"No."

But she took the glass he handed her and gulped it.

"Then what happened?"

"Archie said . . . something like . . . it's a good thing you did that or I woulda. But that was just talk, it was Gaston who'd done it. And he'd sat down and there was no concern or . . . anything . . . on his face . . . and somebody mentioned the police. And I said no . . . can't call them, they'll lock him up and what would I do without him? He was my life, how would I live? So we rolled her in a rug and that night Archie and I took her off in the truck and we buried her."

Off camera, Quintana said, "What about the other people he killed?"

"I don't know." She began to cry again.

"Should we believe that, Mrs. Rigby?"

"I don't care what you believe. My life is over."

Quintana snapped off the machine and rewound the tape. Neither of us spoke until it clicked.

"Did she know Rigby had taken Eleanor?"

"I don't think so. She says no. I believe her." He put the cassette away and pushed himself back from the desk. "I found out a few more things while you were out playing the Lone Ranger. It was Rigby who made that call at four o'clock in the morning. He called the cops on his own kid. I think he was afraid of himself, what he might do if it turned out that Eleanor really had that flawed book. Hell, he was right to be afraid, he'd killed everybody else who ever had one. He tried to hide his voice, but I've got the tape and it was him. He was on long enough for the number to get logged, so we know the call came from that phone. I think he turned on the record at Pruitt's for the same reason. There was a part of him that wanted us to catch him."

I thought of Crystal and Archie and asked what he thought would happen to them now.

"Whatever it is, it won't be anything compared to what they've already been through. We'll see if the facts bear out her story. I doubt if they'll do any jail time; the only charge would be rendering criminal assistance, and the statute's probably run on that. They don't seem to care right now. They waived their rights to a lawyer, gave us statements of their own free will, and the statements jibed and I believe 'em."

He turned up his palms. "You might as well be in on the payoff if I can swing it. There's just one thing. You've got to teach me this bookscouting stuff. Call it one you owe me."

"I'll give you the two-day crash course, teach you all I know."

"I'm a quick read. One day will do it."

In the morning he came to get me. Trish had had a restless night but was upgraded to fair. She was asking for me but her doctors told her not yet, maybe tomorrow.

Quintana and I ate breakfast together and then did a couple of bookstores. I watched him buy without comment, and afterward we sat in a coffee shop and I told him what he'd done wrong.

Never buy a bad copy of a good book. The better the book, the more the flaws magnify.

Condition, condition, condition . . .

We drove to the jail and picked up Moon. He looked old in his jail clothes, and he looked strangely small sitting between the two deputies in the backseat.

We arrived at Rigby's in brilliant sunshine. Moon walked between us as we crossed the meadow. We went along the path I had followed up from the house, dipped into the trees, and stopped a hundred yards into the woods.

An hour later, the deputies dug up the rug containing the bones of Nola Jean Ryder.

In the spring they flew into Denver for Quintana's long-postponed book odyssey. Trish was looking good and I was thrilled at the sight of her. We ate that night in a Mexican place on a hill near Mile High Stadium, and in the morning we lit out for Nebraska, Iowa, and points east. The trouble with Denver is it's a light-year from everywhere, a hard day's ride to any other city with bookstores. The landscape is bleak, though there are those who love the brown plains and the dry vistas and the endless rolling roads. We filled the day with shoptalk, of books and crime and the people who do them. We laughed our way across Nebraska, drawn by the Platte and bonded by the good companionship that makes book-hunting so special and rich. We prowled in little towns where thrift-store people are uncorrupted by the greedy paranoia of the big-city stores. It was in such a place that Quintana made the first good strike of the trip, a sweet copy of Alan Le May's *The Searchers*. It wasn't *Shane,* but it was a solid C-note, which is not bad for thirty-five cents.

We scouted Lincoln and found some gems at Bluestem, an oasis of books just off downtown; then we moved on to Omaha. The weather was grand all the way, and we laughed about it and Trish swore it had not rained a drop in Seattle since I'd been there last October. Quintana made a dubious cough but had to agree that the winter had been unusually dry. We swung north into Minneapolis and spent a day tramping around with Larry Dingman of Dinkytown Books. I still had the picture of Eleanor that Slater had given me long ago, and in every stop I showed it to bookpeople in the hope that someone had seen her.

In Chicago I saw a guy brazenly doctor a Stephen King book, just the way Richard Grayson had done *The Raven*. He sat at his front counter and tipped a first-edition title page—sliced out of a badly damaged and worthless book—into a second printing. The book was

The Shining, an easy deception because the second printings are so much like the firsts in binding, jackets, and stock. The only notable difference is on the title page verso, the magic words *first edition* are at the bottom of a real one and missing from the others. The entire operation took less than five minutes, and when it was done, even a King guy would have a hard time telling. The guy marked it $200. Quintana leaned over his counter and called him a crook and a few other things before Trish managed to pull him away and we headed for Indianapolis.

I had a dream that night about the first Grayson *Raven.* In the dream Richard fixed that one too: changed two letters of type after Grayson had quit work and gone to the pub for the evening. It would've been easy then, in 1949, when it was just the two brothers working alone and a mistake was easy to miss. No glue, no tip-ins to tell a tale years later: just switch the letters and it would always be assumed, even by Grayson, they'd been set that way. At breakfast in the morning I told Trish and Quintana and none of us laughed. For a long time we couldn't shake the notion that the whole Grayson tragedy had been for nothing.

We were out ten days, in all a great trip. They stayed with me another three days in Denver, and the house felt empty when I put them on the plane and watched them fly away.

A year has come and gone. It's winter in Denver, late on a snow-swept Saturday night as I sit at my front counter writing in the little diary that I've begun keeping of my life in books. Far up the street a shrouded figure comes out of the snow, battling a wicked wind that howls in from the east, and I think of Eleanor Rigby. I still have a delusion that one of these days she's going to walk into my bookstore and help me write a fitting end to the Grayson case. Grayson was my turning point as a bookman. I came home with enough of Scofield's money that, for now, I can buy just about any collection of books that walks in my door. I still have Grayson's notebook: Amy gave it to me. Kenney calls once a month and asks if I'm ready to sell it. I should probably do that: the money they're throwing around is just too good to keep turning it down. But Kenney understands when I laugh and tell him how it would diminish the old man's life if suddenly he had that road map to everything.

Among the fallout from the Grayson papers were letters indicating the real identity of Amy Harper's father. The name Paul Ricketts had been one of the pseudonyms used by Richard Grayson in his early writings, and the letters revealed an affair of many years' duration between Richard and Selena Harper. "So we're first cousins," Amy wrote of herself and Eleanor. "Imagine that." The news from the Northwest gradually tapered off. I had to return the Ayn Rand books to Murdock's estate as his last two relatives could never agree on anything. The best guess, the one that seemed most likely to me, was that these were the last of Murdock's really good books, gathered for a wholesale run so he could get some money together to make Amy an offer. The cops found a big batch of real Graysons—all the lettered copies of everything but the 1969 *Ravens*—in the rafters above Rigby's shop. He couldn't resist taking them, holy books made by the hand of God, as he traveled through St. Louis, Phoenix, Baltimore, Boise, and New Orleans. As for his own, they are called the Rigby *Ravens* now and are widely admired by people who have seen them. Scofield wants them but his woman in red doesn't seem to care so much about money anymore. The books will belong to Eleanor, wherever she is.

The New Mexico case is still open. Charlie Jeffords died not long ago and it remains to be seen who fired the gun, if and when the cops find Eleanor. I've just about decided that it's too easy for people to disappear into that street-level book subculture. I keep showing her picture around when I'm on the road. There's a lot of money waiting for her and Scofield's not getting any younger.

It's ten o'clock—time to get the hell out of here and go home. The figure in the street has reached my door, and in this moment, in less than an instant, I think, *Hey! . . . maybe . . . maybe.* At the edge of her hood I see the facial features of a young woman. She turns her head, our eyes meet through the plate glass and she smiles faintly. It's the neighborhood's newest hooker, heading on up to the Safeway after a hard day's night. I give her a friendly wave and turn off the lights fast. In the yard behind the store I look at the black sky and wonder what books tomorrow will bring.

ABOUT THE AUTHOR

John Dunning won the prestigious Nero Wolfe and Colorado Book Awards for his first Cliff Janeway mystery, *Booked to Die*. The sequel, *The Bookman's Wake,* received Gold Dagger and Edgar nominations and was a *New York Times* Notable Book of 1995. His new Janeway novel is *The Bookman's Promise* (March 2004). An expert on rare and collectible books as well as old-time radio, Dunning lives in Denver, Colorado, where he is working on the fourth Cliff Janeway novel.

Visit his website at www.oldalgonquin.com.